Pat Barr

Jade

Originally published as *Chinese Alice*
and *Uncut Jade*

CORGI BOOKS

JADE

A CORGI BOOK 0 552 12281 5

Part One of this book was first published under the title
Chinese Alice, published by Martin Secker & Warburg Limited and
Corgi Books. Part Two was first published under the title *Uncut
Jade*, published by Martin Secker & Warburg Limited.

PRINTING HISTORY
Corgi edition published 1983
Corgi edition reissued 1984
Corgi edition reprinted 1984

This book is set in 10/11 Mallard

Corgi Books are published by
Transworld Publishers Ltd.,
Century House, 61–63 Uxbridge Road,
Ealing, London W5 5SA.

Printed and bound in Great Britain by
Cox & Wyman Ltd., Reading, Berks.

To 'Mother Barr' with much love

The Greenwood Family in 1890

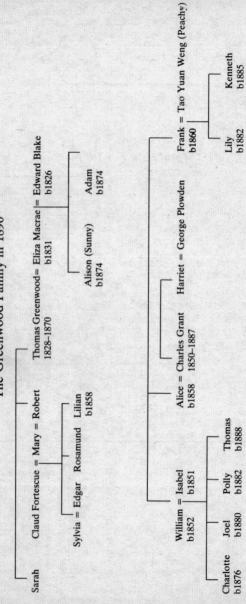

Sarah

Claud Fortescue = Mary = Robert

Thomas Greenwood = Eliza Macrae = Edward Blake
1828–1870   b1831   b1826

Frank = Tao Yuan Weng (Peachy)
b1860

Sylvia = Edgar   Rosamund   Lilian
b1858

Alison (Sunny)   Adam
b1874   b1874

Lily   Kenneth
b1882   b1885

Alice = Charles Grant   Harriet = George Plowden
b1858   1850–1887

William = Isabel
b1852   b1851

Charlotte   Joel   Polly   Thomas
b1876   b1880   b1882   b1888

JADE ...

THE MAGNIFICENCE OF THE CELESTIAL
EMPIRE, THE DRAMA OF AN ANCIENT LAND
ON THE BRINK OF CHANGE, THE PASSION OF
AN EXTRAORDINARY WOMAN TORN BETWEEN
EAST AND WEST ...

JADE ... 'A match for FAR PAVILIONS in rich
cultural ambience, with traces of the lyric intensity of
SPRING MOON ... a grand late-Manchu adventure,
tumultuously plotted and handsomely decorated.'
Kirkus Review

JADE ... 'Move over THE FAR PAVILIONS, NOBLE
HOUSE and THE THORN BIRDS ... Now comes
JADE ... a moving, monumental work standing high on
its own ... Simply said, JADE is exciting and moving as
only the finest of fiction can be.'
Book World Syndication

JADE ... The story of Alice Greenwood – born to an
England she could not love, bound to a China she could
not leave ...

The Chu Family in 1890

Lung-kuang (Dragon Brightness) = Yun-hwei (Hidden Glory)
b1827   (1828–1883)

Tamao
(Eldest Daughter) = Weng

Han-fei
(Eldest Son) = Dull Thorn = Seed Pearl
1855–74   b1857

Hung-mei
(Second Daughter)
b1857

Han-li = Yu An
(Younger Son)
b1860

Hsiao-ping
"Little Piece"
b1866

Eldest Son
b1869

Second Son
(Custard Apple)
b1872

Third Son
(Pepper Seed)
b1875

Book One
Uncut Jade

Part One

1

Thomas Greenwood stood at the door of the chapel with a pistol in his hand. He looked anxiously along the street that was so deserted it made him more uneasy. Usually, at this time of day, the shops along it—selling cordage, netting, fish-baskets for use on the boats in the nearby Tientsin harbour—were filled with customers. But this afternoon's emptiness was unnerving, especially when, in the distance, there was a great deal of noise. He could hear gongs beating, temple-bells clanging, wheels grinding, the shuffle of many feet and above all the sound of a multitude of threatening voices pitched at an ominous and sullen rumble.

Suddenly, two pistol shots cracked in quick succession and the noise of the crowd rose to a shrieking crescendo. Thomas examined his pistol; his hand was shaking; he had never fired such a weapon in his life. Gingerly he stroked the trigger, wondering if he could ever squeeze it, knowing that he might have to, astounded that matters could have reached such a sorry pass. But gradually they had and it was too late to escape. Now the matter was out of his hands and in God's.

He waited, but there was no further sound of firing, so, laying his weapon on a stool in the porch, he walked slowly down the centre of his humble chapel to the table at the end on which stood a silver cross. The only other furniture was some rickety benches on the hard earth floor, a lectern and a picture of the Crucifixion. He looked at it.

'It is nothing,' he murmured, 'to die. . . . There is a green hill far away,' and paused. For it was not the green hill of Calvary that filled his vision but one little more than a hillock and covered with English wild flowers.

It was springtime, and he, Mother, Father, his brother Robert and baby Sarah had gone for a picnic into the country just outside the city of Norwich where they lived, because it

13

was his birthday. Twelve he must have been, the same age as his little Alice was now. And after the picnic, he and Robert had run to the top of the little hill and rolled down the other side shouting for joy, and he smelled again the young crushed grass, saw the sun tippling around him as he tumbled over, heard the larks high in the blue sky and his mother calling, 'Thomas, Robert, whatever are you doing? And in your best suits, stop it at once!' And there she stood on the hill's crest in a bright dress of sprigged muslin looking down at them, vexed, but smiling a little in spite of it.

No Calvary, just a green hill in Norfolk so many years ago. The intensely sweet pleasure of that long-forgotten day pierced him with such agony that he gasped as he stood in the chapel of the Church Missionary Society in a side street of the port of Tientsin, China, on the afternoon of 21 June 1870. If I could just see that hill once more, hear those larks, I would die gladly and with gratitude, he vowed silently. But in his secret self he guessed he never would. He was about to pray for a broader courage to meet the present circumstances when his wife Eliza came rushing in from their living quarters behind the chapel.

'Thomas, there you are! What is happening? Are things worse? Tan-sho has just arrived with the most dreadful tale, something about the French, as far as I can make out, but he's so upset I could hardly understand. . . . Come . . .'

He hurried to the parlour, where Alice, his daughter, stood white-faced.

'Oh, Father, what shall we do? Tan-sho says the people have just killed two Frenchmen right in the middle of town. Do you think it can be true?'

Alice's grasp of Chinese was good for her age; moreover Tan-sho always took time to make her understand him, for he had become rather fond of this quaint foreign child with her large greenish eyes, her merry laugh, her spirit of independence and vitality that was very unlike the obedient passivity of his own granddaughters. Thomas looked straight at the man, an elderly basket-maker and one of his most loyal converts.

'If Tan-sho says that then it must be so, my little one. Frenchmen, eh? I heard shots a while ago. . . . But come over here, my man,' and he drew Tan-sho aside so that the others should not hear.

It was as bad as Thomas had feared, and he was alarmed, though not unduly surprised, to learn that the French Catholic missionaries had provoked this situation, for they had, in his view, been behaving quite reprehensibly. Two years ago they had built a large, pretentious cathedral in the town's centre on the site of a former temple. They had taken into their new orphanage so many sick Chinese children who soon died that the place had developed a sinister reputation as a disease-ridden death-trap.

Apparently, Tan-sho told him, matters had come to a head that afternoon when the French Consul had visited the Chinese magistrate's yamen to demand protection for some Catholic missionaries who had recently been severely harassed by the local populace. The Consul, a choleric man, had evidently lost his temper entirely and stupidly fired a pistol at the magistrate. The bullet had missed its target; nevertheless, on leaving the yamen, the Consul and his assistant had been literally torn to pieces by an enraged mob outside.

Frank, the youngest Greenwood, who had been pretending to read while trying to hear Tan-sho's story, jumped up restlessly and opened the back door. 'Phew—it's hot in here, I'm going into the yard.'

'You stay inside, Frank,' Eliza said sharply, but joined him in the doorway. There, they both heard it—an active, swelling sound rather like the sea on a choppy unpredictable day. But unlike the sea, which was glittering in its usual place a few miles away at the mouth of the River Peiho, this sound was coming nearer, and occasionally, above the general swell, Frank heard wild hoots of fury.

'They're coming this way, Father.' He tried to sound matter-of-fact and manly for his ten years. 'Do you think we should lock the back gate?'

'Or should we leave, Thomas? Go away at once—perhaps to the Consulate? It would be safer there surely?' Eliza appealed. She had had lovely clear blue eyes when he married her and her hair had been as fair and curly as Frank's was now. But she had been a missionary's wife for nearly twenty years since then, and now her hair was scraped back in a lacklustre bun, her eyes dimmed and red-rimmed from so many years of witnessing the heathen ways of the Chinese and their almost total rejection of the Word of the Lord.

'I don't think there's time to leave, my dear—and we can't

15

go by cart because the mule is lamed, remember.' He paused irresolutely, listening, as they all were, to the threatening sounds.

The trouble was that Thomas hated the idea of seeking protection from the odious young whippersnapper of a Consul, Mr. Waters, who, having spent less than three years in China, thought he knew everything about it. 'Tientsin is a potential trouble-spot, a hot-bed of crude xenophobia,' he had grandly informed Thomas soon after his arrival. 'This is where we and the French negotiated the new treaties that the Chinese dislike so much, you know—and we had troops here till '63 which always arouses resentment. Still, in my view it's a pity we don't have any here now.'

Thomas had curtly explained that, as he and his wife had first come to China in 1852, he was indeed aware of the treaties that the British and French had forced upon the country in 1858. However, he did not agree that the generally touchy situation in Tientsin could be improved by stationing a regiment there—far better to allay the people's natural fears by spreading the peaceful message of the Gospel among them.

But, in spite of the efforts of Thomas and missionaries of other denominations working in the district, hostility against them had recently intensified and vile propaganda had been circulating. He remembered with sick incredulity the translation of an anti-Christian pamphlet that Mr. Waters had shown him only the week before. It was entitled 'The Foreign Devils Worship the Incarnation of the Pig They Call Jesus.' Jesus, Thomas read, ' . . . was very licentious by nature. As soon as a woman heard his Pig's grunts, her clothes unfastened of themselves and she would let him satisfy his lust. The followers of the Pig therefore exhort the people to worship him, making use of this as a pretext for satisfying their own unnatural desires . . .' The pamphlet concluded: 'Those missionaries who have committed a thousand times ten thousand malicious acts, who have castrated boys, removed foetuses from pregnant women, gouged out people's eyes, and cut off women's nipples—do you think that the gods will permit themselves to be taken in by their wickedness?'

'You see what we're up against?' Waters had waved the document in his face almost triumphantly. 'Can you wonder at the people being hostile towards you when they read this sort of filth? That's why I'm asking you to be very circumspect and

16

not go preaching where you're not wanted and not keep so-called converts in your house, as the Catholics do in their orphanage. They'll have every foreigner in the town slaughtered if we're not careful—for what common Chinese rabble can distinguish between a Catholic and a Protestant, or a consul and a missionary come to that—in the middle of a riot?'

Obviously Waters had been frightened, but Thomas had been too deeply outraged by the pamphlet to feel any fear and he had stormed from the Consulate after saying that, with eighteen years of Chinese experience behind him, he knew better than to adopt the Catholics' ill-advised tactics and that he was not about to take orders from Her Majesty's Consul on how to conduct the mighty work to which God had called him. Brave words at the time, but now his heart quailed a little as it occurred to him that many of the ignorant people who had just killed the Frenchmen and were even now moving towards his Mission had actually heard and probably believed propaganda of that sort.

'Perhaps you are right, Eliza, I must swallow my pride—we will go to the Consulate immediately, on foot if we can avoid the mob. I'll see which way they're heading.' He hurried to the back gate, Alice and Frank clinging to his arms, for he was a big man with an air of reassurance and they felt safer at his side.

'What's that smell?' Alice sniffed. Accustomed as she was from birth to the numerous, generally unsavoury odours of a Chinese town, this was something different. 'Burning—something nasty?' She looked at him doubtfully.

He too sniffed; it was a sickly, deadly smell and it evoked a vivid memory for him. On the way Home on leave several years ago, he had visited his brother Robert, stationed with the Indian Army at Calcutta. Robert had taken him to see the funeral pyres lit beside the River Hooghley; mound upon mound of smouldering human flesh. He locked the gate quickly and hurried the children back inside; Eliza noticed his face had gone chalky.

'What is it, Thomas?'

'They're burning something ever so nasty,' Alice volunteered.

'I'm afraid some buildings must have been set on fire,' he began.

'Look, I can see the smoke . . . there. . . .' Frank pointed

17

excitedly over the yard wall to a thick black column that was billowing from the direction of the town centre only a few streets away.

'Quickly, children, run to your bedroom and put some clothes in this,' Eliza handed them a calico bag. Thomas, taking another, went to his desk and with a feeling of disbelief threw in his Bible, prayerbook, purse, mission accounts, bundles of letters from Home. As he did so he felt his guilt growing: here he was, suddenly faced with what was perhaps the greatest challenge of his dedicated life, and yet he was bundling together his paltry possessions and fleeing to save his skin just like any small-town merchant with no more idea of salvation than a beast of the field. He should be in the chapel beside the Cross, uplifted by the chance to make a sacrifice of his humble life, inspiring his family to accept God's will for them all.

He stood helplessly as his wife rummaged through the desk drawers. 'William's picture? Wherever is it? Upstairs? The frame broke and we put it by to mend. . . .' Their eldest son, William, was ensconced in an English boarding-school and, at that moment, Eliza thanked God for it. Usually William's absence was the hardest burden she had to bear, for he had been born during their early years in China when she was still resilient and full of hope, and he had never caused any trouble. She had lost a daughter in infancy, and then had Alice and Frank, who were such a boisterous handful that they often made her feel tired and old, though she was not yet forty. She ran upstairs in search of her son's picture and suddenly stopped.

'Thomas,' she called, 'what about Wo-wo?' Thomas dropped his half-filled bag feeling obscurely relieved. How could he have forgotten Wo-wo till now, he thought with shame? Wo-wo was an old woman now; when they had come to Tientsin six years ago she had been their first true convert and they had called her Wo-wo as a joke because that was how her name sounded in the unfamiliar local dialect. For the past four years she had lived in the Mission, faithfully and cheerfully sweeping the chapel and polishing the cross every week, handing out prayer leaflets at the door with a wrinkly smile of welcome, bouncing her favourite young Frank on her knee and giving him sugar plums. But for the last few months she had been visibly failing; her screwed-up little hoofs of

18

feet, bound into deformity from childhood, would no longer support her considerable weight even as far as the chapel, to which Thomas carried her every Sunday. She was upstairs in the box-room now, peacefully dozing the warm afternoon away as usual, undisturbed and unknowing.

'Wo-wo,' Thomas said helplessly to Tan-sho, who had been sitting watching their preparations for departure with a quizzical, bewildered look. 'We can't leave Wo-wo, and I couldn't possibly carry her far and the mule is lamed. . . .' Tan-sho nodded as if he had realized this long before. Thomas put the contents of his bag back into their customary places. Eliza joined him.

'We cannot leave her to the mercy of the mob,' he said. 'You know what they do to converts. The way is made plain. God will protect us, darling.'

She nodded. 'It's not so much us, it's the children.'

Thomas's mind seared with pain as he thought of Alice, his favourite child, so young, vulnerable, alive; the way she jerked her long hair back from her face when she was reading. It was soft-brown and glinted like ripe nuts in the sun just as his own had when he was a lad in Norfolk. How could he not make every effort to save her—at whatever cost to himself, his pride, even to helpless Wo-wo?

'Alice, Frank, come down, we're not going,' Eliza was calling them. 'We can't possibly leave Wo-wo, can we, dears? We'll be all right, Father says so.'

At that moment they heard loud banging and calling at the back gate. Tan-sho jumped up. 'I'm sure that's my son's voice. . . . Let him in please, Mr. Greenwood, he may have news.'

Thomas hurriedly unlocked the gate and Tan-sho's son rushed in, his face terror-stricken. He grabbed his father's arm and began dragging him away, shouting in his rough, dock-side accent. Tan-sho pulled back, his skinny old legs swathed in thin cotton visibly shaking.

'He says the Catholic cathedral and orphanage are all a-blaze, Mr. Greenwood—and the people threw the nuns and priests into the streets and stripped them, and they—oh, may the Lord preserve us all—then he says they cut off the women's breasts and the men's genitals and threw the poor creatures back into the flames to burn. Can you imagine such terrible things? But my son speaks true and he says I

19

must flee with him at once and he'll hide me for I'm a known Christian. He has done a filial deed in coming here, Mr. Greenwood, for it's dangerous to be seen anywhere near a Mission, he says. Oh I don't know . . . Mr. Greenwood, dear pastor, what shall I do?'

'You must go at once, Tan-sho, and may God protect you.' Thomas raised his hand in blessing, then caught up with the son at the gate. 'Tell me, do you think it is possible for my family to get to the British Consulate without being attacked?'

'Oh, you mustn't dare that, sir,' he laid a trembling hand on Thomas's sleeve. 'No, no—your only hope is to lie low here. I've never seen such savagery as is going on in the streets today. The rioters are like wild animals, and they'd pull any foreigners to pieces on sight. No-one seems able to control them. Can't you hear the terrible noise?'

And indeed the noise of the mob was perceptibly closer now and mingled with it the crackle of flames, the thud of timbers falling, smells of burning cloth and that sick-sweet odour that was worst of all. The children ran up, Alice clutching a book, Frank a painted wooden horse. 'Look at the flames now, Father, they're getting nearer. Will they spread to our chapel?'

'Oh, Father,' Alice ran into his arms and buried her face against his chest. 'Can't we go away from here at once? I'm frightened—there's a whole crowd gathered at the end of the street, you can see them from the other window. Wo-wo's awake and she says they may come for us and we should go quickly. She doesn't mind, she wants us to. . . .'

Eliza put her arm on Frank's shoulders. 'Oh let us pray, children, let us pray for deliverance. Surely, Thomas, the people won't harm us? It is the Catholics who've caused this dreadful trouble. . . . Surely it is only they who are being punished for their misguidedness? But, oh the punishment . . . terrible indeed are the ways of the living God and we must all quail before his righteous anger. Let us go to the chapel and pray together.' She shepherded the children inside and Thomas went to reconnoitre again.

'Yes,' he said gravely, when he returned. 'There is indeed a mob coming towards us. I fear it is unwise to go to the chapel, my dear—they're bound to make for it first. I think we must all be very brave and hide quietly in Wo-wo's room which is the least likely place.'

20

He took his Bible from the desk and handed his wife the prayerbook she'd carried on their wedding day. 'Alice,' he asked sternly, 'where is your *Child's Garden of Prayers?*'

'I don't know, Father, but I've got *Alice in Wonderland* instead.'

'And I've got Dobbin,' Frank patted his horse. 'He's not frightened.'

'Surely not "instead", Alice?' Thomas smiled gently, but there was no time for theological corrections. As they ran upstairs, they could hear feet pounding nearer and, to Thomas's dismay, they seemed to be converging on every side. Wo-wo had managed to stagger to the door of her room, her round face tense.

'In here—you must hide here—they are shouting such terrible things outside, terrible. Frank, my poor little one. Come to Wo-wo, she'll protect you.' She engulfed the trembling child in her stout arms and said over his head, 'Get into the store-cupboard behind my bed, Mr. Greenwood. I shall stay in the bed and say you have all escaped. They will believe me, I pray they will, if God is good.'

Thomas marvelled at the true Christian strength that had come upon her, it was deeper and firmer than he had understood. He thanked God for it and was proud.

'But you—what will they do, Wo-wo, if they find you here?' Eliza cried, as a hail of stones and mud came clattering over the wall into the yard.

'They will not harm me, I am an old woman. and if they do—I am still an old woman, is that not so, Mr. Greenwood?' He bowed his head humbly.

'But I shall face them with you, Wo-wo. Eliza, you and the children must hide. . . .'

'If you are seen, the people will know your family is here.' Wo-wo said simply. 'You would never leave them.'

'No—I suppose—'

Another shower of stones landed and they heard the gate breaking as people crashed against it. The burned air vibrated to the sounds of yells, thumps, hoots, and shrills of bamboo whistles.

'Quick, children, in. . . .' Eliza and Thomas shifted Wo-wo's bed and slid open the cupboard door behind. Thomas kissed the top of Alice's head. 'Come, dear, don't look so alarmed. You'll be safe in there—and think of the story you can tell

21

William—about the day when we all had to hide in the cupboard among the jams and pickles!'

Suddenly two more pistol shots cracked in the distance and Eliza jumped, 'Oh Thomas, perhaps that's the troops or the Chinese guards coming to save us?'

'Let us pray so, my dear . . . but my pistol? Oh where is it? I had it earlier this afternoon. . . . If the worst comes I must defend you all. Oh, where on earth did I . . .?' He looked round wildly, suddenly very distraught, for he had earlier comforted himself with the secret vow that he would shoot them all and himself last rather than they should suffer the same fate as the Catholics. And now his pistol. How could he have been so careless? A lack of organisation and forethought had bedevilled him all his life. That it should do so at this most crucial juncture of all was inexcusable.

'Get into the cupboard, Eliza,' he bundled her in. 'And Wo-wo, you sit on the bed . . . I can't . . . I believe I left it in the porch. . . .'

He flew down the stairs, aware of the din of the multitude on every side; the whole of the orderly little world which he, his family and their few faithful converts had painstakingly built was crashing round his head. He pelted up the chapel to the porch and grabbed the weapon from the stool where he had left it. Just as he did so there was a tremendous crash against the chapel door. It splintered like matchwood and a large battering ram came thrusting through. He turned to run, but the faces peering through the hole had seen him.

'There's a child-eater! There's one of the goat-farts! Get him, take his piglet progeny and tear out their livers!'

Thomas stopped, brandished his weapon at the leering faces and fired into the door above their heads. He could not . . . thou shalt not kill. He turned his back on them just for a second and looked at the silver cross on the chapel table. A beam of late afternoon sun, in which danced the dust of all these disturbances, shone upon it from the lattice above, and he knew then with absolute certainly that his hour had come. He had been right; he would never again see the green Norfolk countryside of his childhood. If only they would kill him, just him, there and go away. 'O merciful God, take me and spare the others, my young ones,' he prayed aloud. 'I am ready to die for Thy Sake, O Lord.'

The leaders of the mob were nearly through the door and

Thomas faced them again, his pistol steady and pointed straight at them. They were armed with wooden pikes, swords, and battered shields. It is medieval, Thomas thought; these are medieval people and they will have me for a martyr. There was a pause of confrontation which was, for Thomas, an agony of indecision through which he could not think fast enough. Should he fire? Or should he save the remaining bullets for his family? How many bullets did the pistol hold?

Then he heard Eliza's voice behind him screaming, 'Thomas, Thomas my beloved. You shan't die alone, I can't bear it. Thomas, don't fire at them—we will die here together.' And she rushed to him obsessed with the vision of their joint martyrdom.

'No,' he barked. 'Go back—back to the children, woman.' He pushed her behind him.

She clutched at him blindly, then obediently ran away to the living quarters and he tried to cover her retreat. But the interruption had broken his small threat of defiance and the crowd came pouring through the broken door hooting derisively. They were a motley, ragged collection—casual fishermen, labourers, and loafers—and they brandished sticks and spiked truncheons, while two carried poles tipped with pitch. Thomas knew what those were for.

At the door of Wo-wo's room they fell on him; he could not bring himself to fire the pistol after all and it was torn from his grasp. As he went down before them he heard his children's piercing screams and Alice's cry of agonised disbelief, 'Father, Father, help . . . help . . .!' One of the leaders had a sword, rather rusty, but sharp enough to hack three times through Thomas' neck. The blood spouted in a thick red jet and the head thumped along the floor. Alice saw her father's eyes roll away.

Hands grabbed at her—Mother's and Wo-wo's—shielding her and Frank against the wall. There were thuds, grunts, cries and a rivulet of bright red creeping towards her. Mother screamed 'Thomas, Thomas, Thomas' over and over again. Then she was torn from Wo-wo's arms and saw her mother, her face covered with blood, sprawling across her father's headless body and Wo-wo thrown roughly upon the bed where she wailed helplessly and prayed for death.

'We're to take the children alive,' said the man with the sword. 'There's one who wants to taste the piglets' livers,'

23

he guffawed and aimed a kick at Eliza. 'As for the women, leave them to burn where they are, it's getting too hot for comfort in here.'

And indeed the room was beginning to fill with smoke from the fires that had been lit in the chapel below, and the prayer-benches were crackling merrily. Suddenly came the distant sound of rifle fire and the men looked uneasy.

'Let's go, it might be the yamen guards,' the leader growled as he poked about the room, disappointed at the lack of worth-while loot.

'Or the barbarians landed from the sea,' said his comrade, as he swung the screaming Frank under his arm. A stringy fellow smelling abominably of sweat, blood and ashes similarly caught up Alice and they clattered down the stairs and out of the back gate where a covered mule-cart waited. The children were thrown inside, two men leaped aboard and the vehicle rattled away towards the town boundaries.

For the remainder of that dire day and through the night the children were jolted along inside the stuffy cart, so stunned with horror that they simply sat, clutching each other and sobbing. Once during the night they halted, the mules were fed, the men drank tea; the children were offered nothing and were too sick to ask.

Frank whispered, 'Did you see—Father and Mother?'

'Yes, they killed Father . . .' she began to weep bitterly again.

'But not Mother, she was alive and so was Wo-wo. They'll send soldiers to rescue us.' He squeezed her hand, neither of them daring to remember the sight of the burning chapel, the way flames were shooting up towards the room where Mother and Wo-wo lay.

At dawn, hands shook them roughly; the cart had stopped and light shone through the awning. Guards pushed them down into a courtyard, ropes were thrown halter-fashion round their necks and they were led off like convicts. 'The master says he wants their eyes and livers on a plate,' one sniggered to a stable-boy as they passed. Alice, who partly understood the words, decided to make no further effort to understand anything. They found themselves locked inside a dim, airless room. Light sneaking through a high barred opening let them know day and night, but of how many they soon lost track. Twice a day they ate rice and gruel; at night they

24

drifted through nightmares of such terror that they often woke each other with their screams and cries. In the middle of one such night two different guards marched in and dragged them outside. Alice whimpered and clung to Frank. Our last hour has come, she thought, soon I shall see my Father in Heaven, and clasped hands for a prayer that, panicked, she could not remember. Instead they were thrown into another cart, with a shutter fixed at the back, reaching almost to the floor. One of the men jumped on top, the other on the shafts, the driver cracked his whip, whistled 'Hi, yeh ho' and the mules plodded off.

During the next numberless days and nights they became very used to those sounds of the muleteer's whistle, the rumble of the ancient cart, its smells of dust and dung, and wind, rain and sun filtering through the awning. One guard had the habit of hissing disgustedly through his few teeth whenever he looked at them, so they called him Old Hisser; the other, a jollier fellow, passed the time chatting to a succession of drivers about the state of the roads, the prices of crops. But neither of them would talk to the children, except to bark occasional orders.

'Where are you taking us?' Alice sometimes popped the question unexpectedly, hoping to catch them unawares, but the men simply shook their heads. Frank, remembering early geography lessons, guessed they were heading south; Alice thought Hong Kong lay there and hoped it was their destination. It soon became clear that the cart's shutter was to prevent them from being seen, for they were only allowed out at night—to exercise a little and eat a sparse meal. At such times it was hopeless to guess where they were. Sometimes empty plains stretched as far as they could see, or hill tracks wound away to an infinity of dark mountains; sometimes moonlight glinted on a silver thread of river or wet paddies; they heard owls hoot, dogs bark from distant settlements and, once or twice, unknown beasts roar and growl from the hills and the guards mutter uneasily.

Apart from their nightly respite, their view was confined to the patch of ground beneath the moving cart: pebbles, stones, rocks, white, beige, grey; earth dry and dusty, brown and damp, treacly-black and thick; wisps and tufts of yellowing grass; near habitations it was more interesting—scraps of peel, eggshells, excreta, chicken-bones and broken shards for

25

the wheels to churn over. But it all went on forever.

Sometimes, sitting with her chin in her hand gazing at this low-level landscape, Alice wondered if she had been killed with Father after all. Surely she had seen this same stony track a hundred times before? Perhaps she had entered those eternal circles of purgatory of which she had heard and which would lead her to Heaven after a thousand years of journeying? But no; it was still the earth, the familiar night sky, the real sun beating on the cart-awning. But how could any country, even China, be so huge and never reach an end of land? Surely they must be somewhere near the South Pole by now?

Eventually they came to a watery region where rain drummed on the awning and the animals' hooves sploshed and squelched. That night stars were reflected in vast stretches of water near the track, flocks of disturbed wild fowl clacked in the marshes and the children decided they were approaching the sea. But, at dusk of the next day, they saw, in the direction where they thought the sea would be, the distant lights of a city. The guards pointed at it with unusual animation, and the friendlier of the two put his hands wide apart, then close together and grinned.

'He means we're nearly there,' Frank guessed.

'Wherever "there" is.' Alice's heart thumped in alarm. Later the cart halted and there came the sounds of people arguing; when they moved on, occasional flickers of light showed that the ground below was paved. Strong smells of habitations, people, and open drains wafted to them. Again the cart stopped, again men shouted; hinges creaked and they passed through a gate that was slammed behind them. They were pushed out into a courtyard, more imposing than the one they had left so long ago, and with lanterns swinging at its corner eaves—but just another Chinese courtyard nevertheless.

Frank grabbed his sister's hand, 'I thought we'd be out of China now, but we're not.'

A group of men, obviously surprised by their arrival, stood nearby; one shone a lantern in their faces and laughed jeeringly. The others crowded for a closer look. Alice leaned wearily against the cartwheel now wishing they could just go trundling along forever inside rather than face the unknown hazards of this alien place. After an interval, Old Hisser led them inside a shadowy pillared hall. In its centre stood a

26

lacquer table and high-backed chairs. On one of them sat a dignified Chinese wearing a loose robe and looking sleepy, peevish. Old Hisser bowed low and handed him a scroll. The man studied it, looked at the children over its top, re-read it. Then he gave a deep sigh, came round the table and, twisting his fingers into Frank's hair, tugged hard.

'Ow!' Frank yelped. The man smiled faintly, then gave instructions in an unfamiliar dialect to a servant who ushered them out, down long passages to the back of the house.

'You should have asked him where we are and who he was,' Frank said accusingly as they trotted behind the bobbing lantern.

'All very well for you to say that, but I couldn't think of the right words, and he looked so stern and important. I thought he might be like that Queen in *Alice in Wonderland*, do you remember? If you said the wrong thing, she'd shout, "Off with her head." '

Aunt Sarah, Father's sister in England, had sent Alice a copy of that new story last Christmas, saying every little girl called Alice should have one. Alice had read the story a dozen times and now wished desperately for it.

'Scaredy-cat!' Frank taunted, then had a terrible memory of a certain blood-stained sword.

'Well, why don't you learn Chinese yourself instead of telling me what to say?' Alice countered.

'So I will—now we're still in China,' he retorted grandly as they crossed a small courtyard.

A servant unlocked a door, pushed them through, threw two quilts on the floor inside and disappeared. The room was dark and empty—at least of people, though there were scuffles in the corners.

'Mice?' Frank suggested.

'Rats,' Alice shuddered.

A great weariness swamped them and they lay down close together for comfort between the quilts and fell into exhausted slumber. As they slept, several rats in pursuit of their customary nocturnal activities ran over them, but they did not stir.

Grey light filtered through the door. Alice woke abruptly with a sense of dawn and a shift of relief from the nightmares that had, as usual, haunted her sleep. She stood up, aching from the rigours of the journey, and looked round. They were

27

in a store-room filled with sealed boxes, sacks of herbs, maize, shreds of dried ginger and peppers, jars of sesame-seed oil and red-bean paste, piles of broken utensils, baskets and sieves. The combined smells were quite pleasant, both fusty and sharp, but although she was very hungry, she could find nothing edible. She chewed a leathery scrap of ginger and spat it out in disgust.

Cautiously she opened the door. In a small empty courtyard rain dripped steadily from the eaves of the dilapidated thatch atop the buildings on all sides. The centre was a mess of mud and pebbles through which many feet had tramped; the branches of the one straggly willow tree growing there were bent with the tears of the rain. An early clatter of pots began in the building opposite; beyond a wide gate in the far corner came the snort of pigs, the cluck of fowls.

Behind her, Frank stirred. 'Is it morning?'

'Yes, but there's no one around.'

'I'm hungry.' He inspected the sacks in his turn.

'There's nothing to eat—that dried stuff tastes horrid, I've tried.'

He joined her in the doorway. 'Why don't we try to escape before they all get up? That gate must lead somewhere.'

'But I can hear people across there. . . .'

'They're a long way off. Come on. . . .' Boldly he scurried to the gate, heaving at the heavy latch. 'We're locked in.' He looked back at his sister in panic. 'Will they leave us here to starve? I'm so hungry.'

'Of course not—I can smell cooking. I expect it's our breakfast.'

The cooking of the first day's meal for the entire household of the Chu was indeed going forward and as there were many mouths to feed, it was a lengthy process. On account of seniority and gender, the mouth with top priority belonged to Grandfather Chu, who was enjoying an unmolested retirement in his own apartments. In his private courtyard stood lions on lacquer bases and huge pots of golden-coin and tousled-dog chrysanthemums; plum and cherry trees bloomed in their season and from their branches on balmy days swung cages of brilliant song-birds. The next most important mouth to fill belonged to Chu Lung-kuang, 'Dragon-Brightness,' Grandfather's eldest son, a deputy-governor of the interior province of Hunan and functioning head of the house now that his father had reached an honourable old age. It was he who had briefly inspected the children the night before.

Waiting without impatience for the arrival of the most important breakfast in the senior women's apartments known as 'fragrant' was Yun-hwei, the Deputy-Governor's first official wife. Her name, which meant Hidden Glory, was appropriate, though no one gave it much thought. Twenty-five years before, when just seventeen, she had been carried to the Chu residence in a closed bridal chair and had seldom since left. In the course of the uneventful years, she had borne her husband seven children; two had died in infancy; two boys and three girls survived. Gradually and increasingly since her childbearing had ended, she had become withdrawn, any glory she had once possessed being hidden from others and neglected by herself.

The eldest daughter of the house, invariably known by the affectionate family name of Tamao, 'Big Puss,' and her husband, Weng, had spent the night in their apartments on the east side, where they would breakfast together the next morning. Along the passage, Lung-kuang's secondary wife, Red Jasmine, who could never wear the red skirt of official recognition, offered morning gruel to her baby daughter who cried because it was too hot. In the room opposite, Vegetable Aunt, Hidden Glory's sister, fretted at the crying and jabbed a needle into her embroidery. She was a childless widow who had forsworn the eating of meat when her young husband died; but she looked forward to the morning gruel nevertheless and was impatient because, as usual, she was outranked in order of breakfast precedence.

There were, however, many lower in the household's hierarchy: the younger children of the family, their tutors and personal servants; scribes and secretaries, messengers and guards, cooks and gardeners, gatekeepers and seamstresses, grooms and chairbearers, fowl- and pig-keepers, skivvies, slaves and enfeebled old retainers, an idiot boy, a rag picker and a scavenger—all of these were sustained by the Chu kitchens and were never disappointed. But the portions diminished in size and quality according to rank, so the two barbarian children, lowliest of the lowly, eventually received for breakfast a bowl of much-watered gruel topped with the scrapings from the pot of last night's stewed vegetables.

'I can't eat it,' Frank wailed. 'It looks so horrid I'll be sick.'

Alice set her teeth. 'We'll have to eat it—they won't give us anything else. It will warm you up. Food always does, even cold—so Mama used to say.'

As they slurped dismally at the sloppy mush, a man in a neat dark robe came in followed by Old Hisser. It was Weng who, before his marriage, had twice visited Canton where he had seen barbarians walking about, so he knew just what they looked like.

'Ha, real barbarians,' he said knowledgeably. 'Yellow hair on the boy, you perceive, and the girl—very odd eyes. How old are you?' he asked Alice, who, in her anxiety, understood nothing.

'I thought you said she spoke the tongue?' He turned on Old Hisser in annoyance.

'Only a little, sir, and a very ignorant way of speaking.'

Weng tried again in precise Mandarin and Alice stumbled, 'Twelve—I think.' For perhaps she had had another birthday without even knowing?

'And the boy—your brother?'

'Yes. He's ten.'

Frank tugged Alice's sleeve. 'Tell him we're hungry.' Alice tried to summon the word. 'Food,' she blurted.

'Did they eat?' Weng asked one of the cooks who had come over to inspect the barbarians. 'Yes? Then never mind. They look sufficiently fat. Barbarians eat too much and their food is unwholesome, too much animal fat. See they get enough to keep well. They're only children—younger than they look.'

Weng strode off, disappointed at the extent of the barbarians' ignorance. If he wanted to learn anything useful from them they would have to know more Chinese—but probably they were to die. He must find out.

The cook left lounging in the doorway was joined by other servants. 'Just look at them,' he jeered. 'What disgustingly big feet she has—and their skins are pink as piglets.'

'And his hair—like old yellow goat's wool!' A groom tugged Frank's curls hard.

'Stop it, stop it!' Frank beat his hands away and squared his chubby body into a fighting posture. The servants cackled merrily, pleased at this show of defiance.

The cook reached forward, rapped Frank's knuckles smartly with a wooden spoon. 'I've heard foreign devils have holes in their chests so you can put poles right through them and carry them strung up like hogs. Let's see if this one has!' He hit Frank hard on the chest. 'No hole!' They all guffawed, while Frank, bellowing tearfully, lunged at his tormentor.

Alice pulled him away. 'Frank, don't—he's too strong. He'll only hurt you more. . . . Beasts, leave us alone!'

Then they heard footsteps approaching and, as the servants slipped unobtrusively away, Weng reappeared, accompanied by his wife and two of Chu Lung's children, Han-li, Younger Son, and Hung-mei, familiarly known as Mei, Younger Daughter.

'Why, they're squaring for a fight,' Han-li laughed. 'Look at him, isn't his hair funny, and his eyes?' He danced round Frank, waving his fists.

'Leave them alone, Younger Brother, they're only frightened.'

Han-li giggled. 'What, of me?' That was a novel and pleasant idea. Under-sized and not very robust, and with a bullying elder brother, Han-li felt fright much more often than he inspired it. He was the same age as Frank and the practice of those military arts at which Eldest Brother Han-fei excelled and to which he was just being initiated seemed rough and difficult. That very morning he had been fetched out at dawn for exercise round the field and had first dropped his bow and then fallen from his horse and twice been called a bumble-fisted milk-sop. His legs were still trembling from the experience, so it was good to flail his arms and see the fear in the barbarians' faces.

'Ah, yi, yi, let's beat the filthy foreign devils,' Han-li yelled and Frank, recognising the dread term, shrank back.

'Oh stop that noise, no fighting indoors,' Tamao ordered. She went up to Alice and they inspected each other with mutual interest. Tamao was her father's favourite daughter and she was reasonably happy in her marriage; for a mere woman, therefore, her position was enviable and she thanked the gods daily for it. 'Ask what her name is, you say she understands a little,' she said to Weng.

'A-li-chi . . . ree-woo,' they repeated the strange syllables among themselves, amused at their oddity. Tamao pointed at the boy. 'Frank' was equally impossible.

'Also Greenwood,' Alice added desperately.

'Ah, the same name—brother and sister,' Weng explained importantly.

31

They all nodded solemnly at this point of understanding. Then Frank ran to pick up a green-painted box in the corner. 'See—green wood.'

Alice laughed. 'You know, I never thought of it like that before.'

'Nor did I, till now.'

'Box?' Mei, entering the game, pointed to another container.

'No—green,' Alice pointed to some herbs.

'Whatever does that mean?' Mei pouted. 'She must be half-witted. I thought she was explaining her name.'

'Barbarians are all half-witted,' Han-li chanted.

Alice went up to Weng and pointed at the green button on his tunic collar.

'Ha,' Weng smiled. 'Jade—that's the name.'

'Green Jade,' added Tamao. 'That's what they meant—green box, green herb.'

'Green Jade, that's not a proper boy's name,' Han-li jeered at Frank.

'Perhaps that's only part of it,' suggested Mei, for they all had three names apiece.

'You will remember the words of Li-chi,' Tamao turned to her husband. '"Uncut Jade cannot be turned into a serviceable vessel. So men untaught can never know the proprieties." '

'Just so—Uncut Jade. That is most appropriate.'

The moment of communication had passed. Alice sensed that the name they had settled on was both incorrect and derogatory. She shivered; not even her own name anymore.

'She looks cold,' Hung-mei fingered Alice's grubby frock. 'And she doesn't smell nice either.'

'Barbarians all stink like rotten cabbage,' her brother announced. He wrinkled his nose. 'Phew!'

'They must wash, and I'll send over some bits of old clothing.' Tamao turned to a servant.

'Aren't they going to be killed then?' Han-li asked Weng.

'I don't think just yet anyway. A letter came with them last night. After your father read it, he ordered them put in here. Perhaps I'll find out more later.'

Speaking of Lung-kuang, Weng was always uncertain, mindful of his insecure position in his wife's household. In the normal way, he should not have been living there, but disasters beyond the normal had befallen his own family. Eight years before, soon after he was betrothed, his father and elder brother had both been killed fighting against the rebel Taipings during the battle for Nanking. His mother had died soon after, from shock it was said.

So, when Weng and Tamao married they had stayed in the Chu residence. It was a temporary measure that had drifted into permanence and suited everyone except Han-fei, Eldest Son, who disliked having a male senior in age but inferior in standing competing for his father's good opinion. For Weng was astute and scholarly and made himself very useful to his father-in-law. Yet, aware of Han-fei's jealousy and superior status, he never felt secure and sometimes dreamed of taking his wife and their first-born son to Canton and making his own way, as a few of his contemporaries had. But generations of innate conservatism held him back; better to entrench himself where he had taken root; there was much truth in the old adage that those who run after kites trip over straws.

On the strength of his Canton visits and his vague aspirations, Weng was the acknowledged authority on any peripheral 'barbarian matters' that affected the household and so he wanted to learn what he could from the children. Obviously, he thought, picking his way back over the muddy courtyard, they would be of no use to him dead. Moreover he had heard that the barbarians' military might was practically limitless and their directing of it quite inexplicable. He quailed at the vision of a phalanx of fully-armed Western soldiers storming into this city of Changsha, the Hunanese capital, and blowing it sky-high simply to revenge the killing of two pathetic scraps of Uncut Jade. Clearly then it was in the interest of himself and the family to keep the foreign devils alive. But, as he robed himself for the day's business, he sighed, knowing that the main opponent of this endeavour would, as usual, be Han-fei.

'Eldest Brother—come and see the barbarian monsters! They're so peculiar and they smell awful . . .' Excitedly Han-li dragged at his brother's coat as he returned home in the afternoon of that same wet day. 'You've heard about them? They came late last night.'

'Yes, Father told me. They're no more important than diseased pigs,' Han-fei shook off his brother's enthusiasm. 'I'll see them after I've seen Mother.'

Han-fei didn't like his routine altered. At the end of every day he took tea in his mother's apartments—his visits were always the high point of her day, sometimes of his.

Han-li dropped back disappointed. 'Well, let me come when you go. I want to see them again.'

'Aren't they going to be killed?'

'Weng doesn't seem to think so.'

'Huh—what does he know about it?' Han-fei shook the rain off his head violently and threw his wet cloak to a servant. 'Ugh—it's raining as though a tub had overturned. Too bad for riding even.' Han-li nodded, secretly glad.

In his mother's apartments, Han-fei made the customary salutations to her and Vegetable Aunt, received the customary tray of tea and doughcakes.

'Too wet for riding,' Mother said. 'A pity, Younger Son needs the practice.'

'He does indeed,' Han-fei grinned. 'He dropped his bow *and* fell off his horse this morning!'

'He's not sturdy for his years,' said Aunt in extenuation, for Han-li was her favourite.

'Have you seen the foreign-devil children?' Han-fei inquired.

Mother shook her head in disgust, fixing her attention on her youngest daughter, Hsiao-ping, 'Little Piece,' who was stolidly rolling a hank of twine.

Aunt said, 'No—and I don't want to. Han-li says they've got light eyes and big noses and smell bad! Why doesn't the respected Father have them done away with at once?'

'I don't know, I've not talked to him yet.'

'Why were they brought here, that's what I can't understand?' asked Aunt querulously. 'We've not had any barbarian troubles here before. . . . Mother thinks it must be something to do with that old firebrand Lung-pao, Third Uncle.'

Lung-pao was the younger brother of that elderly grandfather who was happily pottering through his declining years in the flower-filled courtyard. Lung-pao, even if he lived to such a ripe age, would be incapable of pottering. The Chus had not seen him for years, but his bellicose deeds were a family legend, for he had spent most of his eventful life fighting losing battles against the barbarians.

He had been one of the young defenders on the walls of Canton nearly thirty years before when British forces had assaulted the city and forced trading agreements upon his people. And had then watched helplessly when the foreign-devil soldiers proceeded upstream and ruthlessly looted the city of Chinkiang, while hundreds of its inhabitants committed suicide by burning or throwing themselves into wells. Later, as a full commander, he had seen his eldest son and many of his foot-soldiers mown down before the European siege guns that had been brought upriver from Tientsin to storm the forty-feet-high walls of Peking itself, capital of the Celestial Empire. For the last few years, Lung-pao, retired from his military career, sour and ageing with the sense of continuous defeat, had been a deputy salt-commissioner in Tientsin, nursing an abiding, obsessive hatred for the Westerners who were invading and humiliating the glorious Middle Kingdom of his ancestors.

'I thought he'd quieted down at last.' Hang-fei signalled for more tea.

'There was trouble in Tientsin a while ago, Father told Weng,' Mother replied. 'Some child-eating barbarians were killed by our people and their religious places burned.'

'If there were any anti-foreign riots going on near Lung-pao he'd be involved,' Aunt affirmed. 'You know how he feels. Weng put two and two together and decided that's what happened—apparently the devil-children come from Tientsin.'

'Weng's always making five out of two and two,' Han-fei retorted. 'I'll see Father myself and get the full story. But I suppose I'll look at them first. Where are they?'

'In one of the kitchen courtyard store-rooms.'

'Are they boys?'

'One boy, one girl.' Aunt replied. 'Tamao says the boy is about Younger Son's age, but looks older. They're always too big.'

Han-fei tapped his youngest sister on the nose teasingly. 'You're not too big, are you, tiny Little Piece? We come in the right sizes, don't we?' He chuckled and went off towards the kitchens, calling for a lantern, as the damp twilight was thickening to darkness.

For the Greenwoods, the day had been one of misery and fear. Earlier, a servant had brought ice-cold washing water, a couple of frayed tunics, padded leggings and straw sandals; later bowls of rice and pickled cabbage had appeared. They ate in defeated silence, huddled on the mats.

'We should have sprinkled some herbs on to make it taste

35

better,' Alice remarked with forced cheeriness. 'We'll remember next time.'

'Next time! How long do you think we'll be here then? Mama must come and rescue us soon.'

Frank had been saying that, with decreasing conviction, every day since their capture. Alice had always replied that, yes, Mama would come as soon as she was well enough—blocking from her mind that frail and bleeding body on the floor—but that, in any case, William would surely come. Six years her senior, William was certainly capable of charging across uncharted China to rescue them single-handed. She thought about him now, as she had last seen him when he had left for England two years before—solemn and swallowing hard as he bade farewell and ran up the gangplank of the *China Cloud* that would land him in Southampton three months later.

'If only William were here, he'd know what to do.'

Frank tried to look elder brotherly. 'He'd try and escape at once.' He got up and looked round. Rain still poured from the courtyard eaves and into the spreading pool round the stunted willow; wisps of charcoal smoke from the kitchens melted into the indeterminate twilight.

'There's no one about.'

'But where would we go?'

'Out of that gate. We can climb over even if it's still locked. I can hear animals on the other side, it must lead somewhere.'

'But if they catch us escaping they may do even worse things.'

'They won't. Anyway, how are Mama and William going to find us, shut in here? We've got to get out and meet them.' It was transparently plain to Frank that the longed-for figures could be no more than a few miles away by now, on the other side of that gate.

Alice said doubtfully, 'Perhaps you're right. We'll try as soon as it gets dark.'

For a while they listened nervously to the splash of rain, moan of wind, occasional chatter of distant voices; certainly they seemed to have been quite forgotten. 'Come on, it's almost dark—let's go, don't be such a sissy!' Frank tugged at her.

She jumped up indignantly. 'I'm not.' He crept off and reached for the gate's latch which still would not lift. In the

36

gloom he discerned notches in the wooden post and, using them, managed to clamber up, straddling the gate and peering down the further side. Dim clucking bundles were moving in the mire; whitish porcine shapes snuffled and grunted. 'Come on—it's all clear,' he whispered.

Alice started after him, then stopped, heart pounding—a swinging light had suddenly appeared in a doorway opposite, a figure behind it. 'Frank,' she screamed, 'there's someone coming—get down, come back—quick.'

He turned, saw the light, froze to the gate-top. Han-fei glimpsed Alice first, lunged and grabbed her by the hair. 'Where d'you think you're going? A little foreign devil, isn't it?' He shook her head back and forth.

'Frank—jump and run!' she shouted desperately.

He took a deep breath and leaped into the dark on the gate's far side, landing with a great splosh in the mire. Hens and ducks scattered squawking, a goose flapped its wings and hissed. He scrambled up panic-stricken, careered forward into a large, evil-smelling beast that knocked him back into the filth and began to snuffle his face.

'Help me—Alice,.Mama, Wo-wo, help me!' he bellowed. The rays of a bobbing lantern lit up the beady eyes of hens, the sinister close glint of piggy ones. Han-fei and a fowl-keeper converged on him as he lay sobbing.

'That'll teach 'em to try any tricks.' Han-fei, yelling with laughter, dragged him up by the hair and beat him across the back. 'Just the place for a barbarian—wallowing in the dung of the farmyard, that's what Third Uncle would say!'

'I suppose he was trying to escape?' The keeper was deferential.

'Looks like it.' Han-fei jerked Frank's head back and held up the lantern. 'What a sight! Not only a foreign devil but one covered with shit! He's got yellow hair, what you can see of it . . . Well, back he comes, I suppose.' He marched Frank back by the scruff of the neck to the store-room, where Alice cowered in a corner. 'Son of a foreign turtle! That's for thinking you could get away from us!' He kicked the boy inside and went to the kitchens, calling for water to wash, just as Han-li ran up.

'What was all that noise? Have you seen the barbarians?'

'They were trying to escape just as I got here—the boy jumped into the farmyard, but I soon collared him.' Han-fei held up his hands, grinning. 'I've always heard barbarians are filthy beasts—they're covered in shit!'

Han-li giggled. 'He was in the mire then?'

'Yes, and a pig was at him—what a sight! Father will be home now and I'm going to find out about them. Might as well throw them back to the swine, if you ask me.'

Han-fei strolled off and Han-li, about to follow, heard a strange noise across the courtyard. Creeping towards it, he recognised the universal cry of anguish, fear and hopelessness that welled from the dark store-room. It was a very human noise, but in the circumstances there was something eerie about it. He paused, fearful, then opened the door and held up a light. The children were huddled together on the floor in a dirty, damp and trembling heap. Frank shrieked as the light flickered over him.

'They'll kill us now we've tried to escape . . . Oh, Mama, Mama, come quickly. Please come.'

Alice muttered, 'O merciful Father, save us, O God in Heaven protect us.' She tried to recall the pictures she had seen of righteous boys and girls wearing golden haloes and nightdresses as they walked calmly towards some bloody martyrdom, but her courage was not up to it. 'Please don't kill us,' she clasped her hands beseechingly. 'We're not even grown up yet.'

Han-li understood the look though not the words, and his desire to torment them further abated. 'It's nothing to do with me, you're only barbarians,' he muttered, backing away to the safe lights of the kitchen.

'They sound like caterwauling wild cats, don't they?' remarked a servant as he passed. 'Nothing but beasts they are.'

Reluctantly Han-li went to his room where books for evening study were laid ready. From the third of Mencius' seven volumes from which he had to learn long passages by heart, he read: 'The feeling of compassion—that is benevolence; the feeling of reverence—that is propriety; the feeling of discrimination between right and wrong—that is wisdom. Benevolence, righteousness, propriety and wisdom are not instilled into us from without, they are part of our very being. Only we give them no thought. Hence the saying, "You can have them for the asking, or lose them through neglect." '

Han-li had never considered the real meaning of these

words, but now he re-read them carefully. Impulsively he jumped up—he would tell Eldest Sister about the barbarians, she always knew what was best. Tamao was painting her face for the evening; she wore a robe of green satin embroidered with red flowers, and the jet coils of her hair, decked with jewelled pins, shone in the lamplight.

'Did you know,' Han-li blurted, 'that Eldest Brother caught the boy barbarian in the farmyard trying to escape?'

'The serving woman just told me,' she replied calmly. In such normally uneventful households any news travelled fast.

Han-li took a sugar plum from a bowl. 'They're making a terrible noise now—and they're absolutely filthy.'

'The Uncut Jades?'

'Yes, I think they're ever so frightened and cold out there, in the dark. . . .' He hesitated, not wanting in the least to appear milk-soppish.

'Did Elder Brother knock them about then? Weng doesn't want them to die just yet.'

'I don't know, but they're certainly howling loud enough.'

She sighed and summoned a servant, ordering that the barbarians should be given washing water, gruel and a candle. 'Does that satisfy you? This morning you thought it was fun to see them so terrified.'

He shrugged away her teasing. 'I thought they might die, that's all, and there'd be no fun in that, would there? I just saw Elder Brother go in to see Father about them.'

Tamao looked annoyed, for Father had not yet consulted her husband on the matter. She turned on Han-li. 'It's near suppertime. Why aren't you at your studies? Get along now and if Eldest Brother has left Father, let me know.'

As he passed Father's room he heard Han-fei's voice and grinned—know-all Weng would not like that, discussing the barbarians without seeking his expert advice on the subject!

Behind the closed door, father and son had exchanged the usual pleasantries and Han-fei now concluded his account of the barbarians' attempted escape with, 'So—shall I throw them back to the swine, Father? No point in keeping them alive any longer surely?'

'I have to for the time being. A letter came with them from that scoundrel Lung-pao in Tientsin. . . .' Lung-kuang paused to light his pipe. 'Why couldn't the old fool stick to his salt-taxing? But no—still full of the red peppers, that one. So he and his younger son, Cheng-ta—remember him?—got involved in the latest anti-foreign riots there. Now, he says, the foreigners have sent in troops to seek out the instigators, so he'll be in for it. But the worst thing is—Cheng-ta's being held as a suspect by the authorities.'

'You mean our authorities?'

'Yes, they're very careful not to offend the foreign devils in the treaty ports these days. Lung-pao says he had the barbarian children sent to him as he intended to cut out their eyes and livers and dispatch them on a plate to the barbarian consul—a typically scatter-brained idea, not very subtle, I must say. Anyway, before he could do so, he heard of his son's arrest, so he kept them in his summer residence for possible exchange as hostages. But now he's under suspicion himself, which is why he's sent them here secretly. No formal charges have yet been made, so I have to keep them till I hear more. What a mess!'

'When did all this happen?'

'The letter was written late in the seventh moon and took nearly two moons to get here. I've sent a letter back asking for news and agreeing to keep them alive till I hear.' He sighed. 'Why for all the gods can't Third Uncle retire quietly like Father?'

Lung-kuang's father had always been a peaceable man who, in his time, had enjoyed the ceremonials of his office, hunting, chess and women and was now content with his song-birds and chrysanthemums. Lung-kuang took after him, being also content to stay in the province of his birth, performing his duties reasonably and keeping his household in peace. But there was a volatile streak in many Hunanese, who were not called 'the red peppers of the Empire' for nothing. Lung-pao had it in abundance, so, to some extent, did Han-fei.

Han-fei jumped up with an oath. 'But why should Third Uncle lump this barbarian filth on us. Slaughter 'em and be done with it, I say. It's no business of ours.'

Father shook his head. 'Third Uncle's son is in danger. What can I do? It will be expensive and tricky to get Cheng-ta off the hook—he's obviously guilty. So we must await developments. Then you can kill them if you like—if they are not to be ransomed.'

Han-fei clumped about moodily. 'I'll have them publicly executed in the marketplace. . . . And what does Grandfather say? It's his brother who's causing all this trouble.'

'I haven't told him yet. Father is too old for such matters. He is to be left in harmonious peace; it is his privilege. Come, it's time for supper, no more of this unpleasantness. And don't spread this matter about, Eldest Son, it is best kept quiet. The barbarians have spies everywhere and they even travel to the remotest provinces disguised as men of religion, I've been told, in order to learn the secrets of our country's greatness. Faugh! What despicable tricks they play.'

'They'll never reach Hunan, never,' Han-fei said confidently. 'They'd be slaughtered to a man if they set foot on our soil.'

'Many Sons of Han have vowed that. But it has not always been so. The barbarians are wily and persuasive and have much power and wealth.'

'You are only repeating what Weng says,' Han-fei muttered jealously. 'Remember rather the words of Mencius, "I have heard of barbarians being converted to the institutions of China, but never of men being converted by barbarians." '

'Power and wealth are strong weapons for conversion nevertheless,' his father retorted sharply. 'And as for Son-in-Law—he uses his brain to better purpose than you do often. . . . Enough, it is time to eat.'

News, which travelled faster than seeds in the wind within the closed circles of Chinese domestic life, moved but sluggishly from one region of the vast Empire to another. Three moons waxed and waned and nothing further was heard of subsequent events in distant Tientsin. During those moons, Alice was later to say, she shed nearly her whole life's supply of tears—pools of them, enough to swim in or drown a dodo, if she had been in Wonderland. But the kitchen courtyard that was their prison produced no wonders and few comforts.

They were fed, but were usually hungry; they were sheltered, but usually chilled; they were given nothing whatever to do. And that, to Alice, seemed very odd, for her childhood till then had been crammed with things to do, to be, to learn. Yet now she was in a world where no one cared whether she knew when Queen Elizabeth lived, her eight times table, the words of the twenty-third psalm—or whether she washed her hair, mended her dress, cleaned her teeth.

The only person to evince the slightest interest in them was

Weng, the 'green-button man' they called him. Sometimes he would come and stare at them curiously without either warmth or distaste. And he would question Alice in slow Mandarin: How big was her country? How was it governed? Why had her family come to China? Alice struggled to reply, but the questions were difficult. Once she tried to explain that the Chinese were heathens and God had sent her father to save their souls. But Wong only barked a curt laugh and went away in disgust.

In the absence of other diversions, the children noted every trivial happening in their immediate surroundings. Each dawn they woke to the sound of cocks crowing and the shouts of the farm-boys belabouring the animals with sticks as they herded them for the morning feed. Then sleepy-eyed kitchen servants came to piss, hawk and pick their teeth in the yard, and throughout the day there was a continuous bustle: the slicing of turnips and cabbages for pickling; the pounding of beans into curd, the stringing of mushrooms and peppers, the preserving of eggs in salt and lime; the cutting up of fowls and fish for drying—all the processes that would keep the large household in food during the coldest season.

For soon it was truly winter. The stunted willow was hung about with the damp straw raincloaks of the bearers and the frayed baskets piled at its base rotted in the wet. Whenever the sun briefly shone, padded quilts were put to dry on bamboo poles and the servants' babies came out to play—and to stare in alarm at the foreign devils, whom they were forbidden to approach. Ice formed on the thatch eaves and the servants, bundled up like rag dolls, skittered across the yard carrying portable stoves filled with glowing embers; cold winds blew the last leaves from the willow and smoke into the cooks' eyes so that they swore with more than usual violence. And after dark the house closed in upon itself and the children were quite alone.

From early waking to final sleeping the focus of their attention was the farm-gate, through which, they daily assured each other, their rescuers must eventually come charging. In her cheerful moments. Alice could imagine the scene vividly: William and Mama to the fore, backed by a regiment of cheering British redcoats, carrying flags and beaming as she flew into Mama's arms. The scene was similar to the brightly painted pictures of the Relief of Lucknow that Uncle Robert from India had shown her when he had visited Tientsin the previous year. Having inspired the original scenario, Robert too became part of it—a handsome, dashing figure, commander in charge of the advancing soldiers—for, as he had been in the Lucknow siege, he was bound to be experienced in rescue operations of the sort required.

And the farm-gate did sometimes open; but only farm-boys came through, carrying eggs, doomed fowls, animal carcasses for the kitchens. One, a gangly lad called Spots on account of his small-pox-marked face, seldom passed without a ribald comment. One morning he advanced and swung a squawking fowl in their faces.

'Look at the barbarian runts!' he shouted. 'Never mind, ducky, they won't get a taste of you! It's the scrapings of the swill-pots for the likes of them!'

Worse than Spots' taunts was the sustained bullying from the cook One-Eye who had first hit Frank. One-Eye had had his other one rubbed out with quicklime as a punishment for pilfering and his face was set in a permanent leer of remembered agony; his queue was greasy and coated with bits of food and his hands, coarse and pudgy for a Chinese, frequently cuffed the devil-children. They hid at the sound of his voice and his misshapen countenance figured prominently in Alice's next-to-worst nightmares; the worst still centring on that dreadful day in Tientsin.

One-Eye was their worst enemy and they had no friend. The nearest was Kau, a hefty girl who beat mats, scrubbed floors, bundled rubbish for the scavengers. She belonged to the Miao tribe of the Far Western provinces and was despised as an 'aboriginal' by all true-born Sons of Han. Her feet were unworthy of being bound, her hands not clean enough to handle food and her body belonged to the household. She was a slave and had been since her birth fourteen years before.

Recently, Kau's mother had died and the girl was now as much an unloved outcast as the barbarian children. She accepted her condition stoically, moving lumpishly about her tasks when the other servants were about. When they were not, she would dart with surprising speed to the barrels of dried fish against the wall and hide some scraps in her sleeves—for the starveling yellowish kitten with no tail that curled on her quilt each night and was her only friend. When Alice first spotted her doing this, Kau put a hand to her mouth in a gesture of secrecy and Alice smiled—establishing an outcasts' bond between them. Soon after, Kau produced two balls of dirty brown sugar for the children and, a few evenings later, a whole handful of delicious nuts.

It was about the same time the following evening that the children again heard steps outside the store-room. 'I hope it's Kau with more nuts,' Frank said with nervous optimism as the door slid open and the slave came in, followed by Han-li and Hung-mei.

The day after the Chu children had first seen Alice and Frank, Father had issued orders that the barbarians were not to be visited or talked about, for it was a matter best kept quiet. Lung-kuang wanted no part of it and whether they were eventually killed or ransomed it would do him no good. He did not share his uncle's brand of hysterical xenophobia, but he did not want to be labelled a Western sympathiser. And things were changing. The present state of the nation was so uncertain under the rule of the incompetent and oppressive Manchus that it was wise to hold one's fire, not to be seen jumping in any direction. Better, therefore, for the troublesome presence of barbarians in his house to be forgotten.

Indeed, the Deputy-Governor himself, often absent on provincial inspection tours, usually did forget, but his family's younger members did not. 'Are the Uncut Jades still there?' they would ask the kitchen servants. 'Do they still cry? Can they speak properly yet?' But despite their curiosity, Father's instructions had been obeyed—until that evening. Kau had been in the act of stealing a few of Han-li's favourite sugar plums from the study-room bowl when Han-li ran in, followed by his sister.

'What are you doing?' he yelled. 'Abo child of a bastard mother—I'll tell the cook about you!'

'No—no please don't, he'll beat me!' she pleaded in the rough mixture of Miao and Hunanese he could hardly understand.

'Beat you, you say. You deserve a good hiding—cursed thief!'

'I wasn't stealing them for myself.'

'Not for you? Who for then?' Mei asked curiously.

'For the barbarians. They're always hungry.'

'Are they?' she looked uneasy. 'Let's be quiet about it, Younger Brother. Don't tell Cook.'

44

He whistled through his teeth. 'All right. They're still in the store-room?'

Kau nodded and Mei shivered. 'It must be awfully cold there now.'

'Do they still look as funny?' Han-li asked.

'I suppose so—funny coloured eyes, green like the grass.'

'Green you say? Blue as our Nanking vase, I thought,' Mei contradicted.

'Pink as pigs,' her brother teased. 'Bright pinky-red eyes like a hare's in the dark, they have.'

'No they don't. Don't be silly.'

'Let's go and peep at the pink-eyed ones,' he challenged. 'Father's away and no one will know. You can take us, Kau, as a punishment for stealing.'

'Let's take a few plums, anyway.' Mei snatched a handful as they went off to the kitchen.

Inside the store-room the five of them looked at each other in silence.

'Their eyes aren't pink—I knew they weren't,' Mei said.

'They're not as big as I thought,' Han-li remarked uncertainly. And indeed their recent hardships had shrunken them and they were wheyfaced. Mei stepped forward. 'Here, take these plums, Uncut Jades.'

'They might be poisoned,' Alice whispered.

'Don't care.' Frank mumbled, his mouth already full of sugary sweetness. Alice stuffed her mouth also.

'They're still greedy,' Han-li jeered.

'Just hungry,' his sister corrected.

'They look as if they might die soon,' Han-li remarked neutrally. 'And Father doesn't want that to happen, so Weng says.'

'He's probably forgotten about them. Shall we tell Weng how poorly they look?'

'But we're not supposed to have seen them. You won't tell on us, will you, Kau?'

'No, I shan't,' she replied spiritedly. 'I feel sorry for them— I'd rather be me than a barbarian. Why don't you slip me a little food for them sometimes? It would be easy for you—who have so much. They could die of starvation because no one noticed.' And it would well suit Kau, the slave-born, to share a secret with the children of the house.

'Good idea.' Mei turned back to Alice and Frank who sat in mute anxiety.

'I wish we could talk to them.' Han-li was exasperated. 'Father won't tell us anything. Where are your parents— father and mother?' he bawled. Alice began to snivel and Han-li sighed. 'Oh she's such a cry-baby. It's no use, they can't understand a proper language. Come along, Younger Sister, I'm supposed to be studying.'

From the door, Mei gave Alice a sweet smile: 'Don't cry. You'll be all right. We'll send you some bits of extra food.'

The Greenwoods spent an uneasy night wondering what new deprivations might result from this unexpected visit, for nothing seemed productive of good anymore. But, to their delight, Kau brought them two dough-cakes in the morning and, in the evening, scraps of meat spooned from some good soup to which the taste still clung, a tantalising reminder of food's deliciousness. Undoubtedly the offerings came from the girl with the kind smile and it was comforting to think that someone in that noisy, uncaring household was concerned for their welfare.

'Let's include her in our prayers tonight,' Alice suggested as they knelt, just before the candle guttered, and prayed—for deliverance from captivity, for the soul of their father and the lives of Mama, William, Uncle Robert and Wo-wo—and, from then on, for the girl with the smile, that she might be rescued from her heathen state. And the efficacy of at least one prayer was apparent, for food-offerings continued to arrive, usually grubby, having been concealed about Kau's person, but just enough to dull the edge of the hunger that had previously gnawed them.

Then, one fine morning, it seemed for a few glorious moments as if their most fervent prayer was to be answered. They were sitting listlessly on the mats as usual, when a most unusual uproar began in the farmyard beyond the gate. Pigs squealed, goats bleated, ducks, hens, and geese squawked; sticks thwacked, wheels creaked, men shouted. The children ran out to look.

'Oh, what do you think is happening? Could it be . . . could it . . .' Alice was starry with hope.

'It must be them . . . it must . . . Mama . . . William . . . we're in here!' Frank rushed to the gate and peered through its chinks. 'I'm going to climb up and see if they're in sight. . . .'

But Alice shook her head, light draining from her eyes. For two servants sitting against the wall slicing vegetables were

46

paying no heed to the noise, which they certainly would had it been caused by the arrival of a regiment of foreign soldiers.

'What's the boy-devil shouting about, I wonder?' asked one. 'Perhaps he thinks he's next for the knife.'

'About time he was—I don't know what the Honourable Head is thinking of, keeping them still, eating our food for nothing,' the other replied.

'Stop, silly,' Alice called. 'Don't climb up, it's nothing to do with us. Look, no one's bothering.'

Frank looked and came leadenly back as one servant honked at him, 'Watch out, barbarian runt, or they'll cut your throat too while they're at it.'

For a while the sounds beyond the gate continued and the children glued their eyes on it, just daring to hope. Then it opened and farm-boys came through, copiously splashed with blood, carrying bundles of dead fowls, carcasses of goats, and pigs.

'So that's all it was,' Frank said in a small voice. 'Killing animals.'

'It must be a special occasion to be having all that meat at one time.'

And certainly something was afoot. The next day glowing piles of oranges, pomegranates, and pomeloes were dumped along the courtyard walls, old women hobbled in with branches of pine, red berries, and bunches of white narcissus. From the house interior came sounds of vigorous sweeping, banging of mats, sluicing of floors. That afternoon three servants staggered into the courtyard with long lacquer boxes from which they took scrolls of red silk, coloured paper lanterns and decorations shaped like birds, lions and dragons. As they shook the dust from them, Alice cried, 'I know what it is—Chinese New Year coming, when they decorate their houses and have feasts, remember?'

'Of course, that's it—so Christmas is over then, and we didn't even know about it.' Frank added forlornly.

'That's right—their New Year is in February, I think.'

'Last Christmas I got that painted horse, Dobbin, do you remember? Father had it made specially for me by the carpenter in Orchid Street. I still had him that day when . . .' His eyes filled with tears and the bright colours of the New Year decorations blurred together.

'Yes—and for me he made that little rocking chair and there

47

was *Alice in Wonderland*, I had it with me when . . .'

'And I got a toy drum and a whistle.'

'And you put your foot through the drum a few days later and Mama was ever so cross.'

Alice dabbed her eyes. 'It's no use crying. Perhaps we'll get some extra food—the kind girl is bound to bring us something special.' She squeezed Frank's shoulders, thinking, as she often did, that being two years older it was her duty to be brave.

Preparations for the festival continued for several days. Strips of red paper were hung from the farm-gate, the eaves and kitchen lintels. Delicious odours wafted from the huge iron pans on the kitchen's plastered brick stoves; above the largest was hung the picture of the Kitchen God and dishes of candied sweetmeats were set before him as offerings for the household's prosperity in the coming year. Mei, her hair specially dressed in a more grown-up fashion, sang as she hobbled about in new embroidered shoes that fitted snugly round her tiny bound feet. Even Kau laughed aloud as she trailed paper streamers across the yard for the kitten to chase.

'Look, he's grinning at you,' Alice said, coming to join in the fun. 'I read a story about a cat who grinned—he was called a Cheshire cat and kept disappearing, leaving just his grin behind.' Kau looked puzzled. Alice grabbed the kitten. 'Has he got a name?'

'Only "cat." '

'Then let's call him Cheshire, please!'

'I don't mind. Call him what you like.'

Alice hugged the docile ball of fur. 'Cheshire, Cheshire—now you've got a lovely name!'

On New Year's Eve there was the customary feast in the large ancestral hall in front of the house to which all relatives of the Chus were invited. Servants dashed about with piles of food, pots of tea, jars of wine; beyond the courtyard walls bells tolled merrily, firecrackers rattled, gongs banged, smells of incense, burned powder, perfumes and boiled crabs hung in the air. After the feast, family and servants gathered in the hall to celebrate the passing of the old year. Only the foreign children remained outside in the store-room, totally forgotten, without food or light.

'I'm ever so hungry.' Frank sniffed forlornly at the appetising smells.

'So am I. I can't think why we haven't got our meal—not even anything.'

'Everyone seems to have gone away. I don't think there's anyone in the kitchen.'

'Let's look,' suggested Alice, goaded by hunger. 'We might find something to eat.' They crept across to the kitchen which for the only time in the year was empty of people. But, oh, the food, succulent, left-over panfuls of it: barbecued pork ribs, fried prawns, livers in soursweet sauces, golden-brown dumplings, bowls of beancurd, morsels of roast ducks and geese, persimmons, preserved peaches, raisins, spiced almonds. For a moment they stood round-eyed, then fell to recklessly, cramming their mouths.

'We should take some away instead of eating it here,' Alice mumbled.

'Yerp . . .' Frank was munching busily.

Suddenly they heard steps along the passage. 'Run, quick!' Alice gasped. But it was too late—One-Eye lurched into view and, though reeling from a quantity of New Year wine, saw them at once.

'Barbarian scum! Filthy beasts—stealing our food, were you! I'll get you for this—you leavings from the piss-pots, you see if I don't!' He grabbed a meat cleaver from the wall and made to bring it down with full force on Frank's head. The boy ducked under his arm and went flying up the passage, screaming wildly. Alice tried to dodge too as One-Eye raised the cleaver again and smashed it towards her face. She twisted away, but the blade caught her as it fell and blood gushed from a deep nick in her cheek. As he made to grab her, he slipped on the greasy floor. Alice fled up the passage, holding her cheek and screaming in her turn.

'Whatever's that noise?' whispered the head cook irritably. He was standing just inside the great hall with the other male servants, holding a cup of wine and a piece of preserved ginger. The world was warm and lovely, lights from the red and yellow lanterns on the beams danced merrily and there was the continuous rustle of silk gowns as people, flushed and smiling, bowed to each other in formal greeting—for another year had just been ushered in.

The cook went into the passage to investigate and Alice ran sobbing into his arms, her face covered with blood. She closed her eyes, half-fainting from pain and terror as he carried her

49

over to the women's group in the far corner of the hall. There was a buzz of voices, red lights bobbed blurrily above her, then the faces of the kind girl and the woman who had first visited her. Someone tied a piece of dirty rag spread with black paste over the wound and gave her a cup of tea, which she sipped gratefully.

'How did it happen, Eldest Sister?' asked Mei quietly.

'The cook says old One-Eye found them in the kitchen stealing food and went for them with a cleaver. He was drunk, I suppose.'

'Poor things, I quite forgot—I mean, I suppose no one remembered to feed them tonight?'

By this time the gathering was about to disperse, for another day of pleasure lay ahead. 'Where's the boy?' asked Tamao. 'They'd better go back to the store-room.' They found Frank outside, weak and trembling, for he'd been violently sick and lost the best meal he had had for many a day.

'Oh, they can't go back there tonight, Eldest Sister—it's so cold and she's still bleeding and they're both ill!' Mei pleaded. 'After all, it is the New Year.'

Tamao smiled, affected by the general bonhomie. 'Oh all right, as long as Father doesn't know—let them sleep inside.'

She issued instructions to the chief cook who was also in genial mood, having received much praise that evening for the excellence of his culinary endeavours. Not unkindly, he took the two barbarians and led them off, putting Frank above the stables with the farm-boys and Alice in the attic with the junior domestics. And so it was that New Year's Eve 1871, when the Year of the Tiger came in, was the first of many nights that the Greenwoods spent actually inside the residence of Deputy-Governor Chu.

2

As the sun rose reluctantly on that New Year's Day, Deputy-Governor Lung-kuang reached for the soft thigh of Red Jasmine and stroked it languidly. It was a dalliance he seldom indulged in at that hour when so many official duties awaited attention, but today there was time before the rituals of feasting began. Red Jasmine responded eagerly for she had sensed a waning of his ardour since the recent birth of her daughter. She began to touch him knowingly and he relaxed. The fumes of last night's wine clogged any urgent desire, but he drew her nearer nevertheless.

Steps thudded along the passages and a humble voice piped outside, 'Please excuse this interruption at such an hour, my lord, but the matter is of vital importance, I'm told.' Lung-kuang merely growled. 'A letter has just come from Tientsin. It's been long delayed en route, but its contents are most urgent apparently. The messenger insisted I inform you at once.'

'Am I to have no peace, no enjoyment in this life? How dare you disturb me so early on this first day of the year when even the lowliest skivvy in my house is still a-bed?'

'Pay no attention,' Red Jasmine whispered hopefully.

But his small desire had evaporated; he lay scowling at the bed-curtains.

'Tientsin—must be that scatty old pepper Lung-pao. Blast his eye-balls! But he's Third Uncle. Bring the letter here!'

Red Jasmine sighed and drew the padded red coverlet round her whilst Lung-kuang called for tea. He snatched the letter-roll from the servant, who waited while he read. He looked up.

'Tell my secretary to come at once, I must write a reply. And root out those barbarian whelps, they are to be sent back.'

Red Jasmine handed him tea. 'That letter has taken a whole

51

moon longer than it should to reach me,' he grumbled sourly. 'And now it's probably too late to be of use.' She nodded uncomprehendingly, for he did not discuss such matters with her. 'And I'll never find out why—the Empire is falling apart, so much slovenliness, broken bridges, roads like quagmires, people failing in their duties. Why should I alone keep to the right way?'

She clucked sympathetically. 'You need to take more time for pleasure and recreation indeed, my lord. It is invigorating for body and spirit.'

'Ah yes, and when I try you see what happens, even on this most auspicious day? That damned old fool, Third Uncle.' He stared moodily into his cup.

There was another knock and Weng came in, bowing apologetically. 'Please forgive my intrusion, honourable, but I've just heard about the letter from Tientsin and your order concerning barbarians.'

'Well, I'll explain later, it really is intolerable, on this of all days.'

'Indeed yes, but someone has to tell you that the female barbarian has been injured and is now in high fever.' Hesitantly Weng explained what had occurred the previous evening, concluding, 'But the male is well enough, shall we just send him, or risk the female dying on the way, or delay a few days, or . . .?'

'Or, or . . .' Lung-kuang groaned. 'Even today I have to make decisions. Here, read this—what do you think? Lung-pao says the authorities intend executing his son for his part in that ridiculous Tientsin disturbance and the only hope is to bargain his life for the foreign whelps. But see the date—that letter has taken a thousand and one moons to get here and by my reckoning it's too late to prevent the execution. But I shall be rid of them at least—only if it's not too late and the she-bitch dies on the way . . . only the girl though . . .' He paced up and down.

'The barbarians value their females quite highly,' Weng reminded him carefully.

Lung-kuang turned, 'Show me this Uncut Sliver—is she bleeding to death? Why do I have drunken cooks in my kitchen, tell me that?'

Soothingly Red Jasmine draped a fur robe over his shoulders and he and his son-in-law went to the attic over the

52

kitchens where the underservants slept. Alice lay on a string bed with Kau beside her and looked up with unnaturally glittering eyes as the men approached. A wad of dirty blood-stained cloth was clamped over her wounded cheek, the other was hectically flushed.

Lung-kuang stared down. 'Fever, yes—the wound going bad, I suppose?'

Weng nodded. 'Perhaps I should get the doctor?'

'A doctor—to heal a gobbet of barbarian flesh!'

'But if it is to be redeemed for your cousin . . .'

Lung-kuang shrugged irritably. 'Is she hurt anywhere else, I wonder?' He pulled off the moth-eaten quilt, raised her night-gown and gazed at her hot, damp flesh. 'Looks whole enough.' He felt her stomach and between her thighs.

'Has she seen the red snows yet?' he asked Kau.

'I don't think so, my lord.'

'Presumably female barbarians have the same visitations?'

Weng was nonplussed. 'Physically I think they function in the same fashion, yes.'

Alice smiled loosely at Lung-kuang, for his hands felt cool and soothing. Through the pitiless throbbing of her head she tried to remember who he was.

'Strange eyes—like a cat's.'

Weng grimaced. 'Doesn't appeal to me.'

'Ah, but you are yet young, with many chambers still unexplored. However,' he threw the quilt back over her, 'you'd better get the doctor. Ask him her chances for surviving a long winter journey. I've decided they can't go for two days anyway—it would cost a fortune to hire drivers and carts during the Festival.'

As he made to leave, Alice grabbed his hand, placed it on her aching forehead. 'Are you the doctor? Please tell Mama I'm ill and ask her for tincture of iodine. It's for cuts and it's in the blue bottle in the washroom. . . .'

He disengaged her hand gently. 'What an unattractive gibberish they speak. Still, get the doctor—and tell him I won't pay twice his usual fee. All this is not a very auspicious beginning for the New Year, I fear.'

For Alice the year certainly began inauspiciously. The doctor came, scraped off the black paste and put on some yellow, felt under her armpits, pronounced she would certainly die within two days unless she took quantities of his infallible medicine made of powdered hartshorn, rhubarb root, and dried pigs' testicles. He would return on the morrow, he added gravely, realising the pecuniary advantages of a New Year visit.

Through her delirium Alice heard the distant crackle of firecrackers that sounded horribly like flames; then Mama was bending over her with a blue bottle; then it was Papa, his eyes very sad and faraway; then it was the real Frank, gripping her hand anxiously. The next day the doctor returned and pronounced that, thanks to his powerful mix, she had as much chance as any other fever-ridden patient of surviving a long journey.

As he rose to leave, his bearer lifting his medicine box, Han-fei rushed into the attic shouting, 'Doctor—thank the gods you're still here. Come quickly, it's Honourable Old, the Reverend Grandfather, he's fallen senseless in the courtyard. Summon all your skills at once. . . .'

After a while, Frank, still crouched by his sister, realised that the racket of New Year revelry had ceased. Han-li and his cousins who had been flying kites in the paddock were told to fold them away and the many visitors who had called with long red cards of felicitations went home early. The servants returned to the attic, sullen and sober; as each candle guttered it was not renewed and a hush of fear descended on everyone. For already the year had begun with the violent spilling of blood, and if now the ancient head of the house should die before the year was set truly on its course, then the portents were ominous indeed. 'May the gods give him strength just to live through two more dawns,' they whispered to each other.

Lung-kuang, bowing his head in the ancestral hall where the red festive banners still hung, echoed their prayers. If his reverend father should resign his last dignity now, then the demons were truly in ascendancy. He raised his eyes to the proud row of wooden tablets placed upright before him, each carved with the names and dates of birth and death of his illustrious ancestors. The family had long been respectable. Many of its members had laboured diligently to maintain tranquillity in this remote province; only a few years before, two had fallen honourably, fighting the cursed Taipings. They had obeyed the laws, had not ground the noses of the poor further into the mire; he himself had remained close to his

54

ancestral tree and, banyan-like, taken root in its shade; he had never knowingly behaved unfilially towards his reverend father. Why then should the soul of the most elderly be threatening to depart at this inauspicious moment? But, yeh, yeh, old age is like a candle in the wind, easily blown out.

As the incense sticks spluttered in the gathering dusk, his wife and eldest son joined his vigil, their faces equally anxious. No one spoke. But, beyond the gates, the sounds of revelry went on unabated, making the nearer silence heavier. In the hour before midnight a cock crowed loudly from the farmyard and they all quivered, for such a sound at such an hour was a sure sign of approaching death.

Shortly after, at the very beginning of the festival's last day, Lung-kuang was summoned that his presence might facilitate the passing of the spirit from his father's body. White-robed priests from the city's largest temple came to chant prayers for the soul's safe deliverance and in the chill dawn the voices of the household's womenfolk were raised in lament. Lung-kuang and Han-fei went into the main courtyard where they threw coins in the well and returned with bowls of water with which to wash the corpse.

'Frank, is that you?' Alice whispered to the huddled shape beside her. 'I've had so many frightening dreams.'

He smiled sleepily. 'Oh thank goodness, Alice, you're better—you're talking sense again. You had such a fever from that dreadful cut.'

'Did I?' She felt the bandage gingerly. 'It still hurts. But where are we?'

'In the servants' attic. They brought you here. But now Kau says someone important in the house has died. Can you hear the praying?'

They listened to the distant wails of mourning that flowed in sad waves along the dim passageways. Alice shivered, 'It's ghostly. A sort of heathen chant I suppose. Oh Frank, I'm so tired.' And, burying her head to hide the melancholy sound, she fell into a heavy, dreamless slumber.

The lamentations continued until noon when a few relatives arrived, still flushed and flatulent with rich festal fare. They were shown into the ancestral hall already hung with while funereal lanterns to replace the red, its floor strewn with the ashes of wads of paper money that had been burned in reverence. There, Grandfather's cleansed body, a piece of

55

silver under its tongue, was laid inside a coffin made of valuable wood brought from Szechuan for this occasion several years ago. Workmen arrived to seal and varnish it carefully and place it before the ancestral tablets until burial day. Only after this was satisfactorily completed did the weary Lung-kuang and his wife rise stiffly from their knees and withdraw.

Lung-kuang ate supper alone in his apartment, the rich viands cloying tastelessly in his mouth as he remembered the harmless foibles of his father's later years. At the end of every summer Father and four servants used to carry all his caged birds into the hills beyond the city so that they should see the colours of autumn and gain strength to sing throughout the winter, as Father put it. The cages were hung in the trees and Father would stroll about and drink a little wine while the birds sang.

It was near those same hills, Lung-kuang suddenly recalled, that the whole family once went for the Festival of Field-Ploughing. He was a mere lad at the time, and Father, being chief magistrate, was required to break the first clod ceremoniously. The weather had been spring-like, and the people picnicking on the slopes and watching the ceremony had laughed a little at Father, who, encumbered with his stiff, official robes, had struggled ineptly with the recalcitrant plough. But the laughter was good-natured and Father had borne it in good part, for he was a kindly man.

'Yeh, yeh,' Lung-kuang sighed aloud, for that was many moons ago, and now the man was dead. Poor Father, better to be a turtle wagging your tail in the mud than to be dead. But perhaps his soul was now a bird in Paradise, flying free, and Lung-kuang began to wonder what should be done with all those beautiful birds of his—the pairs of silver and gold pheasants, the chirpy grey and yellow thrushes and the songster larks, the 'Hundred Spirit Birds,' Father had called them. And the lovely wicker cages, porcelain feeding-bowls, ivory wands shaped like branches for them to sit on. Then he shook himself impatiently; these were mere trivialities. He had to think of his new position as undisputed head of the house and of arrangements for the funeral.

Distant relatives must be summoned from afar and firstly, of course, Father's only remaining brother, Third Uncle. Lung-kuang swore loudly as he then remembered the previous day's news from Tientsin. What to do now? He would have to send news of his father's death along with the barbarian whelps. He long afterwards remembered that he was actually cursing his firebrand uncle and equally hot-headed cousin when the knock came on the door.

'Another messenger has come with great speed from Tientsin, sir.' The servant handed him a scroll with an unfamiliar seal and Lung-kuang's fingers shook as he broke it open. His forebodings were well-founded. He was informed that his nephew had been executed as an instigator of the murders of foreign god-preachers the previous summer and his head exposed to public view. Worse yet—Third Uncle, utterly crushed by this final humiliation, had retired to his summer residence and drunk the official poison cup two days later.

Lung-kuang groaned and staggered to a chair, his knees buckling. The demise of his reverend father, news of his uncle's and cousin's death all in the first three days of the Year of the Tiger before it was properly set upon its course. This indeed was beyond all reason. In some unknown way he had deeply offended the gods and clearly the coming year must be one of mourning and austerity. He sat for a long while, hands folded inside his sleeves. Tomorrow he would call in the soothsayers to advise him on the form of his public piety. Personally his course was plain and, as he was in his middle years and overwrought with the cares of office, not entirely unpleasant.

The following day, after news of the fresh disasters had been broken to the family, he formally outlined his intentions to Han-fei and Weng.

'I intend to hand in my seals of office for the rest of this year,' he announced to their bowed heads. 'Immediately after the ancient's burial I shall retire to the rural residence at Hang-hsien. It is plain that we have offended, that we must walk quietly and carefully through all the days of the Tiger. Eldest Son, your marriage must be postponed until next year, which I pray will be more auspicious. In my absence you will manage any urgent affairs. Eldest Daughter will order the household. It will give you time to stabilise yourself, for you have yet to learn the exercise of the three universal moral qualities—wisdom, compassion, and courage. There is to be no commotion, no trouble going forth in any direction. Is that understood?'

Han-fei nodded stonily, though the news of the marriage postponement delighted him. He had never set eyes on his future bride, but he had heard that she was a specially 'Dull Thorn' whose only lustre came from being the eldest daughter of a wealthy land-owner in the province. 'Yes, Father, there'll be no violence, even in sport. And I'll endeavour to pass Grade Two of the military exercise.'

'And not only those—remember what I've often told you, "the silkworm spins silk, the bee gathers honey"; if men neglect their book-learning they are inferior to brutes.'

Weng smiled. 'And you can rely on me to preserve harmony in the house, Father-in-law, as is fitting. But may I ask, what is to be done with the young barbarians? Presumably they are of no further use as hostages?'

Han-fei growled. 'I'll have them quietly disposed of.'

His father was sharp. 'No. I've just said, no more violence. The infant year is already sufficiently blood-stained. Let them loose, I suppose, to find their way back to their own people.'

'The difficulty is,' Weng began softly, 'that if they did manage to get back, they'd tell the barbarian authorities how we held them prisoner. It might lead to new trouble.'

'Well, what do you propose then?' Lung-kuang knew that Weng's specially courteous patience foreshadowed some plan.

'Might they remain here? At least until they've been completely forgotten by the outside? Eventually I'm sure I can learn some useful "barbarian matters" from them, and they could earn their keep meanwhile. The boy is strong and the girl seems to know more because she's older—and growing up fast.' He glanced meaningfully at Lung-kuang who nodded dismissively.

'All right, do as you think best. Put them both to menial work and don't bother me about them.'

The sun glinted on the golden flanks of the carp as they occasionally rose to the surface of the circular pond in the women's courtyard. The little splashing swirls of their movements, the cooing of doves on the tiled roof and the scrape of Alice's broom on the flagstones were the only sounds to break the quiet of the long, still summer afternoon. Alice had been sweeping those same flagstones every day for months.

In early spring, when she had first begun, she had listened

58

to the windbells tinkling wildly in the fresh winds and watched the arrival of the swallows that nested in the eaves of the verandah where the bells were hung. Soon the gardeners filled the glazed porcelain vases that stood on tripods along the paved walks with peonies, marigolds and tiger lilies. Alice cleaned the vases regularly, especially the one patterned with pink and lavender tracery of petals, clouds, and dragonflies. It bore an inscription which, Hung-mei told her, meant 'The flower opens. Lo! Another year.' Alice liked that. When the early summer rains came, she often stood in the shelter of the servants' verandah watching the drops plop and splatter on the flat leaves of the lotuses in the pond or nestle into the spotted throats of orchids hung in baskets near the windbells. Now the rain had ceased and the mid-summer heats begun, but otherwise all went on in the same quiet fashion.

Because of the household's state of continued mourning, the usual seasonal festivals were scarcely observed, few visitors came and the occupants seldom left. Only Han-fei, chafing at the bit of too much serenity, often went hunting in the western mountains with a group of vigorous young bloods. He cared little for his father's untended duties and it was Weng who managed things with mild circumspection. The even tenor of his rule had only recently been disturbed by the outrageous behavior of one of Han-fei's cronies who, after an evening of drinking in the house, had formed the habit of sneaking along to Red Jasmine's apartment for more intimate revels. The inadvertent discovery of this irregular union had roused Weng to unusual fury. Han-fei prudently denied all knowledge of it, but the young man was forbidden to enter the house again, and, after consultation with the absent Lung-kuang, Red Jasmine was sent packing to her parents' village with her baby.

The woman's distressed wails of departure had destroyed the peace of the previous afternoon and Eldest Daughter Tamao was thinking of them as she came down the verandah steps into the courtyard. She was attended by servants carrying her first-born son, a bamboo chair and books, and she balanced with more than usual care on her maid's arm, for her new pregnancy had recently been confirmed. Looking very warm and ripe in her embroidered robe, she sank under the shade of a magnolia tree with a contented sigh and began to wonder idly about the fate of Red Jasmine's baby in these unfortunate circumstances. And who, she also wondered, would Father choose instead? She hoped it would be a young and tractable girl, for unofficial wives could cause a lot of dissension if they got above themselves, as Red Jasmine had.

Languidly she took up her favourite volume of the Book of Songs and read again Wu-ti's charming ditty:

At the time when blossoms fall from the cherry tree,
On a day when orioles flitted from bough to bough,
You said you must stop because your horse was tired,
I said I must go, because my slkworms were hungry.

Tamao smiled and looked up, aware that Alice's sweeping had stopped. The little barbarian had dropped her broom and was bending over the pond. She reached far out over the water's surface, then stood up and raised her arm. From her opened palm a purple and crimson butterfly flew, cavorted against the blue sky for a moment, flicking moisture from its wings, then sailed away, higher and higher over the roof tiles towards the distant hills. Alice watched it go and, with a sigh, bent to pick up her broom.

Tamao called softly. 'Come here, Uncut Jade.'

Alice came shyly. She was clad in the faded cotton tunic and baggy trousers, the bound-cloth shoes of the servant class. Her hair, plastered with crude gum, was covered by a grubby kerchief; her tanned, roughened face and hands were not clean.

'Why did you rescue that butterfly?'

'It had settled on a lotus leaf and might have drowned. Was it wrong then?'

'On the contrary—your good deed for the day. We believe that departed spirits sometimes inhabit butterflies just after they die—so we try to take care of them. Li-po has a poem about it somewhere . . . I'll see.'

As she looked through one book, Alice picked up another. 'Oh, I wish I could read this. I can speak and understand most things now but I can't read a word.' She looked appealing. 'You're teaching Younger Sister to read and write. I suppose you wouldn't—couldn't—?'

'You? But that would be most irregular.'

Just then Mei came out with a servant carrying her ink and brushes for the afternoon's study. 'Uncut Jade wants to learn

60

to read and write too,' Tamao greeted her.

She clapped her hands gleefully. 'Oh please let her, Eldest Sister, she'll be even more stupid than I—and I shan't be the dunce anymore. See, look,' she grabbed a brush, 'that's jade—yu. Half your name's that character. You didn't know that, little barbarian?'

'No, but I do now,' Alice replied grimly. 'And I'll soon learn more, if you'll let me.'

'But you must keep up with your other work, or the other servants will grumble and there'll be discord,' Tamao warned.

'I will, I promise. You see, before I came here, I had to learn all the time—but now there's nothing much to think about. It doesn't seem right somehow.'

'I taught you how to embroider my tunics,' Mei said.

'But I'm not as good as you at it.'

'Well, you won't be as good at this either.' She grabbed her writing-brush defensively and Tamao smiled, realising that some competition would be good for her light-minded sister.

'All right, show her some easy characters, Mei, it's good practice for you. But it must stop when Vegetable Aunt comes back with Father and Mother. She thinks educating a girl at all is like sowing corn in another man's field—as for educating a barbarian girl—well . . .'

For Alice it meant that the days took on a shape beyond the diurnal routine of sweeping, polishing, scrubbing, with nothing to look forward to except the evening meal and the hours of oblivion in the attic with the other domestics. There were so many houseservants that Alice was not overworked and was too small for the nastiest chores like collecting the rubbish bins and swilling the chamber pots that fell to the lot of strong-limbed Kau. But there was not much fun in it and before the reading lessons began Alice used often to stand at the inner gate wondering whether to make a bolt for it. But where to? How could she possibly survive as a penniless, friendless barbarian in a city of generally hostile people? So she waited, comforting herself with memories of the moral tales she had heard of young girls who lived in bondage and were eventually released to wider horizons. It seemed a fairly common female fate and one day she and Frank would be fully grown-up and would run away together.

She saw little of her brother, for he worked in the farmyard beyond the outer gate, mucking out the pigs, swilling the stables, chopping corn stalks and churning bran for animal food. His clothes were always filthy and he stank of manure, but he was reasonably happy—especially in the evenings when he and the other lads were let loose in the paddock to kick about balls made of blown-up pigs' bladders. He had become friendly with 'Spots,' the duck boy, and sometimes he would sneak Alice a fresh egg or some wild raspberries picked in the boundary thicket.

'I'm learning to read and write Chinese,' she told him smugly at their next encounter. 'I'm starting with the Three Character Classic.'

'Are you? Whatever for? Here.' He popped a berry in her mouth. 'You can speak better than I can now.'

'But writing's different.'

'Too much like school for me!'

'Father always said you were lazy.'

'I'm not. I just like learning different things. Younger Brother's teaching me to throw the javelin and now I'm better than he is.'

'And I'm much cleverer than Younger Sister,' she snorted, 'but they still call us stupid barbarians because we're British and I suppose they always will.'

Frank rubbed his dirty nose. 'Do you remember, Uncle Robert used to say the British are the strongest country in the world?'

'Yes. But it's hard to believe, the way they despise us here.'

'Oh well, it could be worse, at least I don't have to learn Latin and stuff.'

'You would think that! Give me another berry and I must go, or they'll say I don't work hard enough and the lessons will stop.'

But Alice saw to it that they did not. She always finished her chores in time for the afternoon study and, in the precious leisure hour after supper, when the day-long click of the weaving looms and the stirring of the cooking pots eventually ceased, she squatted in a corner of the kitchen courtyard practising the characters. Apart from an occasional cuff from One-Eye the cook, no one paid her much heed anymore, but her round eyes, unbound feet and stumbling speech all doomed her to remain, like Kau, a permanent outcast. Outnumbered, the two of them presented a united front, sleeping beside each other in the draughtiest corner of the attic, guarding each other's small possessions, managing, between them, to keep scraggy Cheshire fed. Lulled into a sense of timelessness by the monotony of these days, Alice was vaguely alarmed one morning to hear the servants discussing preparations for the imminent return of the house's head, who was planning to resume his official duties and then celebrate the passing of the bad old year and the coming of a more propitious one.

'And to start the Year of the Rabbit really well I must produce another healthy boy,' Tamao remarked as she, Mei and Alice sat together in her room that afternoon. 'So I shan't be doing any more teaching for a while.'

'Because of him inside you?' Alice asked tentatively. She had heard mutterings to that effect when one of the servants had recently given birth.

'Of course, of course, haven't you noticed her swollen belly, you silly Sliver of Uncut?' Mei roared with laughter. 'Here— look!' She untied the sashes of her sister's voluminous gown. 'See—in about a moon it will pop out between her legs and it hurts ever so much, doesn't it, Eldest Sister? You screamed and screamed last time. Feel it.' She placed Alice's hand on the hard mound covered by a white undergarment.

'Do you mind it hurting so?' Alice asked fearfully.

'Oh no. It's not for very long and you soon forget because the baby is so beautiful.' Tamao spooned tranquilly at some rose-jelly specially made for the pregnant.

Mei giggled. 'Perhaps barbarian babies pop out from somewhere else, do you think?'

Alice sniffed. 'My Mama told me years ago that people found them under gooseberry bushes, but I guessed that was a fairy story.'

Mei cackled. 'Gooseberry bushes, heh, heh. I'd like to see a man sticking his thing into a gooseberry bush!'

'What do you mean?' Alice felt uncomfortable.

'With his Stalk—why, you look as puzzled as a pig in the weeds! You mean you don't know about *that*?'

Tamao took pity on her. 'Well, Uncut, the man pokes it up the woman's hole—which we have between our legs—and he leaves a seed there which grows into a baby inside your belly, see?'

'Yes, sort of.' Though, having seen the boys' stalks when

they were urinating or washing, she thought it would be a rather difficult manoeuvre. 'Is it nice?' she asked Tamao.

'Being poked? Sometimes it's lovely—if you like your husband and he's kind, like mine.'

Alice's cheeks burned, for what she heard gave her shivery thrills of delighted recognition.

'It will happen to you one day, then you'll see how it feels and you'll have babies.'

'I wonder what they'll look like?' Mei broke in. 'Will they have funny eyes and mud-coloured hair, like Uncut?'

'I suppose that partly depends on the man who takes her.' Tamao hauled herself upright. 'I must get ready for supper. You two can help each other with the characters if you like, but not a word to Vegetable Aunt. She's returning with Father and Mother.'

That night Alice lay sleepless, restless, and tense. The last candle guttered out. Rats began their nightly scamperings among the smoke-blackened roof-beams, and the warm fug created by the charcoal stove and the steaming supper bowls evaporated into dark, harsh cold. On the other side of the partition separating the younger domestics from the older, she heard vague movements. She had often heard them before, but tonight they took on a positive, purposeful rhythm which made her even more restless. What could be going on? She crept across and peeped round the partition. Several servants were asleep in the room, but one candle still burned and in its light Alice saw One-Eye straddled over the half-clad body of a woman, she lying spread open and he thrusting vigorously into her. He had a twisted smile on his face that she had never seen before and his one eye looked quite jolly. As Alice watched, a fist crammed into her mouth to keep herself quiet, the movements increased, the two bodies jerked closer together, came a spasm, a gasp, then silence. Alice crept back to bed. Her whole body tingled as she imagined a man of One-Eye's size but much nicer thrusting deep inside the warm damp place between her legs.

The fertile seed which in early summer Weng had implanted inside Tamao was a good one. For the bunches of camellias were still in bloom on the New Year festal tables, the piled bowls of persimmons, oranges, and loquats not quite consumed when the midwife was summoned. The birth was easy. It was another boy, and Lung-kuang's face glowed with relief. Now the gods were surely appeased and his policy of quietly withdrawing and waiting for the ill winds to pass elsewhere had undoubtedly paid dividends. The proof was his second grandson, healthy and crinkle-skinned with beamy eyes. Baskets of red-dyed eggs arrived in salutation of his masculinity. He was patted, petted, passed from hand to hand. His 'milk name,' bestowed a month after his birth, was Custard Apple. Now, Lung-kuang decided, it was safe to arrange the delayed marriage of his eldest son; the appropriate horoscopes were consulted, the go-betweens selected and a date in early April was agreed.

'Have you seen the beautiful presents that are going to the bride's house tomorrow?' Mei asked Alice a few weeks later. Since Custard Apple's birth, Tamao had been too preoccupied to teach them. But in the afternoons when the vigilant Vegetable Aunt retired to rest, Alice practised her calligraphy in Mei's room, while Mei embroidered the colourful robe she would wear at her brother's wedding.

'Come and see.' Mei led Alice into an adjoining room where a huge camphor-wood trunk stood open on the floor. It was piled high with silks the colour of peaches, lilacs, roses, and emeralds, and capes lined with the furs of snow leopards and golden monkeys; there were bundles of hairpins shaped like butterflies and peacocks; agate, pearl, and pink crystal earrings, jade and turquoise beads nestling in sandalwood boxes; embroidered and sequinned three-inch-long shoes; a creamy satin robe patterned with chrysanthemums and tiger lilies.

'All that—for her?' Alice touched the satin gingerly with her work-roughened hands.

'It's the custom.'

'Why is she called Dull Thorn, it's such an odd name?'

'Oh, her real name is Unimpeachable Splendour—but people say Dull Thorn suits her better. She's wealthy but stupid, you see. Why, they say she can't even make good pickles!'

'And is that necessary?'

'But all well-born daughters should. My pickles are delicious.'

Alice smiled, looking again at the trunk. 'And will you get presents in return?'

'Oh yes, lots. When she comes to live here she must bring furniture and utensils, bed-hangings and quilts, spices, oils

65

and meats. And when Eldest Brother takes these things to her house, he'll be given a huge feast.'

'It sounds such fun.' Alice felt suddenly resentful. How awful it was to be a menial on the outside of everything, eating the scraggiest offal, drinking the sifted leavings of the tea, stroking other people's fine satins. She remembered a scene from an early story book of a London street with two ragged urchins pressing their noses against a shop window. It was bulging with jars of coloured bonbons and a fur-clad lady inside was buying huge boxes of chocolates. The unfairness of it had stuck in her throat then; now it was much worse, for she felt as ill done by as those beggar children.

'I suppose Dull Thorn will be overjoyed at all these presents?'

'Oh no—she'll weep and wail and beg her parents not to make her leave home. That's the custom.'

'The bride isn't supposed to be happy?'

'Oh no—and she'll hate her wedding day because the men guests will all laugh and jeer at her—that's the custom too.'

'And Eldest Brother, what does he think?'

'He never mentions it—it's his duty to marry her, that's all. Knowing him, I'm sure he'll enjoy all the eating and drinking.'

'And it's the custom for her to live here? So one day when you marry you'll have to go and live with strangers?'

'Yes,' Mei sighed. 'And I shan't like it at first. But I've been betrothed for a long time and I'll probably be married in a year or two.'

'You—married!' Alice was horrified.

'I'm almost fifteen and it's time for me to be a wife soon and have babies.'

Alice picked an ivory comb from the trunk and ran her nail down its teeth. 'I'm glad I'm not Dull Thorn after all. It doesn't sound a happy prospect, in spite of this finery.'

'Oh she'll get used to it, we women have to, and our family doesn't treat daughters-in-law as badly as some.'

Alice shuddered. 'I'm going—it's all too much, Younger Sister. I'll see you tomorrow.' She fled away down the passage, in a nameless panic, filled with desperate longing for one of her own kind. Hurrying along the verandah she noticed that the east gate leading to the park was open, and she slipped through, revelling in the full extent of a view which, till then, she had only glimpsed. In the foreground was the paddock, edged with lean-to huts full of sporting equipment; archery butts were spaced at intervals across it. Beyond lay the fine sweep of the park—spotted deer were grazing on the hillocks and the grounds were dotted with small lakes and pavilions sometimes used as tea-houses. The whole was enclosed within a high peak-tiled wall that snaked away over a wooded hill in the distance. Alice's eyes widened, unaccustomed to so much space. She had forgotten how large the world was, how distanced she was from anything truly familiar. She was about to retreat, almost afraid, when a figure appeared from the stables carrying swill. 'Frank—it's you, isn't it? Come here.'

He came towards her; his hair was drawn back in a stubby queue, she noticed, but its dirty-straw colour was still outlandish. 'Hello, Uncut Jade, is anything wrong?'

'No . . . well, it's just that we talk so seldom now. You don't enjoy working in the stables like this, do you?'

'It's all right. They don't beat me or call me so many dirty names these days. What about you?'

'Oh—I sweep and clean.' They looked at each other awkwardly.

'You look just like a servant,' Frank grinned.

'And you like a farm-boy.'

'Well I am, I suppose.'

'You're not, you're Frank Greenwood, son of a missionary, and don't you forget! Frank, we don't talk of people coming to rescue us anymore, or even of escaping—but we could, they don't watch us carefully now.'

'Well no one is ever coming for us, so what's the point? And where would we escape to?'

'I don't know. Only, sometimes it seems so very foreign here. And I think how horrified Mama would be if she saw us now.'

He snorted. 'We've been forgotten—so we might as well make the best of it here. Eldest Son's getting married soon, did you know? We've reared some special geese—fat as barrels they are. I'm looking forward to it—Spots says there'll be piles of good grub around.'

The day of the wedding dawned grey and chill. This was not particularly propitious, nor was the fact that, owing to exceptionally strong spring gales, no shred of peach blossom remained to adorn the reception hall. But it looked resplendent anyway, hung with red lanterns and banners inscribed with good wishes for the harmonious union, immeasurable prosperity and felicitous fruitfulness of the bridal pair. Crowded in a corner of the main courtyard with the other servants that afternoon, Alice thrilled to the shrill blast of pipes, the beat of gong and drum, the snap of firecrackers that heralded the bride's arrival.

The main gate was flung open and a long procession came pouring through. In front were the banner-bearers and men armed with staves and truncheons, to keep the rabble at bay, then the musicians and grey-robed acolytes from the Temple of the Heavenly Clouds on the hill. Other bearers followed carrying caged mandarin ducks and drakes to symbolise conjugal felicity and lacquer boxes full of the bride's gifts. Bearers of more exalted rank with glittering conical hats carried sedans containing Dull Thorn's relatives and attendants and behind came eight strong men bowed under huge stone tablets inscribed with the generational names of bride and groom. Then a forest of red silk umbrellas appeared, their tassels joggling in the breeze, and in the midst of them a closed sedan chair, decorated in vermilion and gold, borne aloft by four men.

'Look—she's inside there!' Kau pushed Alice forward excitedly as the chair was set down before the door of the reception hall. Tamao, her eyes cast down, stepped forward and opened the chair, formally bidding the bride to set foot in her new home. A small female shape emerged. She was clad in a mantle of crimson brocade with a stiff embroidered skirt below. Around her neck hung long strings of pearls, on her head was a high jewelled tiara. From its front hung a veil of golden beads so thick that her face was completely hidden. She stood there for a moment, a faceless, doll-like figure shivering slightly with apprehension, and Alice's heart went out to her.

Poor Dull Thorn! How dreadful to be brought here like this and be linked to uncaring, irascible Han-fei and to have to let him do the things that men do to women, to have to live in uncomplaining subjection within this alien household for the rest of her days.

Two servants approached, carefully lifted the stiff, red figure up two red-carpeted steps and over the pan of charcoal that was burning on the hall's threshold to prevent the ingress of any evil influence. Inside the hall, Lung-kuang and his family were waiting to receive her.

'How long will she have to wear that veil over her?' Alice asked Kau as the servants dispersed to their duties.

'The groom goes to her chamber and lifts it up later—it's the first time he sees her closely. And she's not allowed to wear any paint on this day, so he'll see her plain enough.' Kau chuckled. 'And it'll be quite a shock for him, so I've heard. Then they'll all worship before the ancestors and the marriage will be officially announced. Then comes the feasting— that's the best part. We'll all eat well tonight.'

And everyone did eat well, except Dull Thorn herself, who, as custom demanded, partook of no food and sat silent and expressionless as the smells of the delicious viands wafted round her and guests chewed and sucked appreciatively, crunching last of all at the white-sugar cocks and hens that adorned the tables' centres. The air of the hall was heavy with fumes of warmed wine, smoky candles, spent firecrackers, incense. Replete people sat together; the young male guests, flushed and raucous, had gathered round to enjoy the customary teasing of the bride. They were pulling at her dress, grimacing in her face, tweaking her hair.

'I should snuff the candles before you lay her,' one shouted at Han-fei.

'And here—make her stand on this,' yelled another, inverting a goblet on the table. 'Let's see how delicate her golden lilies are!'

The groom, his cheeks hectically glowing, guffawed and tried to propel his bride upward. But she refused to rise, seeming indifferent to the whole proceedings.

'She'll be a stubborn vixen, Han-fei,' his neighbour announced. 'Not biddable, you can see that. Make her give you some wine at least.'

Han-fei thrust a brimming goblet in his wife's hand and leered at her with open mouth waiting for a drink. Dull Thorn leaned forward and Alice, crouched with Kau behind a pillar, saw her face clearly for the first time. It was, as rumour had suggested, flat and dull, the eyes that looked at her new husband were those of a stupid, dumb animal, tinged, just then, with fear. Her hand shook uncontrollably as she held the goblet to his mouth and some of the wine spilled down his embroidered robe. A roar of mirth went up, and someone shouted, 'Look at that, the clumsy upcountry clod!—She can't even find the way to your mouth.' Han-fei grabbed the goblet and drained it, dabbing his robe angrily.

Attracted by the noise, Lung-kuang went over to them. He too was wine-flushed, but benevolently so, Alice thought. At his suggestion, Dull Thorn rose, bowed low to her husband and went to join the women at the lower table, while the men, half-mocking, burst into a traditional wedding-song:

> My Lord is all a-glow.
> In his left hand he holds the reed pipe,
> With his right he summons me to make free with him,
> Oh, the joy!
> My Lord is carefree.
> In his left hand he holds the dancing plumes,
> With his right he summons me to sport with him,
> Oh, the joy!

Alice seized the diversion to run up and tug at Mei's sleeve. 'Let me have some of those lovely sugar-cakes, please, Younger Sister.'

'Oh hello, Uncut—isn't it fun?' She was happy and excited. 'I'll make sure I don't spill the wine like that on my wedding day. Here you are.' She slipped some cakes into her hand and Alice and Kau carried them to the attic where other servants were lounging about, munching the banquet left-overs and discussing the unimpressive appearance of the bride.

Later that night there was a fresh outburst of shouting and laughing as the male guests accompanied the groom to the door of the bridal chamber. One tried to trip him up while another drew a cord lasso over his shoulders in playful pretence of stopping him. Han-fei roared, butting them with his head like a young bull and thrusting his loins rhythmically towards the closed door.

'You'll need your bellyful of wine to break that one open!' they yelled, pushing him against the door. 'Go to it, man, touch the fish, she's all yours!'

He stumbled inside, slamming the door, and the guests departed, calling for lanterns and cloaks, for the night was chill, damp, and moonless.

'Ho-ho, the male-rain and the woman-clouds have come down,' they said to each other. 'A good sign for a merry coupling!'

The aftermath of the wedding went on for days, with much ceremonious coming and going between the houses of bride and groom. Dull Thorn's parents, reported those servants who saw them, were up-country bumpkins like their daughter and they wondered at Lung-kuang for blessing such an alliance, even for the money. As for Dull Thorn, she found little pleasure in her new home. Her mother-in-law simply ignored her, as she did most people. Vegetable Aunt found another target for that constant irascibility which, said Lung-kuang, resulted from the consumption of far too much hot pickled cabbage. Even Tamao's good nature did not extend to the bovine, sullen girl whose embroidery and pickle-making were not up to scratch.

And Mei positively hated her new sister-in-law. 'Look at her out there,' she said to Alice one summer day as she sat sewing in a verandah-corner. 'She's fallen asleep right in the hot sun and her complexion will be a mess. Her paint's melting and she'll look like a wrinkled old crone—the silly bumpkin! I shall be careful not to do things like that when I'm a wife.' She turned her pretty face to Alice. 'Have you noticed anything different about me?'

'Oh yes—you've got different paint on.'

'Yes, it's called Nonchalant Approach. And see—Elder Sister's plucked my eyebrows in the one-day-old-moon style, so ... and so. ...' she traced the arched lines with her slim fingers. 'Uncut, you're about my age—it's time you put paint on. You look like a paddy-peasant!'

She held up her mirror teasingly and Alice winced at her weather-beaten tousled appearance compared to Mei's smooth elegance. 'You're right, I do look a fright. Here, let me try some!'

She fetched the make-up box and sat still while Mei, giggling, white-powdered her neck and face, rouged her cheeks, blackened and arched her eyebrows.

'There!' She handed over the mirror. 'That's certainly an improvement—it makes your funny eyes look much better!'

Alice was both dismayed and excited by the suddenly older, masklike face reflected back at her.

'And we'll put some gloss on your hair.' Mei plastered some heavily-scented oil over Alice's hair, drew it back with combs, set off the whole concoction with a pink peony above the ear. 'Now you're beginning to look much too pretty for an outside

71

domestic—perhaps Vegetable Aunt will let you come and be my personal servant at last!'

This had been Mei's hope for some time, but Vegetable Aunt was quite determined that no barbarian should ever be granted a position of such intimacy inside the house. Nor did the enhancement of Alice's attractiveness have any effect whatsoever on Aunt's resolve. But, a few days later, it had unforeseen consequences in another quarter.

'Eldest Daughter, are you there?' The commanding tone of the man's voice set up a little flurry among the females passing the afternoon in the women's courtyard as usual. Dull Thorn was dozing in her chair in the sun. Mei was embroidering and keeping an eye on Little Piece. Alice was desultorily cleaning a bronze urn. Lung-kuang strode through the gate looking rather peevish.

'Honourable Father, is there anything wrong?' Mei jumped up.

'Not really—Weng has sent a message to say he's been delayed at Yin-pu with a slight fever. I thought I'd bring the news. Send for tea quickly, little Second Daughter. It is too hot. And ask Tamao to come here.'

Cursorily acknowledging Dull Thorn's presence, he slumped in a chair, took a fan from the case at his waist and fanned himself languidly. It *was* too hot. The time of Great Heat always went on too long. One yearned for the first yellowing leaves and the autumnal chrysanthemums, though no one cared as much about them as his Honourable Father had. Fragments of long-ago-learned poetry drifted into his mind:

Then from the flutes of the forest came a thousand voices.
The colours of autumn are fresh in the wind and rain.
Though the virgins have all gone their way to the yellow
    graves. . . .
Why is it that paintings still hang on the walls?

Written by the admirable Tu-fu surely? A poem about an abandoned palace? How did it go on?

Standing there, even now, under the hanging cliffs.
In dark rooms ghost-green fires are shining . . .

Lung-kuang shivered despite the heat and opened his eyes upon the young domestic industriously polishing a courtyard urn. What was the name of that eerily beautiful palace? Jade

Flower Palace, that was it. Alice looked up, wondering if she should leave.

'Uncut Jade, come here,' he said.

She approached shyly, bowing low.

'I hear that you've been learning the characters with my daughter? How is it that my domestics have the time to read books?'

'I work doubly hard the rest of the time, Honourable, and Eldest Daughter says it helps Younger Daughter to attend.' She looked at him, greenish eyes pleading beneath her delicately arched eyebrows.

'What do you read?' he asked curiously, as Mei and a servant appeared with tea.

'The wise ones . . . the poets.'

'Ah, I've just been thinking of a poem, it is by Tu-fu, quite well known. The Jade Flower Palace.' He took the tea. 'I cannot remember the end. What is it, Younger Daughter?' Mei hesitated and Alice broke in eagerly.

All the while singing I am overwhelmed with lamentation.
Among these lanes of life disappearing in the distance,
Who can make himself eternal?

'Ah—just so. Melancholy, is it not? You are learning well, it seems.' He stared at her firm young body beneath the faded blue tunic.

'She's very clever, Father,' Mei said, adding timidly, 'Eldest Daughter is feeding little Custard Apple, he is ailing in the heat. Shall I ask her to come?'

'No, I'll go to her in a minute. And now Weng is indisposed and of no use, and while I work myself ragged along these "lanes of life" my domestics learn to read and write!' He barked a grudging laugh.

'But Uncut isn't an ordinary domestic, Father—she's special and strange. I think it would be much better if she were my personal servant instead of a skivvy. Can she be, please, Father?'

'And what does Vegetable Aunt say?'

'She says no, just because—'

'Then there is no question. I do not meddle in these domestic arrangements.' He stood up, looking at Alice crouched before him. 'Why you and your brother are still living under my roof, eating my food, I can't imagine.'

73

'But, Honourable, we've no choice. Would you give us permission—and a little money—to go now?'

'Permission? Money? We'll see. Or perhaps I have something else in mind for you.' He stuck his fan under her chin, tilting her head for closer inspection. 'She paints herself.'

'That was my idea,' Mei said eagerly. 'It makes her look better, doesn't it?'

'Yes, it does.' He ran a forefinger down her cheek. 'Strange and special you say? Well . . . we shall see. Now, take me to Eldest Daughter.'

Tamao's shaded room smelled of hot babies, milk and vomit and he felt indisposed to linger once he had inquired after the baby's health and told her about Weng. But, as he moved to leave, she held him with, 'And you, Father? Are you in good heart? You've had so much work to do since your return and there's been little time for leisure, I think?'

He sighed. 'Very little. The incompetency of my subordinates during my absence was beyond belief.'

She smiled sweetly at him. 'Don't work too hard, Father—do not wait for the almonds till you have no teeth!'

He chuckled. 'You are right as usual, daughter. That girl, the barbarian servant, is she virginal?'

Tamao looked up in surprise. 'Why . . . yes . . . I assume . . .'

'We'll find out, and if her red snows have arrived.'

'But, Father, why . . .?'

'The matter need not concern you, simply send me word.'

She stared after him perplexedly as he left. But she did as she was bid and duly sent word the next day to say Uncut Jade was a virgin with the red snows upon her. She remained vaguely puzzled by the matter for several days, till the morning her maid appeared bringing news just whispered to her by the master's body-servant. The Uncut Jade, the ignorant barbarian, with feet the size of boats and eyes like a wild cat, the foreign bitch from the gods knew what monstrous litter, had been summoned to the bedchamber of the head of the house the night before and was still there.

3

Morning sunlight filtered through the lattice high in the wall of the Deputy-Governor's bedroom. It speckled the matted floor and a black lacquer table edged with golden flowers. Under the red silk quilt Alice lay very tense and still, staring at the light through a gap in the brocaded bed-curtains. Her naked body throbbed with unfamiliar usage, most specially the tender places between her thighs where the man had thrust and thrust. Gingerly she explored the sore region with her fingers, then looked at her hand. He had made her bleed; she remembered the pain of it. Tears rolled from under her closed lids and she wiped them away, leaving smears of blood and rouge on her cheeks. She felt unclean, empty, and she did not know what to do.

The summons of the previous evening had been so unforeseen. And even when the master's body-servant had slapped layers of powder and paint on her face and neck, wrapped her in a blue and orange silk robe and pushed her contemptuously into the master's presence, she had not understood. Then she saw the speculative gleam in his eyes, the way he stroked his small black beard, the large bed in the room's centre with its curtains looped back, and a heave of fear swamped her.

'Oh no, no, no, please let me go away,' she begged in English several times, as the servant took off her robe.

'Leave her leggings on, I don't want to see those monstrous feet,' Lung-kuang instructed.

Waiting on the bed, she tried to console herself with the memory of One-Eye and the woman. It had not looked too dreadful. Indeed at the time it had excited her. But when Lung-kuang drained his wine-cup, came over and looked down at her with a weary smile, she trembled violently. 'Well, little barbarian,' he said, 'let us explore the golden gully of an

Uncut Jade, perhaps it is slightly different.' He examined her pubic hair with cool approval. 'Yes, growing the right way.' She flinched. 'There's no need to be afraid,' he assured her. 'I shall do no more than all men do to womenfolk. It will not hurt you long.'

But it did hurt. She had not thought a penis could grow so big. He enjoyed the virginal tightness of her Jade Gate and called for more wine, though he did not get drunk and was not brutal, for it was not in his nature. Eventually, he rolled away and slept. She listened to his heavy breathing for hours, terrified he would awake and go inside her again. But he did not. Soon after dawn, a servant arrived bearing tea and a copper bowl for his washing.

'You can go back to the servants' quarters now,' he said shortly, as he left for the business of the day. She intended to obey, but, overcome with exhaustion, finally slept, so that the sunlight through the lattice was noon gold when the servant reappeared, hustled her from the bed and back to the kitchens. That evening, when she and Kau gave Cheshire his nightly feed, Alice whispered the story of her night's adventures. But Kau, unbelieving, cackled with scornful laughter.

'You—with the Most Honourable? What sort of cretin d'you take me for? I know where you were—with Spots. He has a taste for barbarians, see how friendly he is with your brother.'

'Spots and me!' Alice sprang up, frightening the cat. 'How dare you think I'd share a bed with that swineherd. It was the master, I tell you. Look, there's still paint on my face and this.' She dug into her baggy trousers. 'There's blood down there still!'

'There always is, when you're a virgin. Spots could make you bleed as well as the Most Honourable—and did!'

'No, he didn't. It was the master. I was called to his room. There's a red quilt on the bed and paintings of mountains and lakes on the walls and a writing-on-wood panel that says, "Because we gaze on flowers, the wine is warmed." And before he did it to me, he said he was going to explore the golden gully of an Uncut Jade.'

Certainly that did not sound like Spots, but Kau remained unconvinced.

'All right—we'll ask Spots, you'll see!' Alice dragged her up and they went to find Spots who was chopping maize stalks for the pig swill.

Kau jerked his queue. 'What were you doing last night?'

'Last night? Sleeping like I do every night—unless I can get my hands on a wench.'

'And you didn't last night?'

'No, more's the pity.' He leered up at her. 'Would you like to try me tonight? I'm free.'

'I told you,' said Alice triumphantly as they walked away.

'But that doesn't mean it was who you said.' Kau was seized with doubt and envy. 'Even if it was, that'll be the only time. Men of the master's age like a virgin now and then. So they can break their narrowness apart with pain and see the blood I suppose. It's called deflowering, did you know? Funny sort of flowers!' She snorted. 'Anyway, you'll never see the inside of the master's bed again, I can tell you.'

And for a while Kau's prediction seemed true. The cooler weather for which Lung-kuang had longed duly arrived. Bronze, crimson, and yellow chrysanthemums flourished in the courtyard urns and he looked at them gratefully before leaving on his autumnal tours of inspection, taking with him Han-fei, who needed much initiation into the responsibilities of future office. Severe storms and floods hit the northern districts that year. Hundreds of fishing rafts, traps and boats were broken up, ruining the livelihood of the lakeside fishermen and trebling the price of fish in the city markets. The common people were disgruntled and hungrier than usual, but it was a recurrent pattern, he told Han-fei; one just had to remain unobtrusive, waiting for a better time.

Yet he found it hard even to imagine the goad of hunger, so extravagantly was he feasted by local officials. Wherever he went, piled dishes of roast pig and succulent river fish garnished with ginger and peppers were put before him, however high the prices. After supper, wine and singing women were available if he so desired. So it was not until he was again home near the year's end that he realised he had neglected to install a replacement for the unlamented Red Jasmine—and remembered the soft young flesh of the green-eyed barbarian.

Alice was called three times to the master's bedroom during the New Year period when the wine flowed freely. She went feeling both scared and exultant. She had longed to prove Kau wrong, longed to explore further that strange and intimate coming-together. Soon, rumours reached the ears of Hidden Glory, whose lips twisted in pained scorn at the idea of such a

77

grotesque coupling. Tamao, however, took a purely practical view of the matter: it was preferable, in some ways, that Father's occasional lusts were being satisfied by Uncut rather than a potentially disruptive, official concubine. But it was insupportable that the most private intimacies of his bedroom could therefore be circulated among his lowliest domestics. Whatever else, she told her husband, the hierarchies of the house had to be preserved, and she must take steps accordingly.

Father was warming himself by the charcoal stove when Tamao went to his apartment. Shadows of snow fluttered outside the paper windows and wind whistled through their crackled frames. He rubbed his hands together.

'It is cold, is it not? And how is Custard Apple faring?'

'He is much stronger, thank you, Father. Snow suits him better than sun, it seems.'

'And Dull Thorn? Is there a pregnancy advancing yet? It is time she started breeding sons. Take some tea, Eldest Daughter. Is anything amiss?'

'No, Father, thank you. I am well contented with my lot, as you know.'

'That is good to hear. Women seldom are—the sex that is moulded out of faults.' He sighed and they exchanged a few more pleasantries, he waiting, knowing she had come for some purpose. She set down her cup.

'Just a small matter—of little moment, Honourable. Second Sister is growing in years and stature, as you know, and she has begged me to allow her a personal servant. Her preference is for the foreign Uncut Jade, which is strange, though she's certainly quicker and more intelligent than the other attic servants. I wonder if this would be agreeable to you?'

'Why bother me with such domestic trifles. Do as you wish,' he replied imperturbably.

'But it is not an arrangement that would ever be sanctioned by Vegetable Aunt, for the barbarian would then sleep in the women's quarters and handle Second Sister's food.'

'Ah . . .'

'Alternatively, Uncut Jade could be cast from the house, which would please Aunt more.'

'Vegetable Aunt does not rule.'

'Precisely. But nor do I without your support on occasions.'

'Then you have it on this occasion, Daughter. The arrange-

78

ment sounds satisfactory, and you can tell Aunt so, from me.'

'Thank you, Father.' She rose and bowed. 'I'm sure Second Sister will be most grateful.'

Returning to her room, Tamao wondered how long this strange predilection of her father's would last; probably this effort on her part was unnecessary; though he did not usually tire quickly of a woman.

The next day, Alice, ignoring the envious, ribald taunts of her fellow domestics, bundled her few possessions into a ragged goatskin and went to the women's apartments. She would in future know and possess many rooms of varying size and elegance, but few so satisfying as the cubbyhole in the corridor near Mei's apartment. It contained a string bed, a bamboo stool, a strip of matting, and a window overlooking the women's courtyard. Branches of an almond that would bloom in the spring hung within touching distance.

It was wonderful and Alice did not much care whether she had Hung-mei or Lung-kuang to thank for it, happy to do the bidding of both in return for the pleasures of her new position. No longer had she to sweep the courtyards. Instead she dressed Mei's hair, mended her clothes, carried her embroidery, books, writing materials, favourite caged cricket, wherever she wished to go. Mei was occasionally petulant, but never very demanding, for her nature was sunny. Alice had time to study the characters, watch the blossoms unfolding in the courtyard, talk with Tamao, Han-fei and sometimes even with Weng, who spent more time than was customary in social communication with his wife.

That spring, a friend of Weng's returned from Hong Kong and described to him the steamships in the harbour, the high stone buildings and how the foreign devils were pressing inland demanding new trading rights as they came.

'I've been thinking—why do you barbarians pile the rooms of your houses one above the other?' he asked Alice one day, coming upon her in Tamao's room.

'I . . . I don't really know. But yes, I remember pictures of London, the houses so tall, with stairs going up inside.'

'Perhaps it's because you have so little room to spread sideways in your miserably tiny country called England?'

'It's not small surely?' Alice was uncertain.

'Oh but it is. I hear that hundreds, perhaps thousands of

79

Englands could be contained within the borders of our Celestial Empire.'

'But we have the British Empire too, and that is huge, Father told me.'

'It is a subject of great puzzlement to me that such an insignificant island can control such an Empire, while we Celestials—' He sighed. 'It is a question of vessels, weapons and trade, I'm told. We should be learning more "outward things." We live like frogs in a deep well here.'

'But, Honourable Husband,' Tamao broke in, 'such things are mere conveniences surely? Our imperial power resides in the ancient wisdom, the splendid deeds of our ancestors. The barbarian races are but uncultured savages in comparison.'

'But we have our history and our heroes too,' Alice protested. 'Kings and queens, poets and writers. There's William Shakespeare, and Charles Dickens and a man who wrote about the Greek gods. A Mr. Thomas Babington Macaulay who wrote the history of England and all the saints in the Bible. . . .' She tried desperately to remember more, but there was only a jumble of school-book pictures—armour-clad Roman soldiers, Jonah and the Whale, poor Ophelia drifting downstream somewhere—nothing one could easily explain.

Tamao looked contemptuous. 'Greek—is that a country near England?'

'Fairly near, I think. On the shores of the Mediterranean.' All these untranslatable names fell heavily and Alice was aware of making little progress. 'And there's *Alice in Wonderland*,' she continued more confidently. 'About a little girl who fell down a rabbit-hole where all the animals talked. And she met a turtle who sang a song that began, "Will you walk a little faster, said the whiting to the snail." '

'Whoever reads nonsense like that?' Tamao's disdain mounted.

'Children do. It's a children's story really.'

Weng looked puzzled. 'You mean foreigners write books just for children? How odd! We prefer our sons to learn the wisdom of the sages from an early age. It is study enough for a lifetime. No, we don't need your children's books, but we need your knowledge in some directions. It still puzzles me, for instance, how your vessels manage to move so fast againt the wind?'

Alice was nonplussed. 'Well, they have engines and steam comes out of their funnels.' But she could find no proper way of translating this, so that Mei giggled, saying she had heard that the foreign devils kept tame dragons under their ships to pull them along and the steam you saw was really the smoke from their nostrils.

Lung-kuang asked no such difficult questions of her when she went to his bedroom. His curiosity about the world beyond the Hunan borders had long since waned. In earlier days he had been an ardent supporter of Tseng Kuo-fan, nicknamed The Python, the vigorous patriot, Confucian scholar, brave general who had led his army of Hunanese braves against the Taiping rebels. Tseng, a Changsha man by birth, used occasionally to return home where he would talk of China's need to have its armies equipped with Western-style weaponry for, he used to say, this was the only means of defence against the barbarians' wily, grabbing games.

But poor old Tseng was dead now and Lung-kuang found he had no time for such abstractions. Did he not have enough to do—arranging and supervising public works contracts, organising fishing taxes, and the storing of food supplies against times of famine or drought? No, a man could not spend his entire life trying to improve the naturally imperfect order of things; wiser, when the opportunity arose, to pass a few pleasurable hours dallying in the warm soft country between a woman's thighs.

The barbarian woman, he soon learned, was little different from the many daughters of Han he had known. Her fleshy parts, like theirs, grew rosy and juicy as the inside of a pomegranate at his expert touch. Her breasts were fuller because they had never been bound and her odd eyes, flecked green like a river, grew moist and dreamy as he stirred her Yin. 'Let your moonflower essences flow freely from you,' he would murmur, as she lay spread wide on the bed, moaning with pleasure at his caresses, watching adoringly as he paused now and then to sip tea or bend to drink from her Jade Fountain.

'Come, it's time for you to bestir yourself,' he said on one such night, putting down his pipe. 'Now you shall straddle the White Tiger.'

She rose obediently above him, varying the speed and depth of her movements in accordance with his murmured instructions. 'Gently and quickly go down so . . . there and then there on me, now think of a sparrow picking at the rice-grass, so and so. . . .'

81

'Yes, Honourable.' She smiled lovingly at him, her young body attuning easily to any motion he desired. 'Is that good?'

'Yes, yes, you are learning well. . . .' He closed his eyes and tightened his muscles, forcing himself back from the brink of expulsion. He was still in good condition for his middle years, he thought complacently. And, correctly performed, these sensual delights were good for a man's circulation, they strengthened his bones and renewed his spirit. 'Now then, turn round, let me see your back, like the mounting turtle.' She grasped his legs, bending forward and feeling his increased size, her whole being concentrated on their point of delicious coming-together.

'Now wait a little, I shall have a rest.' She got off obediently, still trembling with desire, and he walked to the window. 'There's a full moon tonight.'

'Yes, Most Respected.' She got up too, came and nuzzled against his belly, caressing his buttocks. 'Oh Honourable, how strong and lovely you are!'

He stroked his beard. 'You wouldn't find a man like me among your barbarian tribes.'

'I'm sure I wouldn't.' She snuggled and rubbed against him. 'Which position would please you next, Honourable?' for she was now well-versed in the various ways of pleasuring the Jade Stalk.

'I think perhaps we will cleave the cicada.' She shivered in tremulous anticipation, took the hard, silk bolster, put it against the bed's edge and spread herself high over it, face downward. She held tight to the coverlet, waiting, gasping with the fullness of him as he gripped her waist and entered her, thrusting slowly, like a carp moving in a pool on a summer's day. As he did so, he watched the lovely moon through the lattice, grimacing slightly at her gasps of pained pleasure. Again, as her essences flowed, he contained himself, but he was tiring, he must not over-indulge.

'Now you must play the flute.' He offered his uprightness to her.

Their encounters usually ended thus. She knelt, bent over his crimson bird, nibbling and squeezing with her lips and tongue in the way that pleased him most. He continued to stare at the moon for a while but with decreasing attention. Then, with a little growling grunt, he pushed her head right down. 'There— take me there, lick harder.' He held her there for a minute, for his Yang essence was good for her, then he patted her hair.

82

'Bring the cloths and then I must sleep.' She wiped him tenderly, then herself and sank into bed beside him, encircled, enchanted, enamoured of his expert lust.

Alice's days came to be dominated by dreams of these musk-scented night encounters. Sick with yearning, she would wait in the passageways hoping for a glimpse of her lover, even though he invariably passed her by without a flicker of recognition. In the evenings of that early summer, after she had helped Mei disrobe, she would sit in her cubbyhole looking at the sky and longing for the servant's tap, meaning that the master required her presence. When it came, she dabbed herself with jasmine water, powdered her breasts and neck and hurried to him eagerly. When, as was more often the case, no summons came, she would toss for hours in bed, beset by lush fantasies of past and future intimacies.

It was on one such night that she first distinctly heard the sound. It was a half-suppressed low moan that went on and on. She shuddered, reminded of Tamao's tale about the evil spirit of a wailing woman with the eyes and teeth of a fox who reputedly haunted the house when trouble was brewing. Unable to sleep, she crept along the passage towards the noise that she now realised was a very human cry of distress emanating from the room of Third Daughter, Little Piece. Candlelight flickered through the room-screen and she peeped in. A nurse was hunched by the child's bed, crooning a dozy chant. Little Piece lay wide-eyed, her small hands helplessly plucking the quilt. Her steady wail of sorrow seemed more profoundly hopeless than any seven-year-old mortal could rightly utter.

'Is she ill?' Alice whispered.

'Oh, it's you, Uncut. No, it's just the foot-binding trouble upon her. The first few months are always the worst to bear, poor mite.'

Alice shivered and looked pityingly at the child who stared back in a kind of defiant agony.

'There, there, have another sugar plum then, and remember, child, not every night can be a feast of lanterns.' The nurse spoke mechanically, giving a plum to Alice also.

'Is she like this every night?'

'No, she's had the new bandages on today, so it's specially bad. I take the old ones off every few days, wash her and then fold the smaller toes under the big one a little more tightly each time. Well, they say each bound foot has to cost a bath of tears.'

'But it's a slow torture,' Alice stared at the suffering child. She had, of course, seen hundreds of bound feet hobbling along awkwardly, deformed hooves concealed by white leggings and embroidered slippers. She had seen Mei's feet unbound—the grossly swollen ankles and folds of loose skin, the deep cleft across the sole where heel and toes had been forced into unnatural conjunction over the years. But Mei had always treated the matter lightly, as she did most things, dismissing it with her usual, resigned, 'But it's the custom.' Now, watching Little Piece beginning to undergo the same remorseless process, Alice understood her dreadful, helpless wail—the inevitability of a crippled life. 'How long will it go on like this?' she asked.

'Oh, about three or four years only. As I tell Little Piece, look at Number Two Sister, she's all right now.'

'But her feet often hurt and she'll never walk normally.'

The nurse shrugged. She was from the lower classes and not bound. 'Ah well, no gentleman of rank would marry a big-footed woman.'

Little Piece jeered up at Alice. 'There you are. No decent man would ever marry an ugly barbarian like you, would they, nurse? Cos she'll never have beautiful golden lilies.'

'That's right, my pretty blossom—so don't you fret. It's all in a good cause, as they say.'

Alice sighed, realising fully for the first time what a prison the house was for its womenfolk. They left it so seldom, and when they did had always to travel in chairs, be supported by attendants and servants. How could all this have become 'the custom'? She longed to ask Lung-kuang about it—was he not moved to pity by his daughter's wailings? Did he really find those fleshy, maimed hooves desirable? Yet her own naturalness repulsed him and he never removed her leggings.

'We're all going out of the house soon for a whole long day!' Mei announced to Alice shortly after she'd begun to chafe anew at this sense of perpetual confinement. 'It's the Chingming Festival—the first suitable season for going into the countryside, so we make a pilgrimage over the hills to our ancestral tombs.'

'Oh, let me come with you please,' Alice begged.

'Well—all right. It's highly irregular, but with so many of us, people may not notice you. The hairdresser is giving Eldest Sister and me a special hairstyle for the open air, and I must

84

finish my new slippers. You must carry everything proper for me, Uncut—a basket for wild flowers, a cage in case we find more crickets, my Spring-Festival fan, and two umbrellas, one for sun and one for rain, to protect my complexion whatever the weather. But I do hope it's sunny.'

And so it was. Ching-ming Festival day glowed cloudlessly with a warm spring breeze that rustled the manes of the ponies waiting in the courtyard and the paper pennons of the banners for the ancestral tombs. The senior members of the family set off first in closed chairs. Alice watched longingly from behind a pillar as Lung-kuang emerged, wearing a fur-bordered conical hat and a resplendent brocade mantle. He looked so tremendously magisterial. She could scarcely believe that the Crimson Bird which gave her so much pleasure nestled somewhere beneath his finery.

After they had gone, the family's younger members and servants followed in humbler procession led by Han-li riding on horseback. His mount was stringy with buck teeth and sores on its tail, but he was proud of it and so was his groom Frank, who, capitalising on his sister's promotion, had managed to procure the job. Frank's fair hair was concealed by a grubby turban, but his legs, bared to the thighs for running, looked pink and muscular beside the other grooms'.

He grinned when he saw Alice walking demurely behind Mei's chair. 'Isn't it exciting? Have you been out before?'

'No, not once since we came in these gates—and I wonder how long ago that was?'

He shrugged. 'I don't know. I've been out with Han-li several times. Keep your head down in the streets, or the people shout "foreign devil" at you.'

Outside, Alice duly lowered her head, occasionally glancing at the passersby—vegetable-, fruit- and toy-sellers, carriers of water and firewood; men with carts full of excrement bound for the paddies, other trundling hand-carts stacked with grain, trussed pigs or stones. Only a few women were abroad—aged crones selling sweetmeats, scavengers with baskets on their bent backs, ragged girls with pock-marked babies.

When the party reached open country, Alice's spirits soared at the expanses of spring grass, the trill of meadow larks, fresh breezes untainted by city smells. The freshness reminded her of the sea, how she used to walk along the Taku

Road near the Tientsin docks—that glittering expanse of water, junks jostling at their moorings, Papa telling her about the flowery meadows and golden cornfields of his Norfolk childhood.

By the time the junior procession reached the ancestral resting-place, the senior Chus had all assembled to bow, clap hands and pray before the tombs on the hillsides. But it was not in the least funereal, Alice thought, watching from a discreet distance. The white banners on the grave mounds flapped as merrily as sails against the blue sky. Children, dressed in their colourful best, bounded about the grass and, on the slopes behind, masses of yellow, mauve, and crimson azaleas were in bloom. In the far distance loomed a range of forested mountains. Its most sacred peak, Mei told her, called Hensha, was guarded by a bird with wings of flame belonging to the God of Fire.

During the afternoon, trays of watermelons, peaches, and loquats were passed round and a troupe of wandering musicians played ballads on their bamboo flutes. Even Hidden Glory looked less remote as she sat gazing at the flowering bushes and holding in her gold-ringed, long-nailed hand a silver pipe at which she contentedly puffed. As for Vegetable Aunt, she wore flowers in her hair and, leaning on her cane, cracked nuts and jokes with elderly relatives she had not seen since New Year. When the younger males went off riding, Mei went to pick azaleas, moving slowly among the bushes. 'You must choose with care, Uncut,' she instructed. 'Try to see which way each branch expresses itself, that's what Eldest Sister taught me. We want one colour for each vase and an uneven number of branches—three, five or seven is best.'

'Why?' asked Alice, recklessly gathering a multi-coloured armful.

'Because the shapes of the flowers and twigs must form a harmonious whole—and even numbers are unlucky. Isn't that right, Tamao?' she turned to her sister who had just joined them.

'Yes, didn't you know that, Uncut? And why are you here anyway? Keep out of the way of the honourable elderly, they wouldn't like to see a barbarian in their midst on such a day.'

'But my brother's here—with Youngest Son's horse.'

'Yes, and Weng told him the same. Anyway, Dull Thorn

whispered something to me this afternoon—she even smiled—she's podded at last. So we're all adding a prayer today for a first-born son.'

Mei clapped her hands. 'How exciting! I hope he'll take after Eldest Brother and not have her face—flat and broad as the bottom of an old cooking pot.'

Tamao giggled. 'So do I. And he'll be an important little personage, first son of the first son.'

Alice looked over at Dull Thorn sitting near her mother-in-law, staring, with her usual passivity, at the grave-mounds which bore none of her family's names. This day of honouring the dead seemed a strange occasion to announce a coming birth. Yet perhaps not, for, in quick painful vision, the whole of life's little cycle compacted before Alice's eyes. The baby growing in the mound of Dull Thorn's belly would as child and then adult probably come here to worship his ancestors when the azaleas bloomed and be laid to rest in his turn inside another of the hillside mounds. So perhaps, after all, Dull Thorn had chosen auspiciously.

But Senior Daughter-in-Law's advancing pregnancy cast a shadow over the ensuing summer. She became increasingly tearful and petulant and, because of her condition, had now to be humoured. Her younger, equally lumpish sister moved in to attend her, and they made a doleful pair as they tottered round and round the inner courtyard every afternoon looking at nothing. Dull Thorn developed a craving for boiled pigs' bladders, fishes' brains, and bears' paws which she ate in huge quantities, just because they were expensive, in Tamao's opinion. Mei and Little Piece had to keep quiet in her presence and embroider caps and shoes for the coming infant. Alice helped, having acquired a certain skill. And how soothing it was to sit in the shadow of the orange trees in the hot afternoons, twisting and threading the coloured silks whilst the crickets chirped in their cages and she day-dreamed voluptuously of the next night with Lung-kuang.

As the time of the birth approached, Han-fei shunned his wife's presence entirely. Female relatives appeared with coarse red-sugar balls, lichees, mangoes and the flesh of turtles to strengthen her. Her belly strained bulbous and sweaty under its cotton casing as she sat in the verandah chair eating greedily through every offering. But there was never any joy in her deeply-embedded eyes, only a haunting fear that no gift could dislodge. Walking across the courtyard one evening, Alice saw her rotund shape still sitting in the twilight. Dull Thorn was nervously clicking her charm-beads and mumbling plaintively, 'Oh may the gods protect me. . . . Oh I know it will go ill with me . . . oh, oh . . .'

Alice hurried away shuddering, but remembered the scene a few weeks later when the sound of Dull Thorn's screams rent through every closed screen of the women's apartments. Unable to bear the noise, Alice crept into Mei's bed and the two clutched close together, rigid with fear as the shrieks intensified and urgent steps hurried along the passageways.

'I didn't think she had it in her to make so much noise,' Mei whispered, 'She's much worse than Eldest Sister ever was.'

'Perhaps she'll die. Women do die having babies. A friend of Mama's did in Tientsin once. Think of trying to push a huge baby out of a small hole—it must be awful.'

'Well, all our mothers did or we wouldn't be here.' Mei was practical. 'So it's no use worrying—and it may be your turn next!'

Alice put her fingers in her ears and shook. Until then, Mei had not referred to the relationship with Lung-kuang and she did not want to think of it in this light.

Dull Thorn's screams continued unabated till the next afternoon when another doctor arrived looking solemn. Silence fell with the dusk, and soon after the news spread rapidly through the waiting household. Dull Thorn's spirit had unfortunately departed from her torn body. The female she had borne was just alive.

As the ritual wails of lamentation went up from the gathered women-folk, Alice watched a line of white-robed priests arrive from the Temple of Heavenly Clouds chanting obsequies and carrying candles to show the newly-released spirit the way to the land of shades. A chill autumnal wind blew the light flames sideways, scudded clouds across the moon, whipped leaves off the almond tree. Alice murmured:

The sound of her silk skirt has stopped,
On the marble pavement dust grows.
Her empty room is cold and still.
Fallen leaves are piled against the doors.

She fell silent, with a sense of dispassionate pity for the short, dispirited life of poor Dull Thorn. Was anyone truly mourning her that night?

'Were you sad about Dull Thorn's passing, Honourable?' Alice asked Lung-kuang curiously as they lay together under the red quilt. It had been their first coupling since the death, for all the correct funereal proprieties had naturally been observed, including the two-month period of sexual abstinence for relatives. Tonight, in consequence, Lung-kuang was in a particular enthusiastic and relaxed mood and Alice was emboldened to ask a personal question.

'It's a damn-blasted nuisance. I hoped marriage would keep Eldest Son in check a little, he has this peppery Hunanese devil in him. But that woman was useless—a lump of mildewed rice-dough. So there'll have to be another one for him, but it is not proper for at least a year. All that wedding expense and fuss over again and worse yet—the delay in getting a grandson from my first son. There are always women-problems of one kind or another.'

'But not from me, Honourable?'

'No,' he chuckled and began to fondle her again. 'That is the advantage of an unofficial female. How does that feel—like the fluttering of butterflies in you, hey?' He spread her gently, thrust inside her for a while, then withdrew, staring complacently at his still-upright stalk. 'See, I'm not quite in need of the bald-chicken potion yet, am I, Uncut?'

'The what, Honourable?'

'Ha—you don't know? Bring me some fresh tea and I'll tell you. Well, there was this aged Prefect, an old old man, but with the lust for women still him, only he just couldn't keep his stalk up long enough, poor old sod! So he called the doctor who gave him a special potion—black as spiders' bile it was. Well, the old rascal took a dose and lo and behold! His Jade Stalk positively leaped to attention and went down only to spring up again. And ho, what fun they had for a while, he and his old wife. He gave it to her this way, this t'other way, till the poor old duck couldn't sit on a chair or lie on a bed. And "oh mercy on us" she cried, "it's too much, this potion of yours, you should be ashamed of yourself at your age!" But he only spread her again, saying, "Well, if you don't let me have you, I'll have to fetch some lusty young wench from the village who will." And at this she picked up the bottle and threw it into the courtyard where it broke.

'Now, there happened to be a fine young cockerel in that yard and he ran right over and drank as much of that potion as he could before it sank into the mud. Then this cock jumped upon the first hen he saw and off he went—in and out, in and out, up and down, fuck, fuck, cluck, cluck. And that cock wouldn't get off his chicken for twelve whole days. All the while he was at it he kept pecking her head till at last, by the time he did leave her alone, she was bald as a coot—and that's the story of the bald-chicken potion!'

Alice screamed with laughter. 'Oh that's a lovely, lovely story, Honourable! I wonder what the stuff was made of?'

'Ah, no one knows—the man who discovered that would be as rich as the Emperor himself. Well, Uncut, let's see what I can do without the potion in me!' They enjoyed the Kingfisher Union and the Turning of the Yellow Dragon together that night, before Lung-kuang eventually spent his Yang essence deep inside her and then slept, his arm heavy across her body.

Safe in the master's bed and with the master in amiable mood, Alice's position seemed secure and the intense delight of her new-found sensuality usually overwhelmed the shadows of shame and guilt that were the legacy of her childhood. Why should she know so clearly that her parents would have been utterly scandalised by her present behaviour? she sometimes wondered. As she wiped the natural juices from her lover, smiled down at his trim, hairless body, lay relaxed by the close feel of him, she could not understand how it could be wrong. But during his frequent absences she was often afraid. Lung-kuang and she were not married, never would be, and so she was living in mortal sin, and even here, in the deepest recesses of heathendom, was not God watching her?

As for Lung-kuang, he took delight in the supple and lively body of his unofficial woman, even though he was slightly ashamed of his perversity in preferring her to a true daughter of Han. In any case he gave the matter little thought, for, in addition to his onerous duties, he and his fellow officials were deeply troubled that winter by rumours that came from the Imperial Capital. Apparently, the young Emperor, the Celestial One, T'ung-chih, had been visited by the heavenly flowers—a euphemism to conceal the dreaded ravages of smallpox—and his death was daily anticipated. An intense struggle for power was going on in the Imperial Court and T'ung-chih's mother, the Empress Dowager, was plotting to dominate whoever became the new Emperor. It might lead to a rebellion against the much hated Manchu regime. It would certainly mean some shift in power, the formation of new alliances. Between the capital and the Empire's distant regions messengers rode secretly back and forth with the latest tidings and the provincial governors were on constant alert.

Thus it was that, on a cold night in late December, at the Time of Winter's Standing, Alice, wakeful in her cubbyhole, heard a disturbance in the main courtyard. Lantern lights bobbed, horses' hooves clattered on the paving, servants' feet padded along the verandahs. She dozed finally, haunted by foreboding, then slept until a servant called her to her duties.

'Didn't you hear people about in the night?' she asked Mei, who sat waiting for her hair to be oiled.

'Come, Uncut, you're late . . .'

'I'm sorry, Younger sister, but didn't you . . .'

The door slid back and Tamao hurried in. 'Have you heard the news? Father has been called to Peking.'

Alice dropped a comb. 'Father . . . the Honourable. Why? What?'

'The Governor sent messengers during the night—Father is to go to Peking immediately to report on what is happening and who we Hunanese should support. He's about to leave, so you must hurry and bid him farewell—come, Second Sister.'

Dread in her heart, Alice hurried to the main courtyard which was all abustle. The men of Lung-kuang's official retinue sat waiting on horseback, their faces muffled against the cold. In their midst was the master's gilded chair, its ill-clad bearers stamping around to keep warm. Breath steamed from the mouths of every man and beast. Frank hurried to her.

'Look at that white horse—isn't he a beauty? Goes like the wind, and Honourable will ride it once they've left the city!'

'Oh, will he?' Alice stared miserably at the fine creature, its flowing mane and tail festooned with official green and red ribbons.

'Here he comes,' Frank tugged her sleeve as Lung-kuang came outside, saying to Han-fei in a stern voice for all to hear, 'And you, Eldest Son, are in sole charge of all household affairs in my absence. Is that understood?'

The son bowed low to hide his shining eyes, while Lung-kuang looked beyond to where servants were loading the carts with baggage and provisions. Stepping into his line of

91

vision, Alice raised her hand in a desperate gesture of farewell. His eyes swept unseeingly over her. 'Tell the servants to hurry,' he snapped.

Alice long remembered the back view of his rich, brown fur robe as he climbed into the chair without another word. Reins jerked, steeds snorted, and as they raised the master aloft, the bearers gave the ritual groan to signify the magnificence of his weight. The gates opened, houseservants bowed low as the chair was carried out and Alice rushed away to hide her tears.

It was the beginning of a miserable time for her, because many of the household servants were jealous and resentful of her intimacy with the Master and, in his absence, gibed her cruelly. Much worse however, Han-fei also felt at liberty to indulge his long-nurtured hatred of the two barbarian whelps. Taught as a child to believe in the innate superiority of his race and class, he was still blind to any broader, more generous vision, and sensed instinctively that the increasing foreign presence in his country boded no good for him and his kind. To him, Alice and Frank were outlandish freaks and interlopers, portents of unnatural change and future disorder. That the female of them had frolicked in his father's bed outraged and sickened him, even undermined the loyal respect due to his honourable parent. Meeting her in a corridor one day, he shoved her violently against the wall and cuffed her cheeks, his eyes blazing with a fury that was positively murderous.

And so Alice began creeping warily about the house, fearful of Elder Brother and of the servants, and beset by a further anxiety, for her 'red snows' had failed to make their customary appearance. Whatever would happen to her if . . .? She fretted; for serene, secure Tamao babies came as blessings, but it was not always so, and she quailed as she remembered the wailings of Red Jasmine, cast out in disgrace, of Dull Thorn, dying in agony. But what she could do about it she did not know, and so waited, hoping desperately and in vain, for the best.

Days passed, from the farmyard there rose again the squeals of pigs doomed to supply the New Year's pork, and the lacquer boxes of decorations were again brought down from the attics. As the old year drew to a close, news reached Changsha of the succession to the Dragon Throne of Kuang-hsu, the 'Emperor of Glorious Inheritance'—and a puny three-year-old. He was the nephew of the Empress Dowager and she had ruthlessly pushed aside more legitimate claimants so that he should succeed and she could consolidate her behind-the-throne power.

'Now the new Emperor is proclaimed, your Honourable Father will be returning very soon surely?' Alice asked Tamao, on the afternoon of the news' arrival.

'No, I fear not. Weng say he has other business to attend to in the capital on the Governor's behalf and gives no date for his return.'

'Oh,' Alice bowed her head miserably, and Tamao smiled. 'You mustn't let it concern you, Uncut. Men have many women in their lives and they think little about any of us when they're away.'

Alice sniffed. 'But . . . I can't . . . I mean . . . I'm worried, Tamao, because my red snows haven't come for almost three months now. Do you think they'll come back when he does or . . .?'

'Oh dear, I expect it's a baby. What a nuisance, Uncut, especially with Father away. I don't know what course he'd want us to take . . .' She looked thoughtful. A half-barbarian whelp would only be an embarrassment. The obvious thing was either to get it aborted now or send the girl away. But is that what Father would wish? And how could she know till he returned, which might be too late? She must consult her husband, and perhaps even Eldest Brother, though she so disapproved of his recent behaviour that she tried to avoid him.

For Han-fei, restrained by neither father nor wife, was thoroughly enjoying the fruits of his new-found mastery over the household. He spent much of his time gambling and wenching in the city's gay quarter and, when the New Year Festival began, filled his apartments with street entertainers, drinking cronies and heavily-painted women, their high coiffures glinting with flowers and jewels. Weng, stiff with angry powerlessness, spent the Festival in the customary fashion with the usual relatives and friends, though Vegetable Aunt was so incensed by Han-fei's behaviour that she became a martyr to hysterical fits. Falling flat on the floor, she unleashed her hair, kicked her tiny feet in the air and screamed till her cheeks were as purple as her favourite pickled cabbage.

'She'll die if she goes on like that,' Tamao remarked to her mother. But Hidden Glory only shrugged disdainfully, 'It's the Hunanese peppers in her—she's never learned to control herself and never will, at her age.'

By the end of the Festival's third day, Han-fei and his companions were fairly besotted with their various indulgences and the floors of the male apartments were littered with chewed bones, spilled wine, nutshells. In the main bedroom, a woman with flowing hair and white powdered face sat on a cushion playing plaintively on a three-stringed lute. Outside it was snowing heavily. Han-fei leaned out of the window, catching flakes on his hot tongue, then surveyed the scene with a bored sigh.

'I'm tired of her and that dismal caterwauling,' he announced to his friends. 'A man needs something more unusual to rouse his senses by this time.'

'How about the outlandish she-devil with jade eyes that your father has tucked away somewhere?' sniggered one.

'Faugh! the barbarian whelp—not on your life!'

'Let's see her anyway. Has she got yellow hairs top and bottom like the male?'

'I don't know—but that reminds me—get the Uncut Sliver,' he called to a servant.

Pushed into the room, Alice stood shivering, a tatty goatskin over her night-robe. Han-fei went over, jerking her head up by her hair. 'My father's whore—this little dog's fart!'

'I'm not a whore, I'm a proper concubine—and he likes me well enough.'

'Oh he does, hey? What revolting taste. Well, I've just heard you're breeding, wench, and he won't like that, I know bloody well. So you can get out of this house, we're not having any little green-eyed devil-monsters running loose here.'

'Well done!' His companion raised a cup. 'Show a decent respect for the proprieties. I'd roll that rotten egg out of the gates right now if I were you!'

'But Number One Son, please.' She dragged at his sleeve. 'Please don't turn me out now—it's your father's child, remember.'

He cuffed her across the mouth and threw her from him so violently that she fell backwards. 'Out, out, I tell you—you devil-assed whore.'

'But what will the Respected Father say when . . .?'

'He'll thank me for getting rid of you, you breeder of

94

monsters. And I'll have a pretty wench waiting for him who'll give him a proper son of Han! Out I say! If you're still in this house of Chu by this time tomorrow, I'll take a knife and cut that sickening grub out of your belly with my own hands—do you understand, foreign-whore?' He thrust his red face contorted with fury towards her. She scrambled up and fled in terror.

There was no hope of Han-fei's relenting, and Weng, the only one who might have interceded on Alice's behalf, refused to risk another confrontation with him over such a trivial matter. Tamao, whose paramount concern was always her family, feared that, when Alice's pregnancy became apparent, gossip would spread about Father's unnatural coupling with a barbarian, and so simply suggested that the girl should avoid making trouble and go to live quietly in a nearby village.

'You must be patient, Uncut, and promise me you'll tell no one what man it is you have known. Here—take this money, and when Father returns I'll speak to him about you. But you mustn't expect too much. We have been kind to you, but now I think it is fitting that you return to your own people.'

Alice bit her lip and Mei threw her arms round her neck. 'Oh Uncut, I'm so sad to see you go! We have been as dear sisters, have we not? Oh please, Tamao, isn't there anything we can do to make beastly Elder Brother change his mind?'

But Tamao shook her head resignedly. Unofficial females and their unwanted offspring were easily dispensed with at the whim of the dominant male in the house. Han-fei had Father's authority for his power, and she was not about to challenge it in such a dubious cause. Mei, railing against her brother's hard heart, pressed upon Alice two woollen gowns and a moth-eaten fur cloak to wear against the cold, and begged her to stay somewhere close by, where she could visit her in secret.

But Alice had other ideas and the next morning she sought out her brother in the farmyard. 'Number One Son's thrown me out of the house,' she faced him directly. 'I've got to leave before nightfall and not come back—oh Frank, help me, whatever shall I do?'

'But why . . . whatever made him? Oh Uncut, how dreadful!'

She felt confused and ashamed. It was impossible to explain. She had no idea how much he knew. 'He's always hated us, you know that. And I annoyed him yesterday when he and his friends were drunk and he ordered me out. Oh Frank, please

95

come with me! I want so much to find Mama and William, and I don't know how to start.'

'Me? Go away from here? But I'm all right, Uncut. And they've forgotten all about us by now, perhaps they're dead.'

She looked at him miserably. 'Oh Frank, please don't say that, I couldn't bear it. Please come with me, it would be so much easier with two.'

He shuffled his feet in the mud. 'But I don't see why I should, Alice, especially now I'm Han-li's groom. We're good friends and he treats me well and I get plenty to eat.'

'Well, I'm going to try and reach the nearest treaty port, and get in touch with Mama—then you'll be sorry you didn't come too, so there!'

'But I shan't know how you get on.'

'Frank, if I find them alive, I'll come back for you one day. Then you'd leave, wouldn't you?'

'Yes, I suppose so, but . . .'

Just then Kau appeared, carrying rubbish. Alice had seen less of the Miao girl since her own elevation in the house, but she had kept her and Cheshire well supplied with delicacies from the well-stocked tables of the women's apartments.

'Kau, come here, did you know that I . . .?'

'Yes, I've just heard. I'm sorry, Uncut. Where will you go?'

'Oh dear, I don't know. If only Frank would . . .' She looked at him pleadingly again.

'Why don't you sneak away with Uncut, Kau?' he said impulsively. 'You've often said you wanted to return to your mother's tribe in Kweichow, you could go together.'

Alice seized on it. 'Oh please do, Kau. We could go to your relatives first, they'd take us in surely? Only the other day you said you'd never find a husband in this household.'

She smiled. 'That's so. I need a Miao man and there aren't any hereabouts. And I'm growing up, and I've been putting a little cash by. All right, Uncut, I'll come. I was just thinking it would be much worse for me and Cheshire here without you.'

'Good old Kau.' Frank slapped her shoulder and Alice clasped her hand.

'Oh thank you, thank you, Kau. Now we must get ready, and remember, Frank—I'll come back some day for you, I promise.'

'All right, Alice, I feel bad about it, but . . . here, wait a minute.'

He rushed off, returning with a little cloth bag. She felt it curiously.

'Money?'

'Just a little and don't ask how I came by it. Well goodbye, Alice, and good luck.'

They parted awkwardly, having lost the habit of kissing each other.

'I'll meet you at the north gate when they open it for the scavenger cart,' Alice told Kau as they parted.

Early dusk was falling among windswept snow-flurries as the scavenger cart trundled in through the north gate and two wrapped-up little figures, each carrying a basket, slipped discreetly out. In the street, Alice paused to look back as the scavenger threw the rubbish aboard. From Kau's basket came a tiny bleat. 'Oh Kau, you've not brought Cheshire?'

'I had to, Uncut, no one would look after him now we're gone.'

The cat mewed pitifully and Alice shivered. Snow caked her eyelids and she wrapped the moth-eaten fur cloak that had been Mei's parting gift more tightly across her stomach. As the cart creaked away the north gate was slammed shut.

'Which direction shall we take?' Alice asked in a quavering voice.

4

A disintegrating corpse floated out of the thick fog and, borne up by the river's oily waters, jostled against the prow of the trading junk on which Alice sat. She shuddered as she watched it, thinking incongruously—you can't come on here, there's no room. 'No room, no room'—bizarre echoes of a distant tale drifted back to her. 'No room,' they cried as Alice approached the Mad Hatter's tea-party. But Alice sat down anyway and later the Hatter recited the poem, 'Twinkle, twinkle little bat, How I wonder what you're at, Up above the world so high, like a tea-tray in the sky.'

Alice smiled wistfully upwards, hoping for a vision of bats or tea-trays or even stars. But there was no sky, just dense fog pierced only by the crowded masts of the craft moored along the banks of the River Tzu as it went through the town of Shaoyang. Hundreds of 'boat families' always lived there, but now their numbers were swelled by vessels waiting for the fog to lift before negotiating the rapids below the town. So tightly jammed together were they that the water between was insufficient to let a corpse sink decently, and, as Alice watched, the bloated blob of flesh bobbed helplessly away towards the steps leading up the bank, where three leprous beggars crouched, picking with scaly fingers at a hen's carcass.

She and Kau had managed to buy a passage to Shaoyang, southwest of Changsha, en route to Kweichow. Rivers were the main highways of the region and travel along them, though often perilous and always slow, was cheap—except for unforeseen delays such as fog, which could prove expensive, as she was about to discover. For, as she huddled outside to escape the foetid crowd of humans, dogs and fowls crowded under the junk's canopy, she became aware of a nearby disturbance. A rotund, bald man flanked by two flunkeys with stout staves came stamping down the bank steps. The beggars cowered away, but were given passing thwacks nevertheless. The man thudded aboard the nearest boat shouting, 'Mooring dues, how many aboard? Pay up or get out, you litters of water rats!'

'Oh rot his eyeballs, it's the River Boss,' Li-chi, the junkmaster, came running up and pushed Alice inside. 'If he counts heads you'll have to pay.'

A minute later their craft rocked as Boss jumped aboard and stuck his oily pate through the opening. 'All right, how many here?'

'Just me, the wife and kids,' whined Li-chi, holding up a string of cash.

'And who's this?' a flunkey, pushing past, thumped Kau on the shoulder.

'An abo—getting a ride to Kweichow.'

'And this?' he leered in Alice's face. 'Another abo. Pay up you two—double dues for every passenger and you know it, you gobbet of dog's spittle!'

'I can't pay,' Li-chi growled. 'They'll have to pay for themselves.'

'But we've no money,' Alice appealed, which was true for they had paid their last coin to secure their passage.

'Then off the boat and into the debtors' jail—you might discover some cash after a while there.' Boss poked her hard and Kau wailed in horror, for she knew about jails.

'Oh not that—anything else. Please, most kind and honourable sir.'

Boss considered her, scowling. 'You've got a face like the backside of an old goat,' he remarked, 'But you're young. And this one?' He jerked Alice's head. 'Squint as an abo all right, but might do. All right, if you want to earn your dues in a couple of days, come with me. Or it's the debtors' jail, take your pick. You're not staying here for free.'

Alice got together her little bundle of clothes, Kau scooped up Cheshire from behind the stove and they followed Boss along the towpath to where a dilapidated houseboat was permanently moored just offshore. It squatted eerily in the foggy murk. Tatty, unlit paper lanterns hung from its rat-holed roof. Boss strode across the gangplank shouting, 'Madame Plumblossom, here, I've found a couple of wenches.'

A tousle-headed woman in a dirty robe and with a heavily

painted face peered out. 'Ah, Boss,' she simpered, 'wenches—that's what I'm short of, so long as they're not riddled with the pox like the rest of 'em. Another of mine's gone down with it.'

'And have you the pox?' Boss turned on Kau.

'No,' she shouted angrily, 'and nor has my friend—we're clean girls.'

'But they're abos,' Madame sniffed.

Boss scowled. 'Can't have everything and perfect golden lilies are hard to find. Their cunts will be the same in the dark and they can't pay their dues. So I take fifty percent of their earnings in lieu, right? You'll need them during the days of the Dragon Festival, the randy lads'll be along then, fog or no fog.'

'You're a hard man, Boss, but you're right. Here, you, get inside.'

'I'll be back for my cut tomorrow evening and perhaps I'll sample one of your fairy-flowers—the Chinese variety for me please,' Boss called as he stamped off.

Inside the dim, low room on the main deck a girl in a soiled pink robe sat silent beside a smoky stove. Madame Plumblossom lit a lantern and inspected them closely. 'Wenches—brought by Boss, that old sack of turds. Abos, the thick one will do in the dark, and this—' She pulled aside Alice's cloak, grasping at her body. 'Big tits for a young 'un, but healthy. They'll see me through the festival, I suppose.'

Alice looked round in horror, suddenly aware of the grunts and shoves coming from behind a curtain at the room's end. 'Kau . . . does she mean to . . .?'

'This is a brothel-boat and she's the devil-granny,' Kau said sullenly.

Alice went very pale and the girl beside the stove drew her gently towards it. 'I'm Little Willow . . . don't worry. Sit down and have some tea.'

Alice sank gratefully on the mats, feeling sick. Kau let Cheshire out of his basket and he nestled close, purring amiably. The sounds behind the curtain ceased and a stringy river-coolie, grinning toothlessly and re-arranging his dirty baggy trousers, emerged, nodded at them and clattered off down the gangplank. A dishevelled woman then appeared, a robe partly covering her nudity as she mopped between her thighs with a wad of cloth. 'Get me some tea, Little Willow . . . and what strange bitches have we here?'

It was Kau who explained while Alice sat clutching Cheshire, frozen into a helpless panic. Bowls of steaming noodles arrived, but they stuck in her throat. She had to escape. She thought of the coolie's loose mouth, his gnarled, dirty hands groping at his trousers. Madame Plum-blossom peered through the blinds.

'Huh, this fog's dense enough to blunt any man's lust. We'll get no more customers tonight. So you two abos doss down in there and get your strength up—the Dragon Tower Festival's always good for business and the fishermen come early. If they're wine-sodden, give 'em some chrysanthemum tea first, and if they're old and shrunk up, move yourselves about like a millstone and keep your legs close together when they're inside you.' She bustled them into an alcove, taking away the only lantern.

Alice lay tense, waiting till she could hear only the water lapping outside—and the women snoring. 'Kau, we can't stay here,' she shook her companion awake. 'I won't do it—not with filthy low-bred men like that.'

Kau grunted. 'It's not nice, but what else can we do? What with the fog and the Festival, Li-chi won't be able to move for days and we can't pay our dues. This is better than the debtors' jail, I can tell you.'

'I don't care, I just won't.' Alice was wrapping on her cloth leggings with trembling fingers.

'But it's only for a little while—then we'd have some cash by us for Kweichow. The men don't hurt if you do what they want.'

'You're staying then?'

'But, Uncut, what can we . . .' Kau wailed softly as Alice drew her cloak round her, grabbed her bundle and crept out.

On deck she paused in dismay. The gangplank had been lifted and there was a considerable gap of mist-shrouded water between boat and tow-path. When she tried to heave the plank up, it fell from her grasp with a clang and there came a shout from the nightwatchman in the poop. She took a deep breath, then launched herself outward, realising, even as her feet left the deck, that there was no spring in her. She landed on the verge with a sickening thump. As her feet slipped towards the water she threw herself bodily forward, clutching the grass, and lay there panting. As the watchman came running up the deck with a lantern she stumbled away along the path, gasping with fear. Unable to see more than a few inches ahead, she tripped heavily over a mooring rope and simply lay there, spattered with mud, freezing cold and aching with a pain that spread from her lower abdomen. 'Oh Mama, William,' she sobbed helplessly, 'come and help me, whatever can I do?'

She was still lying there, clutching her aching body and crying when she heard Kau's voice calling her. And it was as well she came for, on rising, Alice felt warm blood seeping down her legs. Fortunately, the first hut they came to along the path belonged to the grandmother of Little Willow who lived there in peaceful retirement with seven hens and three ducks. The old woman, knowing a lot about Madame Plumblossom's establishment and not liking what she knew, offered temporary houseroom to the distraught girls. And so, during the three days of the Dragon Tower Festival, while Kau stolidly returned to the brothel-boat to earn money, Little Willow's grandmother nursed Alice through her miscarriage.

Being young and healthy, the physical pain of it caused Alice less anguish than the mental desolation that came immediately after. For she had begun to nurture dreams of a little son, of feeding and cherishing him till he grew into a handsome and sweet child. Then perhaps she would have taken him back and presented him to his father, whose heart would have been quite won over and who would have restored her to the only home she really knew—as a proud mother, a desired mistress. But now there was no hope of ever going back, and she had lost everyone—her beautiful baby and her sensual lover, sister-like Mei and her own brother who had deserted her. No one in the whole world, it seemed, cared whether she lived or died in that poor little hut by the river. Nor, for a short while, did she.

But she had to care, she told herself resolutely, for she was still young, and the future could yet bring other lovers, other babies, other homes. So she made herself get up and stagger outside into one of the first bright mornings of early spring. The fog had completely vanished, washed-yellow light shone on the river waters. The hens and ducks were pecking at the weedy grass and Cheshire was leaping in mad pursuit of the season's young flies. Leaning weakly against the doorpost, Alice was overwhelmed by the conflict of her emotions. She felt the sad tug of her flaccid, fruitless body and, watching

Cheshire, thought how her baby would have one day jumped and tumbled in the sun. And yet she was also conscious of a sweet sense of freedom, and of thanksgiving for the life she'd so recently feared losing.

'The varmints ain't laying much.' The old woman poked about in search of eggs.

'They're too busy finding worms,' Alice suggested.

'Heh, heh, greedy pigs.' She straightened up smiling, a frugal, kindly soul with a scraped-back knot of thin hair and a very clean faded tunic. Cleanliness was a habit with her for she had spent forty years as a washerwoman, and her only indulgence was a nightly pipe of opium. Several times in the last few days, she had offered Alice a few puffs as escape from her misery and it was an experience Alice's young body did not forget.

'Honourable Old,' Alice said with a catch in her voice, 'Kau says we must leave very soon and I want to say how kind you've been to a sick, homeless barbarian.'

'Heh, heh, I had similar trouble myself once. It's one of women's burdens and only women know how it feels—barbarian or not.'

Just then Kau came running along the tow-path shouting, 'Uncut, Uncut, get your things and bring Cheshire. Li-chi says the weather's right for the rapids now and we're leaving at once.'

On their way to the junk, they passed Madame Plumblossom's brothel, which in the sunshine looked sad and seedy rather than sinister. Alice thought of Little Willow trapped inside, waiting or lying spread under yet another heaving coolie. 'Let's hurry,' she urged fearfully, 'I never want to see that woman again.'

'She wasn't so bad, only doing her job and she paid fair as long as you did yours.' Alice shivered at Kau's way of looking at it—and at how she had benefited from that way.

Li-chi's junk, called the Silver Turtle, was fully laden with cassia oil, Hunanese red peppers, lily roots, and bundles of the tough Dragon's Whisker grass grown in the southern districts and used for weaving hats and mats. Its southwesterly route lay down a series of treacherous rapids, across stretches of shallows where fish slid just below the surface and men cast nets to catch them, through deep gorges where the waters were overshadowed by cliffs and whirlpools swirled dangerously round half-submerged rocks.

With nothing to do but enjoy the beauties of the passing scene, Alice began for the first time to relish the freedom she had regained. The ways open to her suddenly seemed limitless, yet she could formulate no plan of action. No one seemed to know how far or in what precise direction the treaty ports lay. No one had ever seen them. Indeed she sometimes doubted the reality of her own memories—of Mama's face framed by an old-fashioned spoon bonnet, of Father in a sombre black suit, of prayer-books and teacakes on Sundays. Was it possible that, somewhere, such a world still existed? Anyway, the river people assured her that she and Kau were heading vaguely in the direction of the 'Island of Fragrant Streams' which positively crawled with foreign devils. So it seemed best to go where the waters took them.

Eventually, as spring warmed into summer, they reached the hill-town of Santu on the River Jung in southern Kweichow—the Precious Province. And to Kau it was precious indeed, for, though she had never seen it, it was where her mother's tribe lived and her stolid face lit up with delighted recognition as they walked into the main square. It was market-day and folk from the nearby hill-villages had come to buy and sell—sacks of maize and peanuts, piles of peaches, musk melons, salted eggs, rolls of coarse cloth and caged hawks and eagles. Itinerant fortune-tellers, barbers, letter-writers waited for custom, and some boy-acrobats were tumbling about, led by a black mountain bear with a brass begging bowl.

By far the most extraordinary sight, in Alice's view, and that which made Kau walk with a new air of jaunty assurance, were the numbers of Miao women like herself. They wore loose blouses, skirts decorated with bands of red and green embroidery and black turbans. Heavy bangles and necklaces of silver and beads swung about them and their faces were round, their noses broad. They walked tall and erect on their normal-sized feet, looking bold, even brazen, and they laughed loudly and often as they lifted baskets of farm produce on their sturdy shoulders.

Within minutes Kau had fallen into conversation, using the tongue of her own Black Miao tribe that neither Alice nor the local Chinese understood. It seemed, Kau reported triumphantly, that her mother's ageing brother and family still

lived nearby, and so, with her remaining cash, they bought
four sesame seed cakes and set off for his house. It stood on
the town's edge, up a dirt track. It was of wattle and daub,
with a pitted yard for fowls and pigs, a clear stream beside
and, beyond, as far as one could see, the magnificent wooded
ranges of the Nanling mountains.

Kau went to the door diffidently, with Cheshire in one hand
and the cakes in the other; she called and went inside. Alice
leaned against the wall feeling apprehensive. After all, even
if Kau's uncle were to welcome with open arms the niece he'd
never met, he would be unlikely to approve of her outlandish,
penniless companion. And if not . . . what next? But she need
not have worried, for the Miao, like most outcast groups,
shared a clannish solidarity more generous and certainly
more informal than the Chinese.

Kau's grandparents, now dead, had not wanted to sell their
daughter into slavery, but there had been an uprising at the
time, when the Miao fought against their Manchu masters.
They had lost; a period of great hardship and famine
followed; it had been a question of survival. Now times were
better. The family's sons had worked doggedly, had produced
children to work also and bought a little land. It was thus
fitting that Kau should return to live among them, marry and
bear children for the good of the tribe. They asked little about
where or how she had previously lived, for they had no con-
cept of such distant parts, having never ventured more than a
few miles beyond Santu. As for Alice, she was a green-eyed
stranger from an impossibly far-off place. But she was Kau's
friend, not Chinese, young and fit enough to earn her keep and
even marry and have green-eyed children in her turn, if she so
desired.

So she was given a sleeping-space in the women's room
next to Kau and through all the clear bright summer days she
worked from cock-crow to sunset with the rest of them—
making sandals to sell, baking buckwheat cakes in ashes,
gathering eggs and shiny green fruits from the wood-oil trees
and apricots from the hill orchards.

It was an open-air, free-and-easy life, very different from
the cloistered courtyards of the Chu. The young men and
women of the neighbouring Miao families worked alongside each other in the fields, harvesting barley, gathering
creamy juices from the capsules of the opium poppies. On the

frequent festival days, they played tubular pipes, cymbals, drums and danced together, drank strong fruit brandy, smoked opium and later tumbled together on the floors of the hay-lofts.

'I'm going to marry with Bao-nyi before the winter's out,' Kau whispered to Alice on the morning after the last summer festival as they walked to the stream. She grinned gleefully, as she often did these days.

'Oh Kau, I'm so glad. Bao-nyi seems so nice and his name's nice too!' Translated it meant 'Hill-Silver,' Kau had explained, because he had been the first boy born in a family of five girls—and as rare as silver in the hills.

'And then you and Cheshire will come and live with us in the hut near his home across the river, Hill-Silver agrees. Won't it be fun?'

Alice assented with an appropriate show of enthusiasm, but, as they began washing clothes, her heart secretly sank, for the news made her face the fact that she could never really belong among these peasant people. By mutual consent, she and the young men avoided any close contact. To them, she remained a mysterious alien, and she found them too rough and bawdy when the brandy was in them, and their hands smelled always of manure. For her, there could be no setting up in a hut by a stream with a man of Hill-Silver's ilk, and she did not relish the idea of living with Kau like a super-numerary aunt and within close proximity of Hill-Silver's five sisters who were reputedly of quarrelsome disposition. So something different had to happen, Alice thought, as she swilled the coloured cloth through the mountain water; and in due course it did.

Autumn came, the distant ranges turned gold and then brown. Mists hung low in the valleys throughout the day and rain beat the country tracks into a reddish mire that spattered the young women's long skirts as they walked to market one morning to sell the last of the season's walnuts and sun-dried apricots. Kau and her two cousins were singing as they came toward the square—about a one-legged mountain imp who, if he met you in a lonely place, demanded three silver pieces. If you had none, he wound the three branches of his arms around you and squeezed. Alice was lagging behind, feeling left out, when an elderly Chinese woman rushed up and grabbed her arm.

'You—you're the barbarian wench, aren't you? A real foreign-devil, not one of them abos? Am I right?'

'Yes, I'm a foreigner from across the waters originally, not an abo.'

'Good, good,' she pushed forward the man behind her. 'This is my son, Fu-to, he's a boatman just come from Tushan. Listen to him—you must go there at once!' The man tugged his queue nervously.

'It's like this, woman. There's a barbarian—a huge male foreign-devil, lying in an inn there, very ill, and he keeps shouting for one of his own kind. He's offered a reward to anyone who'll bring him another barbarian before he yields up his spirit—if he's got one.'

'And my son was telling me this and I suddenly remembered what I'd heard about you. So there you are—go quickly, woman, there's money in it.'

Alice hesitated, 'And for your son?'

'Yes of course. But the man's very ill and he's one of your own kind too. Tushan isn't far—my son will get you there in his boat before dark.' Alice nodded. The words 'one of your own kind' left her no option. It had been long since she had seen such a one.

Kau lent her a shawl against the river's chill and she and the cousins saw her off, waving cheerily and telling her to come back with a crock of barbarian gold.

Twilight and a soft drizzle were falling by the time the yellowish lights of Tushan appeared along the river bank and Fu-to pointed out a long wooden building with its verandahs overhanging the water. It was, he said, the Inn of the Five-Tiger Pass where the barbarian lay. On reaching the inn, its landlord confirmed Fu-to's story, adding that the barbarian was failing fast and causing the devil of a nuisance with his ravings every night.

'He'd have been out on his ear days ago,' he snarled, 'except that he can afford to pay for my best room—the Mandarin's room—so he has money still about him.' His eyes gleamed and so did Fu-to's as he urged her forward.

'Go in and see him, and don't forget it was I, Fu-to the boatman, who brought you and I'm entitled to my reward.'

The man lay on a bed against a boarded partition-wall, his feet sticking out below a dirty quilt. Barbarian feet, Alice thought—so very large, long, bony. His face also looked large and skeletally thin with a stubble of reddish beard and red-rimmed eyes that opened at her approach.

'Good evening,' Alice faltered over words so long unused. 'Can you speak English?'

He focused on her a distressed and fearful glare. 'I am English,' and there was a hint of pride in it.

'So am I.'

'You? You don't look it.'

She glared back. 'I've been living away from my family for years—that's why I'm wearing these Miao clothes. They don't belong to me—I suppose.' She plucked at them uneasily, not having thought that before.

He tried raising himself on an elbow but failed. 'I didn't mean to offend you,' he offered weakly, and then, 'What are you doing here?' they both said simultaneously, and smiled at each other.

'I've come south from the Tibetan foothills,' he explained wearily. 'Trying to reach Hong Kong. I was with the Torrington-Graham expedition, did you hear of it? All dead except me—and I'm on my last legs. We were exploring, mapping territory, got roughed up by tribesmen.' His voice had faded to a whisper and she bent close to hear. 'Then we all got this accursed fever—don't come too near, it's probably contagious, kills you off. Have you any quinine? Opium?'

'Quinine, no . . . but I could get opium, it's plentiful around here. The Chinese sent for me to come, they said you were very ill and wanted to see one of your own kind.'

Forgetting his earlier warning, he grabbed her wrist and drew her down to him. 'Yes, there's one thing you must do for me—a dying man—one of your own countrymen. . . .' He stared past her, as if seeing what she could not. 'Me—dying . . . and I thought it would be in some worthwhile place if it did happen—a mountain top perhaps, or some lovely green valley, not this stinking hell-hole. But can I trust you? What's your name?'

'Alice—Greenwood. My father was a missionary, but he was killed in Tientsin years ago, that's why I'm here now.'

It was a vast, totally illogical leap. The man paused, decided he was too weak to attempt it, said merely, 'My name's Stewart Carr. A missionary's daughter, hey? So you should be honest.'

'Of course I am. I don't tell lies.'

'I didn't exactly mean that. Here, give me some more of that tea, young lady. I must collect my thoughts.' He mopped his brow. 'It's this fever. I keep floating away, not seeing you properly, not remembering what I've said. How old are you?'

'Seventeen—I think.'

'You're not sure?'

'I've been living in a Chinese house for years and their time isn't the same. I was captured when I was twelve, that I do know.'

He stared at her bewildered; it was too much for his mind. 'You must tell me all about it sometime, Alice Greenwood. But first there's something important I must tell you in case anything happens. This fever can carry a man off in a night, that's how poor old Tommy Graham went.' He sipped the tea. 'Mountain fever, dries you up inside. Can I count on you?'

He gripped her again and she looked with aversion at his grasping fingers. 'Yes you can. I told you. I'm English and my father taught me always to keep my word.' Yet that was years ago; now even the sound of such a promise sounded odd. 'Keep a word.' Was it even correct?

Stewart Carr seemed to think so, for he went on, 'Good— now then, what is it? Oh yes—the loot. Listen carefully, Miss, the landlord of this place is a rogue, they're all robbers, these bloody Chinks . . . smile to your face and fleece you behind your back.'

'Not always,' Alice was indignant. 'I've lived with them, and they never stole from me.'

'Well, you speak their lingo and . . . oh dear, ache, ache, ache all over. Now what was . . .? Oh yes, where I've hidden the loot. You see that tin trunk against the wall? Well, it's underneath—in the earth under the mats. I dug a hole when I first came, it's in a box.'

'But what is this loot?'

'Jewels, ornaments and stuff . . . worth a helluva lot. And the Chinks'll rob me of every mortal bauble if they find it.'

'Where did you get it?' Alice prised his fingers from her wrist. 'If you want me to help, you'd better not give me your fever.'

'Yes, you must . . . where did I . . .?' He looked vague, then remembered. 'Years ago it was, from the Summer Palace in Peking. I was a young subaltern then—God, those were the days—pounding into Peking with the five thousand, hey?

109

Eighteen-sixty, I wasn't much older than you are now.'

'So you were there when the British and French burned and looted the Summer Palace. My father told me about it. He said it was scandalous.'

'Oh that—war's war. Anyway, the French froggies got the best of the pickings. But I was lucky and was there in time for some of the left-overs. I've sold a piece now and then to keep going, always got a good price.'

'But what do you want me to do?' Darkness had fallen, the gloomy room smelled ominously of sickness unto death and Alice was finding it all very distasteful. From the courtyard came the cackle of fowls being driven into shelter, which reminded her that, as yet, she had no bed for the night.

'It's Flossie, my little sister. Our parents were killed in the Mutiny when she was a baby and she lives in Calcutta with an aunt. God, I'm afraid I'll never see Flossie again . . . haven't seen her for years . . . should have made more effort. . . .' He stared miserably into space.

'I'm sorry, Mr. Carr, truly I am. But let's look at the bright side. You'll probably recover. I'll bring a good doctor to you tomorrow.' She went to light the candle on the table. By its flickering light his gaunt face looked even more deathly.

'A Chink doc? Kill or cure, hey?' He tried to laugh, but only breathed more shallowly. 'But if I don't recover, Alice Greenwood, I want you to get that loot away from these thieves here. Take it back to Hong Kong, will you? You can sell a piece, anything, to pay for the journey, you don't look as if you're very well-heeled. And you can keep another piece too, as a reward. But the rest must get back to Flossie. She's an orphan with no money of her own. I've always held on to the best pieces meaning her to have them, you understand? Can I trust you, Alice?' He tried to grasp her hand again. 'Swear to me you'll do it—as if we had a Bible. Your father was a missionary so you must be an honourable English girl, though a pretty rum one, I must say. You'll keep your word, won't you? Swear now—it'll be well worth your while. The key of the loot box is under my pillow—and in the trunk you'll find a roll of cash.'

She took it out. 'I have no money at all. This will have to pay for my night here and the boatman—he's claiming the reward for bringing you a barbarian.'

'Oh all right, use it how you like. . . . I can't think straight anymore.' He moaned restlessly. 'Only please don't double-

110

cross me, Alice . . . and tomorrow . . .'

The door was flung open and the landlord strode in carrying a lantern. 'So, what's wrong with the barbarian?'

'A mountain fever he says. Is there a good doctor in town? He'll pay, I promise.'

'So, he's still well-loaded, is he?' he leered. 'Well he owes me a pretty penny for his keep already. Who's that for?' He swung the light on the cash in Alice's hand.

'Some for the boatman, some for you.' She tried to conceal the full extent of the roll up her sleeve. 'I want to stay here tonight and get the doctor tomorrow.'

'All right—being as you can pay, even if you are an abo woman.' He held the lantern over Carr, who had fallen into a feverish doze. 'Looks a goner to me.'

'Let him sleep now,' Alice wiped his forehead gently. 'He's exhausted. Mr. Carr, I'll come back tomorrow—and I won't forget what you've told me, I promise.'

He groaned inarticulately as she left. Fu-to was waiting outside and she gave him half the cash-roll.

'Do you want to go back to Santo with me?' He was suddenly eager for her custom.

'I'll see, I have to look after the barbarian first.'

'Well, I'll be here till the day after tomorrow,' he said as he shuffled off.

In a bare, chill room overlooking the river Alice spent a restless night. The rushing of the waters below echoed through her troubled dreams and several times she woke uneasily thinking she heard the distant cries of the sick man. But she could not make herself find out, and eventually, pulling the quilt tight over her head, she slept deep and late. The sun was high when she woke and went in search of the landlord, whom she found in the courtyard, peering through a pair of field-glasses at a duck and chuckling. Their expensive leather case dangled incongruously over his dirty tunic, the strap clamped across his thick queue.

'Where did you get those?' she asked with foreboding.

'From the barbarian's box of course. He died in the night.'

'Oh no—poor Mr. Carr, he kept saying he'd die.' She stared at him numbly.

'Well when people say that they usually do—the spirit gives up the ghost.' He focused the glasses on her and chuckled again. 'Makes your face look even more rum. That man owed

111

me money, so I shall keep these and the other strange things in his box.'

'You won't keep everything,' she said hotly.

'Who's going to stop me, you?'

'He told me yesterday that I was to take possession of his things if he died.'

He leered. 'Most of them have already been taken possession of.'

She pushed past him and into Carr's room. Flies were buzzing round the shape on the bed, its head covered with the quilt so that the bony legs stuck out yet further. In awful fascination, Alice touched one toe; flesh still and chill. She took a deep breath and lifted the quilt. His eyes, thank goodness, were closed, and his cheeks, hollowed with fever before, had completely caved in. Alive he had been in his late thirties; now he looked as ageless as any other death's head.

'I'm sorry, Mr. Carr,' she whispered, 'but you'd want me to . . .' She lifted the head, took the key from under the pillow and thrust it in her pocket. The tin trunk had already been well rifled; its remaining contents were some travel-stained clothes, an empty brandy flask and a battered letter-case. She opened it: a British passport for Stewart Carr; two old letters posted in Worthing, England; yellowed newspaper cuttings about the setting off of the intrepid Torrington-Graham expedition; a sepia-faded photograph of a girl sitting on a swing on a lawn, on its back the one scrawled word 'Flossie.' There was also a vellum envelope and inside that—oh joy—a map of China and a small bar of silver that the thieves had missed. She put the things aside and cautiously began to move the trunk from its significant place on the floor.

The door opened and the landlord came in accompanied by an official from the local yamen. 'I've reported the death to the proper authorities,' the latter explained importantly. 'The body is now to be removed and a report made to the magistrate in Kweiyang.'

Two coolies came in with a litter; they dumped the lank body on it, its white legs sticking out straight over the end, for Stewart Carr was several inches taller than most Chinese.

'I'm sure not all his possessions are here.' Alice looked resolutely at the official. 'There was a pair of field-glasses for instance . . .'

He stared back at her. 'You're an abo, aren't you? Are you

112

proposing to make a charge of theft? If so, you must come to the *yamen* and see the deputy-magistrate. He'd be interested to know who you are, for a start.'

She hesitated. 'Well, I realise of course that Mr. Carr had been well attended here during his illness.'

'Carr? Is that his name?' The official halted the coolies at the door, and studied the dead man's face.

'Yes—Stewart Carr, and these are his papers.' She handed him the letter-case.

'And that?' He indicated the envelope.

'Oh—just a plan. Surely I can keep it? It's in English and of no use to you.' She handed the map over, holding on to the envelope with the silver inside.

He stared at it upside down, grunted, gave it back to her. Another coolie picked up the trunk.

'Well, do you wish to make a formal charge about the contents of this box?' he challenged.

'No . . .' Alice tried to peer under it; the matting below looked undisturbed. 'But please let me keep his personal letters and a picture.'

The official blew out his cheeks. 'No. Everything must go to the *yamen*; reports must be made. You are not a relative?'

'No, but. . . .'

'Well, come on then,' the landlord grumbled at the door. 'I've a rich merchant from Yunnan arriving any minute and he always takes this Mandarin's room—so out of here, abo woman.'

She stood nonplussed. 'Someone in here . . . tonight?'

'Yes of course, I run a popular establishment and it's always full of silk traders going east at this time of year.'

'But how long will the merchant want this room?'

'How do I know? He's a good customer, stays several days in Tushan every season, the longer the better.' He hustled her to the door and she had no choice but to follow the official, the body of Stewart Carr and his trunk outside.

At the inn-entrance, the official beckoned her: 'So who are you? Have you travelling papers? What are you doing here?'

She extemporised rapidly. 'I was travelling through Santu to join my brother who's a missionary. They told me about Mr. Carr and begged me to come to him. I left my papers behind in the rush.'

It sounded very unlikely; on the other hand he did not want

113

any awkward questions asked about the dead barbarian's possessions. Much better for all concerned if she just disappeared.

'My honourable chief is absent today,' he said heavily. 'But if you're still here tomorrow, he'll want to see you—and your papers.'

'Yes. I understand.' They looked at each other; his eyes were blank. He climbed into his chair and, with a flourish, bade the bearers lift it.

As she stood there considering the implications of that exchange, the main gate opened and a fat man on a fat horse followed by a string of mountain ponies tramped into the courtyard. The landlord rushed out, bowing profusely.

'Oh you are most welcome, honourable sir. How fortunate I am to see you again. The Mandarin's room has been pining for your presence.'

Alice slipped away to her room, took out the map, the silver bar, the key to the loot box and stared at them. What was to be done? The first priority was to get more cash, and fortunately, she discovered, the exchange rate for silver in the Tushan market was high. Her first purchases were a pair of Chinese-style trousers, a padded tunic, an over-jacket, a covered basket to put them in. Then she went to the river bank and asked Fu-to to wait for her there until tomorrow.

By the time she returned to the inn, other merchants had arrived and the courtyard was full of coolies carrying baggage, unladen mules and ponies rolling happily in the dust, servants carrying bags of fodder and bowls of soup. Eventually she found the landlord.

'If I cannot have the Mandarin's room tonight, at least give me the one next door. The hole I had last night is filthy and the noise of the waters kept me awake.'

'You, faugh! An abo woman in one of my best rooms!'

'I'm not an abo, I'm a foreign barbarian woman as you know, and I have money to pay.' She produced a large roll of cash from her basket.

He caught a passing servant by the queue. 'Take this abo ... this barbarian woman to the room there, next to the Mandarin's.'

Ensconced in her comparatively grand apartment which boasted a stool and a lantern as well as a bed, Alice applied her eye to one of many gaps in the board partition between

114

her and her neighbour. The fat Yunnanese merchant was slurping a steaming plate of stew and she noted with dismay that rolls of silks were piled against the wall where the trunk had rested. She sighed in frustration; there seemed nothing to do but wait. As darkness fell and she again heard the fowls cackling in the courtyard, she pondered the sad story of Stewart Carr. If only she had talked more to him, given him more comfort, and above all, if only she had taken the loot away while the going was good.

Hearing voices, Alice again applied her eye to the gap; three other merchants had arrived and the talk was about prices—of silks and mulberries, of white wax, furs and opium, of cart-hire and inns. Soon they gathered round the table under the lantern for a prolonged gambling session. Coins and dice clinked merrily. The men cracked melon seeds, spat, called for wine, roared with laughter when one of them lost a newly won pile of cash. Alice watched impatiently; how could she possibly get into that room unseen that night? But if she was still here tomorrow, the yamen official would surely track her down.

There was a knock on the door and three musicians appeared to entertain the guests. One carried a stringed lute, another a flute, the third a hand-drum; two singing-girls with heavily painted faces accompanied them. The music twanged, while the girls swayed slowly round the room singing in high falsetto voices. The older looked absurdly plump and motherly for her role, but the younger had a natural grace and her eyes glinted teasingly at the men.

'Let's hear just her,' shouted the Yunnanese. 'What's your name, my pretty poll?'

'Golden Persimmon, honourable sir.' She folded her hands in her drooping sleeves and sang:

How sweet this branch of jasmine flower,
On the morning of the day t'was dropped in my house.
I'll wear it myself, yet not out of doors,
But will match it with others to make myself glad.

The men applauded, poured more wine while Golden Persimmon sang again and again by popular request and the Yunnanese watched her intently. At length, the leader ended the performance explaining that other guests waited to hear their melodies. As Golden Persimmon handed round a silken bag for tips, the merchant caught her by the neck and whispered to her, while the other men guffawed bawdily, and the leader, bowing low, said, 'Her musical gifts are needed for the moment, sir, perhaps later there will be a chance to explore her other treasures.'

The merchant released her. 'As you will—let her sing for her supper instead.'

The merchants gathered round the table again, but the heart had gone from their game and the visitors soon departed. The Yunnanese's servant brought his master a chamberpot and washing water. The merchant bolted the door, scratched his belly and crotch, oiled his queue, picked his teeth, blew out the lantern, got into bed. Alice waited a little, then, wearing her new Chinese clothes, tiptoed into the passage and knocked on his door.

'Sir, honourable sir, I've a message for you.'

He opened it. Keeping her face concealed, she said, 'From Golden Persimmon, sir. She will accommodate you now, if you desire. But you must go to her for it's not the usual practice. Down the passage, across the courtyard, take the small passage on the left and through the gate.'

'Huh, that sounds better, wait a minute, wench.'

'I'll see you there, sir.'

As he went to don his cloak, she slipped back into her dark room and soon had the satisfaction of hearing him leave. She rushed into his room, threw aside the rolls of silk and folded back the matting. It was easy to see where a patch of earth had been recently disturbed. Hurriedly, she dug below the surface and lifted out a small square box of inlaid wood. She jammed back the earth and the matting, hearing a distant shout as she did so. As steps thudded along the passage, she threw the silks back in place and scurried to her own room.

''T'was a trick, I tell you,' the Yunnanese was shouting at his servant, 'and now I'll bet a turtle for a tortoise I've been robbed blind. You lazy sod, why don't you keep watch, blast you? That girl was a thieves' moll, I'll raise the roof if. . . .' Alice listened as he and the servant checked their untouched stores of silver, silks, opium and cash.

'I must have been too fast for them,' the Yunnanese grunted at last. 'I'm not a man to be hoodwinked for long. I soon smelled a rat. Still, I'll have it out with that slimy toad of a landlord in the morning,' she heard him muttering to himself as he again got into bed, the servant now instructed to sleep outside his door.

Only when she heard them both snoring did she dare light her lantern, and, with shaking fingers, unlock the box. The loot: two bejewelled gold hairpins, one long pearl and rose quartz necklace with ruby clasp, two porcelain perfume bottles with carved jade stoppers, a gold ring set with amber, a silver opium-holder shaped like a walnut, and a little ivory box studded with turquoise. She opened its lid and jumped, for a tinny tune sprang from its inside, a sweet and merry waltz, so totally unexpected. The ladies of the Peking court, it seemed, had a passion for foreign musical boxes. She played the tune, waltzing a little round the treasures spread out before her, then she scooped them back in the box and slept with it cradled in her arms.

Next morning early, dressed again in her Miao clothes, she paid the landlord and hurried away before the Yunnanese had slept off his disturbed night. A while later, huddled on the deck of Fu-to's boat, she grinned to herself as they passed the Inn of the Five-Tiger Pass and heard the shouts of coolies loading animals in the courtyards. How furious that fat merchant would be if he knew what treasures had lain within his grasp!

Getting out the map, she muttered the unfamiliar English words to herself. It looked a very long way to Hong Kong, and it seemed better to continue on this same river, the Jung, to Jungen in Kwangsi. But first she would return to Kau and her family—or would she? It would be dishonest not to tell Kau of her 'crock of barbarian gold,' but then those happy-go-lucky Miaos would expect her to share it with them as generously as they had shared their smaller bounty with her. They would eat, drink, and smoke it all away. She could just imagine the merrymaking at Kau's wedding. But then . . . how would she get to Hong Kong? She watched the clear waters of the Jung sliding by and all her instincts told her not to return to the Miao again. She went up to Fu-to, who was poling along whistling through his teeth in the boatman's fashion. 'I want you to take me straight through Santo and across the Kwangsi border to Jungen. How much will it cost?'

At Jungen three days later, Alice exchanged the gold hairpins for silver and bought silks for Fu-to to take to Kau as a

117

wedding present, and then, dressed in her Chinese clothes, the loot-box concealed in her farm-basket, she set her face determinedly to the south. The journey took a long time for it lay across sparsely populated country. Winter closed in and as the weather worsened boatmen and carters were increasingly reluctant to travel far, even for good money. Not that Alice felt any sense of urgency, for she had only the vaguest idea of what lay ahead, and was uneasily aware that no one, anywhere, was expecting her arrival.

Indeed, as her destination approached, her rate of progress noticeably slackened and she was happy to pass a prolonged New Year with a friendly family of boat people. But eventually, on a bright, blustery day of early spring, she boarded a vessel of the Hong Kong, Canton & Macao Steamship Company that carried her across the stretch of open sea to the Island of Fragrant Streams or, as its barbarian inhabitants called it, Hong Kong.

Jostled down the gangplank with the rest of the Chinese passengers, Alice walked along Queen's Road in a daze, staring up at the clock tower, the church on the hill, the tall rows of shipping, consulate and mercantile offices with various national flags flying from their balconies. And there was the Union Jack, gracing a very imposing building indeed, standing back from the road behind a wall. Rickshaw men were sprawled against it, waiting for custom, and a large barbarian in red and black uniform stood in the guardbox. She went up to him.

'May I go in please?'

He looked down at her small figure, clad in baggy trousers, grubby tunic, carrying an up-country basket, and grinned. 'Why?'

'Because I'm British and my name is Miss Alice Greenwood. I want to see an official.'

His grin broadened. 'Oh yes—and my name's Mr. Disraeli!'

She looked puzzled. 'But, Mr. Disraeli ... I really am British, you can see I'm not Chinese.'

'What a caution! Do you realise this is Her Majesty's courthouse? I've seen the likes of you before, wench, little bit of the old half and half's been going on, hey?'

Again she did not understand and, in desperation, drew a roll of cash from her basket. 'See here—I've money, if you'll let me...'

118

With a roar he pounced forward, giving her a thwack that sent her sprawling into the gutter. She sat there looking at him for a second, then burst into tears. The watching rickshaw coolies cackled with laughter.

'Scram, you little varmint—scarper—or you'll feel a real genuine British boot up your backside.' He advanced threateningly. She scrambled up and fled sobbing. She ran and ran, away from the Queen's Road and the large buildings into the narrow streets of what the Queen's Road residents called 'the native quarter.'

Exhausted, she sat down at a food-stall, ordered a bowl of noodles, began to dry her eyes and clean the mud from her clothes.

'Had a fall, did you? Never mind—every day can't be a feast of lanterns.' It was the cheery voice of the coolie next to her.

'Yes . . . I . . .' Alice sniffed. 'I'm better now.' The noodles came and as she ate she studied his kindly face. 'Do you pull people about in that little cart? I saw them on the big road near the sea.'

He stared at her. 'Little cart? It's a rickshaw of course.'

'I've never seen one,' she said doubtfully. 'I don't remember them.'

He shook his head in amazement. 'You've not been long in Hong Kong then—I've been pulling fat old barbarians about in them for the past five years.'

'So you'd know if there's a Church Missionary Society here?'

''Course there is—up the Victoria Road.'

So Alice's first-ever rickshaw ride ended at a wide gateway, with an imposing stone house looming in front of her. 'That's it, girl,' said the rickshaw-coolie. She paid him and walked to the door. 'Church Missionary Society. Hong Kong Director: Mr. G. Penfold' announced the brass plate at its side. She pulled the bell-rope and a black-suited Englishman appeared.

'What do you want, missee?'

'I've come to see the director, Mr. Penfold.' Alice summoned the last of her reserves.

'You? Do you have an appointment? Who are you?'

She swallowed hard. 'My name's Alice Greenwood. My father was a missionary of the Society, which is why I've

119

come here. He was killed at Tientsin years ago and . . . I've been away ever since. . . .'

He looked puzzled. 'You're not a native, no. Well, wait here a moment, missee.'

She leaned against the doorpost; her legs had turned to water and her heart thumped wildly. If he does not let me in, she thought, I will lie down on the mat and scream and scream. . . . 'Who are you?' the question echoed in her mind. 'Who are you?' said the Caterpillar, and Alice replied, 'I hardly know sir, just at present—at least I know who I *was* but . . .'

The man returned. 'You are to step this way, please. Someone will see you soon.'

She walked tentatively into the hall and the door was shut behind her.

5

Jimmy Callum, cub reporter from the *China Mail*, was looking eagerly at Alice, pencil poised.

'So, Miss Greenwood,' he framed his last question of the interview carefully for the young lady was obviously ill-at-ease, 'now you've told me the exciting story of your captivity and your brave escape—I'm sure my readers would be most interested to know what you find most surprising and different about the civilisation to which you've now returned?'

She hesitated cautiously, mindful of readers who would hang on her every word. 'Well—yes, it is different. Last evening Mr. and Mrs. Penfold took me for my first carriage drive along the Bund, and everything seemed so large and solidly made—the tall buildings, the macadamed roads, the ships in the harbour. And English people—especially the men—look very large too. I said to Mrs. Penfold that it was like Alice, you know—in Wonderland—who kept swallowing drinks that made her different sizes. Well, Hong Kong makes me feel very small.'

Grand, he thought, framing the headline in his mind: 'Alice returns from a Chinese Wonderland to Hong Kong.'

'And, you know it's a great surprise to find Hong Kong actually here. You see, in Hunan, it's hard to believe such a place could exist in the same country.'

'You know, Miss Greenwood, I've never thought of it like that, never.' Jimmy Callum shut his notebook with a snap that sounded almost irreverent in the Penfolds' drawing-room. Alice rose, but stiffly, for the root cause of her unease was physical. Early that morning, Mrs. Penfold had insisted on taking her to a dress shop in Robinson Road where she had been fitted into what her hostess termed 'proper clothes.' The boned stays, tight-waisted jacket-bodice, apron overskirt,

121

stockings and button shoes which Alice now wore were, she had been assured, of the light-weight summer variety, but she felt extremely constricted and uncomfortable and more conscious of her body outline than ever in her life before.

She felt herself blushing as the reporter shook her hand almost reverently, casting admiring eyes on her shaped bosom. 'It's been a real pleasure to meet you, Miss Greenwood. And I think you are quite a little heroine, I do honestly.'

Her modest disclaimer was interrupted by Mr. Penfold who bustled in waving a piece of paper. 'Alice—here it is—a message from the Consulate. They've checked their files and it is as I thought, your mother, the former Mrs. Eliza Greenwood, remarried four years ago, and her present husband is a Mr. Edward Blake of the China Inland Mission. They are normally resident in Mukden, Manchuria. And listen to this, my dear girl, about a year after the marriage your mother gave birth to twins—so you now have a new brother and sister, as well as a stepfather!'

Alice sat down quickly and so did Jimmy Callum, who re-opened his notebook and scribbled furiously. 'And finally,' said Mr. Penfold, waiting for Jimmy to catch up, '. . . I sent a messenger to the China Inland Mission here and they tell me that your mother, whose health is rather precarious, is at this very moment recuperating her strength in Chefoo with the babies. So you'll be able to see her very soon, my dear.'

'Oh, I can hardly believe it—she's alive and still here in China—oh, that's so wonderful! But . . . but I thought she'd have been too old?'

'To have more babies you mean?' he smiled. 'She was under forty when your poor father was martyred—and mothers tend to look rather old to their children, you know.' He patted her shoulder. 'I expect this second marriage and the little ones will have given her a new lease of life—I'll warrant she'll look ten years younger, and it's you who'll look old to her!'

'Oh, I must go to Chefoo at once, Mr. Penfold. But how soon will she know about me?'

'Very soon—a message is already sent by urgent dispatch to the Chefoo Consulate and we'll arrange your passage there as soon as possible. Our Hong Kong Consul, Mr. Meadows, wants to see you this afternoon, to hear all about your experiences, and your brother's continuing captivity.'

'Does Mrs. Penfold know this? I must go and tell her myself. You've got your story, haven't you, Mr. Callum?'

'Indeed yes, Miss Greenwood, thank you.' He sprang to open the door for her, but she hung back. 'Is there anything else? You'll certainly capture the headlines tomorrow as it is.'

'Oh . . . no, I forgot, about ladies going out first, I mean. It isn't like that in China, you know.'

Callum grinned delightedly as she ran out, remarking to Mr. Penfold, 'It's funny how every other foreigner in Hong Kong thinks he *is* in China—except Miss Greenwood.'

'Ah yes, she has much to learn in certain directions—and she'll need some careful handling for a while. But don't put that in your story, young man!'

Careful handling . . . Mr. Penfold recalled his own words late that afternoon as he penned his weekly report to the General Secretary of his London headquarters. 'Miss Greenwood,' he wrote, 'impresses me as a young woman of considerable character and, more importantly from our point of view, she has acquired a thorough knowledge of the language and customs of the country which is very rare among foreigners here. I feel'—he paused, bit his quill, watched two butterflies chase each other among the magnolia blossoms outside—'that it might be a mis-direction of her valuable talents if she were to become too deeply influenced by the doctrines of the China Inland Mission into which her mother has now remarried. She is very much her father's daughter and I believe her potential for mission work is great. I'm therefore arranging that she travel to Chefoo in the company of Miss Ida Palmer, one of our most zealous recent arrivals from the Islington mission-college. I shall instruct Miss Palmer confidentially to keep me informed of Miss Greenwood's progress and do all she can to guide her towards eventual enrolment in our theological study-centre in Shanghai.' He concluded, 'It would be a most wondrous instance of the workings of the Divine will if Miss Greenwood should turn out to be God's instrument for the Opening Up of Hunan to the Word . . .'

Ida Palmer's thin fingers, encased in pink cotton gloves, gripped tensely round the deck-rail of the China Merchant Company's coastal steamer, *Mandalay*. She was filled with excited anxiety at the thought of leaving Hong Kong for the mysterious China beyond, and it was rather provoking that her travelling companion seemed not to share these feelings. Instead, Alice was gazing with calm detachment at the crowds of wellwishers on the quay.

'You know, Alice,' Ida began in the gaspy voice that had been the despair of her college oratory tutor, 'I am still so often struck by the thought of just how many Chinese there are. One is told in college, of course, but one doesn't quite grasp it—so many millions to be saved, such a gigantic task for one short lifetime, don't you feel?'

'I can't say I've thought of it like that,' Alice replied briskly. 'But then I'm not a missionary.'

'Ah, Alice, not yet—but consider all the valuable work someone like you could do for the Cause . . .'

'Frankly, Ida, the only causes that interest me are seeing my mother again and getting my brother out of Hunan.'

'Yes of course, that is understandable,' Ida plucked nervously at her glove, 'but these are just passing temporal causes. I'm talking of large issues altogether—of causes that can take a lifetime.'

'Well, I intend to take things little by little, in bite-sizes as they come.' Alice was thinking irritably that ever since she had reached Hong Kong a week ago the talk had been of lifetime-size causes: converting the heathen, bringing modern civilisation to the Chinese, conquering new dominions. The English seemed so earnest about everything, but not, how could she put it—not philosophical. That was their trouble.

Ida edged closer, trying to be conciliatory, for she had already decided Alice was a prickly little thing. 'What is going to happen about your brother, Alice?'

'I saw Consul Meadows again yesterday and he's sending a detailed report on it all to Sir Hugh Digby in Peking. Probably I'll have to go there and explain everything myself.' She felt rather grand about this.

'My, that would be thrilling, wouldn't it! And meeting Sir Hugh for a *tête à tête* too! My room-mate Celia saw him at a tea-party once and says he's ever so distinguished-looking. How old is your brother, Alice? Oh look, there goes the pilot boat . . . wave . . . now we're really at sea.' Ida gazed back longingly at the solidly reassuring buildings along the Bund. If only Papa and Mama could see her now, how proud and anxious they would be. Poor Father, he had always wanted to see the world. He had gone to Boulogne for three days once and it whetted his appetite, he used to say. But if you were in Father's position with his business and the family, there was not much point in having it whetted, really. Nor would there have been for her, except that, at the age of twenty-three and still unmarried, she had heard the Call. Ida sighed. 'And how old is your brother, Alice?'

But there was no response, for Alice had moved across the deck and was deep in conversation with a young native wearing a very odd-looking combination of Western and Chinese dress. Ida sighed again; it was not for nothing that her brothers called her 'Ida-the-Sigher.' Really, this Miss Greenwood had very little sense of the proprieties, and she must explain to Mr. Penfold how difficult it was to keep an eye on her.

'You're going to Tientsin then? How strange . . .' Alice looked at the young man, feeling a pang of nostalgic grief at the familiar name.

'Yes—a college is just opening there for the study of Western-style military and naval tactics and I hope to enrol.'

'Goodness, how things have changed since . . .'

'Since what?'

'Since I lived in Tientsin years ago.'

He looked at her curiously. 'Did you? Where do you live now, may I ask? Your Chinese is so unusually fluent for a foreigner, but the accent is unfamiliar to me.'

'It's Hunanese, that's why. You see I . . .' Again she paused, overwhelmed by a sense of bewildered disbelief which she later characterised as 'that rabbit-hole feeling.' For it suddenly seemed as if, for the past few years, she had been down a rabbit-hole in a land that had seemed real enough while she was there, but, once you left, was impossible to explain. Or contrariwise, she thought, I have *now* fallen down a rabbit-hole—for how could she tell this stranger, standing so confidently in his half-Western outfit on this half-Western steamer, about everything that had happened to her? In any case, with Frank still in rabbit-hole land, it would be foolish to breathe a word of it.

'My parents were missionaries, you see, and I learned most of my Chinese from a Hunanese convert.'

'So you're a missionary?' His tone was both challenging and disappointed.

'No, certainly not. My father was. He's dead.'

He nodded abruptly. 'If you'll excuse my saying, and with no disrespect to the honourable dead, it is not your Christian religion we Chinese need—it is your knowledge of mechanical objects and technical skills. We don't even have a correct word for what makes vessels like this move, for example! And we're still making wooden war-junks equipped with lances and pikes!' He banged the steamer rail hard in emphasis, then smiled warmly at her.

I like him, she thought, he's bold and different from any Chinese I have ever met. Quite handsome too. How would he be in bed? I wonder. She looked up at him searchingly and he stared back, confused and startled; both of them suddenly tongue-tied.

'What is your name?' she asked softly.

'Lin Fu-wei, I am from Canton.'

'Ah, a hot-blooded southerner.'

He smiled. 'You could say so. And your name?'

She told him, hoping he had not read the recent issue of the *China Mail*, and added, 'But you can call me by my Chinese name, if you like—Uncut Jade.'

'Ha—very good. From Li-chi—"an unserviceable vessel"?'

They drew up deck-chairs and sat down facing the sea. 'Are you travelling alone?' he asked.

'No—I have a companion and she is a missionary, I warn you!'

'Like most foreigners I meet. They're not really interested in the new China and the urgent need for change. In my view, we must start by improving the material lives of the peasantry.' He spoke as if from a recently learned lesson, but Alice had no idea of its source.

'But why should the Chinese want to change? They seem well enough as they are.'

'The masses are oppressed and ignorant—enslaved by all our ancient customs. No, they must be taught new philosophies by new leaders.'

'Like you?' she teased, but he replied in deadly earnest, confidently, full of his own sense of mission.

'That's why I'm going to college—to learn as much as I can and become a leader of the people.'

'I see,' she picked irritably at the never-opened parasol Ida insisted she carry. 'I feel my education has been much neglected—you make me realise how ignorant I am about what is going on.'

'Well, most girls are. They don't need to know really.'

'Don't they? But I want to learn—so tell me one thing for a start. Would there be more chance for your "new China" if the Manchus were overthrown?'

He raised a flat hand, warning her off. 'That's a very big question, Uncut Jade, and I'm certainly not answering it fully here—to you, a stranger, in a public place.'

'But the Manchus are still very much in control?'

'Oh yes, the Empress Dowager has consolidated her power since the death of T'ung-chih. And her nephew—he's only a child—is on the Dragon Throne.' He bent closer. 'The situation seems hopeless at the moment.'

Really it was too much, Ida thought as she came round the bulkhead, to see Alice and the native whispering secretly and literally *tête à tête*. She straightened her back. 'Alice my dear, there you are. I've been looking for you everywhere. It will soon be supper time and you haven't even unpacked. May I meet your new acquaintance?'

'Good afternoon and how do you do? My name is Lin Fu-wei.' He rose stiffly; his English was very poor.

'How nice to hear you speaking English. Where did you learn?'

'A teacher, I have.' He was near the limit of his powers and a pause followed.

'Well now, Alice, you must come and dress for supper.'

Leaving, Alice flashed back at him in Chinese, 'We'll talk more later, won't we?' He grinned agreement.

'Alice,' Ida broached the subject when they had retired to their cabin for the night and Alice was able, gratefully, to loosen her stays. 'You do realise, I trust, that it is not quite seemly for young ladies to accost strange foreign men on boat-decks, as you did this afternoon?'

Alice leaned her hot forehead against the cool metal bunk. The cabin was airless and she looked with distaste at the appearing details of Ida's pallid, angular body. How much more fun to be sharing a cabin with Mr. Lin!

'I didn't accost him. He asked me the time in his very poor English and I replied in my very good Chinese, so we began talking. And we're the foreigners here, not him!'

Ida sighed with extraordinary depth even for her. 'Of course

127

your command of the language is a great advantage—a gift of tongues, one might almost say. But like all gifts it must be used circumspectly. And you mustn't let it lead you into too intimate familiarities with . . . strangers.'

'We weren't talking intimately, we were discussing Chinese politics.'

'Alice, really—must you contradict everything I say like this?' From her bunk's edge, Ida blinked up in helpless indignation.

'Oh, I didn't mean to—I'm sorry but . . . well, it's hot in here. I'm just going on deck for a breath of air before turning in.'

'But Alice, it's not proper to . . .'

Ida's wail was lost as Alice shut the door. With trembling fingers she pulled on her nightgown. What could one do with such a perverse creature? Alice did not seem afraid of anything in the way most girls were, she was so unpredictable and her Chinese fluency looked like being a very mixed blessing.

A yellow half-moon hung low over the South China Sea and the only sounds on deck were the rhythmic swish of water and thud of engines as the *Mandalay* steamed north-east towards the Straits of Formosa. Alice leaned against the rail feeling both elated and troubled as she thought about her short stay in Hong Kong. She had been made much of. The men had questioned her earnestly about the conditions of the interior provinces and the customs of the natives. The women had petted her, presented her with gloves to conceal her work-roughened hands and bonnets to shade her weather-beaten cheeks— tokens of respectability in the civilisation to which she had returned. One and all had lamented her years of absence from a good moral Christian home and had been too concerned with her spiritual well-being to enquire closely about her material circumstances and how she had managed the journey back. Her lack of social graces had also worried them, and Alice remembered with shamed irritation how, during her first supper with the Penfolds, she had picked up her rice bowl and begun slurping rice into her mouth with a fork till she became aware of their scandalised disapproval. They must have taken me for a little barbarian, she thought wryly, and been most relieved to ship me off to Mama at the first opportunity. For the truth is—no one really knew what to do with me.

Now, as she sailed north, she began to worry about the coming reunion with her mother. Looking up the yellowed file labelled 'Tientsin Massacre, 1870,' Mr. Penfold (who had adamantly refused to let her see its entire contents) read out that Mrs. Greenwood had been rescued from the burning Mission at the last minute by the *yamen* guards and had taken a long while to recover from her injuries and the shock of her husband's murder. About six months later, he continued, flipping over several pages, Alice and Frank had been officially listed as dead and Eliza had been on the verge of returning alone to England when, as he put it, 'she somehow got mixed up with the C.I.M. people.' He did not elaborate, but his tone was clearly disapproving.

Alice had never thought much about her mother's religious beliefs before. Now she feared she would be unable to ignore them. Oh, if only Frank were here! He was Mama's favourite and it would have been so much easier with him by her side. She stared at the mellow, low-slung moon, thinking resentfully of the free-and-easy life he was still leading in Changsha—practising javelin-throwing, exercising Han-li's horse. But a javelin—what an absurdity in this modern China that Lin Fu-wei had talked about this afternoon!

She chewed her lip anxiously, for her short experience of Treaty Port life had convinced her that Frank must be brought 'home' as soon as possible, for his own good. And that was why she had already resolved to tell no one about the 'Carr loot,' now carefully sewed into her reticule lining. Funds would undoubtedly be needed for Frank's escape and where else could she get them? But if she had told the story of that strange encounter with Stewart Carr, she would have had to give up the treasure. So: Carr's little Flossie had to wait till her little Frank was safely out of Hunan! In any case, she comforted herself as she returned to the cabin, Flossie had no more right to the loot than she did—by right it should be handed over to the Chinese authorities.

'Oh Alice, I've been so worried, where have you been, wandering about alone at this time of night? It's not safe, you know.' Ida was dozily reading the latest issue of the *Missionary Gleaner*, having vowed not to sleep till Alice returned.

'Of course it's safe. Whatever could happen to me on a British steamer like this? It's no use, Ida,' Alice peeled off her dress, 'you can't expect me to worry about things like that, when I've travelled hundreds of miles alone in the interior and come to no harm.'

'But then you were disguised as a Chinese—more or less—and now you're dressed properly as a Christian young lady, and that makes a lot of difference.'

'My father used to say that the idea of clothes making the man or woman wasn't part of a good Christian's belief.'

Ida pulled the sheet up to her nose. 'I don't know what you're talking about.' Then she softened. 'It's funny you should say that though. My dear Papa often quotes that phrase, only he says it's the belief that clothes maketh the man which keeps him in business.'

'Really? What does he do then?'

'He owns a drapers and outfitters in Bromley, Kent—it's the oldest established firm in the High Street,' she added defensively.

Alice yawned. 'You must tell me about it tomorrow, Ida. About Kent and all those places in England I've forgotten about.'

'Forgotten about *Kent!*' Ida positively jumped up and the *Gleaner* slid to the floor. Alice picked it up as she climbed into her bunk. 'My father was born in Norfolk, so I remember about that, but I can't quite place Kent. Good-night, Ida, and sweet dreams.'

Alice was asleep in minutes, but Ida lay awake staring wide-eyed into the vessel's thrumming darkness, listening fearfully to the metallic scramblings of the cockroaches, praying that God would show her how Alice could be persuaded to enrol in Shanghai's theological college straightaway. It would seem her only hope of salvation.

However, as the ship sailed leisurely north-east, Ida's vigilance relaxed. The seas were calm, the days balmy and it was pleasant to sit in a deck-chair listening to the waves and the flapping awnings, writing letters eventually destined for the High Street, Bromley. Meanwhile, Alice was profitably occupied in teaching her young Chinese friend more English; an innocent enough pastime, though Ida might have felt differently had she understood everything Mr. Lin—'Lin' as Alice soon familiarly called him—told Alice.

'Father says we Chinese must learn your language because we are so ignorant of Western culture and technology. And that makes us weak and vulnerable—he fears we're in danger of being overrun by the powerful European nations within the next twenty years and must strengthen ourselves to preserve the Celestial Empire.'

'Your father must be unusual to view things in that way,' Alice said cautiously, remembering the Chus' unconcealed, unthinking disdain for all things barbarian.

'Yes, he is. You remember those wars over thirty years ago, when you British came into Canton and insisted on new trading rights—including the import of more opium, which hasn't been good for us? My father was quite young then and went on a delegation to the foreigners with his father—my revered grandfather—who was one of the Canton commissioners. Anyway, my father met a young Mr. Clark who kept boasting about the British Empire overseas and how your small island was just about the richest country in the world. Mr. Clark didn't have much time for missionaries—I remember Father telling me that! Anyway, most of the Chinese delegation didn't believe a word he said. But my father listened—that's why he's unusual, and, to cut a long story short, that's why he's sending me away to college now.'

'To learn how to defeat the British?'

'To learn how to defend our own country against greedy European traders and power-hungry foreign governments.'

Alice looked at him doubtfully, having never heard such sentiments before. He stared back quizzically, then melted into one of his charming smiles. 'What strange and pretty eyes you have—hints of green and blue, like jade out of the far western mountains, cut and polished.' He touched her arm and she leaned receptively towards him. But he dropped his hand quickly and returned to his earlier theme. 'I understand that in your country thousands of people work in factories producing goods that sell in world markets—your industrial revolution sounds so full of promise. That is what we need here—it makes my heart ache to see our poor ignorant peasants bending wearily over the paddies, working so hard for so little.'

' "To only see the sky when it is reflected in the mud," ' she quoted at him.

'Well said. And when I think how much more educated and prosperous your working classes must be . . . aren't they?'

'I hardly know . . . I suppose so. I've never seen them.' He looked amazed and she added, 'You see, I've never been to England. I was born here and I've always lived here—so far.'

He liked that about her immensely, it made her less of a barbarian than most. It also explained her lack of that arrogance

131

which seemed bred in most English bones, he thought, as, soon after, he watched Ida Palmer piloting Alice towards the tea-room. Every movement of Ida's conveyed a shrinking, if covert, disdain for 'the natives'—and yet she was but a small-town shopkeeper's daughter, Alice had told him. What effrontery! And he drifted into a brutal fantasy in which Ida was kneeling bound hand and foot before him, and he, with a chopper in his hand, was telling her quite calmly that he was going to cut off both her breasts unless she immediately recanted her Christian faith, shaved her head and became a Buddhist nun. What would she do in such a situation? he wondered. Would she clasp her hands in prayer and bare her bosom for his blade? He was both excited and repelled by the vision, wondering what he would then do? No, she would have to be rescued at the last minute—by Uncut Jade of course. Who would plead for Ida's life, which he would grant in return for—the sweet little Uncut body of course. But for Uncut he would need no other weapon than his own manhood, and there was something in those strange eyes of hers which suggested the encounter would be a delight.

The next day the *Mandalay* stopped at Swatow, then at Foochow and Ningpo, so it was ten days after their departure that Shanghai eventually hove in view one misty morning. As they moved slowly up the Woosung estuary, Alice could just discern the outlines of the international settlement and the tower of Trinity Church. Her heart sank. More missionaries dwelled here, including one Miss Hilda Stubbs of the Church Missionary Society who was going to show her and Ida around during the day's stay in port. 'And you'll be able to see the work of the Mission School and visit the theological college and I'm sure you'll find it all most inspiring!' Ida had promised her. Alice had prevaricated, hoping Lin might go ashore with her instead, but he was meeting some naval students and was totally uninterested in her arrangements. The breakfast gong sounded just as the ship docked and Alice went below, ponder-ing the day's unattractive alternatives: to see Shanghai with Ida and Hilda, or not to see it at all.

'Miss Greenwood?' a steward approached as she was fin-ishing her toast. 'Please to the Purser's Office, very much important—quick.'

'Oh dear, what can be the matter now?' Alice jumped up.

'Shall I come with you?' Ida offered.

'No thanks—perhaps it's another newspaper reporter.'

At the door of the Purser's office stood a tall, erect man wearing a smart, light tweed morning-coat, his blue eyes set deep in a bronzed face intently scanning each passing face. He stepped forward hesitantly as she approached.

'It is . . . isn't it? Alice, it must be you?'

She started up wonderingly. 'It's . . . it's Uncle Robert! Can it really be?' She clung to him joyously, tears in her eyes. 'But however did you, why are you . . .? I mean, you used to be in India!'

He squeezed her shoulders. 'Oh I'm still stationed there, but I'm here on leave. And I'd planned to go from here to Chefoo to see your mother. Then yesterday a dispatch arrived from her telling me the wonderful news of your return. The Consulate thought you'd be on this ship. Your mother's overjoyed and so am I, my dear . . . it's absolutely astonishing, after all these years!' He stepped back to look at her, eyes shining with joy. 'And you're so grown-up and so well-looking, thank goodness. But come to the saloon where we can talk quietly.'

After hearing the details of Alice's talk with Consul Meadows in Hong Kong, Robert consulted his watch and jumped up. 'Well obviously the best thing is for me to come up to Chefoo with you—see your mother and we'll decide what best to do about Frank. I'm sure I can get compassionate leave in the circumstances—after all, Frank is my nephew and I always felt that not enough fuss was made over that dreadful Tientsin business at the time. But that was the missionary angle of course—turn the other cheek and all that. Anyway, I'll go back to the mess, pack my kit, pay my chits and be aboard before teatime. We sail at six o'clock, I believe?'

'But, Uncle, please let me come with you—I've never seen Shanghai and the other passengers are going off for a look round.'

'Well—all right then. Get your hat and gloves and we'll be off.'

As they climbed into a double rickshaw on the quay, Robert pointed out the workshops and dry dock of the Kiangnan Arsenal where, he explained, the few Chinese endowed with get-up-and-go were learning to make Western-style ships and weaponry.

'I hear they're turning out five thousand rounds of Remington shells a day now—well, good luck to 'em—it's about

133

time they used their gun-powder for something other than fire-crackers!'

Leaving the docks, they bowled past the Public Gardens where carefully spaced clumps of wallflowers wilted in the alien soil, the Seamen's Mission, the Oriental Bank, the Circulating Library, the grand portals of the four-storey-high Shanghai Club and the gilded ones of the recently opened Lyceum Theatre where the farce *You Never Can Tell* was playing to packed houses. At the entrance to the officers' mess, Alice waited while Robert hurried inside, returning shortly with a jolly-looking, paunchy officer.

'Alice, this is a chum of mine, Major Cartwright from Bombay, who's kindly agreed to look after you while I go to the Consulate and set things moving. You'll end up at the Grand for luncheon, then, Basil? And I'll join you as soon as I can.'

'Absolutely delighted, my dear fellow. There's a sorry lack of charming feminine company here.' He shook Alice's hand vigorously. 'And this young lady is famous too, by jove! I'd just been reading all about her adventures in last week's *China Mail* when lo and behold up comes Robert and asks me to escort the celebrated person herself around town.' He climbed in beside her. 'I only wish there was more of interest to show you. Now if this were Bombay—but these Chinese stations are godforsaken backwaters, real mongrel settlements in my view. Ourselves, the French, Germans, Americans and lord knows who else all hugger-mugger. As for the natives, you'll scarcely believe this, Robert, but I was chatting with old Harry Chambers after breakfast—and well, you know that little stretch of railway our engineers are just laying down near the Woosung docks? Well, the local Chinks don't like it, if you please, and they're threatening to tear it up! Nasty noisy iron monsters— that's what they think of steam engines! Can you credit it? As I said to Harry, what hope is there for a race like that?'

Robert tutted sympathetically. 'Well you know what they say, Basil—there's nothing like a sharp dose of John Chinaman to make one appreciate the merits of your common or garden Indian wallah . . . But I must get moving . . . Take care of my precious little niece, won't you? We can't afford to lose her again!'

And indeed it was with the most elaborate and attentive care, as if she had been a fragile porcelain doll, that Major Cartwright proceeded to show Alice what he termed 'the sorry little sights of Shanghai.' The race-course was the first of them, with its new grandstand and the white-railed enclosure to separate foreigners from natives; then to the cricket pitch where, he explained, the Duffers were to play the Feebles on Saturday and it was a pity she could not be there. Inside the dim cool of Trinity Church Alice read some of the older memorial tablets—to Mrs. Agnes Colyer who died of swamp fever in 1848, to Ensign L. F. Smith who was killed aboard ship in pursuit of his duty in 1851. Then, in search of fresh air, they strolled along Bubbling Well Road, past Tundall's the drapers, Boles the saddlers and Fraser & Crawford the grocers who, said Major Cartwright, were guilty of daylight robbery when you compared their prices of Lea & Perrins Worcestershire sauce and Skippers tinned salmon with the cost of the same commodities in Bombay.

As for Shanghai's Grand Hotel, albeit under the expert management of Monsieur Pierre Gastone formerly of the Champs-Elysées, Paris, it was, the Major said, a mere lodging-house compared to the well-appointed hostelries of Calcutta. But to Alice, who had never before set foot in any comparable establishment, the Grand fully lived up to its name.

Quaking inwardly, she tried to assume a thoroughly grown-up and dignified air as they walked into the dining-room where each table had its white starched cloth, glass cruet, hovering waiter. She realised the only Chinese in view were the waiters, bell-boys, and shoe-cleaners squatting behind the potted palms. How furious Han-fei would be to see all these lordly rich-looking 'foreign-devil-barbarians' ordering 'the natives' about, and no one even finding it odd, she thought.

As they settled at table, Robert arrived and set about ordering the local specialities of boiled shad with cucumbers and roasted spring snipe, together with a celebratory bottle of champagne. 'I've sent a dispatch for transmission to Calcutta asking for four months' compassionate to be added to my present leave,' he announced. 'The Consul here agrees with Meadows in Hong Kong that Frank's case is a matter for the Minister and he's told me the legalities of the situation. Doesn't sound too promising actually, but we'll see. Ah,' he smiled as the waiter popped the cork. 'And I think you should have a little too, Alice. Here's to you, my dear. It's a very happy day for me to have my favourite niece returned, almost from the dead, as it were, and such a charming young lady she's become too!' The

135

gentlemen raised their glasses and Alice gulped with delighted surprise.

'Anyway,' Robert resumed, 'the most extraordinary thing is that the present Consul here is Mr. Waters—who was Consul in Tientsin at the time of the massacre!'

'Waters?' Alice looked up. 'I remember the name. I don't think Father liked him much.'

'Not much love lost, I gather. But he seems a decent fellow, and told me things I'd not heard before. I was away up on the North-West Frontier when it all happened, you know, Alice. Didn't hear for months, and a great shock it was, I can tell you.'

'Were any other foreigners killed that day, Uncle?'

'No my dear, just the Catholics and your poor father. The French kicked up the deuce of a row about their religieux but our people didn't do much.'

'But why was our Mission singled out for attack?'

'Oh it wasn't that. It was just damned bad luck that you happened to be situated nearest to the cathedral which was the mob's main target. So when they'd polished that off, they headed for you next. After a while the authorities managed to get control—which was why your mother was saved.'

Alice shivered and Major Cartwright laid a fleshy hand on hers. 'Enough of all that on a day like this! Come, drink up, m'dear. This lovely bubbly will soon buck you up.'

He refilled her glass and she drank readily. Robert also drank, watching her. Such a bright, lively young creature she had become—though her complexion and hair were a sorry mess. And full of commonsense, it seemed, unlike her father who had been so kind and good, but hopelessly impractical and unrealistic. Consul Waters had told Robert confidentially that the Greenwoods could probably have been saved if they had sought the protection of the Consulate sooner, as the other Protestants had. 'But your brother was a stubborn man,' Waters concluded. 'He always thought he knew best when it came to dealing with the Chinese, and that God would always protect him. You see what happened? And what purpose did it all serve? The only ones to profit were the Tientsin shopkeepers who turned a quick *tael* selling 'massacre fans' with scenes of the slaughter in all its gory detail!' With his last sip of champagne, Robert silently vowed to do everything he could to get young Frank out of Hunan alive. It was the least he could do for that poor, dead misguided brother of his.

The remainder of the day passed in a happy haze for Alice, who had never before drunk champagne. During her second glassful, the room ballooned into a golden ball of joy and, by the time they left, she decided the hotel was the funniest place she had ever seen—all those solemn obedient Chinese in their neat black Western suits holding doors open and bowing to large barbarian ladies and gentlemen.

'You know what is puzzling me, Uncle?' she shaded her eyes as they emerged into the glare of the Bund. 'I can't understand why the Chinese let us do all this in their country. It's absurd. If a few thousand of them got together and decided to push every foreigner and all their belongings into the sea one afternoon, they could—and think no more about it.' She giggled. 'It would look funny, wouldn't it? All those knives, forks and cruets sinking straight to the bottom and the ladies' feathered hats bobbing about on the waves!'

Robert smiled grimly. 'I'm glad it amuses you, my dear, but you've forgotten a few points—such as the power of the British Army and Navy. We've had absolutely legal treaty rights to trade and reside here since 1842, don't forget, and I imagine your "few thousand Chinese" would soon regret trying any hanky-panky of that sort. So you mustn't worry.'

'Oh, it doesn't worry me in the least. I just find it hard to understand.'

But then, there's a good deal I don't understand, she thought a while later, as she and Robert stood on the *Mandalay*'s deck waving goodbye to Major Cartwright. A golden sun was setting over the western hills beyond the port and golden circles of lamplight began to flicker from the warehouses and mat-huts along the shoreline as the vessel slid away in the gathering twilight towards the East China Sea. I wonder why it had to be my father who was killed and my brother and me who were kidnapped? Father used to say that things happened according to God's plan, but, according to Uncle Robert, it was just that we happened to be in the wrong place at the wrong moment. And what does Mama think of it all? After seeing Father die like that?

She squeezed Robert's arm. 'I'm so glad you're here with me now, Uncle. I was getting a little anxious about seeing Mama again. After all, I was only a child when I left and now I'm practically grown-up. And she's got new babies and a new husband. But now you're here, it'll be all right, I'm sure.'

Robert chuckled. 'I don't know how much good I'll be. I haven't seen Eliza myself since . . . '69 was it? When I visited you all in Tientsin the year before.'

'Yes, and you told Frank and me all about that Lucknow campaign you'd been in as a subaltern, do you remember?'

'Can't say I do, but I'm glad an old soldier's yarns made such an impression. Anyway, don't worry about your mother. She's longing to see you, and I don't suppose she'll have changed much, except for a few grey hairs, maybe.'

The two of them kept that encouraging thought well in mind when, five days later, they again stood on deck as the *Mandalay* moved towards Chefoo harbour. The remainder of the voyage had been uneventful. Ida Palmer had been most relieved to hand over the chaperonage of Alice to Robert though, as she wrote in confidence to Mr. Penfold, she was not sure his influence on her spiritual development was entirely good. For Alice, the only disadvantage of Robert's presence aboard had been its effect on Lin Fu-wei. To be honest, and Alice always tried to be honest in such matters, the young Chinese had simply transferred his attention from her to Robert because the latter had much more useful information to impart.

To what extent did the British government control the policies of its army, he had wanted to know. What was the firing range of the new breech-loading gun he had heard about? Was anyone in England trying to depose Queen Victoria? In such exchanges, Alice was relegated to the role of translator, and when the discussion ranged beyond her powers of immediate comprehension, both men grew impatient, wishing they could dispense with her services altogether. Nor did Lin evince any further interest whatsoever in the colour of her eyes. But when, as sometimes happened, Robert's enthusiasm for international debate waned, Lin was quick to compliment him on his acute grasp of world affairs and even, on one occasion, on his excellent military posture.

Well, bother him, I don't care. He only wanted to pick my brains because there was no one better available. I don't suppose we'll ever meet again, Alice was thinking rather despondently as the vessel drew near the land and she began trying to identify the distant figures on the quayside. There was a tap on her shoulder and Lin was smiling down at her.

'Goodbye for now, Uncut Jade,' he said softly, 'it's been a

great pleasure sharing this voyage with you, and we'll meet again some day. This is a Western-style farewell, I believe?'

She took his outstretched hand, saying impulsively, 'You think we'll meet again? I was just thinking we probably never would.'

His eyes shone confidently. 'Ah you barbarians have no perception of such matters. We shall meet, and in the meantime, to paraphrase the sage, "I shall wear a hair-shirt for the world to see and carry a jade next to my heart!" ' He bowed, half-mockingly, and she glowed with delight.

Robert jogged her arm. 'Could that be your mother— standing with those gentlemen?'

Alice strained forward. 'No, not possibly, that lady's too tall, and too fashionably dressed, unless Mama's changed a lot!'

There were only six foreigners among the several natives on the quay and, having studied them all, Robert concluded, 'She doesn't seem to be there then. There's no one else possible.' Alice sighed and turned for a parting word with Lin, but he had vanished. 'Let's make for the gang-plank,' Robert said briskly. 'She'll probably arrive any minute.'

As Alice stepped ashore carrying her reticule, a small woman in a Chinese robe of faded blue cotton rushed up. 'Alice—my darling darling child! It is you, isn't it? I thought it was, but then you seemed to be escorted by a gentleman and so I . . . oh, Alice, it's a miracle to see you again, my dear, dear daughter!' They clung to each other, laughing shakily through their tears, though even in her joy Alice was shocked by the grey, weary frailty of her mother's looks.

'The gentleman is Uncle Robert, Mother. He's come up with me.'

'Robert here too! Oh I'm so glad he's come, he'll be such a help. And you look so grown-up, my dear. Why, you're as tall as I am!'

Alice squeezed her thin shoulders. 'But that's not very tall, is it, Mother?'

Robert hurried up, followed by the baggage coolies. 'My dear Eliza, how very good to see you. I'm afraid we just didn't recognise you from the ship in those clothes.' He could not entirely conceal the disapproval in his voice.

She greeted him warmly, then looked up with that mixture of timidity and defiance he remembered as being characteristic of her. 'But you know it is our practice—that of the China

Inland Mission to which I now belong—to wear native dress. Our founder, Mr. Hudson Taylor, of whom you must have heard, firmly believes that by so doing we help to break down Chinese distrust. It is no mere affectation, I do assure you.'

Alice hugged her. 'Dear Mother, I don't know about all that, but I'm quite sure that what you're wearing is far more comfortable than these clothes Mrs. Penfold insisted on buying for me in Hong Kong.'

Robert controlled his indignation with an effort, though his collar felt hot with it. Really, his sister-in-law looked quite dreadful—like a little old peasant woman in those clothes, her weatherbeaten face, and straw sandals, if you please! He turned sharply to the coolie.

'You—wait there, I'll get a couple of rickshaws.'

'There's no need really, Robert,' Eliza protested. 'Rickshaws are in short supply here because of all the hotels, and are very expensive. So I've brought the Mission wheelbarrow.' She indicated an old barrow propped against a wall.

He glowered at it. 'And I suppose you expect me to push it?'

Alice giggled. 'I'd like to see you, Uncle!'

'No Robert, of course not. Our mission boy will do it.'

So they set off, the boy trundling the luggage-laden barrow. Alice suited her pace to her mother's slower one and Robert, stalking ahead, hoped he would not meet any of his fellow officers—to whom he honestly did not want to introduce his sister-in-law. But he need not have worried, for they soon turned away from the foreign quarter and down increasingly narrow dirty alleys into which no sane man would penetrate except in course of urgent duty. He stopped to wait for the women, who, oblivious of their surroundings, were talking animatedly.

'This is our Mission's recuperation home,' Eliza pointed ahead to a building which, Robert was later to tell his sympathetic officers in the mess, looked like a derelict, rat-infested warehouse. 'We only rented it a few months ago, so it's still a bit makeshift, but very clean inside.' Eliza sensed Robert's disapproval. 'There's just Miss Beales, Miss Agnew and me here at present—and the babies of course. Oh Alice, you have heard about them, haven't you? My new chicks—and my new husband. I assumed you knew, but we've been talking so much about Frank.'

'Yes Mother, of course I know. Mr. Penfold told me in Hong Kong.'

'That's a relief and I'll tell you more later . . . but come in. This is our communal room, and we've bedrooms ready for you.'

'Oh not for me, thank you, Eliza. I shan't be staying for more than ten minutes.'

'Oh but Robert, surely . . .'

'I wouldn't dream of imposing on you here. Besides,' he lied, 'I've already engaged a room ahead at the officers' hotel and I must go to the Consulate first thing in the morning. So I'll leave you two to get to know each other again and return tomorrow to discuss our future plans.'

'Well, if you insist, Robert. I certainly want to talk to Alice for hours and hours.' Eliza smiled fondly at her daughter. 'But first you must come and see my precious little ones.'

The two babies lay in their mother's bedroom and a smell of milk, vomit and carbolic soap hung about them. At their approach, the punier of the two wailed distressfully. 'This is Adam,' Eliza picked him up. 'Not yet two, and life's been so trying for him, poor mite. He's always ailing—he's got a rash of some sort now, you see. And many's the time I've thought I'd lose him.'

Alice looked at the damp, spotty creature, feeling nothing. 'And this?' The other baby gave her a broad smile of welcome, waving a chubby fist.

'That's Alison.'

'Alison—but that's almost my name!' Alice protested indignantly, as the baby curled its fingers round hers.

'My dear, it was meant to be. As you must know, we eventually gave up all hope of ever seeing you and Frank again. So when these two little ones arrived, they seemed some recompense for my dreadful loss. Edward wanted the boy called Adam because, though he has a grown son from his earlier marriage, this baby came after his conversion to the true faith. And I wanted Alison in memory of my dear daughter—not quite the same name, but almost.'

Alice picked her up and, as the child snuggled against her, felt a surge of quite unexpected happiness. This little girl, she thought, would need a big sister. Robert peered at her, poked her tummy and the child chuckled.

'Quite a little bundle of sunshine, that one.'

'Sunshine.' Alice held her high. 'That must be her name, Mother. Sunny—the part of her name that's different from

141

mine. It suits her and we can't keep two such similar names in the family.'

'Well, I don't know, it's not a proper Christian name. But if you really like it—and certainly she's a sweet-natured, robust child. But oh, my goodness, how could I have forgotten to tell you? William—he's on his way out here at this moment, from England, and bringing his young bride, Isabel, with him. I've not yet met her, of course.'

'William—coming here and *married*! But he was still a schoolboy when . . . oh Mother!'

'Well, he's a grown man now and he's joined the Imperial Maritime Customs under Sir Robert Hart. It's not what your dear father would have wished, I fear, but there was no persuading him otherwise.'

'A fine career for a young man,' Robert broke in crisply. 'As I wrote and said when I first heard, Eliza. Secure, chance to travel, to climb higher. So where's his first posting?'

'In Foochow, as the chief's assistant. He and Isabel will be landing there any day now and there's a letter waiting with the wonderful news about Alice and Frank. But we can't meet yet, because, when they've settled in Foochow, I'll be hundreds of miles away, back in Mukden, with Edward. It's all so difficult . . . oh, the times I've wished China was the same size as Scotland!'

Robert chuckled. 'And part of the British Empire with decent trains and a telegraph system—that would help a lot!'

'Still it's marvellous news, Mother, and we're all bound to meet again eventually.' Alice was happily imagining a reunion party with Mother, William, Frank, Uncle Robert, herself. But there were these worrying newcomers on the scene: the babies, the unknown Isabel and the shadow of a strict stepfather.

'Well dears,' Eliza touched their arms, 'at least we three have come together, and that's a miracle in itself. But I can hear Miss Agnew playing the evening hymn so it's nearly suppertime. You're sure you won't stay, Robert?'

He grabbed his kitbag firmly. 'No thank you, Eliza. I really must get settled before dark. So I'll say goodnight, ladies.' He chucked Alice under the chin, whispering, 'Hope your supper isn't too awful!' She smiled, thinking how little he knew about her.

'I'm so glad you eat the native food with such relish,' Eliza remarked, as Alice scooped up the last shred of cabbage. 'It's quite dreadful how many Europeans, even some missionaries, I'm sad to say, feel the need for tinned meat and butter and such luxuries. So expensive and unnecessary.'

'But I ate only Chinese food for years, Mother, so I'm certainly used to it. And the Chus are wealthy, so they fed well.'

'You really must tell me everything about them, dear. I know so little of what has gone on.'

Miss Beales, a round young woman who had eaten hugely and said little during the meal, cleared away the bowls, asking sorrowfully, 'I suppose they were quite unredeemed heathens? Has the word of the Lord penetrated to Hunan at all yet?'

'Not to my knowledge, but I was mostly confined to the house, so I don't suppose I'd have heard anyway.'

'Now, Mrs. Blake,' Miss Agnew bustled in, 'as this is your very first evening with your daughter, we'll leave you together. Miss Beales will put the babies to bed and I'll bring some tea—and perhaps a cushion instead of that hard stool, Alice?'

'Please, and I'll put on my comfortable Chinese robe—it feels more homey.'

In the gathering twilight, mother and daughter talked quietly, feeling their way, almost as strangers. 'But one thing is still not at all clear to me,' Eliza said, after Alice had explained briefly how, though not really why, she and Kau had left Changsha. 'Why couldn't Frank manage to get away with you? He is well, I hope? You are not concealing anything dreadful?'

'No, Mother, of course not. But for one thing, we seldom saw each other, he worked in the farmyard and . . .'

Miss Beales came in, looking harassed. 'I'm sorry to disturb you, Mrs. Blake, but I can't get Adam settled and now he's being sick again. Could you just . . . ?'

Eliza hurried away and Alice moved restlessly about the dim room. She lit the brass paraffin lamp so that a pool of light shone over a bowl of wild marigolds on the table, and sighed as she touched their glowing petals. So often during the long, lonely journey from Hunan she had dreamed of an occasion like this. How she would bury her head in her mother's lap and pour out the whole story: her early misery, the beddings with Lungkuang, her pregnancy and miscarriage, Frank's refusal to leave, and the meeting with Stewart Carr. Now she realised with a sinking heart that it was impossible to reveal any of these things. She had not bargained on the extent of her mother's naive piety, nor her middle-aged frailty, nor her obsessive concerns with new babies and a new husband. How could Alice burden her with these distressing, unpalatable truths? It would upset her so much and she seemed often close to tears already. Moreover the full story would only confirm her worst imaginings about the diabolical practices of the heathen Chinese.

As she reached this reluctant conclusion, Eliza returned, rocking a wailing Adam. 'Oh he is such a poor bairn, he ails and ails. There, my wee one, sleep now, don't you cry.'

Watching her bent head, Alice felt both desolate and resentful. Then her mother smiled up timidly at her. 'Oh how glad I am to have you with me, dear. You'll be such a help to us all, you were always a willing little girl. Now where were we?'

'I'll do what I can, Mother.' Alice curled up on the cushion. 'But you've not yet told me anything about yourself, or about my stepfather. Where did you meet him?'

'Well my dear, after the tragedy I was in that little Tientsin hospital for weeks. I really didn't want to live at all—my husband and two children all gone in one dreadful afternoon. But the Lord supported me and reminded me of my duty. When I recovered somewhat, I did all in my power to find out about you both—pestering the Consulate and the C.M.S. with letters and visits. But it was of no use. You'd both just vanished and eventually I was told you'd been killed in retribution for the execution of the riot leaders. After that I felt I couldn't bear to stay longer in such a dreadful country, so I boarded a steamer for Shanghai, intending to return Home.

'As it happened, the Reverend and Mrs. Drew were aboard, friends of ours in the early C.M.S. days. Anyway, at their suggestion I disembarked with them at Nantung to see their mission—I think they hoped to dissuade me from leaving the China field. And it was in Nantung that I met Mr. Blake, who was affiliated to the China Inland Mission. Oh, he was so full of hope and enthusiasm, Alice. It was marvellous to listen to him, after all I'd been through.'

'Had he been in China long?'

'No, less than two years. Before that he was a schoolmaster. He's a very clever man, Alice, and taught Latin and History in a boy's school near Lewes. But there was an outbreak of scarlet fever in the school and his poor wife, Clara, and his baby daughter both died of it. It was the year before your father's martyrdom. Soon after his wife's death he attended a missionary meeting in Lewes Civic Hall and heard Hudson Taylor crying out for people to sacrifice their all to go out to China and save the heathen. And Edward was called. He'll tell you the full story himself one day. But, do you know, he gave up his schoolmastering, sold his house, put his son Theobald into boardingschool, sent his daughter Laura—who must be about your age—to live with an aunt, and, in course of time, came out here. Nantung was his first station.'

She paused, smoothing Adam's brow. 'Bring the lamp over here, Alice, he's asleep now and it won't disturb him.' As Alice did so, Eliza smiled at her. 'How pleasant looking you've become, dear, with those greenish-blue eyes, not really like mine or Thomas's. But you have his hair. And you seem so sensible and grown-up too and I'm very proud of you, my child—how courageously you've withstood all your trials.'

Alice felt a lump in her throat at the remembrance of all her mother didn't know, but said lightly, 'I wondered how I'd seem to you, Mother. I'm glad you approve. But you haven't yet told me what manner of man Mr. Blake is? Is he very schoolmasterish?'

'Well, he's a schoolmaster turned missionary, which makes him a little severe. And when he's sure of a thing nothing will alter his mind. That's how he was about me, you see. I spent only three weeks in Nantung and we talked together about our bereavements and God's purpose in it all. The day I was leaving on the coastal ferry for Shanghai he came to see me off and just before I boarded he drew me aside and . . . well, proposed to me. He felt utterly certain that it would be for my own good, for his and for the heathen Chinese if I stayed on as his wife to help him with his work. He was most persuasive.' She hesitated, remembering the relentless intensity of his sombre, lantern-jawed face.

'But it seemed such a big step to take alone, without advice, and I felt I scarcely knew him. So I said I'd go to Shanghai anyway, and think it over there. As I went up the gangplank, he grasped my hand and said, "There'll be a sign very soon, Eliza. I shall pray for it and it will show you that your true duty lies here with me in China." And do you know, Alice, that very night, soon after we set sail, a typhoon blew up—out of nowhere it seemed. And the little boat plunged about in the storm and I clung to my bunk listening to the terrible roar of the wind and waves, thinking again and again of Edward's last words to me. After several

145

hours, just when I thought the ferry would break in two, the wind abated a little and we managed to crawl back to Nantung.

'The next morning I woke up feeling happy and certain. I simply cancelled my passage and walked back to the C.I.M. It was calm and sunny, I remember, and everything sparkling after the rain. Edward himself answered the door and I said, "Here I am, come back already." And he replied, "I knew you would, Eliza, it is even sooner than I expected that God has shown you the way." And about two months later we were married.' She sighed tremulously.

'He sounds very sure and determined, Mother.'

'Yes—or rather, sure of God's will in him, as he would say. But you'll meet him when we return to Mukden together. I hope—I mean I think—your father would have approved. And I'm sure you'll grow to like him, Alice.' The baby whimpered and Eliza rose, cradling him carefully. 'It's more than time for bed, my dear. You must be tired after all today's excitement.'

Alice was indeed tired. She slept late and was just helping Miss Beales clear up when Robert appeared on the morning scene, looking pleased with himself.

'Everything is going according to plan,' he announced. 'I've seen the Consul here who also advised us to go straight to Peking and see the Minister about Frank—only he can authorise any action. So I think we should leave as soon as possible, Alice.'

'Surely you needn't take her with you?' Eliza looked alarmed.

'I'm afraid so, Eliza. She really is the only person who can tell the Minister about the exact situation in Hunan. So she must come, for Frank's sake. You won't mind, will you, Alice?'

'But I'm longing to go—of course!'

'I thought you would. So we'll be off tomorrow. I'll go and book a passage to Tientsin and we'll travel on the overland cart service from there.'

Eliza sighed. 'Well if you say so, Robert. But please take great care of my long-lost daughter. Also,' she added, as Alice rushed off to tell Miss Beales the good news, 'please remember that Tientsin is full of painful memories for us both. I wept sorely when I had to go through on the way to Mukden last year.'

'I had already thought of that, Eliza. I may be a rough and ready soldier, but I'm not without sensitivity, I do assure you. We shall be there only briefly and I shall see to it that Alice isn't unduly distressed.'

But when, four days later, they disembarked at Tientsin,

Alice insisted they take a walk round the town while waiting for the overland cart. As they strolled along, she was again assailed by that rabbit-hole feeling. It seemed incredible that she and Frank used so often to trot along on either side of dear old Wo-wo to buy fruit and vegetables in this same busy street-market, and there, in the dusty park along the waterfront, she had first bowled a hoop and Frank had pretended to ride Dobbin.

The humble Protestant chapel in Taku Road still stood and inside was the same slab commemorating the birth of 'The first Christian child born in the town' in 1861. She had been called Annie Innocent and had died two years later. Alice always remembered the name; it rang with such sweet melancholy. The Catholic cathedral destroyed in the riot was now rebuilt in the same square, looking even grander than before. Leaving Robert gazing at it, Alice started down a side street.

'Alice, where are you going?' He hurried after her.

'To see if the Mission is still there.'

'It isn't—it's in a different place now, your mother told me. And you're not to go upsetting yourself.'

'I shan't, I promise, Uncle. But I must look at the old street—just once, then I'll never need to come again.'

Outmanoeuvred by her determination, he fell in step beside her and they turned a corner. 'It was left—along there some-where—just there, I think?' She paused, watching a man sitting on a stool in the afternoon sunshine peacefully twisting jute cord to make a fishing-net. For a moment, the scene swam before her misted eyes as she remembered her father's voice telling her that missionaries were like fishers of God who cast their nets upon the waters, bringing up, now and then, a soul to be saved—and that was what made all their endeavours worth-while.

'It *was* there, where that man's sitting. It's a boat chandlers now, not a sign of the little chapel,' where fat, wrinkled Wo-wo used to stand at the door smiling welcome every Sunday, while, inside, Mother played the tinny harmonium, and she and Frank bustled about importantly bringing hymn-books and hassocks for the worshippers. She wished desperately that Frank was here now, for only he, who'd shared her subsequent experiences, could have shared her present feelings.

Yet what made her gulp back tears just then was not Frank's absence but the sudden memory of her father on those Sunday

147

occasions. He had always pretended not to mind when only four or five people arrived for a service, straightening his back and strengthening his voice against the disappointment. After the public worship, there had been what he used to call a 'time of family blessing,' and she remembered the touch of his hand on her head as she bent before the silver cross on the altar table. 'May the peace of God be upon you, and the Grace of God live within you, my child,' he had murmured gently.

The top of her scalp prickled sharply and she jerked her head away from the sight of the man twisting cord in the sunshine. Robert, who had been watching her carefully, put a hand on her shoulder. 'Now come on, Alice, let's go. No tears, you promised.'

As they turned and walked quietly away Alice decided she would never make sense of the world. She looked timidly at her uncle wanting to ask how it all seemed to him. He looked so full of assurance and understanding, but she wondered suddenly if he really was? Did anyone, ever, learn to make sense of the world?

6

It was mid-morning when Alice and Robert first saw in the distance the capital of the Celestial Empire, its bell and drum towers, its circular pavilions, balconied pagodas and gated citadels outlined on the level plain. Strings of mule-carts, laden camels, horses and coolies bent beneath packs were converging on the southern gate, churning the infamous Peking dust into clouds that hung hazily in the warm air.

Robert brushed his spruce jacket. 'It's incredible, isn't it? Here we are, approaching what is supposed to be one of the most ancient and glorious cities in the world, and there's not an inch of macadam or a drain in sight—but you can certainly smell it!'

Alice, oblivious to the dirt, the odours, the sad hordes of ragged beggar children and lepers, thrilled with excitement as they came up to the thirty-foot-high walls and joined the queue of travellers passing through the imposing gateway. Robert, bent diligently over his guidebook, read aloud, 'The city is divided into three sections, the Tartar, the Chinese and the Imperial. The walls enclosing the whole measure a total length of twenty-one miles and the top of the wall that divides the two main cities is broad enough for pleasant evening perambulations by visitors.'

As they approached the centre, Alice saw the tower of the White Ming Pagoda and the yellow-porcelain roofs of the royal palaces sparkling above the red-plastered walls that enclosed the Imperial City itself. Here dwelt the mysterious and unapproachable Son of Heaven, the Celestial Dragon, the four-year-old Emperor of China.

'Can you see two gates in the walls with peaked towers?' asked Robert, still reading busily. 'They're called the Meridian and the Gate of Spiritual Valour. Inside, which we can't see, there's another Gate of Supreme Harmony,

149

apparently, and a Hall of Purity, a Palace of Earthly Tranquillity and a Hall of the Blending of Heaven and Earth. I'd like to see what goes on in there—sounds quite messy!' he chuckled.

About half a mile from the Imperial City they came to the Foreign Legation Quarter with its embassies. In the street beyond, their cart turned suddenly into a secluded courtyard.

'This must be the Mission,' Robert jumped up, 'though it looks more like a temple, by jove!'

And indeed the building in which Dr. and Mrs. Sturgeon had established their first Church Missionary Society station in Peking eight years previously had once been a Buddhist temple, with bronze dragons snarling from every roof-corner. The dragons seemed not to mind their dispossession, however, for the place had a businesslike, settled Christian air—with its plain white-washed chapel, living-quarters and a large shed that served as a dispensary. Mrs. Sturgeon, a plump, rosy-cheeked woman who looked as if she had just emerged from a Sussex farm-kitchen, greeted them warmly, installed them in bedrooms, offered lunch.

While waiting for the meal, Alice wandered into the chapel, and now it all came back to her: the same kind of rough benches, the altar table with its silver cross, dog-eared books and magazines—*Peep o'Day*, *The Messenger*, *Golden Grains of Truth*. She opened the register: Catechists, 5; Dispensary Assistants, 3; Unpaid active workers, 14; Backsliders, 38. Oh, it was all going on just the same, and with just as little success and Alice's heart ached to think of the continual defeats and failures of the Sturgeons' lives, of her father's life. Poor, dear Father. She stood before the cross, hands clasped in prayer, but no words came; just the silver very bright in the sunlight, for there was always some elderly female convert of the Wo-wo type to keep the crosses shining, happy in the new-found knowledge that cleanliness was next to godliness.

'But of course the Mission is doing much better these days, isn't it, dear?' Mrs. Sturgeon comforted her husband who, during supper that evening, had given his visitors his habitually lugubrious recital of their trials, and now left his wife to provide her customary jolly reminders of their small successes. 'We have a core of truly faithful converts, about six regular attenders in Sunday school, and my three Bible women are miracles of faith and perseverance.'

150

Robert, who had informed his elder brother many years before that he considered the business of trying to convert the Chinese to Christianity a thorough waste of effort and money, mumbled an excuse and, leaving Alice to bear the burden of the discourse, went for a surreptitious smoke in the courtyard. It had been a promising beginning, he thought, puffing happily. He had made an appointment with the British Minister for the morrow, and then taken Alice to see some of the foreign sights of the capital, for he felt she had already had more than enough of things Chinese. They had visited the old Portuguese burial ground where some early Jesuits were interred; the Russian cemetery near the Tartar wall containing the graves of twelve Europeans treacherously killed by the Chinese during peace negotiations of 1860; and the Roman Catholic cathedral which housed the famous natural history collection of Abbé David, who had lived there for years and made long journeys north every summer in search of rare specimens.

So far, so good, Robert thought, tapping out his pipe and sucking a lozenge to disguise the tobacco-smell from his hosts. But the most difficult task lay ahead—to enlist the help of the Minister in getting young Frank back to civilisation.

That evening it seemed perfectly reasonable to suppose the Minister would immediately put a small expeditionary force at Robert's disposal for the purpose, but, the next morning, as he and Alice reached the Legation, he was assailed by doubts. 'Now, Alice,' he instructed, 'be quiet and ladylike and leave most of the talking to me—just be sure to tell the Minister what a fine, upstanding lad Frank is and how desperately he wants to be freed.'

'Yes, Uncle,' she said in a small voice, wishing she hadn't come.

Sir Hugh Digby's study was panelled in wood and smelled of vellum and leather; bookish dust danced in the shaft of light that streamed through the dingy velvet curtains.

'Miss Alice Greenwood, I am indeed pleased.' The Minister rose with a courtly inclination. 'My wife was telling me more of your amazing experience only the other day, she'd been talking to some missionary acquaintance, I believe . . . yes . . .' he trailed vaguely. 'And Major Greenwood,' he shook hands, aware of the soldierly grip, the worried, defensive eyes. 'Pray sit down, I've asked for coffee.' Sir Hugh entrenched himself behind his desk. 'You must indeed be delighted to have your long-lost niece so unexpectedly returned to you, Major? From the dead—almost. Though I must say you look uncommonly well after your dreadful experiences, Miss Greenwood.'

'They weren't all dreadful by any means, not after the first few months.' Alice corrected humbly. 'The Chu family was quite kind to Frank and me according to their lights—though they did think of us as "little barbarians." ' She knew that phrase made Europeans smile.

Sir Hugh smiled. 'Quite so—the racial pride of the Sons of Han is beyond belief. Still, it is indeed lucky that you fell into fairly good hands, my dear. But you have no idea why the Chus kept you so long? As I'm sure you know, you were originally captured as hostages for Lung-pao's son, one of the instigators of the massacre. Lung-pao was the uncle of the Deputy-Governor in whose house you were imprisoned—as we've recently discovered. But it is remarkable, to be honest, that the Chus kept you alive after Lung-pao and his son were dead.'

'I think they forgot about us,' Alice said lamely. 'It's a very large household and somehow we were just fitted in and made to work for our keep.'

'Well, it says much for the Chus. For I do believe many of our honourable Celestials don't hesitate to, as it were—quietly put down—any barbarian of whatever tribe they consider superfluous, as indeed they do some of their own female babies. And it is equally astonishing, is it not, that you managed to return to Hong Kong unscathed?'

Robert coughed. 'As to the matter of return, Sir Hugh, you realise that is what I've come about? It's the boy, my nephew Frank Greenwood, who's still a prisoner there, you know.'

'Yes, I do know.' Sir Hugh's back straightened just as a servant appeared with coffee. Both Robert's and Alice's hands shook slightly as they took their cups. Sir Hugh's remained steady as he sipped, saying nothing, not helping.

Robert, burning his tongue, asked, 'Well, I wonder what you propose to do about it, sir? A young lad, nearly sixteen, a British subject, held there against his will . . .'

'Against his will? We are sure of that, are we, Miss Greenwood? You see, I've wondered why your brother made no effort to escape with you.'

'But he couldn't. He couldn't possibly have disguised himself as a Chinese because he's big and blond, and he felt it would endanger my chances.' Her voice was not totally convincing, for she was trying to blot out her last picture of Frank refusing to leave.

Sir Hugh turned to Robert. 'So your nephew left his sister to do the brave thing and return to her own kind alone?'

'You can't judge so harshly, he's only a lad.' Robert began.

Alice added, 'No, it wasn't like that at all. I *had* to leave and . . . he knew little about my plans. We seldom met, you see—he minded the horses and practised military arts with the other boys and I was in the women's apartments. It's the *custom*,' she finished defiantly.

'Quite so, and, Major, please let's not get heated over this. But you say you had to leave, Miss Greenwood? Did something particular happen to make you feel that? After all, you'd lived there reasonably happily, it seems, for several years?'

Alice stared at the rows of gilt-lettered books on the opposite wall. Tamao would have known how to deal with this, she was good at turning things aside with an apt quotation, something from Confucius perhaps. . . . Robert was watching her anxiously.

'No, nothing sudden,' she murmured, 'but I was growing up. When I was a child there it was different.'

Sir Hugh nodded soothingly. 'Different of course. More so for you as a girl than for your brother perhaps?'

'Well he's younger and being a boy was allowed rather more freedom. Yes, different.' She bent her head, staring at her tightly clenched hands, feeling the men's unspoken questions eddying about her. Probably, she realised, they guessed more than they were saying. After all—they all did it, Englishmen just as much as Chinamen. Sir Hugh had a wife, Lady Digby, and he must have been with her many times, as she with Lung-kuang. She looked up at him curiously.

'And difficult for the young lady you have become?' he prodded; she only nodded.

A deferential young man entered with some official papers and as Sir Hugh glanced at them, Robert shifted uneasily, feeling the interview was not progressing well. He did not care for Sir Hugh's questioning of Alice, though he too had wondered privately if anything . . . unpleasant . . . had happened. The Chinese had no respect for the female sex and

153

liked them young, apparently. As the secretary tiptoed out, Robert said, 'We really mustn't intrude too long on your valuable time, Minister, so perhaps we could return to the main point which is—what does the British government and you, as its chief representative in China, propose to do about my nephew? He's been in captivity for nearly six years and now Alice has escaped his position could well be more perilous.'

Sir Hugh brushed the back of his hand with his quill. 'I'm afraid, Major, the short answer is—not very much, at least not yet. We've already sent a strong protest to the *Tsungli Yamen*—the Chinese department of so-called international affairs, and they, with their usual courteous circumlocutions, deny all knowledge of the case. I've suggested that protests be sent to the Governor of Hunan, but we must tread warily there, and frankly the *Tsungli Yamen* has little power in that quarter. The Hunanese, unfortunately, have long been renowned for their strained relations with the Manchus and their special dislike of matters barbarian, so I don't hold out much hope.'

'But we can't just leave it like that, Minister.'

'I fully appreciate your concern, but the fact is that relations between the Chinese government and ourselves are relatively cordial just now, since the Chefoo Convention. So there's simply no question of our upsetting the status quo with any kind of official rescue operation—if that's what you had in mind. It could even lead to an international incident, and that isn't in our present interests.'

'So my nephew is to be sacrificed to political expediency, is he?'

'Not exactly sacrificed, Major. After all, we've every reason to suppose that he's alive and well and will remain so. We'll endeavour to do what we can through the usual diplomatic channels and, probably, sooner or later, there'll be a good reason for arranging something—an unfortunate incident, some loss of life, a flare-up, these things inevitably happen from time to time. Then we can say to the Chinese, well now then, we'll overlook this or that you've done—but there's that lad you've got tucked away in Hunan, how about releasing him? You'll see, there'll be a diplomatic solution eventually, but it will take time.'

His tone suggested that the matter had been amicably

settled, but Robert jumped up angrily, 'Time? How long? Six months? A year? Five? It's young Frank's life we're talking about. And what guarantee have we that he'll survive that long? No, it's not good enough, Sir Hugh, just not good enough.'

Alice looked at him admiringly. His stiff unyielding stance reminded her of dear Father when he used to stand before small groups and preach. The memory brought an ache to her throat. 'My father laid down his life for the missionary cause, Sir Hugh. He was such a brave, good man—it would grieve him deeply to know that Frank was held in captivity and you, his own countryman, were making no effort to release him.'

Sir Hugh smiled tightly, for his sympathy with those whom he privately termed 'the pushy Prots' was strictly limited. He sprang from a long-established Anglo-Catholic family and believed that the Catholics had found a more enlightened way of bringing the Christian message to the Chinese. Sometimes, wearied by the burdens of office, he would take an evening perambulation along the Tartar wall towards the northern city, there to ponder the remains of the old astronomical observatory built by the Jesuit Fathers. Finest among them was the globe of heaven, made of solid copper, with figures denoting the stars and constellations still visible on its surface. That was the way it should be done; he was certain.

He said, 'I take your point, Miss Greenwood. But you must be aware that the British Government takes a somewhat, shall we say, ambivalent attitude to the whole question of missionary endeavours in China. Their excessive zeal and indiscriminate proselytising have led to several unpleasant incidents in the past that could perhaps, with more judgment, have been avoided and which had unfortunate political repercussions.' He turned briskly back to Robert, 'Anyway, Major, there is surely a good chance that Master Greenwood will escape himself, as his sister did? But as for any overt action on our part, no, I'm sorry, it is impossible.' He laid down his quill, signalling the interview's end.

Robert stood his ground. 'Then what about sending a few people to Hunan secretly?'

'It would be wiser, certainly, but I'm just not prepared to commit us at all, for the reasons I've given. In a year or so; things might change, one can never predict the future when

155

dealing with Orientals.' He glanced pointedly at the papers awaiting his attention.

Robert barked. 'That's all you care about it, isn't it? Frank's just a pawn, to be forgotten or bartered or made a cause of to suit the requirements of the moment. Well, he's my dead brother's son, and if you won't do a thing to help him, then I'll go and get him out of there myself, secretly, as you say.'

Sir Hugh weighed him carefully. 'It's not something I would advise, Major, indeed it would be extremely foolhardy. You don't know the country or the language, and the Chinese don't take at all kindly to foreigners wandering about their interior provinces.'

'I am something of a geographer and an experienced traveller and it won't be the first time I've gone into unknown native terrain.'

'And I shall go with him—because I do know the country and the language,' Alice burst in eagerly.

'Come now, Miss Greenwood,' Sir Hugh was brusque, 'of course you will not—a young lady like you . . .'

Robert added, 'No, Alice, it's not a job for you, my dear.'

She shut her lips, for it was pointless to argue here, but the idea thrilled her. Why not? Just herself and Uncle Robert—what an adventure! And how delighted Frank would be to see them and they would all travel back together. She could immediately imagine the three of them bumping along in an ancient cart and Frank telling her the latest news of the Chu household.

'It's not in my power to actually forbid your going,' Sir Hugh was saying. 'But I must repeat that the idea is both foolish and dangerous and you should abandon it before it takes hold of your mind. And I warn you, if anything should go wrong, it would be entirely on your own head.'

'Naturally I could hardly expect a rescue expedition in the circumstances,' Robert smiled dourly. 'So I'll wish you good day, Minister. Come, Alice?'

As she rose to leave, Sir Hugh said, 'Major, before you go, I'd like a brief word—perhaps you'd wait in the ante-room for a few minutes, my dear.'

Alice went out, feeling hot and anxious. What an unfeeling man Sir Hugh was, with all his talk of cold-blooded diplomatic bargains. She kicked angrily at the carpet—probably he considered her own father guilty of, what was it?—'excessive zeal and indiscriminate proselytising.' Oh, what a dreadful man! And he had tried to pry out her reasons for leaving Changsha too, as if he had guessed she was concealing something. She shivered, wondering what they were discussing in her absence.

Sir Hugh had resumed his seat. Robert stood tense, ready for further battle, but the Minister smiled disarmingly. 'No, I'll say no more about your nephew, Major—it's about your niece I wanted to talk.' He gestured to a chair. 'It's a rather delicate point, and you can tell me to mind my own business, if you like. But when I asked her her reasons for running away, she became most evasive, didn't you think? I didn't like her look. I wonder if you know, in complete confidence, exactly why she left? For one thing, if we are to try and negotiate Frank's release, it is best to know the full story, and I've a suspicion we don't.'

'I know no more than she told you, Sir Hugh. I've wondered myself, to be honest, and I did notice her reactions. I think there may be more to it, but I could only hazard a guess.'

'Exactly, I too can guess. As you must know, the Chinese don't treat their womenfolk as we do. And the system of concubinage is very prevalent among high-ranking families of the kind in which your niece was living. How old is she?'

'Almost eighteen.'

'By which time nearly every Chinese girl is betrothed, married, or in concubinage of some sort.'

'And you think that is why . . . ?'

'I should be very surprised if any young female living in such a house were exempt from the system, barbarian or not. But she's said nothing? Not even to her mother?'

'No, of that I'm quite sure. Eliza would have been so shocked, I'd have heard.' He leaned forward, man to man now. 'The fact is, my sister-in-law is, well, very missionary, especially since she remarried into the China Inland Mission.' He did not conceal his distaste. 'One couldn't even hint of such matters to her, and Alice would realise that. She's a canny young lady and she'd keep anything of that nature to herself.'

'Which could be very damaging for her in the long run, in the emotional sense, Major. What she could have experienced as a young girl, then have to keep secret.'

'Well, I'll see what I can do, sir. I'm very fond of Alice, she's

157

got great spirit. But I can hardly . . . as a mere man . . .'

Sir Hugh smiled understandingly. 'May I suggest my wife talks to her? She's a woman of the world, and something might come of it. If what we suspect is true, it's a heavy burden for Alice to bear alone. She might crave the understanding sympathy of an older woman. But it's entirely up to you, this is not really my business, nor my wife's . . .'

'It's a very kind offer, Sir Hugh. I suppose with all the worry about Frank I've pushed this aspect from my mind. But if your wife would see her, it couldn't do harm and it might do good.'

'Quite so.' Sir Hugh rose. 'A private invitation will be sent to her. You'll be here for a few days yet, I assume?'

Left alone, Sir Hugh wrote on his memo pad, 'Talk to Helen about Alice G.' He stared at it for a moment. The young lady in question had indubitably picked up a good deal of Oriental inscrutability during her years en famille chinoise—and perhaps the habits of concubinage to boot? She had certainly looked at him with a bold knowingness quite unlike other young missionaries' daughters of his acquaintance. He smiled wryly—he had always thought concubinage had things to recommend it. 'Give me a child to the age of seven and he's ours for life,' the wily old Jesuits used to say. It had not been quite like that for Miss Greenwood, but she was certainly out of the ordinary run. Interesting—and a meaty tidbit for Helen, who was thoroughly bored with the narrowness of Peking's diplomatic circles compared to their previous posting in Rome. She would enjoy the chance of a confidential chat with the girl from Changsha.

The envelope with the Legation's seal was handed to Alice the very next morning by a liveried messenger. She and Robert had just returned from a discouraging visit to the Tsungli Yamen, where they had tried to find out if anything could be accomplished through those slow-moving 'diplomatic channels.' But, despite Alice's powers of persuasive interpretation, they had been faced with blank incomprehension bordering on hostility. The official Chinese view was that Frank Greenwood did not exist.

Alice opened the envelope wonderingly: Lady Digby, tea at 3.30 P.M. 'But it's today,' she turned to Robert in dismay.

'Just a ladies' tea, my dear.'

'But I don't know any ladies here. . . . Need I go? They'll only ask me lots of stupid questions about the Chinese.'

'Of course you must go, Alice, why, it's quite an honour to be asked. There are ladies in Calcutta who'd give their eye teeth for an invitation like that!'

'But I'm not good at tea-parties and I don't suppose I'll like Lady Digby any more than her husband.'

'Come, don't be childish, Alice,' Robert admonished, knowing she hated the term. 'You mustn't judge people before you've met them, and what's more, here's a chance to put in a good word for Frank. So write an acceptance and give it to the messenger straightaway.'

Alice did so, but when, at the appointed hour, she rang the bell of the Minister's residence, wearing her best blue muslin dress, her body clammy inside a tight bodice, hands clammy inside tight gloves, she ardently wished she had refused. Ushered into a boudoir furnished with chintz-covered chairs and occasional tables, she looked round puzzled, for there was no sign of the formidable array of ladies and silver teapots she had expected. She could not decide whether to be more, or less, alarmed by their absence. Arrayed in a corner cupboard were collections of Venetian glass and French porcelain and Alice went to look at them closely—having never seen such beautiful objects of this sort—and her nose was pressed in covetous admiration against the glass when an elegant, soft-blonde lady in a loose tea gown of beige net bustled in.

'My dear Miss Greenwood, I am delighted, I've heard so much about you and wanted to meet you just as soon as possible. Ah, you're looking at my little European treasures, I see. Now pray sit down. I've asked for tea here, so much cosier than the formal drawing-room when one just wants a chat . . .' She pulled a chair closer to Alice, smiling warmly. 'Now, my dear, I know we haven't met before, but I want you to feel as if we had—I don't want you to think of me as the Minister's wife, tiddleypom, but as someone to whom you can talk quite freely. You must have had such fascinating adventures, but probably only your family has heard of them so far?'

Alice felt rather overwhelmed, then a bubble of laughter rose in her, for she was unaccountably reminded of the Duchess in *Alice in Wonderland* who dug her sharp chin into Alice's shoulder on the croquet ground saying, 'And the moral of that is, 'tis love that makes the world go round.' And Alice had replied, 'Somebody said that it's done by minding your own business. . . .'

'Well now, so how do you like Peking, Alice? I may call you that, mayn't I, as we are to be friendly?'

'Of course—and I love Peking. It's like coming back to China.'

'But you've never left surely?'

'No, not really. But when I reached Hong Kong and then went to Shanghai and Chefoo, it seemed different. The Treaty Ports aren't like China somehow, not real, not properly anyway. So coming to Peking is like returning to China proper.'

Lady Digby looked at her shrewdly; it must have been quite strange to have seen Hong Kong for the first time in one's life through her eyes. 'Yes, I understand, dear, and it must be difficult for you, after all these years away from everybody and everything familiar. Yet now you're expected to behave as if nothing much had happened, isn't that it?'

'Yes, exactly,' Alice agreed eagerly. 'And the Chu family were quite good to me in some ways, but no one seems to believe that, or be interested in them.'

'Well, I'm interested, I assure you, Alice. Quite an important family, I believe? The Deputy-Governor of Hunan?'

The tea arrived and as they drank and ate cake together companionably, Alice found herself talking more freely than she had to anyone else about her experiences.

'Well, Alice,' Lady Digby exclaimed eventually, setting down her cup. 'I think that's one of the most fascinating stories I've ever heard. And in some ways, you're most fortunate. Very few English people in China today, and probably none of your tender years, have as much first-hand experience of the country and its languages as you—and we must see it's not wasted.'

Alice's eyes shone. 'Oh, Lady Digby, thank you for that. Ever since I reached Hong Kong people have been feeling sorry for me and asking about my dreadful experiences. They've never wanted to know how much I've learned.'

The Minister's wife smiled gently, feeling a genuine concern for this intense little person who was half-woman, half-child, half-English and half . . . well, something different. 'Most of the people have been missionaries, I expect?'

'Yes, that's the trouble. They have such fixed ideas about the "heathen Chinese"—as if heathenness were the only important thing about them.'

'Quite so. Well as you grow up you'll make up your own mind on such matters, I've no doubt. Personally, I'm very glad to hear of the good times . . . In fact, from what you've said, I'm a little surprised you decided to leave. You took a dreadful risk, just leaping off into the unknown and away from the Chus, where, as you say, much was agreeable?'

Alice felt herself flushing. 'Well, I was growing up . . . and I desperately wanted to see my mother again.'

'Natural enough too, my dear. But I do wonder, if you'll forgive my asking, if something perhaps less than pleasant made you feel suddenly you had to go, at whatever cost?'

Alice realised that a total lie would not, at this juncture, be believed; moreover, even the telling of a half-truth would be a great relief.

'There was something, yes . . . I haven't told anyone up to now, not even Mama. But one day Eldest Daughter took me aside and told me that Honourable Father, Lung-kuang . . . was, well . . .'

'Go on, my dear. I shan't be shocked, I assure you.'

'. . . that he was intending to take me as his wife—or rather as his third wife, for he already had two, his official wife and another. She told me I'd probably have a baby in time, she explained things like that. But I was shocked of course, I felt I was too young and . . . .'

Triumphant, Lady Digby jumped up, squeezing Alice's arm. 'My poor dear child, so you risked all and ran away to save your virtue? Indeed your mother should be proud of you. There's no disgrace in that, for you did not succumb to the easier but immoral way. It was a thoroughly brave and right thing for you to do! Really, however cultured the Chinese may be in some respects, their system of concubinage is an abomination . . . just think what might have happened to you! Come, let me order more tea, it will cheer you up, dear.'

While she summoned the servant, Alice realised that her half-truth had been a success as clearly the whole truth would not have been. So it was the 'easier but immoral way' she had actually taken? Yet it seemed so natural and right at the time. 'And the moral of that is, the Duchess said . . .' Alice grinned and had another good idea.

'You see, Lady Digby, that's why I'm so dreadfully worried about Frank. He's nearly sixteen, and among the Chinese, boys begin doing things much earlier, well . . . things only men should do . . . And I'm afraid . . .'

'Oh dear me, that hadn't entered my mind. Something must indeed be done. He could become thoroughly corrupted for life in no time at all . . .' She frowned anxiously. 'But it isn't an easy matter and there can be nothing in the way of an official expedition, as my husband has told you. Ah, the tea . . .' She poured fresh cups.

'I think my uncle has accepted that. He's determined to go to Changsha secretly himself, though, but there's the expense—carts, guides, provisions. If he could just get a little financial help, unofficially of course, it would make such a difference. And how can we possibly just leave Frank there, in the circumstances?'

'Well, I'll speak to Sir Hugh, Alice. It might be possible . . . taking into account . . . your brother's youth . . . and so on . . .' She trailed vaguely into the hopeful but non-committal phrases that had become her diplomatic second nature. People were always asking her to speak to Hugh on their behalf, and usually it was tiresome or boring. But this particular case was extraordinary and she really intended to do her best, as she told Alice on parting, adding, 'Now remember my dear, I am your friend, and if you want any help or advice while you're in Peking just let me know.'

It was a relief to emerge into the bustle of Legation Street, for Alice could not accustom herself to the silent, empty spaces in English homes where one did not speak loudly for fear of creating disturbance. Indeed her mother had already told her several times to lower her voice. 'Shush, Alice, you sound like a market woman calling her wares,' she had reproved. Alice sighed, for in the Chu household there had always been people about shouting, laughing, arguing, scolding and one had to speak up in order to be heard at all.

At the corner she paused, reluctant to return to the solemn late afternoon dullness of the Sturgeons' mission. Instead she strolled aimlessly till she reached the street of the fanmakers near the Imperial City walls. Each open-fronted shop was hung with fans, the cheapest made of translucent paper, the most expensive of exquisitely coloured silks decorated with traditional designs—dragons among clouds, carp among lotus, lions among peonies, phoenixes among cherry-blossom. In the shop recesses, the makers and their families, surrounded by piles of bamboo struts and material, were cutting, folding, stitching. Alice lingered, enjoying the scene and the slight stir she evoked by inquiring about prices in a totally comprehensible fashion. Then she espied the fan she wanted—of creamy Hangchow silk, embroidered with clusters of jade-green buttons enclosed in black circles.

'But that is a gentleman's fan,' the shopkeeper protested, 'taken from the design intended for Mandarins of the third rank. But for you, how about this?' and he flourished a brilliant silken arc of gold and crimson butterflies.

She shook her head; it was too complicated to explain. 'It's for my uncle, he's going on a long hot journey to the south,' she extemporised.

'Ah so, very good. . . . A southern journey you say? Where is he going? Has he everything organised in the way of mules, carts, guides?'

'Not really, he's only just beginning.'

The fanmaker grinned. 'Your uncle needs David.'

'David? A foreigner?'

'Not exactly, but not a Son of Han either. David's a Mongolian, the only one I know with a barbarian nickname. . . . Here, you lazy whelp,' he shouted at his second son, 'go and find David. Tell him there's a foreigner wanting to travel. Hurry now. Sit down and wait a while; he'll come soon.'

Alice hesitated; even as she did so a stool was brought and she sat, accepting the course of events. 'So, who is David?'

'He's a real character, everyone knows him. When he was a lad, still wet behind the ears, he went with his father— who was a camel driver—on a long journey to some god-forsaken place with this barbarian Jesus-man called David.'

'Oh I know, Abbé David. I saw his collection in the cathedral yesterday.'

'That's him. Well, he taught the lad so much, all about animals, birds, plants and the like, that when he came back he was always boasting "David told me this or that thing." So *he* got called David and he's been a great traveller ever since, with his own carts and mules. Foreigners often hire him, they're always travelling about, stupid creatures. What's so green about the grass five hundred miles away? Still it's good for business, and David's the man for your uncle, I'm sure.'

And so he was, as Alice knew the moment he appeared. He

had twinkling eyes set deep in a pudgy weathered face; he was stocky, his legs bandy from straddling many steeds, but he walked with a springy vigorous stride as if no piece of ground could hold him for long. He had, he told Alice, been in more provinces of the Empire than any other transport-master and no one could equal him in the provision of strong pack-animals, reliable carts, and knowledgeable guidance. For had he not made three journeys to the northern extremities of the Empire with that strange, clever, old Jesus-man? And had he not learned more from him than most common sons-of-dogs drivers learned in a lifetime? He sat four-square on a bale of cloth. Whenever he grinned he showed rotting yellow teeth and whenever he moved a heavy smell of animal dung wafted from him. But the fanmaker was right—he was the man for the job and Alice promised to tell her uncle so that very evening.

It was nearly dark when she left the fanmakers, feeling inordinately pleased with herself, for, in one afternoon, she had enlisted in the cause of Frank's rescue the sympathies of the Minister's wife and the services of Peking's best transport-master. At the Mission gate, she took out the green and white fan, caressed its smooth silk, stowed it in her bag. It was not for Uncle Robert. One fine day, she promised herself, she would present it to Frank, saying, 'From one Uncut Jade to another!'

Mrs. Sturgeon met her at the door, looking anxious yet oddly excited. 'Alice, at last—where have you been? Do Lady Digby's teas go on this late?'

'No, but we had a long talk and then I . . .'

'Well never mind, dear, it's just time for evening prayers and . . . there's a present waiting for you in the sitting-room. Just go straight in and find out.'

Smiling, she opened the door and Alice walked in, wondering if her mother had remembered her approaching birthday. A man stood in the room's dusk. He was in shadow, but there was something about his stance that made her heart lurch in terror for a half-second. He was like . . . but he . . .

He stepped forward and she ran to him. 'Oh, it's . . . William . . . William. . . .'

'Alice my dear, dear little Alice.' Her elder brother caught her in his arms and held her tightly. They clung together and he kissed her warmly. 'But let me look at you properly, dear.

I hadn't realised how dark it has become.' He went to light the lamp, turning away so she should not see his joyous emotion. The lamp glowed and they looked at each other steadily by its light.

'My, but you've changed, Alice. Mama told me you had—you're a lovely young lady now, though not a very tall one!' He patted her hand teasingly. 'Oh Alice, I'm so very happy to see you and we've so much to tell each other, so many years to catch up on! I don't know where to begin, so let's work backwards, as it were. I'll tell you how I got here, it's rather funny.'

He led her to a chair and she sat, quite weak with delight. He had grown to be a man very like her father—the same build, the same look of earnest reliability. 'Oh William,' she wiped her eyes, 'how wonderful to see you. I thought you were still at sea. Mother said your ship was only just due.'

'It was sheer luck. We had a marvellously calm voyage and reached Hong Kong ten days ahead of schedule. And there we were, all ready to disembark, Isabel and I, our baggage on the deck when . . .'

'Isabel—you must tell me about her. You are married, William. Isn't that strange to think of?'

'It's very nice, I can tell you.' He laughed happily. 'You'll like Isabel . . . but back to Hong Kong. There we stood, when a man from the Consulate came rushing up the gangplank calling my name and I thought something else dreadful had happened. But he said, "This *is* your sister, isn't it, Mr. Greenwood, read that!" and handed me a copy of the *China Mail* with the story of your return from Hunan. You must have seen it?'

'It wasn't quite accurate.'

'But it was you. I could scarcely credit it. Anyway, I rushed off to see the Consul who'd been in touch with the Imperial Customs in Foochow and I was granted indefinite compassionate leave to come and see you and sort things out about Frank if possible. So I sailed straight on to Chefoo—leaving Isabel behind, because she's expecting our first child—isn't that splendid, though? But when I saw Mother she told me you and Uncle had just left, so I followed post-haste, and here I am!'

'That's so utterly marvellous! Now you'll come with us to get Frank, won't you?'

'You bet, it sounds most exciting, Uncle's been telling me. I arrived just after you left—for tea at the Legation, I hear? Well Miss Greenwood, you're a young lady of consequence now, everyone wants to know you!'

Alice laughed. 'But I can't get used to being a young lady of consequence, having been a very low-ranking female barbarian for so long. I'll tell you all about it in time, but just now it's almost too much, and, in a funny way, your arrival is like a dream coming true.'

'What do you mean, dear?'

'Well, when Frank and I first got to the Chus, we were kept inside the kitchen courtyard where we sat for hours looking at the farm-gate because we had this silly dream that one day a whole regiment of British soldiers would come marching through to rescue us, led by you and Uncle Robert. We were only children then, remember, with no idea of the difficulties and distances. But now, you and Uncle and I are going to rescue Frank, so it's like the dream beginning to come true.'

William frowned. 'When I think of the terrible times you've had . . . what you actually saw when, as you say, you were still children. No, it doesn't bear thinking about.' He stared into the Mission's enclosed courtyard. 'And how I wish I'd come to search for you, but we were told so definitely you'd been killed. After a while, Mother wrote to say she was coming home—but then the next thing was, she was marrying a Mr. Edward Blake.'

They looked at each other, then, by mutual consent, looked away. 'I've not met him yet,' Alice said neutrally.

'Neither have I. Apparently he can't be spared from his Mukden mission. But the babies are splendid, aren't they? Fancy, a little half-brother and -sister, that was a real surprise for you, wasn't it? But talking of brothers, tell me about Frank. What's he like now?'

William listened eagerly as Alice diverted him with tales of Frank's prowess in archery and horsemanship. And, 'No, really? Why, we'll have quite a little medieval soldier on our hands . . .' William was saying when Robert hurried in.

'Medieval soldier? No reference to me, I hope?'

William jumped up. 'Certainly not, sir, you're a very modern nineteenth-century warrior. No, Alice was just telling me that Frank is a dab hand at bows and arrows!'

'Extraordinary, isn't it? We must get him away from there. Well, isn't this a grand surprise, Alice? But come—we wanted you to have a short time together, but now supper's ready and the good doctor is waiting for grace.'

It was a merry meal. Alice sat next to William and they kept looking at each other in delighted amazement, while Robert only wished he could have raised a glass of wine to their reunion, but that would have offended his hosts. So much was there to say that the table was cleared before Alice remembered to tell them of David.

'And he's coming to see us early in the morning,' she concluded. 'I'm certain he's just the man we need, Uncle, and he's a really experienced traveller, which is rare, you know.'

At precisely the appointed hour next morning David appeared, which was also rare, as Alice pointed out. And, by lunchtime, Robert was so impressed with the Mongolian's expertise in matters of carts, animals and provisions that he began congratulating himself on his ability to 'spot a good man when he saw one,' as if he, not Alice, had first judged David's worth. But she was too involved in the excitement of their preparations to be annoyed.

Later that day, she and Mrs. Sturgeon's cook went to the market and bought sacks of dried pulses, rice, and spices, and jars of preserves, beef extract, arrowroot, and tins of meats from the German shop in Legation Street. Dr. Sturgeon prepared a medical kit with plasters, castor oil, salves, and tinctures, and Mrs. Sturgeon packed everything in the large 'itineration baskets' for carriage in the provision cart.

Then the blow fell. Late in the afternoon, Robert quietly disappeared and, when he returned, drew William aside and they went into the sitting-room. Watching them, Alice's heart sank, for she recognised the tight-drawn line of Robert's mouth as indicative of some obstinate and unpopular resolve. Summoned to the room in her turn, she found Robert at his most upright behind the writing table, William hunched at the window.

'Ah Alice, there you are!' Robert's geniality was forced. 'I thought you'd like to know, I've just returned from the Legation and with good news. First of all, a dispatch granting me four months' compassionate leave has just come, and then I must say you seem to have worked wonders, dear. The

167

Minister has now offered me a sum of money to help defray the costs of the journey and given me a document saying that I'm a harmless traveller engaged in amateur scientific research. All unofficial of course, and if anything should go wrong, our people will deny any knowledge of my real business. But it's certainly a great help, and many thanks to you, for his change of heart seems mainly due to the chat you had with Lady Digby.'

'But how splendid, Uncle! When I was shopping today I began worrying about the cost of things, but now we can just "set off gladly, regardless of short or long"—as some poet wrote . . .' Her voice trailed uncertainly as Robert drew a deep breath.

'Now that's the other point I want to make—you say "we" set off. Now listen, my dear, Sir Hugh has told me what you explained to his wife—why you felt, and most properly too, that you had to get away from the Chus at all costs. It was an admirable course of action, Alice, and both William and I are very proud of you. But that story has most definitely convinced me of one thing—under no circumstances are you going back to Hunan with us. I absolutely forbid it. I owe it to your mother never to expose you again to the risk of falling into Chinese hands. Their ways are not our ways, especially with regard to women, as you yourself found out. And there is no knowing what might happen if we were discovered and handed over to the authorities. You remember Sir Hugh's warnings of the dangers of travelling unofficially in backward provinces like Hunan from which foreigners are almost totally excluded? One or two who did venture have simply disappeared without trace in recent years, I've been told, and it's rumoured they were executed. Well, William and I are willing to take the risk, and we could defend ourselves to the death if necessary, but for you, an innocent and undefiled young lady, there could be even worse perils. So when we leave, I insist . . .'

Alice broke in with a harsh cry of anguished rage. 'But that's not fair, it's not fair! I'm not frightened of the Chinese, I've lived among them for years. I know them, they won't do me any harm, you're talking nonsense. Oh Uncle, please let me go with you. I can speak the language and be your interpreter and . . .'

'Now hush, Alice, you mustn't shout in that unladylike

way. I remember your mother reprimanding you about it.'

'But I don't want to be ladylike—I want to come with you. If I were a boy you'd take me.'

'But you're not, Alice,' William interposed gently. 'That is just why you'd be in special danger, as Uncle has explained. I was horrified when I heard the fate you'd escaped from. Uncle is absolutely right, we cannot possibly allow you to return to a part of the country where concubinage is practised.'

'It goes on all over China.' Alice snorted furiously. 'It's just their way, that's all.'

'And a very immoral and deeply wrong way, as you surely understand.'

Alice battened down into herself, trying to get a grip on her emotions. She looked at the two men, so kindly, yet so ignorant of what she was really like, of what had really happened. She had a reckless urge to break out entirely and shout at the top of her voice, 'But I liked it, liked it! I was Lung-kuang's unofficial concubine for many a moon and I sometimes long more than anything to go back and spread my legs on that red quilt and feel his caress and the thrust of him.' Such a confused storm of intense desire, rage, and frustration broke upon her that she shuddered and turned very pale, clenching her fists on the knowledge that she must never, never utter that dreadful truth.

'Come, Alice, don't take it so hard,' Robert said briskly. 'Enough is enough. And when Will and I leave you'll return to your mother in Chefoo. After all, it won't be much fun travelling across China in a mule-cart in the heat of summer. Surely you've done enough of that sort of thing?' He tried to pat her on the head, but she jumped away, bristling with rage like a cat.

'Well I haven't, so there! And it's just not fair! I know fifty times more than either of you about the country. I found David for you, I talked to Lady Digby and it's through me you're getting this help—and this is what I get for it! It's hateful . . . it's—'

Robert barked sternly, 'Alice, that's quite enough of your shouting, I won't have it. I thought the Chinese taught their children good manners whatever else their failings, but you don't seem to have learned any.'

'But I'm not Chinese, and I'm not a child . . . I'm, I'm . . .

just me. Please, Will, let me go with you. Frank's my brother as well as yours, and he mayn't even leave unless he sees me.'

'Oh nonsense, Alice, of course he will. No, Uncle is absolutely right. This isn't a job for a young lady.'

'Then I'll have nothing more to do with it, I won't help you anymore, you can manage without me . . . oh, it's too bad!' And she fled to her bedroom where, burying her head in the pillow, she sobbed and sobbed.

The two men exchanged troubled looks and William sighed. 'I feared she'd take it badly.'

'Only a childish tantrum, she's very headstrong, as you see—which is another good reason for sending her back to your mother for some sound, home-based discipline.' Robert began studying a map of Hopeh province, for he was a man who, when relationships became difficult, preferred the more measurable ups and downs of physical terrains. William sighed, vexed by his sister's behaviour. She had shown such courage, everyone had praised her, he had been so delighted to see her again—but now she must realise she was only a girl and he and Robert should take matters over. Only—there had been a wild and passionate recklessness in her outburst that disturbed him.

'I suppose she feels she doesn't quite belong anywhere, just at present?' he inquired of Robert's bent head. 'And that must be upsetting for her?'

'She'll soon get over it and settle down.'

But Alice had no intention of quickly getting over it. Refusing supper, she rolled about on her bed in paroxysms of frustration and anger, berating herself for having confided in Lady Digby. She would never again trust anyone with even half the truth; she cursed in full-blooded native fashion the injustice and stupidity of being forbidden to return to the place that only she knew and loved.

Eventually, after nightfall, utterly exhausted by her emotional turmoil, she lit a lamp, dug a few sugar-plums from her bag and, sucking them hungrily instead of supper, began to think. 'Remember Confucius,' she said aloud, 'what did he have to say? There's always something apt. . . .' She paused and chanted, 'Confucius heard the cattle-boy singing "Is the water of the T'sang river clear? I can wash the tassel of my hat. Is it muddy? I can wash my feet." Make the best of cir-

170

cumstances, clear or muddy, Alice, and turn them to advantage, so says Confucius.'

She pondered a while longer, then took from the lining of her reticule the pearl necklace and put it under her pillow. Still desolate, but consoled by a new resolve, she slept.

'Is Alice still sulking?' Robert asked at breakfast the next morning, noticing her empty chair.

'I'm afraid she must be,' Mrs. Sturgeon replied. 'I knocked on her door as I came down.'

'Shall I call her again?' William asked.

'No, leave her a while longer,' Robert ordered. 'The more attention you pay to young ladies' tantrums, the longer they last, isn't that so, Mrs. Sturgeon?'

'I'm sure you're right, Major. Alice has a sunny nature really. She'll shine again before you leave.'

'And we must be off to the money-changers' bazaar straightaway,' Robert urged his nephew. 'They start dealing early, you say, Doctor?'

'Yes—best go now. Get as many silver sycees as possible or the brass cash, they're the only reliable currency outside the capital. They're awfully heavy and the silver must be broken up and sold en route, but there's no choice—don't be palmed off with paper notes, they may be counterfeits or useless in the provinces.'

'All sounds the devil of a business . . . sorry, ma'am,' he bobbed apologetically at his hostess, 'but let's go to it, Will, my boy.'

Though Robert and William reached the money-changers early, Alice had been there before them. She had exchanged the necklace for two bars of silver and a pile of local paper money which she had just thrown on the table in the shed at the animal-dealers' market where David transacted his business. He looked at the pile, then at Alice, weighing the two.

'It's a small amount of money,' he conceded casually.

'It's quite a lot of money. Count it if you like.'

'All in due time, Miss. And what exactly do you want me to do to get this money?'

'You have to let me travel hidden in the provision cart for the first week of the journey to Hunan so that the two gentlemen don't know I'm there.'

David's round face seldom registered the amount of surprise it now showed. 'In the provisions cart! But why?'

'Because they've refused at the last moment to take me with them just because I'm a girl, and they think it's dangerous ... so utterly stupid, when I've already travelled hundreds of miles through the country all alone, and much further than either of them!'

David grinned. 'You should see the women of Mongolia, they don't go boxed up in chairs or hobbled like the Chinese. They're broad-footed and wear loose trousers and gallop on horseback over the plains like the men.'

Alice's eyes widened. 'I should like to go and see them sometime. Perhaps you'll take me one day, David?'

He grunted non-committally, picked up the bundle of notes and counted them with his dirty, splayed thumb. In spite of his boasts, he knew that the axle of the provision cart was in bad need of repair; there was enough here to buy a new one. He looked at her speculatively. 'And what happens after this first week?'

'When we're so far away they can't possibly send me back, I'll come out of hiding.' She said it confidently enough, though the very thought of her uncle's anger made her quail. But what was the alternative?

'And what about me? When they realise I've been hiding you away, they could dismiss me at once.'

'What—out there in the interior with no other transport-master within hundreds of miles and you the owner of the carts and horses? What's more, my uncle is in a hurry, he has only four months' leave to get to Hunan and back. No, they'll have to accept the position and go on—taking me with them.'

David grunted, counting the money again. 'There's not enough. I'll have to bribe the drivers to keep quiet.'

Experienced in such transactions, Alice took another bundle from her bag.

'There—that's all I have.'

He counted again, and nodded. 'Done—but where will you sleep?'

'In the cart. I've slept in many carts before now and travelled in many provinces. I'll tell you about it, if you keep our bargain.'

'You've been to Hunan already?' She nodded. 'Then I'll be interested to hear about it. I'll bring the carts to the Mission late this evening to load because we must leave at dawn,

172

there's always an early queue at the Tartar gate.'

'I'll get in the provision cart then, so please leave a little space for me!'

'All right—you're not very big, for a foreigner.'

'And it is customary for the provision cart to travel well behind the passenger one, isn't it?'

'Yes, there should be no difficulty. You're a strange one, miss,' he added, as they went across the outside enclosure. It was full of horses, camels, pack-asses, bullocks, mules, oxen and men from far-off parts—Tibetans, Manchurians, Koreans, Mongolians like David. The market had become one of the sights of Peking and foreign visitors often came to contemplate its picturesque disorder, stepping carefully between the piles of dung and holding handkerchiefs soaked in eau-de-cologne to their noses. But Alice, David noticed, paid no special regard to the scene, taking it for granted, like a native. Moreover, she knew how to bargain; she had not pressed him hard enough, but she was no novice.

'Why do you want to go back to Hunan then, miss?' he asked curiously.

'Ah, you'll find out in time. You have your money, I have my secret.' She put her small fair hand into his broad dark one to seal the bargain and hurried away.

The rest of that day was tiresome for everyone. Returning to the Mission, Alice found it in uproar. A dispensary assistant had accidentally spilled some boiling water over the ulcerated leg of a baby boy. The baby was shrieking wildly, his mother was yelling vituperations at every barbarian swine in sight. Mrs. Sturgeon was trying to placate with salves and tea. Alice was called upon to help and by the time peace was restored, her non-appearance at breakfast was forgotten.

Robert and William were also too busy to pay her much heed. They had been to the money-changers and come away with sycees and several thousand cash—heavy brass coins with square holes in the middle, strung on straw twist and worth, Robert estimated, about a shilling a yard. They had also shopped in Legation Street for two hunting rifles, two pistols, two mosquito nets, Goldflake tobacco, Sporting & Military chocolate, six bottles of claret and twelve of French brandy—the last of which Robert, in deference to his hosts' teetotalism, stowed unobtrusively among the provisions.

Supper was tense and uncomfortable. The Sturgeons feared the morning's mishap had lost them several potential converts. Robert was fretful in case anything vital was forgotten. William was feeling guilty about leaving pregnant Isabel. Alice was simply quiet. As the meal ended, David's two carts trundled into the yard and the men rushed off to supervise their loading. Showing no interest, Alice stared moodily at her plate. Why did it have to be like this? She hated deception—why could she not be out there, eagerly and openly involved?

'Come, Alice,' Mrs. Sturgeon said gently, 'I know how you're feeling. But once they've left, you'll realise how right your uncle is. It's no easy journey for a woman, you know, and think how you can help your dear mother with her two little ones—that is where you can do most good now.'

'But I don't want . . .'

'Ah, but Alice, what we think we want for ourselves is not always what God has in mind for us. And sometimes, for a Christian, "I want" must give way to "I ought." '

'I don't think I'm a very good Christian,' Alice mumbled sulkily.

'I'm sure none of us can claim to be that, we can only try . . . So now, put on a brighter face for the menfolk when they come in.'

Alice sighed, but gave an obedient half-smile when William poked his head round the door. 'Come on out, Alice—everything is ready to go—and cheer up!' He chucked her under the chin.

Spring moonlight shone on the canopies of the carts in the yard. The larger contained straw pallets and personal luggage for the travellers, the smaller looked absolutely crammed with provisions—but, Alice thought anxiously, there had to be room for her as well. Not daring to inspect closely, she went to Robert, saying in a small voice, 'Well goodbye, Uncle. I shan't get up at dawn to see you off. I wish you an easy journey and please bring Frank back safely, won't you?'

'Of course we will, if it's humanly possible. Now, that's better, give me a goodbye kiss, dear. Take good care of yourself and give my love to your mother, she'll have had my letter. Dr. Sturgeon says there's a Mrs. someone-or-other, American Presbyterian, going to Chefoo at the weekend, and you can travel with her for an escort.'

'Yes, Uncle.' She clung to William for a moment, longing to confess everything—if only he was not so respectable and straitlaced.

In her bedroom, Alice tiptoed about packing clothes in a calico bag and, in her reticule, her new copy of *Alice in Wonderland*, the poems of Li T'ai, the silk fan and, in its false lining, the Carr loot. When all was ready she threw back the shutters so the cool air might keep her wakeful. Looking out, she could see, outlined against the clear night sky, the distant circular white-marble three-storeyed Pavilion of Heaven, its domed roof, tiled in deep blue, shining silver-azure in the moonlight. Gradually the Celestial City subsided into a brief, dead-of-night silence. It was very beautiful and very mysterious, the hour when all the gods—of the mountains and oceans, of the thunder and wind, of the grass, the rain and the corn-stalks—came into their own and entered the dreams of the two million inhabitants who slumbered within its walls.

At last she heard the distant drum in the tower of the southern palace thudding the end of the night watch. She rose, stretching wearily, pinned on her pillow a letter addressed to the Sturgeons. In it she had written that she could not bear to remain in Peking now the men had left, so she had taken the early mail cart to Tientsin and would go from there to Chefoo. They would worry a little, say she should not have gone alone and then, in the harassed bustle of their days, forget about her.

She took her bags and crept outside. The provision cart creaked noisily as she clambered aboard and the Mission's gatekeeper stirred in his sleep. In the cart's centre, sacks had been stacked and covered with straw to make a cosy nest. She sank into it thankfully, covered herself with her cloak and dozed. Dimly she heard a cock crowing, then the tramp of boots and hooves, the sound of voices; there was a jerk as the shafts were lifted and the mules backed into them, one behind the other.

In her half-sleep Alice slipped back into her childhood, to that first frightening journey with Frank into nowhere. She hugged herself with excitement, feeling happy and secure by comparison, for now the voices outside belonged to Uncle Robert, William, and David. There was the general bustle of

175

departure, whips cracked, Dr. Sturgeon called goodbye from the Mission doorway, and the carts trundled off in a single file towards the Tartar gate and the plains of Hopeh. Before they had left the city, Alice, curled in her straw nest, was deeply asleep.

7

They travelled due south across the plains of Hopeh bright with flowers of yellow rape and white bean. Larks sang, and from the fields came the constant creak of water-wheels turned by buffaloes with pink, fly-encrusted eyes. The main street of each village was a smelly quagmire of broken flagstones and open drains and the inhabitants who curiously watched their passing were mostly old crones, spotty children, mangy dogs, for the able-bodied were working in the paddies. Often they had to fight for space along the narrow tracks against advancing carts and barrows stacked with produce. On windy days, some of the latter sported cloth sails that flapped cheerily and aided the coolies' pushing.

Usually Robert and William sat on a box behind David, feeling increasingly thirsty as each day wore on. And 'Why the deuce didn't we bring beer with us?' Robert asked at least twice every afternoon. Although David pushed the animals hard their progress was slow and 'Why the deuce doesn't any of this water run north and south?' Robert asked each time they came to a tributary river carrying vessels speedily from west to east. And 'Why the deuce haven't the Chinks learned to pep up their food with curry?' he asked each evening, faced with yet another bowl of insipid boiled millet or rice, with vegetables.

William replied soothingly to all these purely rhetorical questions, privately deciding that Indian army officers were not half as tough now as they must have been twenty years ago in the good old Mutiny days. Whether it was the absence of beer and curry or an over-sufficiency of millet, Robert could not say, but before long his indigestion was 'really giving him jip,' as he complained on the afternoon of the sixth day out.

'I'll have to give it a rest this evening, Will—arrowroot in warm water, that's all. Not that I'll be missing any gastronomic delights by the look of things.' He looked glumly at the squalid village shack ahead which, David said, was to be their resting-place for the night.

Robert staggered stiffly down from the cart, a griping ache in his belly. The usual knot of villagers gathered at once, peppering him with questions he fortunately could not understand. One youngster plucked curiously at his trousers, then climbed up the cart-wheel to peer under the awning. Robert grabbed him by the scruff of the neck and threw him away so violently that he fell backwards, hitting his head on a stone. He jumped up and tore off, yelling, blood streaming from his head.

'Thieving little brat,' Robert snarled in self-defence at David, who frowned.

'William, get me into a room quick, I think I'm feverish, this sun is going right through my skull.' By the time William had secured a room off the inn-yard, dislodged a couple of specially audacious pigs and a goat, supplied his ailing uncle with arrowroot, the sun had gone down. He ate his supper inside the cart; every now and then a villager poked his head into the circle of his hurricane lamp, muttered unpleasantly and withdrew. Lord, what a country, William thought dismally. Would he ever take to it? If it had not been for his mother, he might have joined the Indian Service, which was much more civilised, according to Robert. But then he would not have been involved in this expedition. Of course, he would not have missed it, he told himself. Though being a natural conservative, part of him yearned to be sitting, at that very moment, round a well-ordered supper table with Isabel in Foochow.

David pushed through the men still sullenly standing about. 'Not good place, not like you.' He put a hand behind his head in a chopping motion.

'You mean chop our heads off?' William asked alarmed, but David only mumbled vaguely, for his English was rudimentary. He handed William a note from Robert: 'Not feeling good. Please bring brandy—in provision cart I think.'

William, remembering the villagers' mood, slipped his pistol into his pocket before walking to the other cart which stood propped against the inn's back wall. As he parted the awning, a dim figure half-rose before him, and he stepped back, yelling, 'Hey, David, here quick, there's a thief in the provision cart.' He jerked out his pistol in panic, 'Come out, you bastard! No messing about, I'm armed.' He fired a shot in the air that resounded sharply through the quiet night.

'William—stop! Don't shoot for heaven's sake, it's me.'

He lowered the weapon in disbelief and grabbed the small figure who crouched on the cart floor. 'You—Alice—what the devil are you doing here?'

'I've been riding behind all the time. Don't be angry, please, William. I just couldn't bear to be left behind.'

Alerted by the shot, David and some villagers rushed up. 'Oh David,' Alice ran to him. 'I've been found out, but it's all right. I bribed him,' she turned to her brother, 'it wasn't his fault.'

The men were growling angrily at William's pistol. 'Tell him to put that away, they don't like it,' David said to Alice.

She did so, then, turning to the men, explaining in a loud voice, 'It's all right. The shot was a mistake. I'm this man's sister—but he mistook me for a thief.'

They sniggered. 'His wench, I suppose she means,' one sneered. 'He'll be able to fire his little pistol in another direction tonight then.' They shuffled off, disappointed by the anticlimax.

William drew himself up. 'We shall have to send you back, Alice.'

'But how could I possibly go back alone from here?' she mocked. 'Oh, Will, let me come. I've done all this and risked so much. I was going to come out of hiding soon anyway, only I couldn't quite screw up the courage.'

'Courage?' William chuckled, for her audacity amazed him. 'Very well, Alice, I give in without a struggle, but heaven knows what Uncle will say. He's not feeling well, by the way, which is why I came to get him some brandy. You'd better take it to him—that will either kill or cure!'

Alice walked into Robert's room carrying in her shaking hand a large tumbler of cognac. He was dozing on the straw bed, hands locked across his grumbling stomach, and half-opened a weary eye. 'Ah, Alice, you've . . . Alice? What the devil?' He sat upright.

William, apprehensive in the doorway, prepared for a tough fight, but, on that particular evening, Robert had little fight in him. And, as the brandy sent its cheering message round his empty insides and he heard how Alice had got there, his sternness evaporated and he suddenly burst out laughing, 'By jove, Alice, you're a real chip off the Greenwood block, I must say. Stubborn as they come, just like your poor father—or me, when I get a mad idea in my head!'

'So I can come with you now, Uncle?' Alice was demure.

'I suppose so. Damn it, what else can we do with her, Will? And certainly you'll be useful when it comes to getting a bit of sense out of this wretched country. Look at this quilt,' he shook it in disgust, 'crawling with vermin.'

She giggled. 'And this place is called the Inn of Irreproachable Purity, did you know?'

'What a farce! And these yokels keep peering in and shouting; they're the nastiest bunch we've met so far. I suppose this is the village of Unimaginable Harmony? I don't know what the hell's the matter with them.'

'I'll try and find out,' Alice said nonchalantly, though she did not much like the look of the group near the door. 'I can't understand their dialect very well,' she reported back, 'but it's something about an injured child that's upset them.'

'Oh lord, that.'

The trouble was, as David had tried to explain, that the parents of the boy Robert had struck down had had to buy some healing paste from the doctor. 'And they all say you should pay for it, as it was your fault,' Alice grinned. 'You're a very rich barbarian and the paste cost as much as a fat duck in the market.'

'Oh well, if that's all.' Robert counted out the requisite cash and gave it to the child's father who bowed sheepishly and slunk away.

'There—you see how useful I can be!' Alice plonked down triumphantly on a stool, reaching for the glass of brandy.

'Alice—that's mine, and don't start getting above yourself, miss.' Robert grabbed it from her, and she hung her head theatrically.

'But, Uncle, it is my eighteenth birthday!'

William kissed her forehead. 'Goodness—21st May, so it is. I used always to remember it, when I thought you were dead I mean, and feel so sad. But now you're so nicely alive and here—that surely deserves a little celebration, Robert?'

'All right, pour another glass—it's certainly helping to settle my stomach.'

William raised it. 'Happy birthday, Alice, and may your next eighteen years be happier than your first!'

Finishing her ration of brandy, Alice went to collect her reticule from the provision cart. It was a balmy night; plain and village silent and small under the stars. She threw back her head and stared upwards, the starry pinpoints of light doing a little brandy-jig before her eyes, and the thought of the long excitement of life making her tingle with joy. To steady herself, she traced the shape of the Weaving Lady astride her stool who, Tamao used to say, rolled up her sleeves seven times a day as she wove the webs of the years. 'I'm eighteen,' she said aloud. 'Aren't I lucky!'

It was late June before they reached the watery region north of Changsha which Alice and Frank had once assumed to be the end of China. The Tung Ting lakes were dotted with the high mat-sails of fishing-boats, men on bamboo rafts were fishing along with cormorants, and cunningly constructed wicker fish-traps floated among the reeds. Rice sprouted in delicate green, yellow rice-birds pecked at the tender shoots. The journey had been remarkably uneventful, for Robert's money and his official document, allied to David's travelling acumen and Alice's translating skill, had seen them safely across every provincial border. But now Hunan was upon them and they grew quiet with apprehension at the temerity of their undertaking.

They decided it safest to reach Changsha just at dusk, and fortune favoured them for, on the evening they arrived, there was the usual motley of itinerant cobblers, fortune tellers, barbers, apothecaries, herb-, book- and pipe-sellers crowding into the gate. Merchants with strings of porters carried wrapped packages containing larvae of the white-wax insect from the valleys of Kweichow bound for the glossy green trees of Kiangsi where they would multiply exceedingly. The watchmen pounded their gongs and shouted to announce the gate's imminent closure, and in the impatient surge forward past the guards, the Greenwoods' cart went through unnoticed. And that night they remained concealed in the cart, which had come to rest in the stinking yard of an inn called Flowery Happiness.

Till then, Robert and William had remained unruffled by the warnings of danger they'd earlier received, but now, immured inside this populous, alien city, renowned for its insular xenophobia, they both experienced secret qualms. How easy it would be indeed just to disappear forever from such a place—a midnight arrest, a summary trial for illegal entry, an equally summary decapitation at dawn! William felt his throat tighten with fear as he lay sleepless inside the stuffy cart, while Robert, equally tense, was trying to work out a regular plan of campaign.

The greatest risk, in his view, was the unknown factor of Deputy-Governor Chu, obviously a man of considerable consequence who could arrange quick as chopsticks for the secret disposal of three unwanted barbarians. Might not Chu be even now fearing some sort of foreign reprisals for keeping Frank and Alice in captivity, even though none were in fact contemplated? And a powerful man afraid was a dangerous man. Again, though Frank was, according to Alice, a mere stable-boy in his household, surely Chu had some ulterior motive for keeping him there? These mandarin high-ups were devious and ruthless, in Robert's opinion, and here he was, hidden in one of their inviolate domains, totally at their mercy and with a very tricky mission ahead.

On consideration therefore, Robert reluctantly abandoned his earlier idea of simply brazening out the whole matter openly, and decided with reluctance that it was more prudent for him and Will, who couldn't possibly pass for natives, to remain in concealment the next day, while David and Alice, wearing her 'peasant outfit,' went to reconnoitre.

The first stage was easy, for every street vendor knew the whereabouts of the Chu residence. As they approached the stretch of mud-brick wall topped with blue and red tiles, the familiar sound of the Heavenly Clouds temple-bell quivered in the air and Alice's heart thumped with excited recognition. The main gate was open, the same lame gate-keeper was squatting there and gossiping; as they passed, she saw a servant scraping the flags with a broom, another carrying a bucket. She fought back a strong urge simply to run inside, calling 'Younger Daughter—I'm back.' Surely it would be all right? They would all understand and she and Frank could leave openly together. But what if they went for the magistrate instead? And what if Lung-kuang wanted her back in his bed? She shivered and David at her side whispered, 'Don't be afraid, but don't stare so long.'

'I'm not afraid,' she replied crossly. 'I'm just wondering what to do. I think we'd better sit in the cart till I see someone who doesn't actually belong to the house but can take a message in to Frank.'

David positioned the cart where they could see the gate and Alice, having mastered the oriental art of biding time unworriedly, sat on its floor, sucking melon slices and contemplating the scene. The Chu residence was like a shell, she thought, which, when she had been inside, seemed impregnable, but which now seemed very vulnerable to change, to breakage. The people within were living as they had for generations—Lung-kuang and Hidden Glory worshipping regularly in the ancestral hall, Han-li ploughing through the wisdom of the ancient sages, Eldest Son's new wife sitting patiently in the women's courtyard, podded perhaps with the seeds of the future. For they still assumed the future would be like the past. But how could it be when the fringes of their Empire had already been overrun by barbarians who rode in iron-clad ships, sipped wine in grand hotels, pressed up the rivers with their foreign merchandise and Bibles? She thought of Lin Fu-wei on the *Mandalay*. Was he too not a destroyer of all this in his fashion? The shell of the Chus would not be safe in his hands.

In the course of the day the gate opened several times as people passed inside, but Alice had already decided whom to approach. The scavenger's cart arrived at sunset as usual, and there was the familiar clattering as the day's detritus was thrown into it. When it left, Alice and David accosted the driver, drew him aside, dangled before his wide eyes a string of cash longer than he had seen for many a day. A message was handed over and they returned to the inn.

For two long, hot, fly-ridden days they waited, leaving the inn only at night, eating food provided by the inn-keeper who had been told that two escaped convicts from another province lay ill inside the cart. A water-carrier brought the reply on the third day: 'Dear Alice, it was luvly to here from you. I was serprisd. Cum to the outside wall wair it gos threw the litel wood tonite. I will be there if I can. Luv frank.' Robert and William were shocked by its illiteracy; if they needed further justification for this mad endeavour, here it was! The lad was nearly sixteen; he wrote like an eight-year-old.

An owl hooted from a nearby tree and Alice twitched

nervously. They had been waiting for over three hours, spaced out along the boundary wall as it went through the little wood and they were stiff with tension and fatigue.

'Sssh! Here he comes . . .' she heard Robert's warning and looking up, saw a figure straddle the wall further down. As they ran towards it, another figure appeared beside him. 'Wait, there's someone else!' Robert, fearing a trap, pushed them into the wall's shadow. But, as the two figures lowered a rope ladder to the ground, Alice broke cover.

'Frank—it is you, isn't it?'

'Yes, Uncut, it's me.' He sprang lightly down and she rushed at him, throwing her arms round his neck, hugging and kissing him despite his attempt to withdraw.

'Frank, Frank, oh my dear little brother, here you are at last—safe and well and bigger than ever! Oh Frank, I've missed you so much. There's been nobody to talk to who really understands, nobody to compare things with.' She tugged at him. 'Look, here's Uncle Robert, you do remember him don't you? And William. . . .'

They clapped each other's shoulders awkwardly, William amazed to see how his little brother had grown. 'But who . . .?' Robert peered at the figure behind Frank.

'Why—it's Youngest Son . . . how lovely to see you,' Alice slipped easily into Chinese, greeting him with a bow. 'But why are you here too?' For she was apprehensively aware that Frank had brought not the smallest bundle of possessions. But he had brought Han-li.

'Can he be trusted to keep quiet?' Robert asked tersely.

'Trusted? Of course—he's my pal, the youngest son. We hunt and ride together now and I'm better than him at archery, but he's cleverer at books than me.'

'Well say goodbye then and we'll be off. It's damn risky to hang about. David, our driver, is waiting with a cart at the edge of the wood.'

'Goodbye, but you've only just come! And there's so much to ask you. . . .'

'But we're all going, Frank,' Alice grabbed his arm tightly. 'There'll be lots of time to talk once we're safely out of the city.'

He shook her off. 'No, I'm not going with you. I guessed you might want me to, which is why I told Han-li about it. I still want to stay here.'

'You *what*?' Robert exclaimed. 'Stay *here*? After we've come hundreds of miles and risked our very necks for you? Don't be mad, boy, of course you're coming with us.'

Frank's voice took on that mulish tone that William recognised as an unhappy family trait. 'But I'm not, I told Alice when she went away—whenever that was—that I didn't want to leave.'

'You told . . .?' Robert spun on her. 'But you never said . . .'

'Now listen please. I'm sorry, yes, it's true. Frank did refuse to leave with me at that time. But you said you would later, Frank, if I came back for you—you did. And now you've seen us all again and we've come so far for you and we want you back so much. Haven't you missed me like I've missed you? You simply can't carry on growing up out here, dear, away from us all, not learning anything new or useful. Please Frank, it's for your own good. Honestly Frank, I thought you'd have realised that by now!'

'Well it seems he hasn't.' Robert contained the anger he knew was useless. 'Now listen, Frank, since Alice has returned to Western civilisation she's begun to understand how much she needs to learn, how much she's been missing. Isn't that so, Alice?'

'Yes . . . yes . . . in a way. But there's another thing, Frank, Mother is alive and well.'

'Mother?' He looked up from his obstinate contemplation of the ground.

'Yes—she's remarried and we have a new little brother and sister, twins called Sunny and Adam. Frank, how could we possibly return to Mother and tell her you didn't want to see her anymore. . . . She's just aching for you.'

He stood nonplussed. 'I've forgotten what she looks like,' he muttered sullenly. 'And it's more fun here.'

For a mild-tempered man, William then became extraordinarily angry, shaking his brother's shoulders violently. 'Fun?—Is that all you think about in life? Well, I'll tell you something, laddie, life's about a lot of other things, like duty to one's family and one's country and learning to grow up a decent man able to earn your own living and hold your head up in the world! And you won't do that riding around on horses and playing bows and arrows.'

Frank glared back defiantly. 'It's not like that here—you know nothing about it. And why should I come away now, just to please you? You all forgot about me and Alice for years and years.'

'But, Frank, they were told we were dead. It wasn't their fault.'

Han-li, uncomprehending, plucked Frank's sleeve. 'Whatever's the matter? Don't they like you anymore?'

'They want me to go away with them, and leave you—but I won't.'

Alice, understanding, gave a teary sniff. 'It'll just about break Mother's heart, Frank, and mine.'

There was a deadlocked pause; into it fell the sound of a watchtower gong reminding them all that dawn was not far off. Frank grabbed Han-li's arm and backed away, muttering, 'Perhaps I'll come back myself—later.'

'You can't go just like that, you can't,' Alice restrained him. 'Tell me about the family, how are they? Eldest Daughter, Younger Daughter—did the Honourable ask for me when he returned? Did they miss me?'

'Not for long,' Frank said cruelly, again making to leave. Suddenly with one accord, Robert and William fell on him, throwing him to the ground. Frank yelled and fought back, arms flailing. Then there came the sound of someone rushing through the wood.

'By God, someone's heard us—shut up, Frank, you silly sod!' William cuffed him across the mouth.

'Go and raise the alarm, Han-li,' Frank called in Chinese, just as David pounded up.

'Whatever's happened?' He stared in bewilderment.

'Help us hold him—he won't come,' William panted, as Frank, well versed in the arts of self-defence, lunged fiercely upward, knocking Robert off-balance and bringing William to his knees.

'Oh, oh, David—help!' Alice rushed forward, then realised that Han-li had gone. 'David—quick, we must stop him!' They raced after him and David grabbed the lowest rung of the ladder just as Han-li was about to pull it up after him. He teetered on the wall's top; it was too high to jump down the other side. 'Han-li, come back down please,' Alice called desperately. Han-li jerked the ladder; David held on firmly; he came slowly down.

'Youngest Brother,' she caught his hands, 'we were always friends, weren't we?'

186

'But you went away.'

'I had to, Han-li. I didn't entirely want to, but I had to return to my own people, my own family. You could never leave your own people forever, could you? I'd always have been an inferior barbarian among you, and it's the same with Frank—only he's so young and stubborn and never thinks beyond the end of his nose, does he? But you do, Han-li. You're much more sensible and deep down you know it would be better if Frank came back with us. We can all meet again later—when he's grown up and sensible.'

The sounds of the scuffle receded and Alice saw that Robert and William were dragging Frank away. 'See—he's got to go, and please, please, don't betray us. We might be thrown in jail if we're discovered. Pretend you know nothing—and one day you might decide to come and see the world and find us. There's so many modern, different things going on—things you never dream of here. I wish I'd time to tell you. This is such a small pond, Han-li, and Frank and I weren't born in it. You do understand?'

Han-li shuffled his feet. He did understand, though he did not much want to.

'Promise me you'll keep quiet and we'll be forever in your debt, me and Frank too.'

'All right, Uncut Jade, I won't tell. Frank's gone and I suppose his first duty is to his family, as mine is.'

David said, 'Someone's coming back for us, miss. Let him go now, or there'll be more fuss.' He stood away from the ladder and Han-li shinned up.

Alice called. 'How is your Honourable Father?'

'Another son is just born. By the new woman he has. He's pleased, more sons are always good.'

'Yes . . . I'm glad. And Han-li,' she quoted at his departing shape, ' "May you ever perpetuate the fragrance of books in your ancestral home." '

Robert panted up. 'He got away?'

'We let him go—he's promised not to betray us.'

'Huh, a typical Chink promise, I suppose. You believe him?'

'Yes I do. You think all Chinese are thieves and liars just because you've never met the well-brought-up honourable ones!'

Robert ignored her outburst, saying hastily, 'Well, there's nothing to do now but get out of this infernal city at the double.

The east gate opens at dawn and we must be there.'

Early sun glinted on the full buckets of the water-carriers and the piles of lake trout bound for the morning market. Alice, in her peasant's garb, sat beside David. In the cart behind them, Robert, William and Frank lay hidden under sacks—it having been made clear to the last that, if he raised the alarm, all their lives might be forfeit. So he was silent, half hoping for discovery, but also excited at the prospect of the unknown world beyond. It might be good fun.

Above the gate hung cages containing the still-dripping heads of three recently executed bandits; their cart passed below unmolested. Within a few miles the city's clatter fell away and the changeless country sounds took over—honk of wild duck, trundles of wheels, insects humming over the paddy-mud. Alice leaned against the cart frame, sleepy after the night's activity. She smiled at William as he came to sit beside her. 'You know I sometimes feel I've passed more of my life so far jolting along in carts than doing any other single thing! Don't look so anxious—I'm positive Han-li won't raise the alarm, and Frank will soon settle down and make the best of things—he always falls on his feet!'

'Stupid young dolt! What gratitude for you—after we've come all this way. He doesn't deserve to fall on his feet!'

'But he will, he's the type, so there's no point in having another row.'

'I shan't—but that laddie's got a lot to learn.'

And just how much, was brought home to them some time later, when they halted for what Robert called a 'convenience stop.'

'Alice, Frank—get down and stretch your legs!' Robert hustled them out. Alice breathed the fresh air gratefully; Frank leaned against the cart shafts.

'Where are you taking me?' he asked sulkily. Alice looked at him critically. He had grown beefier since she had last seen him and had a certain swagger she had not noticed in him before, though she had seen it often enough in Han-fei and his cronies.

'We're all going to Shanghai,' Robert said crisply. 'By the quickest route—north-east across the Chiuling Shan mountains and reaching the Yangtze at Chiuchiang.'

Frank yawned with elaborate lack of interest, untied the cord holding up his trousers, let them drop and began urinating against the cart-wheel. William pounced.

'Frank—what the blazes d'you think you're doing—right here in front of a lady?'

'Who—Alice? She's seen men do it hundreds of times.'

'Oh Frank, Frank,' Alice burst into embarrassed laughter. 'You mustn't really, not like that, not now.'

Frank reached for his trousers. 'Don't those garments even have flies?' Robert inquired with distaste.

'No, they don't. So where do you all do it then?'

'We go out of sight—at least I do,' and Alice giggled. But Robert did not see the joke for he was busy explaining that, in his view too, Frank, had much to learn.

What Frank came to believe was that he could do nothing right. His social manners were boorish, his posture slovenly and his clothes filthy, Robert informed him. His spelling, William added, was at kindergarten level, his spoken English sloppy, his outlook selfish and frivolous. And all in all, Frank decided on the fourth day out, he would have sneaked away and headed back to Changsha, if it had not been for Alice. But she did not chide him with his shortcomings, for she understood them too well, and he could not resist her pleadings when she talked about Mother and the new babies and the exciting things going on in what she called 'the new China.'

'I've discovered that the Chus are very old-fashioned in some ways,' she told him. 'And a lot of Chinese in the Treaty Ports don't regard foreigners with the ignorant contempt they do. That's what I told Han-li—to come out in the world and see for himself. I bet he's partly envying you, for Hunan really is a backwater, dear.'

She could be very persuasive when she chose, and after she had left, he had missed her more than he had cared to admit. He had felt very lonely and forgotten and, in self-defence, had begun to imitate Han-fei's bullying swagger. But if he went too far, he was simply mocked. 'Look at the barbarian runt!' Han-fei had shouted one afternoon at the archery butts. 'Ordering my servant around as if he were a Son of Han—pick up the arrows yourself, you streak of dog's piss!'

At the time, Frank had tried to ignore such insults, but now, sprawled on a grass verge near the big cart, waiting for William and David to return from the nearby village, he reminded himself that what he had left behind was not entirely sweet. It was pleasant to have Alice's company again, he thought, as he spotted her coming up the bank towards him. She wore her sun-faded tunic, straw hat, open sandals. 'You look just like a peasant!' he called in parody of Robert's crispest bark. She grinned, putting a finger to her lips, for, as he then saw, Robert was toiling behind. Apparently he had not heard, for he threw himself on the grass, took off his hat to mop his forehead.

'Phew—it's hot. Oh to reach the Yangtze! We bought some duck eggs back there. The others aren't back yet?'

'No, David's getting that wobbly wheel repaired on the other cart. It might take some time.'

Robert looked quizzically at his nephew. 'Feeling better about things, young Frank? We are your family, you know, not a bunch of kidnappers.'

'I suppose so,' he muttered evasively. 'Come on, Alice—let's see if we can get some peaches. There are orchards full around here.'

As they walked off, Robert thought despairingly that they looked exactly like a couple of young peasants. But there was nothing to be done about it just then, so he put his head down on his hat and dozed.

'Frank, there's something I've wanted to say to you, and now we're alone . . . but it's a bit difficult, so wait and listen to me.' He did so, looking down into her tanned face framed by the coolie hat.

'When I was turned out by Eldest Brother, did you ever find out exactly why?'

He coloured. 'Not really, but I guessed later. It was because of the Honourable, wasn't it?'

'Yes, but I couldn't explain it to you.'

'No, I understand. But after you left I was allowed to go out more, riding in the hills with the other lads. I suppose they knew I wouldn't run away. And after hunting, we'd go to one of those tea-houses in the plum groves, you know?'

She frowned, puzzled, 'No—I don't know.'

'Well they didn't just serve tea, there were pretty girls there too—for us. So I learned a lot I didn't know before, about what goes on—between girls and men, I mean.'

'Did you enjoy it?' she asked anxiously.

He studied his knuckles, 'Yes, mostly . . . It was exciting and fun. But the girls often teased me, about the yellow hair on my body—and . . . other things. They were quite shameless. So then I put two and two together, about you and the Honourable. It must have been dreadful for you.'

'Oh . . . yes and no,' she shrugged drearily; a conundrum she could not solve. 'But the point is, Frank, that I've not told anyone what really happened to me. And you mustn't either. Do you understand? The English look at these things so differently from the Chinese—you'll find out. But promise you'll keep quiet?'

'Of course, Sis, you can count on me.'

'And if I were you, I shouldn't mention the tea-houses in the plum groves either!' They laughed conspiratorially and continued on their way to the peach orchards.

Supper that evening was merry and satisfying, with eggs, rice, peppers and pork ribs cooked over an open fire, and juicy peaches to follow. Afterwards, they sat on the bank in the warm night air; fireflies darted green and gold across the ditch below and night-jars called in the bamboo groves. Seated a little apart, Alice watched the men's faces lit by the embers of the fire. William had been talking about his father-in-law, who was a merchant in Singapore and held very strong views on the subject of the British Empire. This prompted Robert to describe his experiences of the Perak War in Malaya the previous year.

'But do you think the British might come marching into this country like that?' Alice asked.

'Very different kettle of fish—but it could happen, if the Russians or French started moving in here.'

'That's not what you said to Lin, the young man on the *Mandalay*. You assured him the British hadn't the slightest intention of ever interfering in Chinese affairs.'

'Not wise to tell these ambitious young Asiatics too much, Alice. There's a similar breed growing up in India, heads stuffed with clever revolutionary ideas from France, and they could be dangerous one day.'

'But I thought you liked Lin?'

'He seemed a nice enough fellow, but that's got nothing to do with it.'

'To do with telling him the truth?'

William rose, kicking apart the last embers of the fire. 'That's enough, Alice. You don't understand anything about these international affairs. And it's time we all turned in. There's young Frank fallen asleep with all this political chat.'

They shook him awake, went off to urinate at discreet distances, washed in the communal bucket, then all slept soundly in quilts on the cart floors.

A few days later they reached Chiuchiang from where they were going to Shanghai by river, leaving David to return to Peking with the carts. They had come to rely on his cheery resourcefulness: 'We'll miss you,' said Alice, as they stood on the quayside where the muddy Yangtze rolled towards the distant China Sea. And Robert slapped him heartily on the shoulder. 'Been a great pleasure, David, and I'll give you a written recommendation for any other barbarian madman wanting to go through the interior in a cart. Translate that for me, Alice.'

She did so and a broad grin cracked David's face. 'He says it's the best way of really seeing the country. And remember,' she turned back to him, 'some day when I'm rich I'll pay you to take me to your Mongolia where the women wear trousers and ride freely over the plains.'

He bowed. 'It's a bargain, young lady. I shall be at your service.'

They shook hands on that before loading the baggage aboard the *Red Pearl* junk. Frank had never seen so many sorts of boats and people as he did from the junk's high poop during the week's journey to Shanghai. As he watched the traffic of the great river, he dreamed of spending his days sailing it, bargaining for cargo, shouting at the tow-coolies, commanding from the bridge—a respected junk-master whom nobody would dare call a barbarian dog. Near Shanghai, they passed go-downs proudly emblazoned with the names of successful European merchants—Jardine & Matheson, Guthries, Dent & Co.—and his dreams enlarged. Why the master of only one junk? Why not own a whole fleet? Greenwood & Co. ships would be famed for their speed and size and Alice would help him, and Mother too. Only she was married to someone else.

'Your mother tells me in her letter that she's had to return to Mukden, Frank,' Robert said hesitantly. They were in the hall of Shanghai's Church Missionary Society where Frank and Alice were staying, while he and William put up at the Grand. 'She sends you this letter with much love.'

Frank fumbled it; 'I can't read it very well.'

'Oh dear, of course, here . . . She writes: ''My very dearest

Frank, The thought that you, my long-lost son whom God has returned to me, will read this letter fills me to overflowing with gratitude and happiness. How I wish, my dearest child, that I could be with you at this moment. But as you must know, I have other duties too and my presence is urgently required in Mukden where your stepfather, Mr. Blake, labours alone. I've asked Uncle Robert to arrange for Alice to join me in Mukden, for her help there is badly needed. I long to see you come with her, but I'm trusting Uncle to decide the best course for you. Once the future is clearer, we will I know have a happy reunion somewhere. Please write, my dearest boy, and tell me how you are. I cannot think of you as sixteen, and no longer my curly-haired little treasure whose favourite toy was Dobbin. Do you remember, dear? This comes with much love to you and Alice from your loving Mama." '

Frank turned away. 'Dobbin was the old wooden horse, wasn't he? Fancy her remembering that.'

Robert looked at him sympathetically; having brought his nephew all these hundreds of miles, it was pretty cool of Eliza not to be here. But that was the way with women; new husbands, new loyalties. And it put more of a burden on him, Robert thought later that evening as he enjoyed the last pipe of the day on the balcony of his hotel room. Obviously this Edward Blake fellow had no interest whatsoever in his wife's long-lost children, and William, about to start his own family, had no money to spare for them. It was not so important for Alice, she was just a girl and picked things up quickly anyway. But his nephew—unlettered, uncouth, raw-boned—he needed at least two years' good hard study and discipline if he was to make anything of himself. It was lucky for Frank, Robert told himself, that he had an uncle with a deep sense of family loyalty who had put a few coppers by. A growing sense of virtue suffused him as the half-formulated plan he had been considering for several days became a certainty. There was no alternative—he must write to Elsie and put her off again.

No one knew about Elsie, the daughter of a bookseller in Sheringham, Norfolk. Robert had been sixteen when he first met her—a shy, studious young lady fond of quoting Mr. Shelley's poetry. Two years later, when on holiday at Sheringham, he had walked with her along the promenade one summer afternoon and told her he wanted her to be his wife. She had been wearing a brown linen dress with little blue flowers on it, a straw hat and faded lemon-yellow gloves that did not match the dress very well. He had kissed her cheek in the shelter of the sea-wall and told her he was going into the Army and might be away for years, but one day he would return and marry her. He had promised her faithfully. Elsie had believed him and waited.

He had sent for her to come out to India once, after he had been commissioned, but her father was dying at the time. He continued to visit her in Sheringham on his infrequent leaves. As time went by, her dresses became plainer, her gloves less of a match; she spent years nursing her mother till she died too. But she and Robert continued to correspond and now the date of their union was definitely fixed for two years ahead, when he was to resign from the Army and go Home. Definitely, that is, till this business of young Frank blew up.

Looking along the Shanghai Bund—the rickshaws, carts, sedan chairs with their bobbing lanterns, the stir and bustle of it all—he pondered Elsie and Sheringham. She had always been a quiet woman living in a quiet place and sometimes such peace seemed infinitely desirable. At others it seemed, rather—well, dull. After all, as this recent expedition had proved, he was still a man of considerable resource and stamina—qualities that would find little outlet in Sheringham. But if he were to resign in five years instead of two, he could afford to do something for young Frank now and have more behind him when he eventually went Home and married. Dear old Elsie—she would understand of course; she always had. He knocked out his pipe on the balcony rail, went inside, drew a sheet of hotel stationery from the writing-desk: 'My dear Elsie . . .' he began.

As Robert often said of himself, he was not one to shilly-shally once his mind was made up. The very next morning he acquainted the family with his plan to send Frank to Bishop Hart's boys' college in Shanghai for two years at his expense. William was delighted and grateful, Frank reluctantly acquiescent; Alice went very quiet, then said, 'You're very lucky, Frank. I wish I had your chance.'

'Oh you'll be all right, Alice,' Robert said quickly. 'As you know your stepfather's a former schoolmaster and he's offered to help you catch up with your studies once you've settled in Mukden.'

Alice's mouth snapped shut and the pause was broken by Robert's conciliatory, 'Well Frank, get yourself smartened up, the consul wants to see you this afternoon to hear about Hunan. And probably there'll be a reporter from the *Shanghai Mercury* on your doorstep next.'

'Won't he want to see me too?' Alice asked petulantly.

'You're a bit too fond of the limelight, aren't you, miss?' William reproved.

'But why shouldn't I be included? After all, I made the journey from Changsha alone, I didn't wait for people to rescue me.'

Frank scowled. 'You know that isn't fair. I didn't want to leave when you did. I wasn't scared.'

Alice was saved from his blunder by Robert's reminder that what mattered was not past mistakes but their present happy reunion. 'And I've been thinking,' he continued, 'it might be a very long time before we're all together again like this. I think we should mark the occasion with a short holiday before we separate. My ship doesn't sail for two weeks—how about a few days on a houseboat to the lakes beyond the Sung-kiang hills? Treat on me of course. We can hire a boat in a jiffy, I'm told, and the shooting is excellent just now—the wild fowl gathering to fly south for the winter.' The idea was carried unanimously, and Robert went off to make arrangements.

Their houseboat was moored along one of the artificial canals that linked the lakes together; the shimmering flatness of the paddies on either side was broken only by the humped backs of the peasant women harvesting rice. Reclining in a deck chair, Alice watched dragonflies and butterflies buzzing about the banks, for, having no love of firearms, she had elected to remain on board while the men went shooting in the nearby marshes. Through half-closed lids she saw the women moving slowly through the mud, pausing only to shift the weight of their baskets or brush flies from their eyes. Then a swish of water announced the approach of another houseboat, more imposing than the Greenwoods' comparatively humble craft. A blonde English girl was leaning over the rail and, as they edged past, called along the deck, 'Oh Mother, do come and look at these peasant hats—they're the biggest I've seen yet! Can't we stop while I do a sketch?'

'You'll see thousands like that, Evelyn, so please don't fuss now.' Mother's irritated reply reached Alice as they glided out of earshot.

She smiled wryly—Evelyn looked about her own age, just off a steamer from Southampton probably and China like a quaint picturebook to her. Was it a pity that she herself could never see China like that? She knew only too well about the flies, the mud, the heavy baskets and the sweat that gathered under the picturesque hats. How stupidly the world seemed to be arranged! Until recently, her life too had been a continuous toil as it was for these peasants. But now, as a civilised young lady, no one required more of her than to sit in a deck chair, sip lemonade and sketch, perhaps, like Evelyn. She shifted and sighed; the chair creaked as she moved.

'Anyone at home?' a voice called from the gangplank and a young man appeared, dressed in the customary white ducks of the English sportsman. He halted, smiling pleasantly. 'Oh, I do beg your pardon. Am I on the wrong boat? I'm looking for a Major Greenwood.'

'He's my uncle,' Alice sat upright, 'but he's off shooting.'

'Ah—then I'll explain. I met him on the marshes earlier, with his nephews.'

'They're my brothers.'

'Well that younger brother of yours is a superb marksman—what an eye! I just had to tell him so and we began chatting. Then they invited me back for a drink before supper as I'm travelling alone—just upriver from you.'

'In that case, please sit down. They're due back any time.'

'You're sure? I'm obviously too early.' He hesitated, then held out his hand, 'I'm Charles Grant.'

'I'm Alice Greenwood. Do have some lemonade and take a seat.'

He did so. 'Phew—it was hot on those marshes—and the mosquitoes. You know, I was thinking as I came along—are you *the* Greenwoods?'

She smiled. 'I like to think so. But what do you mean exactly?'

'The brother and sister who spent years in captivity in the interior and have just returned. I read the story in the Mercury yesterday.'

'Yes—that's Frank and me.'

'But how exciting, I thought the names were familiar. Now

please tell me all about it. No one I've met in the Treaty Ports so far seems to know much about the real country—or even to care.'

'You've not been here long then?'

'A few weeks only, and this is my little holiday before returning to India. I came to look at new trading opportunities in Shanghai and perhaps upriver. It's bound to open up more soon. So anyone who's been in the interior interests me—especially when it's an adventurous young lady like yourself.'

'Well . . .' Alice paused teasingly, liking his winning enthusiasm, 'it's a big subject, Mr. Grant. Where shall I start?'

'You're right, I should get my thoughts in order first, as my father used to say.'

Boots tramped up the gangplank and Frank appeared, triumphantly waving a brace of plump teal. 'Look at these—and the boys are loaded with ducks.'

'Not to mention every pin-tailed snipe that didn't take off for India yesterday!' Robert said behind him. 'We'll all grow feathers eating this lot—ah, there you are, Mr. Grant. You found us then?'

'Yes, I fear I'm a duffer in the field compared to you two, so I gave up—and met your charming niece instead.'

Robert clapped his hands. 'Boy, bring more lemonade, beer, glasses.'

They settled down with drinks; flocks of still-unscathed wild fowl wheeled against the sunset over the marshes. While Frank explained why Chinese archery practice had made him such a good marksman and Robert warned that the only real hazard of shooting in China was the stupid propensity of the natives to jump out of ditches without warning and get in the way of the occasional bullet, Alice considered their guest. She liked his crinkly smile, the timbre of his voice; she wondered why he was travelling alone.

'Come along with us tomorrow if you like, Mr. Grant,' Robert was saying, 'and pick up a few tips from young Frank to stun the locals when you get back. You're an India man like me, didn't you say?'

'Not entirely—but I've Anglo-Indian relatives going back three generations. The country's become a family tradition, you might say. That is perhaps why I'd like to break away to somewhere else. So I'm looking for trading prospects up the Yangtze, as I was telling Miss Greenwood.'

'Risky business, trading with these yellow men,' Robert shook his head, 'never know where you stand with them.'

'Inscrutable, hey, Uncle?' William teased.

'Devious and dishonest—think of the trouble we had with bribes on the journey.'

'Oh come, Major, you sound like my father—he talks as if every Indian were a paragon of integrity by comparison. All Eastern peoples have different standards from ours in money matters.'

'Maybe,' Robert was stubborn, 'but you still know the Indian, even when he's robbing you blind. So your father's not keen on your starting up here then?'

'No, I can't say he is. He and George, my brother-in-law, have been in the I.C.S. for years, and my wife's family too. So they all expect me to follow in the jolly old footsteps, but I'm not really a desk man.'

'And your wife, Mr. Grant? What does she think? Isn't she here with you?'

'Not yet. Maria's expecting again and as this is just an exploratory trip, she decided to stay in Madras. I'm not sure she wants to move, but I believe China offers so many more opportunities—it's challenging in a way that India isn't anymore.'

'But it's all very uncertain here,' William warned him. 'I'm about to start in the Maritime Customs Service and the whole question of duties and tariffs isn't yet fixed. What's more, the currency is in a dreadful mess—Hankow taels with different values to Shanghai ones, and that sort of thing is hardly conducive to business. It'll be years before we get things properly organised and controlled. What's more, the Chinese themselves are getting a grip on the upriver trade, I'm told—chartering their own steamers and even going into marine insurance!'

Grant laughed. 'You could say they're entitled to! But anyway, who wants certainty all the time, Mr. Greenwood?'

Alice clapped her hands delightedly. 'Mr. Grant, I so agree with you—Uncle, supper is ready. I'm sure there's ample for Mr. Grant, if he'd like to stay?'

He accepted readily, and as the meal began, Robert continued, 'Now yours is a typical young man's reaction, if I may say so, Mr. Grant. But there's much to be said for certainty—for institutions like law courts, public works departments and so on that we've set up in India. For example, I shudder to think what might have happened to us if we'd been discovered in Hunan. Hauled up before some benighted oriental magistrate, chop, chop, heads off, say no more about it, maybe. Things like that can't happen in India. And take the roads here, scandalous! Your main route south from Peking is worse than a Himalayan hill-track in places. How can you move goods over such terrain?'

'I bet that would be a way to make a fortune, wouldn't it, Uncle?' Frank burst in excitedly. 'Build some decent roads and railways, like in India?'

'It might be, boy, depends how you go about it.'

'Well whatever you others say about risks and difficulties, I entirely agree with Mr. Grant,' Alice announced, 'China is much more exciting than stuffy old India.'

Robert turned on her, 'Please, Alice, you know nothing about it, and don't forget that "stuffy old India" is the main-stay of the British Empire, and where would we all be without that?'

'You're right there, Major,' their visitor smiled, 'but that still leaves me plenty of room to experiment elsewhere.'

Robert signalled the boy to remove the plates. 'Well, Mr. Grant, if your own father can't dissuade you from China, I don't suppose I shall. And you may make a go of it—Will here is about to try and I imagine Frank will too, once he's got some education behind him.'

'I'd like to build railways,' Frank declared. 'I'm going to be a railway millionaire with a stable of racehorses in Shanghai and a fleet of trading ships as well!'

Alice wandered to the boat-rail, all this having little to do with her. If only, she thought bitterly, her relatives would evince one scrap of interest in what her future held. But they did not; nor did this handsome married stranger who was planning his own future in a way she could not possibly do. The boy had lit the lanterns, the men were smoking and sipping a brandy nightcap, there was no point in sulking, she told herself grimly, and rejoined them with a smile. 'I think I'll go to my cabin, I'm rather sleepy. So good-night everyone—and, Mr. Grant, don't let my uncle change your mind about China!'

Charles sprang up. 'Indeed he won't. And thank you for making me so welcome. It's rather wearisome travelling alone and talking pidgin the whole time.'

'Then you must join us again tomorrow. We can promise you some more truly British conversation, I'm sure.'

Charles Grant frequently returned to the Greenwood boat during the remainder of the holiday—days that Alice long remembered as among the least troubled of her life. For the boat was a private, serene world, and, as they moved along the water, she forgot the difficulties of both past and future. Further west, the countryside became more beautiful, with ranges of low hills covered with teabushes, larches and flowering tallow trees. In the valleys nestled thatched huts and Buddhist monasteries. She woke each morning to hear the boys sluicing the decks, and the voice of a tow-coolie nicknamed Beancurd chanting wild songs from his native province of Szechuan. After much shouting and banging about, the vessel got underway before breakfast, as the cook fried eggs over the kerosene stove. In mid-morning they tied up in a backwater and while the men went off with satchels of sandwiches and guns, Alice and the cook strolled to nearby villages for provisions. At sunset, they forgathered with Charles Grant as they had on the first evening, and talked about the day's bags, the strange ways of the East, the vagaries of British politics.

But on the last evening Charles did not come to supper for he was packing up his own boat, and the Greenwoods ate quietly, cast down by the shadow of imminent partings.

'Come on now, you boys, jump to it!' Robert tried to dispel the gloom as the meal ended. 'We've got to oil all the guns and pack the fishing gear—can't trust the coolies with that.'

'Can I help?' Alice asked.

'No, I don't think so—tell you what, can you get it across to the cook that we must leave at dawn for Shanghai, dawn mind you, so they ought to start packing up now.'

She nodded listlessly, knowing that the cook would be smoking his nightly opium, that tomorrow he would dismantle his entire *batterie de cuisine* in ten minutes, that nothing would persuade him to do it sooner. Instead, she went on deck. A low mist hung over the paddies, not dense enough to conceal the beauty of the starlit night beyond. She pulled her cloak round her and, on impulse, donned one of the coolie hats hanging near the gangplank. She walked down and along the towpath, and soon the only sounds were lapping water and frogs croaking in the ditches. A coolie with an ox-halter slung across his back padded past. 'Misty night,' he said. 'Yes, quite thick.' She smiled gleefully to herself; she was still of the country. Then she heard heavier feet and a large shape loomed out of the mist. She bent her back as he approached and pushed rudely past her on the narrow track. She turned: 'Good evening, Charles.' He stopped, peered back, holding up his lantern.

'Good heavens, it's not you, Alice? Whatever are you doing out here?'

'Just taking an evening stroll.'

'But all alone and dressed up like that!'

She smiled. 'I'm not dressed up, I just borrowed a coolie hat because of the damp—I always think they rather suit me!'

So do I, he thought, looking into her upturned face, framed by the simple straw.

'I'm not sure your uncle would approve.'

'He doesn't know. They're packing up the gear and not to be disturbed—very important job, like moving a regiment!'

He chuckled. 'I was coming along to say goodbye, but you think I wouldn't be welcome?'

'Wait a little—the packing won't take long, but Uncle enjoys making a great fuss about it. I was just going to that little temple we passed earlier, why not come too?'

He fell into step beside her, offering his arm attentively at every patch of rough ground. How strange, she thought, five minutes ago he pushed me roughly aside, thinking I was a Chinese peasant; now I seem to need help over every pebble. If I had the lightest bag, he would offer to carry it, but if a peasant woman bent double under a heavy sack passed, he would not lift a finger. So this gallantry in men does not have much to do with their physical strength after all. What then does it have to do with?

She was still puzzling this as they reached the temple steps, up which Charles helped her as if she were lame. As he pushed open its creaking door, a string of flapping bats flew out and they both recoiled. Inside, a peeling gilt Buddha squatted in a niche hung about with cobwebs; there was a fusty smell of incense and bat-droppings.

'Not much used by the look of it.' Charles swung his lantern round. Alice made a quick obeisance which she hoped he would not notice; but he did.

'What does that mean, Alice? You're not a clandestine Buddhist surely?'

'No—but I remember my father's story about a convert who went to all the Buddhist and Taoist festivals as well as attending his mission, because, he told Father, he was hedging his bets. Father had to laugh, though he didn't approve of course.'

'So you hedge your bets too?' Charles was amused by her as usual. What a splendid wife she would make for some lucky fellow out here, with her knowledge of the country, her lively attractiveness. He thought of Maria; his marriage, unlike his choice of career, had been considered eminently suitable by his family.

'My wife wouldn't agree with hedging of that sort either, but she's more devout than I am.'

A silence fell between them, then he moved to the door and looked out over the misted landscape. She joined him. 'It's a beautiful night in its way, isn't it?'

'My wife doesn't want to come to China at all,' he blurted out. 'She's praying that I'll return from this trip agreeing with my father and all the others who say "Stick to India."'

'And shall you?'

'No. For the reasons I've mentioned. So she'll have to put up with it. Shanghai at least will suit her well enough once we're settled.'

'But why doesn't she want to come here?'

'Her relatives are in Madras, you see. And she's not lucky with child-bearing. We've been married four years and Peter, our first-born, is fine. But she's lost a child since and her latest condition isn't proving easy. . . .' He sighed, with a sudden memory of her lying leadenly in their marital bed, nightgown raised, eyes beseeching him to leave her alone. But what was a fellow with normal male appetites to do? He shifted uneasily. For Alice his words had conjured very different thoughts and she shivered, so that he put a protective arm on her shoulder. 'Are you cold? Let's go back, there's an autumnal nip in the air.'

'I'm quite all right, thank you.' She looked up at him smiling gravely and suddenly he had his arms tightly round her, pressing her to him, kissing her gently and then, feeling her warmth, with increased purpose. She fastened her arms round his neck and clung closer, nibbling his lips. Stimulated by her knowingness, he thrust his tongue deep into her willing mouth. Then he pulled back sharply, untwining their arms. 'Alice, we must stop this at once, it's quite wrong. Here am I, a married man, years older than you.'

'Only about eight.'

'So you've worked that out? Never mind, you're an innocent young lady and if your uncle saw us now he'd call me a complete rotter, and rightly so.'

Determinedly he broke from her and started down the steps, stamping down his ardour as he went. He stopped at the bottom. 'Come on, Alice, let's go back.'

He extended his arm and she pulled herself in tightly. 'All right, Mr. Grant.'

'Now please—we've been on Christian name terms for days, don't be so formal. You're not angry, are you?'

'Of course not,' she replied distantly.

He chucked her under the chin. 'We can be friends, I hope?'

'Well we could be, but I don't suppose we'll ever meet again.'

'I hope we will—but that's certainly reason enough for not doing anything we might regret.'

'Yes, and it's nice you wanted to kiss me.'

'Of course I did. I have several times in the last few days, as a matter of fact. But you'll keep it secret, please? Promise?'

She promised. They squeezed hands and returned along the towpath in a companionable but rather depressed silence. Approaching the boat, they saw its lights ablaze, heard the Major's voice barking into the darkness. 'Alice, where are you? Alice, are you out there?'

She giggled nervously, 'Oh dear, we . . .'

'It's all right, Major Greenwood, she's with me,' Charles squared his shoulders as they met him at the gangplank.

'Alice, wherever have you been? I was about to organise a search-party—and in that outfit. I've never known such a girl for slipping away—and turning up in unexpected places!'

'I only went for a walk, Uncle.'

'Alone and at this time—why on earth didn't you ask one of us to escort you?'

'But you were all busy, and then I met Charles and he escorted me.'

Robert regarded them suspiciously. 'I was just coming to make my farewells and share this with you perhaps, when I met Alice.' Charles produced a bottle of brandy from his jacket pocket and Robert looked somewhat mollified, for it happened that the Greenwood spirit supply was exhausted.

'A good thought on your part, Charles. Well, as there's no harm . . . we'll say no more. Come and join Will and me in the main cabin. As for you, miss, to bed at once. I've just sent young Frank off, he nearly blew his head off cleaning a gun—the pair of you are enough to turn a fellow's hair white, eh Charles?'

Charles followed him obediently, but at the cabin door turned to look at Alice where she still stood, under the hurricane lamp on deck.

'Goodbye, Alice, and good luck, whatever you do.'

'Goodbye, Charles, and good luck to you too. And I hope you'll return to China.'

'Nothing will stop me. You can count on that.'

As the door closed on the men's voices, Alice went to her cabin, sat on her bunk and sighed. Charles Grant was the first Englishman she had ever enjoyed kissing; but he was married and going away. There came a quiet knock and her heart leaped hopefully, but, 'Uncut Jade,' a voice whispered, 'may I come in?' Frank slipped inside grinning. 'Uncle and Will were getting in a paddy about you—I kept telling them you'd be all right.'

'Of course. I always am.'

'Yes I know. I felt I had to see you alone before we're packed off—you to Mukden and me to this wretched college. You know I was thinking, Sis, once that's over, I really do want to go into business like Charles Grant with a company of my own—and I'll let you in it too—Greenwood & Greenwood, doesn't that sound grand?'

'It's a fine idea—we'll buy a junk and go trading upriver.'

'We'll only need a little capital to start.'

'Perhaps I can find some,' she said lightly, thinking of the Carr loot. 'Oh Frank—that reminds me. I've a little present for you. I bought it in Peking and vowed to give it to you one day.' From her reticule she took the jade-button fan.

'A memento of our past, dear—from one Uncut Jade to another.'

'It's beautiful, Alice, thank you very much.' He stroked it, swallowing hard. 'We'll stick together, won't we, Sis? We really understand each other because of what happened to us, don't we?'

'Yes dear, we need each other very specially because of it, and perhaps we always will. I'm realising how difficult it is to be completely honest with our family and with friends. But at least we can always be honest with each other and that's a great relief, isn't it? I suppose that was my selfish reason for wanting you away from Hunan so much. It was for my sake as well as yours. But now you're here, thank goodness, and we'll stick together, as you say, through thick and thin.' She kissed him lightly and they smiled at each other, then he heard Charles leaving and slipped away.

Alice stowed the reticule under her bunk. Earlier she had vowed that, once Frank was safely out of Hunan, she would return the rest of the loot to Flossie Carr. But now she was increasingly reluctant to do so. How could she ever explain her long silence over the matter? And how could she possibly trace her? Perhaps Flossie was dead by now or married to a rich man with no need of the treasure anyway . . . at least, not as much as she, Alice, had. For what if life in Mukden proved unbearable? How could she ever leave unless she had some money of her own? It was her only source of independence.

'You're an unprincipled, wicked young lady,' she told herself as she snuggled into her bunk. But her dreams were not guilt-ridden for all that. Rather they wove themselves round the handsome figure of Mr. Charles Grant.

Part Two

8

'To trust God when our warehouses and bags are full and the table spread is no hard thing. But to trust Him when our purses are empty, but a handful of meal and a cruse of oil left, and all the ways of relief are stopped, herein lies the wisdom of Christian grace. For, whatever your wants are, want not faith and you cannot then want supplies.'

Edward Blake's sonorous voice stopped. He snapped shut the book from which he had been reading and announced, 'That passage, from the wise old divine, Mr. Charnock, concludes our little prayer offering. Let us now offer up also our silent meditations to Him.'

In the ensuing pause, he surveyed the small gathering on the school-room benches before him. Doorkeeper Peng, christened Gabriel upon his conversion, was gazing at him with unctuous incomprehension. Equally unreachable was his neighbour, the cheerful widow christened Ruth, their only Bible woman, who also helped in the house. The only native who had understood some of his words was the interpreter Be-dien, a scrawny man in faded silk gown and dingy skull cap who at the age of forty was still trying to gain a literary degree. In the course of an undivulged past, Be-dien had travelled in the Treaty Ports and picked up a smattering of pidgin. It was an excruciating mongrel tongue and, having once heard himself described as 'Number One Topside Heaven Man,' Edward often wondered what versions of God's peerless message were transmitted to the natives through this imperfect instrument. Now Be-dien sat impassive, eyes closed, just sufficiently awake to keep his jaw clamped shut.

Next to him Eliza wore a meditative expression, but Edward guessed that on this particular day she was much too excited to be concentrating correctly. Beside her sat Alice, whose clear greenish eyes were looking glassily past him to the summer sunlight streaming through the open door. Edward had encountered many recalcitrant spirits during his fifty years of life—in his own family home, in the school where he had once taught Latin to unruly boys, and certainly during his six years in China; but never one more so than his stepdaughter's. She was like a prickly new broom that you could take and bend but which always snapped back to its original shape the moment you let go. He had never found a key to her, and so they bargained, he and she. The bargains, begun soon after her arrival those months before, had, as time went on, become more complex, more hardly driven on both sides. Most of the words he uttered at these Sunday prayer-offerings were directed at her—it was she who wanted that faith, that wisdom of Christian grace to which old Charnock referred. But she had not been truly listening, he knew.

Beside Alice, Adam suddenly jumped up, saying, 'Please, Father, 'scuse me,' and waddled quickly out. Sunny watched him disdainfully, then smiled smugly at big sister Alice. She never had to leave in such an undignified rush in case she wet her knickers as Adam sometimes did.

'Thank you, Edward. Come Alice, Sunny . . .' Eliza moved towards the door. 'We have so much to do. . . .'

But Alice was at her school-desk, taking out her text books.

'Oh Alice—not today surely? Must you study? There's the fruit to peel and chop for the cake.'

'I'll help you later, Mother. It's my Latin lesson day and you wouldn't want me to miss that, would you, Stepfather?'

She looked at him boldly; it was one of the bargains that had to be kept or she would leave—as she had nearly done soon after the confines of Edward Blake's China Inland Mission in Mukden first closed around her. It had been winter then, northern, long, lightless and harsher than any she had known. The harshness was inside as well as out. It permeated the bare interiors of the former grain-chandlery where the Mission had been founded three years before. It emanated principally from stepfather Blake himself, whose stern voice was raised day after weary day on the themes of the unregeneracy of the Chinese soul, the proximity of Satan's dominions, the relentlessness of God's righteous wrath.

It was only when driven by all this to the point of reckless departure that Alice realised she held a trump card that could make life a little more tolerable. She could speak and write Mandarin, and that was a skill of inestimable value to a missionary who had no fluency in Chinese but was yet determined to convert several thousand Mukden residents to his uncompromising brand of Christianity. And so the bargaining had begun, tacit and indirect because of the innocent optimism of Eliza who could not accept that Edward was not won over by her attractive, high-spirited elder daughter, or that Alice felt no spark of regard for her worthy, diligent, educated second husband.

The first bargain was that for two hours of every weekday Alice should help Be-dien improve Edward's grasp of the native tongue. The second, that for one hour daily he should teach her—or at least make available books for her from which to acquire—the basics of history, geography, and Latin. The last had been Alice's overambitious mistake, for at Latin she proved stupid. Edward was excellent at it of course, but extremely poor at Chinese. As it was, she usually concealed her satisfaction at his ineptitude and merely pointed out some of the more obvious absurdities of a literal translation of the Bible into Chinese. Edward found this hard to accept, for, he was fond of saying, Wycliffe had pressed Bibles into the hands of England's rude ploughboys, and they had got the message—so why could not the Chinese?

He said now, as Alice reached for her books, 'No, Eliza, Alice mustn't miss her lesson, even today, for she needs the mental discipline that study induces.' And Eliza nodded, for she seldom contradicted Edward.

Left alone, Alice studied her grammar unenthusiastically, then fell to thinking about another of their bargains which was that on her 'free' Sunday afternoons she usually went to visit Dr. and Mrs. Campbell at the hospital of the United Presbyterian Church of Scotland Mission. But today it would be difficult to go on account of the cake-making and preparations for the morrow. Still, her heart warmed pleasurably at the thought. Tomorrow Frank was arriving from Shanghai to spend his first summer holidays with them. She wandered out, staring at the bright, dry sky of the North China summer, and leaned against the warm mud-brick wall of the former grain store wondering how it would be when Frank came. She was longing for his company, to talk and laugh openly together; his lighthearted, uncaring, worldly boyishness would be such a relief. To an extent, she was resentful and envious of the freedoms and opportunities of his present life compared to hers, but that didn't affect her love for him—Frank, her beloved little-big brother, made lonely and confused as she was by their past, and ultimately, more vulnerable than she. Sensing that, she wanted now to protect him from the worst excesses of their stepfather's dour, stern bigotry. For how could Frank warm to him any more than she could?

'Old Tombstone Face' the Chinese called him behind his back and so did she, for it aptly described the straight graven furrows of his brow and mouth. The Chinese thought he had been forced to leave his homeland because of some crime he had committed, for why else would a man choose to live in a foreign land? They thought Alice was his concubine, brought in to console him for the insufficiencies of his grey, often ailing official wife. They felt this arrangement a preferable way of satisfying his wayward desires than plying his female converts with aphrodisiac pills so that they threw themselves lustfully upon him—for did not many teachers of the Christ-religion behave so? And was it not rumoured that Jesus himself had been the son of a prostitute and licentious with both his male and female disciples?

All this Alice had soon discovered because of her thorough understanding of the language, which was not fully realised by the local gossips. She had not passed on any of these horrendous tidbits, which would have only confirmed her parents' opinion of the natives as little better than half-savage degenerates. Also she feared to imagine the effect it might have on Edward, from whose cold eyes a glint of tantalised lust occasionally peered at her. Experienced as she was, she sometimes played on it, mockingly, out of a bored contempt that she then turned upon herself.

For she was bored. After the upheavals and challenges of her earlier years, Mukden was an emotional desert. Its other foreign residents—the Campbells and a few European merchants with whom the missionaries seldom fraternised—were, in her youthful opinion, commonplace souls. But like theirs, her Chinese acquaintances were now limited to servants, shopkeepers and the converts—the 'eaters of foreign rice,' the 'secondary devils' who sought out the

212

Mission for their own dubious purposes. At least, she thought restlessly, as she left the sun-warmed wall and went to help Mother in the kitchen, Frank's coming would enliven the scene.

'What does bruvver Frank look like?' asked Sunny digging a spoon into the cake mix Alice was stirring.

'He's got blond hair, like Mama used to have, dearie, and he's quite tall.'

'Taller than Papa?'

'No, not that tall.'

'And please try to remember,' Eliza said gently, 'that your Papa is not Frank's and Alice's Papa—because he died many years ago.'

The child didn't like being in a minority. 'But my Papa is Adam's Papa, isn't he?'

Adam, playing with toy bricks in the corner, said, 'Stupidy Sunny, of course. The Lord brought us into the world at the same time and it was a gweat twial.'

Eliza laughed, leaving her baking to hug him. 'Fancy you remembering that silly phrase of mine—but the "twial" was worth every minute.'

'What does that mean?' Sunny asked.

'Oh you'll find out one day when you're a grown woman, and so will Alice, I daresay.'

Alice lowered her eyes. Often she was tempted to throw into the complacent pool of the Mission's narrow world some unspeakable truth about her past. The intense dramas that would follow such dire revelations enlivened her daydreams, but she always resisted the temptation for her mother's sake. As she did now and briskly finished the cake and the preparation of glazed sugar plums that were her special offering to Frank. She wiped her hands: 'I'm going to the Campbells' now, Mother.'

Eliza looked resentful as she usually did when they were mentioned. The Campbells were decent and true Highland Scots which was greatly in their favour, but Eliza felt their whole approach to missionary work was deeply misguided. They were far too concerned with healing of the flesh, not sufficiently with the deeper ills of the native spirit. The only Way, as she and Edward knew, was a straightforward going forth with the sincere Milk of the Word. It was an abiding grief to Eliza that, in spite of years of effort, her own ability to offer the Word in the native tongue was still sorely limited. It affronted and saddened her that Alice, whose linguistic capacity was of God-given proficiency, should absolutely refuse to preach directly, yet was willing to translate patients' symptoms for Dr. Campbell's benefit.

'But surely they won't expect you today, Alice?'

'Why not? The doctor relies on me to tell him about the new admissions.' Eliza sighed. Adam comically imitated her. Sunny seized the chance to steal a sugar plum and, turning away to hide her bulging cheeks, mumbled, ' 'Bye Alish . . .' Alice guessed, smiled, and left.

The difference between the Scottish Presbyterian and China Inland Missions in Mukden reflected the considerable disagreements over method that divided the Protestant movement in China. Alice had now heard a great deal about those differences—from her stepfather and Dr. Campbell separately and on the infrequent occasions when they met, in default of other more congenial Christian company, to celebrate the commonly binding festivals of Christmas and Easter. She was thoroughly tired of hearing about them. She sympathised with the C.I.M.'s insistence on unadorned, native-style living (which had the bonus of allowing her to wear native dress) and she shared her stepfather's scorn for those numerous missionaries who confined their labours to the comfortable security of the Treaty Ports. But there was a naive and wasteful silliness about so many of Eliza's and Edward's efforts, an ignorant refusal really to understand the country that often irritated and depressed her. In the Campbells' Mission, by contrast, an air of purposeful endeavour centred on the hospital and Alice had sometimes seen patients' eyes shine with hopeful faith because the foreign medicine had relieved their sufferings.

'He says he feels as if he's got nests of white ants growing in his belly,' Alice reported to the doctor as they stood looking down at a young muleteer on a hospital pallet. He looked most woebegone and distraught, for, as Dr. Campbell often said, the Chinese made the most of their illnesses.

'Where exactly does he feel this?' He prodded the pallid flesh. 'And what's he been taking for it?'

'A special medicine made from crabs' livers and crushed dragons' teeth from his doctor—it hasn't helped.'

The doctor jotted in his notebook: 'Admission No. 3—white

ants; "dragon teeth" ' as they moved through the jumble of rice-kettles, teapots and food bundles that the patients always brought in with them.

'We've seen her before,' Alice said of the next patient.

'Have we? It's dreadful how they all look alike.'

The wizened little woman on the bed held up a withered arm pitted with festering sores. 'The local quack's been burning those moxus of amaranthus on her by the look of it,' Campbell snorted. 'Nothing I can do except heal the burns.'

'You remember—she's the widow with two daughters who says her fingers are too stiff to make firecrackers anymore and they're nearly starving—she threatens to commit suicide by swallowing lucifers.'

'Well, her daughters must do it, I suppose. I'm not gifted with miraculous powers, I can't cure withered arms.'

'Do you wish you could, Doctor—like Jesus?'

'Come, young lady, don't be flippant. I believe, if you seriously want to know, that some people have a certain gift of healing, but it's a great responsibility. Now, let's go and sample May's delicious scones. And I expect it's another of my novels you'll be wanting the loan of?' he continued in his pleasant Highland burr as they crossed the courtyard. 'I see you've returned *Rob Roy*.'

An unspoken bargain Alice had struck with the Campbells was that, in return for her translating help, she had the run of their considerable library. And last winter, by lantern-light and surreptitiously because her stepfather disapproved of such trivial literature, she had read *Pride and Prejudice, Adam Bede, Waverley, Lorna Doone, Pickwick Papers, Lavengro, Henry Esmond, The Mill on the Floss, Northanger Abbey, Vanity Fair,* and, at the doctor's insistence, every air, prayer, poem and song penned by the great Robbie Burns. She now had a richer if still rather quaint picture of that small, distant homeland she had never seen.

'And how did you enjoy the harum-scarum adventures of Rob Roy, gentleman, Alice?'

'Oh well enough, thank you. But George Eliot's Maggie Tulliver is still my favourite.'

'Och well, your tastes will not be fully developed yet—you grow into things, I do myself. Take Emerson for example, Ralph Waldo, an American—never thought anything of him, but I just received a volume of his essays, *Society and*

Solitude, published recently. Now listen to what he says on the subject of books.' He took out the volume, adjusted his spectacles. 'And he's not only writing about the sacred books of Christendom, but of Epictetus, the Buddhist texts, the Upanishads, and your favourite Confucius to boot—they're all, he claims, "the Bibles of the world ... majestic expressions of the universal conscience." He goes on, ". . . These are scriptures which the missionary might well carry over prairie, desert and ocean, to Siberia, Japan, and Timbuctoo. Yet he will find that the spirit which is in them journeys faster than he and greets him on his arrival—was there already long before him. The missionary must be carried by it and find it there, or he goes in vain." Now that's a strange thought, Alice, and I'm not sure how I take it, for to tell you the truth, the "universal conscience" of the Chinese eludes me. But you know, lassie, I read in Blackwood's magazine recently that Emerson's philosophical approach is very similar to the Chinese. He doesn't ever reach for one complete and logical system of ideas, but deals in momentary truths, temporary opinions if you like, refusing absolute definitions, as the Chinese do. Now what do you say to that, Alice?'

Rather out of her depth, she said hesitantly, 'Certainly the Chinese sages seem to contradict each other, even themselves sometimes, but it doesn't seem to bother them as it would us. And they get carried away by flights of fancy, not minding about logic. . . .'

'Aye well, that's a bit Emerson's way too, but he's an eloquent man for a' that.'

'Can I read it, Doctor?'

'When I've finished mulling it over myself you can.'

Indoors, they met May Campbell with the tea-tray. 'Hello, Alice dear. Phew, it's hot baking scones at the stove today—look at my face!' Alice grinned, for May's cheeks were even more deeply flushed than usual. Both the Campbells had retained the ruddy Highland complexion of their youth and were called 'the two purple plums' by the sallower natives. This Alice knew, but, as with many things, felt unable to reveal.

'And I doubt if the tea will be up to scratch—I hung the mare's milk in the well to keep cool, but it's almost sour, it's that hot.'

Alice did not much care for this hard, dry-as-dust inland heat that pounded down on the flat town, cracked its mud tracks and walls, yet left chill shadows. There would be no rain for another month, but the surrounding fields were already parched and the wells too low for the efficacious cooling of milk.

'We've been baking a special cake for Frank—Mother's been saving fruit and sugar for weeks.'

'Och aye, she'll be excited today?'

'Oh yes—Frank was always her favourite.'

Dr. Campbell smiled quizzically. 'Sons often are—with mothers.'

'Yes, Mother always said I was Father's.'

'Never mind, dearie,' May patted her hand. 'Have another scone? And it will be grand to see your brother again, won't it? Is he a bit of a bookworm like yourself?'

'Oh no, Frank's the outdoor type. According to his letters he's best at sports, and he's longing to leave school and go into business.'

Dr. Campbell's scone-crumbs blew in his mirth. 'Oh dear, dear. That won't sit well with your stepfather, I'll warrant. Your brother'll have to mind his Ps and Qs.'

But Frank had never worried unduly about the Ps and Qs of life and did not do so in the company of his family as they all sat round the tea-table the following afternoon. He had arrived off the overland cart from Newchwang that morning—a strapping youth with a loud, easy laugh and hammy hands, his broad physique well set in its manly mould. Only his blue eyes still sometimes held the look of a furtive, bewildered, uncertain boy who knew life could produce some nasty surprises for the unwary—and that wariness was not his strong point.

'More cake, dear?' Eliza leaned to touch him, as she kept doing, in happy wonderment that this really was her long-lost son.

'No thanks, Mama, but I'll have another sugar plum—quite like old times, eh Alice?'

She nodded. 'But have more cake as well—it's a special treat.'

He looked at it dismissively. 'You can get scrummy ones at the new confectioners on the Shanghai Bund—with whipped cream, cherries and thick thick chocolate on top like so.'

He help up two fingers.

Sunny's eyes rounded. 'An' cream, an' cherries an' chocolate all on one cake?'

'Yes—and nuts. I forgot the nuts.'

'I wouldn't like them,' Adam chimed in. 'They make me choke.'

'Stupidy Adam, you could scrape them off and give them to me.'

'You wouldn't be there, you're only a girl. But I'd be there eating lots of cakes with just Frank, wouldn't I?' For Adam had already taken an enormous shine to his stepbrother.

Frank laughed. 'Oh come, Adam, that's not very gallant. When you're bigger you'll all come to Shanghai, Alice and Sunny too. And I'll buy you all cakes, with nuts or without, and ice cream, strawberry or vanilla.'

Sunny sighed deeply. 'I've never had ice cream.'

'Yes dear, you had some in Chefoo once, but you were too young to remember,' Eliza corrected.

Edward Blake coughed, folding his napkin like a prayer-sheet. 'Well I think it's time I returned to my labours. I'm greatly hoping that the carpenter from Sparrow Lane who called at the street chapel yesterday will return, Eliza. He seemed a very genuine inquirer. And I trust we'll soon hear something of your actual studies, Frank? The news so far has been all of cricket matches, rowing contests and the consumption of cake.'

Frank said curtly, 'I study of course, Stepfather, but I'm not clever with languages and stuff like Alice.'

'Well, you are competent in something other than hitting a ball, I trust?'

'I'm not bad at geography, maps and things. Uncle Robert's pleased about that and suggests I might go in the Army. And I'm fair at arithmetic and that's good for business—which I really want to go into.'

'Business, dear?' Eliza clattered the plates nervously. 'Whatever kind of business?'

'Shipping of course, that's where the money is. Sending foreign goods upcountry to remote places like Changsha. That was Charles Grant's idea too—you remember him, Alice?'

'I do indeed. Did you ever hear from him again?'

'Not a word—I suppose he stayed in India after all.'

Edward coughed again. 'Am I to take it then, Frank, that

your ultimate ambition in life is to become an upriver trader, making profits out of selling to the Chinese such items as kerosene lamps, cotton goods, glass baubles, and various mechanical contrivances which they've lived quite happily without for centuries?'

'Oh please, Edward, let's not discuss these matters on Frank's first day here.' Eliza put a timorous hand on his shoulder which he immediately removed.

'My dear, I had no intention of so doing. But when my stepson talks of money-making as his *summum bonum* and this is all his education is presumably fitting him for, then I cannot but express some dismay—which you'll surely share; Eliza?'

'Of course, Edward, I'm disappointed that up to now neither he, nor Alice for that matter, seems to have found the true Path. But they're still young.'

'But I shall be . . .' and 'nineteen's not . . .' they protested simultaneously.

'Yes, dears, that is still young,' Eliza said firmly. 'After all, Edward dear, it was many years before you saw the Way clear to your life's work.'

He bowed humble assent. 'And wasted years they were too in some ways. I only hope your children won't waste so much of God's precious time. But at least . . .' he rose, 'I was never wedded to the notion of making money in trade.'

Frank's lips went into a familiar pout. 'There's nothing wrong in making a little money, Stepfather. It takes a man much further than one without any.'

It was perhaps fortunate that, while everyone's attention was elsewhere, Sunny had been devouring as many sugar plums as possible and now got a stone stuck in her throat and choked violently. In the ensuing diversion, Alice whispered, 'Don't go on any more like this please, Frank—for Mother's sake.'

Edward, thinking similarly, gave a frosty nod and departed to the street-chapel where he spent two hours kneeling on the earthen floor, praying in vain for the return of the Sparrow Lane carpenter.

'I don't know how you bear it, Alice,' Frank said the next morning as they set off on a tour of the limited Mukden sights. 'Stepfather's even worse than our French master and he's the worst in school. And you have to live in the same house.'

'But I shan't always, I keep telling myself. Only Mother does

219

need help with the little ones just now. She's not strong.'

'No—she looks so much older and greyer than I remember, I was quite shocked.'

'I suppose it isn't surprising, after all she's been through.'

'And now married to that man.'

Alice gave a twisted, sad smile. 'She saw it as God's will for her—and who are we to gainsay that?'

'Oh all this praying and Bible-thumping, it's not good for you, Alice. You should come to Shanghai where there are so many dashing young bachelors in the shipping offices and consulates—and even "in trade." ' He imitated Edward's tone of heavy disapproval. 'And not enough pretty young ladies to go round. Why, you could take your pick and have such a jolly time!'

She tossed her head. 'Oh, I don't fancy that sort of gent somehow. I've seen a few—so pleased with themselves with their smart moustaches and smart jokes and smart jackets—they seem so young and silly to me.'

'I always guessed you'd be hard to please, Sis, not like the rest of the English lassies.'

'Well, how could I, after what's happened to us?'

'Did Stepfather and Mother ever find out how we really lived in the Chu house?'

'No, they didn't want to hear about anything pleasant and they still think we were kept in some sort of prison, because that's how "the heathen" would behave, in their view. And there's so much I just couldn't explain—Mother would faint clean away!'

Frank chuckled. 'It's the same at school. I once told a chum that I'd been a groom in the service of a Deputy-Governor's son. He just jeered, but when I swore it was true, he advised me never to mention it because it was letting the side down.'

'So we just have to keep it to ourselves. . . . But I often wonder how they are, don't you?' Her tone was wistful.

'Oh I expect they're all right. Anyway, in a couple of years we'll set up that company, Greenwood & Greenwood, remember? So blow Stepfather! And we'll get rich in no time and buy a splendid junk painted red and gilt and go sailing back to Changsha together!'

Laughing in that golden dream, they turned a corner and were nearly trampled by a string of horses trotting to market. 'Gosh, look at those!' Frank's eyes widened. 'That's what I want, old girl. They're true-bred Mongolians, I've seen them at the Shanghai races—yes, I often go, you see some real swells there, but don't tell Mama! Fierce little brutes they are, they bite and arch their backs like cats when they're angry, but they go like the wind and never give up. We call 'em "griffins"—the same name they use for green youngsters just out from Home. Now if I could only afford one of those—let's find out what they cost anyway—I've still got some of Uncle Robert's allowance!'

They followed the animals to the market, where dealers from the north were bartering mules, sheep, goats and pigs and the pelts of foxes, ermine, sable, squirrel, dog and racoon as well as the sprightly Mongolian horses. Their price, Frank discovered, was less than half the going rate in Shanghai. 'Our first trading venture—we shouldn't miss a bargain like this!' he pleaded with Alice.

She hesitated thinking of her tiny hoard of coins, then smiled. 'Bags I the front half then!' So they returned to the Mission that afternoon with a springy steed called Griffin. He had a bristly tail and mane, wickedly glinting eyes, and had cost their every penny.

But he was worth every brass cash, Alice soon decided, for it was only the fun, first of training Griffin, who had very much a mind of his own, and then of teaching her to ride him well, that kept Frank contented for most of his holiday. Even then, boredom set in during the evenings when, instead of a stroll along the Bund, a cricket or rowing practice, came the Mission routine of prayers, a sparse supper, book-reading, early to bed.

'Let's play checkers again, Alice,' Frank suggested with a yawn as the sun sank in a fiery glow behind the tiled Mission roof. They got out the board. Eliza took up her sewing, happy just to have them with her and hoping guiltily that Edward, who had gone to see a convert, would return late. So her heart sank a little when, within the hour, she heard his heavy tread in the passage. He stood in the door surveying the scene, until Alice, feeling the waves of his rising anger washing over them, raised her very cool eyes to his tired, red-rimmed ones.

'Won't you sit down, Stepfather? Would you like some tea?'

'Tea—what I want is more than tea, miss.'

Eliza looked agitated. 'But Edward, what . . . ?'

'Help, madam, that's what I need and what no one in this

unfeeling household will offer me. Do any of you know or indeed care what I've been doing this evening? I've been trying to bolster the sorely tried faith of our poor ploughman, Lo-shi. He's being persecuted by his neighbours and his farm tools have been stolen—yet he clings to his new-found conviction in the Word. And while I struggle thus, you sit here—playing checkers, if you please!'

'But Edward, they . . .' Eliza was now at his side.

'And you, Eliza, many's the time I've heard you say, "Folded arms will never save sinking souls"—yet here you sit with your arms folded while I labour alone without support.'

'But Stepfather, we do help in many ways,' Alice began mildly, seeing Frank's face darken with rage.

'But not in the way that is more valuable—you should be my interpreter, the instrument through which the most marvellous message in the world could be transmitted to the unbelievers. And Frank too, he can speak the tongue with the utmost fluency—yet he sits here eating the bread of the house every day, yes and the cake too, but won't raise a finger to . . .'

'Well if that's how you feel, Stepfather, I'll leave tomorrow!' Frank blazed. 'I've very little money, but I don't want your charity thrown at me.'

'Please Edward . . . children, stop . . .' Eliza's wail was lost.

'No money?' Edward sneered. 'Just enough to buy horses, hey? And enough time to go riding over the plains all day like a gypsy without a care in the world.'

Frank leaped up, spilling checkers on the floor. 'If it wasn't for Mother, why I'd . . .' He doubled his fists, pushed violently past Edward and out of the room. Eliza hurried after him, flinging back at her husband, 'If these were your children—your Theobald and Laura—you'd never speak to them so, Edward. How dare you send my darling boy away like this?'

'I'm not sending him away, I'm only asking . . .' he shouted as she ran out.

Alice began picking up the checkers with shaking fingers. There was a silence.

'And you, miss?' he towered over her. 'What can be done to break that stubborn and wilful spirit of yours—which has been tainted, yes I use the word advisedly—tainted through too much close contact with heathendom during your girlhood. I pray on my bended knees for you every night, Alice, that God may reveal His purposes to you, that you will realise the hopeless spiritual coma in which you live.'

She straightened. 'Tainted you call it—by something you know nothing whatsoever about. You tell me the people are sinful idolators, don't you? Well, I won't believe it. I've lived among them as you say and I don't think they're any worse or any better come to that than we are. And what you call idolatry is people going to pray and give thanks at the graves of their ancestors. What's so wrong in that?'

'Are you trying to tell me that I don't recognise sin? That I don't know what wrong is—when I see it on all sides, in this town, in this house, in your very eyes at this moment, Miss Alice, I see the powers of darkness lurking, goading me.' He raised his arm dramatically, pushing a greater distance between them. He was deathly pale and trembling with a passion that first repelled her, then stirred her to pity. She stepped towards him and he backed violently. 'Get out,' he said in a low voice, 'begone from my sight this instant, woman.'

She flew out, brushing the checkers-board as she went so that it too clattered on the floor. Left alone, Edward fell on his knees beside the scattered game, grasped his large bony head in his large bony hands and tried to pray.

In response to his mother's and sister's entreaties, Frank did not leave immediately. He told Alice angrily he would only stay on condition he paid for his keep. Stepfather could consign his soul to perdition for all he cared, but he was not going to label him a sponger, so, as Frank's entire allowance was tied up in Griffin, the horse would have to be sold. Alice pleaded, but her brother could also be stubborn, and the result was that Alice slipped off to the money-changers the next day with a perfume bottle from the loot-box.

'Now his hind quarters are mine too,' she laughed, pressing money in Frank's hand. Wisely he did not ask where it came from but simply took it and paid his protesting mother a 'mess bill' for the remainder of his stay. It was short and rather uncomfortable for them all. Edward usually maintained a haughty, wounded silence, interrupted by the occasional, querulous bark at Adam, who had taken to following Frank about like a timorous, adoring lap-dog. Eliza lived in a continual twitter of anxiety, fearing more rows, while Alice simply withdrew, glad of a respite from the front-line of battle, but uneasily aware that, when Frank left, tensions would

223

probably increase. Only Sunny bounced gladly through the days as usual, happy that Frank's presence meant more tea-time treats, happiest of all when, clinging to the front of Griffin's saddle, she and Alice trotted to market.

Two days before Frank's departure the twins went down with chicken-pox, so only Alice saw him off on the Newchwang cart, kissing him lightly and joking about the rigours of his journey to conceal her misery and envy at the thought of his immediate prospects compared to hers. 'It won't be for long, Sis,' he promised. 'One more year of school grind, then I'm going to make a fortune for us both and you can leave Stepfather to stew in his own miserable juices! I hope I never see him again!'

As the cart trundled away, Alice turned Griffin's head and rode north-eastward out of town. Bright morning light flooded the plains and the stony ground was dotted with clumps of wild marigolds, daisies and yellow daphne, about which flitted pale violet butterflies. At the sound of hooves, ground-squirrels skittered into their tunnels and rock-partridges rose cackling into the air. Higher in the sky soared kestrels, buzzards and flocks of magpies bound for the reddish-brown millet fields that were higher than Griffin's head. Heaps of already-harvested grain were piled against the mud-walls of farmsteads and from their yards came the beat of threshers' flails and the tramp of oxen pulling stone rollers. Near the settlements, strip-fields were still planted with late summer beans, barley and tobacco; foul-smelling hemp was steeped in shallow pools; flocks of ragged sheep and goats nibbled at dried turf. As the sun rose higher, she reined Griffin to a halt.

'We have to go back,' she told him, and he turned a wild, disbelieving eye on her, his quivering nostrils exulting in the fresh smells from the distant hills. She sat there numbly. 'You're wondering why? And so am I!'

On the way back, Alice made a detour to the tombs dedicated to T'ai Tsung, a seventeenth-century leader of the Manchus. The tombs, containing T'ai Tsung, his official wife, and favourite concubine, were out of sight behind high walls, but the surrounding park was open—a veritable oasis of trees, flowering shrubs and grassy hillocks. Alice rode slowly down the wide flagged path leading to the tomb-enclosure, flanked by stone statues of camels, horses, lions and elephants. Grey, ruffled doves were cooing in the dark pines, green lizards basking on the camels' humps, and suddenly, a yellowish snake slid over the stones ahead and vanished behind an elephant. Griffin snorted warningly and she halted him. The hot silence enveloped them both.

The place, which she often visited, always spoke to her of death, especially of her father's. Whenever she remembered that dreadful summer day in Tientsin, her heart lurched in sad panic. To her mother, Thomas Greenwood was the very exemplar of the Christian hero who had gone so bravely to his martyrdom in the defence of his faith. But, as she grew older, Alice found this version increasingly hard to accept. There had been such a silly wastefulness about the whole episode— as if God's attention had been elsewhere that afternoon. The first time such an idea came to her, she had felt horrified and guilty; now she accepted its implications. And every time she came to this secluded spot—impregnated as it was with the short-livedness and short-sightedness of all human endeavour—she felt more certain that her reckless, stubborn, dearly beloved father had died in vain, though her heart ached none the less for that.

But then, as she sat on, the sun pouring on her head and Griffin's sweating flanks, and she looked at the graven animals, the trees and sky, she was overcome by an awareness of the beautiful unimportance of her own life and the reassuring inevitability of its passing. She murmured,

> 'Green, green the cypress on the mound,
> Firm, firm the boulder in the stream.
> Man's life within this world
> Is like the sojourning of a hurried traveller . . .'

That made her feel better, put into perspective the small trials that awaited her back at the Mission—the twins' illness, her mother's depression over Frank's departure, her own loss of his company. What did it all matter? She was a young and buoyant traveller with a long road still to explore. A lark burst into a sparkling chain of song high in the blue; she leaned forward and tweaked Griffin's ear, 'Come my lovely, my very own lovely—it's all right to go back now.'

Although there had been no hint of it in the clear sky of that morning at the tombs, the torrential late-summer rains began a few days later and the evenings began to draw in early and

225

chill. Alice slipped away to the furriers' market and, with the money left from the sale of the perfume bottle, bought a fine cloth jacket, luxuriously lined with sable. Because of its cost and beauty, she dared show it to no one. But, in the privacy of her bedroom, she wrapped herself in its elegance, dreaming of a time when she would be draped in furs—in the lobbies of grand hotels, on the way to glittering balls. She hungered for the challenge and excitement of young people's company, longed to find out how she would fare in what her mother termed the 'worldly' world that had so far been denied her.

She had no one in whom to confide her longings, for they would have shocked her parents, but the Campbells at least realised Alice's lack of congenial and eligible companionship. So they produced Josiah Simmons for her as if he were a Christmas present. He arrived on 22 December, and the Campbells decided he and Alice should be properly introduced, for the meeting might be momentous—and what better time than the goodwill season when doctrinal and personal differences were put aside? So it was on Christmas Day, when the Blakes and Alice arrived at the Campbells' for dinner, that May beckoned forward a chubby-cheeked, bespectacled young man with curly hair and a shy smile. 'And *this* is Mr. Josiah Simmons, Alice.'

They shook hands. She had heard of his impending arrival of course. He was the new Mission assistant and May had told her all she knew of him. He was twenty-two, unmarried, the son of a factory-owner in Birmingham. He had spent two years at the Society's Mission at Hankow on the Yangtze and its head had written to Dr. Campbell that Josiah was energetic, willing, devout, and a good musician. May had great hopes of Josiah, for she felt, as she told her husband, that poor Alice was rather a lost soul, though with great promise. What she needed was the guidance, support, and love of a decent, God-fearing young man. So May beamed as she ushered them into the sitting-room, where her little Jenny and Sunny passed round home-made biscuits, young Andrew Campbell played with Adam behind the sofa, and Eliza sat pink-cheeked by the stove roasting chestnuts. Dr. Campbell produced some ginger wine which Edward sipped as if it were cough syrup and Josiah, as was fitting, talked to Alice.

He spoke enthusiastically of the advance of mission-work in Hankow compared to Mukden. 'Why, there are American

Presbyterians, Episcopalians, London Missionary Society, Methodists, Canadian Baptists—as well as pioneers such as the C.M.S. and ourselves there,' he explained. 'Quite a community, and the bolder spirits among us—of which I was one, I may say—formed a "Sowers Band" to work jointly with the young natives. We'd have a sing-song every Saturday evening in one of the Mission parlours with an harmonium, fiddles and several of us singing. Do you play or sing, Miss Greenwood?'

'I'm afraid nothing like that goes on here, Mr. Simmons, and I have no musical accomplishments.'

'Ah well—we must remedy that. We're so few here to "make a joyful noise together" that it's a case of all hands on deck, surely? Perhaps Mrs. Campbell could be persuaded to teach you the harmonium accompaniment anyway—singing is really my forte.'

And later, as twilight fell and they all sat replete from the generous Christmas feast, he showed that it was. As his rich baritone filled the room, Eliza hummed softly in the background, tears just behind her eyes, for she was remembering earlier Christmases when the children had been young and she and Thomas had put oranges, toy whistles and sweets in their stockings. Staring at the orange glow of the wintry sunset, Edward's thoughts drifted in his own similar directions, to a particular Christmas of years ago: fair Clara lighting the candles in the window of their Sussex home; Theobald poking his chubby fingers in a trifle and little Laura shrieking with laughter on finding a silver horseshoe in her pudding. Whatever would Clara think of him now? Of his drab and humble Chinese robe, this harsh, alien city on the Manchurian plains, and he with no comforts, no truly congenial company, hardly any money? He shivered, for he could almost hear the little tinkling laugh of scorn she used to reserve for the less sophisticated members of the school staff. Ah, but Clara had been fair, very fair—but alas very worldly.

To Alice the songs meant little, so she considered the singer. He reminded her of a picture of the young Schubert on May's music sheet, with the same bumbling over-eagerness she felt the composer might have had. One of her stepfather's favourite sentiments was that the Gospels contained 'Shallows where the lamb may ford and depths where the elephant must swim': Edward certainly considered himself in the elephantine class; Alice suspected that Josiah was among the lambs.

227

Whatever Alice's private reservations, May Campbell decided that the first meeting between the two young people had been promising and encouraged Alice to take up the harmonium. From the first, Josiah found time to help her—singing encouragement and explaining the difficult passages. When the weather improved and Alice resumed her riding over the plains in the early mornings, she often heard the thud of hooves behind—and there was Josiah, on the doctor's plump steed, his spectacles steamed up with exertion. To entertain her, he reeled off the names of every plant and bird. He brought lumps of iron-ore or soapstone for her inspection; when the first jonquils of spring appeared, he gathered a huge bunch and presented them to her, smiling shyly. She found his company pleasant enough, and it was a relief to hear little of Christian dogma, for, as Josiah readily admitted, men like her stepfather could soon tie him in theological knots.

'It's enough for me to be here doing what little I can as a practical Christian,' he explained earnestly. 'I think God intends to use me in this way.'

'But Josiah, how can you be so sure of God's intentions?' she asked. 'I never am. What makes you so certain He wanted you to become a missionary? My stepfather now, he vows he received a direct message from God in Lewes Civic Hall where he heard Hudson Taylor preaching. It was only a few months after his first wife, Clara, died, and I've often wondered if he'd have heard that message if Clara had lived, or if he hadn't gone to that meeting.'

'But it's very difficult to explain about Calls, Alice, especially to those who've not yet received them. People are more open to them at certain times of their lives—perhaps your stepfather was made receptive by his bereavement. In my case, I must confess I first wanted to be a singer, but Father disapproved, saying it was no life for a Christian gentleman. So I was feeling very discontented and disheartened when I started attending missionary meetings.'

Sometimes, secretly, Josiah himself wondered why and how it had all come about, though he did not regret his life's choice. He was, however, beginning to repent somewhat of the excessive zeal that had urged him to leave companionable Hankow for this Mukden outpost, where there was such a dearth of charming feminine company—except of course for Alice. And Josiah was a susceptible young man whose emotions tended to bubble over easily like his voice and, on the desert of the Mukden scene, the sight of Alice's trim figure riding over the plains, her merry laughter and teasing, the withdrawn, sometimes harried look in her green eyes, held him in thrall.

There was a certain mystery about her that tantalised him, a strange boldness that slightly awed him. He did not fully approve of her Chinese clothes, of the novels she read, of her merciless derision of her stepfather, or even of her over-easy familiarity with the natives. But he never dared to hint his disapproval, for he had once seen her eyes flash with anger and guessed that, in any battle of words, he would surely be vanquished. So he played admiringly to her tune—which was, had he known, the last strategy to win her affection. And when, after several months, this seemed of no avail, he steeled himself for a more direct approach.

He chose his time carefully, wishing there were some moonlit ruins or picturesque glen as fitting backdrop for his essay. But Mukden was singularly lacking in romantic spots and he had to make do with the strip of formal garden laid out by the foreign residents for promenading. It was located unfortunately close to the animal-dealers' market and, though screened from it by trees, the garden's air was so feculent that promenaders were few. On the evening that Josiah determinedly steered Alice there after an harmonium practice, it was quite deserted. The smell, he realised with dismay, was strongly animal, but there was at least a moon, a few tattered streamers hung on the rose-bushes, and firecracker-cases littered the paths.

Josiah kicked one. 'Looks as if the natives have been celebrating again.'

'Of course, the Ching-ming is just over, when they visit the family graves and pay homage to their ancestors . . . didn't you know *that*?'

He reddened at her asperity. 'Yes, silly of me—they have so many festivals, I get confused.'

'You wouldn't if you'd actually been along to the tombs with a family—as I did when in the service of the Chus.'

He put a tentative hand on her shoulder. 'Poor little Alice, how absolutely rotten it must have been for you.'

'They didn't treat me so badly and it was more interesting than life here, in some ways.'

'But you were so alone and young—then to escape like that

was so brave, Alice—indeed I think you're quite wonderful altogether.' He stopped, pulled her against him and, in a sudden rush, covered her cheeks and mouth with moist kisses.

She drew back in surprise. 'Why . . . Josiah . . . no, please stop. You really must.'

His body trembled violently like an eager puppy's and, for a moment, he simply held her tighter in his shaking arms. 'Oh Alice . . .' he released her with a gasp, 'dear, dear Alice, I've wanted to kiss you so often—please don't be angry with me. I know you must be innocent of a man's feelings, how he has to struggle with himself sometimes . . . I haven't offended you, have I, dear? Please say not.'

'No, Josiah—I'm just so surprised. You see, I'm not . . . well, you mustn't think of me in this way.'

'But how else can I think of you, Alice? You're so pretty and sweet.'

'Josiah, I'm not sweet.' She laughed lightly. 'Why, you've often told me, and quite rightly, that I'm critical and impatient—and not nearly as devout as you.'

'Ah but, Alice, I'm sure you are in your own way and would become more so, if you were to . . . I mean, I don't want to hurry things, but if you could begin to think kindly of me, in this new way . . . I mean I could come and see your stepfather soon . . . if you'd like, now I've kissed you like this and . . .' His voice trailed away, and he looked down at her hand he was still forlornly rubbing.

'Oh no, Josiah, why, whatever has made you think that? We can be friends of course, but I couldn't possibly consider . . .'

'But dear,' he pleaded desperately, still squeezing her limp fingers, 'it's hard for a man not to want something more than friendship when he's with a lovely young lady like you so often. I want everything to be proper of course. I'm sure the Campbells would be very pleased—they've even hinted as much. My prospects are quite good you know, and the Doctor thinks well of me.'

'I'm sure he does, Josiah, and so do I. But I'm not at all a suitable person . . . I mean, I've no idea what my prospects are.'

'Oh I know you must think carefully about such matters, Alice, and perhaps I've been a little hasty, considering your inexperience.' He drew back again, polishing his spectacles. Alice turned away, biting her lip, for his words, allied to a specially pungent odour from the market, filled her with a huge desire to laugh.

'Come, Josiah,' she gasped instead, 'we must go back or Mother will fret. And please let's not say another word on the subject. It's quite out of the question.'

'But, Alice,' he blinked at her, 'I really don't understand why you should say that. What's the matter with me? I mean, your present situation isn't very appealing surely? So why couldn't you just consider growing slowly fonder of me, as fond as I am of you?'

She faced him firmly. 'You don't understand. You know so little about me, really, Josiah, and that's how it should be. I shall never be a missionary, nor the wife of one, and that's that. Everyone's been trying to persuade me in that direction ever since I returned from Changsha—the Penfolds and Ida Palmer, my mother, my stepfather, the Campbells. And it's quite largely because I speak Chinese fluently and they see me as a sort of instrument for conveying their messages. Well, I've told them all to forget the idea and I'm now telling you the same. Please let's go—this garden really has the most abominable smell, haven't you noticed?'

He fell sulkily into step beside her as they returned to the Mission. In their mutual silence Josiah was wishing ever more fervently that he had never left Hankow, while Alice marvelled that the Campbells and perhaps her mother too could imagine she might want to wed Josiah. The thought depressed and angered her, for it meant they did not take her own declarations at all seriously—they had simply assumed that if the 'right young man' came along she would gladly become a missionary's wife after all. Did they not realise how extraordinary she was—or at least felt herself to be? Probably, she decided with a flash of uncomfortable insight, only her stepfather had a perception of that.

What her stepfather did perceive in Alice was an independence of spirit unleavened by Christian humility. He, for one, was not surprised to learn—for the news soon reached him—that Alice had refused Josiah's advances. 'I expect,' he remarked tartly to his wife, 'she doesn't consider him good enough for her. I sometimes fear your daughter doesn't believe that Christ Himself in all His Glory is good enough for her. And I must confess, Eliza, that, considering her age and sex, I find her degree of self-pride quite overweening.'

The desire to humble that pride, to force Alice to accept her manifest destiny as one of God's instruments for converting the heathen, goaded him constantly. As he had said, he prayed for her soul every night. How could she remain totally unmoved by that power that had urged, nay, almost forced him to forsake his all to come and labour in this alien soil? Again and again his mind furrowed along these tracks, but in spite of all his prayers throughout that next summer, Alice showed no sign of 'growing in grace.'

For her too it was a barren time. She saw much less of Josiah, who had been quite shocked by her adamant rejection, not only of him, but of any connection with mission work. Prudently he started writing warm letters to Mildred Thistlethwaite, one of the single young ladies in Hankow and an accomplished harmonium player. From the outside world came tantalising news. William and Isabel, now the parents of Charlotte and little Joel, had been posted from Foochow to Port Arthur on the Liaotung Peninsula where Frank now spent his summers. Alice could not help feeling jealous, for again it seemed Frank had all the exciting opportunities, whereas she had nothing but obligations in Manchuria to fulfil.

The seasons passed. Spring brought jonquils, but also premonitions of heat. During the late summer rains, swarms of mosquitoes hummed above the town's flooded drains and Alice noted with a depression of the spirits the familiar portents of the long, cold northern winter. The tracks where she rode were churned into a yellowish, flowerless mire by the carts of sturdy Mongolian traders already swaddled in their padded sheepskins. Overhead came the rhythmical wing beats of wild fowl flying south. The grazing herds of antelope and gazelle vanished from the foothills.

It was in a mood of nostalgic melancholy induced by the season that Alice sat in the school-room one autumn afternoon practising calligraphy to show Be-dien. She had chosen to copy the poem 'Jade Flower Palace' by the admirable Tu-fu, and, as she wrote, the scene in the Chu courtyard when Lung-kuang first really looked at her returned vividly. 'The colours of autumn are fresh in the wind and rain . . . though the virgins have all gone their way to the yellow graves . . . in dark rooms ghost-green fires are shining. . . .' She shivered at the line, sensing, as she sometimes did, that the Mission itself, the former grain-chandlery, did not like their barbarian presences. The building was reputedly set in an ill-omened *fen-shui*, meaning it had an unlucky relationship to the elements of wind and rain, and certainly it was true that, from whatever quarters they came, they blew with exceeding ferocity through every crack.

As Alice rose to secure a blowing shutter, Josiah came riding through the gate and called to her, 'Oh Alice, come out—there's such a bother. Mrs. Campbell fears she's beginning premature labour and the doctor has just gone off on a two-day itineration. She wants me to go and fetch him back at once and wonders if your mother will come and stay with her till we return. . . .'

Eliza hurried off with Josiah at once, leaving Alice in charge of the children.

'Why is Mrs. Campbell having another baby, Father?' Sunny asked as they all sat round the tea-table. 'Doesn't she have enough?'

'Ah but it is God's will that she should bring forth more fruit.'

Sunny looked puzzled. 'But Father, I said a baby, not fruit.'

He glowered at her. 'It's a manner of speaking, children, fruit of the womb, fruit of the loins. . . . But these matters are quite beyond your understanding.'

'Perhaps we could say that Mrs. Campbell's baby is the fruit of the gooseberry bush—babies are sometimes found under them, I believe?' Alice suggested maliciously.

'It may be the simplest explanation for now, yes, Sunny.'

'But Mrs. Campbell doesn't have any gooseberry bushes in her garden.'

And Adam said, 'There aren't any gooseberry bushes in the whole of Mukden. What do they look like? Do gooses eat them?'

Edward rose hastily. 'I have a return of the colic, Alice, and I don't wish for more tea. I shall go to study some characters in readiness for the morrow's lesson. Ruth will help you with the children.'

Edward had been a martyr to the colic for the past year, due, he decided, to an excess of boiled millet and not enough good red meat. To counteract this, Dr. Campbell had prescribed a brownish tonic and a small glass of port every evening. These Edward now dutifully swallowed before his nightly wrestle with the Mandarin. After a while however, his concentration was disturbed by noises from the nursery. 'It's time they were asleep,' he muttered crossly, going to investigate. Alice's voice reached him through the door.

' "You are old said the Youth, as I mentioned before, And have grown most uncommonly fat; Yet you turned a backsomersault in at the door. Pray what is the reason for that?" '

Edward walked in. The twins tucked in bed were giggling loudly at Alice's lively rendering of 'Old Father William.' 'What balderdash are you reading them? You know that is not what they should be hearing! This is their bedtime book, surely?' He indicated the copy of *Noble Tales for Little Boys and Girls* with which Eliza usually sent them to sleep.

'That's not nearly so nice and funny,' remarked Sunny.

'I like hearing about the White Rabbit much better—"oh my fur and whiskers . . . I'm late, I'm late . . ." ' squeaked Adam, giggling up at his father, holding his hands like paws.

'You see how you've over-excited them?' Edward grabbed the offending book. '*Alice in Wonderland*—ah, that Mr Carroll, I've heard of it, and he's a don I believe? What nonsense! He should know better. . . .' He glanced through it disdainfully. 'And how unfortunately typical, if I may say so, Alice, that you'd choose a tale with a heroine bearing your own name—further increasing thereby your sadly overblown sense of your own importance, I suspect.'

'That's nothing whatever to do with it! I adore Wonderland Alice because she's a real heroine. I'm not nearly so brave . . . why, if I were I'd—'

'And what exactly would you do?' he challenged, throwing down the book in disgust.

'I'd get out of this miserable house for a start, that's what I'd do. It's like a prison, filled with your narrow ideas, so grim and depressing. What's wrong with telling the children a light-hearted fairy story for a change? They don't have much fun, poor little doves.'

Sunny began to cry noisily and shaking Adam buried himself under the bedclothes, for he hated rows. 'Now look at the state you've got them in! And no mother here to comfort them—be quiet, Sunny. Go to sleep like good children, and tomorrow night I'll read you a suitable story myself as Alice's taste is obviously not to be trusted.'

She scooped up her book. 'I wonder sometimes if you've ever really laughed at anything, Stepfather—or if you were ever a child, it's hard to imagine!'

And with that she bolted, leaving him to deal with the children. When they were eventually settled, Edward returned to his books, but now his stomach positively stabbed with choleric bile. Those pictures of a pretty little girl with her silly animals—

234

self-aggrandisement, that's all it was. How dare she fill his children's head with such trivial stuff? The colic gripped him; he groaned and, going to the cupboard, tossed back more tonic and port. But still he could not concentrate, tortured by her gibe about the lack of laughter and light in his house.

The evening deepened into chill night and the town's Drum Tower bell tolled the watches. Edward's belly stabbed relentlessly as he reviewed the unsatisfactory circumstances of his present life, and was only temporarily calmed by further recourse to the port bottle. When at last he rose, his head reeled unaccountably and he stepped into the yard to clear it. He looked at the sky, seeking for some sign, however remotely construable, of God's supporting presence.

All that caught his eye was a light still shining from Alice's bedroom. What could she be doing awake at this late hour? What new unsavoury mischief might she be brewing—that hard, unredeemed, young female spirit? He stumbled back inside, along the passage and burst into her bedroom. His face, though he did not know it, was glowing and he was breathing heavily. She was sitting up in bed, reading by lantern-light, the sable-lined jacket thrown round her shoulders.

'What's this now?' he pounced at her, tearing away the book. '*Wuthering Heights*? So it's not enough to fill my children's heads with romantic nonsense but you fill your own, hey, miss? And this—this finery? How did you come by it? I've never seen this—it's a very expensive garment, I can tell that much. How could you—what devilry's been going on here?' He was bellowing with rage and his words slurred slightly as he slung the novel away, tore back the bedclothes and jerked the coat off her.

'Stop it, stop it!' She clung to it. 'It's mine, mine. How dare you come bursting into my room like this?'

'How dare I?—How dare you sit here in my house reading trash, adorning your person with garments you could never have come by honestly? Oh Alice, I've had my suspicions about you before—there is not enough innocence about you, not enough Christian humility. It is time for you to be forcibly shown the way to repentance, Alice, for your own good I shall. . .' With shaking fingers he untied the thick waist cord of his robe. 'This headstrong spirit of yours must be tamed, child. There is something of evil in you, I fear.' He breathed harshly over her, the cord in his hand, and she screamed, pushing him away, trying to

235

duck under his raised arm.

'Stop it, Stepfather, stop it! You've gone mad . . . how dare you?'

'Dare, me dare . . . why I dare to . . .' He lunged, caught her round the waist, lifted her bodily and, sitting back on the bed, slung her face down across his lap, holding her neck towards the floor with a steely arm. She cried out again, kicking her legs violently till he pinioned them down with one of his stronger ones.

'Don't resist me, Alice,' he panted. 'This chastisement is for your own good—it had to come. I won't tolerate this worldly light-mindedness under my own roof any longer. Humble yourself, Alice, subjugate yourself to my will. You have been contaminated by heathendom and it is my bounden duty to . . .' As he spoke he pulled up her nightgown and began to whip her bare thighs and buttocks with the cord. She struggled help-lessly, clamped down over him, shaking more with rage than pain.

'Stop it—you beast—I hate you—'

'You are still defying me, Alice. Your spirit must be humbled—there and there again. Oh, submit yourself willingly to this punishment, Alice, accept this small pain I'm inflicting on you for your greater good.' He was almost whispering now. 'Ah Alice, let me chastise this rebellious flesh, this sweet but tainted fruit. Let me feel your closed spirit opening to my will, let me just . . .'

As he clamped her even more tightly across his lap, she became aware of a growing bulging thrust against her stomach and, knowing she could not be mistaken, gave a sudden violent upward push of revulsion, tearing at the front of his loose robe and rending it open.

'Look at you!' she screamed. 'Look at you—you filthy old man! Look, that's what you really want! Oh, it's hideous, hideous.'

For a second they both stared in mute horror at the penis which was quite unmistakably in a state of erection beneath his merino-wool combinations. He leaped up in a frenzy, hastily gathering his torn robe over the obstreperous organ with a whimper.

'Oh dear God . . . what have I . . .? How could it . . .?'

'Get out,' she gulped, suddenly very close to tears as the full enormity of the situation struck her and her flesh began to sting. 'Get out—you're odious and disgusting.' He made as if to move towards her in a gesture of conciliation, but she shrank back.

He rushed away, leaving the cord on the floor. She stared at it numbly for a minute, then, putting a chair against the door, examined the weals on her skin. They were pink and sore but the flesh hadn't been broken. She lay face down on the bed and cried softly for a long while. Neither of them slept for the remainder of the night. At the first glow of dawn Edward emerged into the yard, saddled the mule and rode slowly away without a backward glance. After watching him go, Alice too rose, packed her clothes, books, the map of China and the loot-box in her calico bag.

Downstairs in the kitchen where the air smelled of charcoal, soy, pickled turnips, and stale animal grease, Alice stared at the scrubbed wood table where the family had shared so many meals, so few of them pleasurable. She visualised Edward at its head, bony hands clasped in prayer for yet another frugal repast. Never would she be part of that group again; the very thought of him there made her feel sick. She wrote a note to her mother explaining that she and Edward had quarrelled so badly she had determined to leave at once for Port Arthur, where she would stay with William. No one, she added, need worry about her in the least. Then, in a panicky haste lest Edward should return, she gulped down a bowl of purplish sorghum porridge, saddled Griffin and rode away, wrapped in her sable jacket.

All that day she travelled south, forcing herself to keep her sore buttocks on the saddle in case she was pursued. But no one followed and, by the second night, she felt securely enveloped again within the ample lap of the uncaring country. But, as her physical wounds healed, she felt more deeply hurt and out-raged by what had happened. The inescapable conclusion was that her stepfather had been aroused by whipping her and this filled her with a nauseous dread, for it suggested a brutality that she had never sensed in Lung-kuang. So which was the more 'civilised' way—Lung-kuang's unashamed sensual enjoyment or her stepfather's desire to subjugate and hurt her, all mixed up with his horrible secret lust? Surely Edward did not feel the same when he made love to his own wife, her mother?

Questions like these throbbed in her head like an aching tooth and every time she probed them she experienced a burning dis-gust. Again and again, though she tried desperately not to, she saw that large unsightly bulge beneath Edward's underwear;

the way his hands had clawed to cover it; hands she had so often seen clasped in prayer. Stirred and weakened by these thoughts, she longed to lie beside Lung-kuang's trim body, to feel again his gentle knowingness. One morning, waking in a dirty village inn, she got out the map of China with the wild idea of simply riding south-west for hundreds of miles till she reached the gates of the Chu.

But this, she knew, was impossible, for the winds, blasting straight from the Mongolian wastes, were daily more bitter. The tracks between the villages became iced-over mires, and her freedom was but a temporary respite, for the family would be in anxious contact about her, and she had no other home. So she spurred Griffin down the broad mountainous spur of the Liaotung Peninsula until, on the tenth day out, she reached that point where it narrowed to little more than a bridge separating the Bay of Korea from the Gulf of Chihli. Then the land widened to small-island size, and there ahead, on the very last tip, huddled at the base of stony hills called The White Wolf, The Dragon Ridge and The Eagle's Nest; was Port Arthur.

9

Both Alice and Isabel long remembered their first meeting
and learned to laugh about it. But its actual occurrence, on a
wintry evening in 1880 at William's house next to Port
Arthur's Imperial Maritime Customs office, was uncomfortable. Making herself known to the servant, Alice was shown
into the drawing-room and she was tentatively running her
fingers over the luxurious wine-velvet of the armchairs when
Isabel came in. No one had told Alice that her sister-in-law
was beautiful—or at least striking, for her nose and mouth
were too full for classic beauty. But what Alice first saw was
her statuesque figure, splendidly arrayed in an evening gown
of emerald brocade with a sweeping satin train. Silken gloves
covered most of her arms, her creamy shoulders were half-
bared, and a diamanté necklace glittered at her throat.
Above all shone a mass of natural auburn curls, coiled back
from her face in a glowing chignon. In the eyes of foreigners
this was her crowning glory, though the Chinese had a special
aversion to such a hue and her nickname among them, Alice
later learned, was 'Number One Red-Devil.'

Painfully aware of her travel-stained jacket, baggy trousers, and the stench of roadside inn that clung to her, Alice
simply stood and gaped. Isabel too paused involuntarily, then
stepped valiantly forward, silken-cased arms outstretched in
welcome. 'You must be Alice?' It was almost an incredulous
question, and Alice replied, 'Yes, but I don't always look like
this, only I've ridden a long way on a horse.'

Isabel's face lost its majesty as she replied with a broad
smile, 'Never mind, I don't always look like this either, only
William and I are dining with the French Consul tonight.'

Then William hurried in, gathering her into his arms, smell
and all, saying how delighted he was that she had arrived safe
and sound. When the pair went off for dinner, Alice had a

bath, a good supper and slept in a bedroom that seemed a veritable bower of luxury and elegance compared to her room at the Mission. Isabel soon made her feel at home, for she was a kindly, sensible woman devoted to her husband and two children, four-year-old Charlotte and baby Joel, and quite prepared to include within their tranquil circle her husband's sister, who, she felt, had so far spent a rather wretched life. It was little wonder, she told William, that Alice had determined to leave Mukden, for what sort of life was there for a spirited girl in a remote mission station unless she were a missionary? Alice, she declared, had been put upon enough, and what she needed now was a little social polishing, a bit of wholesome fun and a radical reappraisal of her wardrobe.

William seldom contradicted his wife in such matters and Alice was so grateful to be offered a home without the asking of awkward questions that she fell in eagerly with Isabel's plans. So the two spent many earnest hours closeted with Madame Claire, the town's French dressmaker, where Alice was fitted for a tight cuirass bodice moulded to her waist and hips, for a day-dress of astrakhan cloth, for a lemon-yellow tea-gown with ruffled lace sleeves, and a velveteen tie-back walking dress that she wore with an ermine muff and saucy fur hat. And in due course, when it was the Greenwoods' turn to invite the French Consul to dine, Alice appeared in a blue silk polonaise gown, looped at the sides and draped at the back, trimmed with white and rose ribbons. Moonstones glowed at her neck and brown curls framed a face that looked almost too demure, were it not for the mischievous greenish eyes that were always knowing, alert and clear.

Monsieur Félix Fauré, the Assistant French Consul, also present, was much taken with the Customs Inspector's sister, as Isabel guessed he would be, for Félix was intelligent, if a little affected for her taste. His dark moustache was long and droopy, he wore velvet waistcoats and the silk facings of his dress-coats were rather flamboyant, his manner and accented English most dashingly Gallic. But, a Parisian by birth, he undoubtedly possessed savoir-faire and was just the man to teach Alice the social ropes.

Félix too wanted to cultivate their acquaintance, for not only was Alice the most fascinating English sliver of Chinese jade he had ever met, but she was thoroughly conversant with the native tongue, the mastering of which was his only serious ambition. Soon after the dinner-party therefore, it was arranged that Alice should go to the French Consulate every Friday afternoon to help Félix with his Chinese, for which she received generous payment and a lavish pastry tea. As the days shortened, the tea-hour lengthened into suppertime, after which Félix escorted her home. At least that was generally the practice, till the evening Félix suggested they call for a night-cap at Epimoff's.

At that time Port Arthur was little more than a fishing port except for the newly opened Chinese naval college on the out-skirts and the cluster of Western-style buildings near the har-bour. Here stood the consulates of various European nations, of the Americans and Japanese, and the Customs office where William presided. Here too was Epimoff's, the only hotel and known to everyone, though Alice had not been inside before because William did not think it quite respectable. This view would have infuriated its owner who claimed to run the only thoroughly reputable hostelry between Shanghai and Vladivostok.

A kindly Russian Jew of ample proportions and experience, Madame Epimoff had opened her establishment three years before and its dining-room, with huge oak sideboard, glass chandeliers, tinkly piano and a corner bar, was famed for its borscht and brown sourbread. Olga, her daughter, wore tight satin gowns and played French chansons near closing-time and was an added attraction to the regular clientele. Most were of French, Russian, or American extraction and of the male sex, for Madame considered the British, Germans, and most women to be unutterably boring and the Chinese totally inexplicable. Alice, though lacking the requisite qualifica-tions, was allowed in on sufferance at Félix's request, for he was a favourite of hers.

Madame had also been persuaded to offer table-space to some of the Chinese naval students who, in tight-buttoned jac-kets, serge trousers, and peaked caps, provided a touch of comic relief that was irresistible. Earnest, argumentative, puzzled young men, they tried in vain to seem at ease in this alien setting, spooning soup self-consciously, sipping hesi-tantly at the famous Epimoff cocktail made with vodka, melon juice and angostura bitters, losing their shyness in violent poli-tical debate as the evenings progressed, and fleeing instantly when Olga began to play, for they found the noise unendurable.

241

Soon the Friday visit to Epimoff's became a high point of Alice's week. She developed a taste for borscht and vodka and liked the cosy familiarity of the scene on long winter nights when only habitués gathered there and Madame's aged father-in-law, sole witness to the existence of some long-departed spouse, sat in the warm stove-corner playing chess with the Russian doctor.

As the season warmed, the port livened up again. Local fishing boats ventured out into the Gulf of Pechili and trading junks loaded cargoes of soy, bean-cakes, and sesame seed oil from the warehouses. Larger vessels came nosing into harbour from afar and Félix and Alice, arriving at the hotel on the first balmy evening of late April, were surprised by the crowd of new faces.

Two Korean sea-captains and three Russian tea-merchants were eating borscht, and propping up the bar was a portly grey-whiskered man called Harry Snow, owner of a schooner called the *Snowdrop* in which he hunted sea-otters along the Korean and Japanese coasts. Draped at his side was a blonde woman in a low-cut sequinned dress. The Chinese students also seemed more animated than usual, Félix thought as he elbowed a way to the bar, cosily nudging the blonde en route.

'Alice *ma chérie*,' he handed a cocktail, 'there is something in the wind with the students—they are all drawing ships on bits of paper. Find out what it is, my little Jade, and come and tell your old French uncle.' He rolled his eyes at her. Félix was in fact only a few years Alice's senior, but it was a game he had instigated to avoid any hint of seriousness in their relationship. Through the visits to Epimoff's, she had however proved a useful source of information about what was going on among the naval students, some of whom were hot-headed political reformists. It was for this reason that the French Consul was always ready, if required, to vouch for the games of cribbage with which Félix and Alice were supposed innocently to while away Friday evenings. The Consul's reward was the satisfaction of being generally better informed than his rival British counterpart, who had never considered Alice's diplomatic value.

Alice, innocent of such stratagems, simply enjoyed the students' company and their ambitious plans for the future of China excited her. So when she returned to Félix, her eyes were sparkling.

242

'Yes, there is news. Li Hung-chang has finally persuaded the Empress Dowager to go ahead with the building of that shipyard here.'

'Really? It is official, not just another rumour?'

'Official yes. That lecturer, the one they all call "The Leader" who never comes here, has just returned from Peking where he had a meeting with some great man himself and got the direct word. They are to begin building at once and some students have just arrived from Foochow Arsenal to take navigation courses. It will really put Port Arthur on the map at last, they say.'

The blonde leaned over Félix's shoulder. 'Well it's sure time something put this godforsaken hole on the map. And your French friend tells me you live here year round, Miss Greenwood? That's tough.'

Alice smiled. 'Oh I don't mind, I've lived in worse places, Miss . . .?'

'O'Hara, Mrs. Bella O'Hara. Well, at least there's a good selection of real full-blooded gentlemen round here—that must be a compensation.' She looked roguish, but Alice flushed and stammered, 'Oh I don't . . . I mean, I only come here on Fridays with Félix, you see my brother doesn't know and . . .'

Félix grinned. 'Poor Miss Greenwood had the dire misfortune of being born into a missionary family, Mrs. O'Hara. She's on the road to recovery, I'm pleased to say, under the tutelage of her bon oncle, but still has much to learn. . . .'

'Is that so?' Bella, losing any spark of interest in Alice, turned to him. 'Well my gallant Parisian, perhaps you can tutor me a little. . . . Who is this Chinaman, this Li someone-or-other who orders shipyards to appear? Is he the President?'

'Hélas, non, the Chinese, dear madame, do not espouse the enlightened republican ideas of you Yankees and us French. Non, they have their Emperors still, or rather now they have mainly an Empress, the old Buddha, the arch-she-dragon of all times. She is the avowed enemy of all change and progress who lavishes her country's money on the building of yet another grand edifice in the grounds of her glorious Summer Palace near Peking where there are already Halls of Sparkling Brightnesses, Pavilions of Southern Fragrances and what not. Naturally she has no interest whatsoever in such ugly monstrosities as shipyards, but this Li Hung-chang, the Governor of Chihli, is powerful and persuasive. And he sees that if, in ten years' time, there is still nothing more terrible to behold in China than fragrant pavilions and men brandishing muskets, the place will be in a hopeless mess. Someone will over-run it. So—the astute Governor wants his country to be the proud possessor of arsenals and shipyards and vessels made of iron instead of wood, with trained technicians to make them work, and he must have gained the Empress Dowager's ear recently. And *that* is why our young Chinese friends over there are happily designing grand and quite improbable warships and dreaming of the days when they'll all be admirals of the fleet, conquerors of all Asia, and Heaven knows what else!'

Bella, laughing in appreciation of this discourse, proceeded to ask Félix about the scandalous court revels in which the Empress, her intimates and eunuchs were rumoured to indulge, while Alice twirled her glass disconsolately and eavesdropped. People were talking of fishing, buying tea and selling timber, of otters, stormy seas and places she had never seen. Only she had nothing to say, for her life had become lacklustre and static, she thought resentfully. Who would want to hear about Lottie's new tooth, Isabel's new evening-gown, the jam tarts she had made for tomorrow's picnic? Finishing a second cocktail, she lapsed into a discontented sulk, feeling ever smaller and of less account as more people crowded into the bar chatting animatedly and ignoring her. But suddenly she gasped, staring incredulously at a latecomer who had just joined the nearby student table.

'Félix—that student over there ... it's ... it must be ...' Excitedly she pushed through the crowd and tugged his sleeve. He turned.

'Han-li, Younger Brother—it is you!'

Seeing his familiar face, so little changed under its absurd peaked cap, she felt as if a rabbit-hole had opened at her feet. The years fell away from them both and they clasped each other with shining eyes. For a minute everyone quietened at the extraordinary sight till Han-li drew back in embarrassment.

'Uncut Jade—you. Is it possible?'

'And you, Han-li, in that Western uniform. I am astounded!'

'But let's go and talk quietly over there, everyone is watching us.'

After a word of excited explanation to Félix, she joined him, bubbling with curiosity. 'You—a student here? But however did you manage it? What are you studying? Your Honourable

244

Father has actually permitted this? And how is he—the respected Dragon Brightness? And Tamao and Mei?'

He butted in eagerly. 'And your brother, my barbarian horse-groom, where is he now?'

'Working as a clerk in a Shanghai hong—quite a young man about town now, and still mad on horses, But you . . .?'

'It all started with Younger Sister really. She was betrothed to a Changsha man of good family, you remember? But just before the wedding he died and she was broken-hearted.'

'Mei was fond of him?'

'She scarcely knew him, but she desperately wanted a husband and sons. So she pestered and pestered till Father let her marry another man—a young fellow and restless by nature. He took her off to Canton and went into business. Father didn't much like it, but it meant I was able to visit her.' He looked at Alice shyly. 'You remember when we last met you said there were so many things in the modern world I'd never dreamed of? Well when I went to Canton I began to understand, and I begged Father to let me stay there to study after I did well in my Eight-Legged Essay examination—and eventually he agreed.'

'But how is it you are here, in Port Arthur?'

'I studied maths and Western naval science at Canton, then at Foochow, because I'm good at these things. Now I'm here for a short while because of the new shipyard. But you, Uncut? Is that your husband over there?'

'No, Han-li, I'm not yet married. I live here with my brother, the older one you never really met—except in the little wood near the boundary wall!'

'But you're quite old now, Uncut. Surely you should be married and having children?'

His question wasn't intentionally rude, but she replied curtly, 'We Western women don't marry so young, you know.'

He smiled. 'I'm sorry, I didn't mean . . .'

Félix pushed through the crowd. 'Alice, I hate to interrupt this happy reunion, but there'll be a grand confrontation with your brother if you're late.' He held up his watch. 'Fifteen minutes to ten.'

'Oh botheration, and we've only just met. But I'm afraid you're right. I'll tell Will about Han-li . . . but oh dear, I'm not supposed to be here at all. Félix, why is it I always seem to be deceiving people though I never want to?'

'Because you are something of an original, *ma chérie*, you

don't easily fit the mould. But you're not quite original enough to break it altogether, if you see what I mean?'

'Only too well.' She laughed wryly and he patted her arm.

'There are worse fates, I am similar in a way. But come, I really must see you home.'

'Oh dear! Younger Brother, I know—you must come to our family tea on Sunday and meet everyone—my brother, his wife, the children.'

The arrangement was made, though Han-li looked rather anxious about it and Félix, drawing her into the shadow of a verandah on the way home, warned gently, 'This meeting between the Chu lad and your relatives may not be easy, Alice—a great exercise in international diplomacy for you, *hein*? You'll have to be careful.'

'I was just thinking that. It will be so odd to see them together, I'm not sure I'll like it.'

He chuckled, tilting her face to his. 'But it will undoubtedly be interesting, and think, if I'd not taken you to Epimoff's, it might never have happened. So do I not deserve my usual reward, Little Jade?' He began kissing and cuddling her gently, which he regarded as an hors d'oeuvre for his customary Friday visit to the little piece of Chinese porcelain who was waiting for him in nearby Green Peacock Street. Finally he kissed her nose. 'There—does Mr. Jeffrey Winthrop make love to you so nicely?'

Félix was slightly jealous of Jeffrey Winthrop, his counterpart at the British Consulate who'd been courting Alice recently with what Félix considered typical British phlegm. In Jeff's shoes, Félix would have soon made sure of Alice, but he had a fiancée of his own Catholic faith waiting in Tours, not to mention the lady of Green Peacock Street.

Alice tossed her head. 'That's my business is it not, Monsieur Fauré? But he's coming for a picnic on the hills with us tomorrow, so you'd better watch out!'

'Ah, *le pauvre Winnée*, he's somewhat slow, is he not? He'd bore the pretty little socks off you in no time, such a big sack of rugged northern grit!'

Alice giggled; and did again the next morning when they all set off for the hills and she considered the shape of Jeffrey Winthrop riding ahead with William—his solid bottom planted squarely on his horse, his hair, she suddenly thought, very similar in hue to the gritty slope up which they were climbing. Sun sparkled on the wavelets of the distant sea below. The wiry undergrowth was greening and butterflies flickered over it. She sniffed the balmy air and smiled, for spring was her favourite season. On the hill's crest, Will and Jeff waited for the rest of the party: Alice on Griffin, the cook-boy driving a laden donkey, and two covered litters, one for Isabel and Joel, the other for Charlotte and the amah.

'Look down there—quite large trees and even a tinkling brook,' Will pointed. 'What better spot for a picnic?'

On that they all agreed and slithered down into the valley where the cook-boy, resigned to these barbarian follies, unloaded the donkey and the bearers bathed their arms in the water. 'A proper coppice,' Jeff marched about triumphantly. 'Birches in new leaf, alders, gorse, even a bit of grass.' He dug his heels in the tough tufts. 'Reminds me a little of the Dales, know that part of the world, Will?'

'No—but it reminds me of those spinneys near the North Norfolk coast where I used to go on holiday with Aunt Sarah.'

Jeff jeered. 'It's a coppice, not a spinney and it's all Dales!'

Isabel clambered from the litter, brushing dust from her skirt, 'What nonsense you men talk—it's a grove, made for green thoughts in a green shade, ten a penny in the Cotswolds, and the streams smell better there!'

Alice, leading Griffin to water, said tartly, 'Why can't it just be a Chinese wood—as we're in China?'

Isabel smiled gently. 'Oh Alice, I keep forgetting you've not seen the beautiful English countryside yet—meadows of lush grass and wild flowers, the variety of trees. Once you have, you'll understand why we talk so, pretending to be Home for a while.'

Jeff frowned into the budding birches. 'Yes, it's seeing something like this, just familiar enough to make one homesick suddenly. It's more than time you saw the old country, Alice, we'll have to do something about it, don't you think?'

He smiled towards her encouragingly but she was busy with Griffin, for conversations about Home always made her apprehensive and resentful. 'You must come back with us on our next leave,' Isabel had already promised, 'that is, if some handsome young man hasn't already taken you as his blushing bride!' Was that what Jeff had in mind now, Alice wondered, intercepting a meaningful glance between her brother and Isabel.

'Well, we'll not get all melancholy about Dales or

Cotswolds,' Will said briskly. 'As Alice says, it's a Chinese wood and we're about to have a proper Chinese picnic—and you wouldn't get bean-sprout salad at Home, so we should count our blessings!'

They all laughed, then Isabel settled in the shade to feed the baby and William gave Cook-boy a lesson in the art of chicken-carving, while Jeff and Alice mounted again to ride up and look at the hill-top view. As Isabel spooned mush into Joel's mouth, she said, 'Jeff hasn't spoken to you, has he, Will? I wondered when he mentioned Home just now.'

'About Alice? No—I daresay she could nobble him if she tried harder, but I suspect she prefers Félix.'

'Who's oozing with Gallic charm, unlike our solid Jeff from the Dales. Anyway, it's hard to guess what Alice really thinks. You know, we were out walking with Charlotte recently and some of those naval college students greeted her most familiarly, and I wondered then how they knew her. Then last night she tells us she just met this younger Chu son by chance, but I doubt it somehow. She's rather secretive, you know, and I'm not being over-critical I hope, because I love her dearly.'

Will came to kiss her, holding the carving knife playfully at Joel's forehead.

'Papa, don't, he might jump into the knife!' Charlotte squealed.

'I'd like to see him—go and help the boy, Lottie,' and she trotted off, enjoying taking knives, forks and dishes from their padded hamper nests and spreading them around the white cloth.

'Yes, she is secretive, Uncle Robert used to say so—never quite know where you are with her. And I'm not sure it's at all a good thing, this young Chu turning up out of the blue. The real trouble is, she's twenty-three and it's time she was properly settled. Now if Jeff were to propose I'd be all in favour.'

'Well, I doubt if she'd accept. She doesn't look at him in the right way.'

'Oh, you ladies and your looking!'

'But there isn't enough choice for her here, she'd be better off in Shanghai which is bursting with lovelorn young bachelors, I believe.'

William sighed, arranging chicken slices carefully on the plates while the boy watched, apparently lost in admiration. 'But I can't send her to Shanghai without chaperonage and Frank's leading much too wild a life with that horse-racing fraternity to be relied upon . . . Lottie, don't tip the salt on the ground, there's a good girl . . . No, we must wait for something to work itself out.' He looked up the valley where the two had just reappeared, riding leisurely in single file. 'Perhaps something has?'

Isabel, following his gaze, smiled fondly. 'Don't be silly, Will, if any momentous subject had been broached, they wouldn't be returning in that ordinary sort of way.'

Commonsensical Isabel was right of course. Jeff had not proposed, though he had said how he enjoyed riding with Alice and how dull life had been before her arrival. And Alice had been a trifle flirtatious in return, reining close to him at the hill's top where they looked eastward across the glittering sea.

'And beyond the horizon lies the Hermit Kingdom—the last bastion of oriental exclusiveness soon to be broken down because the old king's just been deposed,' Jeff said sententiously. 'The Americans are opening a consulate in Seoul soon and my boss wants to be the first British rep on the scene. He says everyone will have diplomatic relations established within a year.'

'Really? The Koreans I've met don't think so.'

'Oh? Where have you met any, Alice? I can't tell them from Mongols.'

'Their language is awful and they smell of that dreadful pickled cabbage they eat so much. . . . As to where I've met them, wouldn't you like to know, Mr. Winthrop?'

She teased so winningly that he wanted to crush her in his arms and get the truth from her, which he suspected involved that foreign frog Fauré. But his northern caution saved him. 'It's none of my business of course, Alice. . . . Let's go, your brother will have carved the chicken to perfection by now.'

So they had ridden back in their ordinary sort of way to eat the chickens, the salads, Alice's jam tarts, all washed down with claret, and then lounged in the shade of the English-seeming birches while the amah crooned lullabies for the children. As the sun set they had ridden home, and later, as the moon rose, Alice gazed at it from her bedroom window, relieved she had not been pressed towards any decision that day. Jeff Winthrop was pleasant enough, the stuff from which worthy Vice-Consuls are cut, as Will had said in an unguarded moment. But she did not want to be the wife of a life-long Vice-Consul whose grit-coloured hair was already receding to reveal a life-long freckly skull.

So what did she want? Her encounter with Han-li had unleashed the haunting secret memories of lustful beddings with his father. Undressing, she looked sorrowfully at her firm, young, unused body and, shivering with untimely desire, traced faintly on the chilled windowpane the characters Lung-kuang, Dragon Brightness—the only man who had yet penetrated her. Tomorrow, she thought as she climbed into bed, she must discreetly learn more of him from Han-li and oh, how pleased she was to have met him again!

But when he was ushered into the drawing-room the next afternoon her pleasure shrivelled into apprehension as she seemed to see two simultaneous but conflicting scenes. For Han-li, there was large William drawing himself up importantly and smiling with no warmth. Isabel was cool, unknowable, with that dreadfully unnatural-coloured hair, and the children wide-eyed at the idea of a Chinaman come to Sunday tea. And for William there was an undersized student, looking much younger than his twenty-one years in his absurd ill-fitting naval academy suit and twisting his cap in his hands and darting inscrutable glances at them.

Alice made the best of the introductions; Han-li sat on the very edge of a straight chair, and Isabel asked kindly, 'You are studying here at the college, Mr. Chu?'

'Yes,' he mumbled carefully.

'And have you ever been in a real English home before?' William inquired, looking round his heavily furnished room and thinking it must be quite an eye-opener for the lad.

'Yes. In Foochow.'

'Ah . . . We lived there for a while. Quite a fine little dock-yard you Chinese have there now, what?'

Han-li turned to Alice, pleading in his own tongue. 'Uncut Jade, you'll have to help. I've learned a lot of English from books and I can understand, but I can't reply quickly enough, please translate for me. . . .'

After that conversation flowed rather more easily until Isabel took the children to wash before tea and Alice said, 'Will, I must ask Han-li about the family and that's easier for me in Chinese.'

'The family—what an odd expression for you to use. But go ahead, don't mind me.' William began to read a copy of the *Illustrated London News* with ostentatious attention which was distracted nevertheless by the irritating clack of an alien tongue in his Sunday drawing-room.

'Tell me about Tamao and Weng first.' Alice drew her chair closer to his. 'Are they well—and little Custard Apple?'

'Ah yes, they live in tranquillity and lighten the home for everyone. There is another son now—a real scamp. We call him Pepperseed because he shows signs of the Hunanese quick temper already.'

'And Han-fei, Eldest Brother?'

Han-li shrugged. 'He still doesn't please Father—he's so touchy and irresponsible. His new wife is prettier than silly old Dull Thorn, but she too only bears daughters.' He sniggered. 'So he has three now—including the poor little runt who should have died when her mother did.'

'Han-li, what a cruel thing to say!'

He glanced at her. 'But it would have been better. Oh I know you Westerners look at it differently—all babies are sacred, so your missionaries say. But your soldiers think nothing of killing hundreds of babies—and their parents—when they go grabbing other nations' territories.'

Alice bit her lip. 'I suppose I never thought of it quite like that. You're learning the ways of the world fast, Han-li.'

'This is no time for slowness—that's what Father found hard to understand. When I eventually persuaded him to let me study foreign matters he said, "Can you not wait? It will mean losing you forever, my son." And in a sense he was right. I can never go home again, not really.'

He looked at her gloomily and she patted his hand. 'I know just what you mean, Younger Brother, because, when I think of them all—even Vegetable Aunt with her fits and Spots with his ducks—it seems almost like home to me too. A lost home.'

Irritably William threw down his magazine and stalked out saying, 'Tea is served, Alice.'

'I don't think your brother likes me, Uncut,' Han-li whispered.

'Oh it's not you personally—I suppose it's because he's not used to having Chinese to tea.'

Han-li grinned wryly and rose as Alice put a hand on his shoulder.

'And your Honourable Father? Is he healthy? Is he happy? I often think of him kindly . . .'

'Ah yes . . . he has now two sons with his unofficial wife and

251

that gladdens him. But he grows a little weary and it worries him, I think, that Eldest Brother will one day be in charge of the household. How he and Brother-in-law would quarrel!'

'But the Dragon Brightness is not that elderly surely?'

'Not yet—but he shows his few grey hairs with pride and says he wishes he had time to cultivate chrysanthemums as his Honourable Father did before him. The years pass. . . .'

'Yes indeed, and you are a man now, like Frank.'

'Frank, now tell me . . .'

They went in to tea chatting gaily and Alice, ignoring the frost that emanated from her brother, reported defiantly, 'Han-li's been asking about Frank. He's going to call on him in Shanghai when he leaves here. Won't that be a wonderful reunion for them?'

William mumbled noncommittally, thinking it was pretty cool of this Chinese whippersnapper to be claiming friendship on an equal footing with his brother and sister. But they would not see it that way of course. Damn and blast that dreadful Tientsin business; there never seemed to be an end to it. Finishing his second tea-cake, he asked, 'So you're learning something about modern science, are you, young man? It must be a great puzzle? Can you read a compass properly yet?'

Han-li scowled. 'We Chinese have used compasses since the days of the Han dynasty, sir. It's only recently that we've fallen a little behind in these technical matters, but we're catching up fast.'

'Ah yes, I forgot. Still, you've quite a lot of catching up to do at the moment. It seems to me that the vast majority of your countrymen have no desire to learn anything new whatever—poor ignorant wretches. And you few young idealists will find it difficult to drag them into the modern world. Progressive, enlightened civilisations like ours in Britain today are built on solid foundations, you know.'

'And you don't think China has a solid foundation of civilisation?'

Han-li's eyes glinted and Isabel broke in: 'Now, Will, have more cake and stop this political talk, it only causes friction. Cake, Han-li? Now tell me about your father and mother. Are they not curious to visit you and see Treaty Port life for themselves? All the modern changes, the grand buildings and foreign ships?'

Han-li smiled wistfully. 'My father is a very busy man in

252

Hunan; he couldn't be spared, madam. And he wouldn't quite know what to make of it all, would he, Uncut?'

'But your mother, she has more time surely?' Isabel insisted politely.

The very thought of Hidden Glory in Hong Kong made Alice laugh aloud. 'Oh Isabel, no—Han-li's mother only leaves her house two or three times a year. She knows of nothing—nothing beyond Changsha, and precious little of that.'

'But how dreadful, you never told me that, Alice. Really, the way Chinese women are treated.'

'It's different, Isabel. The seclusion seemed cruel to me sometimes and I could never live happily within it, but . . .'

Han-li, partly understanding, added stiffly, 'Please explain to your relative, Uncut, that my mother is quite tranquil in her home. She would be most unhappy in the common bustle of the world that seems so desirable to you Western women.'

Isabel, bridling at his tone, rose abruptly. 'Come children, it's bedtime. Say goodbye to Mr. Chu. He used to play bows and arrows with your Uncle Frank when he was a little boy—isn't that odd to think of?'

Indeed it was and Charlotte and Joel stared in renewed astonishment at Han-li as Isabel and Alice led them away.

William, folding his napkin, wondered how he could make it clear to this young Chinaman that, whatever had happened in the past, he could not expect to be 'one of the family' in this house. 'I hope you enjoyed your first real English tea, Han-li? You must visit us again sometime, though I'm sure you understand that, in my position here, I have to be careful about local contacts?'

Han-li bowed, saying merely, 'The tea was very nice, thank you.'

When Alice returned they moved towards the drawing-room and William decided to reinforce his message. 'I don't suppose you've much time for anything but your studies here, Han-li? And you must stick at them. China's going to need promising young men of vision like you who've realised the errors of the past and broken free from the backward old ways of their families.'

A flush mottled Han-li's sallow cheeks, and the fierce pride of the Sons of Han gave him the ability to say directly in English what had been smouldering in his mind for the past hour. 'You call my country uncivilised and my people ignorant. Our ways are very different—our ways are deep in the past, centuries and centuries. You know nothing about us. My father is an important man, he has power and dignity but you call him backward, and my mother also. You do not want to know me, his son. But when your brother and sister were in our household they were the ignorant, uncivilised barbarians and at that time your brother was grateful to be my horse-groom and your sister my father's woman.'

'What—what did you say?' William grabbed him by the collar while Alice wailed in dismay. 'Oh Younger Brother—what have you said? He didn't know that—oh dear heaven . . .'

Han-li, red and trembling, looked at them both, realising where his fury had led him. He blurted, 'I'm sorry, Uncut, I assumed he knew—and I lost my temper. I cannot stand his attitudes. I must go now, please. . . .'

William shook him. 'Alice, my little sister, and your father. How dare you suggest such a filthy thing?'

'It's true, William. I never told you because you'd have been so shocked. Well now you are. And stop shaking Younger Brother. It wasn't his fault. He was only a boy at the time.'

'And you only a girl, only . . .'

'Fifteen, yes.' Sadly she handed Han-li his cap. 'He'd better go. I suppose it was a mistake his coming here, but I so wanted you all to like each other.'

'Like each other—when his father . . .'

Han-li glowered at William, unrepentant. 'My father is an honourable man, civilised, not backward. He was very kind to the Uncut Jades called Greenwood. Goodbye to you.'

Hearing the front door slam, Isabel rushed down. 'Has he gone? But what's happened?'

Alice's voice trembled with sympathetic rage. 'Han-li couldn't stand any more of your patronising airs and graces about his country and people. And when Will started on his family he lost his temper and I don't blame him. It's never once occurred to you, has it, brother William, that this whole house and everything in it would fit easily into the Chus' courtyard? Oh you just have no notion how proud and fine it all was!'

Her voice broke and she began to sob noisily. Isabel reached for a handkerchief.

'There, there, never mind, Alice. I was afraid this mightn't work out well.'

'But she's not told you the whole—the parting shot from our

dear Younger Brother. Not only was Frank his horse-groom apparently, but Alice was his "father's woman," as he bluntly put it.'

'He said that? Alice—oh dear God—that can't be true surely?'

'Yes Isabel, that's why I ran away from the house.'

'But my dear, how very very dreadful. You just a child and he . . . he forced you to . . .?'

'Yes, but I soon escaped.'

'Oh dear, oh dear. Will, you had your suspicions years ago.' She put an arm on Alice's shaking shoulders. 'But you can't blame her—a mere child and forced to it.'

'No, I can't blame her for that, it's just too horrible to think of. But I certainly do blame her for inviting that insolent lad here, to our house as a friend, after the crime his father committed on her.'

'It was the custom. He didn't see it as a crime at all. No one there did.' She sniffed. 'In their eyes it was far superior to being a skivvy—the other kitchen maids quite envied me.'

Isabel shuddered. 'Oh Alice, how can you think of it in that way? Using innocent girls, keeping them in concubinage, a sort of harem—men like that are not civilised.'

Alice's face flamed. 'Well, what's so civilised about many men of our race? They have their women just the same—I've seen them along the waterfront—miserable creatures often without any homes. At least a proper concubine has a roof over her head. But you're all so hypocritical—pretending such things don't go on among us, that we are whiter than the driven snow compared to the "immoral Chinese" . . . Oh, how I hate that expression, Stepfather used to say it and he . . . ugh!' She shuddered, her tears drying in remembered outrage.

'The men you speak of are foreign sailors and such—the riff-raff of the docks,' William snapped. 'But the subject is closed, Alice. What happened to you was most shocking and you were an innocent victim. It's a thousand pities you weren't completely honest years ago, then this needn't have happened now. Naturally I don't want you ever to see that young Chinaman again—and I say again, you must put the whole unsavoury episode of your captivity right out of your mind. That is the only healthy solution.'

She snorted bitterly. 'Episode—we're talking about years of my life and Frank's.'

William raised his head at a distant wail. 'I hear Lottie crying. Why don't you go and soothe her, Alice? She listens to you.'

'The only one here who does,' Alice muttered as she stormed out and Isabel, shrugging at her husband, followed.

William poured a sherry to steady himself. What a stubborn, argumentative little minx his sister was. No wonder Mother had not tried to get her back to Mukden! So—she was not virginal, somehow he had always suspected it. There was a look in her eyes sometimes. He began to speculate on what had actually occurred in the house of the Chu. Dragon Brightness—ugh! Had Alice really been one of several women in his harem, draped in soft silks, smoothing him wherever he wished, satisfying his every whim? His skin tingled. How much did his sister know about the pleasures of the flesh? Perhaps more than he did. The thought disturbed him profoundly and, for the first time since her arrival, he devoutly wished his sister would go away.

In spite of William's prohibition Alice looked for Han-li at Epimoff's the next Friday and, when he did not appear, sent a note via his friend begging him to come the following week. In the interim, she rehearsed how she could soothe his wounded pride, convince him that she shared none of her relatives' stupid prejudices. And, when Friday came again, Han-li was indeed there, but bursting with eager importance and saying, before she could open her mouth, 'Uncut Jade, I'm to take you to the Leader at once. He's asked me to . . .'

'The Leader? But why ever should he . . .?'

'I don't know. I happened to mention my meeting you again. I didn't tell him everything, don't worry. And he simply instructed me to bring you this evening. One doesn't ask a man like him questions.'

Alice turned in puzzlement to Félix. 'I should go, Alice. There can be no harm, he's a respected college lecturer, and you may learn some interesting political tittle-tattle. But back before ten . . .'

Han-li and Alice bowled along in rickshaws to the old quay where fishing junks were moored near some seedy, two-storey dwellings with overhanging verandahs. He led her up a narrow stair, knocking carefully on a door. 'One and two, three-four-five—the special knock for the Leader's friends,' Han-li whispered as the door opened and the man stood looking at her.

First her scalp, then her whole skin prickled with excitement as if she had known all along who it would be, but dared not think who, inevitably, it was.

'Uncut Jade,' he said softly. 'So we meet again, as I knew we would.'

'Lin Fu-wei, the man on the *Mandalay*,' she gasped.

'You haven't forgotten me surely?' He sounded quite shocked.

'No—but I'm surprised to see you here.'

'And I you—till Han-li told me of his reunion with a certain English girl called Uncut Jade who once lived in captivity in his household. . . . But why didn't you tell me that when we first met?' He drew her courteously inside, saying, 'Thank you, student-boy, it is indeed she. You may go now, but return at the right time to escort her back.' Han-li bowed reverently and fled.

Lin had filled out in stature and bearing since their earlier meeting. His face showed signs of authority, though his eyes were still as bold and quick, his mouth as full and mobile. His room was simply furnished with every chair piled high with books; a writing-desk stood in the verandah window. As he cleared a seat for her, she noticed his hands were trembling and guessed why, for she too was tongue-tied, remembering his exciting nearness as they had talked on the *Mandalay* deck, and his words at their parting. He was considering her carefully.

'You are a grown woman now, Uncut Jade, but you are still Miss Greenwood and unmarried?'

'Yes—it is not a disgrace to be single among us, you know . . . we aren't like the Chinese,' she murmured.

He grinned. 'I am aware of that, Miss Greenwood, or Uncut Jade as I hope I may still call you? I'm sure one so charming would easily find a husband if she chose.'

There was an embarrassed pause till Alice said, 'And you have grown into a position of importance now, Lin? The students call you Leader, do they not? When they spoke of you at Epimoff's I wondered why they used that title—in English?'

'But don't you remember at our very first encounter I told you I wanted to be a leader of the nation? I could tell you didn't take me seriously, but I kept the name in English to remind myself of the ambition I first expressed to you.'

She flushed with pleasure. 'I'm glad I helped in my small

way. But now, five years later, how does leadership feel, Lin?'

'Ah that is the trouble—I'm not a leader of the people at all, only a college lecturer with bright new ideas that I can't knock into my addlepated students! It is all so much more complicated than I thought then . . .' He cleared another chair and sat down. 'There is so much stubborn, deep-rooted conservatism in this country, so many die-hards in powerful positions. I've recently returned from Peking where I met an American, Mr. Martin, who runs a school for the acquiring of Western knowledge, the T'ung-wen Kuan.'

'I've heard of him. Wasn't he once a missionary? My stepfather says he's been seduced from the true Way by the false dawn of modern science.'

'Huh, the stuffy, old-fashioned missionary view . . . No, Mr. Martin's a good man, but getting so dispirited by us reactionary Chinese. I'll give you an example—recently he wanted to teach his students how to operate a telegraph system and had one sent over especially from America. When he demonstrated it to some officials in Peking they thought it was just a great big joke! They were blind to its potential, his students won't soil their hands with it—so now it's mouldering in a school cupboard. He showed it to me there and I felt sad and ashamed.'

'I'm sorry, yes I can see how difficult it must be—you with original ideas among so many without.'

She listened spellbound by that vehement conviction which had first attracted her. 'That one cannot separate the process of change and industrialisation from the fundamental culture of a country. That you in the West believe in this abstraction called "modern progress" which grows naturally from your civilisation. Now we Sons of Han have a totally different civilisation and we don't basically understand or believe in this progress of yours. It is an alien ideal, perhaps we don't even need it in the same way. The government sent me to England and there I . . .'

'You—Lin, you've been to England?'

'Yes, I studied in your famous naval college near London, at Greenwich. . . . But I'm still a bad linguist.' He smiled ruefully.

'But . . . oh, that's dreadful . . . oh . . .' She jumped up in agitation. That she, a true-born English girl, had never been Home, yet the government sent him. It gave him a tremendous advantage and a different dimension altogether. It was, she

258

obscurely felt, terribly unfair. Bad enough listening to her relatives discoursing on the different sorts of English wood, but that Lin also had seen them was too much!

He was watching her in puzzlement. 'I thought you'd be pleased that I've been there but you look downright angry?'

'I'm—just envious I suppose. Everyone pities me for not having been yet, you see.'

'But you'll go soon, with your relatives or your husband when you deign to marry?'

'Oh that's the trouble with being a woman!' she scowled fiercely. 'You always have to wait for a man—relatives or husbands—to make things happen. Why can't I just go Home alone if I want? Or why won't the government send me?' She was teasing now, trying to dissolve her vexation. 'I could be so useful—there aren't many foreigners as fluent with Chinese as I am.'

'Ah that's true enough,' he put a calming hand on her shoulder. 'You're a white jade of rare value, Miss Greenwood. And putting aside the claims of the government which has its own translators, think how you could help me and my students. . . . You see these books? They're full of new, fascinating ideas that we Chinese need to fully comprehend. I struggle with them, but I'm ashamed how poor my English is . . .' Endearingly helpless, he held out a copy of J. S. Mill's treatise on Liberty. 'The sagacious Yen-fu is intending to translate this, for example. But he's hampered and overworked as I am . . . Now if only you . . .' She flipped through the heavy tome.

'I don't know, I mean I've never read this. It looks difficult even in English.'

'But you are unusually intelligent for a woman, Miss Greenwood. I always remembered how interested you were in my ideas. Surely books written in your own tongue wouldn't daunt you? And you could learn from them too, as I try to . . .'

She opened a page he had marked, and translated, ' "The despotism of custom is everywhere a standing hindrance to human advancement." '

'Ah yes, and he talks of the Chinese in that context and what exactly does he say?'

'That their sages and philosophers "impress the best wisdom they possess upon every mind in the community, but they've been stationary for thousands of years, government for them is a staying still . . . If they are ever to be improved it

259

must be by foreigners." '

'There—just as I was saying. Now when your thinkers make arrogant statements of this nature we need to understand exactly why they do—what to accept, what to reject. And you will help me in this, won't you?'

Her eyes shone. 'Oh Lin, it would be grand, but how am I to?'

'We'll think of a way,' he said, and in fact already had, for it was soon arranged that she should meet his college principal who would formally hire her to teach the advanced students and help Lin with translations. 'And we'll work together at the texts, here or at the college,' he added.

'But I'm so afraid my brother won't approve, especially since . . .' she trailed off vexedly.

'He's in the Maritime Customs, is he not? I made it my business to find out when I learned your identity.'

'And if you'd come to Epimoff's we'd have met sooner.'

'Well, the place sounded rather a waste of time—people just drinking and vaguely theorising, I believe? Of course, if I'd known you were sometimes there . . .'

'You'd have come?'

'Yes,' he said deliberately, consulting his French pocket watch. 'But student-boy will soon return for you. As for your brother, don't worry, we'll find a way to him. There's bound to be a little unofficial help we can give, you understand . . .?'

She nodded, though she didn't really understand. Indeed, she didn't bother to understand anything much just then except that he had come back into her life and that all the attraction she'd felt for him at their first meeting had returned in double measure. Here, at last, was a man of conviction, and she yearned to share his certainties; a man with new ideas, and she loved the way his eyes flashed with the passion of them. Lying in bed that night, wide awake, her mind was full of him— what he had said and how he had looked. She longed to know him better, to discuss with him some of her own ideas that had been hardly formed when they first met. Most of all, she wanted to feel again the thrill of his warm and assured presence beside her, and, as she drifted into sleep, she felt him getting closer, until he was holding her gently, then tightly, until he was deep inside her.

Lin had promised somehow to arrange their working together, but how, she could not imagine until one evening the next week, when William announced that he'd been called in unexpectedly that morning to see the principal of the naval college.

'He was most unusually friendly and confidential,' Will reported rather proudly. 'Seemed keen to get my opinion on the plans for the shipyard and the coastal defences.'

'Did he say anything else?' Alice interrupted eagerly.

'About what?'

'About me.'

'He—mentioned you, yes. I suppose he'd heard of you through the Chu lad.'

'What did he say?'

William looked uneasy. 'Never mind what he said, Alice.'

'But I do mind. It's not nice to be talked of behind one's back, you say so yourself.'

'He simply referred to your excellent knowledge of Chinese. I suppose Han-li had told him.'

'And?'

'Oh you're so abominably persistent, Alice. It's not at all ladylike. He asked if you might be interested in doing some translating and teaching there, if you must know.'

'And what did you say?'

'I said you would not. It all sounded extremely dull anyway.'

'But how dare you—just like that, as if you had a right to speak for me. You're my brother, not my keeper, you know, and I've got a tongue of my own.'

'That I never doubted for a moment.'

They had been sitting waiting for the supper bell when William had made his announcement and, at the first hint of trouble, Isabel had slipped out to avoid acting the mediator between the two yet again. Alice drew herself up, strong with a sense of utterly justified indignation. 'It's just the chance I wanted. Here I am—one of the few English in the entire Empire with an absolutely thorough grasp of the Mandarin and the colloquial, written and spoken—and doing nothing whatever with it. At last I can be of some use and earn a little money of my own besides—and I'm going to.'

'You are not because I forbid it.'

'And what right have you to?'

'You are living in my house and under my protection and I have every right.'

'Then I shall leave your house and your protection, as you call it, this instant!'

261

He groaned. 'Alice, calm down please.'

'Calm down yourself.' She was busily collecting together her embroidery tapestry and silks as if about to carry out her threat.

'You know my reasons very well. I simply won't let you mix any more than is necessary with the natives. After what has happened to you in the past it's simply not—fitting. I don't thoroughly trust you in that regard, to be honest.'

'And what do you mean by that?'

He quailed slightly at the intensity of her passion. 'What I say. I think you could easily be led astray—in several directions. You are young, vulnerable and rather too sympathetic towards the Chinese generally.'

'And that's a sin, is it? To be sympathetic towards the people I've lived among all my life?' She had her work-bag over her arm now, ready for immediate departure, and her voice was controlled. 'William, I've thrown myself utterly on the mercy of this land and its people three times before, and I'm quite ready to do it again now. Either you'll allow me to make some good use at last of the only real skill I have—or I shall go to the college tomorrow, take both the work offered and a room in their teachers' hostel, and move in there—much as I should hate to hurt Isabel and leave the children. I shall do it, Will. Short of putting me under lock and key, you couldn't stop me.'

He knew defeat at her hands as he had before and, as before, reluctant admiration mingled with his chagrin. 'Yes I fear you would—if only to spite us.'

'I don't want to spite you, Will, only to have a say in the conduct of my own life.'

He grunted, preferring not to rise to that. 'I'll find out from the principal exactly what he has in mind and then, perhaps—strictly on a short-term, part-time basis, mind . . . At least it will enable me to maintain contact with the college and that could prove useful.'

Two weeks later Alice was appointed as a temporary tutor to the senior students and translation adviser to Mr Lin Fu-wei, lecturer in Western science and philosophy. She enjoyed the teaching, and the students treated her with rare deference, but better yet was the translating work with Lin. Excited both by the ideas in the European texts they studied and by his warm physical proximity at the writing-desk they shared in his lodgings, time passed all too quickly, and she was always reluctant to leave at the stipulated hour.

He went to open the verandah lattice, staring down at the sun-drenched sea. 'Huh—it's too hot to think properly anymore . . . You know, Alice, my dilemma is simple. If I express my own nature at the expense of others—and there is no other way of doing so—I am but a vulgar and ignoble brute, as Confucius says!'

Alice joined him. 'It's the same with me. Often I have to dissemble, to deny my real nature because I'm allowed no space to develop it truly and freely.'

He turned in surprise, unaccustomed to the moral problems of womankind. 'Really? But what is it you want that is not in accord with the moral laws of your society, Uncut?'

'I want—oh so much. Freedom to travel and work at what I like, to meet different sorts of people in my own way. I want to be bolder and more ambitious, like a man, I suppose.'

He put a hand on her neck. 'Come, Miss Greenwood, you've been reading too much philosophy. You wouldn't want to be a man surely? You're much too pretty as you are!'

'No, not be anyone else really, but have more liberty to be myself, as Mill says.'

'Ah sweet liberty, and how would you use it at the moment, little Uncut? Perhaps as I would—in a fashion that isn't entirely in harmony with the moral laws of either East or West.'

As he drew her into his arms, her voice quivered, 'Yes . . . I think, I'm afraid that . . .'

'Don't be afraid, my green jewel, for haven't our bodies made up our minds for us in this one direction at least? Perhaps Mr. Mill would approve, I don't know, nor at the moment do I care . . .' He closed the lattice and half-carried her to his narrow bed; his lips moved over her face and neck as he fumbled with the unfamiliar fastenings of her dress and bodice. She smiled, helping him until he could gather her bare breasts in his hands. 'Ah they are full and lovely as I often thought of them—like plump white gourds topped with luscious cherries.' He licked her nipples.

'But are they too big?' She was a trifle disconcerted by his comparison.

'Bigger than any I've known, but then I've never before fondled the breasts of a Western woman.'

The very idea fired him; with trembling hands he pulled off the rest of her clothes and, slipping easily from his loose robe, spread her thighs and thrust urgently into her before she was ready. Then he withdrew, struggling for control. 'Ah—I am much too excited. I must pause.' He caressed her again and she clung to him tightly. 'My dear little Uncut, you are the only barbarian I've ever wanted.'

'Did you then—when we first met?'

'Yes, but my desire was unformed and seemed almost unnatural; I was a little ashamed, to be truthful. And you?'

'I'd but recently come from the bed of Lung-kuang in the house of Chu, so it seemed natural enough to me then. It was only later I learned the shame. But this between us now is not at all like that, is it, Lin?' She moved under him happily.

'Of course not, we shall be lovers in the modern way and there is no shame in it, my sweet Jade. And now you are with me, are you not? Your red flowers have begun to open and burn?'

'Yes, oh yes my darling.' He poised over her erect, raised her legs high round his waist and went deep inside her till she cried out, kissing and biting his shoulder joyously.

After their union when they had sponged away the dampness of heat and sex, they stood in the verandah watching the sun set. 'Oh Lin,' she grasped his hand, 'we must be so careful, no one must ever suspect this, must they? I daren't imagine what my relatives would think—or the people at the college. It's all very well for Mill to talk about "intelligent deviations from custom," but not so easy in practice, is it?'

He kissed her forehead. 'Exactly so—you see what I guessed in the abstract is already proving true in the personal and particular. We've just enjoyed the liberty of our own impulses—in spite of prohibition, but it would be most foolish to take a public stand in the cause of the future betterment of mankind . . . At least I won't!'

'Nor would I,' she shuddered at the thought, turning into his arms. 'Yet I still want you and don't feel ashamed either, just a little worried.'

'There's no need, so long as we behave as if nothing untoward had happened. And so you must go as usual now.'

'And come next week as usual?'

'Indeed yes—at the same time, but not, alas, before and I hope not later.'

As she walked along the quayside all her senses were quiveringly alive. The junks were setting out for a night's fishing.

Globules of lantern light illuminated the ships' masts and the figures of the men below who were banging about with baskets. There was the smell of fish offal, seaweed, kerosene, the swish of ropes casting off as boats nosed into the dark waves like antediluvian monsters. Primitive craft, Lin said of them dismissively, doomed as the dinosaur in the new world of steamships. But there, 'Things never are the same for ever, nor even for as long as we think they will be,' this also he had said and it was unquestionably true. Her world had changed often already and now it had taken a new direction that she both desired and feared. Her flesh still tingled with the joy of it, but her thoughts sheered away from the new deceptions it would involve. And how could this intimacy possibly turn out well? Even then, right at the beginning, she dreaded the end, feared pain, loss, disgrace, tried hopelessly to imagine how they could be avoided. The only way would be to withdraw now, before the sweet tangle of their lust and love enmeshed her. As she left the sound of the night sea and headed for the Customs House she almost persuaded herself into this prudent resolve, and yet, at a deeper level, she knew she would not and could not keep it.

And nor did she, for once back in Lin's room with his warm eyes and light hands upon her, her only resolve was to enjoy him and be enjoyed, to love and be loved for the first time in her life. The pace of their studies slackened considerably during the long hot afternoons of that summer as the intensity of their lovemaking increased. Entwined on the narrow bed, touching each other towards further excitement, Lin would murmur snatches of popular love poetry:

> Her robe is a cloud, her face a flower,
> Her balcony glimmering with bright spring dew
> Is either the tip of earth's Jade mountain
> Or a moon-edged roof of Paradise . . .

And she, unable to respond in kind, would rub her face against his chest, delighted by such Oriental extravagances.

Lin, proud of his lover's prowess, encouraged her to compare his lovemaking with that of Lung-kuang. 'But I cannot,' she giggled, 'I was so young then too.'

'But was his organ bigger than mine? Of the same mushroom-shape?'

'I don't remember, dear, does it matter?'

He squeezed her nipples. 'Not really, I suppose. Do you know, there was an Empress Wu long ago who had a lover whose stem was so big and strong she called it the "Wonderful Thing" and said the whole Empire was less valuable by comparison. But then she took another lover whose organ was small and she called it her "Little Monk"—but he was as active and subtle as a snake in his thrusting and it was he she made her Imperial Adviser.'

Alice moved her loins against him. 'I don't compare you with a snake or a dragon-brightness, my darling, just be my wonderful thing—that's all I ask!'

As they lay quiescent after their vigorous and tender unions he would talk to her about his family—of his proud, sad, aristocratic father who was disillusioned by the present state of China and harked back to the glorious ancient days, of his spendthrift younger brother who had gone into trade, and of his much-loved mother who kept the old-style family life going. He spoke too of his brief stay in England where he had seen so much to amaze him: cows moving in those lush meadows, railway stations and horse-buses, carriages in Hyde Park; the busy docks on the Thames, and people splashing about in the sea at Brighton just for the fun of it.

He asked little of her in return for he was not used to women's confidences and she was disinclined to speak, for her life seemed thin and pointless in comparison. So she simply cuddled close, listening, aware that all too soon the sunlight through the lattice would fade and she would have to leave—carrying her books in an innocent bag, all signs of their heated dishevelments expunged.

It was with this customary demeanour she returned home in the dusk of a late summer evening and came upon Isabel sewing in the drawing-room. Her auburn curls glowed under the lamp and she looked, as always, orderly and calm. She smiled, asked Alice if the translating was going well, said supper would soon be ready and then, rummaging in her workbox, added, 'Oh Alice, I've a bit of news for you—I think you should be the second to know, after William that is.'

'What is it, what's wrong?' Alice guiltily assumed the news must be bad.

'Nothing wrong—I'm going to have another child, that's all.'

'Isabel—how lovely, for you and for Will!' She kissed her

warmly, feeling, as always, a secret tug of ambivalence on the subject of birth—what she had lost, what she was even now risking. She asked lightly, 'So which do you want? A sister for Charlotte or a brother for Joel?'

'I don't much mind, but a girl would be called Polly after my favourite aunt, and a boy Thomas after your father—Will and I were just discussing it, and he wants your father to have a namesake.'

'I'm so glad he thought of it—and Mother would be pleased too.'

'Oh yes, talking of your mother, this news has made us decide to make the effort to go to Mukden at last before I find travelling difficult. As Will says, it's too bad that she's not clapped eyes on me or the children yet and we've not met your stepfather.'

Alice groaned at the word. 'Come, dear, I know you don't care for him and he sounds dreadfully straitlaced and missionary, but he must have some redeeming features, so we'll go and find out—all of us.'

Alice backed in alarm. 'But not me—you'd have to drag me every inch of the way!'

'Yes, Alice, of course you too. I know you had deep disagreements with them, but that's all over and done with now, and it's silly for families to harbour bad feelings.'

'No, I just can't see him—or that place again. You don't fully understand, Isabel, and I can't fully explain. But I won't go.'

'But, Alice, just think how disappointed your mother and the twins will be if you don't come with us!'

'There's another thing, the college term begins next week and I can't possibly be away then.'

'But, Alice, that's only a little job and . . .'

'Oh yes, all my jobs are little, aren't they? Well, I won't let my students down and I *won't go*.'

The supper bell rang and Isabel folded her sewing with a sigh. 'I can't think what your brother will say—we'll only be there a fortnight because the journey takes so long, so for that short time you could surely bury the hatchet?'

'No, I wish you joy of the place and him, and I'm sorry not to see Mother; but I won't go, whatever you or Will say.'

And though William said quite a lot on the subject it was of no avail and on a bright September morning two weeks later

Alice rose early to see them all off in the Customs House mule carts. As the sound of the wheels faded she looked round the walled courtyard where pots of chrysanthemums and daisies bloomed and stretched her arms above her head with a glow of delight. Dearly as she loved her relatives, it was so pleasurable to be alone for a change, to be the sole mistress of a house. What would it be like actually to live alone? she wondered. How free one could be—going out at odd times, entertaining whomever one liked. And why should she not entertain now? The cook and boy were still here, with little to do. She plucked three chrysanthemums—bronze, ruby, white—imagined them gracing the centre of the dining table with her at its head in her polonaise dress and her guests around her—Félix and Jeff, Olga Epimoff, dear Han-li, Harry and Bella of whom she had grown quite fond, and at her right hand, Lin of course. Oh, it would be so much more fun than the usual stuffy collection of consular and customs officials. Why could she not do things like that sometimes? Because she lived as a dependant in her brother's house; because respectable unmarried young ladies did not have their own establishments. But one day, when she and Frank were rich and living in Shanghai, they would have magnificent dinner-parties with people of various nationalities and Lin, her acknowledged lover, would bring the leading Chinese intellectuals of the day to her table. She tripped indoors, arranging the flowers in a vase and imagining how the conversation would flow at her ideal dinner-party.

When she left the college that morning, Lin fell into step beside her. 'Let's go to a fish restaurant I know near the docks,' he suggested. 'You don't have to hurry back, do you, for your relatives have gone to Mukden.'

She gasped, 'You always seem to know what goes on in our house before we do ourselves.'

'It's part of our Oriental mysteriousness—we get messages through the air much quicker than those through the telegraph wires you Westerners have just put up between Tientsin and Shanghai!'

'Oh fiddle-de-dee—you just have your spies everywhere!' And that was nearer the truth for it happened that Lin's houseboy was a relative of the Greenwoods' cook and both were eminently bribable.

'Moreover,' he continued, 'I hear your Customs House food

is excellent but for the next month you've no one to share it with. Will you not invite me to supper tomorrow, Uncut Jade? You've seen my humble abode many times, but I've never seen yours.'

At first it seemed an outrageous idea, but then, remembering her day-dream of that morning, she laughed recklessly. 'Yes why not? Why shouldn't you come? You're a very respectable college lecturer after all! Tomorrow—at seven.'

At first the difference that the unfamiliar setting made took them both unawares. She was carefully dressed for the occasion in a peacock-blue gown with a low neckline and drooping pagoda sleeves, and he too looked different in a dark stiff Western suit usually reserved for college functions. They sipped sherry awkwardly like strangers and Lin prowled about examining the ornaments and family portraits on the drawing-room tables, then stared at her with a heavy intensity that was both tantalising and vexing. 'I've never seen you look like that before.'

'In this evening gown, you mean? But you've been in England and know what women wear there.'

'Yes, and it's foreign. I never supposed you could look like that.'

He came over and squeezed her encased waist. 'I sometimes wondered in England how hard women's waists were, but never found out.' He began kissing her fiercely, murmuring, 'Oh you foreign bitches show off your shapes—your bulges and curves. Tying yourselves so tightly . . .' He prodded her stays and bodice in a mood of sudden hostility laced with heady desire. 'A fashion meant to tantalise poor men, I suppose?'

She moved away. 'I don't know about tantalise, but men of my acquaintance don't behave like this before supper.'

'Only after—when they've gazed their fill at every part on display I suppose?' Again he grabbed her and again she broke away. 'Oh stop it, please. Don't you like this dress and this room then? You wanted to come, remember!'

He slumped in a chair and began examining the contents of Isabel's workbox. 'I forgot how flaunting foreign women can look, that's all.'

'It's not flaunting, it's just the fashion—but you don't like it?'

He shrugged. 'I am Chinese. Our women don't show off for men in this way.'

'But they bind up their feet to make themselves desirable and that's worse.'

'And you bind your waists so tightly for the same reason. What's the difference?'

'Look, I'll go and change if you want, or you can leave. This isn't a bordello, if that's what you're thinking.'

'No, no, Uncut, keep the dress on, it's very attractive, as I've told you in my fashion. And it will serve as a reminder of the strange temptations of the West. How foreign it is—and you are, to me. Give me another sherry and I'll behave like a proper English gentleman, I promise. But eventually you'll let me unlace that tight little middle, won't you?' he added in a whisper and she had to smile with the pleasure of him, as they allowed the tension to cool.

At the supper table, arrayed with the best silver and a bowl of chrysanthemums, Lin tried half-apologetically to explain himself. 'You see, Little Jade, I deal mostly with the abstractions of your Western civilisation and find much to admire, as you know, particularly the methods you've devised to make the wishes of the masses known to their rulers. But then, when I encounter certain Western-style realities, I'm slightly shocked, almost threatened, and my pride in our Celestial Empire reasserts itself. Do you understand?'

'Partly—but threatened, here in your own country?'

Meditatively he traced with his finger the pattern on the silver flower-bowl. 'I think it is this casual prosperity, these small but certain statements of your imperial power. Much of it dependent on quite ordinary materials like coal, iron, and oil which won't last forever of course. But for the present your people enjoy much economic security compared to ours. And the struggle for existence is being generally replaced by the struggle for more enjoyment, more possessions, is it not? I look around—amazed to see how much is considered necessary for your family's comfort, yet your brother is quite an ordinary, run-of-the-mill Customs Officer.'

'But surely you don't think it nobler to spend one's life just struggling to exist as many Chinese do?'

'No, but what happens to people when they get more money? My family is quite wealthy but our tastes are discreet as have befitted our class for generations. But in the Treaty Ports you find the Chinese nouveau-riche—isn't that what the French say? They are despised by our scholar-gentry for their lavish habits, they have no political influence or standing and are given few opportunities to improve themselves. Yet we

270

need more young men of confidence and ability from all classes of society—Wang T'ao, an early reformer, wrote that twenty years ago, and it's still true. These things depress me, Uncut, as I sit at your table,' he smiled at her wryly.

'So you are rude and pounce on me as if I were to blame? But what about the Japanese, Lin? Jeff Winthrop was talking about them recently. They seem to be adapting very quickly to Western ways and the Meiji Government is full of men of ability, so Will said.'

'Oh the Japanese—pushy, conceited, shallow-minded dwarf-pirates! And I hear they've taken to your silly games and fashions—billiards, lawn-tennis and their women wearing those ridiculous bulges over their bottoms.'

'Oh bustles—yes, I suppose they are rather absurd. But you're certainly hard to please in the matter of ladies' dress, sir.'

He leaned across to stroke her cheek. 'It's what lies beneath the garment that really interests me, jewel.'

She glanced round anxiously. 'Hush, Lin . . . the servants.'

But the servants had discreetly vanished from the scene, almost as if they knew, which indeed they did, exactly what was going on. Lin led her quietly up the stairs, pausing at the top, 'Show me your brother's room, Uncut.'

She opened the door, the lamplight falling on the heavy flowered quilt of the double bed. 'Ah—truly spacious, designed for the couplings of large barbarians, is it not?' He bounced down on it, holding out his arms. 'The very place to unleash the generous breasts of the lovely green-eyed foreign devil!'

'Oh Lin no, not here—we must go to my room . . .'

He pulled her to him, smothering her protests with kisses until the novelty, the recklessness of it fired them both as they tumbled in a state of disarray and soon of nudity on the flowery quilt and at length they slept—entwined in a sticky heap under the fine linen sheets.

The next month passed in a happy dream for them both, each utterly absorbed in the other, filled with an urgent, insatiable need for each other's presence, feel, taste, smell, look, a passion that seemed to grow remorselessly with every meeting. And they met constantly in a way they had never done before; walking and working together, eating and sleeping together, and several times stealing away to the little wood in the hills where they nestled under the birch trees. Often the spacious delights of the barbarian bed drew Lin to the house late in the evening and he came to the side gate, conveniently left open by the cook, and crept upstairs where Alice waited in a fever of excitement and guilt. Their passion, always strong, was the more intense because they knew this period of completely abandoned union was brief and dangerous and must end when Will and Isabel returned to reclaim their bed and regularise Alice's life.

And so the night came, when after their lovemaking, Alice whispered that he must not come again. 'I must go to Epimoff's as usual tomorrow evening, and then they're due back.' She stroked his head sadly.

He turned in her arms, mumbling, 'Such a shame, we are so well together here. But that is the way with human joy, as Li-po says, "ten thousand things run away forever like water towards the east." I wish I could offer you a double bed in my humble place—but you'll come next week as usual?'

'Of course, my precious.' They held each other close and he crept away before dawn as was his custom.

But, on returning from Epimoff's the next evening, she was surprised: Lin stepped from the shadow of the door. 'Uncut— let me come with you, just one more night here.' He pressed inside the hall. 'It's a waste of that good bed to remain empty.'

'But Lin it's risky, they are due tomorrow. . . .'

'Ah tomorrow is tomorrow, tonight, tonight—where's your philosophy, dear?' Her small resistance melted as he ran his hands down her body and they stole upstairs like guilty children.

It was about three in the morning when the Customs cart came into the courtyard and William congratulated the driver on the speed of their progress. He roused his wife, 'Now wasn't I right? Much better to carry on even at this hour than spend another night in a foul inn.'

She yawned. 'Yes dear, I suppose, certainly we've made good time. Now you and the nurse carry the children in and straight to bed, they're so sleepy, poor mites.' They went quietly inside and lit a lamp in the drawing room. 'I'll just take my cloak upstairs, then make a nice cup of tea for us . . .'

Alice sprang awake in instant panic at the sound of steps on the stairs. 'Lin, I think there's someone . . .'

The door opened and Isabel came in with a lamp. 'Why

Alice—you, in here and . . .' Her voice rose to a little shriek as she saw the black head rising from the other white pillow. 'William—William—come here at once, it's Alice and . . . she's, oh my God, I can't believe it, William . . .'

He pounded upstairs, terrified that his sister had been murdered, and there the two of them were, holding the bedclothes round their nakedness, Lin's normally sallow face a deep red, Alice, pale and crying out, 'Isabel, oh, I'm so sorry . . . that you should see . . . oh, what have I done? Oh please, please go away for a minute and let us put something on.'

'But Alice—who is this, this native—you here with a man, a *native*, in our house, our very bed?' William passed a hand over his eyes to wipe out the sight. Then he roared, 'Who the hell are you—you fornicator? Get out of here—'

'Yes, can, but clothes . . .' Lin's English broke completely under the strain as he reached for his nether garments.

Isabel took William's arm, 'Come away for heaven's sake, it's too dreadful to look at . . . so upsetting . . . Let them dress.'

'You—fellow—I'll see you downstairs in five minutes.' Will slammed out.

'Oh dear God, oh help me, oh Lin what have we done?' Alice quivered under the sheet like a terrified animal as he fumbled with his clothes.

'It's my fault I fear, Uncut. If only I hadn't returned tonight. It was greedy of me, and I'm terribly terribly sorry . . . I'll tell your brother I led you astray for you are younger. And I'll tell him who I am—at least he should be glad to know I'm not just a bounder off the streets!'

'But, Lin, what if he throws me out?'

'Oh he mustn't, can't do that. He's a kind man, you always said so. But I must go and face him; it is only right. I'll take what blame I can, I promise . . .' He did not touch her but rushed out with a set face now turned unnaturally pale.

Alice cowered in the bed, feeling sick and weak, listening to the bawling of the thoroughly awakened children. The front door slammed and Will came up the stairs. She met him at the door in her nightgown and they stared at each other in silence for a moment. 'I'm very sorry, Will, it was terribly wrong of me to let this happen here—in your house. I know it was. But you mustn't think it's just a casual sordid thing between Lin and me. He's a very intelligent, charming person and . . . I love him, Will, truly I love him . . .' Her voice broke.

'You what, Alice? Love—a young native like that? It's quite loathsome to think of—this shameful, horrible infatuation between you, and that it should have gone this far, and in my house. I'm utterly shocked, utterly disgusted. I'm ashamed of you as I've never been in my life before. You were terribly corrupted in your youth, my girl, and now it's all coming out— like a festering sore! No, it's no use your saying another word. Go to your room at once. We're wretchedly tired after the journey and as for my poor dear wife, to have returned to a scene like this! She's crying her heart out—she, who's always treated you like a sister, and you repay her, us—with this flagrant immorality, it's . . .'

'Oh please stop, William, please, I can't bear it.' She reached for him wildly, but he brushed her furiously aside.

'Get to your room, I tell you. But I'll just say this, there'll be no more talk of love—it's lust, disgusting animal lust you've succumbed to. And, as I told Mr. what's-his-name Lin, you are never never to see him again. I had grave doubts about your college activities all along and how right I was. If you don't obey me absolutely in this, Alice, I'll throw you straight out into the streets, where I'm beginning to think you belong!'

He clattered downstairs, leaving her looking into the shadows of the hall and shuddering. And there rang in her head not only her brother's harsh words, but her own sad ones—'I love him,' she had told William. Now she was forbidden ever to see him again.

Breakfast next morning was late and sombre. The children were fretful after their late night, the two women pale and red-eyed. William studied with elaborate attention the mail that had accumulated in his absence, only looking up to snap, 'Quiet, Joel' at his son, who had just discovered that beating a spoon on a bowl made a nice noise.

Not until he was about to leave for his office did Alice venture, 'Well at least you might tell me about Mother and the twins? I still care for them, you know.'

He grunted. 'Oh—er, yes. How did we find them, Isabel? Healthy I suppose you'd say, though Mother looks worn out.'

'And the children so peaky and whey-faced,' Isabel added. 'They need building up and some good sea-air. Your step-father keeps Adam grinding away at his studies for hours and the whole place is so shabby and comfortless and grim—you know of course.'

'And what did you think of Stepfather?'

Will shuffled his papers in silence till Isabel upbraided him: 'Come Will, don't pretend you've changed your opinion on that score just because . . . We didn't, couldn't like him, could we? He's overbearing and harsh and his views are extremely bigoted in every respect.'

'He's the worst kind of missionary, I must agree,' Will snorted. 'All that prayer and effort to try and save the soul of some poor leprous beggar he's got there, while he makes life a misery for his own family—ugh! We left as soon as we decently could.' He glowered at his sister, remembering the result of that. 'I must go, there's a lot to catch up on.'

As Isabel wiped Joel's fingers, Alice began timidly, 'Please, I'm terribly sorry, truly. You've always been so good and kind to me, and I'm more ashamed about upsetting you than anything else. Please forgive me if you can! I must tell you, as I told Will last night, that I truly love Lin. Doesn't that excuse it a little in your eyes?'

Isabel frowned, picking up her son to hug. 'I'm not really narrow-minded, Alice—not in the missionary way, as you know. But what you've done is quite shameful and it must never, never happen again. And as for love—I don't think you know the real meaning of the word or you wouldn't have behaved so. Anyway, you must put this romantic nonsense from you immediately. I occasionally heard of inter-racial marriages when I lived in Singapore, they never work out well and as for the Eurasian children that result—well, the less said the better.'

Feeling fresh tears rising, Alice simply hurried away. Such a term as inter-racial marriage had never occurred to her before; it sounded quite unseemly and not in the least descriptive of their passion. But that apparently was how it looked from the outside, even to Isabel. But what right had she or anyone else to decide categorically that it was wrong? She and Lin were different. Every fibre of her being said so.

Impulsively she donned her cloak and, telling the maid she was going to the market, walked to Lin's lodgings. He was out, the boy said, and brought her tea while she waited, staring at the by-now familiar scene of the boats along the quay. A grey drizzle was falling, heightening the sense of a cold raining in her heart; coolies slipped about on wet decks, swinging netfuls of glistening fish ashore. She watched numbly, losing all track of time, so that the catches had all been unloaded and the men gone before she heard Lin's step on the stair.

'Uncut Jade, you?' He looked weary. 'Your brother hasn't thrown you out surely? He promised he wouldn't.'

She came and put her arms round him. 'No, but I had to come, though he's forbidden me to see you again, ever.'

'Yes—he said he would.' He shook his cloak. 'It's a beastly day—pour me some tea, Uncut. I don't know what to say, except that I'm so very sorry. If I hadn't come last night, all would have been well.'

'All? I'm not sure about that now, something was bound to go wrong eventually. We'd have been discovered, or you'd move to another job—and what then?'

'I don't know.' He stared moodily out, till she turned him to face her.

'Lin . . . Lin . . . I love you, truly. I told my brother so, and I want to be with you when you accomplish great things and become a real leader . . . I want . . . Oh Lin . . .' She buried her head in his chest. 'I want to be with you, in bed and out of it . . . I . . .'

He grasped her wrists tightly. 'And I want my sweet little Uncut, in bed and out of it, just the same. Then you must come and live here with me, never mind what people say. And when I move on, you'll come too, wherever I go!' He began kissing her passionately and they clung together like frightened children.

'Oh Lin,' her face was alight with joy, 'I know my relatives will hate it at first—inter-racial marriages never work, my sister-in-law said this morning. But she's wrong, Lin, we'll prove her wrong, ours will.'

He pushed her away, looking bewildered. 'Oh no, Uncut, that is quite impossible. I cannot marry you. I've been betrothed for years. The girl is from a well-known Cantonese family, waiting to be my first wife. In fact, Father wrote recently saying he could allow no further postponement, for he wants the blessings of my sons in his declining years.'

She could scarcely take in his words, they sounded so unlike him. 'But Lin, Lin—you never told me—you don't love this Cantonese girl surely?'

'Of course not, I scarcely know her. But my bounden duty to my honourable parents is to marry her.' He faltered then, realising how little he wanted to do so, and, from Alice's stricken pallor, how deeply he had wounded her. The thought of her wholehearted giving of herself to him, and of how they had both enjoyed it, filled him with anguish and remorse. He should have been more considerate, explained all this much earlier—indeed right at the beginning, before their mutual passion took control. 'A prime quality of leadership is antici-pation,' he reminded himself angrily, and this he had deliber-ately neglected, allowing the pleasures of the moment to rule. It had been unfitting for a man of his stamp, and he hated himself as her next words went home to him.

'But this—this is ridiculous. It's so old-fashioned from you, Lin! You who believe in the liberty of the individual, the break-ing down of traditional barriers between men and women . . . and yet now you say . . .' He took a deep breath and turned away from the painful sight of her distress, persuading him-self of the rightness of his words even as he spoke them.

'Ah yes, but my revered father is far too old for advanced ideas of that sort. It would be a terrible disgrace to the ancient lineage of our family if I were to . . . wed a barbarian.' He used the word gently, but the cruelty was still there and she stared at him in dry-eyed horror.

'So it's all right for me, is it? I offer to give up everything, knowing how my family would loathe an inter-racial mar-riage, but you, you won't sacrifice anything for me!'

'But little Jade, dearest, I'm offering you much—to come and share my life and work, in spite of what people will say.'

'Together with your official wife and your official children, I suppose? What you're offering is concubinage, Lin, a very ancient institution in spite of the modern trimmings you sug-gest—oh yes, I made a good concubine, as you know . . .' She moved away from him, her voice trembling and he came up behind her. He yearned to stroke her bent head, take her in his arms for comfort, but he knew the touching would hurt them both too much. He said quietly, 'Please Uncut, come and live with me. There is such now as free love between men and women, we've talked about it. Think of all we could share, of what we could accomplish together.'

'Oh Lin, Lin, I know, I know. But how can I do that at the expense of absolutely everything else in my life? My family might eventually and very reluctantly agree to our marriage, but if I were to come and live with you "in sin" they would, I know, totally disown me.'

He bit his knuckles, looking at her sadly. 'You're right, it cannot be—for either of us. We are talking across a great divide suddenly, are we not? You with all the family ties and conventions of your culture, I with the traditions and conventions of mine. You don't fully realise what you ask of me— even were I to disregard the feelings of my parents, marriage to a barbarian would ruin my future. Already I'm labelled a Western sympathiser, an outspoken critic of our ancient ways, a slightly suspect person, and I must tread carefully. No, it is quite impossible.'

He turned back to the window, saying huskily, 'I'll leave this town at the first opportunity and you must return to your brother's home, your proper life. We must forget this—this dream of romance. Secretly we always knew it was doomed, did we not? "The time has come to pour the wine in the dust," ' he ended formally.

She could not reply because of the aching lump in her throat, but simply buttoned up her cloak with shaking fingers. In the late afternoon grey they looked at each other without touching anymore, neither of them able to break this last, sad silence. At length he walked to the door and opened it, murmuring, 'Goodbye for a long while, Uncut Jade—but we shall meet again.'

'You said that once before.' Tears welled in her eyes.

'And we did.'

'But this time no, it is all over . . .' She blundered down the stairs.

Outside a rising wind whipped the ropes of the boats, and gulls were squabbling over fish-offal on the quay. The drear, harsh sounds seemed to cut right through her and though it was but chill, her every pore was icy cold.

After a small pretence of eating supper she went early upstairs, and it was only when she lit the lamp by her bed and stared into the rain-flecked night that the full extent of her loss came upon her with such intensity that she gasped. She paced restlessly up and down, hating Lin for causing her this misery and for the burning shame mixed with her pain. For the unvarnished truth was that she had offered all she had, a lifetime's commitment to him, a native—a little yellow Chinaman, the English would label him—and he had refused her. Oh, if only there was someone to whom she could talk, someone who would consider everything in a broader, more

278

charitable light than her relatives ever could. She could think of no one, but the misery of the empty room was too great to bear and the only temporary alleviation she could imagine was a double Epimoff cocktail. She stole very quietly downstairs and out, but in the drawing-room they heard the front door click.

'If she's gone off to join that native again I'll . . .' Will started from his chair.

'Now calm down, dear, I don't suppose she has. But she's undoubtedly very infatuated and very distraught. She's not a child, you know, and we can't control her every movement, even after this.'

'You take it pretty coolly, I must say. I'd have thought you could hardly bear the sight of my sister after that scene last night.'

'It was a dreadful shock of course, and if she'd been normally brought up—but I've been thinking it over all day, and Alice just hasn't had a normal life so far. To lose her virginity so young and at the hands of a middle-aged Chinaman—we cannot know how deeply that has affected her. Then, how did she really live with those primitive hill-folk, I wonder? Then, after all that, to be sent to Mukden. We said on the way back how dreadful it must have been for her there and we were feeling sorry for her, remember?'

'Oh, yes, sorry indeed, till we got back to find . . .'

'Yes, yes. But don't you see that Alice's behaviour now has so much to do with her past, for which she wasn't to blame? I can't quite fathom the root of it, perhaps better not to, but we mustn't be too harsh. If we make life unbearable for her here, wherever would the poor creature go?'

He picked up a skein of her pink knitting wool. 'You've decided it's to be a Polly, not a Tom, then?'

'I shall knit one pink jacket and one blue.'

'Ah, marriage to the right person is such a blessing, is it not, my love? That's what Alice needs, now more than ever—the right man to come along. We'll invite young Jeff to supper. He's due for a posting and I must try and pin him down. I hope to heaven he's not heard rumours about this damnable native and Alice.'

Alice, hurrying through the rain, thinking about the damnable native, was acutely aware that she had only to turn in the opposite direction to be with him again in a few minutes.

But she stuck to her road. It was a slack between-seasons at Epimoff's and in the saloon were only the chess-players and Bella O'Hara flipping through an American magazine called *The Good Housewife*.

'Why Alice—you here, and on a Saturday night. Is Félix coming?'

'No—I'm alone.'

'Well come and sit with me then because I'm alone too and bored stiff. Harry's gone off for the last hunt of the season along the Korean gulf. He wanted me to go too, but the weather is lousy—here, have a stool—and I'm sick of watching those poor silly otters being butchered, to tell the truth. They come right near the boat you know, all friendly and cuddly-looking with their funny little heads and paws out of the water—and then bang, bang, bang, all that blood and muck.'

'It must be quite horrible.'

'It is. Of course Harry says I'm just a hypocrite because I love an otter-fur as much as the next lady and help him spend the profits. But there's a limit and I've reached it. So, when he comes back we're off for the gay lights of San Francisco, thank heaven . . . Would you like a cocktail?'

'Yes please, a double if you don't mind.'

Bella looked at her closely. 'Is anything wrong? Why, Alice, you're nearly crying. . . .'

'Bella, can I talk to you—somewhere private? I feel I must . . .'

'Why sure, honey, come up to my room.'

Alice had not seen an Epimoff bedroom before, furnished as it was with a worn velvet armchair, tasselled lampshades, a stained pink rug and bedcover of a similar hue. The tawdriness, the hint of illicit, unloving sex broke the last shred of her control and she flung herself on the bed sobbing as if her heart would break. Bella lit a cigarette in a long holder, looked at her, went to the cupboard and poured a drink. 'Here—brandy's always good for a crisis.'

Alice gulped it gratefully. 'I'm sorry, Bella . . .'

'No need to apologise, honey, just tell me your trouble, then you'll feel better.'

So Alice told her everything, from the time of her first meeting with Lin on the *Mandalay* deck to their grey, agonised parting that afternoon.

When she had finished Bella lit a second cigarette, poured a second drink, asked, 'And are you pregnant?'

'No—I've no reason to think so.'

'Well, that's a plus anyway. And how old are you?'

'Twenty-three.'

'Well that makes me just ten years older than you, Alice, and now I'll tell you a little story. When I was twenty-three I was living in San Francisco with dear old Pa and Ma, who ran a dressmaking shop for the bar-girls—and did I ever sew on a million sequins in my salad days! Anyway, when I was twenty-three a guy called Cowboy Joe walked into my life, swept me off my feet and into his bed in no time. He was tall, handsome, had a ranch out Arizona way, so he said. Well, time came for him to ride away home and he asked me to go with him, not as his wife, mind—none of that fancy religious stuff for Cowboy Joe. But I'd be his woman, his doll, his favourite lady. Oh I loved that man, Alice, such a fine figure he had and other pleasing masculine attributes, but I thought of leaving Ma and Pa and everything familiar for no security and I refused to go.

'So Joe rode off into the sunset and I cried and cried—just as you're crying now, and thinking my heart had broken in a thousand pieces . . .'

Alice smiled a little through her tears. 'And had it?'

'Nope—at least not for ever. There were other gentlemen after that, and in due course I met nice Mr. O'Hara, a ship's engineer, and we married—you should have seen the wedding dress Pa made for me! Then I had a child and it died of croup and I cried again, and then Mr. O'Hara was blown to bits in the boiler room of the *Hawaiian Queen* somewhere in the Pacific and I cried more than ever in my life before. But why I'm telling you all this, Alice, is that when I was howling my eyes out at your tender age, I thought the world had come to an end, but it hadn't, had it? And now there's no more than a tiny ache in my heart where Mr. O'Hara used to be, and as for Cowboy Joe, I'm sure glad I didn't ride off into the sunset with him. He'd have found another favourite lady pretty soon and I might have found another cowboy. But ten years later it wouldn't have been so good.

'And if you went off with your Chinaman there'd be an end to it, honey, because there always is with these arrangements. Maybe you'd find another Chinaman, but in ten years' time, when you'll be as old as I am now and with a lot of life left to live, we hope, where would you be? Because no respectable white man between Hong Kong and Port Arthur would look at you then and you'd be pretty tired of being unofficial barbarian wife number two, three or four.'

Alice picked at the satin coverlet. 'So you think I've made the right decision, Bella?'

'I'm darn positive you have, honey. And I'm just looking at it from your point of view, nothing to do with your family or even your lover. He'll take care of himself—men always do. And my advice is—marry a nice well-heeled young English gent as soon as possible. For one respectable marriage always stands a woman in good stead whatever happens later. So stick it out, Alice, even if you have to sit and suffer for a while. And right now, come on down and I'll buy you a double cocktail—won't hurt you, they make 'em mainly of melon juice for the ladies anyhow, the crooks.'

Alice went over to the cracked mirror above the washstand. 'I look such a mess though.'

'Here—bathe your eyes, then put this stuff on.' Bella handed her a box of peach-coloured make-up and stood behind her whilst she applied it. As the two women shared their reflections in the mirror, Alice secretly hoped that she would not look quite as old as Bella at thirty-three. She gave a watery smile.

'Is that better? And you promise me that in ten years Lin will be no more than a tiny ache in my heart?'

'Sure I promise, Alice, and I speak with the voice of experience. And you'll have a lot of happiness in your life well before that, I can tell. There's something about you that won't be kept down and under for very long.'

Bella squeezed her shoulders affectionately and the two women went out of the bedroom together arm in arm.

10

The memory of that shocking scene of Alice bedded with Lin caused William such surges of rage and revulsion that he could take no more pleasure in her company. Sometimes he felt she had been let off too lightly; but at other times he decided she looked unhappy enough already and if he said more, she might simply run away—and then what would he do? So instead eventually, and at his wife's urging, he again asked Jeff Winthrop to dine, with a view to making discreet enquiries as to his matrimonial intentions, if any.

The evening did not sparkle. Isabel's pregnancy was trying and she was heavy and listless, as too was Alice, who responded politely but without enthusiasm to Jeff's laborious jokes. It was clear she cared little for him, but this no longer mattered, Will thought irritably. If he could just marry her off to him it would be more than she deserved in the circumstances and she would have to make the best of it. So, when the ladies retired after dinner, Will pushed the port across the table saying, 'So you'll soon be off to Canton, Jeff? We'll be sorry to lose you. When do you go exactly?'

'About a month, the governor says, but these things are always uncertain.'

'You're looking forward to it, I'm sure? Canton's several notches up on this dead-and-alive hole. Wish we'd something else in view. But you know what they say about the I.-G., Sir Robert Hart, he has a chart on his office wall with the names of us hapless officers on it and when he's in the mood he takes a couple of pins, sticks 'em in at random—"Now move him here and him there"—and that's it. A fellow can be in some godforsaken backwater for years, or up to head office in no time!'

Jeff clucked sympathetically. 'I've heard that was the way.

Well, at least if I behave myself I've every hope of being made a Vice soon.'

It was the perfect opening, but William hesitated, moodily reflecting on his right to persuade this perfectly decent chap to marry his sister. He himself certainly would not, knowing what he did. She was not to be trusted, that was the devil of it, time and again she had been slippery as an eel and she would twist round this Jeff chap in no time. But she was his sister, very lovable in some ways, and he no longer wanted the responsibility of her. 'A Vice, hey? That's pretty good going, Jeff. And you'll be setting up your own establishment in Canton, I expect?'

Jeff smiled, guessing the way of the wind. 'I hope to, yes.'

'Anyone particular in mind to ... well ... share it with you?'

'You mean a wife?'

'I suppose I do.'

'You mean Alice?'

'Well nothing pressing of course, my dear fellow ... but you've been seeing a deal of her in the past eighteen months, and I just wondered, as her elder brother?'

'Alice wouldn't have me even if I asked her, Will, as I was once tempted to. But I'm over that now. There's something else worrying her, but it's none of my business. She's got a mind of her own, has Alice, and there's no room for me in it, and that's all about it.'

He settled his broad behind more comfortably and drained his glass. William sighed. 'Some women are like that—it makes for the deuce of a problem. Alice has never been easy and I fear never will be. One more top-up, Jeff, then we'll join the ladies—bless 'em and forget 'em. What'll be your new duties, same as here? More people on the staff of course?'

'Oh yes, several officers and three student interpreters. Canton's a focus for the self-strengthening movement you know, we had a memo round recently—the F.O. wants to know more. . . . Is it gaining widespread support? How dangerous is it to our interests? What sort of people join it?'

'The self-strengtheners haven't got a bat in hell's chance as long as the Old Buddha and her posse of eunuchs hold the reins. In twenty years' time, China will be the same moth-eaten old gunny-sack of ancient tradition, disorder and ineptitude as it is today, I warrant.'

'I'm not so sure. Some of these progressives are quite persuasive and very determined. The principal of the naval college here for one, and Lin Fu-wei, the man they call the "Leader," he's quite impressive.'

Will looked into his glass. The deuce was he could not decide whether Jeff was deliberately going along this track—perhaps the whole town knew of Alice and Lin? Curse the girl. 'Really? I've not met him.'

'He's suddenly resigned his post and returned to Canton, his home town, I gather. It could be an indication that things are hotting up down there.'

'Well, I wish 'em all luck, I suppose,' Will rose, 'but there'll certainly be a bloodbath if they come into the open and try to start a revolution. Shall we go to the drawing-room?'

It was quiet there except for the crackling of logs, the click of Isabel's knitting needles, the occasional rustle of Alice's books. Jeff warmed himself at the fire, regarding her covertly. She was attractive to him still, in spite of his show of nonchalance. 'That's a heavy-looking tome you're reading, Alice. I didn't know your interests extended to the philosophical?' The whiff of a scandalous rumour about her had reached him and he wanted to scent it out.

'I think it's time I stretched my mind a little—it's already overstuffed with trivial chaff, so my stepfather used to say.'

'And you're translating these works at the college, I believe—so you need to understand them thoroughly?'

Her colour had risen. 'I *was* working there, as you must know, but not any longer.'

Isabel broke in, 'More coffee, Jeff? I always think it must be wonderful to have Alice's grasp of the Mandarin.'

'Indeed yes—I certainly wish I had, especially now. I was just telling Will the F.O. want us to find out what we can about the self-strengthening movement and several of its members are Cantonese you know, including that man they call the Leader. I think you helped him with some translating, Alice?'

'Yes, but he's gone away now.'

Jeff's strategy had not been specially subtle, but it took little perception to realise from the Greenwoods' reactions that what he had heard held at least some grains of truth. With this assurance Jeff left the Customs House that night with a lighter heart, comfortable in the knowledge that he was well rid of Miss Alice.

'He must have heard something!' William snarled at his sister as the door shut on Jeff. 'Harping on about your ex-paramour like that!'

'Not necessarily, Will, but we were so on edge when his name was mentioned,' Isabel contradicted.

'Well if he has heard, it would explain why he made it clear to me that he's no serious intentions in your direction, Alice.'

'And I've no intentions whatsoever with regard to him. You've known that for months, Will.'

'But the point is, no respectable young man here ever will if your scandalous behaviour is public knowledge. I really don't know what to do about you!'

She slammed her book shut and jumped up. 'You don't need to do a thing about me—I'll go at once and live in Shanghai near Frank if I'm such a burden to you!'

'You'll do no such thing, Shanghai's no place for an unchaperoned young lady.'

'But you don't really think I'm a respectable young lady anymore, do you? So why not let me go to the dogs—or the horses with Frank—in my own way?'

'Will—you two, stop it!' Isabel also rose. 'Alice is not a burden to us. She's behaved badly as we know, but this is her home and here she stays. Indeed, I badly need her now, you know that, don't you Alice?' She caught her hand. 'You're going to help me and the little ones through this winter, aren't you?'

Alice laughed shakily, putting an arm round Isabel's neck. 'You're a very sweet sister-in-law, Isabel. I sometimes wonder if Will deserves you. If you want me, then I'll stay—unless my brother actually casts me out!'

'Of course I shan't, you women always stick together,' Will growled, stalking out.

Isabel wound up her knitting. 'I like that! We women have to stick together, considering the way men behave! Now calm down, dear, and have a good night's rest.'

In her frigid bedroom Alice undressed quickly, reminding herself of the much more intense cold she had earlier survived in Mukden; yet, in some ways, those drear winters had been preferable to this one. For then life had still seemed full of promise and hope, whereas now she felt sure, with the uncompromising passion of her age, that all the best was behind and she might just as well die, for no possible good lay ahead. But she went through the days doggedly, if resentfully, nevertheless, keeping up a cheerful front before Isabel and helping with the children.

Between times, she worked on the translation of J. S. Mill's treatise which Lin had sent soon after their last meeting, with a formal note telling her of his imminent departure for Canton on both political and family business—and she had bitterly guessed the nature of the latter. He had begged her to continue alone with the work, 'for the sake of the China of the future.' At first, she had angrily put it aside, but had then taken it up again, first as a continuing link between them and also because it held new meaning for her. For was she not a member of 'a subject class,' given little chance to use her talents and kept in a state of economic dependence, at everyone's beck and call? 'If there is anything vitally important to human beings it is that they should relish their habitual pursuit,' Mill had written. But what chance had she to discover a truly relishable pursuit anyway?

Made resentful and restless by the realisation of her powerless position, she sometimes sneaked off to Epimoff's in search of congenial company, but even that had lost its charm. Bella and Harry had gone and Félix was in France, marrying his betrothed. Some naval students still frequented it, but Han-li was no longer among them, for he had returned to Foochow to teach the rudiments of intensely crammed navigational science to others even less knowledgeable. In January, Jeff Winthrop left for Canton, and the following month, to everyone's relief, Isabel was safely delivered of her baby.

'It's a Polly,' she whispered to Will as he crept into the bedroom where Alice, who had just witnessed her first birth, was rearranging the bedclothes.

'Polly—little Polly Eliza—we agreed on that, Isabel?'

Alice came to him. 'Let me hold her, Will please . . . She's lovely, isn't she lovely? Let me be her godmother, please Isabel, please Will!' she begged in a sudden burst of joy.

He hesitated and Isabel said from the bed, 'If you wish it, then certainly, my dear. You've been a great help to us all this winter.'

William mumbled, 'Yes of course. . . . And now I must give the doctor a brandy before he leaves.'

Alice touched the button-nose of the wrinkled creature in her arms. 'Such a wondrous thing, isn't it? I feel so drawn to her—exactly as I was to Sunny.'

'You seem to prefer the girls of the family, Alice.'

'Oh I love the boys too, but the girls may really need me one day, as the boys probably never will.'

The miracle of Polly's birth buoyed Alice temporarily, but then she was assailed by a dire lowering of the spirits. What could she look forward to? Was her future role to be no more than dependent aunt in her brother's house? A steadily aging spinster devoting herself to various good causes as the years went by? Was it for this that she had risked her very life to return to her own people? And now she sometimes wondered to what extent they were her own people—these conventional consuls, customs officials, traders who lived so complacently and myopically on the fringes of one of the world's greatest countries.

Alice's restlessness was inadvertently brought to a head by William who, peering at the sky one morning around the 'Time of Clear Brightness,' announced cheerfully that it would soon be the picnic season again. But the very idea filled Alice with melancholy. The birth-wood—where she and Lin had lain together when there seemed no end to their delight. How could she bear again those long, somnolent family picnics? Mentally she heard Will's meticulous sharpening of the carving knife preparatory to cutting chicken; it set her teeth on edge.

Closeted in her bedroom, Alice contemplated her secret store—the rest of the Carr loot and her savings from teaching. Then she wrote to Frank. Clearly, she began tartly, he was having too good a time to bother about Greenwood & Greenwood Ltd. But she was bored to tears with wretched Port Arthur. She had saved some money, and that, allied to his trading experience, was sufficient for a start. She intended coming to Shanghai that summer. She concluded, 'I'm sorry, dear, if I sound like a bossy old spinster schoolmistress, but I'm beginning to feel like one. I'm saying nothing of this plan to Will till I have your answer. He's bound to raise objections, and it's best to present him with a *fait accompli*. Please reply soon—I'm counting on you now.'

But Frank was never a brisk correspondent and when, a while later, the weather was sufficiently clement for the first picnic, he had sent no word. The birches were in green leaf and Joel toddled about under them while William carved the chickens and Charlotte laid the cloth. When they were all comfortably settled, William went to his horse and returned with a bundle. 'The Home mail,' he announced triumphantly, 'came this morning, so I thought I'd bring it. One for you from Frank, Alice.'

She scanned it, then raised her head with a jerk, but the others were too engrossed to notice. She paused, savouring the drama to come before saying with studied calm, 'Frank's about to get married.'

They both looked up. 'Married—young Frank?' Will frowned. 'Well, he's twenty-one of course. But why the deuce haven't we heard about her before? Who is the lucky girl?'

'Her name is Tao Yuan-wang and he calls her Peachy because "Tao" is the Chinese for that delectable fruit.'

There was a stunned silence. 'You mean she's . . .' Isabel moaned faintly.

'Chinese, yes. Her father is a respectable, quite wealthy merchant apparently, who owns several race-horses as well as the most beautiful girl in the world—according to Frank.'

'My God, whatever next?' William jumped up agitatedly. 'Is this—this arrangement definite? Can I do anything to prevent it?'

'No, it's a *fait accompli*, Frank says. The wedding is fixed for the third of June, which isn't far off. He's sending us all an official invitation by the next mail but wanted me to break the news. He hopes you'll be as delighted about it as he is.'

Will knocked his head against a convenient tree trunk. 'Is that meant to be a joke? Delighted at his—marrying a native!'

'Oh dear, these inter-racial marriages never work,' Isabel wailed. 'Yes I know I told you that, Alice, and it's so true. Oddly enough, the girl's family is probably just as upset as we are.'

'Oh yes, Frank says they've tried to dissuade her for months, which is why he hadn't told us before. But it's Frank or no one for Miss Peachy apparently, and they've finally given in.'

William flopped down and reached for some claret. 'Well I'll be damned—and to think of all the pretty young English lassies in Shanghai. It's not as if he's stuck in a backwater like this with nothing but Chinese girls to look at.'

'What those Chinese did to you two,' Isabel whispered sadly. 'How they altered your lives—for that's the root of it, isn't it?'

'First Alice and now this. I honestly don't know which is worse,' Will groaned.

'Well you can't stop this and I'm glad—yes, glad that Frank at least has got what he really wants.' Alice glared at her brother, suddenly recalling Frank's tale of his youthful excursions to the plum groves near Changsha. 'Yes, that's the root of it, Isabel. But it's not as if Frank were marrying a tea-girl. Peachy sounds very sweet and respectable. And you'll come to the wedding, won't you? Because Frank will need all our support—I suppose there'll be dozens of her relatives, if they deign to come . . . Oh goodness, I wonder what Mother . . .?'

'God—Mother, it'll kill her,' Will gulped his claret. 'I suppose little Peachy-weachy isn't a convert by any happy chance?'

Alice consulted the letter. 'No—because he says there'll be two wedding ceremonies, one Buddhist and one Christian.'

'Oh poor dear Eliza—not only a native but a heathen native! I can just hear Stepfather Blake on the subject, can't you?' Isabel shuddered. 'He'll never allow her to attend the wedding. You see what troubles alliances of this kind cause, Alice? But we'll have to put a good face on it—for Frank's sake, as you say. And it'll be fun to go to Shanghai, won't it, Will? We'll do some shopping and see a lot of new faces . . .'

'And spend a lot of money,' he snapped.

'That's right! We'll go to Madame Claire's tomorrow, Alice, and get some new clothes made—everyone's frightfully smart in Shanghai these days. Come on now, let's have lunch, then we'll all feel better about it.'

Defiantly Alice raised her glass. 'And here's to them anyway—Frank and Peachy!'

They all drank, but then a glum silence fell as they considered the full implications of the news. Alice's feelings were very mixed. She was happy for Frank and jealous of his happiness at the same time. She was both amused and saddened by her relatives' consternation and hated to think how deeply it would distress her mother. Most of all she feared it meant the end of the dream of Greenwood & Greenwood—indeed Frank had hinted as much, but added that she should move to Shanghai anyway. 'We're going to live in a villa belonging to Peachy's father, with stables and a paddock,' he had boasted, 'and there'll be lots of room for you, Sis.'

So once again Frank was the lucky fish of the family. Everything seemed to come his way without any effort, whereas she made so many efforts to no avail. Yet, in spite of its unfortunate aspects, the news of Frank's marriage lifted her spirits. At least it heralded change of some sort, and when, a few weeks later, Alice packed her trunks for the journey to Shanghai most of her belongings went inside, for, secretly, she intended to stay there.

Shanghai of the 1880s was just the place for anyone in search of a bright new future, China-coast hands always affirmed. Stand on the Bund, they proudly bade the newcomer, and look at the view. Westward, the whole of the Old World before you, the largest land mass on the globe; eastward, its greatest ocean, nothing but sea between you and California; in the foreground, plenty of solid, reassuring evidence of the Occident's presence in the Orient: banks and consulates, churches, courts of justice, customs offices, the spacious residences owned by those foreigners who had already manifestly made good.

Frank met them off the Port Arthur steamer, very smart in a suit of white Marseilles drill, check waistcoat, leather button-boots. He ordered the coolies to put the baggage in his buggy. 'We'll ride in grander style.' He nonchalantly indicated a gleaming two-horse carriage with a liveried coachman on the box.

'This your turn-out, Frank?' William asked cautiously as they climbed aboard.

'Not exactly—belongs to my future father-in-law, he's got two landaus and he lent me this to ferry you about in.' William raised his eyebrows. 'I've a little luncheon in the hong mess for you,' Frank continued. 'I thought we'd go straight there, and then to the Dawsons at the Customs House—which is where you're staying, I suppose?'

'But Frank, Polly's feed is due and there's the children and the amah . . .' Isabel protested. It was settled by Alice and William going to the hong, while Isabel coped with the family.

'So this is where you've been holing up. Looks very fine, I must say,' Will remarked as the carriage turned into an extensive walled compound along the Peking Road which was the hong of Guthrie & Robinson Ltd. Facing them was a solid, rectangular, two-storeyed house flanked by warehouses and outbuildings.

'Yes—it's quite large. There's the silk godown, that's the tea and the smaller one's for piece-goods. Then there's counting offices, general stores, rooms for the compradores and the shroffs who check the cash. The taipan's got some grand stables at the back too. My bedroom's up on the left there—it's quite a chummerie and now I'm about to move, I know I'll miss it.' He led them into a huge dining-room where luncheon was in progress—an enormous meal, as Shanghai meals invariably were, accompanied by various beverages and considerable conviviality. (This, perhaps, was why the young men of the settlement spent much time in violent exercise 'shaking up their livers,' while the women, deprived of similar outlets, looked bloated and depressed during the hot summers and suffered much from colic.) It was nearly three in the afternoon before the dessert dishes were cleared, the other hong members left, and the Greenwoods were alone.

An awkward pause fell which William broke with, 'So it's settled then, Frank? You're going to marry a Chinese girl?'

'Certainly—and an extraordinarily lucky fellow I am! You wait till you see her, she's expecting us to call later and . . .'

'Well, I shall have to delay that pleasure. I must go and help Isabel, we've left her to manage everything,' Will cut in firmly. 'But there's something I did want to ask, though not in front of your chums—you do know how much you've upset Mother, I suppose?'

Frank shrugged irritably. 'Of course I know, I had an awful letter from her. She won't come to a wedding between her son and a heathen and what's going to happen to the souls of our children—and all that.'

Alice sighed. 'But it's very real for her, Frank, the basis of her life—though I've every sympathy for you.'

'Well I haven't,' William snapped. 'I just hope you realise what you're taking on—a woman of a different race, different religion as your mother says—different outlook on life entirely. It doesn't work, you know.'

Frank stuck out his lower lip. 'Of course it does. I won't be the first white man in China to marry a Chinese, nor the last. And my Peachy is a little beauty, you'll see. Anyway, I love her, more than I've ever loved anyone in my whole life, so there!' He glared defiantly at his brother. 'And she loves me too,' he added for good measure. 'She refused lots of rich young men to marry me.'

'Then there's no more to be said, but I can't help wondering what Father would have thought.'

It was an unkind thrust as Frank's face showed, and Alice broke in briskly with, 'But that's a silly idea, Will. If Father had lived, things wouldn't have happened like this—no Hunan, no Frank alone in Shanghai, nothing the same. So we might as well forget it.'

Frank smiled in relief, adding, 'But talking of Father—guess who is coming to the wedding? Uncle Robert arrives tomorrow.'

'Oh that's splendid news, I do like Uncle Robert, he's so reassuring somehow.'

'And what did he have to say about it?' Will asked slyly.

'Oh, he wasn't exactly overjoyed—but it's decent of him to come, don't you think?'

'Very, in the circumstances,' William rose stiffly. 'Thank you for an excellent luncheon, Frank. Now I must go back to the family. Alice, you go and meet Peachy. It'll be easier without me anyway, you can all chat together so fluently.'

'That's typical,' Frank sniffed at his departing back. 'In fact, Peachy's been practising her best English greeting for him.'

'Well, you haven't told us much about her yet, dear.'

'Oh, I'm no good at letters . . . that's all my writing's good for,' he signed the meal-chit with a flourish. 'But Peachy's counting on you; she's sure you'll take a broader view than the rest of 'em.' He looked at her shyly as they came out into the driveway. 'I mean, you do understand, don't you, Sis? Why all this rot Will talks about different races and religions cuts no ice with me?'

'Yes Frank, I do understand perfectly.' She stopped to smell a yellow rose by the entrance. 'You see, I myself . . .' But no, Englishmen did not want to hear such things about their women, least of all their sisters. Besides, it was Frank's wedding, Frank's adventure. 'But what Will says is not altogether rot—it won't be easy.'

'Oh I know,' he agreed carelessly. 'I didn't tell old Will, but several of Peachy's relatives have refused to attend the wedding, and there's been a great to-do about the two religious services and the breakfast has to be in a dreary guildhall because it's neutral territory—but what does all that matter? When you really love someone, that's the only important thing.'

His words stabbed her; she wondered, as she had so often,

whether she too should have sacrificed all for love. But there was a difference, she thought bitterly. It was at least marriage, not concubinage, Frank was going into—and one with considerable financial advantages, it seemed.

'You say Mr. Wang has two carriages like this? He must be pretty well off?' she asked as they drove off.

'Oh this is his least grand turn-out. His old man was in the opium trade I believe, though they keep that pretty dark now. Anyway, Wang switched over to tea during the heyday of the clippers. He's a wily bird and made a small fortune. Tea's quietened down now, but what he's lost there he's made up on horse-racing, I reckon. He's got a grand stable and I have the run of it—his pals call me the Golden Horseboy. It's my hair that does it!'

'And Mrs. Wang—is she a lady of consequence in the household or another Hidden Glory?'

He grinned in recognition of their shared past. 'There's nothing hidden about Madam Wang—she's a Manchu for a start, and they're very determined characters. Like the Old Buddha, whom she rather resembles.'

'Manchu—and married to a Chinese?'

'Unusual yes—indeed that was considered a dreadful inter-racial liaison till I came along!'

'So who made the decision about Peachy's feet?'

'Her mother fortunately. The two elder daughters were bound and when it came to Number Three, mother put her foot down—ha!'

'So she's not bound, I'm so glad. I wondered how you could ever . . . I mean I've seen bound feet and . . .'

'Yes, it always rather put me off, I must say. Never looked at them.' He stared out of the window in embarrassment. 'But Peachy is natural from top to toe—all the best qualities of Chinese and Manchu rolled into one!'

And certainly that was an apt physical description of the young woman who greeted them in the reception room of the Wang villa. Peachy's slender form was shaped in a high-necked jacket of iridescent turquoise brocade, patterned with white irises; her wide trousers were of deeper green silk; she carried a painted ivory fan, her jet hair was swept up and away from her pale, oval face by jewelled combs. Her features, of a slightly Manchu cast, were well moulded and her smile eager.

'You are Uncut Jade, Frank's sister,' she spoke in halting English. 'I ver' please meet you.'

'And I you! Why, you are everything Frank told me!'

She looked at him in puzzled adoration. 'That good?'

'Excellent, I assure you.'

As a servant brought tea she reverted gratefully to Chinese and Alice looked round. There was a great deal of mother-of-pearl about, intricately carved lattice-work screens, huge, colourful Ningpo vases. She remembered Lin's disdainful reference to the nouveau-riche of the Treaty Ports. Undoubtedly this was the house of one. But, she checked herself. What right had she to assume his snobbish, aristocratic standards—and what right had he to judge others by them? Oh, he could talk so grandly about the need of equality between classes, sexes, races—yet the traditional divisions still moulded his attitudes. How she would love to tell him that one day!

She smiled warmly at Peachy. 'You know, I've not yet heard how you met each other.'

'It was last spring. My father let me go to the races because his horse with my name was running. And he introduced me to Frank—the only barbarian who knew anything about horses, he said! And after that Frank kept calling on me and I kept stealing away to see him . . .' She giggled, put a hand to her mouth. 'I speak English now, for the walls have ears—my father want me marry Chinese man, but I say no, no, no. I have letter from my sister, is in America with husband. She tell me in that country women not have marry men not like. So I likes Frank, is best man. Many times I say—marry him. My father say no, yellow barbarian, foreign devil, them sillee thing. At las' they say, all righ', you like old ox . . .'

'Ox?' Alice raised an eyebrow.

'Stubborn as a mule,' Frank explained.

Peachy looked anxious. 'You teachee me goo' English, not pidgin, please?'

'Yes, I'll help you to learn good English.'

But Peachy had drawn back, reverting to her own tongue. 'Here's my mother coming, she's been playing mah-jong as usual and has returned early to meet you.'

Frank and Peachy stiffened as Mrs. Yuan-wang swept in. With her oiled hair folded on either side of her square face, her square shape encased in a richly embroidered robe, she was indeed reminiscent of official portraits of the Empress Dowager and the same veiled disdain for foreigners lurked in her hooded eyes. She held out a long red-nailed hand, her deeply rouged cheeks cracking in a polite smile, but conversation was suddenly very hard to make and it was a relief when she was soon called away on what Alice guessed to be a pre-arranged pretext.

Riding back along the Bubbling Well Road, Alice first reflected that she did not care for the atmosphere in the Wang house, then subsided into a wistful daydream wherein she was married to Lin after all, and was warmly welcomed into his aristocratic and cultured family in spite of her unfortunate barbarism. But, 'What nonsense, Alice,' she said aloud, as they reached the Bund and she distracted herself instead with the passing scene.

It was early evening and the Bund was at its sprightliest. The gardens along Soochow Creek were gay with roses, lilies, geraniums, heliotrope; from the bandstand came the strains of a popular Strauss polka, and children were darting about the gravel paths watched over by amahs in white coats and wide black satin trousers. Along the main thoroughfare smart landaus with footmen as well as drivers conveyed foreign ladies and gentlemen to their various evening entertainments; buggies pulled by tough Mongolian ponies like Griffin, and little basket-carriages much used by brokers and commercial agents for the conduct of their peripatetic businesses. Visitors and humbler folk of many nations were riding in rickshaws with their hoods down, for the air was balmy, and the humblest natives trundled slowly by in wheelbarrows with platforms on either side of the wheel for people, packages, and animals.

Alice stared at it all longingly, wondering how she could manage to stay here without again incurring her brother's displeasure. As she drove up to the Customs House where Mr. and Mrs. Dawson lived, she yawned mightily, suddenly realising how weary she was from all the activities of her first day ashore.

But there was little time to rest, for Isabel, having inspected the elegance of the Shanghai crowds, was convinced that the garments cobbled together by poor Madame Claire in Port Arthur were quite inadequate for the coming nuptials.

'We shall look like poor relations from the hills,' she told

Alice at supper, 'and quite let Frank down. So we're off to Mrs. Dawson's own couturière in the morning and she promises she'll have something decent ready for us in a day.'

So the next morning was a whirlwind tour of dressmakers, tailors, milliners, haberdashers followed by a courtesy call at the Wang villa. Then William rushed to meet Uncle Robert while the ladies went to the hairdressers. Late in the afternoon a weary but satisfied Isabel sank into a chair at the Viennese patisserie where she was to meet Robert and William. She patted her newly styled hair, ordered tea, began a critical survey of the ladies' bonnets in view.

'Ah, Isabel, hello, hello, my dear!' Robert appeared at her side. After their greetings, he drew up a chair, and reported, 'Will's got another touch of fashion-fever and has gone to buy some smart shoes. He may join us later. But it's lovely to see you—and as blooming as ever.'

'Thank you, Robert, and I'm glad to see you safe and well. We've been most anxious about you—out there in Kabul fighting those blood-thirsty Afghans. We read about that battle where over a thousand men were lost.'

'Yes, a nasty business. I wasn't there fortunately, but I did march with General Roberts' forces to the relief of Kandahar which was quite hard going.' He took a chair. 'So I feel entitled to a rest—and one certainly gets it on the P. & O. these days. Excellent accommodation and service, better than the old days of sail when I first came East.'

Isabel poured tea and they prodded chocolate gateaux while she described the charms of her new-born. 'I'm looking forward to making Miss Polly's acquaintance,' Robert said, adding cautiously, 'I wish I could say the same about Frank's future progeny.'

She looked at him. The two had seldom met, but they understood each other.

'It's a great shame and we could do nothing about it, Robert, a *fait accompli* before we even heard.'

'Same here, and I was beastly disappointed after all I've done for Frank. But one has to put a good face on it.'

'Exactly. And I'm sure it has to do with their past—his and Alice's—what happened in Hunan, and, when they returned, no proper parental guidance. We've all done our best but it's not the same, and Eliza's so taken over by this mission. Will and I visited Mukden last autumn you know, and met Step-father Blake.'

'From what Will wrote, it couldn't have been pleasant for Alice there. I'm so glad she's now with you—and well I trust?'

Isabel was silent, weighing him.

'What's the matter with Alice? Why isn't she here now?'

His obvious concern decided her, 'Oh she's perfectly fit, thank goodness, having tea with Frank. But I'm worried about her, Robert. You see in Port Arthur last year she . . . well, fell for a Chinese—just like Frank, that's what's so worrying.'

'Good Lord, who? Is it over?'

'Yes. He was a naval college lecturer—quite a young radical.'

'Oh I know the type, have 'em in Calcutta these days—want to throw out the white man, start a revolution, put the world to rights . . . and with a dangerous appeal for clever young ladies! But what happened? Could you break it?'

'Well . . . we . . . found them together . . .' she was blushing.

'Together? What do you mean exactly?'

'In our bed if you must know. We got back from Mukden earlier than expected, and there they were.'

He stared in glassy horror. 'Isabel! I can't believe it—little Alice—a thing like that, good God!'

'Now, Robert, there's no use getting upset. Will was furious enough and it was all most unpleasant.'

'But how utterly disgusting—in your bed and with a . . . a Chink!'

'Well, it's over now. The man left town soon after and has now married his betrothed, thank goodness. But the point is, Robert, I have reason to believe Alice's attraction to the natives is deeply rooted—as it is, you see, in Frank. She's been quite miserable since and we've kept a close eye. But I'm so afraid she'll meet another man of a similar type and before we know it there'll be a second wedding as unfortunate as tomorrow's.'

'Good heavens, this really is appalling, but I'm glad you've told me. The danger's there all right . . . But what's to be done?'

'As Will and I have often said, Alice needs a good steady English husband. But the choice in Port Arthur is very limited. Now if she were here in Shanghai, mixing socially with eligible young men. . . . But the difficulty is, who'd keep a check?

Frank's offered her a home, but it will be full of Chinese, of course, and after what's happened. . . . If there were someone older around, if only for a while, just to . . .'

'I have it, Isabel—I'll stay here myself for the summer! I'm at a bit of a loose end with this long leave until January.'

'Robert, what a perfectly splendid idea. It never occurred to me,' said round-eyed Isabel, who had been thinking of nothing else for the past half-hour. 'And I'm sure you'll thoroughly enjoy Shanghai too.'

'Well, I was thinking as I came here, it's perked up a lot since I was last here. And dash it, I've invested enough in Frank, not to much avail, I fear, so it's time I did something for my niece. We can't have her going off the rails like that again. Then I'll have done my best all round, hey?' He beamed. 'And let's have two of those delectable-looking nut sundaes to celebrate. It'll give Will a little longer. He must be buying up the shoe-shop.'

So they spooned their sundaes and discussed the details of their plan and then, in a relaxed pause, Isabel asked guilelessly, 'Robert, I hope you won't think I'm inquisitive, but when we last met I thought you intended leaving the Army and going Home this year? You've changed your mind?'

'Had it changed for me really, Isabel,' he gloomed into his sundae glass. 'Fact is, I was jilted.'

'You jilted—my dear, you're far too handsome and nice for such a fate!'

'Thank you for saying so, but—I'll tell you, as we seem to be exchanging confidences this afternoon. I had a lady friend in Sheringham, Elsie Massingham—known her for ages, since I was a boy. Always thought we'd marry one day and so did she. But things always kept cropping up to prevent it somehow. Anyway, to cut a long story, when I decided to finance Frank at the college here I wrote and told her I was staying in the Army for three more years after all, then I'd go home to her. Well, that was the last straw, I suppose. Her letters cooled a bit, but I didn't pay much attention, not enough apparently. Then bless me if she didn't write to say she'd married the Vicar of Blakeney, a widower, quite elderly. Said she'd waited long enough and I'd taken her good nature too much for granted. Quite a horrid letter it was, though with grains of truth, I must confess. So there I was—no Elsie, no villa in Sheringham, no point in going Home really. So I've signed up for two more years, then we'll see.'

'Robert, you old dark horse! You never told a soul about Elsie, did you? What a shame—and all through your generosity to Frank too. Ah well, you'll have to see what Shanghai can produce for you as well as for Alice. Come, let's give Will up and go—else the wedding feast will be upon us before we've digested this delicious tea.'

The day of the wedding was a sparkle of sunshine. As Alice tried on the dress of apple-green silk trimmed with white ribbons that the dressmaker's boy had delivered at dawn, she felt almost as happy as if the ceremony ahead were her own. The previous evening, Isabel had told her the plan she and Robert had 'cooked up in the patisserie' and she had been overjoyed. As she pirouetted in front of the glass and tried on her new ostrich feather hat, she felt as if Shanghai was already at her feet and all the worries about Frank's marriage were groundless. Why should he and Peachy not be perfectly happy when they loved each other so much? That, as Frank said, was the only important thing, and surely enough for a lifetime?

She kept that thought uppermost when, a few hours later, she watched the bridal pair climb from Mr. Wang's best landau and go into the guildhall for the wedding breakfast. Peachy wore no white, the Chinese colour of mourning, but looked ravishing in pale pink, a veil partially covering her rouged face, and carrying a bouquet of red roses. There were roses everywhere—in the church, the hall, stuck in the men's buttonholes and the ladies' hair, and ever afterwards Alice associated their fragrance with that day, such a sweet, beguiling scent, yet with an elusive hint of melancholy and swift decay.

Earlier the Greenwoods had attended the Buddhist ceremony in the Wangs' ancestral hall, and Robert and William had been fearfully oppressed by the strangeness of it all—the gongs, incense and chanting of the priests. But Alice had been beset with memories of that other wedding long ago in Hunan. She remembered Eldest Son's flushed face, the cowed features of poor Dull Thorn, Lung-kuang doing all the honours with the proper degrees of courtesy. In some ways, that ceremony had had a magnificent sense of occasion which both this and the subsequent Christian service lacked. For there were too many discordant elements, and which was worse, the sight of Frank's blond head bent before the ancestral tablets, or the senior Wang's pigtailed pate making similar polite obeisance before the altar of Trinity Church?

As they filed into the guildhall, Alice hoped that the secular activity of feasting would create a pretence of fusion—and no expense had been spared to that end, for tables were piled with native and foreign food. While toasts were proposed, Mr. Wang, looking, Isabel decided, exactly like the hundreds of other natives from whom she had bought fish and vegetables, talked about the fostering of links between England and China, a theme embroidered by other speakers in both English and Chinese. Afterwards, Peachy's brothers and their racing friends gathered in a corner drinking hard and laughing loudly, and the older men grunted together in business pidgin. The ladies were reduced to smiling politely and pointing at the roses, to show their shared appreciation of their beauty. Seeing Mrs. Wang and Isabel stranded side by side, Alice was about to go to the rescue when Charlotte tugged her sleeve.

'Aunt Alice, there's a man at the door asking for you.'

'For me—specially?'

'Yes, Miss Alice Greenwood, he said.'

Her heart leaped; it must be—who else? 'But he can come in—there are lots of Chinese here.'

'But he's not Chinese, he's English.'

'Oh . . . oh well, I'll come.'

It took but an instant to place the face at the door in its six-past-past slot.

'Charles Grant! Mr. Grant—why, how lovely to see you.'

'And little Alice—Greenwood, is it?' he cast a surreptitious glance at her left hand.

'But come in and let me get you a drink to the bridal pair. But however did . . .?'

He smiled. 'I seem destined to read about your doings in the Shanghai press. I slipped into the Club for a snack today, picked up a *Mercury*—and lo and behold, the wedding announcement of Mr. Frank Greenwood and Miss Tao Yuan-wang. I wasn't sure it was the same of course, but it seemed worth finding out.'

'What a shame you didn't come sooner. We've been rather short on the English team, as Uncle Robert calls it, and now it's nearly over. Here, Will, look who's just arrived!'

301

William joined them. 'Why it's—of course, Charles Grant, the man on the houseboat, how splendid to see you. You must come and meet Frank before he whisks the bride away. Set up in business here now have you? As you planned?'

'Only just started really—there have been delays . . .'

'And your family is here now too, I suppose?'

He avoided their eyes. 'No, I fear my wife and the new baby died, about a year after I was here.'

'Oh Mr. Grant, I am sorry, how dreadful for you. But what happened?' Alice broke in.

'We'll talk later, shall we? This is a wedding feast, after all.'

William nodded. 'Yes of course—now let me introduce you to my wife . . .'

As he pushed through the throng that was gathering at the door, a sudden burst of cheering went up, firecrackers snapped and Frank and Peachy came running down the length of the hall hand in hand, pelted as they came with rose petals, rice and paper streamers. As they neared the door, Peachy's brothers and friends waylaid Frank, tripping his feet and butting him in parody of the traditional teasing of the bridegroom outside the bridal chamber. Peachy, giggling, fled outside and as Frank tried to follow, a guest caught him from behind, pulling him down backwards. Others fell on him, stuffing rice down his shirt, throwing wine in his face, while one of Mr. Wang's dapper jockeys pranced round thrusting out his loins rhythmically and muttering suggestions about the capabilities of a barbarian cock. Frank bellowed with frustration and laughter and, trying to rise, kneed one of his tormenters in the groin. He doubled up, groaning theatrically. As Frank struggled harder, Peachy's brother punched him in the belly while a friend pinioned his head to the floor and rammed a champagne bottle against his mouth. Frank's mouth began to bleed and a cry of real pain broke from him.

The mask of the day had slipped. The flushed faces surrounding Frank were unsmiling now. The man they held to the ground was a yellow-haired barbarian who was going to put his cock inside one of their own kind. The mouth of Peachy's brother was drawn back in a snarl. As Alice looked desperately for discreet help, Mrs. Wang suddenly surged up in her brilliant robe of vermilion and emerald, the jewels of her headdress shaking in her wrath. She hissed at the youths in a

302

low whisper and they fell back instantly. Frank stood up and his attackers brushed him down, smiling sheepishly. Mrs. Wang dabbed coldly at his cut mouth and he gave her a shaky smile of gratitude as he rushed off to join Peachy in the waiting carriage.

'They're off on honeymoon to the Snowy Valley Lakes,' Alice said to Charles brightly.

He brushed her neutrality aside. 'That wasn't very nice, was it?'

'No—but then the whole affair isn't very nice in some ways, only we all have to make the best of it.'

'Of course, I understand. Look, Alice—if so I may still call you—I'd love to see you again, but I feel I'm gatecrashing on a family affair. Perhaps we could meet tomorrow? How about the Hotel des Colonies in the French concession at noon?'

The date was made and he hurried away. Alice leaned against the door for a moment to regain her composure. The scene she had just witnessed had shaken her and as a result of it, she thought remorsefully, she had been led into her first betrayal of Frank and Peachy. Her words to Charles had been an exact echo of what her relatives had said all along about the marriage. Yet, at the moment of speaking, she had felt them true, and now, at the end of the day, she no longer knew what to think. Indeed, she suspected that its only certain good had been the totally unexpected reappearance of Charles Grant.

Their meeting at the hotel the next day rather confirmed her view, for he was as good-looking and affable as she remembered. 'The chef here is Swiss,' he explained as they went into the dining-room, 'and far superior to the man at the Grand.' The prices, he did not add, were also more moderate.

She smiled. 'You know I've done nothing but eat and drink since I came to Shanghai.'

'But that's exactly what most people here do most of the time . . . so when in Rome, eh?'

She studied the menu closely, remembering her past attraction to him, aware of his close scrutiny.

'It's been six years, hasn't it, Alice? In which time you've grown into a charming and attractive young lady, if I may say so.'

'Oh—thank you,' she raised her eyes. 'And you—seem little changed, which is meant as a compliment.'

'But a lot has happened in the interim. I can tell you, if you care to hear. Only it seemed rather an Ancient Mariner's tale for yesterday's wedding feast . . . But you shall hear. I recommend the duck à l'orange—and a small Graves,' he added to the waiter.

'You returned to India after we parted, did you not?'

'Yes and Maria's baby, a girl, was born soon after. Only, they never flourished, either of them—they just ailed and ailed . . .' He traced circles with his fork on the cloth. 'An arduous journey to China was out of the question. I sent them up to Ooty, but it didn't help. Then came an epidemic of that summer fever which often hits the South—they both got it and died quite quickly. The baby was only eighteen months, poor mite.'

'Oh Charles, how dreadful for you, I am so sorry.'

He smiled twistedly. 'Not such a rare occurrence in India, but the sort of thing you always assume happens to others, like avalanches or earthquakes. I went down with the fever myself then, but pulled through eventually. Thank heavens my son Peter escaped it.'

'And he is well now?'

'Yes and a great comfort. I took him Home to school for a while after it happened and got a job for myself in London. But Lord it was dull, just the sort of thing I'd always tried to avoid. Ah, here's the duck, and here's to you, Alice!' They drank and he continued, 'We stayed with my sister Dottie in Hampshire for the next Christmas and I remember we stood looking out of a window at one of those typically colourless English-winter days and Peter said, "Father, I hate it here, let's go back to the East." He'd put into words exactly what I felt, and it seemed a sort of sign. When you're a bit lost, you pay attention to signs, don't you?'

She nodded with understanding.

'So in due course, we went back to Madras and at least that made Peter happy, he's in school there now. But India still wasn't my cup of tea and Harriet, my elder sister, had really stuck the black sheep label on me by this time!' He smiled charmingly at her.

'But surely it's better to cast around for a while than settle for too little?'

'I'm glad you feel that too,' he poured more wine, 'so I started casting back in the direction of China again, threw up my Madras job eventually and landed here a few weeks ago. I've taken a recce up the Yangtze and I'm now trying to raise more capital, then I'm opening a trade agency in Hankow. Yesterday, I was in the Club, picked up the *Mercury* . . . and now you're absolutely up to date!'

Her eyes held his, warm with compassion. 'Yes, that is a sad story and you were so full of hopes when we met before. It seems cruel you've been so . . . battered.'

'Well I still have my health and am beginning to hope again, whereas poor Maria. . . .'

He looked away at the potted ferns behind her. 'She was lovely in many ways. One always feels guilty afterwards somehow.'

'But you did what you could, I'm sure?'

'Oh yes, at the time.' His face closed. 'But now it's your turn, what have you been doing since we met?'

As she gave him a carefully edited version of her recent past, he listened carefully for clues to the one question he really wanted to ask. Why was she not yet married? She had seemed such a lovable, lively creature at eighteen and to this she had added the graces of young womanhood. Was there some odd quirk in her nature that was not immediately apparent, or was it simply that she had been stuck in out-of-the-way places where few matrimonial chances existed?

'And now Uncle Robert's decided it will be good for me to stay here for a few months and he'll keep an eye on me,' she imitated his sombre tones. 'I'm to stay at the Customs House annexe and we are to have some fun, he assures me.'

'Quite right too,' he grinned. 'And let's kick off right now with a *crème brûlée* and cream—specially good here.'

As he ordered she asked casually, 'And will you be in Shanghai long?'

'Only a few days, then to Hankow to learn the ropes of the tea-trade on the spot. Later I hope to get upriver beyond the Treaty Ports—Ichang, Chungking . . . who knows?' he waved an airy hand.

'It sounds exciting. I've never been up the Upper Yangtze region—the River of Golden Sands.'

'Sounds damnably dangerous whatever its pretty name. Dozens of boats get smashed to smithereens in the rapids every year apparently. Nearly put me off altogether, I admit—not only the risk to life and limb, but many a merchant

305

has lost his entire capital outlay through the breaking of a tow-rope at the wrong moment.'

Her eyes sparkled. 'I'd love to see how they get those junks up the rapids. And you'll go ahead, won't you, in spite of the risks?'

'No choice—I've really burned my Indian boats this time. It's partly a question of how much to gamble in what. The risks are so great that insurance is enormously costly.'

She frowned. 'It must be difficult. Frank and I used to dream that we'd form a company and go trading up the Yangtze one day. But now he's married to Peachy and is joining his father-in-law, which sounds safe and easy, but excludes me.'

'Really? I never imagined you'd be interested in the sordid business of buying and selling. Most ladies aren't.'

'But I don't seem to be like most ladies and I'd love the adventure of it, and trying to beat your rivals—though the best time for that is past, isn't it? When the great tea-clippers used to race from the Yangtze to London with the first of the season's crop.'

'So I've been told and now it's prosaic steam through the Suez. Trouble is, I always seem to be too late for the real thrills—like my parents' tales of the stirring Mutiny days when I was just a little nipper. Yet being a pre-Mutiny baby is quite a sign of age now, when all the bright young lads coming out were born after it!'

'And I was born just as it ended—so where do I stand? In the old days it was before or after Waterloo that dated you. I suppose it was ever thus? And always will be?'

He reached for the bill. 'I wonder what the next great watershed will be, the sort of event historians begin and end chapters with?'

She grinned, '1882 of course—the year Mr. Charles Grant went a-merchanting up the Yangtze and opened the Middle Kingdom to the greatest influx of Manchester cotton goods and Birmingham hardware that the Celestials had ever seen.'

'. . . changing the economy of the entire East and the balance of world trade and becoming a multi-millionaire in the process!' His eyes twinkled. 'And with that cheering thought I must go, Alice. I've an appointment with a junior chahsee at Crawfords—not a very brilliant beginning, I fear.'

'Well, the Chinese say that to build a mountain you have to

start with one bucket of earth. And I'm sure even the humble life of a Yangtze trader will have its excitements.'

He glanced at her keenly. 'And you'll be enjoying yourself here, I'm sure.'

She shrugged. 'We shall see—but don't let me detain you. Oh and Charles—Isabel has asked you to join us for supper tomorrow evening—if you can manage it?'

He did manage it and, in spite of business commitments, joined the Greenwoods on several occasions before he returned to Hankow, and Isabel and William to Port Arthur. The tone of his subsequent encounters with Alice was lightly flirtatious, both of them avoiding the deeper currents of their first luncheon together. Alice felt they might have gone too far too soon, and in any case he no longer had the same dazzle for her as when she had met him at eighteen. She still liked his breezy promise of a recklessness that had not yet been really tested. But perhaps his sister was right—he was something of a black sheep, a rolling stone mossed only with vague dreams of wealth. When he left, he kissed her gently, carefully withholding any hint of the passion that had once sparked between them. It was as if, after the first elation of their re-encounter, they were both a little disappointed—but did not quite know why.

11

There was general agreement among the resident foreign ladies of Shanghai that June was altogether delightful. The weather was warm and dry enough for the lightest muslin frocks, but not oppressively hot, and gardens, both public and private, glowed with flowers. Cross-country racing was forbidden on account of the farmers' rice seedlings, and the spring snipe had flown north, so that the menfolk did not spend all their waking hours galloping about the countryside or peppering it with gunshot. The first race-meetings and regattas of the year were in full swing and the first contingents of globetrotters and visiting artistes from Europe and America brought new zest to the social scene.

Immediately after the departure of William and his family, Robert Greenwood made it his business to find out forthcoming events in the community's social calendar. As an officer and gentleman he obtained temporary membership of the Shanghai Club and from the vantage of its famous Long Bar easily made the acquaintance of various respectable and popular citizens. Very shortly, it seemed to the impressed Alice, he knew everyone worth knowing in the several-hundred-strong British community and there was no shortage of invitations to suppers, picnics and balls for them both.

'I really don't know how you do it, Uncle,' she exclaimed admiringly, as he raised his hat to acknowledge the greeting of yet another passing lady as they strolled through the Bund gardens one afternoon.

He beamed complacently. 'Shanghai's an easy-come-easy-go sort of place, m'dear. But wherever you are, go at it like a military exercise—do a recce, find out who's who, get the right lines of communication going, invest in the right equipment—well-tailored clothes and wallets of calling-cards for example—get up a few treats for the right people, and Bob's

308

your Uncle . . . ha! Needs a bit of *savoir-faire*, but this Uncle Bob's been through many a Simla season and that's a social minefield compared to this. Ladies are often better at it than gentlemen. You should watch Mrs. Dawson of the Customs House or Mrs. Fortescue in action, for example. They only need to keep in trim now for the field is theirs, you might say, but they've certainly employed similar tactics in the past.'

She was amused. 'I don't believe I'd have the confidence.'

'Well you're still young—you need a husband in the background, then you'll be all right.'

It had not been a deliberate barb, but he saw her mouth tighten and wondered whether to soften it. But no—Alice had to understand that, though bachelors might proceed in this way, a woman needed the financial and social support of a husband. Alice, well aware of his attempts to furnish her with one, had conscientiously studied the season's form, as Frank put it, but so far without enthusiasm. There were eligible young men a-plenty: juniors in the consulates, the hongs and banks, the subalterns in the barracks, and several of all types happy to escort her on pleasurable excursions. Like Jeff Winthrop, she discovered, they talked earnestly of their families at Home, their future prospects, their recent successes in various sporting endeavours. The bolder spirits held her hand, pressed kisses upon her, told her how charming she was. But they all seemed mere boys compared to Lin Fu-wei, or even to Charles Grant, who had gone away without another word.

The only exception might have been Clifford White, a student-interpreter at the Consulate, until the evening when she had heard him read a paper to the Asiatic Society on 'The Influence of Confucianism in the Chinese Home.' A stranger and one of few ladies present, she had not dared question him, but afterwards she had informed him at length that his conclusions were both superficial and inaccurate and that she could have done much better. He had stalked off crimson-faced, saying he wondered why ladies were allowed to come and listen to members' papers if all they could do was criticise. And she had gone miserably to bed, wishing she could learn to hold her tongue.

As they neared the Customs House, Robert said, 'Oh, I meant to tell you—Mrs. Fortescue has asked us to be of her luncheon party for the Victoria Cup race-meet, quite an affair apparently. She says—do bring a friend, if you'd like.'

'Next Saturday, isn't it? I might ask Bertie Tarrent, I suppose.'

'I thought Clifford White was the hero of the hour?'

'No—he's abominably self-opinionated and puffed-up.'

He looked amused. 'Please yourself, miss, you usually do. Now I must go and change for the concert tonight. Mrs. Fortescue assures me this orchestral group from Hanover is superb.'

'I never knew you cared a fig for music, Uncle.'

'Well I've developed a taste—a love for cultural activities—it comes later in life to some than to others.' His tone was deliberately noncommittal and, as he hurried away, she did not quite know what to make of it.

The day of the Victoria Cup meeting, last of the spring season, dawned as fair as many before. Its refreshing sea-breeze, Alice was assured, would die away within a week, leaving them to the mercy of the mid-summer heats with positively no air to breathe at all. Foreign ladies on the arms of gentlemen strolled near the grandstand wearing day frocks of lemon yellow, rose pink, or peppermint green, and crowds of predominantly blue-clad Chinese spectators crowded round the track corners where betting was furious. The drum and fife band from the gunboat *Euryalus* played a selection of lively airs. Boys ran in and out of the striped marquees with trays of drinks and the members of the racing fraternity were clustered round the ponies in the paddock.

Frank was among them, giving advice to his father-in-law's jockey while nearby, Peachy watched her husband adoringly. Alice, on the arm of Bertie Tarrent, a senior clerk in the Hong Kong & Shanghai Bank who had a good head for figures and a waspish sense of humour, spotted her from a distance.

'Oh—there's my sister-in-law, near the paddock, we must go over!'

Bertie raised his field-glasses. 'Where—I can't see . . .'

'There, near the mounted pony, in pink and orange . . .'

'Oh . . . er yes, Chinese of course, I forgot . . . silly of me. And a bit rum for you?'

'Not at all. Peachy's very sweet—let's go and see her.'

'If you like, but I think the saddle-bell is about to ring.'

Defiantly she started off, but just then the bell did ring and Mrs. Fortescue claimed them, leading them to her table in the shade with a good view of the last length. Mary Fortescue had quickly become rather important in Robert and Alice's life. A friend of Mrs. Dawson's, she had been delegated by that busy lady to take the newcomers under her wing and was admirably fitted for the task. She was a rather ample, garrulous middle-aged lady with changeless ash-blonde hair and roguish blue eyes. Early the previous year her husband, Claud, a director of the Hong Kong & Shanghai Bank, had dropped dead of a heart attack one morning; instead of going quietly Home, as most women did in such circumstances, Mary Fortescue stayed on. It was the most unconventional step of her life and she still felt obliged to justify it sometimes—though less often recently as people grew accustomed to her singularity. Events like race-meetings brought out the best in her, for she was a Shanghai-hand of twelve years' standing. She knew everyone, liked the majority and was liked in return for her generous hospitality and an irrepressible liveliness that had survived her widowhood undimmed.

'. . . Now Alice, Bertie, whom do you know? Major, a chair for Alice please . . . Why practically everyone, I believe . . . Mr. and Mrs. Wetherby and the Misses Wetherby, Clifford White of course—and Mr. Hinkson, our dear Hink, you know? And Bubbles Parker, well everyone knows him. . . . Then we'll settle down and think about making our fortunes. Hush now everyone,' and she called for silence as, after two false starts, the next race began.

'Lady Luck in the lead yes . . . it is . . . yes, I knew it! No, Petronella—come on Petronella . . . no, it's Lady Luck!' The Misses Wetherby clapped their gloved hands and cried out in excitement as the favourite scampered past the winning post and made them ten dollars richer.

Alice had early realised that she was not to be the most sought-after belle of that Shanghai summer, the position being jointly occupied by Violet and Iris Wetherby, charming, elegant daughters of a newly appointed shipping director. They had recently come from Home bringing the latest fashions and social chat and had already impressed upon the assembled company that today's races were mere comedy compared to last year's Epsom. Still, they had sportingly decided to make the best of it and giggled mightily at the funny little Mongolian ponies bouncing round the uneven course.

'Now who's going to win next, Vi?' Iris ran a finger down the card. 'How about Taiping? What does that mean? Something Chinese I suppose, Mr. Hinkson?'

Mr. Hinkson, librarian from the Consulate secretariat, could scarcely ever have been asked a sillier question, Alice thought, but he answered good-humouredly. 'I wouldn't back a pony of that name, Miss Wetherby—the Taipings didn't exactly emerge victorious from the field.'

'Oh—people, were they?'

'Rebels against the Manchus who wanted to set up a Heavenly Kingdom on Chinese soil. They were causing havoc when I first came out here more than twenty-five years ago—plundering and slaughtering wherever they went.'

'Really, how horrible.' Iris shuddered. 'Then I shan't back him, I'll have more of that delicious salmon mousse instead.'

'Did you actually see the Taipings in action, Mr. Hinkson?' Alice asked. 'My parents did in Ningpo.'

'So did I—unfortunately—at Soochow, not fifty miles from this race-course. I was a young interpreter with the Ever Victorious Army commanded by Major Charles Gordon, "Chinese Gordon" they later dubbed him. The Taipings held Soochow for a month and I was there when Gordon's troops recaptured it. A grisly affair altogether, difficult to know who behaved worst, the rebels or the Imperial Forces storming through the city like animals, firing buildings and cutting up innocent people—the ditches overflowed with blood. Hard to believe now that such things went on not far away, not so long ago . . . But here, some salmon mousse?'

'Thank you. And hard to imagine the sort of life that still goes on among people living not so very far away who'd be absolutely astounded by a scene like this. The drums and gongs of the magistrates' procession reminded me.'

He smiled understandingly, his reply lost in the crowd's roar as the race finished and Iris turned on him reproachfully. 'Oh, it's Taiping I do believe! An outsider too and you told me not to back him, Mr. Hinkson!'

Alice was unsympathetic. 'Never judge the jam . . .'

Iris, looking annoyed, went to join Clifford White and Bubbles Parker, thinking that Miss Greenwood was simply a country-born little person of no possible consequence. 'I gather Miss Greenwood has never been Home?' she whispered to Clifford as he poured lemonade.

'I think not—which is why she feels entitled to have so many decided opinions on things Chinese.' He smiled at her.

'And I gather her brother is actually married to a native?'

'Yes—he's over there, that blond chap with the dandy Chinaman. Here, take a look . . .' Bubbles Parker handed Iris his glasses. He was a ruddy-faced man with ruddy whiskers and was reputed to foam at the mouth with rage at the misdeeds of his houseboys, hence his nickname.

Clifford shrugged. 'Well, old Frank's married into quite a bit of money, if you like that sort of thing.'

Bubbles snorted. 'Not my cup of little green tea, thank you . . . How could one possibly, when there are so many utterly alluring English ladies about?' He bowed at Iris as they moved away from the emptying tables.

Alice felt her cheeks burn, for, though she had not quite heard the conversation, she had guessed Frank and she were its subject. She had just decided to go and talk to Peachy, when Mrs. Fortescue drew her aside. 'My dear Alice—your uncle's been telling me of your little difficulty about accommodation and I wonder if I could help?'

'Oh that—it is rather a nuisance.'

The previous day the Dawsons had heard that the Inspector-General of Customs, Sir Robert Hart, had left Peking on an inspection tour. Sir Robert's tours were renowned for thoroughness, unpredictability and size of entourage. Clearly the whole Customs House had to be held in readiness.

'I've suggested to your uncle that you come and stay with me and he's quite agreeable, if you'd like to? My daughter Lilian and I just rattle round in my place these days. And Lilian is no sort of company anyway—so I should be delighted and it would give the servants a bit more to do.'

Alice's heart leaped with pleasure, for on her one visit she had thought Mrs. Fortescue's house, Fairlawns, quite the nicest in Shanghai.

So it was arranged and Mrs. Fortescue was to send her carriage round the very next day, for, she explained, soon no one, except the indefatigable I.-G., would move an inch in any direction on account of the heat. Only when packing her trunk that evening did Alice realise that, in the excitement of the races and the subsequent whirling away to the Wetherbys' house for tea, she had not even spoken to Peachy. She felt vexed. How easy it was for such situations to occur, how difficult to have introduced Peachy to them all. But she knew that her sister-in-law would be feeling slighted, and there was nothing she could do about it.

Fairlawns, into which Alice moved the next day, was spacious and peaceful, its rooms adorned with scroll-paintings, porcelains, lacquerwork, its lawns surrounded by oleanders, magnolias, palms and tulip trees. On Alice's first evening, Mrs. Fortescue arranged to be in, for, she said as they settled on the verandah at sunset, 'As you are to be staying here, my dear, we should get to know each other better. And,' she continued in her usual rush, 'I expect you wonder why I've chosen to stay on here? My married daughter in England begs me to join her and so does my son, Edgar, in Singapore, but it's Lilian my youngest who's the bother.'

'I don't believe I've met her yet. Isn't she studying for something?'

Mrs. Fortescue's eyes rolled skywards in despair. 'Indeed yes—and of all ridiculous things, she's fixed on becoming a medical missionary. A sort of lady doctor if you please, dealing with all those utterly repulsive Chinese diseases—leprosy, scrofula, elephantiasis, the Lord knows what. It quite turns my stomach to hear of them. Lilian, I say to her, you are a well-born, well-brought-up young lady, it is simply not fitting for someone like you to . . .'

Alice decided to interrupt. 'But what gave her the idea? Does missioning run in your family as it does in mine?'

'Oh dear no, and I'm sure they do most worthy work, but Claud, my late husband, would send her to the mission school here. She was always his favourite pet lamb,' there was no mistaking the venom in the mother's voice, 'and he couldn't bear her to go Home to school as the others had. That's how the missionaries got hold of her, body and soul—oh Claud, if you'd but lived to see the mischief you've wrought, I say to myself. She was already inclined to it before he died, but since then there's been no stopping her. She studies nothing but dreadful medical books and some of their illustrations are positively indecent in my view. She refuses to do anything else and if I leave her here, she'll move into the mission hostel and there'll be no hope for her!'

'But there's another side to it, surely, Mrs. Fortescue? Lilian is obviously doing what she wants—she has found a mission in life, you might say. And I sometimes wish I could.

Are not people with a sense of true purpose the happiest, whereas the rest of us—I speak for myself anyway—tend to drift along rather aimlessly?'

'No, my dear,' Mrs. Fortescue was quite firm, 'there are things a woman can fix upon if she's a mind to and I'm sure you will. If Lilian wants to do good, there's the Benevolent Society, those funds for orphans and sailors' widows and whatnot. But missionaries are hopelessly one-track; they don't give a fig for their own kind. And they often make the most unsuitable marriages. Why, a young lady came here with the C.M.S. recently, daughter of a wealthy Sussex land-owner I understand, but full of the word of the Lord, as they say. Well, would you believe it, within the year she'd married a young blacksmith from Aberdeen—now they're going hammer and tongs at the souls of the heathen somewhere in Szechuan! Nearly killed her poor Mama. And that's what worries me most about Lilian—bad enough being a lady doctor, but she could end up marrying a carpenter to boot!'

'Well Jesus Christ was a carpenter.' Alice bit her lip, realising she had angered her hostess.

'Come now Alice, that's being frivolous. There are carpenters and carpenters. Your uncle warned me you have strong opinions, but I didn't gather you fully supported the ideas of the missionary fraternity.'

'Indeed I don't, it was just a silly joke, Mrs. Fortescue. My stepfather considers me quite a lost soul, I assure you.'

'Then let us drop the subject and have supper. And after, I'll let you see the other reason why I stay in Shanghai—of which Lilian doesn't at all approve, but you might.'

And when Mrs. Fortescue showed her the long gallery behind the house filled with her collection of Japanese works of art, Alice's approval was wholehearted. 'I began buying when Claud and I were in Yokohama in the early '60s,' Mrs. Fortescue explained. 'And the most beautiful things were going for a song then—it was before the Meiji Restoration and Japanese currency was in a sorry mess. It wasn't till we came here in '70 that I realised how clever I'd been, and should have bought more! But it was a start and since I've traded the lesser stuff for works of real quality. See, here's a print of Harunobu's, "Two Girls by a Stream"—look at those delicate colours, the flowing lines ... and here's Shinenaga's "Descending Geese at Katata" ... isn't it droll? But they're

315

only woodblocks, *ukiyo-e*, "pictures of the passing world." Come, see over here: this exquisite screen, irises, reeds . . .'

'Did you like the Japanese as people?' This was a new idea to Alice, for the Chinese spoke of them so disparagingly.

'A wonderful race, my dear, so clean and go-ahead, so admirably effective in every way, compared to slow-poke Chinamen. One day they'll beat the pants off the rest of Asia, as your uncle bluntly puts it. And good luck to 'em. I always wish we'd stayed there, but now I have to be content with occasional buying sprees to Nagasaki and Yokohama. And between you and me, everything I buy sells extremely well to globetrotting amateur collectors with more money than sense! And my favourites, which you see here, give me the added gratification of increasing in value every year. That's why Lilian doesn't approve—quite unprincipled according to her and I should make due penance by donating all profits to the new Mission hospital! So you see my dear, my daughter and I seldom see eye to eye. But would you agree with Lilian in this?'

'Certainly not—it's a marvellous collection and I think you should cherish it, build on it and let others admire it with you.'

Mrs. Fortescue patted her shoulder.

'Well Alice, I'm sure you wouldn't say that just to please me. So please feel at liberty to look round here whenever you like. . . . Some of the works grow on you—you'll see.'

Indeed the gallery did open a new dimension of seeing for Alice, who, while quietly absorbing the beauty of the art, gradually realised that its creators could not be as contemptible as she had been led to believe. The relative coolness of the gallery also attracted her during the long summer days when the social pace slackened as the temperature rose, when, along the Bund, the whitish afternoon sun shone with a metallic glare on the stone façades of offices, the zinc-plated godowns, the motionless sea beyond.

After sunset, people began to move again in a limp way and Uncle Robert, who seemed remarkably content with Shanghai life, would come to take Mrs. Fortescue and Alice out—to a concert, a supper-party, a drive to the playing fields where the sportsmen were practising. At weekends, parties were made up for excursions into the hills or houseboat trips along the Wampoa with the usual contingent of bachelors, the elegant Misses Wetherby and globetrotters with the right introductions.

Late in the evening, returned from various jollifications, Alice used often to stand on her bedroom verandah enjoying the fragrance of blossom, the croak of frogs from the lily pond, and think—for, as everyone said, it was too hot to do so at any other time. Invariably, a light still shone from the room of the industrious Lilian, a quiet young woman pale of skin and eye, who disapproved of Alice as of everything in her mother's household. To Lilian, Alice was just another husband-seeking, light-minded young lady flitting on the social scene, and it was in vain that Alice told her how she admired her determination to acquire a profession against all odds.

'You could do the same if you really wanted,' Lilian had snapped back. 'There's a crying need for qualified medical people in mission outposts throughout the world.'

'But you see . . .' Alice began, then stopped, wondering then, as she did when she stood on the evening verandah, why it was that she could not commit herself as Lilian could—wishing desperately to be in some way taken over. For having fun, she thought dismally, was not enough. But why did she feel the odd one out? The other young people seemed never to be afflicted with the sense of dissatisfaction that so often beset her. It was, she supposed, her missionary inheritance that rendered her incapable of prolonged frivolity and had given her a sense of purpose that she could not quite ignore, though it was undirected by any conviction.

I could spend a lifetime on the sidelines, waiting to be convinced by something—or someone—she thought in despair, leaning against the verandah pillar, watching Lilian turn off her lamp at last and kneel in prayer before sinking into untroubled, virginal slumber. But Alice's nights were sometimes haunted by erotic fantasies wherein her body moved knowingly into one of her favourite positions and she became 'like a silkworm spinning a cocoon' with her hands clasped about the neck, her feet across the back of her urgent lover, whose face was now Lung-kuang's, now Lin's, now an indeterminate amalgam of Oriental manhood. After such dreams Alice would lie awake, damp and troubled in the bright dawn, wondering whatever was to become of her.

The first sign of change occurred on a late August evening when she was dressing for the Mih Ho Loong ball. From outside there came the sound of a thousand beating wings and she went on to the verandah, looking into the clear dark sky.

317

'Hear that?' Mary Fortescue called from the garden where she was standing with Robert. 'It's the snipe returning from the north—they'll be all over the marshes tomorrow and the men will be oiling their guns tonight. It's the beginning of the end of summer.'

Alice listened to the lovely rhythms and then went inside, brushing her hair absentmindedly. The end of summer—and then what? She had made no plans beyond that and still lacked the urge to do so. Downstairs, Mrs. Fortescue and Uncle Robert were waiting for her in the drawing-room, he in his officer's mess kit, she in a ball-gown of pearl grey silk trimmed with harebell blue. They stood stiffly side by side, posed, like a *tableau vivant* or a studio portrait.

'Is anything wrong? You look so solemn.'

The pose broke and Robert handed her a glass of the champagne they were drinking. 'Not at all—quite the contrary. We were drinking a little toast and hope you'll share it.'

'Of course, I love champagne.' She lifted her glass. 'To what do I drink?'

Robert glanced at his companion. 'To us—if you will. Mary and I have just become engaged.'

Alice set down the glass and stared at them, tears springing to her eyes. 'You—why—you two? You pair of dark horses . . . but I never dreamed . . .' She laughed shakily.

Mary came to kiss her. 'You are pleased, I hope, Alice?'

'I'm delighted of course—delighted. But so surprised, I must have been blind.'

And indeed she had been, for, with the self-centred arrogance of her years, it had not once occurred to her that their summer friendship was more than a mild flirtation. She gulped down the inexplicable emotions in her throat. 'Mrs. Fortescue, how lovely for you! I assure you my uncle is a dear man.'

'And Mrs. Fortescue is a very dear lady, I assure you, Alice,' Robert smiled. 'But we needn't be so formal anymore. Wouldn't Aunt Mary sound better?'

Mary laughed coquettishly. 'Oh Robert, please not! Alice is too grown up to suddenly acquire another aunt—and how ancient that makes me feel! I think just "Mary" in the circumstances . . .'

'To Mary and Robert, with all my very, very best wishes for their future happiness . . .' Alice raised her glass. 'And when is the wedding to be?'

'Ah, that was the slight difficulty we've just negotiated successfully. You see Alice, I felt it just couldn't be this year—when poor dear Claud only died last. Widowed one year, remarried the next—sounds a bit fast.' She giggled into her champagne. 'But Robert has to be back in Calcutta by late January. So we've settled on 2 January. We don't want to seem impatient, but that will give us a little time together before Robert leaves.'

'You won't go with him?'

'Oh dear no—that's fully agreed. I'll join him in Simla for a late honeymoon next year, but we both want to stay in China.'

'And once I'm out of the Army I'll settle here with Mary for a few years anyway.'

'So you'll always have a home now with us.' Mary patted her arm reassuringly, aware of how mixed Alice's feelings must be. After all, the original purpose of the Greenwoods' staying in Shanghai was to find a husband for the niece, not a wife for the uncle.

'But come—let's go to the ball and dance the night away!' She tripped to get her shawl, and Alice noted with a pang how Robert put it round her shoulders in a newly proprietorial manner.

The Mih Ho Loong ball given by the Hook and Ladder Company volunteer fire brigade was one of the most select held at the Club. Members of the brigade wore the same scarlet shirts, tight black trousers and leather helmets in which they sallied doughtily forth to fight the frequent blazes that occurred in the foreign concessions. Their dashing outfits gave an extra brio to the evening and encouraged everyone to look their best. Dancing was in full swing when they arrived and Alice was claimed by coolly-waiting Bertie Tarrent for a cotillion; a couple of Highland reels followed—practice apparently for the equally grand St. Andrew's Day ball later. Then the band struck up the popular Shanghai waltz and, over her partner's shoulder, Alice saw Robert and Mary float past, happily oblivious of anyone else.

'Well, well, good for Mrs. Fortescue,' Bertie exclaimed when she told him of their engagement in the supper interval. 'I'd have thought her a bit long in the tooth for your handsome uncle—must be over fifty if she's a day.'

'But he's ... let's see, in his late forties. Not much difference.'

319

'And she's very comfortably provided for, is she not?'

'I hope you're not suggesting that my uncle . . .'

Bertie smiled sardonically. 'Tut, tut, of course not, my dear.' But, remembering the recent liaison of young Frank, he had just coined the term 'gold-digging Greenwoods' to amuse his chums.

He looked at Alice keenly. 'And you'll have the run of Fairlawns now, I imagine? Cunning of the old girl to have you stay there so that Uncle could keep making highly respectable calls, what?'

'Oh Bertie, I don't suppose she deliberately planned it so.'

'Of course she did. A good strategist, Mrs. Fortescue. And your uncle didn't have to fall. She simply recognised he was ripe for the plucking.'

Bubbles Parker, next on Alice's card, lunged up for his polka just then, leaving Bertie to consider Alice's new position, for the name of Fortescue was still one to conjure with in local banking circles where he was making his way. When the time came to claim her for the last waltz, he whispered in her ear, 'The floor's abominably crowded; let's go outside instead.'

It was a balmy, star-filled night, the Club gardens awash with late-summer blossom. Bertie drew her into the shadows murmuring softly, 'You are a lovely creature, you know, Alice Greenwood, a lovely lovely creature.'

His slim fingers stroked her cheeks and neck, pressed gently into her breasts, and she, still in a happy haze of music and champagne, responded gladly. How odd the world was, she thought, unbuttoning his jacket and putting her hot cheek against his cool stiff shirtfront; men and women catching and clinging to each other—on dance floors, in bedrooms—and she giggled at the marvellously ironic joke of sombre Uncle Robert catching, being caught by, the roguish widow Fortescue.

'Why are you laughing, sweetheart?' Bertie murmured into her hair. 'Does what I'm doing only amuse you?'

'Oh no, it's very pleasurable, Bertie. . . .' She wriggled closer, trying to accommodate her small soft body to his tight narrow one.

He kissed her ardently and whispered, 'Isn't it romantic— this beautiful starry sky, music in the background and we two alone here together?'

She stared up at him, wondering if he had reverted to his usual badinage, but his expression was humourlessly intent, though no stir of sensuality came from him. Was he really bowled over by passion at last—the cool, flippant Bertie for whom all women were like bank accounts with credits and debits to be carefully balanced? Then she understood and flung her head away from his nestling arms.

'Why of course—Bertie, you great fraud!' She was almost amused. 'It's not me you're trying to seduce, is it? It's my new prospects, my sudden credit rating, as you'd call it—a sort of step-niece to Mary Fortescue, owner of Fairlawns, widow of your bank's director?'

He drew back, affronted, whipped by guilt into an immediate flash of anger.

'Don't be insulting, Alice—how dare you accuse me of such baseness? It's because I'm so fond of you—or was, but not if you think things like that of me.' He rebuttoned his jacket primly. 'I suggest you apologise at once, Miss Greenwood. As if I cared . . .'

'But you do, Bertie, you do.' She wiped the moisture of his kisses from her mouth. The very traces of them angered her. 'Oh you hypocrite, Bertie. At least the Chinese are honest in such matters—their unions are unashamedly based on credits and debits with none of this foolery about starry skies and sweethearts. But oh—oh you have to pretend you're madly in love with me all of a sudden. But you're not a man who knows how to truly want a woman, Bertie Tarrent, I can tell that.'

'Well, well and I wonder where you acquired so much expertise in the field, Miss Greenwood?' His sneer was icy. 'And where you find your truly wanting men? The streets of the native town are full of them, I'm sure. Why not try there—if you've not yet done so?'

She raised her evening bag and hit him square and hard across the face. The bag was beaded and he yelped. She did not wait to see if she had drawn blood as she hoped before rushing away across the lawn and down the driveway. The ball had ended and couples were streaming out into the night, some still prancing and singing a little as they came with a swish of gowns, crunch of boots, jewels glinting on warmed flesh, glamorous smells of powder and perfume. Globular lanterns bobbing in the hands of servants and on the poles of the carriage-drivers gave the scene a certain enchantment. It was like a stage set, she thought, leaning against a tree to regain her composure. And were they not all actors, these merry revellers, laughing and flirting in groups, then driving off home together two by two? Would the magic of this evening sweeten those marital beds where resentment, boredom, and revulsion so often reigned? She sighed heavily. Why did she know that? See so clearly through Bertie's little stratagems? Why was it that other people—these dancers, Uncle Robert and Mary Fortescue—found it so easy to fall in love and get themselves properly married off? Disconsolately she walked to the gates, looking for the Fortescue carriage. A Chinese in Western clothes passed, then paused to look through the Club railings. Was there not something achingly familiar about the turn of his head? The miracle—how she needed it at that moment!

She rushed to him. 'Lin . . . Lin, can it be you?'

An unsmiling, unknown face stared round at her. 'I'm sorry,' she fell back. 'I thought you were someone else.'

He looked her up and down insolently. 'You were at this foreign festival?'

'Yes—a dance.'

'You barbarian men and women hold each other close to dance, I believe?'

'Yes, it's quite fun.'

'It must be—for the man with you. Will you show me how?'

He came closer holding out his arms and she stepped impulsively into them. 'You move slowly and together like this.' She pushed him gently into a waltzing motion, closing her eyes the better to imagine Lin's embrace.

The stranger's arm tightened round her waist and he chuckled. 'This is worth learning—come to my lodgings and teach me more, foreign woman.'

Why not, oh why not, she thought. Her body ached with tension, rebellion, half-roused desire. Bertie, even her brother William had already suggested she was a woman of the streets in thought if not in deed. Why not live up to their expectations? At least with this young stranger there would be no hypocrisy, no play-acting—just direct sensual sex. She could feel it in his sinews. She looked at him, her eyes glittering.

'Come,' he tugged at her and she melted towards him. Then she heard pounding footsteps and Robert's voice shouting.

'Alice—it is you! What the devil are you doing?' As he ran up the stranger bolted. 'Who was that man? Do you know him?'

'No, I was just showing him how foreigners dance.'

'Dancing—in the arms of an unknown native in the streets!

Really, you are an utterly shameless hussy sometimes. It's degrading . . . disgraceful. Here's the carriage, get in there . . .' He propelled her so roughly inside that she fell across the seat and lay there inert, trembling, dazed.

'This is becoming quite appalling. We must get that young woman respectably married off quick,' Robert muttered to Mary between his teeth as they drove home.

'I'll see what I can do, Robert. Leave it to me.'

'Come here a minute, dear,' Mary called as Alice returned from giving Peachy her English lesson one afternoon shortly after the ball. She was sitting surrounded by fashion plates cut from European magazines. 'I'm trying to decide which of these would be suitable for my going-away. Hong Kong is so smart. But guess who I met in Saxby's this afternoon—he gave me this.' Teasingly she held up a namecard, blank side showing. Alice reached for it. 'No, guess who you'd most like it to be, and that's who it is.'

'But I don't know that . . .'

'In your heart of hearts you do, Alice, I'm sure. See . . .'

'Grant and Co. . . . Why, Charles, back again?'

'Yes, arrived yesterday and asking very particularly after you. So I've invited him to supper with us all tomorrow. . . . Such a charming, handsome man. I've only met him briefly, but . . . anyway, I should wear your lime-green and gold dress, dear, it's most becoming.'

She wore the dress and was glad, for the look of admiration in Charles' eyes when he saw her was the start of a very pleasant evening. He was in high spirits and more than ever convinced that Yangtze trade was full of promise.

'You should see the houses of the tea-men along the Treaty Port bunds—very grand. They've obviously made some tidy piles in very few years. One needs some experience to get in the right swim though, and I've been advised to dabble a little in Eastern exotica for the European markets as well.'

'What a good idea!' Mary bubbled. 'I've always been sure that those jolly little painted fans you see everywhere would sell like hotcakes to English ladies wanting to feel a trifle outré in Bromley. And how about pictures? Not good ones of course—you must see my Japanese gallery, Mr. Grant—but the hideous scrolls of demons and gods they sell at temples. Yes, I think it will soon be fashionable to have a scrap of the

323

mysterious Orient in every seaside villa hall.'

'Why, you inspire me, Mrs. Fortescue,' Charles bowed. 'And what about a few tons of those handbells to summon the maid to dust the scrolls?'

And Robert added, 'While we're about it, why not a few thousand of the brass gongs from the monasteries of various heavenly clouds to summon the guests to dine?'

'Seriously, Mr. Grant,' Mary continued, 'I'm sure you're on the right track. Several traders I first met in Yokohama in the '60s have done excellently exporting Japanese trash to America.'

'You were in Japan that early—before the Meiji?'

'Indeed yes and what a time it was! Fewer than two hundred of us foreigners cooped up in the Yokohama settlement in rickety clapboard bungalows with just a couple of stores, a few godowns and bars of ill-repute. But it was all so *pioneering*—we ladies felt as if we'd won a gold cup if we secured a bottle of Lea & Perrins sauce or a tin of salmon from Baker & Co. when the overseas cargoes came in. And people kept making fortunes and losing them just as fast . . . oh, but it was such fun!'

Charles grinned. 'There you are, Alice—too late for the real thrills again! In India, Japan and now here, I imagine the best of the action is over.'

'Oh that's your grumble, isn't it, Robert?' Mary got in first again as usual. 'To hear him talk sometimes you'd think he'd be glad to have another Mutiny on our hands.'

'Tush, that's putting it too strongly, Mary. But certainly now that Pax Britannica has descended over all and even Afghanistan seems quiet, there's precious little excitement in the military life. I might as well go trading trinkets like you, Charles.'

'But you make it sound so trivial, Uncle,' Alice protested. 'I think it sounds most exciting—merchant-adventuring up the Yangtze.'

'Oh for the visionary glow of youth!' Mary sighed, ringing the bell. 'Now, do show Mr. Grant round the gallery, Alice, and then join us for coffee on the verandah.

'. . . You know, Robert,' she continued, as he lit his after-dinner cigar, 'I think that's the man.'

'What—for Alice? He's rather old, isn't he? Widower, bit of a rolling stone . . .'

'But more likely to appeal to her than these Shanghai sprigs. She's old for her years in some ways and is obviously attracted by his sense of adventure.'

Robert grinned. 'So now you've fixed me up, it's my niece's turn, is it?'

She kissed him on the forehead. 'Exactly so. And I shall be good for you, just as Charles would be for Alice. You'll see.'

As they strolled through the gallery Alice was thinking along similar lines and remarked with a feminine pout worthy of Iris Wetherby, 'I haven't heard a word from you since you left, Charles, and I did hope to.'

'Did you? I thought you'd be much too taken up with all your young beaux and I didn't feel I should interfere.'

'Silly—it hasn't been like that at all.'

'But you've had beaux surely?'

'Oh yes, several.'

'Anyone—important, if I may ask?'

'No.' They stared at the paintings in silence.

'That one would fetch a pretty penny,' he remarked at last.

'You do want money, don't you, Charles?'

'Only because I've much less than the rest of my family and they tend to judge me accordingly.'

They moved to the end of the gallery, tense with awareness of each other's presence, and, instead of looking at the last painting, he put his arms round her.

'You remember that night—the old temple on the hill when I first kissed you?'

'I've never forgotten it.'

'Haven't you? I had to pull myself up then because I was married, but that's no longer the case. So perhaps it's time I kissed you again?' For answer she moved into his arms, feeling her senses stirring as his hands moved round the back of her neck. When they returned to the verandah Mary privately decided then and there that a few prods in the right direction would undoubtedly produce the required result.

These Mary discreetly administered during the next two weeks while Charles lingered in Shanghai, acting as Alice's constant escort and finding it unaccountably difficult to conclude his business affairs. But eventually he had neither reason nor excuse to stay longer. 'I have to return to Hankow on the Friday steamer,' he told Alice as they bowled along in a double rickshaw one evening after a Fine Arts Society meeting.

Her heart sank. 'I shall miss you.' She didn't look at him.
'Will you really?'

They listened in silence to the laboured breathing of the rickshaw coolies who, driven near exhaustion at the end of the day, were craving rest.

'Let's pay them off and walk back via the Bund gardens, shall we?' Charles suggested. 'It's not very late.'

The gardens were practically deserted; moonlight shone on white chrysanthemums in the flowerbeds and Alice commented self-consciously on their beauty. Under the shadow of a magnolia tree Charles pulled her to face him. 'I think I'd better say quite simply what I have in mind, Alice—what has been occupying so much of my thoughts for some time, actually. I am in love with you, dear, and want you to marry me. Will you be my wife?'

She drew in a sharp, thrilled breath, thinking incongruously that she seemed doomed to receive proposals in public gardens. 'Oh Charles . . . well, I really . . .'

'Of course you've every reason to refuse me. I'm a widower, considerably older than you, and with the responsibility of a growing son. I have little capital, no fixed profession or even abode and my future prospects are by no means certain. So I shall quite understand if you . . .'

She felt so happy that it was easy to tease a little. 'So you are advising me to refuse the offer you've just made, I take it, Mr. Grant?'

He paused, nonplussed by her banter. 'I think I . . . No, I'm not. You see I love you very much. I think a little bit of me has loved you ever since we first met six years ago. And that is the most important thing, is it not?'

He took her shoulders, forcing her to meet his eyes seriously.

'Yes Charles, I do love you. I know I do, very much. And I shall be very happy, very pleased to become your wife.' It was a formal moment. Then embarrassed and pleased, they fell into each other's arms, kissing and touching tenderly, while Alice assured him that her family would certainly approve.

After a while they pulled apart, Alice straightened her hair and they walked away together arm in arm. 'And you realise, Mr. Grant, how useful I shall be to you?' she asked lightly. 'There are few Englishwomen in China today with my knowledge of the language and people. And you will let me help you, won't you, dear? I can translate documents for you and

326

manage the compradore and I'm excellent at bargaining.'

'You'll really enjoy doing things like that, Alice? It would be a tremendous help of course, for I know so little . . . but I wouldn't expect . . .'

'Yes, of course, we shall be in business together and—oh Charles, I was getting so bored with all these frivolities here—they become pointless after a while. And now this—I told you I'd long dreamed of trading up the Yangtze and I'd much rather do it with you than Frank. But there's one condition if I'm to help you whole-heartedly.' She tugged him to a halt.

'What is it, sweetheart?'

'The firm Frank and I dreamed of would have been Greenwood & Greenwood. I want our firm to be Grant & Greenwood.'

He frowned. 'But I don't see why . . . I mean your name will be Grant too.' It had not occurred to her and she felt a pang; Greenwood was her name; Uncut Jade stemmed from it. 'Well I shall keep my maiden name too then, Greenwood-Grant, some women do.'

'But, Alice, I've just had all the cards and letterheads printed—you saw them—and it's not usual for wives to . . .'

'But, Charles, I'm not quite a usual sort of wife and several very unusual things have happened to me, as you know. You said the other day you like my having a mind of my own, so I want my own name on the firm, our firm.'

He sighed, feeling it was a bad omen to wrangle so soon after plighting their troth. 'All right, but it will be expensive to get everything reprinted.'

'I'll pay for it. I have some money.' She tucked an arm into his. 'And you must admit that Grant & Greenwood has a grander ring to it?'

He grunted noncommittally, comforting himself with the reflection that once the firm got on its feet and she had children and domestic duties to see to, the 'Greenwood' could be quietly dropped.

As Alice guessed, Robert gladly gave his formal blessing to the proposal and Mary capped it with an inspired idea: why not make it a double wedding on 2 January? Half the expense and fuss, double the pleasure and purpose, they all agreed, so the new engagement was announced forthwith. Bertie Tarrent, his nose much out of joint, opined that Charles Grant must be a wealthy man because Greenwoods only married into well-feathered nests. Clifford White said it was a blessing Grant

327

knew little about China and was thus a willing empty vessel to receive his fiancée's many fixed views on the subject. The Wetherby sisters thought that Alice must have been rather desperate to marry a widower senior in years and a trader to boot. But the other Greenwoods were delighted; Isabel wrote to congratulate Robert on his cleverness. Frank harboured vague dreams of Greenwood, Grant & Wang Ltd. that would one day monopolise the Yangtze trade. There was a touching letter from Eliza expressing her gratitude that Charles was apparently a Christian gentleman and offering to come to the wedding with the twins.

Charles' people were less pleased, especially his sister Harriet in Madras who feared that the new bride would immediately lay claim to Peter, of whom she was extremely fond, and fill him with all sorts of Chinese nonsense. To his parents, recently retired to Hampshire, Charles sent a photograph of Alice sitting in a basket chair on the Fairlawns verandah. She looked, decided his mother, quite a presentable creature, but her jaw was too set and her eyes were not looking directly into the camera, giving a somewhat shifty impression. One must not, of course, expect too much of a missionary's daughter of totally unknown background, but, all in all, it was a thousand pities Charles had not stayed in Madras and married dear Belinda Dodds who had discreetly doted on him for years.

When Alice studied her photograph she had the disquieting sense that only part of her was there—like a painting of a half-moon by one who had never seen it at the full. She looked demure and lady-like enough, in a pretty muslin dress, ankles carefully crossed; but she too noticed that her eyes were averted from the camera, detracting from the happy smile on her lips. For she had felt thoroughly happy at the time, as relieved as everyone that the problems of her future were suddenly solved. She did not have to fight against the barriers of race or religion after all, did not have to worry about where to live, what to do next, whom to love. She was not going to be an old maid, or a supernumerary aunt or the mistress of a struggling revolutionary; she was going to be a respectable lady with an English husband, just as everyone had hoped. And in a few years, Charles had promised her, when the firm would be thriving, he would take her to Europe at last and they would see all the sights. Such had been the stuff of her conscious thoughts when she posed on the verandah, yet she could not meet the camera's eye in case it saw through the things she most deliberately was not thinking about, of which her fond fiancé had no suspicion.

These things seemed to have accumulated over the years and were a burden to her as never before, because she believed Charles to be an honest man and yearned to be equally honest in return. Often, that autumn, when he had returned to Hankow and she and Mary were engrossed in preparations for the double wedding, she imagined that, when he returned, she would tell him all: the delights of her early concubinage; the distress of her eviction and miscarriage; the wild scenes she had witnessed among the Miao; the meeting with Stewart Carr and her continued guilty possession of his loot; the feel of her stepfather's 'jade stalk' rising as he whipped her buttocks; the delicious joys and searing pains of her love affair with Lin. 'Only those who are their absolute true selves in the world can fulfil their own natures,' she sternly quoted Confucius to herself. But there were so many factors in her life which the sage could not possibly have reckoned with, and she feared to see the love-light die from Charles' eyes, feared to be left alone again with all the problems his reassuring presence solved.

So, when he did return to Shanghai a week before Christmas, her resolve faltered though in one respect she found it hard to keep her secrets intact. His passion for her was noticeably increased by their separation, while vigilance of the securely affianced pair was noticeably relaxed. Thus they were often alone together, and once he pressed and caressed her, murmuring his desire for her, and she, roused in spite of herself, retreated into a coy, girlish teasing that bewildered him. The next day she crept to Lilian's bedroom, consulted her textbooks on the subject of female virginity and decided that something must be done.

'Charles,' her approach that evening sounded more tentative than she had intended.

'Hmm?' He was engrossed in the *Mercury*'s list of silk prices.

'Charles dear, will you listen a minute please, there's something I must say.'

He looked up reluctantly. 'It's quite important, dear, and you mightn't like it.'

'Don't tell me you're going to marry a millionaire instead!' He was jocularly confident.

'No indeed, but when you hear, you might wish . . . well, I'd better say it quickly, only it's embarrassing.' She felt her cheeks burning. 'You see, Charles, the fact is, I'm not virginal . . . not a virgin. I, I've . . . there was a man earlier, only I couldn't help it, I was powerless . . .'

'No! But, Alice . . . who? When? You must tell me everything—at once.'

She averted her eyes. 'It happened when I was in captivity in Hunan. I was only fifteen and the master of the house took me as one of his concubines. I was forced, I couldn't help it, please, Charles, I really couldn't and then I ran away just as soon as I could.' She raised pleading eyes. 'You will forgive me?'

'Oh Alice, how simply dreadful—how awful . . .' He jumped up and patted her head. 'There, there, don't get upset, little one—what anguish it must have been for you, at that tender age. The brute, the uncivilised savage—and you, an innocent, undefiled little girl—ugh!' He shuddered with disgusted rage.

'You can't blame me, can you, Charles? There was no one to help or protect me.'

'No, no Alice I can't blame you—rape, rape, the savage yellow beast!' He spat it between his teeth.

'I've never told anyone before, Charles, but it has been a secret burden to me and now we are to marry, I felt I owed it to you.'

'Yes quite right, dear. It's something of a shock of course. A man naturally expects his wife, when she's single as you are, to be unsullied. But the circumstances are quite exceptional and it would be most unfair of me to hold it against you. I'm sure you escaped from the dreadful situation just as soon as possible?'

She came and twined her arms round his neck. 'Of course I did—and it was horrible in every way.' He kissed her and she tightened her grip on him. 'Well now that's over—and I feel much better for telling you—we can talk of more cheerful matters.'

Retreating from their mutual embarrassment, he retrieved his newspaper. 'And I'm glad you were honest with me, Alice. Now we shall proceed as if I didn't know and it didn't happen. I can't be fairer than that, can I?'

'No, dear, and thank you. It was many years ago and now I'll try to forget it too. Let me show you Mary's latest additions to the guest list—she really is quite impossible, saying it's to be a quiet wedding while inviting most of Shanghai to come!'

Going to get the list, Alice felt relieved that her way into matrimony was now a bit easier, but, she thought wistfully, even if Charles magnanimously chose to forget, the memory of those early joyous sexual unions must be with her for life and remain with her untold. For she simply couldn't risk a change of course now, caught up as she was in the momentum of the approaching festivities, paddling, as it often seemed, in the wake of the indefatigable Mary. And Mary was in her element. Not for many years had every bedroom in Fairlawns been aired ready for use, the finest porcelains brought from her glass cupboards, all the silver polished, provisions of every delectable kind filling the pantries for the glut of jollities ahead.

Isabel, William and the children arrived first, wrapped in furs against the colder Port Arthur winter, bearing gifts of Russian caviare, French cigars and painted wooden toys from Korea. Then came Mary's son Edgar from Singapore with his wife Sylvia and their children, Lawrence and Grace. Edgar had followed his father's footsteps into banking, a lean, saturnine man whose wife did most of the talking, as his mother had before her. They brought charm bracelets of Malayan silver, tortoiseshell knick-knacks, and a thick tiger-skin rug for Alice, which was her favourite present in that present-filled time.

And at dusk on Christmas Eve, just as Mary and Isabel were lighting the candles on the pine tree, Eliza arrived with Sunny and Adam. They brought hand-painted Biblical texts, hand-carved models of Mongolian camels for the children, and for Alice Eliza had worked a tapestry with the words 'God is Love' framed in a border of pansies, lilies, roses. But Alice's heart ached to see them—her mother's bent frailty, her hands so work-roughened in a company where those of the other ladies were soft and white, and worse were the skinny, pallid children who laughed far too seldom. Sunny retained shreds of her natural vivacity, but Adam seemed totally cowed, his skin clammy with perpetual fear—of his father most of all, of a vengeful Christian God, of all the devils and heathens in China, and now of the imminent prospect of sailing alone to England where he was to go to school.

On Christmas morning they all went to Shanghai Cathedral where Frank, Peachy, and Charles joined them, coming back to the liveliest and largest Christmas dinner Alice had ever known. Such a gathering it was, with Mary and Robert at the head of a table laden with stuffed birds of every variety, sides of roast ham and pork, potatoes, pies, puddings, jellies, tarts and fruits—and both of them aglow with a joy that was infectious. For Mary it was a return to the days of her first prime when her own children were young, and for bachelor Robert it was a belated celebration of the family life he had earlier missed. They joined in the children's games with gusto—charades, consequences, hunting the slipper and thimble, passing the packet and, in the Boxing Day *tableau vivant*, Mary was Queen of the Fairies, Robert her Oberon.

By comparison, Alice and Charles seemed a lacklustre pair. 'You'll have to exert yourself if you want to outshine the other bride-to-be!' Isabel had laughingly warned Alice soon after her arrival. But Alice had no desire to do so, for she lacked both the older woman's aplomb and her confident adoration of her intended. Clearly Mary and Robert harboured no doubts about their union, but, as the days of festivity reeled by, Alice and Charles felt increasingly strange together. Almost they avoided each other, on the unspoken understanding that their relationship was too fragile to be tested further in case, like property deals, it might collapse before completion of contract.

Charles sought refuge in what Robert jokingly called 'the business team' that also included William, Edgar Fortescue, and Frank, who gathered solemnly in smoke-filled corners and exchanged views on the inequalities of export taxes and customs dues, while Alice, seeing her fiancé so involved, glumly realised that this would be the pattern of their future social gatherings. Most of the ladies were in the 'mothers' team,' headed by Mary, with Isabel, Sylvia and on occasion Peachy. She was heavily pregnant, but her condition was ignored by all except for Alice who recited, smiling,

> 'Buxom is the peach-tree
> How its fruit swells!'

For Eliza that Christmas was the worst of everything that she disapproved of—the silly games, the copious quantities of food and wine, the other women's frivolous conversations about fashions and recipes. Eliza did, however, find one unexpected ally in Lilian Fortescue, for whom her mother's precipitous liaison with a dashing army major was an unmitigated disaster. Lilian shrank appalled from the spectacle of Mary's flighty joyous flirtatiousness and vowed deep inside her thin, tense frame that she alone would keep loyal for life the sacred memory of her beloved father who had so recently died. The heady seeds of martyrdom were sown in quiet Lilian that Christmastide.

On the last day of the old year, Alice and her mother took Adam to the P. & O. wharf and consigned him to the care of a missionary family bound for Home. As he went up the gangplank his peaky, elfin face was whey-coloured with distress while on the quay Sunny shrieked hysterically. 'Hush dear,' Alice patted her head. 'Adam is being braver than you and he's the one who's leaving.'

'But I want to go too, I don't want to stay at the Mission without him—whatever shall I do?'

Having no good answer, Alice's heart ached for her, and for the memory of her own childhood when William had gone Home and she had been left crying on the quay. Eliza turned away from the painful sight of Adam's tiny figure, her mouth working. 'Partings like this are always so dreadful! I always wonder when . . . if . . . you know.'

'Yes, Mother, but I'm sure all will be well. Everything is much safer these days.'

'Yes dear, and in about two years we're due for home-leave at last—so you'll soon see Adam again, Sunny. . . . And I'm sorry you won't be coming with us, Alice. But it will rest with your husband now. Perhaps he'll take you Home soon?'

'He says he will, before too long. And I'd love to go—though his relatives sound so stuffy and proper.'

Eliza took her arm, they waved to Adam for the last time, and moved off. 'Well I'm glad he's a nice gentlemanly sort of man, dear, and I'm happy for you . . . even though he's not in the field of work I'd hoped. But I shan't need to worry about you anymore, as I do all the time about Frank.'

'Because of his marriage?'

'That, yes, and his general attitude to life. Ah Alice, I can hardly bear to look at Peachy now—to think of that baby's future, the grandparents it will have, an owner of racehorses and a heathen Manchu woman who plays mah-jong every day. Frank told me about them himself. He seems to take a cruel delight in shocking me since I've been here, have you noticed?'

Alice had indeed, and replied carefully, 'I don't think he's quite forgiven you for not coming to his wedding, Mother. He was very hurt underneath.'

'Oh dear me, I felt it deeply too, but Edward so adamantly forbade it, it nearly caused an open breach between us. And then there was the expense. I had to scrimp and save every penny secretly to come here now. . . . If only Peachy were a convert . . . that was the bitterest blow of all . . .'

Alice, thinking with renewed hatred of her stepfather, could utter no word of comfort to her mother and, in silence, they walked past the foreign shops along the Nanking Road. Red and white lanterns glowed above the doors and the lintels were emblazoned with English translations of cheery New Year messages, a good-natured Chinese salutation for the foreigners' festival. 'For your New Year—guaranteed Prosperity Dumplings and Lucky Grasses' read one; 'May the bounty of the Five Happinesses be yours throughout the Year'; 'Cast out the devils of the past, welcome the blessed gods of the Dragon Year.' Alice read them carefully, as if they were intended for her alone. And did she not require some special blessing, when, with the year's turning, she would become a different person—Mrs. Charles Grant?

'It is better to be married isn't it, Mother?' she asked in an agonised whisper as they turned into Fairlawns' drive. Her mother blinked in surprise.

'Of course it is, my dear child. . . . Well, there are things that men . . . that husbands sometimes desire to do with their wives that are not always entirely agreeable to us women . . . I trust you know a little about matters of sex, Alice? I haven't said anything to you, but . . .'

'Yes, Mother, I know. I meant that just being married is better for a woman than being single, is it not?'

'Certainly it is, Alice. Very definitely.' Timidly Eliza patted her daughter's hand. 'You will have a good Christian man to protect you and you will see how pleasant and comforting that can be. And I hope every one of the Five Happinesses will attend you, my dear, for all the days of your married life.'

334

12

Mr. and Mrs. Charles Grant stood on the deck of a Chinese Merchant Company's vessel waving good-bye to Mr. and Mrs. Frank Greenwood, who had come to see them off. The rest of the family had dispersed immediately after the wedding: to Port Arthur, Mukden, Singapore, and the other newly-weds to Hong Kong. Charles and Alice had spent a short honeymoon on a borrowed houseboat moored in a creek near the Snowy Lakes and were now bound for Hankow. Alice watched the receding figures on the quay: 'So many comings and goings ... it will be a relief to just settle down quietly for a while, don't you think, Charles?'

He grunted warningly, 'But you might find life pretty humdrum after all these excitements.'

'Oh I'm glad they're over, I assure you.'

She huddled in the shelter of a cabinway, hands clenched in her fur muff. It was drear and chill, raindrops spattering on the muddy waters rolling below. Yes, she was glad it was over and that everything had gone according to plan. Fortunately, 2 January 1883 had been crisp and clear, pale sunlight on the weathered stone of Trinity Church, the inside decorated with ferns, glossy evergreens and winter jasmine. Mary Fortescue had looked splendid in pearl grey silks, with handsome uniformed Robert at her side. Charles had looked equally well-groomed and assured, while she, presumably, had lived up to expectations—the fledgling by comparison, tentative in a gown of creamy satin, clutching a bouquet of camellias, Sunny and Charlotte treading solemnly behind her in rosy tulle. William had given her away. Edgar had given his mother away. No one had cried except Polly, who was teething. When Charles smiled warmly at her as they left the vestry she could have wept for joy. All the Wangs came to the wedding breakfast at Fairlawns and behaved impeccably, and, in

335

Mary's gallery, Mrs. Wang had tapped the pictures with her long red fingernails, grunting with envy.

That night, on the houseboat, after she and Charles had stood on deck entwined together and congratulating themselves on the rightness of spending their first night of marriage in a vessel similar to that on which they had first met, Charles had led her to bed. There he had made love to her with slow, gentle consideration as if she were the virgin he had fondly imagined. And she had cried out obligingly at his thrusts so that he could murmur endearments, assuring her it would not hurt for long. His love-making had not hurt at all, nor had it much pleased her, and afterwards she propped herself, wide awake, on an elbow, staring at his still boyish face as he slept, wondering how it would be in their bed in future.

But already the wedding and honeymoon seemed slightly unreal to her, as such occasions often do to their protagonists, though living undimmed in the memories of relatives and friends. For to Alice all the excitement lay ahead—six hundred miles upriver at Hankow. Several wedding guests had commiserated on her exile to such a place where, they said, the racecourse was shocking and society entirely limited to missionaries and merchants. And she remembered their words with amusement when, three days later, the city hove in sight: miles of low wooden habitations crowded across the grey alluvial plains on either side of the yellowish mile-wide tide that divided Hankow from Wuchang, the capital of Hupeh, and Hanyang.

From a distance the three cities looked equally featureless, but Hankow—the Collecting Place of Nine Provinces—had been a Treaty Port for the past twenty-two years and was distinguished, on closer approach, by its waterfront bund bordering the hundred and ten acres of the foreign concession. Loyal residents claimed it was the finest in China, with a broad promenade chained off for the sole use of foreigners, a high stone wall pierced by steps, rows of willow trees and an extent of half a mile, giving everyone the chance of a daily constitutional.

No one was taking that chance on the afternoon Alice and Charles landed, for the weather was at its wintriest, the sluggish waters at their lowest, flanked by filthy mud-banks, the willows wind-stripped bare and most of the finest porticoed houses to the west of the Bund, locally known as 'Nobs' End,' shuttered, for their residents had briefly fled to cheerier climes. The only people in sight were boatmen, customs officials, coolies, and a crowd of particularly diseased and ragged beggars crouching on the steps, holding up skinny, pleading hands.

Charles had been subdued that morning and, as they disembarked, said uneasily, 'The house is no mansion, Alice. I did warn you, and it may look worse after being shut up.'

She was cheerful. 'Oh you told me you weren't at the smart end of the Bund! I'm not expecting anything grand.'

And certainly the rickety dwelling at the concession's very edge to which Charles led her was not that. Sounds of scuttling rodents, smells of mildew and bad sewage greeted them as he pushed open the ill-fitting door. 'Where's the boy? He should have got things warmed up for us!' Charles roared in embarrassment. He led her down a dark passage with a rotted floor. 'The work's done on that side—and we're here.' He watched apprehensively as she looked around the main room. It was furnished with two shabby armchairs, strips of shredded matting, two battered bamboo tables that Charles had bought from a departing consul. He had also acquired an old brass bed, washstand, some chipped chinaware and cooking pots stacked in the small, dirty kitchen, and a tin hip-bath now full of dead centipedes. It was propped against the wall of the privy, which stank horribly.

But the place had its bonus—a sizeable verandah which, owing to the risks of summer floods, stood raised on piles, accessible from the living-room by a flight of covered steps. It was, Alice decided, like a top deck, a secret eyrie higher than the rest of the house and with a view of the nearby Yangtze. The view was bounded by the dilapidated Grant & Greenwood godown and the more substantial wall of the Russian factory from which brick-tea was exported to Manchuria and Siberia. The smells and sounds of tea-dust being sieved, pressed and dried arose from it continually and to the end of her days, Alice had only to sniff the inside of a teapot to be reminded of her early married life.

'It looks even worse than I feared, dear,' Charles apologised as he came on to the verandah. 'The boy's obviously done a bunk and he's stolen the bed quilts to boot, the scoundrel—Heaven knows what we're going to do for food and warmth tonight!'

'Oh we'll be all right, I've had lots of training in native household management, you know!'

And so she proved. Within a few hours she had swept the floors, been to the market, got the stove going and that night they dined on vegetable soup, broiled eels and rice, and then enjoyed a most successful lovemaking warmed by the tiger-skin rug and the glowing charcoal embers. As he sank into satisfied slumber Charles congratulated himself heartily on his choice of a resourceful wife and she, equally content, thought how pleasant it was to have a home of one's own, however humble, and be able to decide for herself the colours of the bed-quilts she intended buying on the morrow.

For the next few weeks Alice busied herself happily with the creation of a comfortable nest. The quilts, chosen on account of cheapness rather than colour, were of padded indigo-blue cotton from Chungking, and for the floors she bought strips of scarlet felt and local grass-cloth. The walls she hung with wood panels painted with writing and bordered with flowers and trees; one read 'The sun moves, bamboo shadows steal over the grasses. The wind blows, fir-cones fall on the robe of a guest.' Carpenters came to make tables and shelves on which she set bowls of bright pebbles from the Rainflower Hills, writing brushes and perfumed ink-tablets. In the verandah Alice arranged pots of ferns, small orange trees and two long lounging chairs for when the weather improved.

She hired a fat cook-boy who coiled his pigtail twice round his head and spoke with a thick Hunanese accent. His parents were boat-people who hailed from that province and he was called Snow Duck for the literal Chinese reason that the first thing his mother had seen after his birth was a duck with snow on its back floating past a porthole. Snow Duck adored Alice from the moment he heard her speak his very own tongue, he cheated her less than he had ever cheated an employer and, on her behalf, mercilessly bullied the coolie called Number Eight Son who swept the yard and privy.

As the winter retreated, the shutters of the Nobs' End houses were taken down for their owners' return and Alice, the newcomer, was obliged to call on the community's leading ladies. First on Mrs. Wilcock, wife of the Commissioner of Customs, then on Mrs. Amelia Telford, wife of 'Tommy the

338

tea-man,' as he was jovially known. It was rumoured that Tommy had made a cool £10,000 profit in the vintage year of 1873 by putting all his teas aboard the clipper *Ariel* which won the race to reach the London market. Amelia Telford however, who wore an habitually pained expression, never discussed matters of trade either in good times or bad. She found the whole subject of tea quite lowering, drank only imported coffee, and spent many waking hours in a secret dream wherein she was married to a handsome diplomat instead of Tommy, lived in Vienna by the Danube instead of the Yangtze, and visited the opera regularly instead of playing operatic airs on her tinny piano.

For to be in Hankow at all was bad enough, as she remarked to Mrs. Wilcock, but it must be unutterably dreary for poor little Mrs. Grant in that pokey hole next to the tea-brick factory. So the resident ladies did what they could, presenting Alice with cast-off cushion covers and saucepans, inviting her to tea and assuring her that the first year in Hankow was always the worst.

Goaded by their well-meaning patronage, Alice soon decided to take more active interest in the other side of the house, where the infant firm of Grant & Greenwood was struggling to grow. The tea-season did not begin till May and the godown thus contained a strange assortment of stranded items: sacks of broken aniseed, lily roots and dogs' skins; bundles of rattans, straw hats and iron rods; barrels of glue made from boiled seaweed, of liquid indigo and Szechuan oil; bales of material labelled 'grey shirtings,' 'bunting' and 'turkey red cloth.' The pervasive smell was a heady mixture of the fragrant, the fusty and the simply horrible, and the pervasive impression was of immobility—unused rods rusting, frayed hats, and several rat-chewed sacks, their contents spilled on the earth floor.

'But where is it all going and why is it so long here?' Alice demanded of her husband, who sat at an old roll-top desk adding figures. He frowned.

'It's waiting shipment to the interior or Shanghai. But it's a bad time for transit, the waters are still low, junks can't get alongside to load or through the gorges.'

'And the material labelled in English, imported from Lancashire? Do the Chinese actually buy shirtings and turkey red cloth?'

He shrugged. 'Some of them seem to.'

Persistently she leaned over his shoulder and giggled. 'Iron: nail ditto, hoop ditto, pig; bones: cow, broken, ditto, tigers . . . That's rather funny.'

'Yes, I remember I thought so at first.'

'But not anymore?'

'Well, it isn't a joke that bears much repetition.'

She twisted a piece of copper wire round her finger. 'Don't you think we might do something definite instead of waiting for the river to rise and the tea-season to begin? Why can't we explore a little upriver ourselves and find out what the merchants want? You said you wanted to pioneer beyond the Treaty Ports.'

He put down his pen. 'It had occurred to me, but . . .'

'But what? Where's your sense of adventure? Not gone already, has it?'

He flushed angrily. 'But it's the money angle. I'm in debt already, Alice—new firms invariably are—but I've money to find for my son's education and it's cost a bit to set the house up nicely . . . I'm not grumbling but . . .'

'Charles, I do wish you wouldn't talk as if it were just your firm—it's ours, you agreed. So why can't I be included in these decisions? Please, Charles . . .' She rubbed against him, hiding her irritation under a show of coaxing. 'Let's go upriver and see for ourselves. Nothing venture nothing win, you know.'

He drew her on to his lap, stroking her hair. 'You are a determined little madam, aren't you? The firm's called Grant & Greenwood remember, not t'other way round. But I admit things are slack and I'm tired of listening to rats chewing up our tiny profits—so perhaps this once we'll let the junior partner have her way. But only as far as Ichang, mind. There's an English couple living there I'd like to meet—a Mr. and Mrs. Archibald Small. Old Wilcock told me about them. Apparently they've managed to get a sound business going even though Ichang isn't yet a Treaty Port. Rum couple, Wilcock said, dyed-in-the-wool China hands, and both very large which is rather a joke. Anyway, I'll send a message with one of the junk-captains that we're coming. They're bound to welcome a bit of company at this dead time of year.'

On a windswept morning a week later they boarded the stern-wheel riverboat *Chang-wo*; the below-decks were packed with Chinese and the Grants shared the small saloon with two Belgian nuns also bound for Ichang. The river was still low and the vessel crept along, lurching from one just-concealed gravel shoal to the next. At every grounding, the melancholy note of the leadsmen rose to a wailing crescendo and at every re-floating the nuns raised their eyes to Heaven in gratitude. But the only real excitement in Alice's view was their passing of High Peak Islet that marked the entrance to the Tung T'ing Lake, the great stretch of water that flowed towards Hunan. Hunan. She had never been so close since she left and she stood in the cabinway as they passed and murmured,

'He is going to the Tung T'ing Lake
My friend whom I have loved for so many years.
Spring wind startles the willows.
And they break into pale leaf.
I go with my friend as far as the river-bank.
And my mind is full and overflowing
With the things I did not say . . .'

Later, in her cabin, she wrote a long letter to Tamao which she doubted would ever arrive, and that night tossed in her bunk in half-frightened, half-sensual dreams.

As they sailed west along the Great River the plains gave way to terraced slopes and wooden hills, cliffs and promontories reared where gulls and cormorants nested. Some of the rocks were enlivened with poetical exclamations in large whitewashed characters: 'The river and the sky are one colour' announced one. At dawn on the fifth day they passed through the Tiger Teeth Gorge just below Ichang where ochre-coloured waters poured through a two-mile-long channel. The entrance to the town was spectacular: flanked on the left by a high peak and opposite by a craggy range topped with a Buddhist monastery, its roof gleaming in a shaft of early sun. 'All change at Ichang' was always the cry, for only the sturdy, high-sterned junks could negotiate the treacherous 'Thousand Rapids' beyond in which dozens of craft came to grief each year.

When the *Chang-wo* anchored in mid-stream, its passengers were poled ashore in hooded sampans, where just one foreign woman stood among the native throng. Her large frame was clad in a sage-green gown that struck Alice as pleasantly exotic, though of no recognisable style. She extended her hand, 'You must be Mrs. Grant? And I am Mrs. Daisy Small . . . You might as well laugh at that name once and for all!'

Alice smiled. 'Indeed I shan't. In any case I'd already heard you were . . . not small.'

'So my fame goes before me. When we first came I made a point of translating our absurd name to the Chinese and they were tickled pink. Now I do believe we're known as the size-of-two-elephants-foreign-devils in every port between Ichang and Shanghai. But I've often wished to meet you, Mrs. Grant.'

'Oh—why me?'

'Ah, here comes the baggage coolie with Mr. Grant—it must be? How do you do? I was about to tell your wife, Mr. Grant, that I heard of her sometime ago in Shanghai. We were dining with Mr. Dawson, the Customs Commissioner, and he said, "Well Mrs. Small, there's only one English lady I've ever met with as much grasp of Chinese, both Mandarin and vernacular, as yourself—and that's Miss Alice Greenwood." And he told me a little of your early captivity in Hunan—I long to hear more about it.'

Charles smiled dismissively. 'Oh that's ages past, Mrs. Small, time Alice forgot all about it. Is that your cart the baggage-coolie's making for?'

'Yes—could you see to it, Mr. Grant? Our humble temple-abode is up the hill there. You'll stay with us of course? There's nowhere better here, I assure you. And we ladies will walk behind and begin to know each other, for I'm sure we've much in common. Are we not both China-born for a start?'

As they walked, Mrs. Small explained that she too came from a missionary background.

'But my poor mother died giving birth to me—fifth and last of her oversized brood. Father was more of a linguist than a proselytiser and so I grew up in Hong Kong spoiled and cosseted by amahs and disciplined by the moral laws of the Chinese classics—just like a little Son of Han! But your early experiences sound much more exciting?'

She beamed and thus unusually encouraged Alice was still talking when they reached the former temple on the Hill of Four Prosperities where the Smalls lived. It was a wooden dwelling, with a crumble-tiled roof and an air of aged serenity, set in a grove of pine and bamboo. After luncheon, when

Charles went off to meet Mr. Small at his office, Daisy took Alice to see the locally famed view from the hill's top. Its dominant feature, she pointed out, was the Pyramid Peak, which had long had an adverse effect on the fortunes of Ichang, and to, counteract its sinister influences, a monastery had been built, at great expense, on this peak where they stood.

'But you will be familiar with such superstitions?' Daisy eyed her inquiringly.

'Oh yes, there were some rounded green hills near Changsha supposed to be of a most benevolent disposition, and I never doubted it, at the time.'

'Indeed why should you? Children don't doubt such things, which is one reason, I suspect, foreigners often consider the Chinese childish. But now you're grown-up, how do you feel? Such an extraordinary experience must have influenced you profoundly and I'm sure you've made much of it since?'

Alice faltered. She liked Daisy's directness, but was unaccustomed to it.

'Oh—I've done very poorly with it I fear. I seem to be different in all the wrong ways as a result. I find I'm much too critical for one thing—of many foreigners' narrow outlooks for example. It's quite uncomfortable really.'

'But I make similar judgments, so does Archie, and we don't consider it a fault. I've never subscribed to the dictum of judging not that you be not judged—one's simply got to stand up and be counted sometimes, don't you think?'

'Well I always admire those who do, certainly. When I lived in Port Arthur before my marriage I came in contact with some of the young self-strengtheners—I sometimes wish I'd had the courage to be counted with them.'

'Ah—such confused, ambitious, arrogant, clever, young men! My heart bleeds for them—doomed to all the frustrations and tribulations of reformers the world over, but with the fearful likelihood, in their case, of ultimate failure and disgrace, if not the execution ground at the end. . . .'

Alice looked alarmed. 'Do you really think so? I didn't realise it was so dangerous.'

'It could well become so, though up to now the Government is too firmly in control to worry much about such hotheads. Do you know any of them well?'

'Not really—not now. I helped one of the lecturers at the

naval college with some translating. J. S. Mill's treatise on Liberty mainly . . . then he . . . went away. I've nearly finished it off alone, but I don't quite know what to do with it next.'

'But my dear, that's perfectly splendid—Mill's *Liberty*, what more stimulating and dangerously incomprehensible book to offer inquiring young Orientals! We must talk to Archie, he can put you in the way of getting it published, I'm sure. There'll be a tremendous demand—no,' she chuckled in self-correction, 'not enormous. That's my enthusiasm again. Archie's always telling me off about it—discriminating demand which could be more influential. And oh Alice, I've a marvellous idea for your next translation—you won't mind my speaking so familiarly so soon, will you? Mill again—on the Subjection of Women, you know it of course? The perfect background text for my League for the Abolition of Foot-Binding. . . . But I've not yet told you about it, have I? There I am running away with myself again.'

She paused, staring at the younger woman with shining eyes. Alice was leaning against a rock; behind her the budding yellow tassels of a glossy-leaved tallow tree swung in the breeze. Far below a bend of the sunlit Yangtze glittered. Her outline was very sharp to Daisy suddenly, the tilt of her head very determined, her greenish eyes very bright and clear. In the silence they both heard the simple tolling of a distant bell and the monotonous chant of the Zen monks who lived in the nearby monastery. Daisy drew in her breath sharply.

'Oh Alice—I've just had such a feeling about you—one of my inexplicable intuitions, that's what Archie calls them, and they're nearly always right. You're going to be an important person in my life, you're going to see and do some of the things that have eluded me—my heiress, just apparent. And not only mine, you will go beyond that—forgive me, but I've just seen it clearly!'

Alice coloured uneasily, for her instinct was always to withdraw from such impulsive enveloping. 'I . . . I wish I had your gift of vision, Mrs. Small—but I feel no such sense of certainty, in any direction. . . . But please tell me about Mr. Mill's book on women and the league you mention—it's all new to me.'

'Come then, it's time we went back for tea,' Daisy hooked her arm as they walked back down the hill. 'Mill's book you must study for yourself—he puts the case for our emancipation so much more forcibly than I ever could. What a magnificent man he was! As for the league, it began because I just couldn't understand how we foreign women can bear being in this country, constantly closing our eyes to the fact that all around us thousands of our own sex are being crippled for life. . . . Those diseased, deformed hooves of the old tottering grannies, and, even worse, the haunting pallor, the morose suffering on the faces of the little girls as they hobble past, their cries of woe in the night. Have you never heard them? Have they never touched you?'

'Yes,' Alice muttered. 'In the Chu household, the youngest, Little Piece—I used often to hear her, but the elder daughters seemed quite resigned. It was just the custom, they used to say.'

'Ah, several influential Chinese I've spoken to on the subject have said the same and I've reminded them, as I do you, that one of the three universally recognised moral qualities according to Confucius is compassion. And how can any person of compassion look upon such youthful pain without wanting to alleviate it?'

'So you've formed a league? But isn't this more a matter for the missionaries?'

'That is just where you and other well-intentioned foreigners are wrong!' Daisy stopped in her tracks and rounded on Alice. 'Missionaries do not have a monopoly of the milk of human kindness and their efforts are often so misguided anyway. We had a pair of fire-and-brimstone Scots here recently, handing out wads of free tracts to all and sundry—which, I heard, made excellent thick soles for the coolies' sandals! Not the sort of soles they intended to save! No, it is just because the people associate the abolition of footbinding with Christianity that they don't take to it. Now my league is based simply on our common humanity— transcending every religious creed, and I'm collecting much supporting medical evidence from enlightened Chinese doctors. You will help me in this, won't you, Alice?

'But what can I do? I doubt if I'd find any kindred spirits in Hankow, and I'm not sure how Charles . . .' She trailed off, aware of Daisy's quizzical look, and added, 'Perhaps I could write something in Chinese about it?'

'That would be an excellent start and I'll show you what

we're already doing. . . . But look, there are the men returned already—I've been carried away on my pet subject as usual. Archie, are you showing Mr. Grant the view? I suppose time has got itself late again?'

She smiled unrepentantly at the broad, placid-looking grey-haired man ahead, and they all walked back together. The Smalls' dwelling was sparsely furnished, though they did not seem to notice, its only luxury being an extraordinary revolving desk made to special specifications. Divided exactly into two, each half had shelves and cubbyholes and each Small owned half—the revolving mechanism allowing whoever was working there to survey the pleasant view from the window. Their only arguments, Archie joked, occurred when they both wanted to work and look outside at the same time. It seemed to Alice an ideal arrangement, having never before met a married couple who shared their interests so equally. Nor had she ever been in a foreign home where Chinese came and went so freely—the most frequent callers being local merchants with whom Archie dealt direct.

'The whole system of foreign trade is wrongly organised here,' he told Charles as they sat round the stove after supper. 'We behave as if China were a colony like India or Singapore, and we keep our white man's distance—negotiating through compradores and middle-men who hold the whip-hand. Look at Telford and his merry tea-men, they can't speak the language, scarcely even venture beyond the racecourse and only survive at all because of the few faithful compradores they've employed since the clipper days. They're cruising along on two illusions: first that the English demand for Chinese tea is going to grow, which it isn't, and second that the Chinese are never going to manage the interior and international trade for themselves—which of course they are. Competition is going to get fiercer and . . .'

'Oh hush Archie, enough of this mercantile gloom,' Daisy interrupted. 'Now let me make a suggestion instead—Mr. Grant, why don't you and Alice consider starting an agency up here? I'm sure there's plenty of scope, and we know the ropes . . . I warrant Ichang will be a Treaty Port in a few years, then you'll be in clover, as the Yankees say.'

'Oh Charles, why don't we?' Alice pleaded. 'Look what a help I could be here, and we'd really become part of the place instead of being stuck in a concession as we are now.'

She saw the lines of dogged refusal set on his face. At such moments he looked beleaguered, uncertain, and she did not like what she saw. Looking at him, Archie interposed smoothly, 'Come, come, ladies, surely you don't expect Mr. Grant to uproot himself from Hankow on the instant. He's only been there a year and he'll want to prove something of what I've said on his own impulses. But bear it in mind, my dear chap, and don't get too much in hock with the Hankow gentlemen. They're cliquey, old-school-tie, stick together sort of thing, and their heyday in tea is over.'

But Charles only frowned noncommittally, for he was quite impressed with Tommy Telford for one thing and, for another, as he confirmed in the course of their Ichang stay, the very thought of living permanently as the Smalls did filled him with secret dismay. They seemed to have so little contact with their own kind, so few amusements of any sort. It might be all right for Alice, she was so close to the country anyway, but, by the time they boarded the east-bound steamer, he was rather looking forward to such civilised company and amenities as Hankow could offer, deciding that his first encounter with life beyond the Treaty Ports had been less romantic and more uncomfortable than he had envisaged. The Smalls saw them off, the men shaking hands briskly, the women parting like old friends.

Daisy pressed a parcel into Alice's hands, 'Take care of it—my only copy and I want it back eventually. But read, mark, inwardly digest!'

As the snow melted in the distant western ranges, the Yangtze waters were rising and the squatters on the mud-banks were uprooting their bamboo hovels stick by stick. Water rats too, their winter holes flooding, were burrowing to higher ground and, higher yet, along the overhanging gorges, men were scurrying in and out of caves collecting saltpetre.

'What's the present?' Charles asked idly, contemplating the men's precarious activities as the steamer chugged away.

Alice stowed it firmly in her reticule. 'Oh just a book.'

'So I gathered, but whose?'

'Some of Wordsworth's poetry. Daisy loves it and thought I would too.'

He nodded dismissively and she slipped to their cabin, unwrapping the volume tenderly, flattered Daisy should entrust her with it. She opened and began to read at random:

'What is called the nature of women is the result of enforced suppression . . . for women have to hide and dissemble most of their mental life from men. . . .' She gasped, seeing the little scene between her and Charles in quite a new light. Why had she lied about this very book? Because she had known instinctively he would not like it, would have questioned her—she could just imagine his teasing indulgence, 'Subjection of who? You—an Englishwoman living in the nineteenth century, and with the Married Women's Property Act in full force? What rot, Alice!' She did not feel strong or sure enough to contradict him, but once she had inwardly digested Mr. Mill's theories it would be different, she promised herself, as she went to join Charles, wishing that their stay with the Smalls could have been longer.

But it was indeed time to return, for one morning soon afterwards Alice awoke to the sounds of unusual activity along the Bund—and there was the first procession of coolies, each with two brightly painted chests of freshly picked tea dangling from poles over their shoulders. They had jogged along for miles from the western hill-plantations, crying 'Ahoi, Ah-hoi' all the way in a manner peculiar to their calling.

Later that day, silk-robed Chinese merchants arrived in blue sedan chairs with green lattice blinds and yellow curtains through which they seldom deigned to peep. But the sure signal for the opening of the tea-season came the following evening when steamers from Shanghai and Odessa hove into port, decks a-twinkle with lanterns, holds crammed with lead spars, cotton piece-goods and copper wiring to be all speedily unloaded to make room for the first tea consignments. European, American, and Russian tea merchants and hong-clerks hastened ashore bringing transit forms and order books, but the most important passengers were the chahsees. Pallid, thin men mostly, who had spent years of apprenticeship in the art of tea-tasting, they were highly voluble on the subject of 'that blasted vegetable' as it was jocularly called, habitually silent on most others, as if the development of such excessively sensitive tastebuds in the single cause had circumscribed their general conversational powers.

For the next month Hankow was at its liveliest. Every guest room in Nobs' End was occupied, the old hulks moored along the quay, deserted for much of the year, thrummed with mercantile activity, and every godown was stuffed with tea—Scented Orange or Flowery Pekoe, coarse Congo, Lotus Heart, and Autumn Dew. In the shaded godown offices, the solemn chahsees held court, surrounded by rows of white porcelain cups and several spittoons. They scrutinised and sniffed each variety of leaf, then, for the crucial testing, sipped a sample quantity of every brew, rolled it about their tongues, squelched it through their teeth, spat it out, and pronounced a verdict that could make or break an upcountry merchant and grower for a year.

In the evenings when the day's sniffing, spitting, and selling was over, everyone gathered round the Nobs' End dining tables where the talk was all of tea—its price compared to five years ago, the iniquity of some native middlemen caught cheating in the weighing sheds, the excessive caution of the big London firms, Twinings and Coope, who usually ordered the bulk of the first crop. After the meal, guests strolled outside to take the air and watch the Yangtze tides heaving magnificently in the moonlight, and many a man breathed a fervent prayer to the stars that the season's crop would bring top prices in London even though the omens were not auspicious. Charles was one of these, standing beside his wife on the Telfords' lawn one evening, wishing that he could afford a fashionable Parisian-style gown like Amelia's for her, and that they had a house grand enough for lavish entertaining on the Telford scale. Looking at Alice, he felt a gush of warm love, wanted desperately to make her happy, marvelled that, in their present straitened circumstances, she put such a brave face on it, and seemed content.

And, in large measure she was, for she understood intuitively that the actual business of trading was more enjoyable than spending the profits thereof. So, for the rest of that summer, after the chahsees and clerks had gone, she remained serene in the having of her own man, keeping the house pleasant for him, lying close to his firm male body every night with no fears for the future. Often they would work together in the office, damp towels round their heads to keep cool, arranging for shipments of tough Hupeh grass-cloth, nutgalls and firecrackers to Shanghai, of dried clams, Shensi rhubarb and tobacco to Nanking and, to Changsha, kerosene lamps and aphrodisiacs made of ground ginseng and labelled

'Penetration Hard Powder.' The last invariably led Alice into an amused, lustful reverie in which she was again spreadeagled on Lung-kuang's red silk coverlet while he, by the light of a new-fangled kerosene lamp, and fired by the powder . . .

The news from the London tea-sales was not good. It was rumoured that Tommy Telford lost so heavily he cancelled a proposed European tour and certainly Amelia looked more than usually vexed. Grant & Greenwood also lost ground, but it was offset somewhat by some small successes in local trade and bric-à-brac. Though Charles did not admit it, this was mainly due to Alice's directly personal dealings with the merchants and shippers who, though highly suspicious of her at first, soon dubbed her 'Number-One-Business-female-devil'; it was a compliment earned by her patient haggling over sums that most foreigners considered too trifling. But haggling was a noisy process, and Amelia Telford, calling at the office one day with a special delivery letter from Shanghai, shuddered as she overheard it. Mrs. Grant, she later told Mrs. Wilcock, sounded like nothing more nor less than a common Covent Garden market-woman, and she felt bound to mention the matter to Tommy that evening, for such behaviour could not but lower the dignity of all the foreign ladies in Chinese eyes. And what a blessing it would be, Amelia concluded, if little Mrs. Grant were to begin a family so that her mind should have a more suitable occupation.

The letter Amelia brought was from Frank announcing his imminent arrival, and just two days later he bounded off the steamer, greeting Alice with his usual enthusiasm. His athletic frame was thickening already, she noticed, for he spent more time at his desk these days, less shaking up his liver with the lads. He had developed an air of rather flamboyant well-being and self-satisfaction, for he was enjoying his present life to the full—good food, drink, sex, the excitement of the racecourse, the accumulation of possessions, babies, hopes for the future. And yet, when Alice looked at him she saw first, as she always did after a period of separation, the frightened blubbering boy whom Eldest Brother kicked, the stocky groom running beside Younger Brother's horse, the sulky lad they had brought out of Hunan. And he too, though not blessed with her vivid recall, did not

350

really see, at first, the young woman in a high-necked, smocked blouse, broad-sashed navy skirt who was his married sister, but some smaller, blurred version of the same, who had sobbed and screamed as he once had, been hungry, cold, and cowed—he and she despicable runts in the land of the proud Celestials, part of them forever unrescued.

So it was no surprise when he said, as soon as they settled in a double rickshaw, 'Han-li visited us recently—it was grand to see him again.'

'Han-li—how lovely! Is he still at Foochow? How is the family?'

'Yes, he's doing very well—lecturing in navigation. But there's been a sadness in the house . . .'

'Oh dear—who?'

'The mother, Hidden Glory, died—just slowly faded away over the months, Han-li said. No specific cause. And just after the funeral Han-fei's fourth daughter was born—ill-omened that one will be.'

'Yes, poor mite. And Lung-kuang, how has he taken it?'

'He's quite well—his secondary wife and their two young sons keep him happy.' He grinned a trifle lewdly.

'I suppose she must have been in her fifties? Hidden Glory? What a melancholy life, Frank—no one knowing or caring about her right to the end.'

'Well, Eldest Brother was very upset. He was her favourite and now he's more ill-tempered than ever. Weng and he often quarrel and Weng keeps threatening to leave.'

Alice thought of the house, the courtyard with the carp in their pond, the flowers in their urns, the hall where Hidden Glory's death tablet would now be added to the proud ancestral row; the same passions and contentments among the same people, only fewer of them as the years went by.

'And Han-li lives in Foochow then?'

'And he's married, though he didn't say much about her. The men never do.'

'Married! Well, it happens to us all. And Little Piece? I've often thought of her recently, is she still at home?'

'He didn't say, but he sees Mei in Canton occasionally.'

The Grant & Greenwood establishment, Frank noted, was not in the right part of the concession. 'So this is where you are? Jolly fine view of the river, hey?'

'Yes—splendid.'

'And business—is it good?' He stopped her in the doorway.

'Could be better, could be worse.'

'Well, you need to know exactly what you're doing in these days of increasing competition.'

'And you think we don't?' she snapped.

'Now Sis, I didn't say that. But I want you to know first—I've come with a proposition from Father-in-law. A very generous offer I promise you. I can count on your support, can't I?'

'Depends what it is, Frank.'

'It's very sound—good for you, good for us. I'm assuring you that in confidence, you know you can trust me.' She nodded tentatively as Charles came thundering down the passage shouting a welcome.

It was not Frank's way to beat about many bushes; and once they had settled on the verandah with their pre-luncheon sherries, he broached the subject.

'Well Charles, I expect you're wondering why I've come?'

'My dear chap,' Charles protested, 'delighted to see you any time, you don't have to have a special reason.'

'Nice of you to say so—but the fact is I've come partly on my father-in-law's account.'

'Yuan-wang? Doing very well for himself these days I hear?'

'Yep, on the up and up—and taking me with him, I'm pleased to say. He treats me fairly enough and I've no head for the big deals—that's the Eldest Son's line. But that's what I want to talk about now—they ... we ... are thinking of expanding up the Yangtze here. The river's going to be thrown wide open in the next decade, everyone says so— limitless trading opportunities right into the interior, up to the Tibetan border maybe.'

'Yes—I keep hearing about the marvellous future.' Charles was terse.

'Well, the long and short is—Grant & Greenwood already being established here in a fairly small way—he's wondering if you'd like to join up with us, under our joint names, with you as sole agents in these parts? All legally arranged and above board, only we'd have the monopoly with you of course.'

Charles brooded. 'I should have thought there were enough tea-men here already.'

'Oh not tea—that's past its peak. Wang's a wily bird and he

swears our tea will lose out to the cheaper Indian stuff. The European barbarians, he says, simply haven't fine enough palates to appreciate the subtle native brews that are delicate as sparrows' tongues—and he may well be right.'

'I hope to God he isn't.'

'Be that as it may, he's not interested in it—it's native manufactures and bric-à-brac he wants to export with some importing of pig-iron and such.'

'Good old muck and truck, hey?'

'But that's just what Archie Small and Mary . . .' Alice broke in eagerly.

He turned on her icily. 'Why don't you go and see if luncheon is ready, Alice? This is very much a business discussion.'

'And I'm not part of it?'

'Not really, no.'

He turned back to Frank. 'So your father-in-law really believes this miscellaneous trade will do better than tea, Frank? But how could I. . . ?'

Fuming, Alice retreated to the kitchen, poured another sherry, grabbed the spoon from Snow Duck and stirred the soup vigorously. Returning to the verandah after a few minutes, she heard Frank saying, '. . . for your own good, yours and Alice's. Honestly, if it wasn't for your being here and part of the family, so to speak, Pa-in-law would be in like a shot and . . .'

'But here's Alice to say luncheon is served, I hope?' Charles' smile was bland.

'Yes it is. And what's been decided in the absence of your business partner, Charles?'

'Nothing. Frank is going to show me some figures after lunch, and figures, you've always admitted, are not your forte.' He took each firmly by the arm. 'My dear good young Greenwoods, it's time to eat and I'm going to open a bottle of the best French white I've been saving for a truly appreciative visitor. I want to hear the latest Shanghai gossip, Frank, and I want my dear wife to relax and listen too. We sadly lack for frivolity in these parts and it makes her too serious by half! Come—to the wine . . .' Determinedly he steered them to the table and the conversation away from any business topic throughout the leisurely meal.

At its conclusion, the men disappeared into the office

353

while Alice, mellowed by the wine, snoozed on the verandah, dreaming lazily that all was bound to be well, and that, with Mr. Yuan-wang involved, their fortunes would soon be made. But when they reappeared, it was apparent no such happy conclusion had been reached and the subject was again deliberately avoided during supper. Pleading tiredness after his journey, Frank excused himself early.

'See what you can do, Sis, he's so stupidly suspicious of the idea,' he whispered as Alice handed him a night-light in the kitchen.

She grimaced. 'He hates me to interfere, as you've seen today, and anything I suggest he always takes as criticism. But I'll try.'

Charles was reading the trade reports Frank had brought and sipping a brandy. She picked up her embroidery, feigning calm till his air of unruffled occupation defeated her. 'So you've looked at the figures—the agency terms? What do you think? It seems an excellent idea to me. The tea business is overcrowded and uncertain, you said so yourself.'

'Maybe, maybe, but it's well organised and we Brits are all in it together. As for this trash trade, I don't like it.'

'But the terms, Charles?'

'Oh fair enough on the surface, I admit—but could I trust them?'

'Not trust Frank—my own brother?'

'Oh, Frank's honest of course—absolutely and transparently so. But is he the innocent being used by Wang to persuade me into this? Remember, Alice, you've often warned me against relying too much on the native traders, saying they'll do a barbarian down any day in favour of their own countrymen. . . . Yet now . . .'

'But Charles, don't you understand? To Wang, as you insist on calling him, we're not just any old barbarians—I'll spell it out for you: Peachy is Wang's favourite daughter. Through Frank and me she's linked to our firm. Therefore we've become part of his family network—and that, to a Chinese, is crucial. And so, even though we're foreigners, he'd never do us down, and we could trust him implicitly because he'd use a different set of rules with us. I'm positive his offer is generous and honourable. He intends to make money of course, but not at our expense, though it could be at the expense of some other Hankow merchants, if they're not sharp enough.'

'Ah yes that's the point, isn't it?' He poured himself another brandy. 'You want me to go into open partnership with a Chinaman even if it does mean doing the dirty on some of our own.'

She realised her mistake. 'I'm not suggesting any sort of crookedness, just that we seize this opportunity to expand honestly and accumulate more capital, which we're not doing at present.'

'We're honest.'

'Yes, and poor.'

They glared at each other. 'What do you really know about all this?' He drank moodily. 'You're a woman with no head for business and are just being ruled by your emotions as usual. You want this arrangement because Wang is Frank's father-in-law and you're devoted to Frank.'

Her tone was icy. 'I love Frank of course—but my devotion in this case is to the success of Grant & Greenwood. No, Charles, it's you who's not looking at it logically because you've got a snobbish bias against any sort of alliance with a "native trader" or moving out of tea—after all, it's so much more respectable and jolly isn't it—trailing on the coat-tails of Telford and his merry tea-men? That's the truth, isn't it? Now give me a brandy.'

He handed her a very small quantity in a very large glass, and she gulped it. 'Now come, dear, let's stop quarrelling and accept the offer. Go into it gradually if you like; talk it over with Wang in Shanghai—would that put your mind at rest?'

'Nothing will put my mind at rest, because I'm simply not going into it, so there!' he snarled. 'You're getting too uppity in these business matters, my dear. You spend far too much time in the office as it is, instead of keeping company with the other ladies.' He swigged his drink and looked at her with unusual venom. 'I suppose it would suit your book to have more natives around the place and you hand-in-glove with them, talking their lingo? Why, you might eventually be able to move me out entirely in favour of Greenwood, Greenwood & Wang Ltd. . . . All your childhood dreams come true!'

'Charles—you . . . you . . . how dare you suggest that I—oh it's too much!' Her voice broke with angry tears. 'You're a short-sighted fool in business matters and I just want to help you, help us both . . . But all right, have it your own way—you will of course. But if things go wrong after you've refused this offer, don't expect me to help. I'll be too busy playing croquet with the ladies and spending your money on dresses and parties and all the things I don't do now—because we can't really afford them! So be sure to make a fortune for me, won't you?' Tears streaming down her face, she slammed out. He poured another drink, flung himself back in his chair.

The reasons Alice had given for his refusal were right to a point, though she didn't know the extent of his indebtedness to Telford, who had so manoeuvred matters that he could buy him out any day if he chose. Sometimes Charles hated Tommy's chummy bonhomie, his arrogant confidence in his superior business acumen, but he was not going to admit that to Alice. We men have to stick together, Telford had said only the other day—and it's not a good idea to let the little wife have too much to do with business, old chap! Women soon get above themselves and the natives hate doing business with 'em, don't think it's natural. And Telford was right. Alice had just given more proof of that. From now on, he vowed angrily, he would see that she had enough money to join in all the ladies' entertainments, even if it meant going further into hock.

He swilled the liquid round his glass moodily. Dash it, indebtedness seemed an inevitable part of life in China—like the constant noise, the stinks, the gawping filthy crowds. But more depressing still was the sense of being relegated to the barbarian fringes, a mere interloper in the Celestial scheme of things, without power, privilege or even much knowledge of what was really going on. This, he realised, was just what his family had warned him about. 'So you think you'll be a swashbuckling merchant-adventurer, do you?' his father had snorted. 'Sailing up the Yangtze and making a glittering fortune. Well there's no room for that sort of caper in China. Once a barbarian always a barbarian there and you'll end up in some mouldy back-of-beyond concession built on a mud-bank plagued with dishonest traders and riddled with debt—you mark my words!'

In the late-night quiet of his sitting-room Charles did mark his father's words, and a flood of guilty, reluctant nostalgia overcame him. He thought of Madras, its stately offices, the orderly, consequential lives of its British administrators. And he had a sudden painful vision of dear dead Maria in a sprigged dress, standing on the trim lawn of Government

House during some official function with little Peter beside her. He would write to Harriet about the boy coming here. It would give Alice another interest for one thing and compensate for their own lack of children.

Why Alice had not yet conceived they did not know and found it hard to discuss. Charles, assuming his second wife's attitude to her marital duties was as unenthusiastic as his first's, pressed his claims fairly infrequently and with a half-apologetic briskness that seldom roused her. During the early months, she had occasionally tried leading him towards some of the inventive, leisurely, uninhibited ways of pleasuring that she knew, but her initiatives only embarrassed him. Not the proper feminine behaviour for an English lady, he felt sure, and it only served as a reminder for that confession about her past which he had carefully expunged from his consciousness. And so they soon fell into a mutually acceptable pattern of polite intercourse that sent Charles quickly to sleep afterwards and left Alice wide-awake, her half-aroused flesh longing for what she had once enjoyed.

The coolness that followed their first bitter quarrel was not therefore melted in the warmth of the marriage bed, but instead accentuated by a letter from Daisy Small that arrived soon after. Now the tea-season was over, Daisy wrote, she felt sure Alice would have time to consider the Anti-Footbinding League and she enclosed pamphlets illustrated with real-life photographs of bound feet in all their ugly deformity. Charles shuddered when she showed him. 'How disgusting—really, it's too much.'

'But just what's needed to shake the matrons of Hankow out of their apathy, as Daisy says.'

'Mrs. Small should leave this sort of thing to the missionaries.'

'No—that's just the point. As Daisy says, our best chance is to convince the people on purely humanitarian grounds.'

He handed the pamphlets back. 'Oh those—my dear Alice, what about the lepers on the quay with their noses and fingers falling off, the numbers of baby-girls drowned like kittens or put out for the dogs to chew, the criminals starving in cages and spattered with human ordure—with all that going on around us every day, why worry about bound feet? Your so-called humanitarianism doesn't make sense to the Chinese, you know—they're not even quite human in the way we are.'

'Oh don't be absurd, Charles, of course they are. I've lived among them and I know. They've had so many more dreadful things to contend with, that's all. Listen to this, apparently Daisy tackled an Ichang magistrate on the subject and he said, "Yes, poor little mites—they have but five years to run" . . . Think of that, isn't it awful? One's got to make a stand somewhere, as Daisy says, and she wants me to start a branch of the League here, and distribute these to the foreigners and some Chinese officials and . . .'

'Daisy says, Daisy says,' he mimicked tartly. 'Well, Daisy can say what she likes in Ichang, but here she's considered an eccentric busybody if you want to know and I'm not having your name associated with her damn fool league. Amelia Telford's already hinted that your behaviour isn't always up to snuff apparently and . . .'

'Amelia Telford, Amelia Telford! What do I care about that snobby cow?' Alice snorted. 'Why, Daisy's worth . . .'

'You'd better care about Amelia's opinion,' his voice rose in competition, 'I'm enough in hock to her husband. So now you have it, Alice. And no, I'm not giving you any details. All I'm saying is that I absolutely forbid you to get on some ridiculous hobby-horse that would antagonise the whole settlement.'

'That's all you care about it, isn't it, Charles? People's good opinion—and I thought you were an adventurer.'

'I have to care, we live here—this is our livelihood.' His tone moderated. 'Let's not quarrel again, Alice. Just reflect for a moment, even putting the community's views aside, you know the native officials would be affronted by these pamphlets and, given the present political situation, the last thing we want is to stir up trouble.'

That, she knew, was true. For the past few months popular feeling against Westerners' presence in the country had been running high again due to the crisis between the Chinese and the French over the tributary kingdom of Annam where the Vietnamese tribes lived. Bands of Annamese peasants had started a guerrilla war against the French who wanted control of all Cochin China. The conflict, though distant, had aroused China's awareness of its vulnerability to foreign aggression. Anti-barbarian tracts were again in circulation; some foreign houses in the Treaty Ports had been stoned. Knowing this, the flood of conviction inspired by Daisy's letter ebbed from her and she mumbled, 'Oh, I suppose I'll have to wait. Things will quieten down soon.'

The subject was not mentioned again and Alice wrote a shamefaced letter to Daisy promising to take action when the political situation improved.

In the meantime it worsened. The French captured two Annamese cities and this prompted anti-barbarian riots down-river at Wuhu. In Hankow, the force of native constabulary detailed to protect the Concession was increased from eight men to twelve, and the foreign men formed a volunteer brigade which met once a week to oil guns stored in the godowns and to inspect barriers which, in any uprising, could be used to block off the settlement from the native city. As there seemed no imminent danger of this however, volunteer meetings were quite convivial, lasting into the early hours. At breakfast the morning after Charles would assure his wife that she was protected by a fine set of fellows ready to lay down their lives to a man if need be. But by this Alice was politely unimpressed, for the idea of any such eventuality seemed absurd.

However, the unsettled international situation adversely affected trade. Several of the foreign merchant houses refused to invest more in the China market and the upswing that usually began in March simply did not materialise. Even Tommy Telford was worried and eventually he and Charles decided to visit Chiuchiang to investigate possibilities of going into brick-tea like the Russians—who seemed to do very well with the stuff. Amelia, frightened of being left without male protection, went with them, but Alice stayed behind to 'mind the shop' as she put it, and welcome Frank who was coming to inspect the Wang Agency now flourishing in Hankow.

Expecting his arrival the day after Charles' departure, Alice made noodle soup, glazed some sugar plums, ran up to the verandah time and again watching for the steamer from Shanghai. When it had not arrived by lunchtime. she coiled in her basket chair and took up her embroidery. A mist began to form, clouding water and sky to pearly grey, blurring the red sun to a stained haze, disembodying the usual river noises.

Row her to bite the water-side and make her fast,
In rain and wind we must always find anchorage,
When the sun sets, I'll buy a bright cloth for my woman to
wear.

The song of a poling boatman drifted to her through the mist.

For thousands of years, she thought, similar sounds and songs had rolled over these ancient waters, and bent old women had stood ankle-deep in the mud fishing. The one below Alice's verandah now lived in a mat hovel propped against the factory wall; her little net circled in the air as she threw it out, and each time she drew it in, a few, flat, oval fish flapped inside.

Inconsequentially, a verse of Yu Hsiang rolled through Alice's mind:

> *Turning without end,*
> *Heaven and earth shift secretly.*
> *Who is aware of it?*

She remembered the day she had returned to Tientsin with Uncle Robert and seen a man weaving nets where the Mission had once been. She got up restlessly, wishing Frank would come, a sense of foreboding strong in her. At length, as the sun set and the old woman coiled away her net, she heard a knock and hurried down in alarm. 'Frank—is it you? Thank goodness—but I didn't see the steamer?'

'Hello, Sis. They're not running, haven't you heard?'

'Heard what?'

'A French naval squadron attacked Foochow three days ago, bombarding the Celestial Navy and its dockyard out of existence. Reprisal for the Annamese mess . . . Shanghai's up in arms of course and the Chinese have commandeered the river steamers—going to turn 'em into gunboats overnight they say. Poor fools haven't a hope, just making the appropriate cries of outrage, as old Ben Smythe put it. He was coming this way too, so we got berths on a Russian coaster, and here I am.'

'Oh, Frank, how dreadful—here, sit by the stove, Snow Duck'll bring tea. Every single Chinese ship sunk, you say?'

'Yep—the entire navy, such as it was. Not many lives lost, but an awful lot of face.'

'Oh, how furious the self-strengtheners will be—they've been calling for the build-up of coastal defences for years. And Han-li, I hope he's all right.' She remembered how proudly he had once described those Chinese warships to her—the power of their engines, the Whitworth guns bristling on their decks. Lin, Han-li and thousands like them would be hating the guts of every foreign devil.

'Oh curse the French—what right have they to. . . ?'

'Nothing to do with rights, as Ben says. Just the biggest

bullies showing their muscle. ''The ambition of the barbarian nations is long, hard and deep, while the stupidity of our scholar-officials is boundless''—or something like that, in the words of a Chinese minister reported in the paper last week. He's right, this goes to show . . . Give me a brandy and soda instead of tea, Sis, it was cold on the river and this sort of thing always upsets me. Puts me in a beastly position at home, you can imagine.'

'With all the foreigners toasting the exploits of the victorious Froggies?'

'Exactly,' He took the glass. 'One reason I determined to get away. There's no danger, just a lot of huffing and puffing— there'll be another peace treaty eventually and the Chinese will get the worst of it, as usual. But it's crippling for trade.'

She sighed, stirring the embers of the stove. 'And things are shaky already.'

'Really? Well, Charles should have agreed to Pa-in-law's proposition. Our agency here is doing very well. Did you know that feathers—on hats, dresses, boas—are very fashionable in Europe just now? We're exporting them by the hundred-sacksful each week. That's what I admire about old Wang— his eye's for the main chance, whereas men like your Charles wouldn't stoop to that sort of thing. Anyway, Sis, I've got to see our compradore Old Cho at the Golden Phoenix. I'll unpack later.'

'But, Frank, you've only just come.'

'Well, I expected to be here much earlier, didn't I?'

'Oh don't leave yet, we've not talked for months.'

'You're not frightened of the big bad yellow men like the other fluttery ladies surely?' he teased.

'Of course not, but I'm tired of being cooped up in this Concession as if we were in an enemy country. Since this situation, we aren't supposed even to venture into Hankow proper.'

'Well, I'm certainly going . . .'

She faced him in the doorway. 'Then take me with you. I'm bored with behaving myself.'

'But people are bound to . . .'

'That's what I hate about these foreign communities—the spying and tittle-tattle. Where are all the adventures I used to dream about?'

'Oh, you always had high falutin dreams, Uncut Jade. But tell you what—put on your native togs like you used to, remember? And we'll go in closed chairs . . .'

She ran to her bedroom and soon emerged in a drab-blue robe, hair tucked under a kerchief, face powdered white, eyebrows black.

He surveyed her. 'Not bad—more like an abo than a true Daughter of Han, but never mind.'

'Better than you can do with that yellow mop—like an old straw horse-box, Eldest Brother used to say.'

'Ah, but to Peachy it's royal gold. By the way, she's going to have another child. And daily prayers are going up for a son this time . . . You don't seem to be doing much in that line?' he looked at her curiously.

'The doctor says it might be difficult because of—what happened in Hunan I suppose. I didn't give him the details of my miscarriage . . .'

'Oh dear, I'm sorry, Alice.' In the ensuing awkward pause, he said, 'I've sent Snow Duck for two chairs . . . Er, have you heard from Mother recently?'

'Yes—she seems quite cheerful. They're receiving more money from wellwishers recently because of the revival going on in England, led by those American evangelists, Moody and Sankey.'

Frank sang mockingly, ' "Hold the Fort for I am coming," etc., etc. . . . And the children?'

'Adam's settled in school, but poor Sunny's so lonely. Mother's hoping to go on leave with Will and Isabel next year and take her. Stepfather won't leave the Mukden Fort, but she certainly needs a holiday.'

Snow Duck arrived with the chairs just then and they jogged off in the gathering dusk—across a hump-bridge, through a small gate in the crenellated wall of the 'million-people-city' where China began. Their way lay through the street of the druggists whose gilded signboards proclaimed the efficacy of various herbal aphrodisiacs, of dragons' blood tablets and alligator pills. One shop had a special display of liquid extracted from the gall bladders of recently executed bandits—an infallible cure for boils. Of more sinister import was a hastily scrawled poster on a nearby wall: 'Death to the dog-faced barbarians of France. They have invaded our western tributaries, destroyed our magnificent war-vessels. Their heads are monstrous, their dispositions fiercer than tiger or wolf, their hearts greedier than snake or hog.'

The news of the attack on Foochow had reached the city that afternoon, and the Golden Phoenix was unusually animated as a result. Its rooms, some more secret than others, were all designed for the entertainment of the city's business men. Its portals shone with red lanterns. From its ornate restaurant drifted succulent smells of sizzling pork and fish. Across the passage in the Good Fortune Hall gamblers stood tense round tables, and through the lattices of the Flowery Chambers came the pluck and whine of romantic song, the scent of women's bodies, and along the passages to the inner courtyard the heavy, bittersweet smell of opium hung in the air.

Old Cho met them in the restaurant. 'I wondered if you'd get here,' he greeted Frank.

'I got a ride on a Russian coaster. This is my sister, Old Cho, come to dine.' He concealed his displeasure under a bland smile that cracked his smooth yellow cheeks.

As they settled at a table, Frank asked, 'There are anti-foreign posters up, I see—does it mean real trouble, do you think?'

'The filthy French toads,' Old Cho spat in disgust. 'I wish we could blast them all to searing hell!'

Alice was startled by his violence. 'Are you of the anti-barbarian faction then?' She was half-joking, but he turned narrow, cold eyes on her.

'I've been of that faction ever since I was a lad, foreign woman. Since the day—and more than two cycles of the Rat have gone by since then—when I first saw one of your god-rotting vessels rolling on the waters of our Great River. We all went to watch the big-nosed barbarians step ashore as if they owned Hankow. There was a wily linguist from Canton aboard and we asked who those vulgar monsters were. Men from some tin-pot island beyond the far western horizon, he answered. Their leader was a lord in his country—El-gin was his name. Fat as a pig with good living he was, face red as a turkey-cock's. His boat was in the service of *her* majesty, because these barbarians were ruled by a female, and it was called *Furious*— Furious!' Old Cho sucked his mouth into a humourless chuckle. What the hell have they got to be furious about? I asked, being a cocky youngster. How dare they sit out there, all primed and prickly with guns like an angry little wasp—Bzzz, bzzz, we should swat 'em straight under the waters, mister, that's what I said to the interpreter. We, the Sons of Han, *we* should be furious . . . Well, if we'd taken a stronger line in those days, we might not be in this damnable mess now, with the French toads overrunning our western tributaries and battering our navy to bits. Cost us millions of taels to build those ships—and I'm so furious my hair is on end under my cap!'

'But you can't keep China closed away from the world forever, you know,' Frank protested.

'Why not, why not? Our Imperial dynasties did well for thousands of years without the rest of the world . . . Yes, yes . . . bzzz, bzzz—throw all the foreign devils back into the sea, I say.'

Frank grinned impishly. 'I don't think my Peachy would thank you for that, Old Cho.'

He snorted. 'Well—I might pull just you out again, if you grow a proper Chinese tail . . . Ah, here's Mr. Shen from Szechuan, I told you about him—the upriver trade and all that . . .'

He ambled to meet the newcomer, and Frank sighed. 'Fancy, Old Cho—he isn't usually so disagreeable, this French business has certainly upset him.'

Returning, Old Cho introduced his friend, then turned to Alice, 'I fear I'm asking you to leave us now, Mrs. Grant. We cannot discuss these things before you—a woman and one whose husband has a rival firm.'

Alice jumped up, flushing. 'The mistress of this establishment has agreed to let you wait in her private apartment.'

Frank pulled an apologetic face and Alice followed a servant across a courtyard and into a dimly lit room. The bittersweet smell of opium enclosed her; a middle-aged woman reclined on a couch smoking, and a younger woman was crouched over her, next to a spirit-lamp, plucking a lute and singing in a low sweet voice,

'You and I in the same boat,
Long leaves bending in the wind,
Plucking rushes at the Five Lakes.
We started at dawn from the orchid island,
We rested under the elms till noon,
. . . You and I plucking rushes,
Hadn't plucked a handful when night came.'

At the song's end, the singer raised her face to Alice. It was a smooth, beautiful oval in the lamplight but its eyes were sightless. 'Who's there?'

'My name is Uncut Jade. They said I could wait here while my brother talks business.'

The woman bowed. 'Then please sit down. This is the mistress of the Golden Phoenix, but she's dreaming.'

Alice sat gingerly on another couch next to a white Pekinese dog and watched as the blind woman took a nut of opium from a box on the table and teased it over the lamp. When it was soft she inserted it in the small silver bowl near the pipe's end. Keeping the bowl over the flame, she handed the mouthpiece to her mistress who drew it into her lungs with one long satisfied breath, then reclined again on her porcelain head-rest. As the blind woman replenished the pipe again, Alice said,

'You have a most melodious voice, may I ask your name?'

'Flowing Spring—because I was found wandering by the river one spring day when I was young. I was so lucky because a kind boat-man brought me here—where I've lived ever since . . . And you? There is something different—you smell strangely?'

Alice chuckled. 'You must please excuse me, I'm English and it is the smell of the barbarian, I'm told we all have it.'

'Flowing Spring, pretty dear,' moaned the woman from the couch, 'sing again . . .'

Obediently she took up the lute and began.

*'The monk of Szechuan on the heights of Mount Omei,
Comes down westward, under his arm a Lu-yi lute.
He plays for me, fingers brushing the strings,
And the sound is like murmuring pine-trees in ravines.
So with the flowing spring song he recreates my soul.'*

As the soft voice chanted and the poppy-fumes swirled, Alice felt herself drowsing. 'Would you like one?' Flowing Spring was holding a pipe for her and Alice hesitated, her senses remembering a strange dream of long ago, when she lay ill in Grandmother Willow's hut.

Flowing Spring smiled. 'Come, take it, Uncut Jade. The flowers of your childhood will bloom again. You will walk through gardens you had forgotten you abandoned and see the shadows of strange bamboos under moons of amber.'

Alice took it, inhaled, swallowed, sucked till the pipe was empty. Flowing Spring inserted another pellet. 'Don't worry—this is no adulterated mix, it is pure Benares. You have smoked before, I think?'

'So long ago, I'd almost forgotten.'

'Ah but the poppy is patient. It knows how to wait.'

In the inert half-light two moths circled slowly above the opium tray with its box of pellets, pipes, water and lamp. The box was pink with a yellow design that flared as intensely as a rape-field in full bloom; the moths were liquid white like water-lilies, but powdery too with blue edges like the lamp flame. Alice watched them, totally relaxed and at peace with all the world. Flowing Spring's lovely face smiled sightlessly down at her as she circled into a landscape where a monk stood on a green mountain. He beckoned to her, but she knew he was waiting like the poppy and she had not yet met him. Behind the monk she sensed a black dwarf lurking, his mouth full of blood. She could scarcely see him though and he went away behind a flat silver cloud.

When she woke her mouth tasted harshly acrid and her eye-lids were too heavy to open. When they eventually did, it was on her familiar bedroom and she remembered how Old Cho had bundled her and Frank into closed chairs late the night before. He had been sodden with wine and pleasure, she with the spell of the ancient poppy. A foolish episode that she must never repeat, she told herself sternly, and it had only happened because Frank had lingered long in the Fragrant Chambers.

The next day the river steamers resumed normal service and Frank, returning to Shanghai, passed Charles and the Telfords returning from Chiuchiang. It had been a thoroughly wasted trip, Charles told Alice gloomily, for no one would consider advancing capital for new ventures in the present tricky international situation.

'We got pelted with mud when we went to the Consul's for supper and old Tommy kept shouting, "But we're not French froggies, you stupid sots, we're true blue British bulldogs!" If they understood, it made no difference—Amelia's hat was knocked off and I now know exactly what mud in your eye feels like!'

'Oh dear, how oafish these mobs are. Did they shout "kill the barbarians" at you—that's a dreadful sound.' She shivered.

'I expect so—luckily we couldn't understand. But they have killed a barbarian elsewhere—the French Consul in Foochow was murdered the night after the attack on the dockyard, and that will worsen the situation—see, here's an account of it.'

He handed her a copy of the *Mercury*.

'Oh Charles—no, no, it was Félix, Félix Fauré, I knew him in Port Arthur—oh dear oh dear, oh no!' She sat down, reading with blurred eyes how Félix had been dragged from his house, kicked along the street, beaten and stabbed to death. His wife and child had been saved by the authorities just in time. She buried her head in her hands and Charles stroked it comfortingly.

'My dear—I'm so sorry. I'd no idea you knew him, or I'd have broken it gently.'

She sniffed. 'That doesn't matter, I had to know. But Félix—he was so lively and handsome . . . so French. . . . To think that . . .' Too vividly she conjured that last horror—the pain and humiliation, those flashing eyes ground into the dust, blood soaking the dapper facings of his jacket. She clenched her fists in sad anger. The incident was a hazard of diplomacy of course and Félix dead would, the *Mercury's* editorial said, prove more useful to the French in subsequent bargaining than Félix alive ever had. The wry wit of the living Félix would have appreciated that.

There was nothing to be done of course. 'n Hankow the Concession's constabulary was redoubled and some foreigners slept with pistols under their pillows. Alice felt the sense of imprisonment keenly and, with time on her hands, drafted a translation of Mill's treatise on women which she sent to Daisy Small, 'in the hope,' she wrote, 'this will serve to show you I'm not quite lost to the cause of women's various subjections. When this dreadful French business is settled I promise to do something for the League. I feel the worst is over, don't you?'

And indeed it was, for neither side wanted full-scale war. That summer the Chinese signed a treaty by which the French gained suzerainty over Annam, and Li Hung-chang, appointed Associate Controller of the Admiralty, set about re-building the country's shattered naval defences. Trade improved and money flowed back into Shanghai, but in Hankow there was a tremendous row between foreigners and local officials over the imposition of new customs levies which held up shipments, so to Charles it all seemed one damn thing after another. In September, just as trade really picked up, a junk named *White Wings* that had always been lucky broke its tow-ropes at the Yellow Cow Rapids and sank with all hands, plus quantities of Grant & Greenwood's dye-stuffs and lead spars. On the same day that the news of this disaster arrived, the Shanghai steamer brought a letter from sister Harriet in Madras. Charles whistled through his teeth as he read.

'Good Lord, Alice, they're all coming to see us!'

'What—your family?' Her dismay was unconcealed.

'Yes, I told you Harriet and I have been in correspondence about Peter's future and though I'd like him here, it's more than time he went to school in England. Well, George is due for leave next spring, so they propose taking Peter home with them and . . .' he read aloud, '. . . "we're hoping to make a Chinese excursion first—to Hong Kong, Shanghai, then up the Yangtze to see you and meet your wife at last. Won't that be exciting, dear? By the way . . . I hope you won't mind if we bring Florence Plowden with us? She's married to George's brother Ian you know, and he's going to be up at the North-West Frontier for months a-railway-building . . . Quite a pretty creature, a bit flighty—and country-born unfortunately." '

Alice bridled. 'Like me . . .'

He glanced up. 'Oh don't mind that—Harriet's a bit of a snob I'm afraid, but very kindhearted.' He continued reading: ' "Seems rather cruel to leave Florence alone where she's no relatives, so we're suggesting she share our China trip, then return to India when we go Home." '

He flung down the letter. 'All sounds perfectly splendid and well-planned—just like Harriet—but they can't possibly come to this pokey little hole.' He prowled about agitatedly.

'Charles, how mean of you—I think it's a sweet place and after all I've done.'

'Oh you've done wonders, my dear. But it's not the sort of scale Harriet and George are used to in Madras. And there's simply no space—why, we'll need three more bedrooms.'

'But can't we explain that now? Before they confirm their arrangements.'

'My dear Alice, Harriet and George have given my son bed and board for about five years—the least I can do is offer them generous house-room here for a holiday.'

'Yes dear, of course, I'm sorry. But wouldn't the Telfords help out?'

'It won't do, Alice. I've got to put on a better show than this. Harriet would be horrified—it would confirm all her worst fears about my coming to China—oh, she'd be so scathing!' He shivered.

'You sound quite frightened of her. She's your sister after all.'

'But ten years older and very elder-sisterly, and I want to show them I'm making good in spite of their warnings—even if I'm not.' He laughed mirthlessly.

'But we're doing all right in our small way.'

'Oh yes, we can afford to pay Snow Duck and hire a buggy occasionally.'

'And Harriet would look down her nose at all this?'

'Yes she would—and rightly so, Alice. The fact is, my family's standards are—higher than some, and I won't let them down any further.'

'As you have by coming to China and marrying me, I suppose?'

'I never suggested that. All I'm saying is that we must move into a house big enough to accommodate my sister, her husband, my son and this half-sister-in-law, whoever she is. They're not due for months yet and there's time—in fact, I've got an idea already. You remember that house beyond the Telfords' where the Ukrainian merchant, Markov, lived?'

'Till his wife died of fever caught from that pestilential swamp behind. . . ?'

'Oh pooh, that was a silly rumour. Anyway, Markov left after the funeral and now I hear he mayn't come back, so the place would be for rent. I'll find out.'

A few weeks later the permanence of Markov's departure was confirmed and the Russian Consul half-heartedly cleared the house, leaving behind a worm-eaten table, some tea-chests, and a cracked chandelier dangling from a rusty rod in the hallway. The chandelier was the first thing Alice saw when she and Charles looked the place over, its dusty glimmer only adding to the general air of neglect and melancholy. The rent was higher than Charles could afford, repairs were badly needed and most of the rooms overlooked the dreary swamp behind Nobs' End. But it *was* at that end of the Bund, it had five bedrooms and a large dining-room, so, over-riding his wife's misgivings, Charles took it.

Workmen went in to mend floorboards and leaking windows, but, Alice realised, their knocked-up bits of local furniture, their cheap draperies, even the beloved tiger rug, were going to look small and second-rate in the gloomy, lofty rooms. At the market one day she sold the silver walnut from the Carr loot to buy a heavy sideboard, bedsteads, dressing-tables from the Russian dealers, using, she told Charles, money she had saved in Port Arthur against a rainy day.

369

The day they finally moved into the house was very rainy; cold mid-winter rain that crept through the crevices the carpenters had not sealed, and positively poured into the fuel store. Wet wood and charcoal spluttered dully in the unused grates, wind whistled through shutters, and on their first evening in residence the chandelier, shaken from its tenuous mooring by the unaccustomed activity, fell and shattered in a thousand fragments.

'What the devil's that?' Charles shouted from the bedroom as the sickening tinkles of glass exploded below. He rushed downstairs till his feet crunched as into breaking ice. Alice snatched a lamp and hurried after him, then stopped with a scream. A long brown and black spotted snake, shaken in turn from its winter retreat under the floorboards, reared its flat head at her from the top stair. Its yellow eyes glittered and its forked tongue flicked out with a hiss.

'Charles—help, quick—there's a snake! Call Snow Duck, quick.'

Charles grabbed a walking stick and pounded up the stairs, Snow Duck behind him. He was about to crash the stick down on the creature's head when Snow Duck lunged past and grabbed it by the throat.

Alice shrieked, 'Careful, careful—he'll bite you!'

'No killee master, him no bitee . . .' Snow Duck panted as the snake twisted in his grasp, flailing its tail angrily.

'Oh kill it anyway, it's horrible!' Alice moaned.

'No, lady—this is the death snake. Not poisonous, no, but it's an evil spirit snake, always attracted to a house where there's been a death. But if you kill it inside the house there'll soon be another death—Here, help me, master, it's getting a grip on me . . .'

Shuddering Charles loosened the scaly length that was binding tightly round the boy's arm; its yellow eyes glittered with greater ferocity.

'I'll get a box and carry it back to the swamp,' Snow Duck said, as Alice translated for Charles.

'Damn superstition,' he grunted. 'Tell him to just get rid of it fast.'

Snow Duck ran down the stairs holding the snake from him; at the bottom he skidded on the chandelier glass and fell. The creature thrashed out of his loosened grip and slithered across the floor in a series of horrible tinkling slides. Charles pounded after it, picked up a chair and crashed it down on the snake's head.

'No! Stoppee, stoppee, master,' Snow Duck cried, but Charles paid no heed. When he lifted the chair, the death snake was dead, its head mangled to a mash of reptilian flesh and glass. Alice rushed down and helped Snow Duck pick slivers of glass from his shaking hands. 'Master makee very bad, very bad. No good house now.'

'Oh nonsense boy, it's just an old superstition,' Alice snapped, but her voice trembled. 'I'll get some ointment. Are you all right, Charles? I'll sweep up—and get rid of that horrid creature outside please.'

It took hours to clear the glass fragments from every cranny, and Snow Duck, hands bandaged, sulkily refused to help. The fires would not stay alight and they went to bed tired and cold. Lying next to her sleeping husband, Alice was gripped rigid in a paroxysm of terror. The scene of the evening rolled again and again through her mind: the harsh crash, the yellow eyes glittering, the last glassy slither, Snow Duck's bleeding hands, the snake's mashed head. Beyond it in the dark she seemed to see the face of Mrs. Markov who had died of swamp fever—a dark-haired woman with a put-upon, wistful look—the dead one who had attracted the snake to the house. And Alice hated and feared the place from that first night on. It was gloomy, pretentious, costly and withdrawn from the everyday bustle of the river that had given her such pleasure before. Worse than all this, though, was the coiled shadow of the death snake that had died inside, the death that was still inside waiting.

13

Alice moved round the dining-table checking each place-setting yet again, blowing dust-specks from its polished surface, ears straining for the whistle that would signal the arrival of the steamer with Charles' relatives aboard. She had secretly dreaded this day ever since she learned of their coming and the dread had not lessened because the occasion had been delayed. Harriet had written that a most inconvenient famine had struck the southern provinces that spring, just before they were about to leave, and poor George had to organise the distribution of emergency supplies, relief works, and the usual botherations that occurred in the *mofussil* when the crops failed and people starved.

It was all a great nuisance because they would miss most of Queen Victoria's Jubilee celebrations in England and were now arriving in Hankow at the very fag-end of August, the Limit of Heat, as the Chinese called it, when the flotsam of the year was stranded in stinking piles on the receding water-line and everyone was plagued with lassitude and mosquitoes. Because of the delay, Harriet wrote that they could spend less than three weeks there, for their passages Home were already booked.

'That long,' Charles had moaned. 'What on earth can we do with them?'

Alice tried to cheer him. 'We can visit the Hills of the East Dragon; there's the September race-meeting and the Telfords' croquet-lawn for Peter.'

'Oh Peter's all right, it's the adults . . .' So they sent for cases of wine and brandy from Shanghai, hired an extra cook, a maid-of-all-work and hoped for the best.

'Snow Duck,' Alice called. 'Are you sure everything's ready for luncheon?' He came in, sweat rolling down his fat cheeks, looking cross. 'That new cook's useless, Missee, more damn trouble than he's worth. I could do it all better myself.'

'But there'll be six of us at every meal.'

'And my new coat's too tight—like a suit of armour round my middle.'

'Please, Snow Duck, don't complain—for my sake—you know Master wants us all to look specially smart.'

As he shuffled off, hang-dog, she heard the steamer whistle and her heart plummeted. Her sole wish was to take herself off to the Golden Phoenix, there to receive from Flowing Springs' soft hand a pipe that would very soon reveal the inanity of her worries about servants, place-settings, unknown relatives. For, since her first visit, she had secretly returned there sometimes in the dark winter evenings when Charles was away. Flowing Spring greeted her warmly, only she had to pay for her opium as any customer, and the spending of precious money so illicitly saved her from undue indulgence.

But today escape was impossible. Instead she pinned a new green hat atop her head, drew on new gloves, hurried to the landing-stage. Charles was already there, fussing around the hired buggy. Occasions like this, Alice thought, brought out the most boyish in him—enthusiastic, wanting to please, but lacking the resources to do it properly. The steamer was nosing to shore and as Alice came up, Charles waved his hat and cheered.

'There they are—there's Harriet, looking every inch the memsahib.'

Alice's sister-in-law came down the gangplank slowly, mindful of her voluminous skirt, her back erect, swept-up hair, greyed by many Indian suns, concealed under a light travelling veil. There was a look of faint disdain on her face that Alice first thought was occasioned by the sight of unpretentious Hankow, but which, she later realised, was as permanent as her other strong features.

'Charles—my dear boy, at last! And Alice—I've wanted to meet you for so long!' Her grey eyes surveyed Alice from head to toe quickly, missing nothing, revealing nothing.

As they embraced, Peter scampered towards Charles who cried, 'My, but you've grown tall, lad—where are you shooting up to, hey?'

So like Charles he was, Alice saw, with that boyish charm in its proper boyish place—curly brown hair, freckled face, but with a pensive, withdrawn look characteristic of many Anglo-Indian children. Then came florid, amiable-looking George and clinging to his arm, his sister-in-law Florence, who was slender and held a parasol to shade her delicate skin. So they all stood exchanging pleasantries while coolies shouldered their several trunks, portmanteaux, hatboxes, and Alice wondered briefly if she had, after all, just taken opium, for the whole scene seemed at one remove. Who were these strangers? Who was she among them? And why did she feel they boded ill?

When they reached the house and Harriet had politely praised the flowers in the hall, Snow Duck hissed quietly to Alice that the new cook had just dropped the best tureen filled with the luncheon's consommé. She hurried to the kitchen; the cook was not even repentant. She and Snow Duck guiltily scraped it back into a bowl and hoped for the best. In the dining-room they were sipping sherry, Harriet and Florence on the sofa, the men in the window-alcove.

'Not a major disaster, I hope?' Harriet raised a sympathetic eyebrow.

'No—the cook broke the tureen, but luckily it was empty,' she lied gaily.

'Oh cooks are dreadful nowadays, not a patch on my mother's time when they really had the interest of the household at heart.'

Alice asked politely, 'I expect you've quite a large staff to manage?'

'Not really, let's see . . .' she counted on her dry, many-ringed fingers. 'There's the head bearer, the khitmager who waits at table, George's valet and my ayah who also does needlework, the dhobi, the mali—that's the gardener . . .'

'And don't forget the bhisti who carries water, the tailor and outside people like grass-cutters, sweepers and stable boys,' Florence chimed in merrily.

'Why, that sounds like a regiment. We can't begin to compare with it in humble Hankow, I fear.'

Harriet pursed her lips. 'Florence and I were just wondering however you manage—and there doesn't appear to be much to entertain the ladies?'

'No, there isn't really, but,' Alice said defiantly, 'I was born in the country so I'm used to things just as they are.'

'Quite so,' Harriet sighed gently.

'But once you've been to other parts of the world doesn't it make you feel that China is just too ten-thousand-miles-offee?' Florence trilled.

She was, Alice realised, something of a porcelain beauty, with fair curls, blue eyes, but marred by the pout of her rosebud mouth and rather square jaw.

'I've not yet been abroad, so I don't know.' Alice smiled determinedly.

'Not anywhere?—how awful for you.'

'And you—you've travelled? I believe you were born in India?'

'Well yes, but I've seen Europe now—London of course, Paris, Rome, Vienna . . . Ian took me for our honeymoon.' She listed the cities with the same air of proud possession as the servants had been counted.

'Well, I'm sure Alice will soon be seeing the world too,' Harriet interposed. 'I gather you and Charles are planning a European tour—at least I hope so,' she lowered her voice, 'I told Peter he'd see his father over there before too long—he's counting on it.'

'Oh yes, next year perhaps . . .' Alice spoke confidently, wondering how they could afford such an excursion. Such calculations obviously did not enter Harriet's head.

They looked across at Peter, standing quiet beside the men, and Harriet said, 'He's a very pleasant young creature, more studious than his father. I hope you'll take to him, Alice.'

'I'm sure I shall,' she replied truthfully as they went to the table. The consommé seemed none the worse for its contact with the kitchen floor, indeed amiable George pronounced it excellent. 'Ah,' Charles looked at his sister for approval, 'my little wife's an excellent housekeeper, not going to be put off by a broken tureen, are you, dear?' He raised a glass vaguely at her. 'But things have a habit of breaking in this house. The chandelier in the entrance crashed down the very night we moved in and Frank, that's Alice's brother, broke a whole tray of glasses during a tea-season party, remember, Alice?'

She duly made light of it, but had been furious at the time, for Frank, arriving after a visit to the Golden Phoenix, had been unsteady on his feet.

Harriet leaned forward. 'Oh yes, Frank—I must say, Alice, how sorry we were not to see him and his wife—what's her name?—in Shanghai, but everything was so hectic, wasn't it, George?'

'Yes m'dear, no time to see anything much really.'

Florence said, 'Your brother's married to a Chinese lady, I believe? How fascinating. Has she got those quaint little bound feet?'

'No—her mother's a Manchu and they don't bind, luckily.'

'Got quite a bee in your bonnet about footbinding though, haven't you, dear?' Charles drew the talk away from his Chinese sister-in-law. 'There's a lady in Ichang wants to start a league for abolishing the custom throughout the entire land.'

'Rather ambitious, don't you know,' George muttered.

'Ah but she's an enthusiast, like a missionary only not one.'

Harriet sighed. 'Oh these enthusiasts, we have them too—want to change everything that doesn't fit their notions.'

Alice felt both cold and hot, thinking of Daisy's fine fervour. 'But there are certain things one must condemn simply on humanitarian grounds surely. I mean take suttee—we outlawed that, are you saying we were wrong to?'

Harriet appraised her like a patient headmistress. 'No I'm not. But I believe one meddles with the customs of the country at one's peril. And there's a great gap between binding feet and burning widows.'

'Anyway, I've heard the Chinese ladies bind willingly, even though it hurts, to please their menfolk?'

Florence shivered theatrically, glancing at Charles who rose to her look with, 'Oh men are brutes aren't they, Florence? I often wonder why you ladies try to please us at all. But as for those hideous hooves called "golden lilies"—how they can appeal, I don't know.'

'*Chacun à son goût* I always say,' said George, 'Moslem, Buddhist, Sikh, Hindu—*chacun à son goût* ... That's not bad, is it, Harriet?'

His wife, a fork of pâté near her lips, gave him the briefest of acknowledgments. The meal progressed slowly, the sun pouring unremittingly through the lattices, and soon a heavy lassitude fell upon them.

'One misses punkahs so,' Harriet gasped, moving the tepid air with a fan.

'The houses here just aren't equipped for them,' Charles apologised.

'Well they should be. Really, Alice, will you excuse us.

We're so fatigued after the journey, we really must rest, mustn't we, Florence. And we haven't unpacked yet. Do you take a siesta, Alice?'

'Not often. And I must go to the market for another tureen, we're rather short.'

'You actually go and buy things there yourself, Alice?' Florence marvelled. 'But how adventurous of you—we seldom venture to the native markets, do we, Harriet?'

'Ah well, Alice knows the language and that makes a difference. You're probably good at bargaining, dear?'

'Almost too good,' Charles interrupted. 'But let me show you upstairs. . . .'

'Oh please don't bother,' Harriet yawned. 'Just send a housemaid up later, after we've rested.'

Alice wondered if she might buy a housemaid along with a tureen; but the visitors would discover the full humbleness of their circumstances sooner or later.

'And are you up to having a look round the godowns, such as they are, George?'

As the men rose, Peter jumped up. 'Let me come too, Father!'

'Oh well—not much to see, you know.'

Alice took his arm. 'Why not come to the market with me, Peter? Lots to see there, I can tell you.'

He hung back, then seeing the men deep in dull conversation, nodded. 'Please, Stepmother Alice.'

'Oh dear, I can't bear that word, Peter. It sounds so elderly. Why not call me Aunt? I'm that several times over already. Don't you agree, Charles?'

'Whatever you prefer, dear. Stepmother certainly has a rather sinister ring.'

The market-bustle usually lifted Alice's spirits and especially so that afternoon following the dignified somnolence of the dining room where words had to be so carefully weighed. 'I'll show you something of the real China,' she promised, leading Peter down narrow alleys where strips of matting sunblinds stretched from opposite roofs so that business was conducted in a curiously dappled twilight. In the streets of the idol-makers she showed him the straw, cloth and tinsel models of possessions and animals that were bought only for burning as funeral offerings.

'It's better than burning the widows themselves, isn't it?' he asked solemnly and she hugged him for that.

In the street of lacquerers, the smells were resinous with jungles of oiled-paper umbrellas hung for sale. Nearby, in the street of the potters, Alice haggled over tureens while Peter watched a barber shave the front of a coolie's head. On the way back, they passed the street of fortune-tellers where elderly bearded men kept caged birds trained to pick out lucky cards. Alice paused. 'Would you like to try one?'

He shrank back. 'No—I'd only be unlucky.'

'But what makes you think so?'

'I usually am, that's all.'

'Oh come Peter, just think how lucky you are here and now. I always try to remember that about myself.'

'But I'm not. I'm just being sent to England though I'd much rather stay with you and Father. I like it here—the people laugh a lot, don't they? More than Indians.'

'Peter, I'm absolutely delighted you like China, but you must go to an English school for a while—then you can come here to live with us if you like.'

'It will be years and years.' He stared moodily at the fortune cards. 'And I might never get back.'

'Oh nonsense—let's see, how old are you?'

'Nearly thirteen.'

She winced, remembering the raw pains of that age when every year seemed eternity. 'Let's try your luck anyway.' She turned to one of the fortune-tellers.

He opened the cage and a skinny yellow bird hopped among the cards, beady eyes flicking as it lifted the edge of one card repeatedly. Its owner picked it up.

'Very good—mountains of golden fortune for the boy.'

Alice snatched it from him. 'Dog of a liar . . . It's a long-long-delay card—grey years ahead.' And then in English, 'Come, Peter, let's get back.'

'It wasn't good was it?' he asked as they hurried away.

'Not good, not bad, a nothing card.'

He spoke with conviction. 'I told you—I'm not lucky.'

The ladies had revived when they returned. Alice put a fixed smile on her face and supervised supper. When bedtime eventually came she was too exhausted even for customary finger-crossing as she passed the top stair. In the bedroom, Charles was unbuttoning his shirt. 'All going rather well so far, don't you think, dear? And that Florence Plowden's a bit

378

of an enchantress, I must say.'

'Really?'

'Oh I suppose she's the kind of woman who appeals more to men than other women. But don't worry, I've my little resident enchantress, haven't I? And I'm sure Harriet approves of you.' He hugged her and she smiled wearily.

Certainly Florence had looked most fetching at supper in a low-cut gown, her fair curls perfectly arranged in an intricate style that Alice could never manage.

'I'm not surprised she was the one to catch old Ian, though,' Charles continued, removing his trousers. 'Several ladies tried, but he's one of those chaps who talks, lives, breathes railways and he never even noticed.'

'Rather dull for Florence. But I wonder what his attraction was?'

'He's got a good position, good prospects, and perhaps Florence has changed him. She's the sort to get under a man's skin.'

'Quite.'

'You don't like her, do you?' He kissed her as they climbed into bed.

'Not much, admittedly. But I quite like the others and Peter's a splendid little fellow, Charles, and so well-behaved.'

'I imagine he's had to be with Harriet around.' He began fondling her breast till she said wearily, 'Oh Charles, I'm so tired, it's been a wearing day . . .'

He obediently desisted. 'Yes, we must get some sleep—picnic to the Yellow Crane Tower tomorrow, isn't it?'

The Yellow Crane Tower was famous for its bright green roof and the view from the hill on which it stood. Its main feature was the mighty flood of the tributary river Han, opaque yellow in the sunshine, dotted with brown and red junk-sails, flowing to meet the Yangtze. A thick heat haze hung over the pullulating cities of the plains, foetid smells of human ordure rose from the cultivated paddies below, mingled with the more sickening stench from the decaying corpses of girl-babies left to rot in the tower's purple shadows. Florence wrinkled her pretty nose, and Harriet's disdainful expression lengthened.

'Might as well start back, hey?' Charles glanced at the time, calculating that the awkward before-supper hours could be filled with the return journey. He and George set off downhill, heedless of Florence's plaint for an escorting arm.

Politely, Alice waited for her.

'Really—it's all right for gentlemen, but one's skirts get so torn and dirty they drag one down!' Pouting, she hoisted her skirt over the prickly undergrowth, holding her fashionable boater in place with the other hand. 'My brother was just the same when we were young—off he'd stride in his strong boots and then laugh at me for being a slowcoach. I used to get so cross.'

'I didn't realise you had a brother, Florence.' Idly, Alice watched a striped lizard run under a stone.

'Oh, I don't now, he's dead. He was a sort of explorer, quite useless at anything sensible. He'd take off into the Himalayas for months, leaving me in Calcutta with my old aunt, which wasn't at all amusing. . . . There's my skirt caught again, bother . . .'

Alice helped her free it, saying sympathetically. 'Oh I know how it is with brothers, they always seem to do as they like and get away with it!'

'And the annoying thing was, he was supposed to look after me, being several years older. Our parents died when I was a baby, you see. Oh I'll leave you well provided for if anything happens to me, he'd say as he went off on another mountain climb.'

'What happened then?'

'The fourth time he went on an expedition—about twelve years ago now I suppose, he just didn't come back, and didn't leave me any better off either. Worse in fact, because Stewart was my aunt's favourite and once he was dead, she didn't even pretend to care for me . . .' She sighed. Those long, dull hours spent in Aunt's stuffy parlour making pin-cushions for the next charitable fancy fair. While Alice, leading the way down the path, suddenly seemed to see the bright gravel coming up to meet her, for the ground ahead threatened to lurch entirely out of place.

'You never learned what happened to your brother Stewart then?'

'Eventually yes, we were notified by the consular authorities that he died of fever in some remote spot in West China.'

Alice's lips were stiff, a prickling sensation in her scalp. 'Stewart?—I seem to have heard—What was his name, not Plowden of course?'

'Stewart Carr—oh this awful path, at last we're nearly down. Whoever would choose to be a mountaineer, such a stupid occupation!' Her laugh tinkled out as they joined the others waiting at the bottom. Alice stood, numb-cold in the hot sun. Already the words, the moments for confession were slipping away; absolute confession—now or never. Her mind refused the full implications of such a totally unexpected dramatic challenge. If she could just turn the clock back that little space—see the lizard run under the stone again, not ask about Florence's brother, have time to think. But she was bound, doomed, to have learned the truth soon, the black hand of divine retribution had clawed down on her out of the blue sky and she shuddered.

'Whatever's the matter, Alice?' Harriet looked concerned. 'You look quite pale—are you feeling ill?'

Charles put an arm round her waist. 'You do look peaky, dear, not like you . . . Here, stand in the shade for a minute.' She did so, knowing the decision had been made. Charles fetched her a parasol from the buggy.

'Is she—er—perhaps in a certain condition?' Harriet whispered to him.

He paused. 'Well I'm not aware—but this could be an early sign, yes.'

Rather to her surprise, Alice did not have to make any further explanations. Charles tucked her into the buggy and they drove quickly home, not seeming to mind her silence. That evening, pronouncing herself recovered, she joined the party on the verandah before supper. She found it impossible to keep her eyes off Florence, summoning back to her reluctant consciousness the face of the dying man in the Inn of the Five Tiger Pass, the girl in the sepia photograph. Poor little Flossie—Stewart had died feeling guilty about her; Alice should have told her that.

'You were talking about your brother this afternoon, Florence?' She sipped a sherry. 'Did you ever hear any more details?'

'Oh, the whole expedition died one way or another—Stewart last of all. Such a waste of young men, and I was miserable for ages afterwards. But Stewart was like that—reckless, never caring much about others.'

'I'm sure he cared for you really, Florence. Brothers do, in their fashion. And at least all is well with you now?'

381

She pouted. 'I suppose so—but Ian's so often away and thinks of nothing but railways.'

'Not when he's with his charming wife, I'm sure,' Charles said gallantly.

'Even then quite a lot—though I do what I can to distract him!'

'Lucky fellow,' he murmured and Alice, overhearing, thought it would serve her right if her husband fell madly in love with 'poor Flossie.'

'Florence was telling me earlier that her brother died on an expedition, Charles, did you know?' She tortured herself relentlessly.

'Yes, Ian told me I remember—they went to Ladakh, didn't they? Rum part of the world. I met a chap who'd been to Leh once—absolutely priest-ridden he said, thousands of those filthy lamas wandering about the place carrying prayer-wheels and muttering something that sounded like "Oh mother pat me tum." '

Florence giggled. 'But what were they really saying?'

' "Om mani padme hum," I suppose, it's the universal Buddhist prayer meaning "Oh Jewel in the Lotus O," ' Alice explained.

'How clever of you, Alice—but I like the English version best.'

'And so do I—let's see what Cook has for our tums tonight.' Charles steered her towards the table, giving Alice the chance for another sherry to steady her nerves.

After preliminary discussion of the continuing difficulties with the troublesome Dacoits in Burma, the dinner conversation again turned to India, for the visitors had scant interest in China. And Harriet was determined to remind her brother of all he was missing by living there.

'You should have joined us in Simla last summer, Charles—a splendid season, wasn't it, George? The Dufferins have improved the general tone immensely, so much more fun than that earnest Lord Ripon who was always grumbling about the "frivolities of hill-station life." But dear "Lady D."—Marchioness of Dufferin and Ava you know—is quite charming, with three delightful daughters. And Lord Beresford is still Military Secretary, such a witty man—organising everyone for picnics, hunting trips, fancy-dress parties—a mad whirl, wasn't it, George? You'd have loved it, Charles—and Alice too, I'm sure.'

'The hill monkeys used to swing on my bedroom verandah in the early mornings, Father,' Peter added, 'and tap on the window. And I had a pony and went up Jakko and sometimes wished you were there.'

Charles laughed off the little silence with, 'Well when I've made my fortune here, we'll come and spend a summer in Simla with you, Harriet, promise. You'd like that wouldn't you, Alice? Alice, did you hear. . . ?'

'Yes dear, sorry, it would be lovely. . . . Have some more chocolate pudding, Florence?'

'Oh no, Alice, thank you, I'm sure you're determined to make me quite fat.' She preened her slim shape.

'Oh you need have no fear in that direction, I'm sure nothing could spoil your lovely figure,' Alice said sweetly, and Florence was a little puzzled by such compliments from one who, being female and of a similar age, she could only regard as a rival for any man's attentions. Alice was very lucky to have such a handsome, pleasant husband, but she seemed to take him very much for granted. It would do her good, Florence thought spitefully, if Charles were to be a tiny bit distracted from his habitual marital bliss. He was undoubtedly susceptible to feminine charms; indeed most gentlemen were, she had discovered. She tossed her fair curls in the lamplight and saw that Charles noticed, though he was again discussing the dreary subject of Indian politics with George.

Alice, pleading a headache, soon slipped unobtrusively away. Alone in her room, she paced about, holding a clenched fist to her mouth. She went to the window; a moonless night, low mist over the swamp, distant mutter of water, boats at anchor; just as usual, yet all changed. In fact, she comforted herself, she was no more nor less deserving of punishment today than yesterday. But yesterday she had not known her victim. How could she have borne the knowledge of her crime so lightly for so long? Truly it had bothered her conscience but little and since her marriage she had scarcely thought of it. Oh, she was even more wicked than she had realised before—was she really the unredeemed creature that Stepfather thought her? Would it have been better or worse if she had liked Florence? But she could not like her, even though she had wronged her. She was vain, shallow and capable, Alice suspected, of considerable hysterical vindictiveness if the truth came out. If only she had never come here . . . but that was Fate. She shivered.

Was the guilty remorse she now suffered sufficient punishment, or did worse things coil in wait?

She unearthed her reticule from the wardrobe, took out the three remaining pieces of loot: a perfume bottle, the amber ring, the musical box. Carr's ravaged face and pleading eyes came to the very forefront of her vision. She had heartlessly betrayed the last wish of a dying man, and a surge of self-disgust overcame all other emotions. She picked up a pamphlet recently delivered by the China Religious Tract Society and read: 'Sin is Satan's work; forgiveness is God's great prerogative and most glorious act. But our God is a jealous God, jealous of the honours of mercy as well as of His Holiness. Let us fear to sin against so holy a God, but let us also fear His Wrath, lest we provoke Him by doubting His infinite Mercy.'

Heavy words she had heard so often in the past: fear, jealousy, wrath. She was surely doomed. The paper slipped from her fingers and in its place came an ordinary Chinese proverb: 'Only watch how the flowers bloom, how the flowers fade. Say not this man is right, that man is wrong.' At that, and with a surge of her usual resilience, she made ready for bed, having decided to ameliorate her crimes by contriving to give something to Florence without letting her suspect the truth.

'Harriet, Florence—such a strange thing in the market this morning . . .' Alice joined the two ladies who were putting new trims on their ball-gowns in readiness for the first of several farewell functions being held by the Telfords, who were about to leave China for good.

Tea prices were even more depressed this season, which had led to a spate of suicides among the Chinese merchants, bankruptcies among the foreign, and Tommy decided it was time to leave the field open for younger men. Amelia had become quite cheerful thinking of promenades by the sea at Eastbourne, where they planned to settle, knowing that never again would she have to watch the filthy river-tides rising so rudely over the croquet lawn.

Harriet raised a politely inquiring face as Alice tripped up, holding out three rings of amber and gold.

'Look at these—from my pet jeweller in Plum Street. He bought them from a pedlar who said one of them's worth a great deal more than the other two, but no one seems to know which. They're quite similar, aren't they? So Harriet, here's one for you, and yours, Florence, and I'm keeping the third. We'll see which one is really good.'

Florence slipped hers on, regarding it disdainfully. 'Oh I'm sure it won't be mine!'

'Well, promise to get it valued anyway—it's a gamble and I wanted to share it with you.'

Harriet laughed. 'But what if mine turns out to be valuable? I'd feel quite guilty, Alice.'

'Oh no, you mustn't—it would be just luck and you should keep it.'

Florence told Charles about the little transaction that evening and, in bed later, he tartly inquired of his wife why she felt they had money to throw about on amber rings. 'I wanted to give Harriet something nice without making it obvious, she's been so good to Peter—I think she's got the valuable one,' Alice explained, thinking how tangled webs of deception became. Oh if only their visitors would leave so she could gradually resume that state of relative contentment which had been customary before their arrival.

The halfway point of their stay was marked by the Telfords' party, held after the last race-meeting. It would be quite dismal, people kept saying, not to see Tommy and Amelia in the grandstand anymore. For Tommy was such a lucky card and generous too, and Amelia was—irreplaceable. Nevertheless, by Calcutta standards their parties were quite provincial, Florence privately decided, rather like functions in the Indian *mofussil*. Feeling unaccountably chilled, she drew her Kashmiri shawl closer, looking round the Telfords' crowded drawing-room. Not a single army officer to flirt with; even the remotest Indian outpost could furnish that. Hiding a shiver, she went to join Charles and Alice, guessing that their conversation, with Customs man Wilcock and his wife, would be quite uninteresting.

'Ah Florence, there you are . . .' Charles drew her into the group. 'We were grumbling about our local missionary enthusiasts again.'

'Government keeps 'em well under control in India I believe, Mrs. Plowden?' boomed Wilcock. 'And quite right too. A letter in the *China Herald* recently suggested the whole missionary system is simply a charitable scheme for keeping lowly qualified professional persons from Europe and America in overseas employment—strong words, but I sometimes feel inclined to agree.'

Alice murmured, 'But many of them are very sincere, Mr. Wilcock, and feel a genuine call. They're not just looking for work, I'm sure.'

'Maybe not. But the Call can be remarkably intermittent I may say, considering the time some of them spend resting and recuperating in pleasant seaside resorts.'

'But that again depends on the individual—my mother, for instance, has just gone Home with my elder brother and family, and it's her first proper leave for twelve years.'

'Ah yes, Mrs. Grant, I'd forgotten you come of missionary stock, or I wouldn't have spoken so freely.'

At this the group uncomfortably dispersed, leaving Alice to reflect that one of many disadvantages of her missionary connection was having to justify her way of life in their company, yet feeling obliged to defend them in their absence. By now Charles and Florence were talking animatedly and, resolving not to interrupt, she wandered over to the piano where Amelia was playing operatic airs, her guests standing around humming nostalgically and exchanging reminiscences of operatic performances in London and Vienna. Having no ear for European music, Alice went to the window, tracing, in her mind's eye, the course of the moonlit Yangtze southward through the lakes and into Hunan. One could go from this very quay to Changsha by water. How old was Lung-kuang now? The chrysanthemums would be blooming in the courtyards, the owls hooting in the park beyond—how many nights she had heard them—and in the kitchen quarters the servants might be singing their weary, after-dark songs.

Charles found her there, leaning against a curtain, a slightly forlorn figure in a slightly faded dress of delphinium blue. She did not look happy, he thought, but it was no time to wonder why. 'Alice—I fear we must leave at once. Poor Florence isn't feeling well, touch of Chinese liver perhaps.'

Relieved to be off, Alice collected her cloak and they all went home, where Florence was put to bed and dosed with quantities of curative camomile tea. But in the morning her condition was noticeably worse. The Russian doctor came, prescribed quinine pills for fever. By the following day Florence was delirious and the doctor, suddenly concerned, prescribed his special fever mix of barley water with eight grains of sal-ammoniac and three of aconite every four hours. By the fourth day the fever was at its height and the doctor shook his head, pronouncing it definitely malarial, of the type quite common at this season when the swamp was at its pestilential worst. Mrs. Markov, the merchant's wife, had died of it in this very house, he reminded Charles gloomily.

Alice had long since remembered both that and the snake on the stairs as she sat for hours by Florence's bed, dabbing her brow with lavender water and watching her body feebly tossing, her eyes wandering frightened and stricken as her dead brother's once had. In anguished panic the scenes of the inn rolled repeatedly before Alice's inward eye, her leaving him during his last night on earth, the anguished cries she had pretended not to hear. Oh, she had been young and raw at the time—but that was not really sufficient excuse.

'Do take some rest now, dear,' Harriet crept into the dim, sick-smelling room. 'Snow Duck has some hot supper for you. I'll sit with her.'

'No, I'd rather stay, I'm not in the least hungry.'

Harriet sighed and sat down opposite, lips pursed with worry. It was all so very sad and provoking—their homeward passages were booked from Shanghai in less than a week. Harriet had never thought much of silly little Florence—perhaps if she died tonight, they could just, decently, make the boat? But if she did not? She shook herself from this outrageous wish and dabbed the patient's head guiltily. 'You mustn't get too upset, Alice—you should look after yourself, particularly at a time like this you know . . .' It was half a question, but Alice ignored it. 'After all, George and I realise things aren't easy for you here. It's proving a struggle to make ends meet, isn't it? We always guessed that, but Charles would try. His judgment isn't always—well, he's easily led, or misled, as I'm sure you've discovered. Not that he isn't a most delightful man.'

'Yes, I suppose . . . his judgment, yes. . . .' Alice trailed off, her spirits, already low, sank further for this was not what she wanted to hear just now about her husband who was supposed to protect and guide her—leading her into adventure and perhaps fortune. She knew there was some truth in it, but continued defiantly, 'Oh we manage—the business is growing gradually.'

'I'm sure, dear, and you've a good head for it, I can tell. You'll help Charles in the right direction. Maria used to—in her quiet fashion she usually had the last word. So I just want to remind you, dear, if this venture does prove impossible, there's always a welcome for you in India.'

'Thank you, Harriet,' Alice tried to sound grateful, but her heart sank at the idea of such a fate: she a minor memsahib in Madras; Charles in some dull office. A sense of being trapped yet again overcame her as there came a gasp from the bed.

'Where's Ian?' Florence muttered feverishly. 'Why isn't he with me? He's never here when . . . oh dear, is that you, Harriet? Where's Ian?' Tears oozed from her glassy eyes, and Harriet wiped them away.

'There, there, dear, Ian'll be with you soon, don't worry, we're looking after you.'

Florence's eyes focused on Alice. 'Who's she? Oh yes, Alice—but where's Stewart? He's never here either . . .' She sank back on the pillow and Alice shivered uncontrollably.

'Alice, you're looking quite ill—I insist you go and eat some supper at once.'

Alice stood up, clutching the bed quilt in distress, 'Harriet, I . . . I . . .'

'What is it, dear?' Harriet's face showed the smooth, absent concern of a worthy headmistress.

'Nothing—yes, I must be hungry.' Downstairs Alice fell into exhausted sleep by the fire and was thus spared the last few hours of crisis when the doctor, summoned in the early hours, announced that the worst of the fever was past and that, if given careful nursing, Florence would eventually recover. The verdict, though most welcome of course, put Harriet and George in a great dilemma, only resolved by Alice's insistence that they stick to their travelling plans, for she would be quite delighted to undertake the task of restoring Florence to full health.

'It's extremely good of you, Alice,' Harriet's dry hand clasped hers as they stood on the quay the next day. 'I feel quite dreadful leaving you with such a burden—for I fear Florence won't be an easy patient.'

'Well, just as soon as she's fit enough to travel you must arrange for her to return to India, Charles,' George added. 'Any expenses we'll meet of course. I've written telling Ian what's happened and I'm sure he'll drag himself away from his engines for a while in the circumstances . . . We can go aboard now, Harriet . . . Now, now, Peter, be a little man . . .'

Peter, his head buried in his father's chest, did not feel in the least manly just then and the mouth he raised for a farewell kiss quivered. 'I'm not lucky you know, Father,' he said thickly. 'It might be ages and ages before I see you again.'

'Oh nonsense, son, we're coming to England next year, aren't we, Alice? And we'll take you on a European tour—promise.' Charles pushed him up the gangplank. 'Mind you get on well at school now.'

Harriet put a protective arm on his shoulder and they mounted together. Yet another parting; another increasing distance as the ship, whistle blowing, pulled into the main current. Alice, hating to see Peter's receding figure, squeezed Charles' hand. 'We must manage to go Home next year, it would be such a treat for Peter—and me.'

'Oh we will. Things are looking up and now Tommy's going there'll be more room for the rest of us. He's a bit of a monopolist, you know.'

She glanced at him. 'I'm glad you realise it. But you owe him money, don't you—and now he's leaving. . . ?'

'Don't worry your little head about it. I'll sort that out, you just concentrate on getting Florence better as soon as possible.'

And, in a spirit of dogged penitence, Alice did. She was not a nurse by temperament and, as Harriet suspected, Florence was not an easy patient. In due course, she managed to totter to the drawing-room and her rosebud mouth resumed its habitual pout, made more woebegotten by her present misfortune. Alice, having sold the last perfume bottle in the cause, stuffed her with beef tea, arrowroot and calves' foot jelly ordered specially from Shanghai, kept every fire in the house roaring for her comfort, listened with all the tolerance she could muster to Florence's tales of the various gentlemen admirers whose hearts she had once captured.

'But weren't you tempted to accept his offer?' Alice asked one afternoon, after the story of some particularly dashing and ardent suitor.

'Oh yes, and he was such fun—but absolutely penniless, dear. And I'd been too long scrimping and saving every anna in my mean old aunt's house. I was so tired of genteel poverty as they call it—no, I wasn't going to marry a man like that. Whereas Ian has good prospects, and a good family background as you see. Quite honestly,' she leaned forward confidentially, 'I sometimes wonder if I'd have married him if I'd had money of my own—but what else could I do? Only Ian's always so wrapped up in his railways—he even snores like a steam-engine!' She laughed bitterly. And Alice sighed, for there seemed no end to the twists in the screw of her guilt. 'Keep mum about that, won't you?' Florence continued. 'Ian's not so bad as husbands go, only not as handsome and amusing as your Charles. . . .'

It was lightly said, but Florence's attraction to Charles was quite apparent. When he returned home in the evenings her face immediately brightened; she shook off her hunched dejection, lifting soft, wistful, blue eyes to his.

'Oh Charles, there you are. What dreary weather, isn't it? And I fear I've been dreary too, haven't I, Alice? Now you must play the gallant gentleman and cheer us both up!'

Usually at this juncture Alice went to help with the tea, while Charles warmed himself by the fire, telling Florence the small annoyances of his day while she clucked in sympathy. As he did so he felt the closeness of her frail and feminine dishevelment, while she was equally aware of the masculine pulse of his body standing over her. Sometimes she leaned forward carelessly so that her flimsy robes of convalescence loosened to reveal the swell of her breasts, sometimes he would shift his leg casually against hers, keeping it there, hard-limbed against her softness. And Alice, returning with the tea, noted their quick readjustments of posture, and tightened her jaw in pained resolution. Oh, it served her right. Let them flirt if they wished; they deserved the pleasure, she the pain. Florence had suffered unknowingly at her hands; let her suffer knowingly at Florence's.

And this thought was uppermost in her mind on the day that Charles, coming to take her tea-tray, said, 'Florence has been telling me of Ian's letter—excellent news, isn't it? He'll be back in Calcutta to meet her well before Christmas.'

Florence tossed her curls. 'And you'll be rid of me at last, Charles! For Alice thinks I should leave in two weeks.'

'Rid of you? Why that's not what I meant at all, Florence. Indeed I was just thinking—before you go—I've to make a short business trip to Ichang. So why don't we all go? At least you'd see a bit more of the country beyond this dreary hole and the upriver gorges are magnificent. Then you could just trans-ship straight down to Shanghai. What do you think, Alice?'

'Why it's a splendid idea, and the fresh air would buck you up no end, Florence.'

Florence was already looking excited at the prospect when Charles' next words added another spark: 'Of course it's a bit risky leaving the new compradore here to deal with everything alone but . . .'

'Oh but there's no real need for me to go too, Charles. I've been before. No, I'll stay and mind the shop—but it would do you the world of good, Florence,' Alice added persuasively. Not that Florence needed much persuasion at the thought of days alone with Charles. 'But I'm not sure it's quite proper. . . ?' she looked coquettish. 'I mean people might imagine . . .'

'What people? No one here to know, and the Smalls at Ichang aren't that small-minded are they, Charles?'

'Heavens no, and we'll be either on the steamer or staying with them . . . Well Alice, if you really think. . . ?'

'Yes, you two go.' She was firm. 'And when you change ships here on the way down I'll bring the rest of your luggage to the quay and see the roses in your cheeks again, Florence.'

'Alice, you're an angel, really!' Florence smiled in genuine gratitude and Alice, bending over the teapot, thought that the vengeful gods must now be satisfied. What if Florence and her husband did flirt and kiss a little in the secrecy of their cabins? No harm would come of it, and she would never seek to know, for her only consuming desire was to see the last of those fair tossing curls at the earliest possible moment.

The weather was unusually clement for November when Alice waved goodbye to Charles and Florence sailing away upriver. Light-heartedly she watched them out of sight, then went for a long walk—along the Bund, into the native city, out towards the Pagoda Hill; but on the way her buoyancy evaporated. She had optimistically assumed that once Florence's burdensome presence was removed, all would be as before. Instead she was filled with disquiet, still fretted by the unconsidered, long-term results of her youthful dishonesty, still beset with superstitious fear at the odd coincidence that had brought it so closely home to her. And somehow the visitors had seemed to diminish Charles as well as herself. She remembered what Harriet had said of him, how often he had seemed unsure of himself—rather weak and vacillating, though she was reluctant to frame the words.

Like most men, Alice decided drearily, Charles simply wanted money and social standing. If he got them they would simply move to a larger house, perhaps in Shanghai, eventually even to Eastbourne in the footsteps of the Telfords. Their house, she noticed as she came back, was firmly shuttered, its croquet law quite gone to pot—how Florence had turned up her pert nose at it, explaining that croquet was dreadfully old-fashioned these days when everyone was playing lawn-tennis.

Alice turned in her own gate, reminding herself the house was now free of that presence, so why did the future still seem lack-lustre? Before leaving, Charles told her that Harriet had thought her pregnant, and was obviously disappointed to learn she was not. It seemed another failure for them both. And that led to a sudden undiminished ache for Lin. How he would scorn the conventionality of her present life after so much fine talk about the regeneration of all China! Were he to see her now, standing in this empty drawing-room, he would consider himself well rid of her. But what was he doing? Certainly the self-strengtheners had not produced a new dawn. The Manchus were still securely in control, the barbarians ever more aggressive. Perhaps Lin too found himself relegated to some confining backwater? That thought depressed her more than any, for she drew inspiration from his glowing, if distanced, enthusiasm and could not bear to doubt it.

As darkness fell the house closed round her with its custom-ary sad chill, the death snake not banished from the stair. It was long since she had been there alone, and, after a solitary supper, the resolution that had kept the one tempting thought at bay snapped. Donning her blue robe and padded winter jacket she bade Snow Duck call a chair. Soon after, she received from Flowing Spring's hand the first flaring pipe of oblivion, drawing its smoke deeply into her. The price of pure Benares opium was going up, Flowing Spring told her the next morning when she paid her surprisingly large bill. Merchants were blaming it on the depression in tea, but were probably just making more profit for themselves.

'That's what your husband should go into if he wants to make money,' she smiled innocently. 'There'd be ways of selling to us direct, without middle-men.'

At the time Alice rejected the suggestion out of hand, but it returned to her later when she sat in the office studying the firm's accounts that Charles usually kept locked away. Plainly the business was in a worse state than he had admitted, partly because of a large loan recently repaid to Tommy Telford. Alice felt angry as the ledgers revealed many misjudgments he had not told her about, and she knew it was because he would not trust the trading instincts of a mere woman. But the fact was—hers were keener than his. Damn him, she thought, when he returns I shall tackle him about this.

Restlessly she prowled about the godown, sniffing its multifarious odours, touching its strange substances, trying to recapture the glamour it had once held for her. But now it seemed no more than a messy shed full of absurd things. She had often been told that the Chinese devoted more energy to the pursuit of wealth than any other people, but was it not also true of foreigners here, whose main aims were either to save money or souls? Well, she could not share either of these passions. Back in the office, she slammed the drawer savagely shut on the ledgers. No, let Charles get himself out of this mess, he had already spurned her help. Instead, when he returned, she would at last throw herself wholeheartedly into the work of Daisy's league.

Having made that decision, time hung heavily on her hands and two days before Charles was due back she gave herself one last escape to the Golden Phoenix. It was particularly busy that evening and Flowing Spring was so in demand that Alice received her pipes from lesser hands. The state of disembodied calm was as always, but in the middle of the night she woke and vomited violently. There was a rustle of skirts and the blind woman was at her side.

'Oh dear, Uncut Jade—the girl must have given you inferior mud, not knowing you are a valued customer. I'm so sorry. It won't happen again, I promise . . . I'll get you a chair, you must go home and sleep for hours—it's dirty stuff you've been given.' Solicitously she helped the groaning Alice outside. The freezing night air bit through her clothes like a ravening dog and the bearer's lantern exploded inside her skull like a firecracker. Dumped at her front door, she took what seemed hours actually to get herself inside as the handle slipped from her grasp. Upstairs she stared in the mirror at her dishevelled hair, bloodshot eyes, her mouth sour as a clogged drain, and then huddled miserably into bed, vowing that, from that moment on, the poppy would wait for her in vain.

The torpor into which she pitched seemed endless, but it was only a few hours before she was roused by an urgent thudding. Pale light seeped through the curtains and the sound that she imagined to be inside her head was a pounding on the front door. She lay fearful, calling for Snow Duck, but he slept behind the kitchen and would not hear. Who could it be at such an early hour? Groaning, she tottered downstairs and opened the door, blinking up into a familiar face.

'Daisy—why what time is it?' Mrs. Small looked distressed, Alice thought vaguely, and a wave of guilt swamped her. 'I'll do something about the League—really, I've just decided to.'

'Tush, my dear Alice, it's not that . . .' Daisy came hesitantly indoors. 'You don't look well, dear, is anything—already—wrong?'

'No, no, a touch of fever I think . . . I'm still half asleep. But is it really you? I'm not dreaming, am I?'

'No dear . . . no it's really me, but . . .' Daisy's voice trailed away as she unpinned her hat, turned to face her, then her courage temporarily failed. 'Before I explain why I've come, could I beg a cup of tea, dear? I've been sitting on the deck of a salt junk all night and I'm frozen stiff.'

In the kitchen Alice struggled as if from a remote distance to light the stove, put the kettle on. Only then did she realise the oddity of Daisy's appearance, and called out, 'But haven't you seen Charles and Florence? They went up to Ichang last week.'

There was no reply and in sudden apprehension she ran along the passage.

'Daisy—Daisy . . . Charles and Florence? Haven't you seen them? Has anything happened?'

Daisy met her at the door, caught her in her arms and half-carried her to the sofa. 'There, there, dear . . . sit down. Oh my poor Alice, I've the most dreadful news—you must prepare yourself : . .' She paused, staring pityingly at Alice's fearful face. 'They . . . they're . . . they were both drowned, in the rapids above Ichang. They would go—just a little excursion really, but dangerous at this time of year when the waters are low—all the rocks and shoals and . . .'

Alice began to scream, she put her hands over her ears so as not to hear herself so plainly, and screamed and screamed. Her mind, first opium-dulled, now enflamed with anguish and disbelief, seemed to be splitting, parting at its very seams. Daisy dabbed at her eyes, tried to rock her like a baby. Alice wished she was a baby.

Snow Duck rushed in, twisting his pigtail round his head, and Daisy told him her news. Hearing the words said again and in Chinese, seeing his fat face collapse into woe, Alice howled the more as the actuality of it penetrated even more. The kettle boiled over and Snow Duck made tea which Daisy sipped gratefully, until Alice groaned and vomited on the carpet. Daisy, distressed, sent Snow Duck for the doctor and Alice, her throat stripped raw with the cheap opium, the vomiting and the screaming, could eventually only gasp piteously, hating to face the silence that would fall if she quietened. 'But tell me everything . . .' She clutched Daisy's hand. 'How did it happen? How could it have—just like that? In the rapids you say?'

'It must have been quite quickly over . . . for them both. They stayed with us, of course, but Florence so wanted to venture upriver a little. It would be exciting, she said, her last chance to see more of the country. Archie warned them of the dangers but—oh my dear, I'm so very very sorry, such a stupid, stupid accident . . . Anyway, to humour her really, Charles agreed.'

'So he wouldn't have gone if she hadn't been there?'

'Well . . . no, but you can't really blame . . . he was just being kindhearted and she wanted a little adventure . . .'

Alice began to scream again, rending the membranes of her throat.

'Hush, dear, calm yourself a little, please . . . They went in one of old Chin-ling's boats, just for two days, intending to return in time for the downriver steamer. But then they didn't turn up,' Daisy dabbed her own eyes. 'And we were just getting anxious when Chin-ling and his captain arrived with the terrible news.'

'Not everyone was drowned then?'

'No, the tow-ropes broke at the Sorceress Gorge and the boat went out of control, bashing downstream against the rocks. The decks were awash and the captain advised them to jump for the shore, which was quite close. Florence jumped—but not far enough and she was not strong enough to fight the current and got carried away instantly. Charles and one of the crew went to her rescue and all three were drowned in those fearsome whirlpools below the rapids.'

'And the rest of the crew?'

'Struggled ashore—and the boat sank.'

'So if Florence hadn't been there . . .' Alice shrieked at her again and Daisy began again.

'But you can't really blame . . .'

'No I can't blame Florence . . . not Charles—it's me, me to blame . . .' She thrust her face into Daisy's, whimpering, 'Me,

I'm the criminal, the murderer, I killed my husband, I killed them both.'

'You—Alice, my dear, that's madness, madness. Why, you had nothing whatever to do with it.'

'I did, I did . . .' Alice rushed out into the hall pointing up the stairs. 'There—see, the death snake, it's been there all the time waiting, waiting for me, knowing I had to make it all happen . . . aagh!' She spun round in a shivering arc of terror, and fell, scrabbling the tiles with her hands.

Daisy rushed to her. 'Alice . . . my dear dear girl, there's nothing there—no snake, no nothing . . . please calm yourself.'

As she tried to lift her, the door opened and Snow Duck rushed in with the doctor. They carried her up to bed thrashing wildly and the doctor mixed a sedative.

'Now, Mrs. Grant . . . take this . . . hush now . . .'

Daisy held her head while she swallowed, the room spun again and Alice fell back listening to the concerned voices receding. But she must not let things recede yet, and she held doggedly on to her distress till Daisy crept back into the room.

'Daisy, you must listen—I'm not mad to think it was this way—I must tell you everything please, or I shall never rest . . . come here . . .' Her fingers closed over Daisy's wrist and she pulled her down by the bed.

Telling of her long-ago encounter with Stewart Carr for the first time was a great relief even in her agony and in spite of its eventual consequences.

'And now,' Alice concluded, 'how can I ever face life with this burden? For if I hadn't felt so ashamed, so guilt-ridden about Florence, I'd never have let them go off together like that. They were having a mild flirtation, weren't they? It doesn't matter now, but I knew she'd enjoy the trip better without me, and I was so tortured about her . . . Oh Daisy, Daisy, I've killed my husband and ruined my life—oh I wish I were dead too!'

'My poor, poor dear, you mustn't talk like that for an instant.' Daisy, shaken but in control, smoothed her hair. 'Now you must listen quietly to me. You're making far too many assumptions, jumping to conclusions—can you not see, even in your present distressed state, that causes and effects are more complex than this? My dear, how can I put it simply—our whole lives are made up of a series of "ifs" and "buts" and "if onlys," and it is simply not given to us to make sense of them or of our place in the universe. Certainly you behaved dishonestly by telling no one of the Carr loot—remember though it *was* loot, his theft before yours—and I can see that this coming of Florence into your life years after would seem a fateful coincidence. But there are many other imponderables—of accident, timing, people's feelings, sheer bad luck, over which you'd no control. Clearly you never wished Florence any harm and you must never, ever blame yourself for this tragedy.'

'But they were having a little flirtation, weren't they, and if . . .'

Daisy pursed her lips. 'There you go—if. Well, if the rapids hadn't been specially treacherous all would have been well. You can't persuade me that the state of the rapids at the Sorceress Gorge the other day was directly connected to an incident that occurred at the Inn of the Five Tiger Pass twelve year ago!'

'No—but perhaps to bring home to me . . .'

'Come, Alice, you're getting above yourself. Nature may sometimes be relentless and cruel, but not personally vindictive—your theory would suggest an arm of justice longer and more avenging than even the devoutest missionary would wish!' She smiled gently. 'When you were young and were in fairly desperate straits you kept what didn't belong to you. That is really the beginning and end of the matter.'

'But if I'd confessed as soon as I discovered who Florence was . . .'

Daisy sighed. 'Here we are again, faced with the tantalising "would have beens" of our lives! You won't puzzle them out today, Alice, I've been trying for years and expect to carry on doing so . . .' She had lowered her voice, for the sedative was at last taking effect and Alice sank into hours of feverish, troubled slumber.

For the next week Alice lay inert trying to absorb the shock of her bereavement and, in her stronger moments, writing sad letters to relatives containing the news. Daisy, understanding, treated her like an invalid, offering tempting morsels and sympathy, reading the sonorously comforting lines of Wordsworth to her on grey afternoons. The care of her fell wholly to Daisy, for Eliza and William were in England, while Robert, recently out of the Army, was on a tour of the Middle East with Mary.

Frank hurried to Hankow when he heard the news and begged Alice to return to Shanghai with him, but the thought of Treaty-Port life depressed her unutterably and she chose instead to return to Ichang with the Smalls. And this, to Daisy, seemed part of an inevitable pattern, for had she not first seen this gifted young woman as her heiress apparent? Was it not now up to Daisy to mould one so unexpectedly and tragically bereft towards a newly fruitful, thoughtful future?

Archie Small arrived to help with the process of clearing up. All the assets of Grant & Greenwood were sold to pay outstanding debts and Alice, practically penniless, kept only the firm's seals in Mandarin and English. That Christmas at Ichang passed Alice by almost unnoticed. Cards from Home with scenes of coaching inns stood about on the Smalls' tables and on Christmas Day the few resident foreigners gathered for a service with the Belgian priests and nuns. Throughout it Alice sat numb, beset with memories of that jolly Shanghai Christmas five years before when Charles had been so winningly, appealingly alive.

How she had under-rated him, she castigated herself, when he had been so anxious to make her happy and comfortable! Why had she often been so critical of him? Achingly she wished for him back that she might make amends, but the ache was not only on her own behalf but on his—for the years of life he had counted on. Daisy, knowing there was no short-cut through bereavement, simply let her huddle for hours in their sitting-room, which she left only to walk up the hill, from which she could look down at the waters of the Great River that had drowned her husband. Sometimes as she stood there, the chant of the monks came from the nearby monastery and, attracted by the sound, she would walk to its entrance and stand in the shadows of the cypresses listening.

One afternoon, greatly daring, she opened the wooden door and quietly slipped inside. Shaven-headed priests in patched gowns were shuffling in procession round the interior of a dim hall, their cast-down eyes showing no awareness of her presence. The leaders were sounding drums, bells, gongs in a ding-dong rhythm, the air was heavy with incense burning on the altar at the far end, where a dusty-gilt Buddha sat, surrounded by tutelary gods.

'We pay homage to all the Buddhas of the present and all the Buddhas of the future . . . we pay homage to the Buddhas of the past. . . .' This repeated chorus Alice eventually deciphered, though the mumbled verses eluded her. After a timeless monotony of repeated sound had washed over her, each priest genuflected before the altar and disappeared through a door behind. Alice stayed on, chilly and disappointed. They must have seen her—would no one acknowledge her unspoken need? As she reluctantly prepared to leave a monk appeared through another door and bowed at her.

'The Reverend Abbot will see you now.'

'But I . . . I have no appointment.'

'It is not always necessary.'

She followed him into a cell-sized room where an elderly man robed in black sat reading in a high-backed chair. As she approached, he gestured to a cushion on the floor. She bowed and sat. 'Reverend Abbot, I must apologise for . . .'

'It is all right, you don't have to explain yourself. The foreign woman who lives in the old temple told me of you—she said you might come here one day.'

Alice smiled at the thought of Daisy's warm caring. 'Then you won't mind if I come again?'

'As you wish, but what could you be seeking here?'

'I hardly know—my spirit is so heavy. I suppose I'm wondering about the meaning of this place—of your faith, of the Zen?'

It was half a question and he sighed gently. 'Our Master tells us that to seek the truth of Zen is like looking for an ox when you are riding on the back of it. Has no one explained that to you?'

She shook her head dumbly and an unhurried silence fell. At length she said, 'Would you let me come and stay here for a while in your guest-room as travellers sometimes do?'

'But who are you? You are not a traveller?'

'Yes I am—I think I always have been and always will be.'

The answer pleased him, but he hesitated. 'You are a woman and this is a monastery. It would be irregular.'

'But I'm a barbarian woman and therefore the irregularity is not relevant.'

He chuckled. 'Or the two irregularities cancel each other out?'

'That's it—and make the way smooth.' She smiled back boldly. 'I've a little money to pay for my keep,' she added, knowing the poverty of monks.

'You may come for a while, only don't rush about seeking enlightenment in every corner. If you stop looking, stop talking, stop thinking, there is nothing you may not eventually understand.'

'I do not understand you, Reverend.' she murmured sadly.

He clicked his beads in sudden impatience. 'It is the message of a poem by Seng Ts'an. Read it, even if its meaning is beyond you. The guest-room will be ready for you tomorrow and for one hour each day an acolyte will try and teach you a little something. We're quite strict here and live sparsely. Won't that worry you? For I believe you barbarians thrive on the oily fats and fleshes of animals?' He wrinkled his nose.

'In my youth I lived long on rice-gruel and vegetables. Now food is tasteless to me.'

He nodded, satisfied, waving a dismissive hand.

She had spoken confidently to the Abbot, but when, overriding the Smalls' misgivings, she moved into the monastery she soon found her constitution quite unaccustomed to its frugal regime. The meagre diet sapped her low vitality and the chill cell gave her a feverish cold so that, instead of being lulled into meditative oblivion by the monks' prayers, she had to concentrate on the stifling of disruptive coughs.

And the meaning of the place eluded her, as the acolyte Fa-yen, who came to her every day warned her from the start. He was quite young with a long bony head and hooded eyes. Sitting cross-legged before her, usually concealing the contemptuous outrage he felt both for this intrusive female presence and his order to speak with it, he slammed between them a thick book entitled *Platform Sermons containing the Doctrine given out by Hui-neng, the Great Teacher Sixth Patriarch, at Tai-fan Ssu*. This was usually sufficient to reduce Alice to that silence in which he hoped to pass their obligatory hour, but occasionally she tried to question him:

'You believe in the Buddha, don't you?' she asked one afternoon. 'Will you not try to explain it—him—to me?'

His eyes flipped wide for a second. 'What is not the Buddha?'

'I don't understand you.'

'The Buddha is to be made within the self-nature and is not to be sought outside the Body.'

'But how do I . . . one, begin to see the self-nature?'

'It is by the discipline of Zen.'

'Which you are learning?'

He shook his head. 'If you wish to learn Zen, Zen is neither

400

in sitting cross-legged nor in lying down.'

'Then we are wasting time here, doing this?'

He bowed his head in silent assent and she asked him to leave. But the next day she tried again. 'Can't you explain a little more?'

'The simplest text I know,' he replied, 'is that of a lamp and its light. As there is a lamp, there is light; if no lamp, no light. When you have understood the Oneness of those two you will have taken the first small step towards emancipation.'

'Emancipation?' The word, with its connotation of social subjugations, surprised her. 'From what?'

'From thought into thoughtlessness, from form into formlessness—in essence, from the realm of opposites in which we customarily live.'

She considered this. 'But are these not merely emptiness, nonbeing?'

'No indeed. Emptiness is not merely negative, it is always within us, not grasping, it is the other half of suchness. Suchness and emptiness make a whole.'

He rose to leave and she caught at his robe. 'But this suchness—what does that word mean?'

For answer he banged his fist on the wall. 'The stone in the wall, the air in the sky, the crack in the ice, the pain in the heart—these things have the original nature of suchness. In the deep mystery of things as they are we are released from our relatedness to them.'

After he had gone, Alice would sit cross-legged, chilled, overwhelmed sometimes by the sense of having fallen down a rabbit-hole and eaten from that side of the mushroom that made her bigger than all the creatures around. The figures and scenes from her past scuttled through her mind in a series of distant miniatures. So large was she that the two ends of the rabbit-hole seemed almost united—a bright lamp and its light. But the euphoria of this mood was easily shattered and more often she sat looking at the wall, seeing nothing but wall, unable even faintly to discern the meaning of Fa-yen's words. For she possessed an inborn reluctance to contemplate turning herself inside out for the start of that strange journey between subjective and objective that had to do with the meaning of this place.

Nevertheless the monastery was, in some fashion, balm to her troubled spirit. As the weather warmed, she strolled through its groves, taking pleasure again in the dark green of cypresses, translucent pinks and whites of sunlit blossoms against a spring sky. Daisy visited her often, bringing fruit, buns, news of the outside whether she wished to eat and hear or not.

'Alice will come back to us soon,' she told Archie confidently. 'But I must admire her perseverance. She's not cut out for the contemplative life, but she'll have to understand this for herself.'

'Get her involved in the League,' he suggested. 'It will give her a practical purpose, something outside herself.'

But Daisy shook her head. 'In her présent state she's not interested in native women's feet.'

He shrugged, bowing as usual to her womanly intuition, and merely commenting that something was sure to turn up for Alice soon.

Alice, waiting half-consciously for some sign of resolution, lacked Archie's conviction. Her mind, extended or perhaps obfuscated by grief and her spartan monasticism, pláyed with unaccustomed metaphysical speculations. When the sparse doctrines of Zen proved impenetrable, she turned for help to her favourite Taoist poet, Chuang-tse. It was he who had once dreamed of being a butterfly, fluttering about on a summer's day and conscious only of his butterfly happiness. When he awoke he no longer knew if he was a man dreaming he was a butterfly or a butterfly dreaming he was a man.

'Between a man and a butterfly there is necessarily a distinction. The transition is called the transformation of material things,' the poet had written. Alice looked at her cell-wall for a while, then took from her bundle of possessions the only book she had brought with her. And there were Tweedledum and Tweedledee in the dark green wood and the Red King snoring in his red nightcap—dreaming of Alice. Tweedledee said, ' "And if he left off dreaming about you, where do you suppose you'd be?" he demanded of her, and "Where I am now of course," she replied. "Not you," Tweedledee retorted contemptuously. "You'd be nowhere, why you're only a sort of thing in his dream." '

Also contained in Alice's bundle was a small mirror into which, shunning all vanity, she had not looked since her arrival at the monastery. She looked now, startled to see how thin and wan she had become, understanding suddenly why

Daisy worried about her. And then her musings on the nature of reality led her to a rather frightening idea: that there was someone somewhere dreaming about her—staring pale-faced in a mirror, in a cell in a monastery on a peak at Ichang overlooking the River Yangtze in the spring of the year 1888. Just as Lewis Carroll dreamed Alice in Wonderland (or as the Red King did?) or as Chuang-tse dreamed he was a butterfly. But perhaps, her scalp prickled, there was someone else on the other side of the mirror into which she stared so fiercely, who was dreaming them all?

She got up and banged her fist against the wall as Fa-yen had done. Then she put the mirror and book away, knowing that, in some instinctive way, there had been a moment of mind-flower-opening as the Zen masters put it, but that it was time to leave the dark green wood, for she had gone in as far as she could.

And the next day Daisy brought a letter from Frank. William, the family and Eliza were en route for Shanghai, he wrote, and Robert and Mary soon due back also. 'Robert asks anxiously after you,' Frank wrote, 'saying that if you're not out of that monastery by the time he arrives, we'll get up another posse and come to drag you back to civilisation as you once did for me. . . . He means it, you know, so please come away, Sis, and save us the trouble!'

She frowned angrily at the vision of the three men marching into the monastery, grave and heavy with a sense of duty. She toyed with the idea of running away before they came, throwing herself entirely on the mercy of the country that had never yet let her down. Or perhaps she should become a Buddhist nun? And she giggled at the thought of their horrified faces as she met them in black robes with shaven head. But these were merely wild ideas she knew the period of retreat was clearly over. The following day she bade a grateful farewell to the abbot and left, knowing, as she closed the monastery door for the last time, that she had made no more ripple on its contemplative life than a fly alighting on the Yangtze below. But, like a fly, she carried away with her a draught that gave her strength to travel further.

When Mrs. Charles Grant, dressed in sombre grey, disembarked from the Yangtze steamer at Shanghai, she stored her few belongings in the Customs Shed for later collection and took a rickshaw to the Grand Hotel. Luncheon was being served, the dining-room was completely filled and she steeled herself against the cold eyes of the head waiter who did not approve of young women who walked and ate alone. It was, she told herself firmly, something to get used to.

'I'll wait for a table,' she told him, 'and please bring me a glass of white wine on the verandah.'

She sat, sipped wine, flipped idly through a copy of the *Shanghai Mercury*. The names caught her eye at once—on the passenger list of arrivals from England yesterday: Mrs. Edward Blake, Mr. and Mrs. W. Greenwood, Charlotte, Joel, Polly, and Thomas Greenwood. She gasped with pained pleasure at that last—so another Thomas Greenwood was born to tread the soil of the Celestial Empire as his grandfather had. She longed to hold the baby in her arms, to see if she could puzzle out any likeness to her father's looks. She glanced at the paper again, its date, 18 May, a reminder that her thirtieth birthday was nearly upon her, and she recalled the words of a Sung poet, 'At the age of thirty my renown is small as dust raised by the feet of galloping deer.' Never mind; she was not seeking renown.

Leaning back, basking in the sun, she decided to celebrate the arrival of the new Thomas Greenwood and her approaching birthday with more wine instead of lunch. As the drink warmed her, she suddenly recalled with the vividness of yesterday rather than twelve years ago, that spring day when she had first seen Shanghai. How she, Robert and Major Cartwright had drunk champagne in this very hotel, how afterwards, bubbly with it, she had rashly inquired of Robert why the Chinese did not throw every barbarian into the sea and get on with their own celestial business? She smiled, thinking there was much she did not know then that she now knew—and much else presumably, which she did not yet know but one day might, if she lived long enough. She thought dispassionately of Lin, wondered where he was, what he still had to teach her. For she realised that she badly wanted to live in spite of everything—to find that out and much else besides.

When she paid the bill she realised she had but a few taels left in all the world. An almost penniless widow, she thought, without home or children, owner only of a sable-lined jacket, some books, a few clothes, and a long-ago stolen musical box.

And yet, as she left the hotel, her feet were winged with the reckless buoyancy of those who travel the world lightly. Spring flowers glowed in the gardens and a merry crowd of American globetrotters just arrived in the mysterious Orient for the first time off the steamship *Mississippi* were bowling along in rickshaws, clutching their hats and calling gaily to each other. The sight made Alice feel mature and wise, but in a way that enhanced the serenity of her mood.

As she walked up the driveway of Frank's villa she heard his voice calling to a servant at the back of the house. In the stable courtyard she saw her brother bent earnestly over the raised hoof of a racing pony. Unobserved, she paused, feeling the years slide away from her even further until the grown man before her was a lad again, a groom with a grubby kerchief twisted round his head standing beside Han-li's horse in the courtyard of the Chu, and she a skivvy in faded blue cotton with a broom in her hand. The bottom and top of the rabbit-hole came together.

'Frank,' she said softly.

He looked up and rushed to her with his arms outstretched. 'Sis—it's you, at last. We've all been so worried about you. Oh my dear, how are you?' He crushed her to him in a great bear-hug.

'But surely you didn't worry, Frank? You knew I'd be all right, didn't you, *really*?'

He gave her a rare look of love, admiration, and understanding. 'Yes, Uncut Jade—I knew you'd be all right *really*.'

He linked arms with her, she smiled and they walked into the house.

Book Two
Polished Jade

Part One

1

Money was the raison d'être of Shanghai which, by the early 1890s, had become the unrivalled commercial centre of the Far East, the 'Charing Cross of the Pacific' through which flowed the currencies of the world's great trading nations. It was an energetic, flamboyant, cosmopolitan city divided into three foreign setttlements—British, American, French in order of size and splendour. Its broad, well-lit main roads were lined with banks, mercantile and marine offices. Private mansions, many of them in the grandiose Anglo-Oriental style of architecture, bore witness to the fact some of its residents had rapidly made and lavishly spent fortunes there. Others, moderately successful, accumulated comfortable nest-eggs while many more remained in the hope of so doing.

Among the last were the owners of businesses in the busy commercial quarter bordering Hongchew, the American settlement. Salt Alley was in that area, a narrow thoroughfare lined with small enterprises—printers, tobacco-cutters, marine chandlers, a wholesaler of 'Cabin, Ship and Assorted Biscuits' and dealers in 'upcountry purchases'—grass-cloth, feathers, dyes, vegetable tallow, goat-skins, straw braid, and pigs' bristles. In comparison to these humble commodities the legend on the brass-plate fixed to the freshly painted door of the corner building had a rather superior ring—Grant & Greenwood, Curio and Jewellery Specialists.

Alice's office was on the second floor, an unpretentious, business-like room furnished with a second-hand roll-top desk, two bamboo chairs and a charcoal stove that the boy lit on chilly mornings. On the shelf above it stood the music box that had once graced the Imperial Court and the original drawing of the company's brand or 'chop'—an oval piece of green jade. On a damp winter morning of 1890 the stove had been duly lit and Alice sat at her desk sipping tea and studying recent accounts. Her air of quiet, assured command was not assumed, but had not been easily achieved. Her determination to carry on the firm single-handedly had been generally considered a most unsuitable step for a youngish, attractive widow.

Indeed she'd soon discovered that the only way to proceed was to behave as if she were a man—a white man in a business suit with a perfect God-given right to run a firm, hire, and fire. So she had had made several sober-coloured tailored jackets with plain revers and matching skirts, with which she wore starched, pleated, high-necked blouse-fronts, her hair drawn back in a simple swirl. Mary said sorrowfully that she could have been mistaken for a prissy governess from somewhere quite dreadful like Accrington, but it was the right guise for the job in hand.

Her first job was to find a Chinese comprador, an invaluable class of men who acted as brokers, stewards, agents, treasurers, and buyers for the main foreign firms. Most European bosses relied on them so totally they could almost name their price. Prestigious, 'big-faced' men of this ilk were beyond Alice's means, but she was able to hire an intelligent clerk from a leading British firm. Dubbed 'Benjy' by his white superiors, he was a poor relation of a well-known comprador family and eager to gain experience, even at the cost of swallowing his pride to work for a foreign woman.

Following her hunch that the boom in staples such as tea and silk was declining because of Japanese competition, she and Benjy had made two excursions to the upper reaches of the Yangtze beyond Ichang and purchased wares brought into the westernmost provinces from Nepal and Tibet. These relatively exotic novelties were very popular with the increasing number of globe-trotters who called at Shanghai on the new Oriental Cruises offered by the major shipping lines. Usually, they had quite a lot of money, little time to spend it, and were greatly taken with the Nepalese and Tibetan chunks of turquoise and coral, or the subtle opalescent moonstones that Alice sold to local jewellers. In her private opinion, such stones suited the darker skins of the East much better than the pale freckled arms and necks of pampered Westerners, but what happened to her merchandise concerned her little.

For Alice was not especially enamoured of the items she

traded, nor did she want to devote her life to accumulating money and its consequent privileges and possessions. What she did want for herself, however, was a certain measure of independence and security, and this the firm was giving her. But, even in cosmopolitan Shanghai, respectable English-women were seldom 'in Trade,' and Alice would surely have been ostracised by the higher ranks of the foreign community had not Mary and Robert offered her a home at Fairlawns. There, she was naturally included in a social circle of people with impeccable, if not very exciting, credentials; so the ladies chose to ignore her business connections, while the gentlemen teased her about them with fine masculine condescension. After all, her firm was small, harmless, and created no threat or resentment among them. This was not the case with Frank. Every time he saw Alice's brass-plate on the outer door, as he did that wintry morning, he felt a secret stab of rancour, remembering his youthful dream of the firm Greenwood & Greenwood that was to have cornered the bulk of the Yangtze trade with its fleet of upriver steamers. The name of Greenwood did not appear on the letterhead of Wang & Co. and was never likely to, for his father-in-law's three sons ran the firm and paid him reasonably well to do not very much—because he was married to their sister.

'Morning Alice. Made your first million yet?' Frank strode past the offending name-plate into the office. 'You might use some of your vast profits to warm this place up a bit.' He blew on his hands.

'Oh it'll be better when Snow Duck arrives. He's a dab hand with stoves.'

'Snow Duck? The Hunanese boy you had in Hankow?'

'The same. He was so reliable, I've sent for him. He's got a wife and two little ones now. They'll live in the back somewhere,' she waved a hand. 'And he'll be Number One.'

'You always like a bit of the rough country tongue about you, don't you? Nostalgia, that's what it is. A decent gathering last night?' He drew a chair by the stove.

'So-so. The French musicians played beautifully, only I don't understand their modern music very well. Several French there, and one's handicapped not speaking even a word of their precious lingo. Most well-brought-up English ladies can at least manage a "parlez-vous".'

413

'And you're not a w. b. E. lady! Too bad. Meet anyone interesting then?'

Alice had been cornered by one Mr. Bellamy, Deputy Commissioner of Customs whose wife had died of cholera in Swatow several months before. He'd dwelt much on the hapless plight of his three motherless children, a habit which she'd discovered was common among widowers when in conversation with single women of anything like marriageable age.

'No,' she replied.

'Well there's someone interesting just passing through. Younger Brother—he's bound for Peking, came to see me off his boat last night. Thought you might like to join us for luncheon at the Hotel des Colonies today before he sails?'

'Han-li! How lovely! We haven't met for years, not since the Port Arthur days. He's still teaching?'

'Yes. Still full of mad ideas for a perfect world too.'

'And what's wrong with a little idealism? Better than the way you and I spend our time simply trying to make money.'

'Trying is right. The brothers Wang will make sure I never make a fat lot, even if they do. No, I've got to branch out on my own a bit, Sis. There are a hundred ways of getting an excellent return on investments these days, if you pick the right ones. And I'm pretty sure I'm on to a winner this time,' he gnawed his knuckles. 'Has Robert said anything to you about our proposed venture into railways?'

'No. I thought the government had decided against any rail development being undertaken by foreigners?'

'Well, things are improving and a foreign-owned Syndicate is being formed here. Robert and I are both buying bonds. It's an excellent proposition, Alice, and I wondered about your joining us?'

'Me? Well, I might be interested certainly.' She regarded her brother a little suspiciously, for, like many Shanghai citizens, he was in the habit of plunging into risky, hare-brained schemes that promised a quick fortune. 'There's a prospectus? Well, bring it along to the hotel today, will you please?'

The Hotel des Colonies was in the French concession next to the native city, where streets, as in Paris, were called rues and marked in blue and white tiles. It was a small, shabby establishment, but knowledgeable Shanghai residents patronised it because its Swiss chef produced the best French food on the China coast. Dusty potted plants crowded its corners, cut-glass decanters stood on tablecloths with wine stains starched into them; at this season a log fire blazed below the massive marble mantelpiece in the dining-room.

Han-li sat near it, the only Chinese present except for the table-boys, affecting an unconvincing air of disdain, as his compatriots usually did in such alien surroundings. He still looked absurdly young, Alice thought as she approached him, wearing her sober business suit—which, in turn, made her look mature and awesome to him in a very foreign way. So he answered her questions stiffly at first: yes, he was still teaching western sciences to naval students; and yes he had two children now and a third expected.

'And the family at Changsha, Younger Brother? The honourable Lung-kuang? Tamao, and Weng?'

He relaxed at the familiar names and her use of the Hunanese. 'Ah, the Honourable Father relinquished his official duties several moons ago. He lives quietly, reading much. He wrote me an instructive letter recently saying he feared he would not attain that tranquillity of mind his father enjoyed in retirement. "The chrysanthemums bloom in the same way every autumn, but too much else has changed," he wrote. That's true, isn't it, Uncut?'

She nodded. 'He is a most civilised man, your father.'

'Civilised in the old ways, yes. But Eldest Brother Han-fei is not of his heart and never will be. And I, his favourite son—yes, he confided that to me, which is a great benison—have duties that keep me from his side. It has to be so, as he said. "Intelligent men must not hide away in these provincial interiors any longer, living as frogs at the bottom of deep wells when the Celestial Empire is in such hopeless disarray." Those were his very words.'

'Do you remember, Han-li, I told you that too, years ago?'

They smiled at each other and he continued. 'Now even the girls are leaving home. Little Piece too has left. You remember her?'

'Of course—the tiny one whose feet were being tight bound so she sobbed and sobbed in the night. I have never forgotten the sound.'

'She was never tractable, and when it came time for her to marry she kept refusing eligible young men. Can you imagine such a thing? She would not obey her Honourable Father. Eventually he lost patience and simply arranged a marriage—quite reasonable, the man was wealthy. But one night just before the wedding Little Piece ran away—two years ago it must have been. Search parties were sent out, but she's never been seen since.'

'Oh poor, poor Little Piece.'

'Poor! It's a disgrace to our family, shameful that she, a daughter of good breeding, should behave so. The Honourable Father never mentions her name.'

Frank hurried up to them. 'I'm sorry—spot of trouble with a cargo-master. Isn't it grand to see Younger Brother, Alice? Here—let me whistle up the menu.'

While Frank launched into conversation with Han-li, Alice pondered the news: Lung-kuang retired, it seemed absurd, and made her feel quite old. How she'd love to meet him again on adult terms. But would he ever countenance it—with a female barbarian? The appearance of Han-li, ill-at-ease in his ill-fitting western-style suit in this alien dining-room, stirred her profoundly. The son of a proud, cultured family—how could he have guessed the world would change so much, so soon, and mostly to his disadvantage? Her reverie was pierced by a disdainful voice at the next table.

'Oh, they're dab hands at the native lingo, but I doubt they can muster a word of French between them.'

Alice stiffened angrily, realising that Frank was trying to translate the French menu to Han-li while the French waiter deliberately wasn't helping. She glanced balefully at the speaker whose face was half-concealed by a large, ostrich-feather hat. There was nothing one could say. Han-li handed her the menu. 'French-English, look alike to me.'

She glanced at it. 'Just order the set meal all round, Frank.'

The waiter sniffed as he took that down.

'This is a proper French restaurant, isn't it?' Han-li asked. 'Owned by Froggies in the Froggy concession, and here we are paying to eat their food. Yet only a few years ago their devil-ships blew our Celestial Navy out of the seas at Foochow. I was there and saw it happening—the destruction of all we'd just built up. The waste and shame of it. So why are they allowed here now? Making money from our land, our people? I can't understand it—we Chinese seem so helpless to prevent anything, or profit by developments, or take revenge.'

416

'But Han-li,' Alice protested. 'All civilised peoples frater-
nise with each other, and trade together, even after wars.
You can't put the clock back to the days when the Celestial
Empire was inviolate and other nations came only to pay
tribute.'

'Oh I know, that's not what we want anymore. . . . What's
this?' he poked suspiciously at the *hors d'oeuvre*. 'As you say,
there should be give and take between nations, but that's
another thing. For the past thirty years our poor people have
been emigrating to America to build railways, working like
slaves, hacking down forests, tunnelling through mountains
so that white men can travel faster between New York and
Sacramento. Many died—I've heard dreadful stories, none of
them made fortunes. Now the white men are coming over here
to build our railways, and still they make the profits. Our
people will still be the slaves. Why do we always give, always
lose, while others take? We have few engineers now, trained
in America, but no capital for these enterprises, and our
people don't understand them.' He pushed his plate away
untouched and scowled at them both.

Alice said, 'Younger Brother, you are right to be so critical
and angry. But please don't blame us personally for what's
going on between China and the West!'

'No, no . . . But I seldom meet foreigners I can talk to and
know as well as you. So when I see you, which isn't often
enough, it all comes bursting out like a furious fire.'

She smiled as the waiter brought the main dish. 'Well, try
some of this to cool you down. As to why foreign investors are
getting so much control these days, I don't understand myself.
Where's that prospectus, Frank? You brought it?'

He hesitated. 'Yes . . . but . . .'

'Well, show him, it might explain a little,' she commanded,
adding in rapid English, 'He is our soul brother.'

Frank handed Han-li the document. 'It's in business jargon,
but basically it invites people to buy bonds in the Central
China Railways Syndicate that's planning to build a one-
metre gauge line from Shanghai to Nanking. You see, the Syndicate puts up the money in the form of a loan and the security
of the loan is the railway itself, its properties and rolling
stock.'

'And this—what's this?' Han-li frowned as he read.

'Oh that—the Syndicate will also have the mining rights for

417

coal and iron on each side of the proposed lined, "for a distance to be determined," it says.'

'Ah—so that's how you get your hands on our mineral wealth also. You see how we're being exploited, Frank? All our resources going to unscrupulous foreigners?'

'Now that's not quite fair. Uncle Robert and I aren't unscrupulous for a start. All this is perfectly legal and above-board, and it's been going on all over the world ever since railways were invented.'

'Yes, yes. Let the waiter remove this, Uncut. I really don't much care for this Froggy food. Can I have a delicious sweet pudding with ice cream instead?'

Frank ordered, adding, 'And your own government is encouraging railway building in a half-hearted fashion. It's part and parcel of modern progress and I thought that's what you and your self-strengthening friends wanted for China?'

'It is, it is. But how are all these developments going to help the lot of the ordinary people? That also must be considered.'

Alice smiled wistfully. 'I remember when I first heard someone ask that . . . must have been fifteen years ago now.'

'Lin Fu-wei, the Leader?'

'Yes. It was when I first met him, aboard the *Mandalay* going to Chefoo.'

He looked at her sideways. 'He's teaching at the School for New Learning in Canton, which was founded by Kang Yu-wei. I'm wondering whether to apply for a junior post there myself.'

'Oh do, Younger Brother, it would be marvellous for you. And does Lin Fu-wei still support Kang's views?'

'More or less I think. Certainly I've seen his name on a list of supporters of the Anti-Footbinding League that you're concerned with.'

'Oh I am glad. He's such a right-thinking man.' She sighed, thinking how wonderful it would have been to work beside him in the League's cause. 'He doesn't allow his own daughters to be bound I trust, as some supporters do?'

'He doesn't, no.'

Frank nudged Han-li. 'And your daughter, Younger Brother?'

He looked down. 'She is being bound, yes. My wife insisted on it, saying she'd never find a good husband otherwise. But I am now persuaded that it's an uncivilised custom and if we

418

have another girl, she'll have natural feet. My wife is not cruel, you understand. She simply accepts things as they are—most women do. They are not like you, Uncut Jade.'

'Many more women would question things as I do if they were allowed the same sort of education and experience as men, Younger Brother.'

Though she was quite prepared to argue the point, Han-li was embarrassed at the thought of doing so with a foreign woman in public. It was, he decided, time to return to his ship for the afternoon sailing. He hurried away, promising to keep in closer touch with them in future.

As Frank escorted his sister to a rickshaw, she held out a hand, 'I'll take the prospectus.'

'You're sure you want it, considering what Han-li thinks?'

'I'm trying to be practical—like the native entrepreneurs who invest in foreign concerns and don't worry much about the fate of the peasantry. Anyway, this railway business isn't a black-white issue, is it? I'll think it over.' She stowed the document in her bag.

Frank looked suddenly dubious. 'Mind you, I don't know how the Board would take to the idea of a lady investor.'

'I'm not a lady. I'm Grant & Greenwood. No law against that I hope?'

'No, sister mine,' he grinned and touched his hat. 'Anyway, I'll see you tomorrow evening. Ken's birthday party, remember. We can talk more about it then.'

She nodded, the runner lifted the shafts with the customary grunt and carried her off to Fairlawns. He wheeled her along the British Bund, past the offices of the P & O, the Canadian Pacific, the long-established trading firm of Jardine, Matheson & Co., the porticoed façade of the British Consular buildings, where mounted Sikhs guarded the gate. Along the fashionable Bubbling Well Road, carriages full of ladies and children both Chinese and Western were out for their afternoon drives, arrayed in the expensive garments appropriate to their race and class. The tree-shaded, well-swept avenues that led from it were lined with substantial private houses, mostly built during the past twenty years in the wide-verandah, oriental-colonial style.

Fairlawns was one of these and its main verandah, leading from the drawing-room, had recently been extended to form a spacious p'eng, an enclosed court, roofed and curtained with matting roller blinds and lattices to be raised or lowered, opened or closed with such variation that the temperature was pleasant in every season. Here were comfortable, cushioned bamboo chairs, yellow-marbled occasional tables, a profusion of potted plants. The steps leading to the drawing-room were guarded by two rows of curly blue-green dragon-dogs, some with mouths open to take in the luck, others closed to keep it there.

And indeed Fairlawns always seemed charmed with luck, Alice thought when, the next evening, she waited in the p'eng for her brother and family to arrive. Treasures and comforts accumulated there, servants seldom left, visitors returned, and she, living there, was aware of her good fortune. A carriage drew up outside and she frowned as she heard Frank bellowing irritably at a stable-boy. She felt he didn't appreciate his own luck and had learned little from his years spent in a Chinese household. Hard to imagine now that he'd many times emptied the manure buckets over the vegetables in the Chu's gardens, been proud to scrub the flanks of Younger Son's pony.

Frank, however, felt he'd learned a most important lesson—those who have once seen the inside of a manure bucket must take good care never to do so again. His secret nightmares of poverty and servitude were kept at bay by his new-found money, in the pursuit of which he didn't much mind what he did for his father-in-law. Frank's nickname in the foreign community, first bestowed by Wang's eldest son, was Golden Horseboy, and habitués of the Shanghai Club wondered why he didn't tie his lovely golden hair back in a pigtail and be done with it.

Frank didn't care. It was the metal that mattered, as he'd told Ken earlier that day when he'd presented him with a tiny gold replica of a race-horse. Now the child sat docile on a silk cushion in Fairlawns drawing-room, temporarily stunned into sleepy silence by the amount of food he'd stuffed that day and the numerous presents he'd received. He had deep, narrow black eyes and hair of an odd gingery-brown, which didn't make a pleasing combination. His sister, Lily, had all the looks, everyone agreed, but that hardly mattered, for Ken was showing early signs of business acumen, and Mary, looking down on him, noted that he was clutching the little gold horse tight in his chubby fist.

Across the room, Alice sat with her sister-in-law on the sofa. The beautiful bloom of Peachy's youth was not wearing well. She had borne Lily, sitting curled at her feet, and Ken, as well as another son who had not lived; now she prayed daily for a second male child. Thick white powder was smoothed over the facial lines of her recent tribulations, but her eyes followed Frank anxiously while she was talking. He didn't once glance at her, Alice noted sadly; it used not to be like that.

'. . . And so Father's calling this horse Kenneth the First. We feel quite honoured by the Honourable Parent because he paid a great deal for it,' she laughed, glad to be speaking in her own tongue at a foreign gathering.

'How splendid. I suppose they'll be hoisting the little chap into the saddle soon?'

'They already have and he takes to it well.'

Mary joined them. 'Lan-sho is about to sound the gong, ladies. If we don't dine soon, I fear our little guest-of-honour will be asleep.'

'I hear from Frank that your up-and-coming plan for the '90s is railways, Robert?' Alice inquired as Mary supervised the serving of the sole à la mandarin. 'You really think the time is right?'

'I'm positive. Viceroy Li Hung-chang let it be known recently in his usual roundabout fashion that the construction of a few lines will be most graciously permitted. His main concern is strategic of course. Wants to get something going in Manchuria—the menace of the Russian bear again. He fears they're planning to run a line from Vladivostok.'

'Syndicates are popping up like mushrooms,' Frank interrupted, 'though I didn't mention that to Younger Brother yesterday. And the competition's heating up—Belgians, French, Americans, Germans all wanting to get in at the start. We Brits and the Belgians have cornered a section of line from Tangyang to Wusieh.'

'But what about the people? How do the junkmasters and traders along the Yangtze feel about the threat of the iron monsters? Won't their livelihoods be ruined?'

'Nonsense Alice,' Robert replied brusquely. 'Canal and bargemen said the same thing when railways started in England, but everyone managed. In any event, the Chinese have simply got to get railways going—it's a matter of economic and military survival in this modern age. But there's only a handful of Chinese with the right sort of know-how to get on with the job, so foreigners are being called in. The idea is—I won't bore you with the details—that we and our Belgian colleagues start a joint-stock enterprise with the Chinese under foreign supervision.'

'With most of the profits going to foreigners, I suppose?'

'Not that clear-cut—foreigners are taking most of the risks too.'

'But the risks are quite small,' Frank assured her. 'Foreign investors in other parts of the East are making a mint out of railway development already and there's no reason it shouldn't happen here.' His tone was persuasive, particularly because, in the genial flush of a dinner party with two Syndicate directors, he'd promised an investment beyond his own means. 'Oh I know you're always concerned that the Chinese get a fair deal and so am I,' he continued. 'But no point in missing a chance like this. Pa-in-law, who's a fully-pigtailed, yellow-as-a-guinea Son of Han after all—sorry Peachy—is all in favour of this particular venture. Wants to put money down in my name because of the tax angle.'

Peachy, hearing her name, smiled vaguely, only half understanding. She kept trying to improve her English, but the men's talk was so dull. It used to be tea-markets and horse-racing, now it was railways and horse-racing. Ken was getting fractious and she tried to catch her sister-in-law's eye. But Alice was preoccupied, thinking that, whether idealists like Han-li approved or not, the scheme would undoubtedly go ahead and probably prosper. The idea that she might, perhaps, be China's only lady investor was an additional spur. The underlying irony—which she drew to no one's attention—was that she'd never even seen an actual train, much less ridden in one.

She smiled, 'All right Frank, I'm with you. But I can't afford to lay out a great deal.'

'Bully for you, Alice,' Frank raised his glass to her just as Ken let out a tearful howl, for he was feeling very neglected after the birthday attention he'd received earlier.

'There, there,' Peachy soothed, preparing to take him out of ear-shot.

'One minute, Peachy,' Robert signalled for the butler to pass the wine.

'A toast to the birthday boy. May four-legged Kenneth the First win the Shanghai Gold Cup and may little two-legged Ken have a happy year. Indeed, may his next six be even happier than his first.'

'Seven,' said Peachy with unexpected firmness, as glasses were raised.

'But he was born in . . .'

'Yes, but we count the womb-time, remember, so children are a year old when they're born.'

'Peachy and I don't agree on this,' Frank scowled at her. 'I thought we'd compromised—seven in your family, six in mine. And now you—'

'But this is a blessing, isn't it? With the wine? It's very unlucky to give the wrong age when it's important. He could be cut off for such a thing.' She was upset and obstinate, her lip trembling. 'I cannot drink blessing to a six-year-old boy when he now seven,' She broke into a clatter of Chinese. 'He must have all the correct blessings at the right time, not your time, or he will not be lucky. I know that, Frank.'

'Oh you and your dam' fool superstitions.' They both stared at the child who was bellowing more loudly. Peachy scooped him into her arms. 'There, there. I'll take him away, then perhaps it won't matter. He's so tired, poor baby.'

She carried him off while the others moved to chairs in the lantern-lit p'eng. The reed blinds were pulled down for the night was chilly; from outside came the comforting clickety-clack clappers of the household's nightwatchman patrolling the grounds. Alice leaned back in her chair, wondering if she'd made the right decision that evening, feeling, as so often, the dual tug of her loyalties between Chinese and European. And yet, again as usual, there was no simple answer; all she could do was to wait and see how her investment in the Syndicate developed. In any case, the instinctively superstitious Chinese part of her nature suggested there would eventually be a 'sign' to tell her whether she had been right or wrong, wise or foolhardy.

In the meantime, Alice seldom mentioned her financial interest in the railway, though she occasionally indulged secret daydreams of future riches: her own Shanghai villa staffed with servants in jade-green liveries; herself as owner and publisher of China's first magazine devoted to women's rights; herself as wealthy globe-trotter swanning round St.

Petersburg in sable furs, Paris in fashionable gowns. Though not entirely convinced by the ultimate desirability of these fantasies, they helped to fuel her enthusiasm for her business and its continuing success kept her reasonably happy and well occupied.

It was not the style of life her family would have chosen for her, and yet, as Mary said to Isabel one afternoon the following summer as they sat together in the drawing-room, 'At least I can understand Alice to an extent. There's great fascination in the buying and selling of beautiful objects, even though I wish she'd be more discreet about it, as I always was with my Japanese print collecting. Still, better Alice's occupation I must say than what my own daughter Lilian has set herself to. You'll remember her?'

Isabel nodded vaguely. Arrived that morning from Foochow where she and William now lived, and on her way to England to put her two eldest children in schools, she was rather fatigued and irritable, what with the heat and the thought of all the travelling arrangements that had to be made.

'Lilian is the religious one?'

Mary sighed assent. 'And now she calls herself a qualified medical missionary, if you please, and has stuck herself in some filthy little hole in Shansi where she ministers to the needs of lepers, beggars, and the great unwashed, not to mention running what she calls an "opium refuge" for drug sots. So far there seem to be no unattached men at her station and one can only be grateful, for any there would obviously be wildly unsuitable. Truly I see little hope for her—I mean in the normal way of marrying, having children, enjoying one's domestic responsibilities and comforts.' Mary looked round her complacently. 'And to think she could be living here at Fairlawns, meeting pleasant civilised people, not to mention young men of honourable intent.'

'How old is she?'

'Early thirties, about the same age as Alice—perhaps that's why I've specially taken to Alice, as a sort of daughter in lieu.'

'Well, William and I are most grateful that you have, Mary. I suppose there are no young men of honourable intent in the offing for her?'

'There could be. But Alice is extremely selective in the way of gentlemen—always was, Robert says. She has one or two

424

faithful escorts, and there was a most amiable Mr. Bellamy a while ago. Widower, youngish, well set up in his work, who paid her a lot of court. But Alice could scarcely bestir herself even to flirt with him. What with her decided partiality to the Chinese and her independent business ventures, she does tend to frighten some gentlemen off I fear. And her interest in the Anti-Footbinding League doesn't have much appeal either. That dreadfully earnest friend of hers, Mrs. Daisy Small, one of the League's founders, is due here any minute. I so hope she doesn't arrive before Alice gets back ... Ah. .' Mary sighed with relief, 'there she is with the children now, so that's all right.'

Charlotte Greenwood came in first; with her fine features, fair skin, and a cascade of fiery auburn hair, she was destined to be the beauty of the family, and knew it. 'Aunt Alice showed us her office,' she began. 'It's not in a very nice district.'

'Isn't it dear? Well, it's only a small firm. What did you think, Joel?' Isabel's stolid, ten-year-old son shrugged awkwardly, 'S'all right.'

Alice came in, holding by the hand the younger, dark-haired Polly.

'Did you have a nice time Polly?'

'Yes, thank you, Mama. There was a horrible smell near the docks.'

'Fish gone bad in the heat—ugh!' Joel explained.

'And rats,' added Charlotte. 'We saw one crawling with huge white maggots just outside Aunt's office door.'

'Dear me,' Isabel frowned. 'Doesn't sound very salubrious, Alice.'

'It's the heat just now, brings out the worst.'

'Like maggots,' Joel snorted with laughter.

'Well there's nursery tea ready for you all upstairs,' Mary said, and Charlotte pouted, 'But I'm too old for nursery teas now.'

'Well you have one today, dear,' Isabel said crisply. 'So take the young ones to the amah to wash their hands.'

As they left, Alice sank into a chair. 'Phew, it is hot. They're growing so alarmingly fast, Isabel. It's been a while since I've seen them. Polly is a serious little girl, isn't she?'

'Much too serious. She listens to everything, says little, then

425

gets het up about nothing. Maybe you'll find out what goes on in her mind while she's here.'

'I'll be happy to try,' Alice smiled, for it had been arranged that Polly should stay at Fairlawns while Isabel took the other two Home.

As tea was being served, Daisy Small was shown in and introduced to Isabel. She was puffing slightly from the heat, damp grey hairs wisping from her bun, and she carried a bulging, faded, calico bag.

'Oh . . . that's better,' she gulped tea gratefully. 'And now Mrs. Greenwood—both of you—I must show you how clever Alice has been. See—' she dumped a sheaf of papers from her bag on the table and patted it. 'You should be proud—her most excellent translation of J. S. Mill's book on the *Subjection of Women*. Archie and I have checked it over thoroughly and she's done wonderfully well, especially considering how totally alien the whole idea of women's subjection is to most Orientals.'

'Which women is Mr. Mill referring to then?' Isabel inquired, puzzled. 'European women? We don't suffer any great hardships surely? Certainly nothing disabling like foot-binding. Most of us lead very satisfactory lives alongside our menfolk.'

'But we are *not* alongside, Isabel, in many, many ways we are subordinate to them,' Alice broke in. 'Our position in society is inferior to men's, can you not see that? We have no equal education, no political rights. Let me read you what Mill says about . . .'

Mary raised a hand. 'Alice please, no. I read about the late Mr. Mill and his extraordinary views on women when that book first appeared, must be twenty years ago now. And I concluded then that he must be an extremely misguided gentleman. Why, if he had his way, there'd be women pontificating in Parliament, women with judges' wigs atop their curls, and heaven knows what else.'

'And why not, if there are women capable of doing such things, as I'm sure there are?'

'My dear, of course our constitutions are not fitted for tasks of that nature,' Isabel intruded dismissively.

'How do you know? How do any of us know what we could be fitted for?' Alice exploded. 'As Mill says, our natural vocations are thwarted, our active faculties suppressed. How many of us, I wonder, have this feeling of the 'wasted life' he talks of because we have been denied education and a career?'

Isabel stared at her coldly. 'Well I certainly do not and neither do most of my women friends. You really are an exception in this, Alice, and perhaps one that proves the rule.'

Alice stared at Isabel and Mary, thinking fiercely, and for the first time coherently, that they and all her relatives and the people she met at Fairlawns, were limited, self-satisfied, closed to new ideas. And if she was an exception among them, then she was glad. And yet . . . was she not being uncharitable and presumptuous? She glanced at Polly, who had crept into the room un-noticed and was listening wide-eyed to the conversation.

'Things have to be changed,' she said firmly. 'Polly and her generation have to be given more opportunities, more freedom of action to express their talents. And the Chinese Pollys are even more oppressed. It's for them I've done this translation.'

'I hope you're not implying that William and I suppress our daughters?' Isabel bridled.

'No, no, not you in particular, Mrs. Greenwood. It's social attitudes towards womenkind that have to be changed,' Daisy interposed.

Polly, staring up at her large robed form, began to whimper and Isabel drew her close. 'There, child, don't worry. We're not really talking about you. Run along.'

There was a small, cool pause, then Isabel rose, saying with distant politeness, 'Well, I've promised myself a little stroll in the Public Gardens now the air is cooling. Mary was telling me earlier how lovely the gloxinia and begonia are in the conservatories this year. Have you seen them yet, Mrs. Small?'

Daisy, reluctant to cause more dissension, yet sticking, as always, to her guns, replied, 'I'm afraid I don't go into any Treaty-Port gardens—on principle, Mrs. Greenwood.'

Isabel's eyes opened wide. 'Principle?'

'I think it's quite wrong that these gardens which cost money from the common purse to maintain and are on native soil should be reserved for the pleasure of white people only. We are living in China after all and while I allow that people may choose to exclude whomsoever they wish from their homes, I don't think we have a right to exclude the

427

natives from public open spaces.'

'Come now, Mrs. Small,' Mary turned on her crossly. 'Surely you, with your long experience of China, know full well that without some such ruling there wouldn't be any gardens—there'd be rubbish dumps, full of wheelbarrows, street hawkers, pigs, hens, ducks, rats, goodness knows what filth.'

'But Mary, that's not quite true either,' Alice felt hot. 'The Chinese keep their own gardens and temple grounds quite well. No, what we are really doing is "keeping them in their place"—as sweepers, garden boys, coolies doing menial tasks. We don't want them sharing beauty spots with us on equal terms.'

Mary looked weary. 'Really, Alice, I think we've had more than enough disputation for one hot summer afternoon without going into the vexed question of whether the yellow race is equal to the white.'

And Daisy, who felt the same, quickly took her leave. Alice saw her out, half apologising for her relatives' views. 'Well, it's given you something to mull over,' Daisy patted her shoulder. 'It's about time you took a few definite stands on such matters if I may say so. It's so easy to drift with the current, as we all know.'

'Yes, and I feel guilty when I find myself doing so. Life here makes one both frivolous and acquisitive I fear, but I will try and improve.' She smiled apologetically, knowing Daisy expected rather more of her. During her prolonged stay in Ichang after Charles' death she'd been much influenced by the older woman's ideas and had resolved then to do more than she actually had for the Anti-Footbinding League and the general amelioration of the female lot.

So, after Isabel had left, Alice decided to start with the education of the nearest candidate—her youngest niece and god-child, who had stayed behind. Resolving that Polly should learn more about the land in which she lived than the usual platitudes offered to foreign children, she began to teach her spoken Mandarin and the formation of basic characters.

At night, she lulled Polly to sleep with Chinese legends of pretty ladies who were foxes in disguise, of armless people who picked flowers with their toes and people who sent their hands flying round at night to steal for them, of the Green Dragon King of the Yellow River whose daughter guarded his caves of pearls, and the Golden King of the North who had leopards and bears to fight for him and buzzards and hawks for his standard-bearers.

The very recounting of these familiar tales, some of which she'd heard from Eldest Daughter Tamao, filled Alice with half-ashamed nostalgia. On first returning to the Western settlements, she had deliberately turned her back on her experiences in Hunan in order to survive and had acquiesced in her family's and husband's pretence that nothing much had happened in what they called her 'lost years.' But a deliberate rejection of the past didn't come easily, and now, thrown on her own emotional resources, she dreamed, occasionally by day and often by night, of life in the Chu household.

In her dreams, the house which was, in reality, large, became all-enveloping. Servants' voices, babies' cries, the swish of brooms echoed along distant corridors, Second Daughter's crickets chirped in their cages, doves cooed on the roof-beams and in the attics, weaving looms clicked. Sometimes she would start from sleep in terror, the whimperings of footbound Little Piece magnified to harsh screams; at others she would surface wearily as if she'd spent the night sweeping and polishing; or she'd drowse awake lustfully, having lain again under the red coverlet in Lung-kuang's bedroom and felt his skilful hands mastering her.

The only men's hands to touch her these days were brotherly or avuncular, Alice thought one evening as she stood on her bedroom balcony, smelling the Japanese lilies and night-stock, hearing frogs croak beside the lotus pond, crickets click in the groves of ornamental bamboo. Despite the beauty of the evening she felt a little desolate, her knowing body so untended. But who did she want to penetrate this sensual isolation? She knew of no one. How was she to break through the limited horizons of this present, pleasant life? She paced the balcony in a state of emotional and mental restlessness, yearning as romantically as any young girl for the excitement of different people, different places.

2

Early reports issued by the Central China Railway Syndicate suggested that the initial construction at Tangyang was forging ahead, and, about a year after the venture was launched, the first stretch of line was completed. To demonstrate its potential to local officials and reassure bondholders that progress was satisfactory, an opening ceremony was arranged that autumn to which Robert and Frank were invited. Alice, asserting her prerogative as the only lady investor, insisted on going with them.

Tangyang was situated on a curve of the ancient Grand Canal, a featureless township typical of thousands. Its main street was paved with broken flags, lined with smelly open drains. The only buildings of any pretension were the public Hall of Felicitous Understanding and the magistrate's *yamen*, which had a curved roof of dusty vermilion and an imposing gateway emblazoned with yellow and green dragons cavorting among tipply blue waves.

The only overt sign of its new designation as First Grade Station on the proposed Shanghai–Nanking line was the Foreign Goods Shop in the main street which sold tins of condensed milk, cheap clocks, packets of Sheffield needles, matches from Trieste, and kerosene oil for the new-fangled foreign-style lamps. The empty oil tins were much used by water-carriers and were on sale at the shop entrance; Alice stared at them, disliking their ugly indestructibility compared to the traditional earthenware jars. They were a discordant element, in her eyes, in a scene where, for centuries, only local, hand-moulded materials had been used.

The town's inhabitants too seemed imbued with a new sense of discord, and looked sullen and suspicious. For, in recent months, many foreign intruders had appeared on the local scene—large men, wearing thick serge jackets and high

430

leather boots with straps below the knee-cap; clumsy, short-tempered, purposeful creatures who snarled at the coolies and kicked the street-dogs. Peasants from the hinterlands had travelled miles to see them and to watch in awe as the first tracks were laid on the raised embankments of the canal along which the iron 'devil-monster' was to ride.

More sightseers than usual had come to Tangyang that day, for the news of the ceremonial opening had spread, and most of them had congregated outside the *yamen* where, in default of any tolerable inn, the visiting foreigners were being accommodated. The Greenwoods pushed through its main courtyard crowded with the usual motley collection of petitioners, prisoners awaiting trial, clerks, writers, and guards in tattered uniforms. A sudden cacophony of gong and drum beats signalled the offices' closure for the day, and wails of protest and despair came from the unheard petitioners, untried prisoners and unaided beggars as they were hustled outside.

'The number of times I've come to this wretched place in the past months to try and calm things down,' grumbled one of the railway engineers as he conducted them to the comparative quiet of the guest-rooms behind.

'The locals are kicking up more than the usual fuss over moving the ancestral graveyards because, unfortunately, there's some very old ones hereabouts. Then there's the trouble caused by slippery Mr. Sheng who's been contracted to acquire land and get graves moved where necessary. An absolute crook, if you ask me. Our contract states we must pay expenses and compensation to the families of the bones concerned, and Sheng does the negotiating. We don't know exactly what deals are made, but his pockets are being well-lined, I'll be bound. Then these so-called benevolent societies muscle in and collect fees supposed to be used for the removal of those numerous departed whose families are untraceable. And what do they do? Hire coolies to shovel up the bones and dump 'em on the nearest waste land, and charge us a pretty penny for it. But if we make any protest, we're smartly told by the higher-ups that we must "respect the ancient traditions of Chinese culture." Culture—bloody hell . . .' He spat on the ground, then added grudgingly to Alice, 'Pardon my French, madam.'

He turned his back on her. 'And talking of French, here comes M. Doumer—our Belgian colleague.'

They were introduced and then Alice, much to her chagrin, was ushered away to take tea with Madame Doumer while the men continued to discuss railway matters. Retiring early that night, she was uneasily aware of the crowds gathered outside the *yamen* gates. Such people, whose usual toil was tuned to the seasonal rhythms of rice and cotton growing, knew even less than Alice about railways. To them, a train was an iron-clad 'fire-cart' that would belch flames and smoke as it tore through their lands with no regard for the crops of the living or the peace of the dead. Having nowhere to stay, most of them huddled in makeshift shelters, hooting and calling to each other throughout the hours of darkness—restless, angry, sinister sounds that threatened trouble.

Nevertheless, the ceremony went off without a hitch the following afternoon. An engine and two box-cars, brought up by canal boat and assembled on the spot, appeared from the locomotive shed exactly on schedule like a genii from a bottle. The driver, a cocky, stocky Glaswegian, blew the whistle loudly and the engine chuffed and puffed merrily along the line in a cloud of steam. Alice, standing on the bunting-bedecked platform with the wives of two Belgian engineers, clapped politely; both she and Frank careful to conceal the fact it was the first train they'd ever seen. As such, they agreed afterwards, it was rather a tin-pot affair, compared to pictures illustrating the mighty monsters that thundered out of Europe's grand terminals.

The ordinary Chinese gasped with suitable awe however, while the richly robed mandarins on the platform looked on with the cool detachment befitting their rank, though the eyes of a few flashed angrily. Further down the line, a group of boatmen yelled derision and threw clods of earth at the driver who tooted his whistle in defiance. That evening, the mandarins of Tangyang moved in solemn procession through the many-tiered memorial arch in the main street, preceded by uniformed lictors banging gongs, twirling ceremonial staves and shouting, 'Make way for the illustrious Great Men.' Arriving at the Hall of Felicitous Understanding they shared a banquet with their foreign guests. Wine cups were raised to herald the co-operation of Chinese, British, and Belgian enterprise and the day when 'the iron-roads of progress would stretch from shore to shore of the colossal Celestial Empire'— as the chief magistrate put it, his eyes positively watering with good will.

Lulled by the wine and the seeming bonhomie, Alice fell into a deep slumber that night, only to be wakened after a few hours by thudding steps in the passage outside. Grabbing a candle, she opened the door; Robert and Frank were just emerging from the next room. 'Whatever's happened?'

'Soldiers came for us—they say men are digging up the tracks down the line.'

'Oh good heavens—here, wait for me.'

'Go back to bed, Alice, we'll see to it,' Robert ordered, as they hurried away.

Alice snorted, pulled on her serge riding habit and followed them down to the courtyard where her relatives and M. Doumer and his assistant were just riding out of the gate behind some soldiers.

'Saddle me a pony, double quick,' she shouted at a stable-boy, throwing some cash to encourage him, and within minutes she'd caught up with the others.

Frank reined to her side, 'It might be nasty.'

'We've been in nasty spots before,' she grinned at him. 'But I wonder who on earth . . .?'

'Doumer was telling me at dinner he'd heard rumours that local farmers have been badly cheated over the compulsory purchase of their land and the canal men are up in arms. They're probably being stirred up by political agitators or secret societies.'

The officer-in-charge decided they should ride quietly through the fields adjoining the embankment rather than conspicuously along the track itself.

'This is a fool's errand if you ask me,' Robert joined them. 'So you're here, Alice? I might have guessed.'

'Yes you might, Uncle,' she smiled unctuously. 'Why a fool's errand?'

'If people are destroying the track they'll either flee before we can catch them or put up a fight—in which case we bolt and let the Chinks have it out between them. We've only got a few soldiers armed with medieval muskets. Something fishy about it altogether, if you ask me.'

They fell silent. A strong icy wind blew at their backs and disturbed wild fowl flew off, squawking angrily; the ponies slithered along the muddy paths between the paddies. Eventually, the officer in front halted and pointed ahead—lanterns were moving about on the embankment, eerie as will-o'-the-wisps in the blackness. Alice shivered; she still found it ridiculously easy to believe in spirits.

The soldiers consulted and decided to creep closer through the paddies, then charge along the embankment; Robert, who had a pistol, insisted on going with them. As they mounted the embankment one of the ponies stumbled, whinnying loudly; the lanterns bobbed rapidly and were extinguished even before the men charged. Muskets cracked and following the report of Robert's pistol, a piercing scream rang out. The men followed the sound and, as Alice and Frank rode up, returned, dragging a skinny old man, bleeding copiously from a shoulder wound. The others who had been engaged with him in tearing up the just-opened line had melted away into the dark. Raising a lantern, M. Doumer showed Robert a pick-axe. 'Ours, no? Same tools they make the line, now dig up . . . *Ils sont foux!*'

The wounded man groaned loudly and collapsed against the soldier holding him.

'Better make a tourniquet, it's a nasty hole,' Robert observed. 'Any good at that sort of thing, Alice?'

'Not much. You can use my scarf though.' Shuddering, she held the man as Robert tried to bind the wound. As blood seeped darkly through the material she turned away her head and saw a light in the sky behind.

'Oh God, look—there's a fire in the town!'

They all stared back towards Tangyang where a red glow was spreading across the black sky faster than blood through a scarf.

'*Mon Dieu! C'est le depot. Allons-y, tout de suite!*' Doumer leaped on his pony and went galloping back, everyone following as fast as they could. Alice, looking round, saw a soldier bending over the wounded man who had fallen to the ground, but whether he was giving succour or dispatch, she couldn't tell. 'Frank, the man . . . he may die . . .'

'Let him for God's sake,' Frank snarled. 'There'll be other heads to roll if they've fired our depot.'

And that was precisely what had happened. As they neared the town the ponies shied in terror at the sight and smell of the flames that were sparking towards them in the high wind. 'Let the beasts go, or they'll bolt,' Frank called back as he and Doumer dismounted and raced ahead.

Alice, hampered by her riding skirt, was the last to reach the scene, but it didn't matter, for the fire had already done its

434

ravaging worst. The locomotive shed and the work-shops were in ashes, the engine that had puffed proudly along the line a few hours before was a twisted heap of molten metal. A gang of firemen in stagey coloured jackets were dribbling water from leaky buckets on to the blaze haphazardly while yamen guards, leaning on their staves, shouted encouragement from a safe distance. There was a suspicious absence of high-ranking officials.

'Deliberate arson, not a doubt about it,' Frank came up to Alice. 'Look——recently emptied kerosene tins and oil-soaked rags. They must have set fire to the matting roofs and the high wind did the rest. A total loss.' He sat down heavily on a tin and put his head in his hands.

As the heat subsided, vagrants began to salvage bits of charred timber, iron rods and sheets of tin from the debris—anything that would add substance to their own flimsy dwellings. Numbly Alice watched them. As long as they lived they would never know one iota about bondholders, syndicates, capital investments; this was their only bonanza and, chuckling with glee, they darted recklessly close to the fire's core, happy as millionaires with this unexpected bounty from the devil-monsters' iron-road. These men, and millions like them, eked out their subsistence by carrying sacks of salt, coal, logs, rice, cloth on their backs for miles every day. What would happen to them when the land was banded by the rails of modern progress?

Robert stamped up, his face twisted with rage in the fire's light. 'The whole bloody thing's a put-up job,' he roared. 'I thought there was something fishy, didn't I? We were decoyed out of town while the real damage was being done. Doumer reckons local officials are behind this and I'll wager he's right. The crooked bastards! I'm getting out of this goddam country in short order I can tell you. Bloody yellow-skinned Chinks! What century do they think they're living in? Here we are trying to help 'em out of the Middle Ages by their bootstraps and this is the thanks we get for it. Let 'em go back to the trees where they belong, let 'em swing by their fucking filthy pigtails . . . We should never have trusted them for an instant. Barbarians, that's what they are, bleeding barbarians!'

Alice and Frank stared at him horrified; never before had they seen him in such a towering fury, never heard him use such language. A large dark figure, trembling with passion against the fire's dying redness, he had become more than himself. He was the voice incarnate of Europe's rampant imperialism—arrogant, contemptuous, aggressive, implacable, self-righteous—and Alice hated to hear it. Eventually he quietened, surveying the surrounding destruction with grimly turned-down scowl. 'Yes, it's all up with China after this as far as I'm concerned.'

Frank, still sitting on the kerosene tin, simply groaned, and Alice knew better than to argue just then. She suggested, 'We might as well all go back to bed for a while. It's icy out here.'

As they left the scene, one of the salvagers who'd been watching Robert's outburst with considerable amusement, shouted after them, 'Stick your iron rails up your backsides, you barbarian animals.' Frank grimaced at Alice; Robert, fortunately, did not understand.

The fire, headlined as the Tangyang conflagration, was widely reported in the Treaty-Port press. The *Shanghai Mercury* professed sympathy with investors who would get their fingers badly burned, but suggested that those who trusted the natives were rather asking for it. An editorial in the *Hong-Kong Mail* said the affair only lent support to the view that the Chinese should be left to push their ancient sampans and wheelbarrows into the dead abysses of the past, there being no future hope for them. Robert, interviewed as the man-on-the-spot, thoroughly agreed, expressing the same sentiments as he had on the night of the fire in language fit to print.

Police were called in to track down the culprits and allegations were made against certain local mandarins, for it was well known that many of their kind saw railway development as a threat to their somewhat tenuous hold on power. If foreign troops or gangs of dissident rebels could move easily and quickly about the country, how many sinecured heads might topple? And, in any case, was it not against the natural order of things to travel faster than the leisurely speeds set by men and animals on their own legs? Whatever the underlying motives, guilt proved harder than any mandarin's button to pin on the higher ranks, and instead, to appease foreign opinion, a few scapegoats were accused of arson and executed with much ceremony.

This did not help the Syndicate, which collapsed totally soon thereafter. Its directors had been counting on international support to provide capital for expansion, and the effectively disruptive, unexpectedly violent hostility of the local populace did not inspire confidence in its future. Moreover, it was felt the Syndicate had been ill-advised to build alongside a busy waterway in obvious competition with thousands of boat-men and in a region strewn with ancient burial grounds.

Personally, Alice took a certain perverse satisfaction in the knowledge that the Syndicate itself, in its ignorance of local conditions, had helped to ensure that a considerable amount of investors' money had fallen into Chinese hands. Albeit the particular hands were probably undeserving, she discovered an ironic sense of justice in what had happened. By ignoring her own deeper instinct and linking herself to patent foreign exploitation in the name of good business sense, she had lost about a third of her working capital. But she accepted the loss stoically as a lesson learned. Robert, his ire cooled, was persuaded by Mary to remain in Shanghai after all and turn his attention to the collecting of ancient Chinese weaponry. Frank, the most severely 'burned,' did not reveal his plans for recouping his losses; the Shanghai community as a whole simply forgot the whole silly business, concentrating instead on celebrating its fiftieth year of existence.

To mark the occasion there were Jubilee Races with prizes of Jubilee cups, concerts featuring Jubilee marches and a grand Jubilee procession through the foreign concessions ending in a firework display with the legend 'Shanghai 1843–1893, The Model Settlement' stabbed in fiery colours against the night sky. Old China hands waxed nostalgic over its grand old days when the magnificent tea-clippers, with their sails billowing, used to leave for Southampton; more recent arrivals waxed equally enthusiastic about their future plans for improved public amenities including a theatre that would rival any in Drury Lane.

Not long afterwards, however, the increasing prosperity of the port was threatened by international tension over Korea. That troubled, secretive land was a long-standing bone of contention between Chinese and Japanese, and for the past ten years, the former's hold there had been paramount. During that same period however, Japan's armed forces had been undergoing thorough modernisation along Western lines, and were now ready to challenge China's ascendancy. In the spring, the Tonghaks rose in revolt against the Chinese-dominated Korean government—but who the Tonghaks were very few foreigners in Shanghai could say.

Alice, however, whose commendable knowledge of Asian politics was balanced by a lamentable disregard of European affairs, spent a thoroughly enjoyable evening when the news broke, explaining the situation to assembled dinner-guests at Fairlawns. The Tonghak Movement, supporting Eastern as opposed to Western learning, had been founded by a scholar who claimed to have discovered the 'pill of immortality' (which didn't save him from being executed as a rebel at the age of forty). Originally religious, the Movement had become political and revolutionary following persecution and was being encouraged by the Japanese who wanted to upset the status quo in the country.

After the ladies had retired and the port was circulating, a shipping director out from Liverpool opined sulkily to his neighbour that it was bad enough having to listen politely while old bores of the masculine gender pontificated on the complexities of Oriental politics, but when presentable ladies did the same it was truly insufferable.

'Who is she anyway?' murmured his companion sympathetically.

'A Mrs. Greenwood-Grant, niece of the Major's I believe. China born and bred into the bone by the sound of it. Chatted to her before dinner. She's all set to take on the Jap army single-handed apparently if war is declared. I guessed she'd start again at the table.' He stifled a yawn. 'Another little nip before we join the Fair?'

In the drawing-room, Alice, standing with Peachy who was noticeably and happily pregnant again, realised she had overstepped the bounds of feminine decorum by expressing her political views so eloquently. For, as the gentlemen drifted in, they tended to avoid her, seeking instead less demanding converse with the other 'Fair' who clustered in wait for them. As Peachy left her, she was about to slip away to bed when Frank bustled up and introduced the burly, silver-haired gentleman at his side.

'Alice—Mr. Bill Risley from Chicago originally—and many other places since.'

He gave her a flourishing bow, 'Delighted, ma'am. I was interested to overhear your opinions on Korea. And when Frank told me you were his sister, I begged an introduction.'

'Bill's one of our freelance sea-captains,' Frank explained, 'and if there's anything to be shipped from A to B in good short order, he's the man for the job. Remember that circus fellow, Bill, who paid you handsomely to take a couple of leopards, a Chinese pangolin, and a troupe of jugglers from Canton to San Francisco?'

Bill groaned theatrically. 'Do I? However handsome he paid it wasn't enough, Frank my boy. Have you ever seen a seasick pangolin, Mrs. Grant? Not to mention ten queasy jugglers all in the same boat!' He chuckled at the memory. 'Anyways, I just wanted to say how much I agree with you about the present situation in the north. I've just come down from Nagasaki, and the little Jappies there are jumping about with guns at the ready longing for a scrap.'

'You don't sound especially partial to them, Mr. Risley.'

'Nope, give me John Chinaman any day—slow-moving and peace-loving by comparison. Philosophical and common-sensical.' He perched on a sofa's edge, ran a fleshy hand through his abundant silver hair. 'Get to my age, you begin to appreciate the slow-movers of this world. Not that I'm one myself, mind. Always been a bit of a hustler, haven't I, Frank?'

'You have, Bill, and not finished yet by the sound of things. Bill's just off to Rangoon with a cargo of ours,' Frank explained. 'He showed me round his new little tub this afternoon.'

Bill snorted, 'Tub! A real swell little screw-steamer called the *Dolphin*, ma'am. Leaps through the water as merrily as her namesake.'

'How exciting! Perhaps you'd show me over her sometime? I seldom get aboard anything speedier than houseboats these days. In the meantime though, I wonder if you'd do me a small favour, Mr. Risley? I'm in the jewellery trade as you may know and I'd dearly love to find out the price of good Burmese jade in the Rangoon markets. It's very expensive here and I've often wondered how much gets marked up in transit.'

'Delighted, Mrs. Grant. Gives me a good excuse for wandering round the bazaars in the old city. I'll bring you back a few samples—No, don't want any money now—pay me if you like 'em. You can count on me for a fair deal.'

And so she could, Frank assured his sister after the other guests had gone. He'd known Bill for years—a big-hearted, genial fellow with fingers in several pies and friends in every port.

As summer progressed the international situation worsened, though no one seemed inclined to do much about it. The Korean government begged the Chinese to help them crush the Tonghaks, and in response some ill-equipped troops of the Imperial Forces were sent to Seoul. Soon after their arrival, eight thousand Japanese soldiers appeared in Korea; Viceroy Li Hung-chang appealed to several Western nations to find a diplomatic solution, but failed. On 25 July the steamer *Kowshing* with nine hundred and fifty Chinese soldiers aboard was sunk in the Bay of Korea by ships of the Japanese navy. A week later the two countries were at war and the Empress Dowager was so certain of victory that she planned to have Emperor Meiji brought to her in a cage to celebrate her sixtieth birthday that October. The powerful nations of the West remained neutral and the Japanese, quietly confident, assured them that no warlike operations would be carried on in the vicinity of Shanghai.

So life there went on much as usual. It was the Time of Great Heat, and a sun-sodden languor spread like syrup over the coastal plains round Shanghai that precluded the taking of any initiative whatsoever. Alice succumbed to the prevailing lethargy and was just emerging from it as the weather began to cool when the news came one evening that Peachy had gone into premature labour. On such occasions, Peachy's female relations took complete control, dealing with matters in their time-honoured fashion, and so Alice was most surprised and concerned when, in the early hours, a servant brought an urgent note from Frank, asking her to come at once.

He met her at the door of his villa, his puckered face in the early grey light immediately suggestive of disaster. 'Oh there you are. Thank goodness.'

'Whatever's happened?'

He drew her inside. 'It's a boy . . .'

'But that's wonder . . .'

'No, it's not right. There's something very wrong with it. The mid-wife keeps shaking her head, two doctors have examined it—the head's wrong-shaped somehow.'

'Oh my dear,' she put a hand on his arm. 'And Peachy?'

'She's all right. Sleeping and doesn't know yet. The Wangs are here in force, muttering together. I think they'd like to . . . like to . . .' He turned away, then said in a rush, 'Do away with it. Like a puppy or something. It's unbearable and they won't say a word to me. That's why I sent for you.'

He drew out a brandy flask, swallowing fast.

'Thank goodness you did, Frank. I'll go and see Mrs. Wang, shall I? And is the baby dreadful to look at then?'

'Not exactly. Wrong, that's all.'

She took a large gulp of brandy before going to Peachy's room. Mrs. Wang sat by her daughter's bed, a bulky, square-faced Manchu. The passing years had heightened her resemblance to the Empress Dowager, which she now sedulously cultivated, and, even at this unpropitious hour, she could have held imperial court in her silk robe patterned with blooming pink peonies. Similarly imperious was the look of venomous hate she cast on Alice—sister of the white-skinned barbarian-demon who had married her daughter and fathered this deformed runt that lay in a cradle in the room's darkest corner.

'Where is he?' Alice whispered. 'Frank tells me all is not well with him.'

Mrs. Wang rose; expressionlessly, she lifted the strange head, opened one of the unfocused eyes, uncurled a tiny pink fist, tracing with her long red fingernail the single deep crease right across the palm. Alice shuddered. As she did so the infant emitted a rasping bellow and Peachy sat up gasping.

'Where is he? Where's my little son? Mother, where?'

Mrs. Wang folded her arms in her sleeves and remained silent. Alice looked from one to the other in dismay. 'Alice, that's you, isn't it? Please, he's crying. Bring him to me.' She held out her arms. Alice picked up the slobbering bundle and carried it over. Peachy held it lovingly to her breast. Mrs. Wang walked out of the room in silence, except that her very robe rustled in fury.

Alice kissed Peachy's damp forehead. 'I'll call Frank. I'm so very glad you're all right, dear. It's all over now.'

In fact the difficulties were just beginning. Relatives and friends who would normally have called that day bringing red-painted eggs and almond doughcakes to mark the birth of a male child, discreetly kept away. For word spread fast that this child was wrong—strange-headed, monkey-handed. The reason was obvious of course: an unsullied daughter of Han had coupled with a yellow-haired barbarian and their progeny was accursed. Three generations of Wangs had come into the world unblemished, now this idiot with tainted blood was a just retribution for his parents' monstrous deviation from the rules of correct behaviour. The eyes of all Wangs accused Peachy herself, Frank, and, by extension, Alice. The atmosphere in the house that day was almost palpably poisonous.

'But Good Lord, how could I help it? It's not my fault is it?' Frank appealed desperately as he escorted his sister to the waiting Fairlawns carriage late that afternoon.

'No of course not, dear, and you must never blame yourself—nor Peachy. It's just something that occasionally happens I'm afraid, and you'll have to be very loving and caring of her for a while because, in some ways, it's worse for her.'

He sighed fretfully. 'Here, come to the stable-yard where we can talk quietly for a minute.'

The horses were having their evening feed, chewing and shuffling contentedly, and Frank took a deep breath, 'Bran, hay and horse-dung—best smells in the world! There, see my new little beaut. Lil the Second? A real goer. Had to pay a whacking price for her though, that's the trouble. Ever since the railway fiasco it's been a struggle to keep the stables up to scratch.' He kicked the dust moodily. 'Which brings me to the matter of Bill Risley. You remember, I introduced you a few months ago?'

'Of course—he was going to Burma.'

'Well, he's back—has some samples for you by the way. I'm meeting him at the President Fillmore Hotel tomorrow evening so I'll collect them for you. We're going to join forces in a little venture, he and I . . . or at least that was the plan before this happened with Peachy. Means my leaving town for about a month very soon though.' He glanced sideways at her.

'But Frank, you can't possibly . . .'

'Now just let me finish and you'll see it's in a good cause. The fact is—and this much you've probably read in the papers—that owing to the usual, one might say traditional, incompetency of our dear old mandarins, there's a dire shortage of seaworthy vessels capable of carrying weapons and supplies north for the Imperial Forces fighting in Korea. And so, soon as Bill's *Dolphin* dropped anchor the other day, he was called in to meet a blue-button "topside man" with a great golden peacock embroidered on his shirt-front, as Bill put it.'

'Civil, third rank,' Alice murmured.

'Show off! Long and short of the meeting was—they want him to take a cargo of military supplies to Port Arthur, the main base of Chinese operations. Well, gun-running isn't Bill's usual cup of tea as he told them and some pretty tough bargaining started. That was when he pulled me in to act as interpreter, not trusting the Chinese johnnies. Now he wants me to make the trip with him. I'll get a good share of the profits, which will be considerable, and it will really help the Chinese. It was just about settled, but now this trouble with Peachy . . .' He gave her a pleading, little-boy smile. 'I was wondering, Uncut, if you'd come and stay here, help her through this difficult patch while I'm away?'

'Excitement for you and duty for me again, hey Frank?'

'But come now, Alice, you're a woman and understand Peachy's condition much better than I.'

'Look Frank, she's your wife, your responsibility, and you should be here to protect her from her own family's most unpleasant reaction to what's happened. It's you she loves and wants, not me. Anyway, why should I?' She looked at him speculatively. 'Bill's staying at the Fillmore and has that jade for me, you say? I'll go and call on him.'

'But Sis, why should you?'

'If I may say so, Frank, you're rather prone to get mixed up in fly-by-night ventures and I'd like to form my own opinion of the whole enterprise.'

'Oh, Bill's true-blue, I'm sure he wouldn't let me down. But the main point is—will you do your bit to help me out?'

'Oh yes, Frank, though it mightn't be quite the bit you expect. But I'll let you know tomorrow.' With that she hurried off, refusing to say more, for she had another call to make.

The President Fillmore Hotel in the American Concession did not attract the smartest of the globe-trotting set, but did lay claim to the biggest bowling alley west of San Francisco and the best bourbon bar in Asia. Performing 'artistes' on the eastern circuit stayed there, along with freelancers and free-booters of various kinds, newspaper men, raffish-looking ladies from California and Melbourne and seafaring men like Bill. Having sent a note to his room, Alice waited in the lobby, pleased with the unstarched, unbuttoned ambience of the place compared to the highly-starched, buttoned-up dignity of such hostelries as the Grand, and thinking it sadly indicative of her recent conventional life that she'd never been there before.

Bill hurried over to her; a dinner jacket of midnight-blue velvet was creased across his bulky middle, against which he

443

clutched a small packet. 'Mrs. Grant—a real pleasure. But I'm sorry you had to come in search of your jade.' He held out the packet. 'I was planning to bring it over, but I've been unexpectedly busy and. . . .'

'Please don't worry, Mr. Risley. I'm glad to have it of course, but I didn't come on that account really. Let's sit over here,' she indicated a secluded corner where she could quietly explain Frank's new difficulty.

'Oh but I am sorry, a damaged baby—it will be a great strain.'

'It will indeed and I've told Frank he shouldn't on any account leave his wife alone for a while.'

'He's told you about our proposed venture then?' He signalled a waiter. 'A glass of wine, Mrs. Grant?'

'Thank you. Your venture—yes. And I'm so pleased that it's actually something positive to help the Chinese. I feel myself a part of this country in so many ways, you know, and it's dreadful how people here are just sitting back and wringing their hands. The provincial mandarins blame the central government, the government blames the army, and nothing goes forward. Yet the poor men fighting in Korea are so badly equipped. It's shameful.'

'It is, Mrs. Grant, and I'd sure like to see the Chinks beat the Japs myself. Though I must admit to a more pressing reason for taking this hot little load to Port Arthur—they call it cash, taels, dollars, dimes, and so on.'

'Quite. But you're sure you'll get it?'

'Ah, that's the rub. The "topside men" and I don't really trust each other. So it's half pay before leaving, half on delivery. But I guess they might try a bit of funny stuff at the other end, especially as I don't speak the lingo. That's why I asked Frank . . . still, if he can't come, there it is,' he sighed, signed a chit for the wine. 'Your good health, Mrs. Grant. Trade prospers, I hope? Now, about the jade . . .'

She took a long drink and said, 'Before we come to that, Mr. Risley, may I make a suggestion? As Frank can't, or certainly shouldn't leave Shanghai just now, will you take me with you instead? I have a command of the "lingo" just as good as his, and a sound business head as you know. I lived in Port Arthur years ago, so I'm familiar with it and would love to look up my old haunts, the people I knew there.'

'You? But Mrs. Grant, this really isn't any sort of job for a lady.'

'When people say that about my business dealings, Mr. Risley, my reply is that I'm not a lady but the director of Grant & Greenwood. And in that capacity I can go with you.'

He looked doubtful. 'Well, I don't know, ma'am—we might even run into what you Brits call a "spot of martial effervescence" before we're through.'

'Oh? Why should we? Hostilities are still confined to Korea surely?'

'Just about—but one never knows.'

'I would then take the share of the profits you were offering Frank and we'll divide them. So I'll benefit, he'll benefit, and so will Peachy because he'll stay with her, as he ought. And we'll be helping the Chinese cause into the bargain!'

She made it sound so cut, dried, and perfect that he looked a little hunted.

'But what about commitments here, Mrs. Grant? Your business and . . .?'

'Frankly I'm bored stiff with the frivolities of Shanghai, Mr. Risley. It truly is a national crisis, but no one here gives a fig, which is typical. I've been longing desperately to get away, do something to help—and now this. After all, it's only as far as Port Arthur, all perfectly straightforward. And when you sail for America, I'll give myself a little holiday in Chefoo across the Gulf before returning here.'

They considered each other: she deciding that she could, and would, trust him: he warming to the idea of having an attractive, competent young woman aboard the *Dolphin*.

'It's fixed then,' her words were half statement, half question.

'Well . . . er . . . what about Frank? How does he take to this?'

'He doesn't know yet, but I agreed to help him through his present difficulty, and this is my way of doing it. He'll have to agree.'

And Frank, though extremely put out by Alice's 'solution,' finally did agree; as did Bill, who concluded that he'd never met a little English lady with so much Yankee get-up-and-go, and that, had he been twenty years younger, he could have taken to her in a big way.

On a brilliant autumn day, the *Dolphin*, its warlike cargo stowed belowdecks, steamed away northwards. To ensure a safe passage the crew lit incense sticks and threw into the water handfuls of rice and written messages that read, 'May the sea never wash over this vessel.' Alice, standing on the top

445

deck, added her own propitiatory offering of roasted peanuts. The men smiled up at her, approving.

Her departure had been made easy because both Robert and Mary happened to be away, the former on an upcountry snipe-shoot, the latter visiting her 'benighted' daughter Lilian in Shansi. So Alice had simply left a note saying she'd gone for a holiday and would be away about a month. When taking a last look round her Fairlawns bedroom however, she suddenly wondered if she'd ever return. The golden sun shone on a polished blackwood table by the window, a bowl of chrysanthemums in its centre, and she stood helpless, the room's familiar charm tugging at her. In spite of the mild weather she stuffed into a last-minute bag the sable-lined winter jacket she'd bought in Mukden, along with her favourite book of Li Po. Instinctively she was preparing for a real journey and later wished she'd trusted that instinct further.

On that first day out, all the omens were auspicious. Sun glinted along sea-lanes that were busy with coastal barges and ramshackle fishing junks with mat-sails, hemp-rope rigging and huge wooden anchors. On their high decks lines of clothes flapped, hens clucked, potted plants grew and children played fearlessly, for they and their parents knew no other homes. To starboard, the *Dolphin* passed a liner of the Messageries Maritime Company; lilting music wafted from it and Alice could see passengers playing deck games, lounging on striped chairs. It seemed impossible to believe that a war was in progress a few hundred miles away—or indeed anywhere in the whole bright and beautiful world.

Alice had been allotted a single cabin on the main deck; its brass fittings and wood-panelled walls gleamed in the dappled light through the porthole. Starched towels on a rail and a lantern on a chain swayed to the ship's motion and the slap of waves outside attuned to the nearer cheery rhythms of shipboard routine—the bells of the watch, the slosh of deck-swillers, men whistling and shouting as they worked. The *Dolphin*'s chief mate, to whom Alice was introduced that evening, was one Matthew Chubb, a spindly, sandy-haired New Englander who, like many of his calling, was habitually taciturn, with a gaze that seemed always reaching over the nearer prospect in favour of some distant, more satisfying horizon. Strolling with Bill around Rangoon recently, Chubb's gaze had unaccountably focused on a balding, ancient-looking monkey wearing a

446

red-beaded cap which was jigging sadly along a bamboo rod at the command of its owner. Chubb had bought the animal, removed its cap and it now sat on his shoulder all day with a newly acquired air of contented dignity.

'Meet Wilbur,' Chubb said. Alice took a peanut from her bag and Wilbur took it daintily from her.

'He'll like you for that. Want to see the ship?' She nodded and he took her on a conducted tour—to the wheel-room, the chart-room where code and log books, nautical maps and barometrical readings seemed to reveal all possible mysteries and hazards of the surrounding waters, and the engine-room, where gauges hissed, oiled cylinders, rods and discs moved purposefully and a large dial proclaimed in black letters the range of possible action: Ahead, Astern, Slow, Half, Stand-By, Full.

'It seems a very ship-shape ship, Mr. Chubb, you must be proud of her,' Alice smiled up at him.

'She's got a bit of a sick boiler that the Chinks can't seem to cure. But she'll do, providing the weather holds.'

'Well it looks fine enough at the moment.'

He shrugged laconically, 'You can never tell with weather, ma'am.'

As the only woman aboard, Alice was mightily cossetted; her deck-chair and footstool were placed under an awning's shade the next morning and a white-uniformed steward brought beef broth.

'Why this is simply heavenly!' she greeted Bill as he came down from the bridge. 'So much more luxurious than your common P & O I'll warrant!'

He grinned. 'And a sight more peaceful. Oh, the razzle-dazzle that goes on aboard those monsters of the deep. As for the stuck-up officers with shiny buttons who do nothing but drink and dance with the ladies and call themselves seafarers—huh!' He bit a cheroot's end and spat it overboard.

'You've been a seafarer all your life, Bill?'

'Yep, and a good life it is for a man—always on the move, on the alert. Gives you something of a philosophical turn too as the years go by. So many nights spent alone in the open looking at the stars and listening to the wind.'

'I think I'd have liked it if I'd been a man, but it's not really possible for a woman—so I aim to be a philosophical landlubber.'

'And what's your philosophy, young lady?' He drew up

447

another chair that creaked mightily as he settled into it.

She shrugged, 'Oh, bits and bobs of various kinds. Buddhism, Christianity, Confucianism, Utilitarianism—a proper old ragbag, that's my trouble. I stayed in a Buddhist monastery for several months once and perhaps that's the nearest I've yet come to the "attainment of philosophical serenity." ' She chuckled at herself. 'But I decided I wasn't cut out to be a nun.'

'I'm sure you're not, little lady.'

'So I suppose all I really believe in is the need for a measure of individual freedom to do the best one can—and that's hard enough for me usually. But out here, sailing over the waves, it seems quite simple, doesn't it? Oh, I *am* glad I came, Bill . . .' She leaned back, eyes closed, raising her face to the benison of warm sun and sparkling breeze. He watched her, liking what he saw and that she'd so naturally called him 'Bill' today for the first time. She was a woman of unusual character, he realised; but he would not easily fathom her; moreover, she had no wish, just then, to have further depths plumbed.

The next day the sportive breeze dropped and the air was sultry, without sparkle; a blurred sun spread flat, brassy light over water that moved in strange, sluggish, heavy lumps. Coming on watch after breakfast, Matthew Chubb stared intently at everything in sight—the odd patches of mist in the distance, the increasing cross-swell, above all at the chart-room barometer that had fallen to an astonishing degree.

'Mucky stuff about somewhere, Wilbur my boy,' he murmured. 'But where exactly?'

'Ouf, ouf,' the animal replied sympathetically, pulling Chubb's freckled ear.

A seaman of long experience, Chubb seldom referred to the dusty volumes on matters meteorological and maritime ranged on the lower shelf, but now he pulled out the *Book of Rules for Storms* and began to read. He learned that once a ship's master has discovered where he is in relation to an approaching storm, he can take evasive action, bearing in mind that 'to be caught between the land and an advancing typhoon may be dangerous enough to satisfy the most adventurous.' If a landfall could only be made at such hazard, it was wiser to head into the weather and 'get behind it'—having ascertained from readings of wind, wave, and sky where it was coming from. But, on that morning, there was no wind, the sky bore no sign except its ominous all-over grey-gold and there were no waves, only the swells from the south-east that were mounting fast, so that, when Chubb threw down the book in disgust, it slid slowly away to the furthest wall, then back past his feet.

'Never quite seen the likes of it, Wilbur,' Chubb said, wondering how they could 'get behind' weather they couldn't find.

Meanwhile, Alice's stomach, that had never felt the likes of it, began to churn sickeningly as the vessel rose and dipped higher and lower with every passing hour. She lay on her bunk, clinging to its edge, and fell into a nauseous, rolling doze, from which she was jolted by a particularly violent lurch that nearly threw her on the cabin floor. Outside, sailors, tripping with little steps as the decks fell away from them, and climbing sturdily up the same boards a minute later, were double-lashing the boats and winches, battening the hatches, securing all moveable gear. In the engine-room where the dial pointed to 'Full' and the thermometer registered nearly a hundred degrees, sweaty-black stokers shovelled anthracite into the furnaces.

There was a knock on Alice's door and Chubb called, 'How are you faring, Mrs. Grant?'

'Not too bad,' she tried to sound seaworthy.

'Wonder if you'd do me a favour? Keep Wilbur down with you for a while.'

'Yes, of course,' she opened the door, hoping she looked less pale than she felt.

'We're in for a few willywhaws I fear, ma'am.'

'Willy what, Mr. Chubb?'

'Whaws—squalls, you might say. Nothing to worry about, but could be rough for Wilbur on the bridge.'

'Will it last long, do you think?'

'Hard to say just what's happening. We're heading for the nearest sizeable harbour on the Shantung coast. Only about two hours' steaming with luck.'

'But if we're making for land it must be serious. It's a typhoon coming, isn't it? I've seen the sky and sea look like this before— only I've been on land and thanked heaven for it,' she grinned weakly.

'Ah, yes . . . well, a typhoon. But we're outmanoeuvring it, getting behind it, you might say. Only it means full steam ahead, which will be a bit rough going.'

The cabin lurched sharply at that moment, Wilbur squealed in panic and dug his nail deep into Chubb's shoulder, while Alice, losing balance, banged her head against the bunk.

'Damn!' they both exclaimed and Chubb smiled warmly at her for the first time since they'd met. 'Sorry about this, ma'am. Best thing is just sit tight and don't worry. We'll make a landfall before dark.' He hurried off, leaving Wilbur and Alice clinging to the bunk, staring sombrely at each other.

Had the *Dolphin* been able to maintain its full steam ahead, landfall would have been made, but, in the middle of the afternoon, the second engineer saw the steam-gauge falling despite the stokers' heroic efforts. The sickness of the boiler had considerably worsened. Speed was reduced to eight knots and, as lustreless-olive twilight fell, the Shantung coast was still distant. Low, dark cloudbanks were humped against the horizon and the wind was coming up fast from the south-east between ship and land. At first it seemed a blessed relief—gushes of damp air that came puffing through the ventilators cooling the sweat-soaked skins of the stokers.

Sniffing the freshness, Alice ventured into the open air where she felt a little better, and, clinging to the deck-rail, watched the vessel tip and reel against the skyline. As lights began to flicker atop the masts, in the wheel-house and bridge, a roaring wind suddenly sprang like a panther out of the darkening sky, and solid, black, foam-crested cliffs of water began rearing high above the funnels. As waves cascaded in torrents over the low decks, Alice realised she was screaming, though she couldn't hear the sound, for rain, wind and sea together drove hard into her face, obliterating all else. Now the ship began plunging, leaping and jerking in a series of headers from crest to trough, behaving less like a dolphin than some leashed and terrified land-creature. Water poured into its every crevice, soaking her to the skin as it passed, while the tearing gale threatened to wrench her apart and toss her overboard in separate pieces. Too frightened to move, she clung on to the rail till she saw Bill careening towards her with a lantern.

Grabbing her arm, he half pulled, half threw her into the comparative safety of the cabinway, 'Stay in there for God's sake, you little fool!' he yelled, fighting mightily with the door to shut and bolt it from the outside.

Miserably she lurched back to her cabin where Wilbur was gibbering in a corner. At the sight of her he began to screech in angry panic, obviously blaming her for the whole nasty situation.

'Shut up, Wilbur,' she gasped crossly, 'it's not my fault.'

450

He blinked at her morosely, both of them soon battered into silence by the outside clamour of crashing waves, deeply roaring wind, of loosened objects clattering overhead, bilge water thudding below and rain slashing violently against the porthole. Towards the end of that dreadful night Chubb burst into the cabin, his oilskins streaming, face and eyes red and puffy from the weather's onslaught.

'Don't worry,' he roared, as he'd been roaring at everyone for hours. 'We're only on the fringes, and the wind's veering right round so we reckon the eye's passing.'

Alice groaned. 'Lord save us, if this is only a fringe, I'd certainly hate to be in a centre.'

'How's Wilbur?' Chubb held out his arm and the monkey took a flying leap at him, landing on his slippery oilskins and slithering with a screech to the ground. They both laughed at his woebegone expression, and Alice, who had spent the last few hours fearing she might never laugh again, continued giggling hysterically with the idea that she might survive after all.

Survive they did, but at considerable cost, as Bill and Chubb realised when, in the light of a pallid dawn, they surveyed the scene. Huge grey waves still curled and peaked angrily on every horizon, and the *Dolphin* was wallowing low and slow among them. Its formerly ship-shape decks were strewn with debris—ragged tarpaulins, shredded ropes, loose gratings, hunks of seaweed, broken covers and fittings, a few bedraggled, broken-backed seabirds. One boat was staved in, doors and shutters splintered, but the really serious damage was below decks, where two pumps were choked and the sick boiler was totally out of action.

Late that afternoon the battered vessel with its exhausted crew slipped past several smugly-anchored fishing-junks into the harbour of Antungwei on the Shantung coast. Alice insisted on going ashore in the first boat and, in a burst of joyous relief as her feet scrunched satisfyingly on the shingled beach, felt all their troubles were over. In the end, however, their enforced stay at Antungwei proved irksome and tedious. Pompous officials were summoned and poked about the cargo asking suspicious questions, their scribes writing down every answer in triplicate. Curious locals gathered to look at the strange barbarians and their ship, but few of them were capable or willing to work on its repairs. While Bill and Chubb fumed impatiently at the incompetent backwardness of the rural Chinese, Alice remained calm, enjoying her role as interpreter-go-between and pleased to find her services invaluable.

'You must cultivate a little more philosophy, Bill,' she reproved her companion one afternoon as he sat on the stone jetty scowling at the desultory activity of the hired men. 'I remember your saying that, in your mellow years, you could appreciate the Chinese virtue of "slow-movingness."'

'Huh, that's as may be in the general way of things. But right here and now and in the particular, I'd like to stick . . .' he swallowed the rest in deference to her sex, and she left him to glower, comforting him with the thought that they were bound to be away before Christmas.

It did not take that long, but the season was certainly well advanced before the *Dolphin* was fully seaworthy again. Little news had reached the backwaters of Antungwei about the progress of hostilities in the north, but the surrounding coasts remained quiet enough and, on the day they sailed, Bill predicted that, with a little overdue luck, they would reach their destination in three days.

This time the weather was kind, and on 19 November the *Dolphin* nosed slowly into Port Arthur's West Port, the natural harbour that was cluttered with junks and provision boats, but not a single man-of-war. Alice peered ahead eagerly looking for landmarks but found scarcely any, for Port Arthur had grown greatly in size and population since she'd left twelve years before. A new dock basin had been built to the east of the natural harbour on the narrow spit of land called Tiger's Tail; there were wharves, repair sheds, steam-cranes and a special dock for torpedo boats. The deep-water channel near the harbour entrance was defended now by torpedoes and submarine mines, the latter, Bill remarked, so wrongly laid that their sinister humps showed above the water.

The land defences looked much more formidable: twenty-two military forts were perched along the range of surrounding hills with such un-military names as Cockscomb, Golden, Chair, Two-Dragon, Pine Tree. Redoubts, rifle pits and trenches had been made around them and a number of quick-firing Krupp guns stood inside. Coloured banners patterned with rampant dragons flew boldly from the forts' towers and Alice, seeing them, felt her spirits lift with pride, and a conviction that the invaders would surely be beaten back in no time. Bill however was much less optimistic.

'God save us, are these fellows supposed to be soldiers?' he muttered as they came ashore and left the quay escorted by two yamen guards.

Troops of men were milling about dressed in padded tunics, baggy trousers and cloth boots soled with quilted rag. Some were equipped with Mausers and Remingtons, but more carried old-fashioned muzzle-loading muskets or one-inch-calibre, locally made guns. Others were armed with staves, bayonets, rusty knives, and a few bore nothing more terrible than painted poles to which bright singing birds were tethered. They had been pressed into service from many provinces, given little training in the use of arms or the harsh disciplines of the battlefield. So they were buying up supplies of fruit, tobacco, crude opium, joking roughly with local shopkeepers, and generally behaving, as Bill said, more like yokels than soldiers.

All this did not bode well for the town's defences, nor did what they saw next. Threading through a line of commissary mule-carts, they rounded a corner into an open space where crude shelters had been put up for the common soldiery. Gallows had been erected nearby and from them swung the naked corpses of two Japanese soldiers captured during earlier fighting in the Liaotung Peninsula. They had been hideously disembowelled, eyes gouged out and throats cut; a gaggle of children were pelting the bloody remains with stones and laughing. Alice cried out in horror and Bill pulled her back.

'Jeessuus—don't look. Here, come this way.'

As they hurried off, the children threw a few stones at their backs, shouting, 'Dog-faced foreign devils, kill 'em all.'

After a while they paused for breath and Alice knuckled her eyes to wipe out the ghastly sight. 'Oh Bill, how dreadful. How terribly cruel.'

'Yeah, it's a barbarous business. I never reckoned on coming to anything like that right in the town.' He drew a harsh breath. 'Do you know anywhere we can get a drink and sit down after that little eyeful?'

'I'll ask the guards to take us to Epimoff's first, if it still exists. Used to be the only foreign hotel in town and they served delicious vodka cocktails.'

'Oh boy, could I do with . . . hey, tell those guards that's where we're going.'

After some argument, the guards led them to the old port on the west of the harbour and, 'There it is!' Alice shouted with relief, for Epimoff's was not only standing but, unlike most of Port Arthur, looked about the same. This, however, was an illusion, for the cosy old-fashioned saloon was crowded with army officers talking loudly or slumped in exhaustion before cups of rice-wine. Heads turned in surprise at their entrance, but luckily Alice immediately spotted Olga, Madame Epimoff's daughter, behind the bar. Her face was heavily rouged to conceal deeper wrinkles, her form encased in larger measures of bright red silk, but she was unmistakably Olga.

She shouted over to them, 'Good Lord no! You here?'

'You remember me then?' Alice shouldered to the bar.

'Of course, you used to come with Felix Fauré, the poor lamb was killed, no? Many years ago, but what on earth are you . . .?'

'I'll explain. Olga, this is my friend, Bill Risley from Chicago.'

'And praying to the Almighty I'll get back there in one piece some day. . . . My pleasure, madam. Our most urgent need is for two double vodka cocktails for which Alice tells me you are renowned.'

'No melon juice anymore. But vodka yes, with bitters?'

Some officers politely vacated a table and Olga joined them, happy at the sight of friendly white faces.

'But the crowd who used to be here—merchants, sea-captains. Where is everybody?' Alice looked around uneasily, the cut-glass lamps were cracked, the once-immaculate cloths messy.

'Oh they all ran off as soon as Jap patrol boats started appearing. Chin-chou and the forts on that narrow neck of land to the north are already in Jap hands you know. We're caught like cats in a bag here. It's no place to be if you value your skins.'

'And we do, madam, we do. So our stay will be pretty damn short—all being well.' Bill drained his glass. 'One more, then we must go along to the big yellow chiefs and get things moving.'

He explained the reason for their unlikely presence and Alice concluded, 'So if it hadn't been for that blessed typhoon we'd have been safely in and out of here three weeks ago.'

'Act of God,' Olga said lugubriously.

'The Wrath of God more like,' Alice shuddered. 'One of the most terrifying experiences of my life. I don't know who was more frightened—me or Chubb's monkey Wilbur. We just clung there gibbering at each other!'

Olga drained her glass. 'I've gotta go serve all these Chinks drinks. Ma would turn in her grave if she could see Epimoff's cluttered up with this riff-raff.'

'So she's . . .?'

'Two years ago. Just as well. Things have got worse ever since. The new dock basin opened and now we've men-of-war around all the time. There's a garrison of some 20,000 Chinese here now who don't know one end of a gun from the other, and the Japs limbering up for the attack. So you'd better get away smartish.' She stood up.

'And you?' Alice wondered if Olga had any life outside this hotel bar, where she'd always seemed a permanent fixture.

'Oh, I stay to the bitter end. Nowhere else to go. As long as the Chinese hold the forts I'm all for the Imperial Dragon, come the Japs I'll bow to the Rising Sun. That's the way we Epimoffs have always survived.' She glared at them defiantly, and Bill patted her silky buttocks.

'Wise woman, them's my sentiments exactly.'

'Well count me out. I'm not a turncoat,' Alice said firmly, as she rose.

'Let's hope it doesn't come to that, Alice. Madame Epimoff, could you put us up for tonight after we've seen the men at H.Q.? It would be a nice change from bunks on the *Dolphin*.'

Olga looked sly. 'Separate rooms?'

'Yes,' said Alice firmly, adding, 'What about Chubb? Wouldn't he like a shore-break too?'

'I've only two rooms free, but he can doss down in a cupboard or somewhere if he likes. This place has gone to the dogs, what's one more fella in a cupboard?' She shrugged her large white shoulders dispiritedly as she returned behind the bar, the brief pleasure of their unexpected arrival overlaid again by the worry and muddle of the present.

At the Chinese military headquarters near the parade ground to which Alice and Bill were then conducted, confusion reigned and no one seemed to know anything about their mission. Eventually, a meeting with a high-ranking officer was arranged for the next morning and they retreated in low spirits, first to the *Dolphin* and then, accompanied by Chubb, back to Epimoff's.

'I've heard the Chinks are slaughtering every prisoner they bring in,' Chubb said worriedly as they sipped watery soup that bore no hint of the nourishing borscht of earlier days. 'If the Japs get in here and see what's been going on there'll be a blood bath.'

He called for a bottle of vodka. As the evening wore on more officers arrived, each newcomer greeted with soldierly bravado, swelling their sense of security in numbers. By the arrival of the second bottle, Alice was overcome with sentiment for the good old days, when, she told them, Epimoff's was secure, quiet, clean; she fondly recalled the old father-in-law and the Russian doctor playing chess by the stove, Olga playing French chansons on the piano.

'Come, sing us a good Yankee song,' Chubb pulled Olga on his knee and plied her with vodka till she sang 'Wait till the clouds roll by, Jennie' in a melancholy quaver that cheered no one. Then Bill fell asleep with his head on the table and Alice retreated to her bedroom, her head swimming.

She drew back the dusty damask curtains and leaned her forehead against the cold glass. Groups of soldiers were wandering about shouting and scuffling together, their weapons gleaming in the light of the hotel's lanterns. It seemed incredible that she was still in the same country as Shanghai, where the races would be in full swing, late chrysanthemums glowing in orderly rows round trim lawns. She thought again of her early visits to Epimoff's when Olga had seemed fascinating, sophisticated, a little wicked. On those hills behind the town now bristling with fortifications, she, Will and Isabel had gone for picnics, she and Lin Fu-wei had lain together in the summer grasses.

A clatter of arms and shouts recalled her to the present; a rifle fired twice, someone screamed. Had her life come to its full circle already and was she doomed to die here, in the town where she'd first known the passionate agonies of love and loss? She shivered, drew the curtains and retired to bed, wishing for a miracle—that the young Lin she'd once known would materialise beside her, would hug and love her, holding at bay the fears of the night and the morrow.

And the next day did indeed bring trouble. During the morning, three soldiers escorted them back to the military headquarters where they were shown into the presence of Officer Chang-shun. After some preamble, Alice, as interpreter, had to explain to Bill and Chubb that Chang-shun most deeply regretted his inability to pay in full for delivery of the *Dolphin's* precious cargo, because the military coffers were empty. Bill stormed and ranted, finally jammed his hat back on his head, swearing that he'd set sail again with the guns aboard and get a decent price for them in California. It would have been a rash attempt in the circumstances; certainly it was a rash statement. Alice had much cause to regret that, in the heat of the moment, she defiantly passed it on to Chang-shun, whose eyes closed briefly as he heard. Then he rose, bowing stiffly, and Bill flung out, describing as he went the nature of the Sons of Han in words that Alice wisely didn't translate.

Overtaken so suddenly and completely by the muddle of war, they huddled against a wall beside the parade ground to decide on the best course of action. It was raining; mule carts loaded with provisions, animal fodder and ammunition were trundling off to the hill forts; the whole area was one vast temporary bivouack for arriving soldiers.

'I tell you—we sure gotta get out of this rat trap pretty dam' fast.' Chubb stuck his hands deep in his serge jacket. 'Look at those stupid bastards over there—I wouldn't give a monkey's paw for their chances.'

He pointed to some soldiers gathered round a pile of cartridges of varying sorts and sizes which they were trying to fit into their equally ill-assorted weapons, and throwing the unsuitable ones back on the heap. Bill watched thoughtfully, then said, 'All right—we head back to Chefoo and fight it out with the top brass there, where at least we'll be safe. Let's go pack our bags and then get aboard. We'll stay on the alert tonight and sail at dawn.'

Returning disconsolately to Epimoff's, they shared a farewell vodka with Olga, then went by hired cart to the west harbour. As they rounded the corner to the quay, an icy rain-filled wind blew at them from the choppy sea where junk masts were wildly bobbing, where the sturdier funnels of the *Dolphin* were not visible. Alice felt a sickening thump of terror.

'It's gone—oh my God, she's not there!'

'The bleeding crooks! Bugger your mother-fucking

Celestials—the bastards!' Bill bellowed.

'Now we're really in the shit,' Chubb muttered. 'And oh Lord, what about my poor Wilbur? They'll cut off the top of his head and eat his brains for supper.'

'No—they only do that in the South and not to Wilbur's kind,' Alice reassured him, as angry and worried, they hurried back towards military headquarters. But it was late evening before they were granted another audience with the implacable Chang-shun, who very deeply regretted that the exigencies of the time had forced him to take temporary possession of the vessel in order to transport back to Port Arthur a detachment of infantry stranded near Korea. Also, he pointed out, the present shortage of arms was so acute, that it would have been foolish indeed to permit Mr. Risley to remove his cargo to San Francisco as he'd threatened. He appreciated that his action might cause some inconvenience to the honourable foreigners, but he could assure them that the *Dolphin* would soon return. In the meantime, he offered them the sum of two hundred taels so they could enjoy the amenities of the place until the Celestial Army had driven every dwarf-Jap dog off the Liaotung Peninsula and into the sea, which he promised, would be accomplished in a matter of days. Finally he suggested that, the town being in something of a turmoil, it might be safer if they spent the night in the barracks. And now he must be excused, for many urgent matters awaited his attention.

Faced with the utter collapse of their plans and the considerable hazards of their situation, Bill and Chubb were suddenly filled with reckless, mindless exhilaration. They'd been in some pretty tight spots before, they assured each other, life had had its ups and downs and probably would again. Having no choice, they might as well buy some booze, sit back and enjoy the spectacle of this oriental scrap from as safe a distance as possible. From a prison-like room in the barracks, watching the confused preparations of the Imperial Army in the parade ground, they were willing to wager Alice ten to one that, within a week, the Japs would be marching there. But Alice couldn't enter into the spirit of their mood; all her instincts repudiated the martial excitement that gripped the town that night. Battle to her meant blood, death, suffering, and the prospect frightened her. Moreover, she was feeling increasingly feverish. She rolled herself miserably into a dirty quilt and fell into troubled slumber.

About 7:30 that next morning, 21 November, Alice woke, as did most of Port Arthur's inhabitants, to the distant roar of artillery fire. The sound came from the First Infantry Division of the Japanese Second Army led by Marshal Oyama, who had spent the previous two nights stealthily advancing over difficult terrain to position their field guns within range of the town. Within the hour the first *banzais* of the Japanese soldiers rang through the air as they scrambled up to the outlying forts on Chair Hill which they captured practically unopposed, and from which they could fire down on other forts.

After their meagre breakfast, Bill prowled about restlessly.

'I'm not staying here listening to the fireworks. Let's go and see the show, Chubb. You'd better stay here, Alice.'

'If you're going, so am I.' She pulled the fur-jacket from her bag.

'But you say you don't feel well.'

'No. But I'll feel worse staying here alone listening to the Jap guns getting closer.'

'Ah, but the impregnable forces of the Celestial Dragon will soon be throwing them into the sea, remember,' he teased, not taking her loyalty to the Chinese too seriously.

She frowned anxiously. 'Oh, I pray so.'

'Well, let's go see who's winning,' Chubb urged them out.

The shops near the parade ground were all shuttered; Chinese militia were trotting about on rough-haired ponies; anxious citizens stood in knots listening to the distant battle sounds. The men decided the safest vantage point was a chalky hill-top just beyond the town boundary but within the protecting perimeter of the inner forts. They scrambled up, Alice lagging behind, feeling weak and scared.

From its summit they could see the East Port to the right, the sea beyond dotted with Japanese warships. In the absence of an enemy the ships were reduced to taking pot-shots at the coastal defences. On their left were the north-west fortifications from which Chinese troops were blasting away with their old-fashioned mortars. The air pulsed with the roar and flash of cannon, scream of shells, the occasional crack of a single rifle. They had scarcely settled themselves between two sheltering rocks when a terrific blast of flame and thunder shook the whole hillside as the large fort on Pine Tree Hill was blown skywards by shells that had ignited its magazine. When the smoke and rubble cleared, they could see men and ponies fleeing down the distant slopes.

'Look at 'em, running like weevils from a biscuit,' Chubb jeered. 'There they go, the brave Sons of Han, their pigtails flying behind them. "Sing *lietea*, my sly John Chinaman, No fightee, my coward John Chinaman".'

'But you'd run away in their shoes,' Alice protested. 'Poor fellows, they haven't got the right weapons, haven't been properly trained.' She buried her head in her hands, longing to run away from the dreadful scene. Yet she hated to show any cowardice of her own, so she clenched her fists, determined to sit it out a while longer. This proved increasingly harrowing, for the battle of Port Arthur was fast turning into a rout.

Two Dragon Hill fell next to the men of General Hasegawa's brigade, and from then on the Japanese forces, who by noon had accomplished more than their commanders had considered possible even in two days' fighting, pushed ahead with ruthless efficiency. While the Chinese sounded pitiful gongs and roared defiance as they formed behind their colourful banners in traditional medieval fashion, their enemies advanced quietly, with only a company officer's whistle or an occasional shrill *banzai* to be heard above the tumult of the guns. Their howitzers easily picked off the colourful standard bearers, and sharp-shooters made short work of two Chinese commanders on caparisoned white horses who tried to rally their men for a stand.

Soon, from the valleys between the hills, where grey gunsmoke had settled thickly, dark columns of infantry, bayonets gleaming, came steadily towards the beleaguered town, supported by mortar fire. The rifle-pit trenches on the hill nearest the three spectators that had earlier been empty began to fill with a rabble of Chinese infantry firing in disorderly fashion at the fast-approaching enemy.

'We must go—oh please let's go. I can't bear anymore,' Alice tugged Bill's sleeve at last.

'Yeah—reckon we better make ourselves scarce. It's getting too hot for comfort.' He glanced at her white face. 'Don't be frightened. These Japs are proper fighting men who know the rules. They won't harm us neutrals.' She shuddered away from him, drew her jacket round her and went scrambling down the hill in panic.

Earlier that afternoon the Japanese Mixed Brigade under the command of a sour-faced martinet called Lieutenant-General Yamagi, nicknamed the Dragon-Eyed, had entered Port Arthur to the north-west. Stuck on poles above the town gate were the bloody heads of some of their former comrades; the mutilated remains of others were spattered on the road. Filled with demoniac rage, the invaders surged madly up to the coastal fort on Golden Hill, one of the last still in Chinese hands, and seized it in a single furious thrust. By the time Alice and her companions reached the town, bands of Chinese soldiers were in full flight from every captured fort, tearing off their uniforms as they ran and leaving a trail of sword belts, cartridge boxes and powder pouches behind them.

'We'll make for the parade ground barracks,' Bill yelled above the din, thinking they would find an officer of the victorious forces there to whom they could commit themselves for protection.

As they struggled through the oncoming tide of fugitives, roars, screams and shots rang out ever more loudly until, turning into a narrow street, they saw ahead a band of Japanese soldiers pressing down on a panic-stricken Chinese throng. For a moment, Alice just stared, having never before seen Japanese soldiers at close quarters. They wore western-style military uniforms with high collars, high-buttoned boots, high-peaked caps fastened with straps under the chin. Armed with bayonets, cartridge belts, well-oiled weaponry, they looked like machines made specifically for slaughter compared to the ragged, ill-equipped Chinese. They were yelling wildly and firing indiscriminately at everyone in sight and, to make sure, hacking to pieces the bodies that were falling in heaps before them. The blades with which they were cutting swathes through the helpless citizens were clotted with blood, their uniforms were spattered with it. Clearly they were in no mood to distinguish among their victims, and the three of them fled with one accord down an alleyway.

'Let's get back to Epimoff's, surely they won't attack a foreign hotel,' Alice gasped. 'Oh, the butchers, oh Bill, Bill, it's a bloody massacre!'

He nodded grimly. 'Jesus, Alice, I never dreamed we'd get into this mess, I really didn't.'

'I'm not blaming you, Bill, but let's get away from those Japs, for God's sake. It's hell.'

They crept away from the ghastly grunts and shrieks of murderers and murdered. Night had now fallen and street lanterns bobbed in the cold wind, their incongruously festive rays shining on piles of hacked corpses. Alice, trying to keep up with the two men, stumbled over a long object and fell on a spongy pile. She jumped up instantly, feeling the warm blood of a legless corpse on her hands, seeing the leg over which she'd tripped.

'Oh help . . . please help me . . .'

The men ran back and grabbed her arms. 'Keep going, sweetheart, not much further.'

What kept Alice's aching limbs moving through the ghoulish nightmare of that night was the feverish fantasy that if only she could push open the glass door of Epimoff's saloon, she'd find everything as it had been twelve years before—the stove crackling merrily, the piano tinkling. Round a corner near the harbour, however, yet more horrors waited. The Japanese had driven numbers of Chinese soldiers into the water and were firing on them as they splashed about. Some, streaming with blood and mud, kept trying to struggle back on land, where the crazed victors cut them to pieces. Retreating hastily, they threaded through back streets again and eventually reached Epimoff's, which was still intact, a light glowing through its glass door. Alice rushed recklessly in and shrieked. Olga lay slumped face upwards across the bar. Her throat had been cut and a gaping wound slashed her from breast to bowels; the blood seeped red-black over her parrot-red dress. From atop the carved posts at each end of the counter glared the dripping sightless heads of the cook and barman respectively.

'Christ almighty! Oh the fucking bastards.' Bill shouted into Alice's screams of agony. He shook her shoulders and half carried her upstairs to the bedrooms.

The place had been relentlessly looted; curtains slashed, glass ground underfoot, furniture smashed. But amid all the chaos Chubb unearthed from a cupboard two bottles of vodka, jars of olives and caviar that the wreckers had overlooked. With shaking fingers Bill opened a bottle, drank deeply, handed it to Alice who crouched gibbering in a corner, her fists in her eyes.

462

'Here, drink this.'

'Oh, poor, poor Olga . . . Oh Bill, they'll get us next. They're killing everyone. Oh, I'm frightened and I feel so ill.'

He held the liquid to her lips and she drank obediently.

'It's a bloody slaughterhouse, never seen anything like it.'

Chubb took the bottle. 'What the fuck are the Jap officers doing allowing this massacre? We'd better sit tight here till morning, Bill. Chances are they've done their worst here and won't come back.'

The men opened the jars and chewed silently, the sophisticated flavours at odd variance with the surrounding barbarism. Bill held out a jar to Alice.

'I can't eat anything,' she choked, the liquor churning violently inside her. She buried her head in her arms, seeing only the pool of entwined entrails splashed across the bar below. Nausea overcame her and she staggered away to vomit in the nearest wash-bowl. Eventually the sounds of her retching lessened and the town quietened as the Japanese command managed to recall their maddened soldiery to the just-captured forts, leaving the citizens of Port Arthur to count their dead. Feeling increasingly ill, Alice sank into blessed oblivion on the floor, while the two men drank themselves into a miserable stupor.

Before they awoke the next day the flags of the Rising Sun had been raised over most of the hill forts and detachments of Japanese had assembled on the parade ground shouting 'Long Live the Emperor Meiji.' Within a day the invaders had gained possession of the most important strategic naval base in the Far East, and neither victors nor vanquished could quite believe in the rapidity of it all.

Bill, the first to wake, was looking out of the window when a harmless local family—father, mother, child—came skulking cautiously past from doorway to doorway. They disappeared from sight, only to come fleeing back a few minutes later pursued by three Japanese soldiers. They were cut to pieces outside the hotel; Bill saw their arms reach skyward as they tumbled to the earth. Chubb woke and Bill passed him a jar.

'Caviar again,' Chubb mumbled. 'Know what I'd like right now? Hot biscuits, corn bread and honey with three easy-over eggs.'

Bill shook his head. 'There are three new easy-over corpses down there, cut up just a few minutes ago. They're still at it.'

Alice woke reluctantly, realising sleep had cured none of her woes; indeed she felt worse than ever. She smelled of vomit and the world around smelled of blood. Refusing food, she dragged herself away to wash and when she returned the men were calculating their chances of reaching Japanese headquarters alive, where the neutrality of their white skins would surely be respected.

'How far from here to the East Port barracks, Alice?' Bill asked as she lay down again.

'About a mile, I should think.'

'You know the way?'

'Yes, but I'm not going.'

'For Christ's sake we must. It's our only hope. We can't just stay here.'

'We can try to hire a boat and escape by night.'

'Cat in hell's chance. Look, if we can just get to the right top brass. . . .'

'The *right* top brass—among these monsters who hack off heads sooner than look at you! Don't you remember them yesterday—their mouths snarling like animals? You think I'm giving myself up to them, to grovel for mercy, pretend I've nothing to do with the Chinese? Our poor silly creatures armed with rusty guns and ancient banners. Part of me is Chinese even if I don't look it, and I'm going to escape from this hell-hole or die trying.'

She sat up and glared at them. 'Oh this is just a little Oriental scrap for you, isn't it? You don't care who wins as long as you save your skins. Well I don't blame you—go and deliver yourself to a smart Jap officer, scrape your foreheads on the ground and you'll probably be all right. But count me out, that's all. I can look after myself.'

Bill scowled. 'Don't be crazy, Alice. How the hell can I do that? I got you into this mess, I admit it, though it was none of my making. I might be a roughneck Yankee but I can't leave you here alone in a tight spot like this. If we give ourselves up you'll have to come along too, even if I have to drag you by the hair.'

'And you would have to—every inch of the way. Do you know what I'd do then? I'd jump at the first Japanese dwarf-monster I saw, grab his gun and blow his brains out before he could *banzai*—that's what.'

Chubb chuckled appreciatively. 'She might do too, Bill.

Then where would we be? To be honest, I'm damned if I want anything to do with these butchers after what we've seen. Look at Olga down there—a white skin didn't save her.'

The thought of the macabre scene below silenced them all. Eventually Chubb sighed into the gloom; he'd joined his first whaler twenty-five years before, at the age of fifteen, and still preferred the hazards of sea to those of land. 'How about your idea, Alice? We could have a shot tonight and if we do get nabbed, then is the time to go on our knees before the Rising Sun.'

Bill shrugged. 'It's outsider's luck either way. I'm game. You'll have to deal with a boatman, Alice, if we can find a living one. I'm sure loaded with dough by their standards.'

Alice had slumped back on the bed, eyes closed. 'She's asleep again. Unlike her. She doesn't look at all good.' He stroked the hair off her face.

'What woman would after all she's been through?' Chubb said. 'But she's got guts enough for a real Yankee. Let her sleep.'

And she did, throughout the long, grey, troubled day while bands of victorious soldiers wandered around the town looting, drinking, raping, and shouting *banzais*, and bands of fugitive Chinese militia slipped north through the hills and were mostly shot down later by the Japanese Second Brigade. When dusk fell early and chill, they wrapped up in warm cloaks and slunk downstairs through the grisly silence of the bar. As they stepped outside, Bill's lantern shone on the head of the young child he'd seen killed that morning and Alice stared at it. The tied-up top-knot of its hair was still perky; its face distorted still in a last grimace of anguished disbelief.

The western harbour at first seemed totally deserted; further inspection soon revealed the presence of the dead. Uniformed bodies lay spread-eagled on the quay-side, a few wallowing bloated in the shoreline water. Moored in a creek above the yard they saw a large sampan and Bill jumped aboard to see if it was seaworthy. As he thudded on deck a terrified face peeped from the awning and a shaking hand levelled a pistol at him.

'Don't shoot, we're friends,' Alice called quickly, and the man lowered his weapon. His name, he told her, was Ah-cheng, master of a fishing junk stranded in the nearby shallows in which some Chinese soldiers had tried to escape. He led them to it; a few bodies were lying on the decks where they had been gunned down. Tied against the bulwarks was an open boat in fairly good condition and on seeing it, Bill produced the first of his silver taels, which shone with sudden brightness like a promise for them all.

The bargaining began, and it was eventually concluded that, for a considerable sum, Ah-cheng and his two sons would row them round the southern edge of the Peninsula, then head due west across the open stretch of the Gulf of Liaotung to Chuangtao, a small port in Chihli which was unaffected, as far as they knew, by the war. If the seas were calm and the gods good they could reach it in two or three days—otherwise it could be the last voyage for them all. It was after midnight by the time they'd managed to procure a few provisions, lower the boat into the water, and head for the harbour mouth, the men pulling slowly against a strong on-shore wind.

In the deeper channel Alice again saw several half-submerged mines bobbing, but she felt so ill that the idea of being blown up in a moment was not really undesirable. Lanterns flickered here and there from the captured coastal forts and, far out, she could discern the outline of Japanese warships riding at anchor. Having had no chance to prove their worth in the recent battle, they were undoubtedly manned by alert gunners with trigger-itchy fingers. But this peril they eluded, and by dawn the desolate, blood-stained town was out of sight and the rowers were battling with the choppier waters of the open sea.

Son Number Two brewed tea on a charcoal brazier under the mat cover at the boat's stern and handed them all a cup, bowing ceremoniously as he did so. As Alice reached for hers he drew back sharply, pointing to the skin of her arm, revealed beyond the end of her sleeve. She looked down; it was covered with a rash of reddish spots. She stared at him fearfully, 'What is it? Do you know?' He pointed again at her eyes and she touched them, feeling a puffiness.

'What is it?' she appealed again.

'The dirty red disease,' he said stolidly, and then she knew, for she'd seen victims of it long ago in the mission hospital at Mukden, many of whom had died. 'Bill,' she said in a shaky voice, 'I've got typhus.'

'What?' he turned sharply from his gloomy contemplation of the Peninsula they were leaving.

'Typhus—look here's the rash. And my eyes are odd. That's why I've been feeling so wretched.'

'Oh no! Jesus God, what next? Yes, your eyes are all swollen.'

'I'll die of it,' she said, putting her violently aching head in her arms.

They put her under the mat cover wrapped in old sacking. An icy wind laced with sleet blew through it and her; wavelets lapped at the bottom of the boat round her feet. Soon it seemed to her as if she were going to float entirely away from them, the frightening, aching world mercifully distancing, men's voices and the creak of oars fading. But it didn't matter; she was too ill ever to move again. But it must matter, half her mind told the other half sternly. Because Alice Greenwood was in grave danger of slipping away altogether—stricken with typhus in a winter sea in an open boat.

'Bill, you've got to get me ashore,' she whispered. 'I can't live in this boat for two days, Bill. I'm too ill—I can hardly see you. I think I'm getting delirious, that's what happens with typhus. Please don't let me die here, Bill. Put me ashore.'

In fact, that was precisely what Ah-cheng had decided, utterly refusing to carry the sick woman any further. To cut down the risk of infection, the best thing was to dump her overboard at once he said, because she was doomed to die anyway. This both Bill and Chubb adamantly refused to do but it was agreed to turn back to shore and leave her in the nearest fishing village.

'What are you going to do then?' Chubb glanced at Bill, as Ah-cheng pointed ahead to a cluster of fishermen's huts. Bill groaned, looking at the pathetic heap slumped under the mat cover.

'I'll tell you one thing, Chubb. If yours truly ever sets his sights again on the shores of good old U.S.A., I'll never leave no more. I never want to see another yellow mug as long as I live.'

Chubb grinned sympathetically. 'So you'll stay with her?'

'I'll bleeding have to, won't I? Get yourself to Tientsin double quick. Go to the American Consul, tell him everything, spin any yarn to make it sound good. Make the bloody Chinks do something for us—come and get us out of here.'

Chubb nodded gloomily; it wouldn't be easy. Landing on the beach, they carried Alice, who was scarcely conscious, to the largest hut wherein sat a scraggy old couple pottering round a charcoal fire. Ah-cheng explained. Bill produced some taels, and the woman reluctantly cleared a space among the clutter of blackened pots and fishing gear for Alice to lie down. Bill, covering her with a ragged quilt, noticed that the rash was spreading rapidly.

I'll probably get it too and that'll be the end of us both, he thought sourly, as he leaned against the hut's rickety doorpost watching Chubb and Ah-cheng run back to the boat and pull away quickly. Chubb waved and Bill snorted.

'What a goddam mess,' he said aloud, going back inside and staring down at the sick woman. She opened her eyes, trying to focus his familiar face through a feverish mist.

'It's all right, Alice, you're ashore now and I'll look after you.' She raised a hand and curled her small red fingers round his large fleshy ones.

'What a goddam mess,' he said again, marvelling the while at the extent of his self-sacrifice.

3

Typhus reached near-epidemic proportions in Port Arthur that winter, spread by rats that grew big as cats feeding on unburied corpses. Many died of it; Alice, whose constitution was strong, did not, but she was dangerously ill and spent several days in a semi-conscious state when Bill feared greatly for her life. Hearing from a fugitive Chinese that hostilities in the immediate area had ceased and that foreign warships had arrived to reconnoitre, he set off with Alice in a mule cart to find medical aid. Fortunately he was directed to an International Red Cross field hospital set up in a village hall near the port. Its medical team of European doctors and nurses, hurriedly brought from Chefoo on a British warship, was headed by Doctor Spencer Eliot, and it was to this skilled man whom Alice probably owed her life.

The makeshift hospital cared for wounded of both sides, though most Japanese were soon tranported home on medical ships. Its main hall was a general ward and a side-room had been converted into an operating theatre, its walls and tables covered with unbleached calico. The suffering moans of the men going to and from it prickled the battle-torn nerves of the other patients as they lay shivering on hard pallets with only a blanket apiece. Alice, as the only woman and typhus patient admitted, was in a curtained recess and given three blankets. Nevertheless, once her fever subsided, she was constantly cold as she watched snow falling outside the flimsy, paper-covered window that gave on to the yard. Noises of creaking carts, shouts of stretcher bearers and drivers filtered to her, punctuated by the barked commands of Japanese officers that made her shiver more than the cold.

But she need not worry on that score, Bill assured her, the conquerors weren't such a bad lot after all. The murderous excesses of their first victory had soon been controlled and

Port Arthur was now designated the main base of operations for Japan's military forces. Towards Bill, an innocent American whose ship had been commandeered by the enemy, the Japanese authorities showed considerable sympathy. They offered him a billet in the officers' barracks and promised to try and find his lost vessel. At this, Bill's natural optimism began to revive, though Alice, debilitated by illness, remained in low spirits.

She was lying thus one afternoon, in a soggy doze, vaguely conscious of the discomforts of hard bed, chill air, and smells of carbolic and disinfectant, when she became aware of someone's presence. She stared up at an unknown face, fringed with a curly brown beard, twinkling eyes looking down.

'Mrs. Greenwood-Grant? Please excuse my intrusion, but could I have a word with you?' His accent was cosy, warm Scottish, and she tried to struggle up. 'Please don't disturb yourself, you are unwell I know. Let me explain—I'm James Galbraith, Far East newspaper correspondent just arrived to cover the war.'

'Oh . . . Mr. Galbraith, I'm afraid I'm not very . . . still do please,' she gestured to a stool.

'I've just come off a troop ship from Nagasaki and Dr. Eliot told me about you—that you were actually in Port Arthur when it fell? It must have been quite a terrifying experience?'

He leaned forward keenly. 'It was—bestial, a nightmare, a living hell, the worst things I've ever seen in my life.' Her lip quivered and he tutted sympathetically.

'I'm truly sorry to hear that, Mrs. Grant, but could you give me a few details—what you actually saw. For my readers you understand.'

'Oh dear. Why don't you ask my friend Mr. Risley? He was also there, only he's not been so ill. It's just my present weakness that makes it difficult.'

'Oh, I do understand, Mrs. Grant. Please take your time. But Mr. Risley is American I believe? And to hear a first-hand account from you, an Englishwoman actually there—why that's a story in itself! And one the Japanese would prefer kept quiet, if I'm not mistaken?'

He had his notebook out. Dr. Eliot had told him something of her history, so he knew on which side her sympathies lay.

'Oh they'll keep quiet about it, they certainly will,' her voice gained angry strength. 'The Japanese soldiers were murderers, brutal butchers, mowing people down like animals—women and children,' she gulped. 'There was—somehow it's the scene I most vividly remember, when we left Epimoff's hotel. They'd killed Olga Epimoff, left her slung over the bar with her throat cut. When we came out there was the head of a small child in the gutter, sort of tilted up, its face showing such torment . . . surprise, almost.' She began to cry then and he gave her a large white handkerchief into which she gratefully blew her nose. 'Thanks. Hankies are hard to come by here. I'm sorry, it's this silly illness really.'

'Mrs. Grant, pray do not distress yourself, let us wait a little,' he put a comforting hand on her shoulder as Bill Risley came through the curtain.

'Hello, what's this, Alice? Crying? And who may I ask . . .?'

James Galbraith introduced himself soothingly, adding, 'So you'll understand I'm sure Mr. Risley that as Mrs. Grant is the only foreign woman who can actually tell me of her dreadful experiences during . . .'

'She's not to be bothered further, Mr. Galbraith. You can see how ill the little lady still is, and the memory of that terrible time is very distressing to her.' Bill came to stand by the bed. 'Maybe in a few days, when she's stronger.'

The correspondent looked disgruntled. 'But I'm hoping to get this dispatch off with the next boat to Chefoo. The hotter the news you know, Mr. Risley.'

'Damn your hot news, sir. The health of Mrs. Grant is of far greater importance. So I'll trouble you to leave her alone now.' He gestured to the curtain as Alice whispered, 'But Bill, it's my only chance to be quoted in the papers and I think people ought to know what the Japs did to . . .'

'They'll hear well enough without your bothering Alice.'

James turned to him. 'It was something of a bloodbath, I believe?'

'It . . . well . . . there was certainly unnecessary violence. The Japs had been provoked of course—their own captured men strung up. It was a battle situation and these Orientals are pretty barbaric towards losers.'

'Bill, it was worse than that, the Japs hacking everyone to pieces and . . .'

'Alice, I won't have you getting upset in your present state.' He glared defiantly at Mr. Galbraith who put his notebook away with a sigh.

471

'I'm sorry I troubled you, Mrs. Grant. I wish you a speedy recovery. But in the meantime I must point out you are forfeiting your chance of getting into the history books. Good day to you, Mr. Risley.'

He swung out and Bill muttered, 'Impudent jackass,' as he did so.

Alice slumped back on the pillow. 'I'm not going to keep quiet about what the Japs did, even if you are, Bill.'

'It's none of my business, nor yours. It's the Japs in charge now whether we like it or not and no damn point in rubbing them the wrong way. All I want is to get the *Dolphin* fixed up and get to hell out of here.'

'Well, it's not like that for me, as you know. So just leave me to manage my own affairs.' She rolled over with her back to him and he swore under his breath. But then she looked so frail and thin under the blankets and her hair in such a sorry mess that he simply patted it and left her.

Having so quickly captured Port Arthur, the Japanese forces spent a while consolidating their position and planning their next move. Their commanders were determined to keep on the right side of the West by keeping international shipping lines open and protecting the interests of any foreigners caught up in the conflict. Thus, when a Japanese patrol boat discovered the *Dolphin*, little damaged, on an isolated shore near the Korean border, it was brought back to Port Arthur, arriving the same day as Chubb who had got to Tientsin and hitched a ride back on a Red Cross supply ship.

'Things are looking up at last. Chubb got some money out of the Chinks and our Consul is looking into our case,' Bill told Alice, as she sat on her bed's edge, wrapped in a wool robe and feeling more perky. 'And can you believe this? When the Chinese commandeered the ship in the first place, the steward ran away and took Wilbur. Brought him back to Chubb safe and sound this morning. You should have seen the reunion—strong men would have wept. So now I reckon we'll be heading for home before Christmas. Oh boy, to think of it, the bright lights, the bars and the bourbon! This rice wine rots your innards. So there's something saved out of this bloody fiasco after all! Bit of cash, the ship . . .'

'And our lives, which we almost despaired of for a while. And you saved mine, Bill. I've never thanked you properly for that.' She put her hand on his. 'You could have just dumped

472

me off that boat and left alone in the village I'd probably have died . . . I do appreciate it, dear.'

He shrugged. 'That would have been a pretty low-down trick even for a Yankee. Anyways, the tide's turned and it's time we got out of here. The doc says you'll be fit to travel out of all this mess very soon. He'll get you a berth on the next hospital ship going south.'

She nodded, plucked dispiritedly at her robe. It seemed so cowardly and unenterprising to leave all this exciting action for the dull safety of convalescent Chefoo. However, the very next morning, Alice was called to Dr. Eliot's office. He sat at a desk littered with papers and waved one at her, smiling; James Galbraith, who was also in the room, jumped to offer her a chair.

'Mrs. Grant—I'm glad to see you on your feet again.'

'Mr. Galbraith, yes I'm better thank you. A little wobbly.' She sat down gratefully.

'I don't know what you'll think about this,' the doctor indicated the paper. 'The most recent list of foreign persons missing in the area of hostilities. And can we help to trace any of them. I can certainly report that one lost sheep is found.' He beamed at her.

'I'm on it?'

'Yes. Person to notify, your brother William Greenwood. But there's also,' he hesitated, then read, 'Mr. and Mrs. Edward Blake, stepfather and mother of William Greenwood.'

She gave a cry of dismay. 'Mother!'

'The couple, who are elderly, were among a party of missionaries who left Mukden in mid-November owing to the danger of attack from Japanese forces in Manchuria. At Newchwang the party boarded a ship for Chefoo, but Mrs. Blake was too ill to attempt the voyage and she and her husband remained behind. Since then, there is no word of their whereabouts.'

'Oh dear heaven. Mother in Newchwang—which is ice-bound now of course. I must go there overland and see if . . .'

The doctor grimaced. 'It's over a hundred miles across mountain roads covered with snow, not to mention soldiers sniping at each other. No, it would be extremely foolhardy in your present weakened state, Mrs. Grant. But Mr. Galbraith has a suggestion,' he glanced at the newspaper correspondent.

'You see, Mrs. Grant, I've just received orders to go north and join the Japanese Second Army in Manchuria—my editor seems to think the next advance will be there. So I leave tomorrow with a detachment of Japanese cavalry. As I told the good doctor, I'll certainly keep a lookout for your relatives, and if I hear anything, I'll try to get a message to you here.'

'Oh but Mr. Galbraith, couldn't you . . . I mean, couldn't I? Will you take me please? I'll be quite all right, honestly. I'm very used to rough travel. Why, I once rode alone from Mukden to Port Arthur on a pony, about this time of year.'

'I'm sorry, Mrs. Grant, but that's quite impossible. I'm accompanying the cavalry in an official capacity and they simply wouldn't permit.'

'And I don't think it's fair to ask,' the doctor interrupted. 'Your constitution simply isn't strong enough, and you'd certainly be a liability to a fast-moving body of troops. And Mr. Galbraith has already offered to do more than is in the line of his duty.'

She looked suitably contrite. 'I see, yes, I'm sorry Mr. Galbraith. It's most kind of you indeed. I think you spring from North of the English border, if I'm not mistaken? A noble, true-blooded race of men always ready to give a helping hand—at least, that's what my mother always says, for she's a Scot herself, born Eliza Macrae from the Hebridean Isles.'

'Why, I'm delighted to hear that now, Mrs. Grant—it will put an extra spur to my endeavours to know she's a countrywoman of mine. And it helps to explain the stout-heartedness of yourself, if I may say so!' His eyes were admiring, and Dr. Eliot coughed discreetly, 'May a mere Sassenach venture to interrupt? I've much else to do I fear and . . .'

'Oh I'm sorry, Doctor,' Alice sprang up and Galbraith escorted her to the door, where she offered him her hand, thinking as she did so that he was a well-built Scot indeed. His muscular frame, of medium height, and his open, alert face conveyed a vigorous, confident experience of the world and its ways that was specially attractive in her present state of anxious frailty. She wished very much that he wasn't leaving or that she could accompany him, but she knew the doctor was right and sighed, 'So be it, Mr. Galbraith. I'll wait here for a while to regain my strength and pray you'll send me good news.'

He smiled, continuing to squeeze her hand reassuringly.

'Give me about ten days to get any message to you. But I hope you understand that the news could easily be bad? An elderly couple, ill, cut off in a place like that.'

She looked at him. 'Yes, Mr. Galbraith, I'm realising that quite clearly, even as you say it. I just want the facts, whatever they are.'

He bowed, 'And let us hope they'll be good. So goodbye, Mrs. Grant. I hope we may meet again in happier circumstances. I'm often on the China beat.'

'Then maybe we shall, for I know no other "beat," Mr. Galbraith.'

A few days after, Bill also bade her goodbye, presenting her with a fairly sizeable sum of money that had been 'well-earned in the firing line,' as he put it. And she was duly grateful, thinking how useful it would be if she received any definite news of her mother's whereabouts.

As her strength returned, Alice took on the useful role of interpreter between the hard-pressed medical team and the Chinese patients, who were a motley and depressed collection. The proudest among them were the Manchu bannermen, some descended from soldiers who had conquered China two hundred years before; there were miscellaneous volunteers from many provinces and men of the Green Standard, skilled only in the quelling of local riots. Alice's special care was for the Hunanese, to whom she spoke in their own dialect. They had sailed cheerily to war in Yangtze junks—proud of their red and orange uniforms, black turbans, their warrior ancestry. Solid, invincible-seeming men who called themselves 'Braves' and whose fathers had helped to defeat the Taiping rebellion, they had now been deserted by most of their officers, left to rot in cold beds, destitute, sick and a thousand miles from home. Morale among all the Chinese was at a low ebb, they had little stomach for the fight and blamed the government for sending them into battle so poorly equipped. It was a kind of murder and they knew it.

Despairing now of the war's outcome, Alice often thought with some bitterness of the idealistic self-strengtheners. Wasn't it time they left the security of the Treaty Ports and the capital and came to find out how weak the country's forces really were? But none of them did.

The only newcomers, who arrived on Christmas Eve, were several officers from the British warships *Undaunted* and *Centurion*, come up on a neutral inspection tour. They brought medical supplies, letters from Home, brandy, wine and Christmas goodies made for those in the front line by the ladies of Chefoo. So it turned out to be a merry day. After the hospital's meagre diet, the food was ambrosia, the drink nectar. Inspired by it, the nurses gave renderings of popular carols, then one of the officers produced a fiddle and all the foreigners went jigging up and down the aisle between the beds. The patients watched in bewilderment, which verged on horror when a young lieutenant dangled some greenery from a roof beam, called it mistletoe, and dragged every lady in sight for a kiss beneath.

The morning after these welcome jollifications, when Alice was still in bed, an orderly arrived with a message from James Galbraith. 'Dear Mrs. Grant. The news I have of your parents is, I fear, rather inconclusive. I've found it very difficult to glean much, travelling with a Japanese escort through disputed territory. I've sent my personal Chinese servant to inquire wherever possible, and yesterday he got into the fortified town of Kaiping, still in Chinese hands. He was told by *yamen* officials that an elderly English couple, "givers of books"—I presume missionaries—were lodged in the largest Mission. They were thought to be ill and had arrived originally from Newchwang. That was all he could ascertain in the time available. I fear I can do no more as we are now heading north directly. Perhaps Dr. Eliot or Mr. Risley can help you. My best wishes for the New Year and may your parents be safely returned to you.'

'Whatever the state of the roads and my health, I have to go to Kaiping. How could I ever live with myself if I didn't?' Alice, looking very determined, sat in Dr. Eliot's office. He re-read Galbraith's note as if for guidance, then sighed. 'As you may be aware, Hai-cheng to the north is already in the hands of the Japanese First Army and we've every reason to believe they're planning a further offensive, using troops stationed here. They're going to push north, capture Kaiping, then join forces. This will be disastrous for the Chinese and makes Kaiping a key strategic point. I cannot possibly spare an escort for you at this juncture, but if you will just wait a while . . .'

'How can I delay, even for a day, when my mother might be dying there, doctor? And I'm not asking for an escort.'

'I admire your courage, Mrs. Grant, but I have to think of your welfare.'

'I know you do, and I'm most grateful. But now I will go to Kaiping. And you could certainly promote my welfare by providing me with one of your Red Cross carts. That would probably get me through whichever side is in control—and I am on a sort of mercy mission.'

In such fashion was Dr. Eliot persuaded into co-operation, and the next morning Alice left the hospital in a Red Cross mule-cart, carrying bedding, medical supplies, provisions and a letter requesting her safe conduct. In normal conditions the journey could have been made in three days, but it took much longer, and was only possible because the mountain tracks were being cleared of snow for Japanese supply carts to advance, loaded with boxes of gunpowder, tents, field ovens, saddlery, cauldrons for boiling water.

The labourers press-ganged into the clearing work were pitiable to behold, their skinny legs flaked white with cold, noses and lips frost-bitten, blackened stumps of toes and fingers protruding from filthy bandages. The soldiers supervising them whipped any slackers mercilessly and several stiffened corpses lay by the wayside. But to Alice they were extremely courteous, offering her food and shelter in their rough bivouacs, which was all the help she received, for the local inhabitants, having heard of the Port Arthur massacre, had fled the district in terror.

In times of peace, Kaiping was a flourishing centre of coal-mining and one of China's first railways ran from the mines to the coast of Chihli. When Alice reached it however, railways and mines were closed, and the town had become a fortress guarded by high walls and redoubts. The river in front of it was frozen solid and the Chinese had cut the ice into huge blocks to make crossing more difficult. In her earlier state of confidence, Alice would have imagined the town impregnable, but she'd quite lost faith in the Chinese powers of resistance, and went through the guarded south gate with a sick heart, knowing she was again walking into a trap that the Japanese would soon attack and capture.

Dusk and snow flurries were falling when Alice's cart drew up outside the town's main Mission. It was of the kind that aroused considerable criticism among the secular foreign community—brick-built, pretentious with verandahs and walled grounds as richly exclusive as any mandarin's residence. An old woman answered Alice's knocking and a few

477

words confirmed that she'd indeed come to the right place—
Mr. and Mrs. Edward Blake were in an upstairs room.

Creeping up, Alice saw an oil-lamp shining from an open
door; by its light a grey-haired woman was reading to an aged
man who lay on a narrow bed, his eyes closed. 'Ye shall find the
babe wrapped in swaddling clothes, lying in a manger. And
suddenly there was the angel and a multitude of the heavenly
host praising God saying, Glory to God in the Highest, and on
earth peace, goodwill towards men . . .'

The scene blurred before Alice's eyes as she listened to the
serene, soft tones; for a moment, the mysterious strength of the
faith she'd so long resisted touched her spirit and a great surge
of love and pity welled in her heart for the woman by the bed
who was her mother. The frailties, the bigotries of Eliza's past
were as nothing compared to this sight of her—an old woman
alone with a dying man in a beleaguered oriental town and
most evidently strong, unafraid, buttressed by faith.

'But Mary kept all these things and pondered them in her
heart,' Eliza continued, then paused. 'Edward?' The man on
the bed didn't stir.

'Mother. Mother, I'm here,' Alice said quietly.

The pale blue eyes blinked unbelievingly as she came forward and took her mother in her arms and smoothed her hair
while they both cried a little and Alice explained how it was
she'd come, 'like a miracle,' as Eliza kept saying, plucking her
daughter's sleeve.

'A miracle. I knew there would be one, if we are to be saved.
But I never dreamed it would be you. I often consoled myself
with the thought that, whatever happened to us, and we are old
now—my children would all be safe. You and the boys in the
Treaty Ports, Adam and Sunny at Home. But it is what God has
chosen for us—see, Edward, Alice has come to help us.'

His eyes opened briefly and shut with firm incomprehension,
and Alice did not meet them. It had been over fourteen years
since she'd last seen her stepfather, standing in her bedroom
at Mukden, pulling his robe across his shame.

Eliza whispered, 'I fear he's sinking, Alice. Pneumonia, in
this dreadful cold, at his age. I succumbed first, but the Lord
helped me to recover. But now there's no medicine left for him
and all the missionaries have gone.'

'Don't worry dearie. I've brought some medicines and he
shall have them. But how could they leave you here alone? And

478

I heard you were in Newchwang?'

The missionaries, Eliza explained, had already left when they reached Kaiping, to which they'd gone in hopes of getting a train out. 'But the Japanese had blown up the line—it was being used to transport Chinese soldiers to the front—and everything was in such a muddle. Then no sooner did I feel better, than Edward became ill. So we just stayed, what else could we do? How long I don't know. It's past Christmas, isn't it?'

'Yes dear, it's January 1895.'

'I thought so, but wasn't sure. So I kept reading the wonderful message of Christmas to Edward over and over again.'

'I heard you, Mother. "Peace on earth, goodwill towards men." '

She thought of the slaughter she had witnessed, committed by the same troops who were about to invade this very town. She said merely, 'I saw men dead on the way here, wounded soldiers and coolies frozen in the snow. There's a verse of Li T'ai-po's I kept remembering, "Soldiers lay in the mud, in grass, in undergrowth. Helpless the General. Yes, incapable before this. We have learned that soldiers are evil tools, But wise men have not accomplished the end of strife and still employ them." '

'Ah dear me, so it is. Most Chinese hate war, despise soldiers do they not? And this is to their credit. Yet wars still come and they lose battles.'

Eliza bowed her head till Alice said, 'Mother, I'm really quite hungry and very cold. Do you think there's . . .?'

'My dear child, of course. We must call Mr. and Mrs. Li-yuan, the caretakers. Such good souls, not even Christians, but they have succoured us both. Yet I fear Edward is not rallying,' she bent anxiously over her husband while Alice went to fetch medicines from the cart.

A snow-laden wind slammed at her as she stepped outside and she leaned weakly against the wall, overcome by the strain of the journey, the emotion of reunion. If only her stepfather would die quickly, she thought savagely, then she and Eliza might still escape before the Japanese came. However, she took the medicines to Edward and they seemed to revive him, though Alice suspected they only slightly prolonged a life already spent. The fact that he had once laid her across his lap and whipped her bare buttocks now seemed to her almost incredible and not a little ludicrous. Yet, she still

479

remembered the stinging shock and shame of it and could scarcely bear to touch his shrivelled flesh.

In periods of consciousness, his pale, hard gaze followed her anxiously about the room as if she were an avenging spirit come to haunt his final hours. Sensing this, Alice frequently removed her disquieting presence and went into the town to get food, and the latest news of the Japanese army's inexorable advance. Eliza meanwhile, unafraid and uncaring of anything but Edward's condition, ministered to him constantly, snatching only brief sleep in the adjoining room that she and Alice shared. It was on such an occasion that the sick man suddenly opened his eyes, stared at Alice and tried to struggle upright.

'There, there,' she didn't touch him. 'Go to sleep, Stepfather.'

'Sleep? How can I sleep with you here?' he said distinctly. 'Can't you let me die in peace? Why are you here?'

'I came to try and rescue Mother from the Japanese forces, not to worry you.'

'The Japanese are coming here?'

'Yes.'

He breathed heavily, his chest rattling. 'Take her away from here.'

'It is impossible. She won't leave you and you are too ill to be moved.'

His breath became increasingly agitated as he thought about that. 'It is time for me to die,' he said finally. She remained silent. 'You have been sent as a judgment on me.'

She marvelled anew on the egocentricity of the missionary spirit. 'That is foolish. I told you why I've come. It's not to do with you.'

His eyes closed with the pain of her harshness and he said after a pause, 'I sinned against you. Oh how many times have I sought repentance on bended knee.' He struggled to rise again, his thin arm creeping over the coverlet towards her. 'Can you—will you forgive a dying man?'

She fought back her rejection. 'Even if I forgive you, will God?'

He gave a rattling groan. 'His mercy I crave. His mercy, and yours. Your forgiveness, do I have that?'

She rose, stiff with revulsion at the sight of him—his weakness and pleading, the fish-white, decaying skin. 'I don't know what to say to you, Stepfather, only that I never wished to see you again. Not only because of what you did to me, but because of Sunny and Adam—you blighted their childhood. That's something I can't bear to think of. Between us there is nothing now, nothing. I don't hate you anymore, but I cannot find in my heart any tenderness towards you either. May you die in peace, that is all I can say.'

She went into the other room, ignoring the pleading grope of his hand.

'Mother, Stepfather is restless. Could you give him more chlorodyne?'

She hurried at once to his side, soothing his deeply hollowed cheeks with trembling fingers. The tenderness of her gesture stabbed Alice and she went downstairs and outside, shivering with emotion and the icy pinch of the wind. Would God, she wondered, forgive her those words, her presumption, her lack of charity? She stared into the darkening sky. Should she not mitigate her harshness, not only for Edward's sake, but for Sunny and Adam who weren't here to pay their own last respects?

But she had no chance of mitigation, for Edward fell into a deep coma that night and died during the afternoon of the following day, having lingered seven days after Alice's arrival. During that week their last chance of escape from Kaiping vanished. At dawn, when Edward's covered corpse was stiffening on the bed, the last rigor, Alice thought, of a totally rigorous life, the Japanese Second Army under General Nogi launched its attack. Alice, hearing their guns, as she had nearly two months before, could have screamed with panic, for, this time, there was simply nothing to do but stay and await the outcome.

During that morning an advance battalion of infantry scrambled and slithered across the frozen river and, though under heavy fire, occupied a commanding hill position on the other side. When a second battalion followed, the Chinese retreated into the neighbouring fields and were felled by artillery fire. By mid-morning the town was in Japanese hands; their casualties were small, but about a thousand of Kaiping's defenders lay dead in the snow or along the parapets which their comrades had then abandoned. Throughout the afternoon small-arms fire crackled spasmodically and soon orderly platoons of conquering soldiers came marching along the main streets, methodically searching all official buildings en route.

The two women waited tensely in the empty mission, Alice

taking what comfort she could from the uncanny silence that lay over the town. Surely, if brutal slaughter was being done, it would be heard?

'Mother, we must make it clear to the Japanese at once that we are Westerners and should be protected as neutrals.' Alice spoke reluctantly, having rejected just such a course earlier.

'We must simply put our faith in the Lord my dear child. My only hope is that He will contrive a Christian burial for Edward.'

'But we must be a little constructive too. God helps those . . . in short, I think you should put on English clothes.'

'But my dear, I always wear these, they are part of my faith.' Eliza plucked agitatedly at the long, thick native robes which all China Inland Mission members wore, in deference to Chinese feelings on the ugliness of Western attire.

'But they're only the outward show, Mother. I'm not suggesting you change your faith, only your clothes. So, let's see if there's something.' Alice rummaged in the tin trunk the Blakes had brought with them from Mukden and produced a dowdy black dress, with a cut-in bodice, high neck and small bustle that had been fashionable in provincial England some ten years before. 'There dear, see if this still fits,' she held it up.

'Oh that! Goodness, I bought that to go to Scotland when I was last at Home, and so unsuitable it proved for walking over the bogs. I've scarcely ever . . . surely you don't think . . .?'

'Try it on, Mother,' Alice said briskly and Eliza obediently did so, her shaky fingers fumbling with the unfamiliar hooks and buttons. 'Really you know Chinese dress is so much more sensible and comfortable—all these silly bits and pieces and the tight waist,' she puffed a little.

'I quite agree, that's why I often wear it. But for the present occasion . . . Here, let's do something more dignified with your hair too.'

Gently she brushed Eliza's wispy grey locks into a neat bun under an old lace cap. 'There now you look quite the grand dame. I'm sure there's not a soldier in the whole Japanese army would dare hurt a hair on your head.'

Alice was sure of no such thing and, in the late afternoon, when she saw a group of the conqueror's soldiers halt in the street outside and knock on the outer gate, her heart pounded with terror. The caretaker let them in, bowing almost to the ground and the two women stood together, clutching hands as army boots thudded up the stairs. A soldier appeared in the door, rifle at the ready. He gave a grunt of surprise, and Alice said loudly, 'We are English. Please help us.'

Four more soldiers crowded into the room, talking volubly and staring at them; Alice saw with relief that they had left their weapons outside. As none of them spoke any English, she gestured to Edward's body in the other room, pointed to her mother.

'He was my husband,' Eliza's voice quavered.

The leading soldier bowed, seeming to understand; then he barked an order, and they all went, except for an armed guard outside the door. Nothing more happened that night and the town was quiet except for occasional distant rifle shots, the thuds of snow sliding from the roof. Alice heard every sound, her thoughts racing haphazardly between the details of getting her stepfather's body buried before it became unpleasant and the overwhelming notion that the coming day might be her last on earth.

The next morning three soldiers appeared with two carts; the two women were ushered into one, Edward's body dumped on the other . . . At the main *yamen*, now the Japanese headquarters, an immaculately-uniformed officer wearing a jewelled sword, held out a white-gloved hand to them. 'The foreign ladies. Please to sit. Tell me of you.'

Alice explained as simply as possible, ending with a plea that Edward be given a decent burial. To her amazed relief, the officer bowed.

'It is all right. I am Christian. My parents too. This afternoon, we do.'

And so it was done. The ground was so hard-frozen that coolies used pick-axes to dig the grave in the Mission cemetery, the pallor of a wintry sun shining into it as Alice read the service, her mother beside her. It seemed fitting—this harsh, cold end and she, who had hated Edward, mouthing his last rites. Eliza stood kneading a damp handkerchief in her mittened hand, the Japanese officer at her other side standing to stiff attention as Edward was lowered into the unyielding soil.

It was almost incredible that the well-behaved troops now in possession of Kaiping were the same as the butchers of Port Arthur, but the disciplines of warfare had now been re-imposed, their savagery sheathed. The next day, the commanding officer explained courteously to Alice that because

Kaiping was near the front line, they were to be removed to Feng-huang, near the Korean border that had been in Japanese hands for three months, where there was what he termed 'A Settlement' for foreigners. It had a slightly sinister ring, but they had no choice in the matter and set off by cart the following morning.

Though winter still gripped the land, Alice found the journey exhilarating now that she'd lost her terror of the Japanese, but to Eliza it was a great ordeal, and she often spoke, almost wistfully, of death.

'Alice dear, I'm quite ready to go and you mustn't grieve if God decides that my time, like Edward's, has come.'

'Nonsense Mother, you're not nearly so old and there is to be no talk of dying. Think how all your children would miss you, we in China and the twins in England.'

'Ah Adam! He is so sweet and kind, yet I fear for his future. When he comes out here as a medical missionary—and he will soon—promise you will take special care of him, Alice? If anything happens to me. He is, I fear, rather ill-fitted for this cruel world.'

Adam's ill-fittedness was hardly surprising, Alice thought, considering his cheerless childhood, haunted by the unpredictable wrath of God, the uncleanliness of little boys' souls, the fears of the benighted heathen. 'I'll do what I can, Mother, but you're going to be all right for years yet, and so is Adam. Please don't keep worrying.'

But Eliza would not be jollied so easily from her lugubrious themes to which she reverted the next day.

'After all, what is the point of going on? I'm too old to labour in the field of the Lord. And what will become of me now Edward has gone?'

'We'll sort something out with Will and Frank, dear, once this awful war is over.'

'But I don't want to be a burden on you all. Edward and I were thinking of going Home at last and I keep dreaming of it—my country, the little island in the Hebrides. We went there when I was last Home you know.'

'Yes, Will told me. He said your family made much of you all, especially Joel.'

'He loved it—cutting peat, catching fish. It's such an honest, frugal life. They don't bother much with money, just weave and knit, bake bread, eat tatties, fish, oatmeal. I kept wondering if I was right ever to leave. How it would have been if I'd stayed.'

Alice patted her hand. 'Well if you had, there wouldn't be me, or Will or . . .'

'Yes, I'm glad I did. I've learned so much more of the world. But they seem happy in their way, and really know little more about China than these poor peasants about Scotland. Do you eat birds' nests and puppy dogs, they kept asking me!'

Alice laughed. 'But they read books surely?'

'Oh yes, they're great readers of history and the classics, and my brother Hamish is quite the island philosopher. But they're not much good on foreign parts. After all they've never travelled. Brother Neil went the furthest—to Glasgow—and the young Morag, the flighty one, goes to the mainland sometimes. But the others stay put, and why not? Hamish still runs the croft with his sons, Duncan and his wife keep the post-office, then there's Katie, my favourite. She's had it hard with her husband drowned and three children to bring up. Perhaps I could go and help her.' Eliza's eyes misted with memory as she thought of the flat, damp, windy land of her youth, wondered if she could endure it now, in her old age. She sighed herself back to the present.

'You know, Alice, I always hoped you'd marry a Scot. Solid, reliable men just right for you. And perhaps you will yet . . .'

'Oh, I can't see myself marrying again, Mother.'

'Why not? You're an attractive woman still, with many good years ahead. But promise me one thing, dear. If I do slip away from you soon, you'll go to my home-country one day. The family would love to see you—my eldest daughter.'

Alice grinned. 'And I could find some solid Scot to take me on, hey? But I can't promise that, Mother. It's such a long way off, a different world. Perhaps we'll go together one day. Wouldn't that be nice? Because you're going to live for years yet, you'll see!'

And certainly when they reached 'The Settlement' in Feng-huang Eliza began to pick up, almost in spite of herself. They were lodged in the town's mission-house together with other foreigners caught up in earlier hostilities, when the Japanese had captured part of eastern Manchuria. There were three Russian tea-merchants who played chess all day, a taciturn German railway surveyor who refused to state his business there, and Veronique and Karl Blum, who were usually resident in Peking.

Veronique was slim and tensely bright-eyed, blonde-greying hair dressed stylishly as if for the Champs Elysées, and she crowed with delight when Alice first appeared. 'Ah, *enfin*, another woman! It has been so dreadful, nothing but men, men, men here.' She spoke English with a charming French lilt. 'Even the sweepers are men.'

Her husband shook Alice's hand. 'Don't know what she thinks she'd do without *les hommes* I'm sure.'

Wiry black hair fringed his balding pate and framed his heavily bearded face. Alice couldn't place his accent; it was, he later told her, 'wandering Central European Jewish.'

'And how is it you are here?' Mrs. Blum asked.

'It's rather a long story . . .'

'Well, we've plenty of time to listen. You are alone?'

'No, my mother is here in bed, recovering from the journey. She was doing mission work in Mukden when the war began.'

'And you, Mrs. Grant, are you also a missionary?'

'No. Definitely not.'

They smiled with relief, and Karl asked, 'Then perhaps you are the Mrs. Greenwood-Grant whose name I recognise—the only she-devil with a proper business in Shanghai and a sharp young comprador called Benjy?'

'Yes indeed, but how . . .?'

'Ah, your fame spreads in the trade. Veronique and I have an antique shop in Peking. "The Establishment of Ten Thousand Glories" was its original name, and we try to live up to that.'

'It's the only decent, foreign-owned shop in the place,' Veronique added. 'But come to the stove and let's talk. The worst thing here is the cold.'

'No, the food's the worst,' Karl corrected. 'How I abominate raw fish, seaweed and cold fried eggs—that's what we get.'

'And whose fault is it we have to eat such muck? I will tell you, it is such an absurd story, Mrs. Grant. We came to Manchuria in October looking for Korean celadon—wonderful pieces they sell in these border towns. Then poor Karl develops an abscess in an unmentionable place,' she poked her husband's bulky buttock. 'And it was impossible for him to ride a mule, or sit in a springless cart, or a carry-chair, pure agony, *n'est ce pas*?' Karl nodded gloomily.

'So we waited for him to get better, pottered about, bought

more pieces, never dreaming, a bit out of touch. Then suddenly, pouf! The Japs thunder over the Korean border, sweep all before them. Not to be trifled with, very good shots. So here we are, all because of a boil on the *derrière*. Can you beat it?'

Karl grinned. 'Part of life's rich tapestry. And you?'

'I wish I could beat it with a funnier story, but mine's rather ghastly. Still, I'll tell it, if you don't mind. I haven't told my mother much, and it's all bottled up inside still.'

When she'd finished Karl shook his head in sympathy. 'You've had a thoroughly nasty time, Mrs. Grant. Incredible people, these Japanese. Take your common soldier, the sort who, as you say, butchered hundreds in cold blood. Yet when they brought us here and searched our trunks, making sure we weren't spies I suppose, they came upon our celadon pieces. And you should have seen them! Handled each piece like an eggshell, passed it around, positively hissing in admiration as they do, like a bunch of art connoisseurs, weren't they, Veronique? Your average British Tommy certainly wouldn't behave like that.'

Alice, disbelieving at first, found that the Blums were right—there was another side of the Japanese that was highly civilised, kindly, humane. She even grew to like the orderly who cleaned her room so industriously each day and showed her tinted photographs of his daughters in kimonos, and the officer who sent Eliza special delicacies and extra supplies of fuel for her bedroom fire because she was elderly and worthy of respect. Above all, every Japanese was unquestioningly, unswervingly loyal to his country's cause.

'And that's why they're soon going to win this war, hands down,' Karl predicted one day, as he, Veronique and Alice sat in the enclosed house-verandah. 'They all fight for one Emperor, all shout *banzai* together. But your average Celestial Tommy hasn't an ounce of *esprit de corps* in him by comparison. He thinks only of his own clan, or his province. And at the top—Manchus against Chinese, progressives against conservatives. And all the different factions at the mercy of the Old Buddha playing hide and seek with her eunuchs in the royal pleasure gardens! No, the Chinese had best admit defeat, settle for peace at any price before the Japs march into Peking itself.'

'You think that's a possibility?'

'Certainly. They've captured Wei-hai-wei in Shantung and if

the Chinese don't capitulate, that's their next move. Sooner the better, so we can all pack up and go home.'

'You'll return to Shanghai and business as usual, Alice?' Veronique asked curiously. She and Karl had become interested in Alice, a restless soul, they decided, a little lost, but sympathetic, and rather admirable.

'Oh I suppose so. But I was getting fed up with Shanghai.'

'It's the ultimate Treaty Port, isn't it? And the foreign community such a boring mixture of petit bourgeois, nouveau-riche, don't you think?'

'Perhaps so. It suited me well when I was building up the business.'

'But now you need a new challenge. Why not come to Peking and open up there?' Karl suggested. 'The intellectual *ton* is much higher. The legation set are a bit stuffy, but knowledgable, and there are some interesting scholars and mandarins who actually like talking to foreigners.'

'And the radicals will be sounding off mightily after this war fiasco,' Veronique added. 'The self-strengtheners, as they used to be called.'

'I knew one quite well once. A Cantonese.'

'The Cantonese are the liveliest bunch, and very sharp. Why not come, Alice? Get out of your mercantile rut and go in for quality instead of globe-trotters' knick-knacks.'

'But why should you want me to? I'd only become a competitor.'

'Ah but you're wrong,' Karl explained. 'If there were thirty foreign-owned antique shops in Peking vying for trade we'd pay you to keep away. But there are very few at present and we want to build up the capital's reputation as the place for the connoisseur.'

'So, at present, the more of us the merrier,' Veronique concluded. 'It's a grand opportunity, really Alice. Think about it.'

Alice was soon prompted to think on the subject of the future because, a few days after that conversation, news came that a temporary armistice had been signed between the opposing forces and peace treaty negotiations had begun. The Japanese had earlier sent details of the foreigners in their care to the consulates concerned, and now letters began to arrive, including one from William, saying he and Frank were coming to Manchuria the moment they were permitted to travel. This happened surprisingly quickly. On 17 April 1895, Viceroy Li

Hung-chang, representing the Empress Dowager, signed the peace treaty of Shimononoseki with Count Ito, representing the Emperor Meiji. The war was over.

In Manchuria, migrant birds returned from the south, pale sun melting the snow on hills and roads revealed all the ugly aftermath of battle: unburied corpses with blackened limbs; rusty weapons marked with blood; pathetic scraps of soldiers' mementoes—letters from wives-now-widows; 'lucky' amulets that had proved false. The Japanese helped the Blums pack their precious celadon ware in straw-padded crates, and Alice saw them off, promising at least to visit them in Peking. Soon after, William and Frank arrived to escort their relatives to Chefoo, where Isabel, recovering from a late miscarriage, was staying with the younger children. It was an emotional reunion, and Alice was faintly amused to hear Eliza telling her sons several times how she owed her life to her daughter, to which they could only grunt reluctant approval, uneasily aware that they had done nothing to help.

'But one thing I cannot understand, Alice,' said Will, after Eliza had retired to bed, on the first evening of their journey, 'is what on earth you were doing in Port Arthur with that American? Such a joy-ride seems extremely foolish at the best of times, but to land yourself in the middle of a war—well really!'

'It was not a joy-ride,' Alice replied curtly. 'Naturally I didn't tell Mother, nor let the Japanese suspect, but most of the cargo on Bill's ship was guns and ammo for the garrison in Port Arthur, which we tried to deliver even though we were delayed by that typhoon.'

Frank whistled admiringly, 'Gun-running?'

'Exactly—we were trying to help, which is more than could be said of most people on China's side is it not?'

Will frowned angrily. 'Like Frank and me I suppose? Well, it's just not given to us all to be able to dash off on wild adventures. And though that puts a better complexion on it, I must say you've caused the whole family a great deal of anxiety.'

'And saved Mother, as she keeps telling you! But it really is time you stopped thinking of me as a little girl whose every move must be accounted for and worried over by the family, Will. What I do is actually my own affair, you know.'

'That's true, Will,' Frank agreed warmly. 'I didn't worry much. I kept telling you—Alice always comes through in the end!' He winked at his sister, and Will said stiffly, as he often had in the past, 'Oh, you two always stick together.'

However, when they reached Chefoo after two weeks travelling, Alice found she couldn't depend on Frank's support in all family matters. They joined Isabel at a hotel on the sea-front and, at first, simply relaxed—walking along the sheltered promenade, lounging on the hotel verandah, playing clock-golf and, most exquisite pleasure for Alice and Eliza, eating large four-course meals. But between them all was the unasked question: what was going to happen to their mother?

To Isabel the answer was clear, as she told her husband one evening as they dressed for dinner. '. . . After all, Will, Alice has got off very lightly recently. Dashing away on madcap jaunts, managing her own little business, with none of the cares of raising children. Surely she'd be willing to look after your mother now? They're fond of each other and Alice is ideally placed.'

Will did up his top trouser button with difficulty; he was getting a little stout; middle age creeping up. 'An excellent idea in theory, but I can't see Alice giving up her business for it.'

'Then she can care for Eliza and continue the business. The point is that Alice always seems to have it her own way. We did a lot for her in the past, and it's time she took on some burdens most women have to bear, instead of this airy-fairy stuff about women's rights and anti-foot-binding. It is, in my view, her duty. She's the only daughter here and has no other ties.'

Isabel pursed her lips. She too was beginning to feel the thickening of middle age, especially when in company with Charlotte, who was a very pretty little thing and well aware of it. Only that day, strolling along the promenade, three subalterns had greeted her with great enthusiasm and Charlotte gracefully responded. Isabel's recent miscarriage, about which she felt a certain guilty relief, had pulled her down; her mane of auburn hair lacked lustre beside her daughter's. . . .

Really it was too provoking—the easy lives some women seemed to lead. 'Well, Will,' she said as she straightened the folds of her skirt with a silken rustle. 'Please put it to Alice most strongly. I really don't see why we should have to take in your mother, and what's the alternative?'

'What about Mary and Robert?' Will mumbled.

'Oh come now, Will, they're getting on in years themselves and have done a great deal for Alice already without having to take on the burden of her mother, who, after all, is no relation of

Mary's. In any case, they're considering going Home to retire in the not too distant future, I believe. No, that wouldn't be fair. And as for Frank, I daren't think how poor Eliza would fare in Frank's Chinese establishment with that awful Dowager Wang in command.'

Later that evening, after Eliza had retired, and Isabel discreetly vanished, Will did put it strongly to his sister and was warmly supported by Frank, who pleaded that Peachy couldn't possibly be expected to help now she had poor Little Nut to look after. Alice listened, staring into her lap; she'd half expected it to come to this. Then she said in a low cold voice, 'So now you expect me to give up my life for Mother, do you? You don't think it much of a life anyway, probably. A single woman living in other people's homes. Do you suggest I give up the firm too?'

'Not at all. I'm sure you're capable of managing both. And Frank and I will help you get a little bungalow for the two of you.'

She turned on Frank. 'I thought you at least might understand the struggle it's been for me to become even half independent.'

'But Sis, I really don't see. . . . There would be just you and Mother living together, and only for a few years probably. She's getting on after all . . .'

'She may live for another decade. I hope she does. By which time I'd be—oh, you men. It doesn't bear thinking about.' She flared into sudden anger.

'Well we're her children, we have to think about it and it's a question of considering the alternatives. At least you can do that much,' William said, icily, refusing to match her temper.

'Oh, I'll think about it. Give me a day or two.'

'Say a day. Frank and I must get back to our respective duties very soon, while you ladies relax by the seashore.'

He tried to raise a smile from her, but she turned away, thinking about her duties, which her brothers never really took seriously. 'We'll talk again tomorrow,' she snapped as she went out.

Summer was just beginning in Chefoo. Through the reed blinds on the hotel balconies the morning sun shone from a blue sky over a blue sea. After breakfast, the lady guests sat in open sedan-chairs along the promenade, perspiring and chatting gently, while their children scampered nearby. Leaving Isabel, Eliza, and the children, Alice wandered off along the shore towards the cliffs. The only people she met were two Catholic nuns clad in ash-white robes who looked from a distance like moving shrouds. As they approached she saw their faces were also ash-white, as were those of most of the foreign women who led such unhealthy lives in this health resort—sitting about all day in tight clothes waiting for the next meal. Women, Alice thought, spent so much of their lives waiting—for husbands, for babies to arrive, for elderly parents to die. Initiatives were seldom expected of them and they seldom took them.

But had she, Alice Greenwood, behaved so very differently? Had she not spent most of her life so far toeing lines drawn by men—father or stepfather, brothers or husband? For Charles, as she admitted to herself now, had not lived up to her expectations. Yet his premature death had not truly freed her from the ingrained habit of waiting for a man to come along and tell her what to do next. If it hadn't been for Bill Risley, she reproached herself, she'd have spent the recent war cosily in Shanghai, just like Frank. So what had she done off her own bat? Kept the firm going, spoken in the anti-footbinding cause, organised a Fancy Fair to raise funds for it.

She wrinkled her nose in self-disgust. In such puny endeavours her life was slipping by and the scenes of slaughter she'd recently seen reminded her how fragile and short it was. And here she was, thirty-seven years old, and still she had not fully justified her existence, had not committed herself with conviction. But the cause of commitment was here—nothing less than China itself, land of her birth and upbringing, reeling from defeat, deeply humiliated and riven. The country needed strong, loyal citizens, and she thought with a familiar ache of Lin Fu-wei and the self-strengtheners. In his company she had enjoyed an exchange of ideas, begun to grasp the wider implications of politics and society, but in Shanghai such issues were seldom discussed.

Things were better in Peking, the Blums had assured her. Peking. Yet now her brothers were drawing new lines for her to toe, the picture inside that of devoted widowed sister caring for widowed mother in their mutually declining years. Was this truly her moral duty—and her only choice? She kicked the pebbles underfoot irritably, thinking it was, in the opinion of both the filial Chinese and her relatives.

At the end of the beach she walked up a steep incline.

Dragon-flies and swifts flew in the bright air on the hill-top; the town lay behind her, bored in the noon heat. Hotel guests would soon be making tracks for the dining-room. 'Where on earth is Alice?' Isabel would soon be asking. She so often sounded peevish these days. The years were passing for them all. Alice, watching one particular bird cavort and swoop against the sun, prayed for strength.

That evening, she pointed out to William and Frank that, as they each possessed commodious houses with staffs of servants, they were much better placed than she to undertake their mother's care. In any case, she was moving to Peking very soon and Eliza certainly would not want to live there. She had, she added, recently saved her mother's life, which should surely count for something. If it did, her indignant brothers were not about to acknowledge it, and Alice left Chefoo the following day, unforgiven and feeling very much on her own.

Part Two

4

On a sunny day during the late spring of 1896, Alice sat reading in a Peking courtyard under a just-blooming mimosa tree
beside a tiny pond wherein darted a shoal of three-tailed gold
and silver fish. The courtyard was behind her shop, 'The Polished Jade,' in Pumpkin Lane, one of a network of narrow
alleys to the west of the Ch'ien Men Gate in the south wall of
the Tartar City.

The square tower of the Ch'ien Men was a landmark. Its
magnificent rafters of Burmese teak had been brought by
Mongol rulers to the capital six centuries before, and from its
many square windows, its defenders had once fired arrows on
the invading hordes without. The tower rose above the low-
lying, sprawling caravanserai called Peking, or 'northern
capital.' But it was viewed also as the exact centre of the earth
in the eyes of the ancient Chinese. Looking north from the
tower, one saw the curved yellow-tiled roofs of the palaces of
the Forbidden City wherein dwelt K'uang Hsu, the young
Emperor of China and his formidable aunt, the Empress
Dowager.

To the south, on the other side of the high Tartar Wall—
wide enough for three carriages to be drawn abreast—was
the densely populated Chinese City. Here were boisterous,
busy markets and a Pleasure Quarter with gaming and opium
dens, restaurants, theatres, the 'Flower and Willow Lanes'
lined with brothels. Young Manchu and Chinese nobles, and
Emperors more secure and stalwart than the present frail
incumbent, had long been accustomed to disguising themselves as commoners to go whoring and gaming there, just like
medieval European princes. In their official capacities,
Emperors seldom emerged from their resplendent private
residences, except to pay seasonal homage at the twin temples of Heaven and Agriculture, whose bright-tiled roofs were

also visible from the Ch'ien Men.

On the gate's east side, opposite Pumpkin Lane, was the Legation Quarter where, in earlier times, embassies from subject nations such as Korea, Tibet, and Mongolia used to lodge when bringing annual tribute to the Celestial Emperor. The Chinese would have preferred it to remain that way, but now the foreign diplomats of the world's most powerful and modern nations dwelt there in residences appropriate in size and splendour to their international standing. The French Embassy was smart and perky; the Japanese boasted a Western-style entranceway; the Germans occupied a dignified palace; and to reach the British Legation one passed through a particularly massive, portentously carved gate. Not content with these spacious dwellings, each set in large compounds with servants' rooms and stables, most families of the diplomatic corps also kept summer residences in the cooler hills to the west of the capital, where the Empress Dowager had also built a Summer Palace for herself, with funds originally earmarked for the modernisation of the Chinese Navy.

Indeed, the writer of the article Alice was just reading actually dared to hint that if the money concerned had been put to its proper use, the Chinese might not have been defeated so disastrously in the war. 'See what contempt the world holds us in now,' he wailed. 'We are called the boneless giant, the headless dragon, the cracked kettle, the large soft melon waiting to be carved into pieces by more powerful nations. Russia, Japan, France, Germany, and Britain are like vampires come to suck our national blood, like butchers sharpening their knives ready to dismember us, while China is soundly sleeping on top of a pile of kindling.'

The writer, though typically prone to muddled metaphors, was clear sighted enough in his essential diagnosis of China's present situation, for, since the humiliating defeat of its Imperial Forces at the hands of the despised Japanese dwarfs, the country had suffered considerable loss of international power and prestige.

By the terms of the peace treaty, Korea became independent, China had to pay a crippling war indemnity, and the battle-scarred Liaotung Peninsula was ceded to Japan—though this last was soon rescinded following intervention by three Western powers. Viceroy Li Hung-chang, held chiefly responsible for the country's military defeat, was stripped of his Yellow Riding Jacket—a cape of golden silk with peacock-blue sleeves that was the highest imperial honour. Though the war convinced the government of the superiority of Western-style arms and the need for strengthening military defences, the spirit of reaction still reigned in high places. In growing opposition to this was the movement for much more radical, deep-seated reform and progress and its acknowledged chief exponent was Kang Yu-wei.

Kang, a doctor of philosophy, dubbed sincerely by his supporters and ironically by his enemies 'The Modern Sage,' had founded the School for New Learning in Canton five years before. He was a leading authority on 'foreign matters' and his theories for change attracted a number of clever, well-connected young men like Lin Fu-wei and Han-li. Following the débâcle of the war, it was these men who formed the nucleus of the Reform Movement, urging the need for fundamental change in China. The Movement favoured the establishment of a constitutional monarchy along European lines—unlike the outright revolutionary, Dr. Sun Yat-sen, who preached the overthrow of the Manchu dynasty. His reckless attempt to capture Canton and set up a liberal regime with himself as president failed miserably and Sun fled to Japan with a price on his head.

Dissociating themselves from such violent tactics, the Reformers set up a club in Peking for influential men with progressive ideas, but it had been closed earlier that year by a fearful and insecure government. However, the spirit of change was still abroad, several reformist associations had been started in the provinces, and various publications dedicated to the dissemination of radical ideas were in circulation.

Alice put down the one she'd been reading and stared into the sulphur-bright glow of the mimosa against a blazing blue sky. The heats were about to begin, and she wondered vaguely who would call at 'The Polished Jade' in the next few months when rich foreigners sought the cool of hills or coasts and China was about to be sucked dry, cut up, or burned down.

Yet she was optimistic; she had been ever since following through her resolve of the previous summer and moving to the capital. It had taken several months to dis-engage and re-establish herself. Mary and Robert had been hurt by her departure from Fairlawns; Frank had said the new enterprise was doomed to failure; Isabel and William, who took Eliza to live with them, had not tried to conceal how put upon they felt. But Alice had persevered and, leaving Benjy in Shanghai as her chief buyer and agent, eventually reached Peking in a mule-cart, on a grisly-cold winter's day, her baggage, Snow Duck and his family in the cart behind.

'The Polished Jade' itself was narrow and ill-lit, its walls lined with box-filled shelves. Rooms were ranged round three sides of the courtyard behind where Alice sat; on the furthest side a gate led into a yard with a well in the centre and smaller rooms round for all the Snow Ducks, known as Mrs. Duck, Ducklings first to fourth. Duckling Number Three came toddling into the sunlight, waving a painted paper butterfly on an osier twig. The ginger-tawny striped kitten recently retrieved from a nearby drain and dubbed Tiger Blossom leaped in the air in pursuit of this colourful prey, and Alice chuckled as she watched.

'Number Three,' she called. 'Go and fetch your father.'

Snow Duck was gasping sulkily as he emerged from the kitchen, beads of sweat on his shaven pate. 'The heat's going to be terrible here, dries up the bones.'

'Well we all have to get used to it. You must find an ice-man to deliver daily. You know I'm expecting a visitor? Mrs. Small from Ichang. You remember, you met her in Hankow?'

He nodded. 'Big lady, little name.'

'That's right. Anyway, make sure there's a good tea—honey-ginger cakes.'

He shambled off, whisking flies from his round face with an off-white cloth. The child and the kitten continued their game and Alice watched, thinking vaguely about Daisy, who was coming on a farewell visit, for Archie's health was failing and they were going Home to retire. Alice would miss her, for the older woman's support had helped her define her own attitudes, prodded her conscience. Daisy's wholehearted commitment to the anti-footbinding cause and outspokenness on the subject of women's rights often made her feel a weakling by comparison. She sensed she hadn't quite lived up to Daisy's expectations. 'But our personal circumstances are very different,' she was thinking to herself, when she heard the shop door open.

'So this is where you are? Phew, it's warm!' Daisy's voluminous shape filled the shop; she removed a floppy pink sun-hat as Alice kissed her.

'You must be exhausted, come into the courtyard where it's shady.'

'Let me poke about first. 'The Polished Jade'—a good name. And you deal only in that hard and lustrous stone?'

'More or less. I've left all the trinkety stuff in Shanghai and joined the quality market, as the Blums say.'

'The Blums?'

'French Jews. I met them in that Japanese internment settlement I told you about. Cultivated people and rather Bohemian. They own an antique shop here too, but the authorities don't like foreigners setting up here. The Blums showed me the right palms to grease and introduced me to jade connoisseurs who can tell the age of a good piece by its temperature and touch only—a certain coolness of years, they say.'

'You're enjoying it, obviously?'

'For the present yes, because I'm still learning, and less easily fooled by soapstone or glass imitations than I was! But I don't intend making it my life's work. On the other hand, I do have to earn my own living—unlike most women of my age, after all.'

Daisy picked up a mottled-green jade inkstone, rubbing her thumb in its central hollow. 'Beautiful stuff. Like me you mean? Yes Alice, I do understand, and I admire you for sticking at it instead of looking around for a suitable gentleman to keep you in idle wifely style. Of course, marriage can be wonderful, as it has been mostly for Archie and me. But there's always a price to pay, as I'm realising.'

'Price—for you? Let's go and sit down.'

Alice led the way into the courtyard and called for tea while Daisy looked around appreciatively. 'It's quite charming, Alice. Your very own place.'

'Apart from the years shared with Charles, I've always lived in other people's homes. It's so interesting being alone— a little worrying too.'

'At least you're the mistress of your own destiny, and that's worth a great deal. I occasionally wish. . . . You know, it's absolutely infuriating having to leave China just now. I can't tell you how it pains me. But what can I do? Archie's nearly ten years older than I and the doctors say he must go Home.' She stared into her teacup, puffing with frustration. 'His spirit and enthusiasm have just drained away, and here am I, in my mid-fifties, wanting to carry on with so much—the League, the even more exciting issues of the whole Reform Movement.'

'Well dear, the League will carry on now without you I'm sure. You've given it so much impetus over the years.'

'Oh everything will carry on famously without me. I don't imagine myself indispensable. But how will I carry on without *it*? Without all the causes and controversies that have been my meat and drink for nigh on thirty years? What on earth will I *do* in the idyllic little Sussex hamlet Archie's set his heart on?' She grimaced and Alice put a comforting hand on her shoulder. 'Oh my dear Daisy, I never quite realised. I'm so sorry and it does seem most unfair.'

'Well it is, and it's one of the injustices we women have to bear. If it was t'other way around, I'd have to stay here for Archie's work, but as it is I can't. It would kill him off in no time if I didn't go Home with him. I can't even talk frankly with him about it as I am to you now. So I keep pretending to be madly enthusiastic about taking tea on vicarage lawns and walking along leafy lanes in the twilight.' She laughed bitterly. 'So that's why you are fortunate in some ways, Alice, having only your own life to consider.'

'But it's not always easy. Indeed most women think my solitary state is greatly to be pitied, if not scorned.'

'Oh most women! I really despair of them sometimes. They are so indolent, so accepting, and the young ones, with more opportunities than I ever had, don't take advantage . . . but change is a long, slow progress, is it not? Well, that's enough of my moans. Tell me what's going on here in the seat of Celestial power? What are the Reformers actually accomplishing? I feel quite a country bumpkin.'

'Well, I've not settled here very long, but through the Blums I've met Hanlin scholars of the so-called "conservative-reform faction." China needs an infusion of western science and technology and all will be well. It's the old line. They want to keep the Confucian institutions intact, because they still secretly believe the Sons of Han have a monopoly on civilisation and true culture. But the self-strengtheners were saying that years ago, weren't they? And it doesn't really work. I haven't yet made any contact with the core of the Movement, I'm afraid.'

'Such as our Modern Sage, Kang Yu-wei?'

'I suppose that's aiming rather high, but . . .'

'Why not? He could probably put your linguistic talents to good use. And if I were staying . . . Anyway, ask Archie about it.'

'He's here with you then?'

'Oh yes, I forgot to say. He's visiting Timothy Barlow, you've heard of him I'm sure? And then coming here to pick me up and see you.'

'Barlow—"Baa-high," the other missionaries call him I believe on account of his contacts with leading intellectuals in high places.'

'Oh, that's typical missionary sour grapes. Timothy's quite a rarity and so lays himself open to criticism from lesser breeds. Archie's no lover of bible-thumpers generally, as you know, but he makes an exception there. Why, speak of the devil, I do believe . . .'

They heard the shop door open and Archie Small came into the courtyard, greeting Alice warmly. She hadn't seen him for a very long time and in the interim his large frame had become wasted and shambling, his hair white.

'And how did you find Timothy?' his wife asked as Alice ordered more tea.

'Jubilant. Positively cock-a-hoop. According to him, the Reformers are thawing the icebergs of centuries and sweeping China towards a new-minted, free-flowing dawn of personal liberty and political freedom.'

'You sound very sceptical?'

'Suppose I am. I just can't imagine it will be nearly as easy as that. Two months ago one of the Ministers asked him to compile a list of China's Most Needed Reforms. He went at it with a will, of course.'

'And why not? He's being positive and active as we all should be,' she challenged him.

Archie munched silently on a cake.

'And what was on the list?' Alice asked.

'I can't remember in detail—foreign advisers for government departments, building of more railways, factories, ships, modernising education. And, I quote, "The establishment of an intelligent Press with experienced foreign journalists to assist Chinese editors for the better enlightenment of the masses." I certainly can't see the Old Buddha and her reactionary cohorts wearing that one.'

'Oh, perdition on the Old Buddha, she's had her day surely?

And the reformers are right to pin their hopes on the young Emperor?'

Archie settled back, looking into the sky. 'So they are, but I'm afraid she's not finished yet. The whole Manchu dynasty is at stake—generations of entrenched power and ancient custom, of die-hard corruption and self-interest. It isn't going to be easily overturned.'

Daisy twitted him irritably. 'You're such a pessimist these days, Archie. You've lost all your fight.'

He crossed his legs and yawned. 'I think I'm a realist these days, but perhaps that's what growing older does. You know we're retiring Home, Alice?'

'Yes, and I'm sorry. I shall miss you. Very much.' She looked at the old couple, and her eyes misted over.

'Oh, I'm quite ready to go. Things aren't what they were ten or fifteen years ago. You remember Ichang in the early '80s? Those magnificent junks on the river, just a handful of foreign residents? Now the Yangtze's awash with mail steamers and gunboats as it's supposed to be "within the British sphere of influence." What infernal cheek! And the riverine ports are chock-a-block with foreign merchants, globe-trotters, missionaries. No, it's time to leave.'

'Some people might find that more exciting than it was,' Daisy commented tartly.

'Well, I've never yet met an exciting missionary, except Timothy Barlow.'

'Oh yes, Archie. I was saying to Alice she ought to meet him. I'm sure he and the Reformers could use her linguistic skills.'

'Absolutely. Why not come along tomorrow evening, Alice? He's invited me, and you Daisy, to a meeting in the Hall of Particular Brilliance, wherever that edifice shines. Some leading reformers are speaking. You'll join us, Alice?'

'Er . . . yes, I suppose . . .'

'Come now,' Daisy said with asperity. 'It's an excellent opportunity to do something useful, get into the political swim.'

Alice swallowed her hesitation, the reason for which Daisy couldn't possibly guess: she'd heard that Lin was an active member of the Reform group in the capital. But, she told herself sternly, how ridiculous and petty it would be to remain aloof during this exciting time of national change, merely because of the high, sweet risk of encountering her former lover. Somewhat guiltily, she felt a tingle of excitement.

'I'd be delighted to come along to meet the renowned Mr. Barlow,' she replied decisively.

The Hall of Particular Brilliance was located in the centre of the Chinese City, and Timothy Barlow, who met Alice and the Smalls outside it the next evening, was a shrewd-eyed, black-haired stocky Welshman with thirty years' experience of China behind him. Over the years, he'd reached the difficult conclusion that his special mission was less to convert the natives to the narrow Baptist dogma of his youth, than to, as he wrote, 'liberate them from the bonds of ignorance and harmful custom and show them the broader light of scientific and religious education.' Consequently he had severed his connection with the Baptists and was now Secretary of the Society for the Diffusion of General and Christian Knowledge. His dedication to reform had won him the confidence of many Chinese intellectuals and the scorn of many missionaries, who felt he had no business getting involved in political intrigue. But he was, to the hilt, and clearly thrived on it.

'Delighted, Mrs. Greenwood-Grant. I've heard much about you from Daisy,' he shook her hand. 'I only wish my wife Grace were here, she'd like very much to meet you too. But she's at Home with the children just now. Now, let me see, someone else mentioned you. Oh yes, your relative, half-brother I believe, Adam Blake. Came to see me in Shanghai on the way to Changsha, in search of up-to-date translations of medical works.'

'How is he? I missed him, having just moved here. He's at Changsha's new medical mission I believe? I imagine he's as earnest, shy and sweet as ever?'

Barlow smiled. 'I'd not met him before, but the description fits.'

'I'm glad he's in Changsha, it gives me an extra reason to go there again myself one day. I spent much of my childhood there, strangely enough.'

'Did you indeed? You must tell me some time, but now they're ready to begin. A short talk from the platform, followed by open discussion, is the order of the evening.'

The hall was crowded but Alice saw Lin the moment she entered. He was sitting on the platform with two other men and talking animatedly in a manner she remembered well. His frame was fuller, creases of experience apparent on his face, but the eyes were as bright, the brushed-back hair the same lustrous ebony. The sight of him quite unnerved her and she clung to Daisy's arm as, being the only foreigners present, they were ushered courteously to the front. Lin looked up, smiled at Timothy, then saw her. There was no hesitation in his recognition; he started visibly, paused, then smiled briefly at her before resuming his conversation.

'You know that man?' Daisy asked as they sat down.

'Yes. Lin Fu-wei. He was the lecturer in Port Arthur with whom I started translating Mill's *Liberty*.'

'Really? And you've not seen him since?'

'No, not once. Till tonight.' Alice hoped the emotions she felt surging through her were not obvious to everyone around her.

The meeting began and Lin did most of the talking. Alice sat with her hands clenched tightly in her lap, scarcely daring to look at him; he didn't once glance at her. He sounded breathless, stumbled occasionally, but she hardly registered what he said. If he rushes off without speaking to me, I shall follow him she told herself; I couldn't bear not to. I can't let him go away again, not after all this time.

Then Lin stopped abruptly, saying he wanted to hear the audience's views before leaving for another engagement. He's going to slip away from me, she thought. As the discussion began, Timothy whispered to Daisy.

'Lin's not quite on his usual form tonight. I hope nothing's happened behind the scenes.'

'You know him well?'

'Fairly. One of the brightest of the Cantonese contingent and a friend of Kang Yu-wei's.'

'Alice tells me she met him in Port Arthur years ago.'

'Oh? Then they must meet again.'

Yes, please, oh *please*, Alice prayed, overhearing. But she could make no move, and sat rigidly still, her mouth dry with the tension of wondering what she'd do if he hurried away without a word to her.

Lin cut the discussion short, saying he had to leave soon, but first wanted to talk to an old friend who'd arrived unexpectedly. He left the platform and came straight to her.

'Uncut Jade,' his voice was low, a private tone.

'Lin . . .'

'I told you we'd meet again.'

'I didn't believe you.'

506

They simply looked at each other as if the hall was empty. Daisy watching, understood much that had always puzzled her about Alice Greenwood.

'It's good to see you again,' she murmured.

'And you. You are with Timothy?'

'And my friends. Let me introduce Mr. and Mrs. Small.'

'Ah, Mrs. Daisy Small, the founder of the Anti-Footbinding League. I'm honoured, madam. I was convinced of your views several years ago. Indeed I'm a member of the League in Canton.'

They shook hands and chatted for a minute, then Lin turned back to Alice.

'And your husband? Is he here?'

'My husband was drowned in a boating accident several years ago.'

He bowed his head. 'Please accept my belated condolences. It is good to see you,' he repeated helplessly. 'I simply have to go to another important meeting. Are you here long?'

'I live here now. I own an antique shop—'The Polished Jade,' in Pumpkin Lane.'

He smiled then. 'The Jade is polished? But of course, all rough edges smoothed.'

'Of that I'm not sure.'

Timothy Barlow broke in on them. 'Mrs. Grant is an excellent linguist, Lin. I thought perhaps . . .'

'Oh, I know, Timothy. We began translating together years ago.'

A man plucked at Lin's sleeve telling him he'd be late for his next appointment. 'I have to go now,' he took her hand with a boldness that surprised her. 'But soon . . .' he bowed with a Western-style courtliness he'd not used to practise. 'Au revoir.' He spoke the last, oddly, in French, then, with hurried farewells to the others, disappeared.

Alice wanted to sit down again, to laugh, or cry, but the meeting was over and the audience dispersing. Evading Daisy's natural curiosity, Alice left her friends outside and rode home in an open rickshaw. A full spring moon hung in the sky like a luscious fruit ripe for the plucking. Her spirit bounded with joy and she wanted Lin with a recklessness beyond her wildest imaginings. He would surely come to her tomorrow, and her mouth tingled at the thought of their first kiss.

But he did not come the next day and by the afternoon of the second one she was reduced to an uncharacteristic state of tense irascibility. A dust storm had blown up; the rush and swirl of the wind grated harshly on the paper windows of the shop and on her frayed nerves; the whole city was blanketed in a mustard-coloured cloud of particles straight from the deserts of Central Asia. The acrid dust seeped into noses and throats; those who had to go out swathed the lower part of their faces in cloths, which made them look strange and sinister. Thus, when Lin came out of the yellowish twilight into the shop she thought for a panicky second he was a bandit come to rob her.

He took the cloth from his face and smiled. 'Good afternoon, dear Uncut. I'm sorry I couldn't come yesterday.'

'I was beginning to wonder if you'd come at all.'

'Of course I would.' He looked round. 'So you are selling off bits of our imperial heritage to Western tourists now, hey?'

She couldn't quite remember how his voice sounded when he teased. 'I'm trying to turn an honest penny, Lin, and my wares are good.'

'I'm sure—you were always that, honest and good.' He stepped up to her, eyes shining with admiration.

'Oh, I wouldn't say . . .'

He took her into his arms, and it was as if she'd never been held since he'd last kissed her, some fifteen years before. They clung together, gasping with the passion of their mutual need and he fondled her in ways her body instantly remembered. 'Do I have to be polite and restrained, take tea and cakes, talk of this and that and nothing at all?' he murmured.

She snuggled against him. 'No, my lover, the first thing that we both remember will be first, and then we'll try and talk some sense.'

Leading her inside, he took off his outer jacket, his warm eyes not leaving her face as he began to undo the silk buttons of her high-necked blouse. Slipping his hands inside, he murmured, 'Ah, the soft, full breasts of a Western woman . . .'

She kissed his lips, 'I hope you've not become too familiar with them since we parted?'

'Oh no, no others, but I never forgot yours,' he assured her, as they moved with one accord towards her bedroom.

In earlier hope, she had put a hard, red-silk Chinese bolster on the bed, and now, just as she'd hoped, she could caress the dramatic black of his hair against the red, smiling as he pulled her down over him. He bunched her breasts, rubbing his cheeks luxuriously between them, then taking her nipples deep in his mouth. She gasped with the pleasure of it, feeling him rising urgently beneath her.

'It's been a long, long time,' he said, half-apologising for his haste as he rolled her down under him, spreading her wide open, moistened and ready to receive him. When he went inside her it was as if no one else had since he had last and she couldn't experience enough of him. Sometime in the late evening when the wind had died and the dust settled, they separated their damp bodies, put on robes, and walked entwined round the courtyard where the mimosa was tipped with moonlight. Alice brought crispy puff-cakes and preserved fruits, and they sat feeding each other and, after a while, talking in coherent sentences instead of the soft sounds of their recent sweet congress.

'So tell me what you've been doing all these years without me, Mr. Lin Fu-wei, leader of men?' she stroked his neck.

'You mock me with that ambition I first told you about. As you see, I'm still no leader, though closer to it, perhaps, than before. At last the reformers of China are moving in the right direction. But what have I been doing? you ask. Teaching, writing pamphlets, agitating, speaking.'

'And learning?'

'That most of all. So much to learn. As one of my colleagues wrote, "We Chinese can no longer expect to excel others merely by sitting upright in a dignified attitude." Westerners know this and I've been trying to understand their ways.'

'But at least you went to Europe once and that must have explained much.'

He laughed shortly. 'Once—for a few months, when I was young, callow, undiscerning. But ever since I am labelled a "returned student"—a supposed expert on the whole Western world. I've learned how complicated it is, but little else.' He squeezed her. 'I should have had a Western woman to help me all these years.'

'Ah, but you chose to marry a Chinese.'

'That had to be so, Uncut. I married very soon after leaving you. My wife and children live in Canton—three boys and a girl. My eldest son is very clever and I have great hopes of him. Perhaps it is he who will be "The Leader" one day.'

She stared into his face. 'It's hard to believe—you, a father,

509

with a promising son. It seems only yesterday that we parted—
that cold, grey afternoon in Port Arthur. I was there again the
winter before last, during the war. The old house where you
lodged has been pulled down, the hills behind covered with fortifications. It was dreadful, Lin, when the Japanese invaded.'

'What on earth were you doing there then?'

'I was translating for an American who was gun-running for
the Chinese,' she was quite proud of that.

'Honestly? Tell me.'

She kissed him. 'Some other time, it's too horrible for this
sweet moment. And your wife? Is she very beautiful?'

'She is my wife.. And "her every hair is always in place."
Four years older than I. And that is that. We'd been betrothed
since I was eight. My father died three years after our marriage, but was vouchsafed the sight of his first grandchild. But I
am puzzled, Uncut Jade. You have not met another Englishman
to marry? You have no children?' He touched her nose. 'It is
very strange, considering you are lovely as green jade in moonlit water.'

'Oh, Englishmen don't queue up outside my door, nor say
things like that to me! But, yes, I could have re-married. Only
the ones I've met are so very settled-down, so sure of themselves. Usually I disagree with them, which they don't like. And
I'm getting very used to my independence, only I wish I could
find my own sureties.' She tweaked his ear, thinking that one of
her few sureties was her continued love for him, which must
always remain outlandish, outside of convention. 'As for children, they just didn't come. Rather ineffectual, am I not?'

'You? Never. And now you have something to believe in—the
reformation of China, a big enough cause surely? Come along to
our next meeting and offer your services as a translator. So
many Western ideas circulate among us that are not being
properly expressed in our language, and you can help in this.
You will, won't you?'

He lay her back down on the bed, and she felt his weight coming over her again. 'You know I can't resist such a request—
especially just now.'

'Why should you resist? The cause is good, the man is capable.' He began unfastening her robe.

'But won't I seem very strange there, among so many Chinese
men?'

'One or two other women are involved. And as my woman,

510

you will be all right.' His possession of her then was total and they both revelled in it.

To Alice, the act of becoming Lin's mistress—in the eyes of Westerners, his 'unofficial concubine' among the Chinese, which had once seemed so scandalously reckless—now seemed quite natural. The years had taught her the rarity of passionate love and the integrity of her own emotions; she was not again going to deny them for the lesser claims of conventional opinion. Moreover, she was growing older, and so was Lin; the times were uncertain and fleeting and she was determined to make the most of them. With this resolve and in the role of Lin Fu-wei's woman and translator extraordinary, Alice was permitted to attend meetings of the Reformers and share the spirit of heady if somewhat insubstantial optimism that moved them. As Daisy Small said enviously when she and Archie left Peking for good, it was the chance, the challenge of a life-time that would bring her into contact with some of the most original minds in the country. Original they certainly were, compared to the built-in conservatism of most of their compatriots, but they were also floundering, struggling to make sense of alien political concepts.

As Alice realised when she actually began listening to Lin as well as touching and seeing him, the Reformers' vision of an ideal China was radically progressive even by most Western standards, and certainly beyond the wildest imaginings of its masses. They wanted popularly elected central and regional governments, state hospitals, and educational foundations, communal living places.

'No more families, but men and women living together for a year and then changing around if they want to,' Lin told her mischievously.

'Sounds marvellous, providing women are well educated and able to earn their livings like men so they can move off too. And who's to look after the children?'

'There'll be state nurseries and kindergartens.'

'You know, I can't quite see your average son and daughter of Han taking to this.'

'But human progress is inevitable and that is what we must teach our people. Human institutions are perfectible; that is what the West believes.'

'I'm a Westerner, but I'm much less sure than you on that score,' Alice admitted, yet she desperately wanted to believe it

511

for Lin's sake, and when she was with the Reformers, she did.

They met throughout the summer in a stifling room in an alley off the Pleasure Quarter in the Chinese City. It was next to a theatre, garish posters advertising the next performances hung outside the lattice, through which drifted the falsetto notes of singing girls, musicians' flutes, shouts of the audiences, and where the heavy air was spiced with the jasmine-oil perfumes of prostitutes, the delectable odours of fried cabbage and sizzling pork-strips from the nearby food stalls.

The Reformers, magnificently disdainful of all these temptations, were hungry only for knowledge, and zealous as missionaries. Their bibles included translations of Darwin, Marx, and Thomas Huxley, the just-written *Study of Benevolence* by T'an Ssu-t'ung, and the iconoclastic writings of Kang Yu-wei. Tirelessly they asked questions, of themselves and each other: Is not reform essential for the health of any nation? If the weak are the prey of the strong, then is it not only through change that China can manage to survive? But how could one reconcile Darwin's theory of the survival of the fittest with Kang's ideal of an all-embracing, non-competitive, Universal Commonwealth?

Some of the Reformers greatly admired what they saw as Westerners' public-spiritedness, dynamism and political realism compared to which, they, the Chinese were still 'deeply entangled in the nets' of official corruption, ignorant superstition, and clannish loyalties. Others were less sure. Westerners to them were clever but not wise, wealthy but not discriminating, powerful but not compassionate. Was that really the worthiest model for all mankind?

And womankind also? A controversial recent pamphlet on women's education stated that, in future, both sexes must be involved in public life, using their intelligence equally. As the writer put it, 'In the struggle for existence, all capable should produce.' So the Reformers congratulated themselves on Alice's presence among them. She was both a 'woman scholar' and an early example of the new breed of women who would move freely around Kang's ideal universal commonwealth dropping babies in nurseries, parents in old folks' homes, and mates if the mood took them.

Alice, however, did not avail herself of all these options just then, for she was happy and busy enough. The business prospered and she sometimes travelled in search of rare items to build up her stock. The translating she did for the cause of Reform made her think more deeply than before about the basic conflicts of the human condition. When Lin was in the capital, she discussed her ideas with him and other Reformers who came to 'The Polished Jade' in the evenings, together with other 'new women.' Most striking of the latter was a well-borne Manchu, nicknamed The Princess, who, after some education abroad, was a convert to the Republican ideal. Though her mind was new-minted, her body was comfortable only in its traditional trappings; she wore sumptuously embroidered robes of orange and emerald, tottered on high jewelled clogs and dressed her hair in large bow-shaped wings, decorated with pearls and flowers. Occasionally, Timothy Barlow also joined them, made somewhat uneasy by certain attitudes and practices which he, as a devout Christian, could not possibly approve, yet the Celt in him was beguiled by the fine, free hopefulness of it all.

Timothy, liking Alice, pretended not to notice that Lin stayed behind when the others left—when they could be intimately close, talking about their friends, he initiating her in further ways of what he termed 'the turning of the white dragon.'

'Now I am older I understand better the polarity of the Yang and Yin, the sunny and shady, the firm and the yielding, the masculine and feminine,' he told her. 'Oh, I know you'll want to protest, thinking your part sounds lesser. But can you not see our needs and our capacities are equal? We are like two sides of a roof, each needing the other for support. Of what use is my out-standing if there is no in-standing? So when we make love it is as a "flowery combat" with neither winner nor loser, dear.'

She smiled, finding enjoyment easy because of the natural unselfconsciousness of his words and movements, which she had never experienced elsewhere, even with Lung-kuang. For she had learned little of true sensual pleasure at the hands of her Western lover, Charles, who had been deferential, hasty, unsure of himself. Lin, by contrast, knew how to refine his own and his partner's enjoyment in a leisured and guiltless fashion, and so successful was he that sometimes, lying beside him in the warm afterglow of love, Alice was beguiled into dreaming of a rosy, shared, future. First, there would be a peaceful revolution, during which the policies of the Reformers would be gradually but effectively implemented; then Lin would be summoned to serve in the new Government, and she would be

513

at his side, sharing his hopes, schemes, the burdens of his office.

But all that was head-in-the-clouds, for months went by, winter came, but nothing decisive occurred. When travelling became more difficult, Lin spent more time in Peking—the main focus of Reformist fervour, where the company was altogether congenial. The city closed in upon itself; dark, northern, isolated. Teams of two-humped camels with long furry coats and bells round their necks clumped through the northern gates bearing loads of frozen game from Mongolia, and coal from the mines; coolies with blue-cold legs delivered the coal in baskets slung from poles across their skinny shoulders. Indoors, the coal fired *kangs*, the hollowed brick benches topped with padded quilts on which people lolled or slept, savouring the warmth below.

Homeless beggars and lepers, bereft of *kangs* or coal, often froze to death in the bitter nights as they huddled in gutters or under mat awnings. Their ragged bodies were robbed early of any small possessions by collectors of night-soil who spooned the precious faeces of humans and animals into brown-encrusted carts, or by sellers of salt, who whipped the sore-covered backs of their donkeys to rouse them into morning activity. The more fortunate of the capital's inhabitants did not venture abroad till later, when the sun had melted several inches off the long icicles hanging from the low roof eaves, and even then they wore several jackets, one over another, so they looked like plump top-heavy dolls made of wadding and fur.

Younger Son, Han-li, arriving at the Tartar gate in a covered mule-cart, saw the changeless, miserable, medieval squalor of it all, and could have cried. He'd spent the previous months in Japan, sent there on an educational exploration by the progressive Governor of Hunan who was planning to open a college for the study of new learning and Western technology in Changsha. It was a bold move on the Governor's part, and he needed the support of men like Han-li—Hunanese by origin and with some Western education. As his cart ploughed through the deep mud of the streets, Han-li was pondering whether he should commit himself to a provincial posting at a time when so much was going on in the capital, so much needing to be changed.

His arrival was a pleasurable surprise to Alice, who'd known of his stay in Japan, but hadn't expected him in Peking afterwards.

'I shouldn't have come really, a difficult journey at this

season. But I so wanted to talk to people here—about Japan, about what I should do.' He'd gone to stay with a reformist friend who'd told him that Alice was right in the centre of things. 'He heard rumours that your shop is just a blind,' Han-li was admiring, 'and the house in Pumpkin Lane a positive hotbed of revolutionary intrigue.'

'Nonsense. My shop is serious business—it's my livelihood. Certainly the Reformers come here sometimes, may turn up later in fact. They come mainly because of Lin Fu-wei, the Leader.' She put it in deliberate quotes, adding, 'He lives here with me when he's in Peking.'

Han-li averted his gaze. He'd long known of the liaison, but he didn't want to hear it. The very thought of bedding a Western woman appalled him; he couldn't understand how Lin could bring himself to do it.

'Relationships between the sexes are changing nowadays, Younger Brother,' she challenged him.

'I suppose so,' he mumbled, embarrassed.

'It's part of the reform process—men and women working and living alongside each other, women having equal rights.'

He said in a rush, 'I had my daughter's feet unbound, so she will not be permanently crippled.'

'Oh, I'm so glad—what a grand thing to do. Did your wife object?'

'Yes, but I over-rode her. I don't believe women do have equal rights to make certain decisions.'

'Oh come, just because she's wrong in this instance. Women are more bound by tradition and superstition, but that's because they've not been equally educated yet. I've told you before.'

'Perhaps, perhaps.' He got up and stared into the courtyard. Fluffy shreds of snow clung to the mimosa's branches, cold parodies of summer's brightness. He liked Uncut Jade very much, but she showed her whole mouth when she laughed, which was unseemly, and she spoke more boldly than any woman he'd known. How could the Leader . . .?

Sensing his displeasure, Alice changed the subject. 'How is the family in Changsha, Han-li? My half-brother Adam's in the medical mission there now, by the way. Is all well there? I haven't heard for a long time.'

'Weng died—of a lingering fever in the summer heats. Did you know?'

515

'Weng! Oh, I'm sorry. Poor, poor Tamao.' She couldn't imagine Han-li's eldest sister, Tamao, without her husband Weng; it had been a true, rare, love-marriage. 'And Weng was such a kind, sensitive man. Not old either. Oh dear, I wish I could see Tamao again. And now she'll be entirely at the mercy of Eldest Brother?'

'I fear so. I'll be there—that is, if I take the job at the new college. It's so hard to decide. Just the few of us among all China's millions who know what must be done to save the country. Such a gigantic task. That's what I came to talk to Lin and the others about. It's all most urgent, yet nothing is happening.'

'There's quite a lot of activity behind the scenes and the Reformers are speaking out openly now. You'll hear—Lin will explain and give you sound advice.'

On this Han-li counted, for Lin was still the master in his mind, he the former student. But, later that evening when Lin arrived with a friend nicknamed Crabbie (because of his cautious, sideways approach to radical issues) and the exotic Princess, it was Han-li who did most of the talking, for the main topic was Japan. The Japanese, he explained, hovering edgily between contempt and admiration, had opened their arms wide to embrace the teachings and technologies of the West.

Trains, postal and telegraph services connected their main cities, efficiently organised by officials wearing white gloves, peaked caps, starched uniforms; in the Treaty Ports were banks, colleges, commercial undertakings of all kinds. New factories, shipbuilding companies, and steel works were being developed, and the constitutional government, first elected seven years before, had united the country under one head. Most ominously, that government was encouraging the buildup of military forces on land and sea. The people hadn't forgotten their easy victory over the Chinese—nor that most of their gains on the battlefield had afterwards been lost at the negotiating table due to foreign intervention.

'In politics, as in war, they understand that might is right,' Han-li said, 'but we, the Celestial elite, still disdain the hubbub of international and commercial competition, do we not? Well, the Japanese have learned better. Samurai have become successful business men, provincial nobles statesmen of the world, even ordinary peasants leave the land to work in factories. That is how to become strong.'

'And the women? How do they take to all these changes?'
Alice asked.

'They just get on with things as usual—working in the fields,
cleaning the big new buildings and factories. Wives of top
officials wear those obscene Western-style evening costumes
with tight waists and low necklines that show too much. They
look ridiculous. So do the "new men" of Tokyo in their stiff
black suits, wing collars and gold watch-chains dangling round
their puny little chests. They've developed a craze for French
champagne—drink it by the bucketful. So bloody cocksure,'
Han-li's voice trembled with anger and frustration. 'But why
not? They're acquiring the right skills, they've got the drive, the
intelligence—above all, the masses are behind them.' He
banged his fist on the table. 'What we must have here is a
popular government and a constitutional monarchy with an
Emperor like their Meiji at its head.'

The Princess broke in, 'And would Kuang-hsu become a
Meiji for us if he were given the chance?'

Lin answered her. 'We just don't know—an imponderable
we have to test.'

'Sun Yat-sen thinks we'd be wiser to overthrow the Manchus
"swift as a clap of thunder" and set up a republic,' Han-li told
her.

'You met him in his Yokohama hideout?'

'No, he's in London—a conspiratorial revolutionary always
on the move. I met some of his associates who are hand-in-glove
with some Japanese reformers. They believe we Chinese and
Japanese should band together to get rid of all foreign
oppression. Asia for the Asians is their battle-cry.'

'Asia for the Japs, more like,' muttered Crabbie. 'Sun's little
better than a peasant, a wild man with no respect for the
ancient verities. And he's mad to trust those double-crossing
dwarfs. Look how they deceived us at the beginning of the last
war, then tightened the screws.'

In the silence that followed, Alice wondered what the next
twenty years had in store for the Celestial Empire. She sensed
that changes would be dramatic and her inability to foresee
their substance depressed her. Indeed, the awesome uncer-
tainty of the future seemed to have oppressed them all. The
Princess sighed and stood up, restive to leave. A jewelled pin
fell from her hair and, after waiting in vain for Crabbie to
retrieve it with Western-style gallantry, she picked it up,

asking, 'Do you think we'll be the last generation of Manchu women to wear these ridiculous shoes and hair-styles?'

Crabbie quoted softly, ' "No longer will the leisurely Chinaman oil and plait his queue before the day's toil, Nor the Manchu lady spread her lacquered tresses wide as jewelled wings in the morning sun. The samurai's top-knot is already chopped . . ." etc. A modern poem, composed by a court reactionary, of course.'

'Ha! Consider the millions of our pigtails out there, bending over each day's humble task, oblivious of the knives of the future.' Lin waved his arms dramatically.

'We seem to have become rather portentous,' Alice smiled at him.

'It's the wine,' he drained his cup. 'Time for bed. Speaking of the great beyond out there, are you taking the Changsha post, Han-li, or staying here?'

'It's a most difficult decision, Leader. My inclination is to stay here, but the claims of my family—my elder sister is recently widowed, my father ages. If I settled my wife and children in the ancestral home it would please him.'

Lin nodded understandingly. 'For me too—my family waits in Canton. I must return soon, when the snow melts and the roads open.'

Alice knew this, but the saying of it made her speak with asperity, 'Strange isn't it—how all these grand schemes of changing family structures are forgotten when it's you and your own relatives involved? I thought you Reformers were going to stage your peaceful revolution here in the capital, not in Canton or Changsha?'

'I told you, the Modern Sage is submitting another Memorial to the Emperor begging him to follow the examples of Meiji and Peter the Great. We must wait for the outcome and meanwhile spread the word of Reform through the land, including Canton and Changsha.'

Lin's tone of rebuke vexed her and she turned away as Han-li rose to leave, looking from one to the other. 'If I may suggest, Uncut Jade, as Lin is to be away for a while, why not come to Hunan? I shall definitely go for a visit and you said you wanted to see my family again and your half-brother.'

'Younger Son, that's a wonderful idea! I'll think it over.'

For a while, Alice did not think, because it also involved contemplation of Lin's departure; but then she received an unexpected letter from William: 'Mother went down with flu . . . pneumonia set in . . . doctor said she'd never regained her strength after that terrible time in the war. . . . Sank so fast . . . no time to send for you . . . terrible shock, dear . . . little in the way of worldly goods, but a package for you here . . . buried in . . .' Alice's eyes blurred as she read, stricken with the loss of one who had been kind, gentle and loving all her days. Why *hadn't* she agreed to look after Eliza for what had been, after all, her last years? Her cheeks burned with guilty remorse, and the undercurrent of satisfaction in Will's letter. He had done all he could for her, right to the end; *he* hadn't neglected his responsibilities. But Alice, who had vaguely planned to look after her mother when she became really frail, could now do nothing.

There was one thing, though, a duty Eliza had charged her with—to keep an eye on Adam, who, she imagined, must be feeling very melancholy, alone in a strange city with no one to share his grief. She would go to Changsha and comfort him, Tamao too if she could, and she would look once more, with the eyes of an adult, on the house of Chu where much of her youth had been spent, and much of her future forged. In March, Han-li set off for Hunan and Lin also prepared to leave.

During the past months, Alice had pushed from her mind the very existence of his wife, whom he scarcely ever mentioned. But now, as they faced a parting of several months, she felt a surge of bitter resentment against this official spouse, woman of his own race and mother of his children to whom he was now returning and who must, in some respects, know her lover better than she ever could.

'Must you really go?' she said, in an uncharacteristic tone of peevish pleading.

'Dear Uncut, I must—there is so much work to do in Canton.'

'And people to see, your wife's bed to share?'

He looked away. 'I do not enjoy sharing it.'

'But you do?'

'It is my marital duty.'

She laughed shortly. 'I wonder what she thinks of that attitude?'

'She doesn't know it. We speak little of such matters, unlike you and me.' He came up and kissed her head. 'I'm sorry that all this has to be—as it is. Things will change for the better between men and women one day, though maybe not in time for you and me.'

Irritably she shrugged off his soothing abstractions, beset with the actual here-and-now parting. She put her arms round his waist and held him tightly to her.

'Why don't I come with you?'

'Dear . . . I . . . we . . . it mustn't be.' He wrestled to disengage from the temptation of her. 'I'll be back soon—I couldn't stay too long away from you—but you must let me go now. Please don't sour what we've already enjoyed—and will again.'

'Very well,' she stood back from him then, drawing herself to her full, small height in a way he knew and loved. So well did he love it, that he could hardly bear to leave her there, alone at the door, waving sadly. And he too was sad, for behind each parting was always the fear that it could be their last.

After Lin's departure, Alice pulled herself together and made preparations for her own journey to Hunan. She left in early April, travelling first to Shanghai, Foochow, then by road and river to Changsha. Her earlier visits to the Hunanese capital had been fraught with fear and secrecy, but this time, arriving on a lovely late-spring day in a hired passenger cart, she saw the city stripped of its mystery and awe for the first time. It was rather ordinary, just another prosperous trade centre of about half a million inhabitants. Timber from the western mountains was sent there by river and made into solid furniture; tea, grown in the nearby valleys, was fired and packed there, and its local specialities were preserved fruits and eggs. It was the military and cultural centre for a people long famed for their courage in battle, their scholastic achievements, their dissident politics. In the past, most of the scurrilous and sinister anti-foreign pamphlets had originated there; now the pendulum had swung the other way. Changsha's New Learning Centre was attracting students from all western China; schemes were afoot for linking it to other cities by railway, and postal and telegraph services were already in operation.

Adam, apprised by telegram of Alice's arrival, had a room waiting for her in the nurses' annex of the Mission hospital, and greeted her warmly. The wispy boy who had spent his childhood cowering over Latin texts had grown into a lank young man with earnest grey eyes and a habit of twitching his nose when he was anxious, which was often. Here, however, he appeared more relaxed than she had ever seen him, working diligently in the hospital, spending his scant leisure with gifted students selected for training in Western medical techniques. Alice was both relieved and a little piqued to discover that, on the one occasion she'd spent considerable time and effort to offer comfort and support, he didn't especially need it. She'd failed him in the past, and might again, but in this matter of his mother's death he seemed remarkably resilient.

'I saw little of her in recent years.' He cracked his prominent knuckles as if in extenuation. 'She was always in Father's shadow, wasn't she? Must have been dreadful for you— Edward not being your father.'

'I suppose, yes.'

'When you wrote to me about his death in the war, you didn't say, was it easy? More or less?'

'More or less.' She hadn't come to talk about Edward, couldn't bear to, even now. 'You've survived very well, considering how he brought you up,' she touched his hand. 'Don't keep cracking your knuckles, dear, it's irritating. Haven't others told you about it?'

'Oh yes—and about twitching my nose like a rabbit. Two of Father's little legacies, probably. But he left better ones—that absolute, fanatical dedication. Almost frightening wasn't it?'

'It certainly was!' They smiled at each other. 'Never mind,' Alice said.

'I don't. I'll do my best.'

'His standards were extremely harsh, Adam, and ... hypocritical. But let's forget it. The man is dead and so is his devoted Eliza who tried so very hard and long to please him—at the expense of us all, really.'

'That's how Sunny feels.'

'How is your little twin? I haven't heard recently.'

'Still devoted to the brother of her friend Hetty I think. Don't know if anything will come of it.'

'Oh dear, if she marries him she might never come to China as she's promised. Still, I mustn't be selfish. And what about you, Adam? Any fair prospects yet?'

He rubbed his twitching nose. 'Certainly not! I'm much too young and earning a pittance. It would be years before ...' then he bridled. 'Remember your grumbling about relatives always trying to marry you off?'

'Sorry, Adam. Just a silly tease. What I did remember was

521

Mother hoping you'd find a "nice sensible wife" to look after you.'

'She never believed I could look after myself,' he said stiffly.

'Well, many men can't, and she spent years looking after others. I've thought a lot about her since she died. The toil and struggles she always had. She left me a few mementoes—a jet necklace, embroidered texts I don't know what to do with, and these photographs. Have you seen them?' She produced a faded little bundle, showing men in rough farmclothes with flat caps and gnarled sticks. They stared ahead grimly, an elderly woman in voluminous black sitting on a stool with a spinning wheel before her; 'Old Morag' was scrawled on the back.

'This one says, "Katie and the wee bairns"—but the bairns are so wee you can scarcely tell them from the rocks. It looks very stark, doesn't it? Mother hoped I'd go there one day. Perhaps you would too?'

'I don't think so. I don't feel in the least Scottish. Nor does Sunny.' He handed them back and she wondered if he was being deliberately hurtful, but his eyes were gentle, eager to please. 'Shall I show you our lab? We're doing lots of interesting experiments, and the students are wonderfully keen. There's one nicknamed Glow-worm because he keeps his light on studying all night. He'll be a famous physician one day.'

'And a good Christian?'

'I hope so, yes. I know you don't approve of that. I'm not bigoted as Father sometimes was, but I do believe Christianity has a great deal to teach the Chinese.'

'Perhaps you're lucky in your faith, Adam. It makes life easier.'

'That's not why I hold to it,' he stood up defiantly. 'But yes, I am lucky, just being here. Let me introduce you to Glow-worm.'

'Our word would be book-worm I suppose?'

'That sounds dry-as-dust, but glow-worms are alight and interesting, you'll see.'

He took her on a tour of the hospital where she met the other foreign doctors, the nurses and the illustrious Glow-worm, who was shyly monosyllabic in her presence. Everyone seemed capable, busy, happy, and that evening, as she listened to them singing a final evening hymn, Alice pondered wistfully, and not for the first time, the mystery of a faith strong enough to sustain a life's work.

The next day she sent a note to the Chùs and received in reply an invitation to tea from Tamao. She was carried through the portals of the house in a closed chair; gatekeepers bowed, two maids assisted her to alight; the courtyard vases she had cleaned so often were in their same places. It was an old dream materialising before her eyes. She was led to the seat of honour in the ladies' reception room which was only occasionally opened, though its carved blackwood chairs and lacquer tables were highly polished. She looked at the scrolls on the white walls—mountains, pine trees, butterflies, and a written panel: 'Because we gaze on flowers the wine is warmed.' It used to hang in the Master's bedroom; she recalled her first sight of it.

Alice picked nervously at her skirt wondering if she'd worn the right clothes. It had been so difficult to decide; fashion had no dictates for a foreign lady of mature years returning to a household where she'd once been both barbarian skivvy and unofficial concubine. Eventually she had chosen a sky-blue robe with embroidered sleeves, high neck, a white sash. Glimpsing her reflection in the lacquer table, she decided it looked rather fetching. Would he remember her? Lung-kuang, the Master who had taken her virginity before she was old enough to lament its passing.

Tamao came tottering in on her hoof-size feet, supported by a maid, and they embraced quietly. Her clothes were sober, her face, unpainted to indicate her widowhood, was worn and expressionless. When Alice offered condolences, she lowered her eyes, plucking her sleeve ends to show her grief. As servants came with tea, she said with an effortful smile, 'I have three sons and two daughters. They all do well.'

'Oh how fortunate in that. Tell me about Custard Apple. I remember him being born.'

'My goodness, so you would! He's in the Governor's office here, but yearns to leave Hunan. That is the way nowadays. The young men are restless, dissatisfied, seeking hither and yon. Number One Daughter is soon to marry a local boy and live here in the customary fashion, thank goodness.'

Alice bit her lip, thinking of Number One daughter—her feet as bound as her mother's and her horizons equally so.

'Do you remember sugar plums?' Tamao handed a bowl. 'Younger Brother remembered your fondness for them, so I had some specially made.'

At the sight of the familiar fruit in a familiar bowl, Alice gulped hard.

'Oh thank, thank you. . . . You saved our lives, Frank's and mine, you Chus. Many others wouldn't have done so.'

'Father is a compassionate man.'

'How is the Honourable Father?'

Han-li came in smiling. 'How good to see you here, Uncut. I remembered the sugar plums you see. Father you say? He will see you shortly.'

'He remembers me then?'

'Oh yes, but vaguely. He is ageing.'

They talked of others in the family, till Alice asked hesitantly, 'You have not mentioned Han-fei, Eldest Brother?'

Han-li replied bitterly. 'What is there to say? He is as always, only more so because he's cock-of-the-walk now. He and I will never be able to live in accord under the same roof. Now I've returned here I'm often reminded of Kang Yu-wei's teaching on the burdens of the private family. "In every household in the world the overflowing of jealousies and the clashing of will is more poisonous than yellow fog." '

Tamao bridled. 'Oh nonsense, Han-li. It wasn't like that when we were children. It's only recently—all these new-fangled ideas and machines from the West have broken in on us and we are out of joint.'

'No, Elder Sister, I don't believe you. There's always change, times are always out of joint and families always quarrelling in yellow fogs. Only as children we don't realise it. . . . Isn't that so, Uncut?'

'I think so, yes. Yet we in the West also set great store by family life—the Christian foundation of hearth and home. And I'm not sure Kang's proposals for alternatives would work well either.'

'And what does the Modern Sage suggest?' Tamao asked sarcastically.

But Han-li jumped up, patted his sister's head, 'If we tell her, Uncut, she'll grow ten thousand grey hairs overnight! No, I'll take you to the Honourable Father instead.' Alice touched Tamao's hand and followed him out of the room.

'So what have you decided to do? Stay here?' Alice asked as they walked to the Master's apartments.

'For a while. But I doubt it can last.' He pushed his father's outer door. 'I don't know if he wishes to see you alone or . . .' He asked a servant who returned saying, 'Master says the foreign woman may enter unaccompanied.'

Alice drew herself together, feeling a tremor of anticipation as she was shown into his presence. Certainly Lung-kuang had aged, but with gracious dignity. As he moved to greet her she saw the lineaments of the younger man who had been her first lover.

'Uncut Jade, you are welcome.'

She bowed formally and he scrutinised her. 'You have not grown very tall.'

'No. I . . . er . . . attained my full stature before I left your household, Honourable.'

'Indeed? I don't remember quite when that was. But most Western women seem to grow tall—very tall.'

'Then I'm sorry not to have lived up to your expectations.'

He chuckled appreciatively at her colloquial turn of phrase and motioned her to a seat. 'You haven't forgotten our language of Hunan?'

'I've a Hunanese servant who keeps me up to scratch. And I met some of your Braves in the recent war.'

'You were at the war?'

'For a time—in Port Arthur.'

'A terrible business. You will have tea?'

'I've just had some with Tamao.'

'Then we will drink a little wine. It is evening after all.' He offered some, settled back, looked at her again. 'Younger Son tells me you are a widow and childless?'

'That is so.' She met his eyes, wondering if he'd ever been told of his child she'd started to bear and lost. Perhaps, after a little wine, she would say . . . But would that be wise? The wine came, with dishes of nuts, sunflower seeds, dried peppers. Lung-kuang's singing birds cheeped in their cages, and, at first, lulled by the familiar charm of the man, the surroundings, Alice wondered if they might be as former lovers sometimes are—matured, mutually respecting, the flame not entirely spent? But such thoughts were totally beyond his ken she soon realised; to him, she was no more than an aberration, the only barbarian woman he'd known, or wished to know.

He peered over his wine-cup, 'And how is your brother, the Horseboy?'

'He is well, thank you, working in the firm of his father-in-law, Mr Wang. He and his wife Peachy have three children.'

He frowned. 'He married a Daughter of Han? The mixing of blood is not good.'

She gave a small bitter smile. So much she could have said then that would have been simply impertinent, irrelevant, in the eyes of this elderly man, sitting at ease in his loose silks surrounded by his favourite scrolls, books, flowers, birds. She said instead, 'I hope you're enjoying your well-earned retirement, Honourable?'

'Ah, you know how it should be with me now? In the words of Po Chui:

'Lined coat, warm cap and easy felt slippers,
In the little tower, at the low window,
Sitting over a sunken brazier.
Body at rest; heart at peace,
No need to rise early.'

'Should be?'

'How can it be when the world beyond is in such disarray? The teacher Lao-tzu tells us that the wise man withdraws from the political scene in times of disorder and weak government like the present. And so I do, but my sons, my friends' sons do not, indeed cannot. They lead disturbing lives in distant places. How can I contemplate my chrysanthemums in peace as my honourable father did? One's progeny fasten to the heart strings and pull on the liver. What are all these rooms in my house for, I asked Younger Son the other day, if not to give living space for my grandchildren? But there are not enough here to fill them. Younger Daughter Mei is with her husband in Canton, Younger Son crosses the ocean to learn from the Jap dwarfs. You remember the attics where the shuttles clicked from dawn to dusk? They are usually silent now because it is cheaper to buy your imported cotton trash, and there are few children to make clothes for.'

He poured more wine and continued, 'But what is even worse, those that are here no longer live in harmony. The Great Learning tells us that men who wish to bring order to the state must first regulate their own families. And I have failed in this it seems. My sons will not be reconciled, Eldest Daughter is bereft and her sons yearn to leave, of Youngest Daughter we hardly even speak.'

She said diffidently, 'When I lived here years ago, Honourable, there seemed to be harmony, but I was a young outsider and perhaps there was discord then too?'

'Discord occasionally, but no breakdowns as now. Then

everyone knew their spheres—the women, the sons, the daughters, the servants, and stayed within them as was meet to do. It is no longer so, and will be less in another generation.'

She was aware of the dangerous ground, but had to attempt it, 'Don't you think there can be other, perhaps better ways people can try? To give them greater opportunities of moving round freely, changing their own lives as they wish?'

He glanced at her sharply. 'Change? From what to what? And why? From peasant to landowner? From merchant to minister? From woman to man, you might suggest next? So what will the humble do? They will band together in rebellious groups as they do in Europe I believe, all wanting to be master. Is that why you want change? But human beings cannot dominate the current of change towards the good. They can only adapt to what befalls, as a man cannot escape his lot, as metal cannot leap up and insist on being made into a special kind of sword.'

'You have studied the teachings of the Tao in recent years, Honourable.'

'They give me most solace now. Confucius would have us strive towards moral excellence on this earth. I'm no longer sure that is possible, or even . . . necessary.'

'Rather a melancholy conclusion, is it not?' Alice murmured sadly.

He didn't answer. Twilight had fallen and a servant entered with a kerosene lamp; its white glare glinted harshly on surfaces of lacquer, porcelain, and silk where only soft wick lights used to flicker. He had not suggested more wine and she knew it was time to leave, yet she lingered, dissatisfied.

'You have a modern light now I see?'

He glanced at it irritably. 'It's better for reading, but it is graceless and smelly. Electricity will come to Changsha soon I expect, and railway trains. My grandsons will soon be travelling rapidly inside little metal boxes from here to Canton.'

She protested quietly, 'But there is nothing in the universe that does not change. Even in China, the revered historian says, "Through the span of two thousand years, there have been myriad changes." '

He rose, exaggerating a stiff tiredness. 'I know, I know, but I am too far in years to adapt to all of it.'

Reluctantly she also rose, realising the naiveté of hoping she could influence him in any new direction. He was, as he said, as entrenched as millions of his generation. She bowed. 'It was most kind of you to see me, Honourable. I pray you might live many years in enjoyment of the five great blessings.'

'Longevity? Peace?' he quoted two of them. 'I think not. It is of little moment either way. You stay in the city?'

'With my half-brother in the Mission.'

'He is a missionary?' The question was cold.

'A medical one, a doctor really.'

Clearly that did not mitigate the case. 'Farewell,' he said abruptly. 'I wish you a safe journey home.'

As she stumbled down the dim passage she realised he hadn't bothered to ask where her home was or much else about her, for there was nothing she could say of any import to him. What pained her more, however, was the obviously unbridgeable gulf between his views and those of Han-li, and the realisation that all the grand schemes for reform, which seemed so eminently practical and sane in Peking, took on a different hue here.

Alice often pondered that theme during the remainder of her stay in Changsha. When she left, summer had come and the peasants were toiling sweatily in the fields, precisely as their ancestors had for centuries—weeding the paddies, watering the buffaloes, gathering wood for the kitchen-fire, pig manure for the soil, fruits for the table. Unchanging figures in an unchanging landscape. Alice watched them as the passenger cart creaked along the dusty roads, and remembered the words of Lung-kuang, 'Change from what to what? And why?' The cart moved far too slowly. She wished it was a metal box on wheels so anxious was she to get back to Lin, to Peking, where her new-found certainties had their roots.

5

Travel by cart, junk, and steamer across the vast spaces of
China was, however, a lengthy process and by the time Alice
reached the northern capital, the worst of summer's heat was
over. Street-vendors were selling sour-apple dumplings,
strings of pinkish-brown mushrooms from the Western Hills
and nuts roasted in pans filled with black sand. Mrs. Duck
had produced Duckling Number Five for Alice's admiration,
which was not forthcoming because their servants' quarters
were already overcrowded.

A piece of more disquieting news awaited her: Sir Robert
Hart, the Inspector General of Customs, had offered William
a superior position in the recently formed Imperial Postal
Service, also under his control. 'As you know it is said of Sir
Robert that he putteth up one and setteth down another in a
divinely incomprehensible fashion,' Isabel had written. 'And
he's setteth poor Will down for long enough, so now at last
he's setteth up as he richly deserves. We're quite delighted,
and so is Polly. She's nearing sixteen and would have gone
Home soon, but now I think a year or two of "finish" in the
capital will do well enough. Tommy comes with us of course,
and Lottie for a while, before going to stay with Mary's relatives in Singapore. (Did I tell you Joel is hoping to get his first
bank posting there?) Sir Robert likes to look his "postal
recruits" over, so Will and I will be coming for a brief visit
soon. We'll be guests in his bungalow—a humble name for a
grand establishment, I believe? Is it really shaped like an
"H"? What an egotist the man is! Anyway, it will give us a
chance to look over our own home. It's in Customs Lane
apparently and sounds quite in keeping with our elevated
station! Isn't it exciting? I'll let you know when we're
arriving. In the meantime, I wonder if you could arrange for
me to meet a few ladies? American and French as well as

Brits, if poss. I wonder what fashions are like in the capital? The *corps diplomatique* thrives on formality, I'm told. And they say the new Chief's wife, Lady Maclaren, is *un peu formidable?*'

Alice bit the paper's edge, wishing her pleasure at the news could have been unalloyed. She was delighted for William of course and would enjoy showing them all Peking; but she could foresee considerable difficulties in her relatives' proximity. So she put the matter from her mind, concentrating instead on the urgent need to make some money, for her extended trip had been expensive, and trade had fallen off in her absence. Luckily Benjy, acting on his own initiative, had bought some stock from a bankrupt Shanghai dealer and arrived at 'The Polished Jade' one day with samples sufficient to convince Alice he'd secured some excellent bargains. They were just the sort of thing to appeal to the influx of well-heeled visitors to the capital that autumn—diplomats, politicians, railway magnates, minor nobility from several European capitals, often accompanied by their wives, often priding themselves on their knowledge of oriental *objets d'art*.

Russians were in the majority, for the resilient Viceroy Li Hung-chang (upon whom the Yellow Riding Jacket had been re-bestowed) had attended the Coronation of Nicholas II in St. Petersburg and a secret Sino-Russian alliance had followed. Former Chinese fears of Russian encroachment were forgotten, and the two nations were co-operating on railway development in northern Manchuria. Such a measure, the Tsar's envoy assured Viceroy Li, would enable Russian troops to move quickly to help China repel any aggressor—that is, it went without saying, the Japanese.

Alice took a strictly pragmatic view of these international political turn-abouts, for the burly, fur-clad Slavs could be easily persuaded that jade vases, perfume bottles and incense holders were the perfect adornments for their heavy northern drawing-rooms and that high prices must be paid for them. When they were surfeited on jade, she assured them that porcelains and bronzes were also extremely desirable purchases and sent them to the 'Establishment of Ten Thousand Glories' nearby. The Blums reciprocated in kind and sometimes invited Alice to supper to gloat over their mutual spoils.

There she met quite different foreigners—rich, sprightly,

talented young men-of-the-world mostly, well-versed in the latest literary and artistic fashions, who quizzed each other about the secret, esoteric pleasures of other capitals—Saigon, Vienna, Cairo, Paris—Peking being the latest exotic addition to their select list. They collected dreams woven by the best opium from Szechuan, beautiful Chinese boys, whose pigtails they unwound at night, girls with golden lilies small enough to stand on saucers, erotic novels of the Ming dynasty. They wore embroidered waistcoats, tucked silky-haired Pekingese dogs under their arms, and their moustaches were long and waxy. Posed thus they took photographs of each other, painted likenesses of themselves in full mandarin fig, and of nude girls who had to be bribed heavily to submit to such indignity. They smoked and quaffed brandy till dawn, discoursing eloquently on the subtlety of the oriental soul compared to the crass occidental, ending with sleepy murmurations from the Tao: 'The great Tao floats everywhere to the left and to the right. All things depend on it to exist, and it does not abandon them.' Alice enjoyed their occasional company as light relief from her heavier concerns and Lin marvelled at their assured freedoms, their spiritual indulgences, and was secretly jealous of what they took so readily for granted.

One late autumnal day however, Alice was jolted from all this by the arrival of another note from Isabel, announcing their imminent arrival. 'A flying visit only, so we're leaving the younger two behind. Quite a social whirl is promised, with a Reception Ball for us ex-Customs people at Sir Robert's. Please come as our guest won't you—on 25 November.' The date hung sombrely in Alice's mind. She had a new ball-gown made of pale lavender silk with a low-cut bodice, the skirt flaring in a shaped flounce to the ground. As she wriggled uncomfortably into it on the appropriate evening, she thought wistfully how she would have enjoyed the occasion if Lin could have accompanied her. An impossible, preposterous notion of course, flouting all the social conventions of both their worlds. It was just as well he was absent from Peking, and so would not even see this rather absurd get-up.

She delayed dressing till the last minute, then lingered over a fortifying brandy, then had to find cashew to sweeten her breath, and so, by the time her chair reached the Inspector General's spacious compound, the ball was well underway. In the entrance hall a servant took her cloak and gloves, another flicked dust from her shoes, a third handed a dance-card with a pink-tasselled pencil attached. She looked at it glumly. Pink was the only colour she didn't like; it didn't bode well.

Sir Robert Hart's own band of Chinese musicians, trained in Western music by a Portuguese bandmaster, was playing a lively polka, and for the first few minutes, she saw the whole colourful scene through her Chinese eyes. The over-dressed, over-fed bodies jumping and thumping up and down, each partnered with the opposite sex, so that they rubbed, bumped, even caressed in awkward fashion, though the stimulus seemed to end when the music did. Then the music changed to a stately waltz and Alice recognised a few people, among them the British Ambassador, Sir Donald Maclaren, dancing with his wife.

'That little woman in lavender who's just come in. Mr. Greenwood's sister, isn't it?' Lady Maclaren murmured.

He circled diplomatically into focus. 'Mmmm, Mrs. Grant-Greenwood. Has that rather good antique shop in Pumpkin Lane.'

'And a liaison with a native I've heard?'

'Ah, but a *reforming* native, my dear.'

'A distinction without a difference, surely?'

'Oh, a great distinction in her mind, I imagine,' he chuckled drily.

'Anyway, we don't need to make a point of . . .?'

'No, I think not.'

They circled away. Alice, unaware, had just seen William and Isabel on the floor—a well-preserved, middle-aged pair. Isabel looked magnificent as always on such occasions in a gown of Soochow brocade, trimmed with lace, not a grey hair in that brilliant auburn coiffure. How did she manage it? Will, getting definitely portly, was holding her from him, displaying her for inspection rather than dancing with her. Alice suddenly remembered Isabel mumbling something in Chefoo about the need for separate bedrooms after her miscarriage. Perhaps that was why they looked so stuffy—public figures rather than private people, their eyes darting about, assessing this new milieu, sorting out the importance of faces. Then they smiled at each other, and Alice realised they were happy. All the years of minor disappointments, the moving around, the lack of promotions, the saving to keep up a good front—and now this due reward, what they'd hoped for. Who was she, Alice, to judge its worth meanly?

Charlotte circled near, leaning across the arm of her handsome partner to speak to her father. She was, as Isabel said, quite beautiful; her slender frame tightly encased in low-cut ivory satin was positively springing to the music. She wished the tempo would quicken, the night go on forever. Alice, on the other hand, feared that it might; but she was claimed for the next two dances, then came the welcome supper interval. She pushed through the throng to Isabel.

'So there you are, Alice. We looked for you in the reception line. Will decided you'd forgotten us altogether and gone off to some political meeting.'

'Not at all—sorry. I had a late customer.'

Isabel didn't reply. Alice's involvement with trade was a continuing vexation and would be more so now, considering Will's position. She steered her sister-in-law into a corner so they could talk quietly.

'Such a lot of new people to meet. More sophisticated than Shanghai certainly. Could you introduce me at all? I need to learn the ropes quickly.'

'I'll do what I can, but . . . Oh, there's the consulate librarian and his wife. Shall we?'

'No, don't bother. There must be others you know?'

'But this is rather the diplomatic and Customs set and . . .' she trailed off.

'I'm well aware of that, but it's a "set" that's quite important to me. Which is why I asked you to arrange for me to meet some ladies, you remember?'

Alice had forgotten, or had chosen to. 'I . . . oh dear. I'm sure when you come to live here we can . . .'

Isabel slammed her plate on a nearby table with unintentional force. 'You forgot, didn't you? And that's so typical, if I may say so. You've never done anything for me have you? Not for years. It's always the other way round—including who looked after your mother in the last year of her life. You just do what you like, when you like, a bit of trade now and then to keep going. You realise I suppose you were only accepted in Shanghai society because Robert and Mary backed you? Glossed over your business connections? The family has always stood by you, through thick and thin—and I remember one very thin time. After all we've done, I come here and ask you to take a little trouble on my behalf, and you haven't even bothered! Too involved in Chinese politics I suppose to think of trivial matters like ladies' teas? Well, they're important to me, and your brother. You know, Alice, Sir Robert is a stickler for the social niceties, I'm told, and the sooner one makes a mark the better. You think the people here this evening aren't important, I suppose? Well, they're the ones with power and influence, my girl, and I wouldn't brush them aside so lightly if I were you!'

She paused for breath at last, an angry flush mottling her cheeks down to her low neck-line. Alice, standing flat back against a pillar, was staring at her in horror.

'Oh dear. Oh Isabel, please don't say . . . I'm sorry, I didn't realise how important . . .' It was all true, she supposed, looked at in that light, which she never had. She couldn't defend herself because she wasn't angry. Only, a great sadness welled in her. A loving bond she'd presumed for life was severed, and its breaking had revealed long-pent-up resentments whose seriousness she'd never even guessed. The music struck up again, jolly, uncaring; but Alice continued to stare at the other woman white-faced, as if she'd been punched, her shock so obviously heart-felt that Isabel began to soften, for she was not cruel. And she was not being cruel now, she told herself firmly, only giving Alice a few home-truths; not the most suitable moment, but then home-truths were often delivered inconveniently.

'I . . . I think I'm going. I'll see what I can do tomorrow about the ladies,' Alice said in a small voice.

'Oh, it's much too late now. We're only here three days and our programme's very full. If something had been arranged in advance . . . but please don't trouble. Think no more of it.'

She drew herself to her full height, just as a Customs Commissioner came to claim her for the next dance. Alice glanced at her card; several dances booked, but with no one she cared about. She felt a little sick; the whole evening had been even worse than she'd anticipated. She gulped a glass of champagne, while standing behind a pillar; the bubbles pricked her throat as she recalled Isabel's hurtful words. The music finished, and if she didn't leave Mr. Somebody-Smith would come for his beastly polka. She hurried to the cloakroom—one of the last ladies to arrive, the first to leave, the attendants noted, looking with pity as they summoned a chair.

Alice called on her relatives next day to make amends, but nothing could be done, though, from Will's amiable demeanour, Alice guessed his wife hadn't told him of their quarrel. This was scant comfort however, for they had not yet found out how she conducted her present life, which they were bound to do soon. Her heart sank at the thought, for she was fond of them both, but she would not renounce her allegiance to Lin and the Reformers for their sakes. She was a grown-up, independent woman, and had already spent too many years compromising and, as Daisy put it, 'not taking stands.'

Nevertheless, Isabel's outburst had wounded her deeply, as she explained to Veronique, who clucked sympathetically, 'Ah, these family resentments—they blow up so unexpectedly, like whales spurting from a sea that seemed calm. And there are always several causes. Your sister-in-law is ageing a little, n'est-ce pas? Good-looking, with new social obligations, and her beautiful daughter dancing the night away, her whole life before her? And her sister-in-law who is her own mistress, not tied to this social milieu, a little supercilious of it perhaps? So she feels hard done by, is tired and pouf . . .!' Veronique threw up her hands, '. . . up comes the raging whale. But now she goes down again, and will plough her own deeps as usual.'

Alice took what consolation she might from that, but Isabel's words still rankled and she repeated them again to Lin when he returned from Canton. He listened impatiently, thinking she was almost as bad as his wife, who'd recently spent an entire evening complaining that his mother abused her because she couldn't make a decent pickle. Really, how could women bother with such trivialities when the whole Empire was trembling on the brink of disintegration or renewal?

For that seemed to be the case during the fateful year of 1898. It began momentously when Kang Yu-wei was actually allowed to air his views to Tsungli Yamen officials and the Manchu general, Jung Lu.

'The institutions of the ancestors cannot be changed,' Jung Lu apparently stated, to which Kang boldly retorted, 'The institutions of the ancestors were used to govern a realm that had been theirs. Now we cannot preserve the realm of the ancestors, what is the use of their institutions?' The interview proceeded along those lines, but most of the officials remained unconvinced, indeed appalled by Kang's radicalism.

So the government did nothing and political unrest increased. Rumours of eclipses, thunderbolts, monstrous births were rife in the countryside; in the towns the *Imperial Gazette* published accounts of quickly suppressed revolts by rebels castigated as 'bandits,' while dissident pamphlets urged the overthrow of the Manchus and street-singers recited tales about the overthrow of the Ming Emperors—an obvious parallel to the historically-conscious Chinese. Within the court, tensions worsened between conservatives loyal to the Empress Dowager, known as the 'Old Mother's Party,' and the 'Young Lad's Set' around the Emperor.

Foreigners, taking ruthless advantage of China's internal weaknesses, had already earmarked certain parts of the country as 'concessions' or 'spheres of influence.' The Germans started by seizing a naval base in Shantung in 1897, the French plumped for parts of western Kwangsi and Yunnan, while the British made for the Yangtze valley and Kowloon— both with great trading potential. The young Emperor was said to be so mortified by all this that 'his very hair stood on end in fury,' and then, most hair-raising of all, the much-fought-over Liaotung Peninsula was appropriated by the Russians on the pretext of protecting it from the Germans.

'Protecting it from the Germans, if you please!' Lin sat, head in hands, in the courtyard of 'The Polished Jade.' It was spring and the news of this latest foreign take-over had just reached the capital. 'It is as the papers predicted, we are being sliced up like a melon, the Manchus are selling our national heritage cheap in the market like second-hand goods.'

Alice stared at the gold-fish in the pond. 'To think of it—Port Arthur, where we fought the Japanese only four years ago, now handed to the Russians on a plate. International politics are simply mad, Lin!'

He stood under the mimosa, throwing its bright blooms into the water, and didn't answer. They heard the shop door clang, and Timothy and Grace Barlow came into the courtyard. Alice sprang to greet them. 'My, what a nice surprise. Whatever are you doing here? But sit down. Tea?'

'Oh please,' Grace sank into a chair. 'Timothy has a meeting with Kang and the *Tsungli Yamen* people. Things are really hotting up.'

'About time, or there won't be any China left to get heated over.'

'Exactly, it's dreadful.'

'So Kang and I have drafted a Memorial to the Emperor on educational matters,' Timothy was saying grandly to Lin, who looked rather sour. Mr. Barlow was certainly able, and had China's interests at heart, but he was rather full of himself these days—hobnobbing with Kang and court officials, drafting Memorials which he, Lin, was surely better qualified to do?

'What does the Memorial say?'

'Abolish the eight-legged essay system, make education more practical and technical, establish a modern University here, grade schools for Western teaching in every province.'

'And where's the money coming from?'

Grace laughed. 'A good question, Lin. Where indeed? And where the teachers?'

'Temples must be converted into schools,' Timothy began.

'Which will be fiercely opposed by the priesthood and many ordinary worshippers,' Alice interrupted.

'We have to face opposition. Christians always have.'

Lin looked annoyed. Grace, seeing it, deflected the discussion. 'Come, Timothy, that question we really needn't explore now. Your cakes are always so delicious, Alice.'

'Oh Mrs. Duck makes them. She's invaluable, only she *will* keep producing babies and there's no more space for them. I'm thinking of getting a larger place.'

'Is business doing well? I've never yet seen you behind the counter.'

'I hope you never will. I don't go in for "casuals" now. Buyers come by appointment. A very civilised way of conducting business, though not sufficiently so for my brother, I fear. He and his family have recently moved here, and he disapproves of his sister's dabbling in trade now he has an exalted position in the Imperial Post.'

Grace smiled sympathetically. 'Oh men—they never want women to do things by themselves. But I hope you'll just carry on?'

'Oh yes, I spent too many years toeing the family's line. Life's too short for that.'

Grace glanced pointedly at Lin, who grinned impishly, 'When brother William hears about me, I'll send him Kang's

537

treatise on "Abolishing Sex Boundaries and Promoting the Independence of Women." '

Grace smiled thinly, for neither she nor Timothy could approve of the Reformers' positively libertine proposals on that subject. Indeed it was, as she confessed to her husband, a conscious struggle to accept Alice's way of life without overt censure. To which Timothy replied that he did censure it in his heart and prayed for her salvation, but would leave it to others to throw the bricks—as they assuredly would.

Of this Alice was also aware, and it was partly in hope of softening such missiles that she made every effort to help her relatives settle down—mustering suitable ladies to meet Isabel, hiring servants, mule-carts, carry-chairs, and taking the younger children to see the sights. Their first excursion was to the famous Observatory on the eastern wall, designed by seventeenth-century Jesuits. The beautiful instruments and dragon-shaped bronze stands on which they were mounted stood proudly against the sky-line, and Alice was reminded of the teachings of the early Manchu Emperor K'ang-hsi, a patron of the Jesuits who, though fascinated by their astronomical lore, still cautioned, 'Now that we can calculate eclipses with absolute precision, we must still make the reforms necessary to avoid trouble and obtain peace.'

From the Observatory platform they could see over low buildings towards the further plains where fields of cotton burst white in the golden afternoon sun; nearby courtyards bloomed with pomegranate and lilac, suggesting, erroneously, that Peking was something of a garden city. Only the crows circling over specially noxious piles of rotting garbage, and the smells of sewers that wafted on the breeze, testified to the filthy squalor of the reality below.

'Mother told me that buildings in London are much higher and grander than here,' Polly remarked.

'I'm sure they are, dearie. But the Chinese don't like very high buildings because they would get in the way of good spirits travelling through the air.'

Polly laughed derisively and Tommy asked, 'Where do bad spirits travel then—underground?'

'Yes, and only at night,' Polly teased him.

'How do you know? Have you seen them?'

'Lots of times.'

'Now Polly, don't lead him on. Let's look at the Examination Halls.'

They moved to look down into an enclosure filled with rows of cell-like cattle pens. 'This is where the ten thousand top students from eighteen provinces come to be examined for the first literary degree,' Alice explained.

'If you were a Chinese boy, Tommy, that might be your life's ambition. Each candidate is shut in one of those cells alone for two days and nights to compose learned eight-legged essays.'

'Why are they shut in?'

'So they can't cheat. They don't even sleep—they're too busy writing. It's a ridiculous system, and will be changed soon when the young Emperor rules the country. Come, we must get back, your Mamma will be ready for tea.'

Isabel had remained cordial since her outburst at the ball, which had not been mentioned again; but when Alice returned to the customs bungalow with Polly and Tom that afternoon, she was aware of a chill in the air. Her sister-in-law seemed disinclined to talk, but when Alice prepared to leave, said, 'Oh do stay till Will comes—he'd like a few words with you.'

Alice's heart sank, but knowing the evil hour couldn't be long postponed, settled down with a book until he arrived. They went into the drawing-room, its soft blues and golds looking very tranquil and home-like in the evening light and Alice wished she could just have an inconsequential chat with her brother. But it was not to be.

'Sherry?' William asked sternly.

'Please. I like the new furnishings, don't you? Isabel's taste is always excellent.'

'Yes it is—very,' his heaviness implied that certain others' was not.

He sat down opposite her, drank gloomily, and began, 'I know you're a grown woman leading your own life, Alice . . .'

She raised her eyebrows in feigned puzzlement. 'So?'

'Nevertheless, certain social conventions always have to be upheld by white communities living in racially alien countries.'

'Like not consorting with the natives?'

'If you choose to put it that way.'

'I assume some kind friend has told you of my long-standing liaison with Lin Fu-wei?'

'Wasn't sure it was the same fellow as before, but thought it likely.'

'At least you can say I'm consistent in my consorting.'

'You can be flippant if you like, Alice, but both Isabel and I were very upset to hear it. You realise, I suppose, that your . . . goings-on will do nothing to help my career here?'

As he failed to offer another sherry, Alice poured herself one. 'I'm extremely sorry if that's so, Will, but I can't lead my life in relation to your career.'

'I didn't really expect you to take my interests into consideration—you never have.'

She winced. 'He is the man I love, Will—for years—ever since, well, you know when.'

He stared through his glass. 'Extraordinary, quite extraordinary. Well, if that is honestly the case, perhaps you should marry him? At least it would be preferable to the present irregular arrangement.'

'He is already married, with a family. There is no question of his changing that, and I wouldn't wish him to.'

He also returned to the decanter. 'So you're going on your own sweet way and that's all there is about it, hey?'

'Yes. We are always discreet, but I'd guessed you'd find out.'

He burst out. 'Why the deuce can't you behave like other women, Alice? I've never understood you in the least and it seems I never shall. You could have a very pleasant life here in China, or at Home. You're attractive enough to find another husband even now, and most capable in many ways.'

'I've asked myself that many times, Will. I really don't know why I can't be content with the sort of humdrum existence that satisfies many other women—not all, by the by.'

'Humdrum existence? Like Isabel's I suppose? Not nearly good enough for clever you.'

She flushed angrily. 'I wasn't thinking of Isabel personally. I'm simply saying that I have to lead my own life, by my own lights, and they're not always the same as yours, unfortunately. What are you going to do, disown me?'

Her tone was light, but he sensed the pain behind it. 'No, but we shall keep our social distance sometimes, I warn you.'

'So be it.' She plonked down her glass. 'I'll put a distance between us now, for a start.'

'Oh, if you'd like to stay to supper . . .'

'No thank you. Please say goodbye to Isabel for me.'

She hurried out, not giving him a chance to mitigate his sentence, even had he wished. 'I ask for no quarter,' she'd once said to him. No, she didn't, damn her, he thought, as he went to tell his wife what had transpired.

Though deeply distressed by the family rift, Alice refused to let it divert her attention from the many hopeful events of that momentous summer. On a bright afternoon in mid-June, Lin hurried into the house in a state of exhilaration.

'It's really beginning at last, Uncut. I've just heard that the Emperor's been completely won over to our cause and has appointed Kang Secretary to the *Tsungli Yamen*. What's more, he's promised to issue a decree stating that the whole country must adopt Reformist policies. Dear god, it's exciting . . . and hot!' He mopped his brow. 'Let's have a cup of wine to celebrate, then I must get busy. Kang wants concisely written summaries of all our individual ideas, and I'd like you to help, by translating our submissions into proper English. So when we're asked questions by foreigners, we can express things clearly and correctly. You'll help, won't you, my clever polished jade?' He hugged her.

'You know I will. You don't have to butter me up,' she pecked him on the chin.

Only when Alice began translating the Reformers' actual programme, did she realise just how sweeping and drastic it was. Agriculture, industry, law, administration—all were to be modernised along Western lines; large-scale public works were to be carried out in every province 'for the use and benefit of the people,' while useless sinecures were to be abolished, including the Banqueting Court, the Imperial Stud, the Supervisory Office for the heir apparent. This last had been a particularly cosy post as, for years, there had been no such heir.

When these radical edicts began appearing in the *Imperial Gazette* with the vermilion seal of the Emperor himself, crowds gathered in public halls and tea-houses throughout the country and there was great excitement among officials and literati. The Empress Dowager remained quietly at her Summer Palace, reportedly engaged in her habitual holiday pursuit of painting peonies and lilies on silk screens. Meanwhile, the international press reacted with some scepticism, pointing out that, in spite of the numerous imperial instructions, nothing much was actually changing.

So the diplomats and their families went off to the Western Hills as usual to escape the summer heat, and only a few foreigners, like Alice and the Barlows, remained, determined to be on the spot when history was made. Han-li returned to the capital and was given the task of organising naval colleges in every maritime province, but Alice saw little of him or Lin, who had been instructed to 'promote cultural exchange between nations.' In this cause, high-ranking officials were to go abroad to study foreign institutions and even the Emperor was to embark on an extensive foreign tour, accompanied by his formidable aunt. When Lin told Alice that, she burst out laughing—the idea of the Old Buddha surveying Europe's capitals with her basilisk stare seemed so totally improbable. But Lin was quite offended by her reaction. The world, he felt, had suddenly become an open book and what might not the Sons of Han accomplish once they'd learned to read it? The prospect of a Reformist government in Peking was heady wine and made perfection almost attainable within his own lifetime.

In the middle of this hectic activity, Frank arrived unexpectedly from Shanghai with his daughter Lily, come to spend a holiday in the hills with Will and Isabel. It was important for her to be in a real English home sometimes, Frank explained, as he settled in the shade of the courtyard mimosa, fanned himself and called for lemon tea.

'I took her straight to Will's as they're off to the villa tomorrow. You've been there?'

'No, I haven't been asked.'

'Why ever?'

'Can't you guess?'

He toyed with his fan; it had a pattern of jade-green buttons in black circles and Alice smiled as she noticed. 'I suppose so. Damn shame, typical of Will. Not sure he really likes introducing slant-eyed Lily as his niece.'

He sighed and leaned back, reflecting, as Mrs. Duck brought tea and cakes, 'You know, Sis, I've thought recently about Will and many others in China like him, for he's no worse than most and better than some . . . Ordinary men doing ordinary jobs—that's all they'd be in this marvellous Home-country we're always hearing about. But out here they're little tin gods—loads of servants, horses and carriages, parties and clubs. . . All well and good. But why should they stick up their contemptuous noses at the natives? And get away with it the whole time? Most of them don't know a dam' thing about the Chinese. We do, you and I, half brought up by them—and a fat lot of good it's ever done us! Because the likes of Will don't want to learn

542

don't want to understand. Doesn't it make you angry sometimes?'

'Yes, it does, Frank. And no one else understands my anger
—except you of course.' She laughed shortly. 'Oh, that's
something we'll always have in common—our embarrassing
penchants for "the natives," and, I suppose, our anger. . . .
Trouble is, there's not much hope of changing people like Will,
or Isabel for that matter. So what about your slant-eyed Lily?
And how does she feel about . . . things?'

'Doesn't fully realise yet. Leads a sheltered life. But she will
of course, she has the makings of a stunning good-looker.'

'That's two in the family—so is Charlotte.'

'Ah, the all-English, auburn-haired Lottie will have an
easier time than my Lily, I'll warrant. Whom will she marry—
one of them, or one of us?'

Alice frowned. 'You didn't used to think of it that way.'

'I know—all for love and to hell with the world's opinion
when Peachy and I married, wasn't it? But now . . . there are
lots of places in Shanghai I can't take her to you know, and
others where she's only accepted on sufferance, so we won't
go anyway. As for the Wangs, they're dead against me ever
since Little Nut was born. They blame me for it. And I can't
even like the creature, though Peachy dotes on him. But he's
caused a rift between us . . . in several ways.' He avoided her
look of enquiry, and she knew then he was going elsewhere for
his sexual pleasure.

'Poor Peachy.'

'Well I certainly don't want Lily to end up in a similiar situation. I suppose if she had a large dowry . . .' he bit his nail. 'It's
so damnably expensive keeping up big face these days. Servants, carriages, Ken's education, nurses for the baby, contri-
butions to clubs, and all their dam' festivals.'

'You're short?'

'Damnably.'

'I suppose I could help a little.'

'Oh I didn't mean that, Sis, thanks all the same. Only told
you because there's no one else I can talk to. I'm here to sniff
out this new railway syndicate in Manchuria. The Russians
are involved and I feel it's a good bet.'

'Remember what happened last time.'

' "Once burnt with hot soup, blowing ever after even on
cold salad," hey?' he quoted, grinning. 'That was different—

543

before the war when people hadn't understood the importance of railways.'

'I suppose so. Anyway, the men who'll soon be in power are all in favour of modern development—railways, factories, mines, the lot.'

'Ho-ho, you do sound confident. But don't get too involved with these Reformist hotheads, Alice, they haven't got a chance.'

'Don't be ridiculous, Frank. Of course they're going to succeed.'

'Well they won't. You may think so, you and your intellectual set here in Peking feeding that poor sod of an Emperor with big ideas so he churns out high-sounding decrees. But the crux is—what's actually going on in the provinces? Take Changsha. You really imagine that grasping stick-in-the-mud officials like Elder Brother are running round putting into practice all these modern hare-brained schemes? Not on your life! They're sitting quietly with their hands in their sleeves waiting to see which way the wind blows, who really wields the big stick. There'll be a confrontation between the Old Mother's party and the Young Lad's set, and I know who I'd put my money on.'

She looked alarmed, for he was voicing her own secret misgivings. 'But these hare-brained schemes are Imperial Decrees, which are always obeyed.'

'Depends who signs them, m'dear. No, the Movement's going to fail and you better watch out.'

'Me?'

'You think you're not marked as a Reformist sympathiser? The city's crawling with government spies and they know where the chop should fall when the time comes. Be careful and don't go too far in, despite Lin Fu-wei.'

'So you do know who . . .?'

'Known for ages. Don't blame you. I'm hardly one to throw stones. Sensible of you not to marry him, in my view.'

He winked, but she only asked, 'And how is Peachy? You haven't really said.'

'All right. We don't talk much these days. Which brings us back to Lily and how I worry about her future . . . full circle. Must be off, having lunch with a Russian railway engineer. Look after yourself, Sis, and remember my words of peerless wisdom.'

Frank's warnings lingered disturbingly, for she knew he meant them well, having her interests at heart, as she did his. As a result, for the next month, though continuing to work tirelessly in the Reformers' cause, she'd somehow lost the zealot's edge of total conviction. 'We command the Bureau of Arts and Commerce to purchase models of various kinds of machinery in modern use so as to educate the masses and they may learn to manipulate it for their own use.' So ran part of an Imperial Decree urging the adoption of modern agricultural methods. Alice considered the words—surely rather naive? She remembered those thousands of peasants toiling in Hunan, tried to visualise them using a modern machine. Who would show them how to use it? Who would pay for it? She sighed and went on to the next paragraph, unable to banish her uneasiness.

But Lin too was having qualms and arrived that afternoon looking unusually dispirited. 'The Emperor has dismissed the Secretary of the Board of Rites,' he announced gloomily.

'Isn't that all to the good?'

'The man was a lazy dolt, but the Old Buddha is furious, sees it as part of a campaign to oust her sympathisers. It's turning into a power struggle between conservatives and reformers.'

'You think the old bitch might suddenly show that terrible iron fist of hers?'

He didn't reply, fanning cooler air into a chair before sitting in it, looking over-burdened. She touched his cheek. 'Why not take a day off, Lin? Just one. Let's take a little holiday tomorrow, we both need it. Just the two of us.'

'Oh if you like. What do you want to do?' He seemed not to care, flipping listlessly through some papers. Then he looked up. 'I know, we'll go to the ruins of the old Summer Palace. The public aren't allowed in, but I'll wangle a pass through my imperial connections. Take a chair there in the morning. It's about two hours' journey beyond the west gate, and I'll meet you at noon.'

Even though Alice left quite early, the sun was already hot. Clouds of insects hummed over the open drains and the fetid canal round the Tartar Wall. Pedlars were doing a brisk trade in fly-whisks, cheap perfumes, and juicy white melons, of which she bought four. Lin awaited her at the entrance to the grounds and she was pleased to see him wearing a silk robe of pale beige. Too often these days he wore dark, stiff, Western-style suits, even though he said the tightly-cut

545

trousers made his genitals feel captive and low-spirited. But today he was in relaxed holiday mood, bandying light insults with the guards who were reluctant to let them enter, and, once inside, further exhilarated by the beauty of the enclosure.

Tangles of sun-bleached grasses and flowering weeds partly concealed the artificial hillocks, the debris of bright-tiled pagodas and arched stone bridges that had been created by the early Manchu Emperors for their private pleasure. Now, lizards basked in the sun on hot stones, pigeons knobbed the top of a marbled wall; overgrown ditches and water-holes were all that remained of a charmingly designed network of canals and lakes.

'The Catholic missionaries called this an earthly paradise, you know,' Lin said. 'Here were enchanted pavilions set among groves of flowering trees and filled with treasures—vases, screens, gold and silver artifacts.'

'I know what you'll say next. That the English and French then sacked and burned the Palace down in 1860. August, wasn't it? Thirty-eight years ago.'

'And as you were about two then I'm not blaming you personally.' He smiled and pointed ahead. 'That must have been the fan-shaped lake with a marble terrace. See the yellow-robed Emperor and his lovely ladies with silken parasols floating among the lotuses . . .'

Metallic blue dragonflies and scarlet butterflies dipped and soared over an expanse of dried mud; along its edge, a row of crumbling pillars were entwined with violet and yellow creepers.

Alice said, 'I once met a man who took part in that Anglo-French expedition. He gave me a musical box he stole from here.'

'You never told me. Do you still have it?'

'It's in my strong-box in Shanghai, a sort of talisman.'

They left the lake-side and mounted a hill topped with a pagoda, its seven storeys still just countable.

'Phew, it's hot,' Lin motioned her to sit on a plinth beside him, looking up at a row of bronze windbells hanging motionless along an eave. 'Not enough breeze to stir three hairs. I once read about a grand fountain somewhere here—the First Spring under Heaven, it was called. Wish it was playing now, we'd feel cooler. Look, right over there you can just see the Hill of Ten Thousand Ages and behind it is part of the new Summer

Palace where the Old Buddha sits like a spider.'

'She really terrifies the Emperor, doesn't she? What's he really like? Can he put up a fight against her?'

'He tries, but he's not naturally commanding, speaks so softly you can hardly hear, Kang says. And always looks so sad, as if a dark cloud of melancholy were fixed above his imperial head. No wonder, really, he's always been so isolated.'

'Poor man. It must be terrible being Emperor unless you're very strong in mind and body.'

'Oh, he's intelligent enough, reads all our pamphlets and is intrigued by Western things—clocks, mechanical toys, bicycles. He lacks the stuff of leadership, but perhaps he'll grow into it when we've guided him in the way of governing.'

She touched his sleeve. 'Part of your task? A Leader at last?'

'I hope so. The reform of this country will be long and difficult.'

'But you'll be part of it, Lin? You'll get a government post surely.'

'I hope so.'

She stared at a yellowish lizard blinking on a stone. 'And what about me? Will I have a job?'

'But of course. We'll need lots of foreign advisers. Which would you like—office for girls' education or the translation bureau?'

'You're not taking me seriously. Here, have some melon.'

She cut half for him and they sucked the cool juices while looking towards the distant outskirts of the city. It shimmered ominuously in a heat-haze; the capital, the whole country perhaps, poised on the brink of a grand upheaval. She asked with seeming lightness, 'And are you thoroughly confident—of the outcome?'

'I am today; yesterday I wasn't. Tomorrow who knows? I only know we're in over our heads now, and I'd give my life for the regeneration of China. I may have to,' he said softly, as if to himself.

She shivered, staring at the decisive masculine line where black hair met pale skin, wanting to trace it with her finger, as, in bed, she sometimes traced other meeting points of his hair and flesh. But signs of affection in an open place embarrassed him, even though, here, they were alone. So she said simply, 'You know I'll stay with you, whatever happens, for as

547

long as you want and need me? You see, I've loved you more than any man, ever.'

He turned to her, his eyes glowing, then briefly touched her hand, their skins sticky with melon juice and heat. 'Thank you, Uncut Jade. And I have loved you . . . strange though this coming together was for both of us.'

He threw away the rind, rubbed his fingers and lips with a silk kerchief, then strolled to look at the ruined pagoda behind them. She watched him, apprehensive at his use of the past tense; it seemed to make every last moment there so infinitely precious and poignant. She moved towards him.

'It's so unusual—we two alone in a place like this. I'll never forget it . . . the heat and the lizards, the melons, and the ruins.' She was almost talking to herself, and if he heard he made no sign, but simply started walking away down the hill, not waiting to escort her in the gallant Western fashion. This she did not expect and simply followed him.

Jogging leisurely back to the city in the sunset their spirits revived again and, as they passed the Temple of the Miraculous Ball, Lin spun her a yarn about a ninth-century monk who owned a wooden ball that carried messages for him to the far corners of the Empire and bounced up and down courteously before important visitors. They ate supper at their favourite restaurant of the Four Pomegranate Trees, and when they eventually reached home, sipped honeysuckle-flower tea and made long deep love in celebration of the day just past.

It was the last week of August when Alice and Lin strolled in the grounds of the old Summer Palace. The following week the Modern Sage urged the young Emperor to decree more radical reforms than ever before, and the conservative faction, realizing the threat to their authority, voiced their outrage and alarm.

From then on a power struggle became inevitable, and the Reformers, realising this, planned a coup d'état intended to depose the Empress and her leading henchmen. They sought the support of Yuan Shih-kai, commander of a newly trained military force and an earlier sympathiser of their cause. The Emperor summoned Yuan to the capital and proclaimed him also Chief of Army Organisation, secretly instructing him also to crush the Empress's supporters and take her prisoner. On 20 September, Yuan, 'for the good of the country,' as he later put it, betrayed the Reformers' plot to Jung Lu, the Empress's loyal general. Immediately the Empress showed her iron fist, and Jung Lu ordered his troops to march into Peking 'to save the Empire.' Neither the mass of the people nor any part of the Army rallied to the Emperor's side and he, afraid and helpless, could only beg the Reformers to 'devise some measure to rescue' him from his aunt's wrath.

It all happened so quickly, so ruthlessly, yet so bloodlessly that Alice couldn't credit the extent of the débâcle until Lin rushed into the house saying the Reformers had received a secret warning from a very high quarter that they were marked men and their lives in great peril.

'Kang's planning to flee the capital tonight and I must go too. It's our only hope.' He strode past her into the study and began sorting rapidly through his papers. 'Burn all the documents I leave behind, Uncut—incriminating evidence. Tell Snow Duck to go for a cart.'

She stared at him in wild disbelief. 'You're just going? Now? All of you? Without a fight?'

'How can we fight with no troops? We've been betrayed and the Empress is in command of the Imperial Forces.'

'But where are you going? How?'

He looked up. 'I'm not telling you where or how, because men may come here in search of me.'

'You think I'd betray you?' she asked fiercely.

'I know you wouldn't, my dearest. But it's better you know nothing—for your own good.'

She clung to him. 'Oh, let me come with you, Lin please, please. I don't care where we go.'

He pried off her grip. 'Now please be sensible, Uncut. We must go quickly, secretly, perhaps even in disguise. But you, a foreign woman, could not possibly . . . Please do as I ask now. They are waiting for me.'

'They?'

He didn't reply and she went to find Snow Duck. When she returned he was standing in the courtyard biting his fist. 'I hope I haven't forgotten anything, better to leave no evidence of my presence here.'

'But Lin, this is incredible, so fast, so final . . . and you're all just running away?'

Her voice broke and he winced. 'Oh, people will say that, I know. But alas, "when the nest falls there are no whole eggs."'

If we stay here we'll all be killed and what hopes for Reform then? Alive, somewhere else, we can at least fight another day. . . .' Lin paused, but did not meet her eyes. 'I always knew it might turn out like this, Uncut—exile, failure, for a while at least. But I must try and save my skin—for the sake of the cause, for my sons who still need a father.'

And for me, she thought desperately, for me? But he didn't say that, nor anything else. And she knew that, in some deep oriental recess of his soul and in spite of all the fine words about free will and forging the future, he had accepted this calamity as his fate. The wheel of fortune had dipped, and he would simply have to wait and see if it ever rose again. So they stood, in hopeless, broken silence together, not quite looking at each other, already separated, till Snow Duck came to say the cart was waiting. She watched numbly as he took Lin's luggage to it. Only then did he take her into his arms, his cold lips brushing hers gently, his voice very tight.

'I've left a trunk full of papers for you to dispose of, don't forget. Pray for me, to whatever gods you choose. Say nothing to anyone about any of us—mention no names. But don't worry about me.'

'Not worry?' Her eyes filled with tears, and she shuddered with a tiny sob.

'I'll write, if I can. Goodbye, my sweet Uncut Jade.'

He squeezed her shoulders and was gone. Sobbing violently she flung her arms round the trunk of the mimosa, rubbing her cheek heedlessly against its rough surface.

'He didn't say we'd meet again this time,' she wailed. 'Oh God in heaven, he didn't say that—not this time.'

6

During the night of 21 September all the gates of Peking were
guarded by troops loyal to the Empress Dowager. That same
night, she, heading a procession of soldiers, courtiers, and
eunuchs, quietly returned from the Summer Palace to the Forbidden City where she accused the terrified young Emperor of
treason and forced him to compose a decree of abdication.
'From this day forth Her Majesty will transact the business of
the country in the side hall of the Palace and we shall perform
obeisance before Her in the Hall of Diligent Government,' he
wrote abjectly in the vermilion ink of his former sovereignty.
As the dawn mists rose over the lily pads on the waters of the
Imperial Palace gardens, the deposed Kuang-hsu was
marched to the Ocean Terrace, an island promontory jutting
into the Winter Palace lake. The drawbridge between it and
the mainland was heavily guarded, all the Emperor's personal
servants and concubines were killed or banished: the Old
Buddha had regained power with a vengeance and those who
had incurred her august displeasure would be wise to make
themselves scarce.

The shutters of 'The Polished Jade' remained closed that day
and Alice stayed quietly behind them while Snow Duck brought
the latest rumours and counter-rumours circulating in the disturbed city. That afternoon she went into the study where Lin
had left his trunk; tenderly she stroked the lid of lacquered
pigskin, the ornate brass handles, remembering the day he'd
brought it to the house. She'd been so happy, seeing it as a sign
of his staying—at least for a while. Well, he had stayed for a
while, and now had gone; leaving nothing tangible behind but
this, full of working drafts, outlines, shreds of the reforming
measures he and his friends had tried in vain to urge upon the
country.

Here was a summary of the ideas of the brilliant young

radical from Hunan, T'an Ssu-tung, with Lin's queries in the margin. Here was a note from Kang Yu-wei suggesting ways in which ownership of private property could be abolished, and Lin's reply raising practical problems. At the bottom of the trunk was a calligraphic scroll-text decorated with flowers, which read, 'In general there is nothing in the universe that does not change. The change between daytime and evening makes the day; change from winter to summer makes the year.' Kiang Chi-chao, on Reform, 1896.

Change yes, but why did its advocates always presume it would be for the better? Alice wondered sadly as she rummaged vaguely through the trunk again. Should she destroy the papers as Lin had instructed? She rose with a sigh and closed the trunk deciding that she would not consign to ashes these pathetic remnants of so many bold, brave ideas. In a sense they were already part of history—documentaion of yet another of man's failed endeavours. She pushed the trunk into a dark cupboard; certainly its contents were incriminating, but if they were discovered, so be it. In her melancholy frame of mind the idea of martyrdom was almost appealing.

At least, that was how she felt in the safe daylight, but, the following night, when she was awakened by a thudding on the courtyard gate, her mouth dried in panic. They're coming for me, she thought instantly. I shall be seized, cast in a dungeon, and executed tomorrow. She lay quaking, wishing desperately she'd burned every scrap of Lin's papers. Then she heard a familiar voice in the yard,

'Uncut Jade, wake up. I must see you. It's urgent.'

She opened the door. 'Han-li, Younger Brother, it's you. Dear God, I thought it was soldiers come for me.'

'Oh they won't touch you, a foreign woman, but as for me . . . Can I stay a little, or dare you run the risk?'

'Come in, of course. This way.' She led him to the study, where he flopped down, looking tired and dishevelled.

'I'm more or less on the run, Uncut. Been hiding in the Chinese City since the blow fell, but it's not safe any longer. I must get out of Peking somehow. And the old hag's guards are at every gate.'

'So I've heard, but why didn't you go with the others? I assumed you had.' Actually, in her distress, she'd scarcely thought of him at all, and touched his hand guiltily. 'I'll see you're all right. Lin's gone, but he wouldn't tell me where. Do you know?'

'The whole Cantonese contingent, headed by Kang, were going to make for Japan. I just couldn't face that—back to the Japs, pigtail between my legs. So I've decided to go to Hunan and lie low there.'

'Oh I'm glad you've stayed. It's dreadful, how they've all fled, like rats from a sinking ship. Here, I'll get you some tea.'

As she moved to the door he said, 'Will you help me escape, Uncut? That's why I've come to you.'

'Of course I will. But what do you think is the best way?'

He gave her a sudden, amused smile. 'I've a plan—quite funny considering all our past—how about me going through the gate disguised as your servant?'

Alice burst out laughing in spite of herself.

'Han-li, younger son of the house of Chu, how crazy! What tricks life plays on us poor mortals, as Shakespeare said more poetically. But if you really think that's best, then let's. And Snow Duck will help. He'd do anything for a fellow Hunanese.'

And so it was arranged. The following afternoon Alice and her servant, huddled in a mule-cart driven by Snow Duck, joined a queue of similar vehicles at the city's western gate. Raindrops were plopping noisily on the vehicle's canopy, on umbrellas of passersby, the stiff oiled-paper covers over donkeys' packs, street stalls, and pedlars' baskets. At the gate, some of Yuan Shih-kai's soldiers armed with modern rifles were examining papers, shouting questions at every traveller. Alice's heart thumped nervously as their turn came to pass through. She was dressed for the occasion in thoroughly Western style—a voluminous cloak, an ugly but awesome feathered hat. Drawing herself up, she explained that her brother had been taken ill in an inn outside the city; she and her servant were going to fetch him. They waved him through without another glance; behind her, Han-li bit his fist hard to contain his relief.

They rode fast till night fell, and ate supper in a squalid inn. It was only about ten miles from the capital, yet it was as if nothing momentous whatsoever had occurred; and that, she remarked to Han-li while they spooned rice-gruel, was one reason the reform had failed.

'I suppose so,' he said sadly and pushed his plate away. 'I'm going on in another cart, Uncut. I won't feel safe till I've put several hundred miles between myself and that old She-Dragon in the Forbidden City.'

It was still raining when they said good-bye in the inn courtyard. Tethered animals stood patiently soaked in broken-roofed stables, and bristle-backed hogs were snuffling for garbage in the mud. From a lantern-lit opening came the sounds of men laughing and shouting; a high-pitched female voice, accompanied by a flute, was plaintively singing.

Han-li looked round in disgust. 'I wonder where it will all end, Uncut Jade? Will things in this ancient, backward, filthy land ever improve?'

'You mustn't despair, things are moving forward, little by little.'

She blinked raindrops from her eyes, feeling despondent at another parting from someone she loved. 'Take great care, Younger Brother. Give my love to Tamao, my kindliest regards to your Honourable Father—Tell him . . . tell him he is to be proud of his younger son, even though all is not yet going well.'

'The Honourable Elderly won't be surprised. He didn't expect a successful outcome, for the Movement, or for me. "Those who follow big chariots to the capital won't be able to see for dust," he quoted before I left. I expect he'll remind me of that and return to the contemplation of his chrysanthemums. Goodbye, Uncut Jade, and thank you. Lie low—an evil season is upon us.' He swung his bag on to the waiting cart and rode away into the wet dark. She went inside, her attempts to sleep long thwarted by the melancholy notes of the pipe and a song that sounded like a dirge.

It was indeed an evil season. A few days after Alice returned to Peking huge crowds gathered outside its walls to witness the summary decapitation of six leading Reformers, among them the brilliant T'an Ssu-tung who combined his belief in the intrinsic benevolence of mankind with a last declaration that no revolution ever succeeded unless martyrs' blood was shed. Kang Yu-wei's brother was also among those executed, though Kang himself had managed to escape to Japan. The Empress, furious that he had evaded her wrath, put a heavy price on his head and for a time it seemed likely that the Emperor, who was entirely at her mercy, might pay for his allegiance to the Reformers with his own life. It was, however, eventually deemed politically expedient to allow the wretched ruler to continue living, or rather languishing in his chilly dwelling on the Winter Palace lake, where he remained for the next year.

Meanwhile, most of the reform decrees he had issued were reversed, and many adherents of reform were 'graciously commanded to go away,' that is, banished for life. Nor did all foreign sympathisers escape unscathed. Timothy and Grace Barlow were peremptorily ordered Home to explain to their Society superiors why they had committed so much effort to a political movement; government-employed translators of New Learning books were dismissed and their works destroyed. In addition the Board of Punishments was re-instated, as was the eight-legged examination system—much to the relief of scholars who had spent years studying for it.

So, throughout the Empire, gainers became losers, losers gainers. Riots in the South—land of desperadoes, salt-smugglers and revolutionaries in the Empress's view—were cruelly suppressed. In the north, where the conservatives' return to power was absolute, many felt it safe at last to show their suppressed hatred of barbarians. Foreigners were jostled in city streets, and even some of the Legation servants became quite uppity, said Lady Maclaren, and had to be dismissed.

Despite feeling as if everything that mattered had collapsed around her, Alice's instinct for survival made her pretend both to herself and others that all was comparatively well. She re-opened 'The Polished Jade' and summoned Benjy from Shanghai, for she'd allowed the business to slide and suspected that its profits weren't reaching her. This Benjy blandly confirmed, explaining that, as he was now a highly competent comprador with a big face to keep up, she could either find a cheaper man or expand the business so that she, as well as he, might benefit from its profits. She chose the latter course and, at his suggestion, began searching the Peking markets for bargains.

'You have a good eye,' Benjy told her smoothly. 'Get the stuff restored here where workmanship is better and send it me to sell. I promise you we'll both do well.'

She disliked his only half-veiled assumption of the boss's role, but lacked the will to challenge him just then. Indeed, she had little heart left for anything: what she had might as well go back into the business.

Humbly clad in a dark blue gown and a tattered fur cap, she sallied forth with her calico bag. Dry winter was approaching; chill sunlight whitened the marble bridge over the Jade Canal to which lepers and starving beggars clung for support, dirty palms outstretched. She prowled through the Chinese City bazaars, glancing at snuff-bottles, rough pots, glazed brush-jars, rock-crystal ink-stone, drinking vessels, marbled vases. Initially, she refused to say what objects she sought, for, faced with the canny city merchants, it was wise to assume disinterest.

Eventually, the dealers, recognising her as one not easy to fool, produced their more select wares for her regard; she, in similarly reluctant fashion, let it be known that jade was her quarry. Cautiously, hesitantly, pieces began to appear and only then did the bargaining begin. Many times she stalked off empty-handed shouting that the price suggested was monstrous, daylight robbery that even a thief would be ashamed to ask. And who did they think she was—a foreign princess, a barbarian millionaire's wife with money to burn? And sometimes they would call her back, bring her tea and honey-cakes to soothe her while the prices were lowered.

And thus, in leisurely, crab-like fashion, over several weeks she bought some prizes. Each had the motif of a living thing, which pleased her most: a greenish-white feline with a single horn, crouching on a seal-block; a light grey duck mottled with black, its head turned back, a weed in its beak; a pale-yellow three-legged toad with polished warty back, symbol of wealth; and, her favourite, an eighteenth-century vase of greyish-brown jade, delicately carved as a lotus plant, with two crested birds perched on its leafy rim. At night, alone, she examined each piece carefully under the lamp-light, imagining its history, taking strength from its hard beauty. But in the mornings, her weakest time, her mind dwelt achingly on the recent past, pondering the fate of those who had gone.

Eventually a letter came from Lin. He had reached Yokohama safely and was staying with Cantonese friends. They and Kang Yu-wei were in consultation with Sun Yat-sen and his followers. 'They want us to join forces with them, but there are fundamental disagreements between us. Now our attempt at peaceful reform has failed, at least for the present, they are even more certain that total revolution is the only answer. Our Modern Sage cannot agree to that; he still supports Kuang-hsu and wants to form a Society for his Preservation. Is he still dreaming? Perhaps, yet I too abhor the thought of what blood would be shed if revolution comes.' He said little about Japan, less about himself personally, only bade her be of good heart, for one day the Movement would take root in China again and he would return.

With that small hope she tried to be content, but depression gnawed her as the threat of winter became a cold reality. Into that bleakness came a note from William inviting her to join them and their friends, the Lawsons, for Christmas Day. The tone was of carefully measured friendliness, and she guessed how he and Isabel had talked it over: how could they not ask her at such a season of goodwill? She had behaved disgracefully, but now she must have been left alone. Alone, Will's sister, for Christmas. It would have been churlish to refuse, and, having accepted, she rather enjoyed buying presents and making boxes of candied fruits as her contribution to the seasonal fare.

She arrived at the Customs bungalow after the family had been to morning service. Polly rushed to kiss her welcome and Tommy blew a new toy trumpet in her ear. She was introduced to Lydia Lawson—short, plump, with a ready smile—to her husband, Hubert, her children, Hilda and Dickie, her brother, Arthur Rawlins, a well-scrubbed loquacious young man recently arrived from Home to take up a junior Customs post.

'And I only hope to succeed as well as your brother one day,' Arthur looked admiringly round the elegant drawing-room as they sipped fruit punch. 'You must be proud of him, Mrs. Grant?'

'Oh I am indeed. Yes.' Alice fixed on her face the first of many false beams the day demanded.

Isabel, determined to be pleasant, added, 'And Alice has her accomplishments too. She's an extremely good linguist and very knowledgeable about Chinese culture.'

'Really? Then I must pick your brains, for I'm only a neophyte. I understand the country is reduced to such decadence that culture generally is falling into disgraceful neglect? Isn't that so?'

'Well, I'm not sure of . . .'

'I went to look at that Tibetan temple yesterday—the lamas' robes were utterly filthy—and the Confucian temple too—those votive tablets needed a good dusting! I'd say the whole city needs a thorough-going clean-up for a start. Don't you think?'

'Well, I suppose I'm rather used to . . .'

'And as for the streets—I've never seen such quagmires in my life, by jove. I hear ponies have actually drowned in the drains in the rainy season!' He snorted with mirth as the gong summoned them all to table.

With a sense of purpose appropriate to the day they ate their way through a considerable number of courses, beginning with salmon pâté sent from the Army & Navy Stores, then roast ducks, partridges, and venison. The meal ended, eventually, with oranges, persimmons, dried date-like jujubes, and crab apples preserved in honey, à la Mongolian, as Isabel explained. They drank the Queen's health, followed by Hubert Lawson's toast to her nearer Majesty, the invincible Empress Dowager, 'the only real man in China.' Will, laughing dutifully, hoped his sister would, for one day, keep her mouth shut on certain subjects. Alice looked down, pretended to drink. I'm a born turncoat, she thought miserably, a female Judas Iscariot—sitting here quietly while people raise their glasses to the one who had the six reformers executed recently, and who'd have Lin's head too if she could.

There was worse to come, for the Lawsons had got up a little tableau vivant for the general entertainment. They hung a curtain across the drawing-room alcove, and disappeared behind it with much giggling and scuffling. Eventually, Hilda appeared, thudded out a march on the piano, and announced in a prim voice,

> 'The Conquering Heroine I should have played,
> For here she is, in all her finery arrayed.'

She drew back the curtain to reveal Lydia, her squat shape draped in an embroidered Manchu gown, topped with a winged wig of black ornamented hair; she waved three-inch-long red artificial nails at the audience and scowled forbiddingly. Golden-robed Hubert, her Chief Eunuch, knelt at her feet, padded to grotesque fatness, with a long pigtail and a chalk-white face, while Dickie, his attendant, blew tonelessly on a bamboo pipe. A poster behind the ensemble announced that this was the 'Honourable Hall for the Cultivation of Magnificent Culture.'

Oh, how funny it was! Isabel and William chuckled mightily, staring straight ahead, while Arthur Rawlins was set fair to split his sides with mirth. Polly clapped heartily, glancing uneasily at Aunt Alice who sat stiffly, as if she were also part of the tableau. There was a pause for full effect, then Lydia Lawson tottered forward on high shoes and recited,

> 'Here am I, the dear old Buddha,
> Back to rule the whole of China.
> 'Cos my nephew is a twit
> Who thought he could reform it.'

Then shrilled Hubert in a piping tone,

> 'Here am I, the eunuch Chief,
> A lack I have that brings me grief.
> Yet I wield the mighty po-wer
> Of the Empress Dowag-er.'

Dickie, bursting with giggles, finished,

> 'A humble minion here am I,
> And oh, the goings-on I spy!
> But what they are, I dare not say,
> . If I did, you'd faint away!'

At this, to much laughter and clapping, Hilda closed the curtain with a flourish and Will and Isabel hastened to congratulate the performers.

'Oh, ho, ho, lord love us, what a laugh!' Arthur wiped his eyes. 'That was really clever, wasn't it, Mrs. Grant? I didn't know old Lydia had it in her, by jove.' He looked at her and noticed her ghostly pallor. 'Bless me, it was only a joke you know.'

'Yes, I realise that.' She turned to Polly, who was hopping about in embarrassment. 'I've brought you a little book of poetry translations. It's in my bag upstairs. Shall we go and look while they're clearing up?'

'Oh, Aunt—yes please show me.' They went out together, while Arthur, thinking what a miserable bluestocking Mrs. Grant was, went to add his congratulations to the performers.

When Alice and Polly returned, the tableau had been dismantled, Tommy and Dickie were running about blowing on trumpet and pipes, and Hubert was helping with the Christmas lights on the verandah.

'How pretty they are,' Alice joined him, beaming fixedly on the wrought-iron candle-baskets, the transparent red-tasselled horn-lanterns that glowed against the approaching dark.

'Yes, aren't they?' Hubert turned a still-powdered face. 'Listen, isn't that a carol?'

Sure enough, a rendering of 'Hark the Herald Angels Sing' drifted to them from a nearby bungalow. 'Makes you feel quite homesick,' he said.

'I suppose it does,' she answered distantly, and went inside. What a touchy woman, he thought; his wife had whispered they had offended her, but heaven knew how.

In the drawing-room, the damask curtains drawn, the fire blazing, tea was served—blancmanges, jellies, jam tarts, mince pies, iced cake. Alice hoped for some diversion, her digestion quite unused to so much rich fare. As she reached for a jelly it came: a ring on the front bell.

'Why, whoever's that?' Will got up, and met Adam coming in, looking cold and apologetic.

'Adam! You here!' Alice sprang up joyously.

'Alice hello. And a very merry Christmas to you all.' He smiled round shyly, was introduced, given a fireside seat. Warming his hands, he explained, 'I've been moved from Changsha to Mukden. But being Christmas, I decided to come here en route and see you all. But the train from Tientsin was hours late—I honestly believe the Chinese did it on purpose to spoil Christmas for all the foreigners aboard.'

'Oh Adam what a shame! You've missed Christmas dinner,' Isabel exclaimed.

'And our little tableau,' Lydia tutted. 'You must be frozen, travelling all that time. Really, the pig-headed natives are so unco-operative these days.'

'But why have you moved, Adam? I thought you were so happy in Changsha?' Alice asked.

'Oh, one goes where one's sent you know. They decided I'd be of more use in Mukden, as I know the place and speak the dialect.' His nose was twitching terribly she noticed.

'It seems a shame. Mukden's so dreary. But how's everyone in Changsha? I keep hoping to hear from the Chus. Han-li left to return there soon after the coup failed. Did you know?'

'Oh well . . . I went to 'The Polished Jade' first, Alice, and heard you were here.'

'Yes, quite. And the Chus?'

'Oh well . . . Could we talk later, Alice? It is Christmas Day. And yes, I will have another mince pie, thank you, Isabel. It's good to see you all, I must say!' His cheeks started to glow with the warmth of fire and fellowship, but still he didn't meet Alice's eye.

She, tense with foreboding now, felt the day would never end. They played 'Hunt the Ring,' 'Consequences,' 'the Minister's Cat,' but it was not until the last, when Adam was sent outside while the others conferred, that Alice could seize her chance and slip after him. He was standing by the dining-table eating nuts, and when she appeared he looked like a guilty schoolboy, a nervous rabbit.

'I'm sorry, Adam. I know it's Christmas and all that. But what's wrong at Changsha? What's happened? Is it Han-li?'

He nodded. 'Alice, couldn't you wait till . . .'

'Tell me. Suspense is worse than knowing.'

For answer he produced a letter from his pocket. 'It's from the Eldest Daughter of the Chus.' He turned away as she took it.

'Dear Uncut Jade, I write at the request of your relative who kindly came to offer his condolences when he heard the dreadful news. He wanted me to tell you what has happened, though I can hardly bear to write, for my sleeves are wet with grief. Poor dearest Younger Brother arrived here safely and told us how you'd helped him escape from Peking. Father and I were most grateful. But soon afterwards our progressive Governor was banished, and oppressive officials returned to full power. We warned Han-li to go away, but he was proud, saying he was no guilty fugitive. A few days later, soldiers went to the college where he and three others were still trying to teach, though most of the students dare not attend. They arrested the four of them, and put them in prison. It all happened so fast, we hadn't time to realise. The very next day they were all taken to the common execution ground and killed, the slice-in-half death, so . . .'

'Oh no, no no!' Alice doubled as a searing pain ripped through her middle. 'Oh my God!' She bent over, clutching her stomach. Adam put a hand on her shoulders.

'Alice, I know . . . it's so dreadful. I'm so sorry . . .'

She gazed at the letter, eyes swimming. 'It goes on. Can there be more, worse? Read it for me, Adam.'

'Can't understand the characters very well,' he mumbled.

She brushed her eyes and continued, '. . . so very terrible. The news was too much for the Honourable Father. He had a seizure in the courtyard that evening and died a few hours later, just like grandfather all those years ago. I am in a frenzy of grief and despair, Uncut, and even Elder Brother is quite distraught. The authorities have cut off all our monies for

561

having a traitor in the family. I'm only relieved that Father had a coffin made for himself years ago—the best Szechuan timber. We couldn't have afforded it now. Many people stayed away from the funeral out of fear. Everyone is on edge, pretending they had nothing to do with Reform. I've sent my boys to Canton for safety and keep Daughter Number One as my sole consolation. For myself, I no longer care. I am totally bereft.

> 'Sad at morning, I lie in bed till dusk,
> Weeping at night, I sit and wait for dawn.
> The fire of sorrow has burnt my heart's core:
> The frost of trouble has seized my heart's root.

'I send you what salutations I can at this time of deepest woe.
'Tamao.'

The letter fell to the floor. 'Both of them dead, Adam. Both of them. The dear, good, brave Younger Brother sliced in . . . two separate parts . . .' She clutched the table for support, seized with the agony of a sword thrust. From a long distance she heard Isabel calling,

'Come on, Adam, we're ready for you now.'

The air of the dining-room was still heavy with the fumes of roast meats, stuffings, puddings, punches, and when she tried to move the pain churned into an increasing, irresistible nausea and she began to vomit. All the unaccustomed rich fare she'd consumed at the table splattered back on to it, and dripped on the carpet below. She doubled over helplessly while Adam rushed for a bowl and Isabel came in search of him.

'Alice! Whatever . . .?'

Alice fumbled desperately for a handkerchief, sobs bubbling through sickness. 'Oh I'm sorry, Isabel . . . so sorry . . . It's . . . Adam, tell her what's . . .' As he handed the bowl she retched into it, leaving him to explain. 'She's very, very upset naturally,' he concluded, as they looked at Alice's bent head.

'How very dreadful,' Isabel said distantly. 'You'd better go and rest, Alice. Take her to the spare room, Adam, and I'll get someone to clean up this mess.'

She swept out; Alice groaned and, clutching Adam's arm with one hand, the bowl with the other, shuffled obediently to the bedroom.

She stayed there for the remainder of the evening and Adam mixed her a sedative that brought blessed sleep. She woke in the early hours, and a dead-weight depression settled inside her like a dark ravening monster. Over-riding Will's protests, she dragged herself to Pumpkin Lane and went to bed; Mrs. Duck brought her gruel and kept the *k'ang* warm. Days passed; showers of snow whirled from grey skies and fringed the mimosa's bare branches. City sounds drifted to her, disembodied as snowflakes: first the scraping of the night-soil men; neck-bells of the Mongolian coal-camels: the knife-grinder's tinny gong and the merry horn of the sweetmeat seller; the occasional clackety-clappers of a travelling show-man with two skinny monkeys on his shoulders and a perform-ing dog on a lead. Being in bed all day, she slept but fitfully, counting the watches of the freezing nights as they sounded distantly from the Drum Tower in the northern Tartar City. On comparatively good days she read a little poetry and made one translation of a Cantonese love-lament:

> The tree of love is planted in sorrow city.
> Branchless and leafless, bleak and alone.
> Flowers are the primal life of love
> When e'er flowers droop it's because of you.
> When spring is chill, flowers strike no firm root.
> So they are changed into duckweed and drift elsewhere.

Veronique Blum was the first to break through her self-imposed isolation, arriving on a cold afternoon, her thin ringed hands curled inside a sable muff. 'Whatever is the matter dear? See, I've brought you some special chocs. Marzipan and violet creams.' She sat by the *k'ang*.

Alice sniffed. 'Oh Veronique, thank you. It's nothing really. I have a cold.'

'And something of a broken heart? My poor *cherie*. Certainly more than a cold, you have lain there for a month.'

'I just don't have the strength to get up somehow. There seems no point. A broken heart? Yes, I ache for Lin, but I kept going till Christmas, and that was the last straw . . .' She told her friend the events of that day, concluding, 'And when I fin-ished reading the letter, I was frightfully, obscenely sick over everything. And crying at the same time. For Han-li most of all. I still feel a sharp pain when I think of it. Do you think there's a split-second agony when the head knows that it's separated forever from the feet?'

Veronique patted her hand. 'There, there, don't think . . . don't. Poor poor Han-li. He was a good man.'

563

'Oh he was, and that very afternoon those daft people had put on that ghastly tableau and everyone else thought it so funny, and I just sat quiet like a damnable hypocrite . . . Oh, I wanted to vomit up my whole life at that table, Veronique! I felt then that everything the Reformers had dreamed of was over, utterly collapsed.'

'No, no. Men like Han-li haven't died in vain, honestly. It's more a case of *reculer pour mieux sauter*. Sorry, to step back in order to leap further forward. See, it's much clumsier in English. Anyway, there will be another step forward eventually, I'm convinced of it. You must begin to think of that.'

'Oh, I shan't be involved, I'm beginning to feel my age. Looking in the mirror the other day I saw for the first time how I'll be if I get really old—even smaller, all shrivelled up and bent . . . ugh!'

Veronique laughed softly. 'Oh Alice you are in a hole, aren't you? Come dear, you are tough really, even though you may suffer more because of it. But you can't give up.'

'I suppose not.' Alice took a marzipan chocolate that tasted better than anything she'd eaten since that disastrous Christmas dinner. 'But I *am* in a hole. You know, long ago when I left Hunan and returned to Treaty-Port life, it often seemed to me as if I were Alice who'd fallen down a rabbit-hole, with a world at each end, and not being sure which was the real one. Then, eventually, they seemed to merge, but now that Chinese world I knew in Hunan is crumbling away. And that makes me very sad because, unconsciously perhaps, I always counted on it remaining intact. But look what's happened to the Chus—and thousands like them. The Honourable Father Lung-kuang I knew in his prime is not just dead, but his kind is passing from the face of the earth.'

'Alice, you are dwelling too much on the past. You're not shrivelled and old yet, by a long chalk. So come . . .' Veronique patted her cheek. 'I've found an excellent polisher to deal with your jades by the way, and it's more than time you got your stock moving. Promise me you'll get up soon?'

Alice snuggled back under the warm quilts. 'I will eventually. Promise. But this *k'ang* is the only warm spot in the house and for the present I'm staying on it. There'll be a sign, and I'll come bouncing out like a squirrel from hibernation.'

Soon after Veronique's visit the first double-almond blossoms appeared in the city's gardens; Mrs. Duck arranged several branches in tall blue and white vases, and Alice looked at them. In the pale sun of the afternoons, three younger ducklings waddled about the courtyard in their padded tunics, squeaking, chuckling, playing 'catch,' chanting,

'Something for all, a pip for one,
Four little seeds and a pineapple bun,
Pears and peas and powder—run!'

On one such afternoon, when the sky was truly blue, Alice got up, for, as she said to herself, the next round.

Spring had thoroughly arrived by the time Grace and Timothy Barlow, having received what the latter called 'a proper wigging' from his London headquarters, returned to Peking.

'The Board had gathered in force,' he told Alice, settling in a chair. 'And the ancient Secretary, who's always disapproved of my methods, wanted to know how I could have been so foolish and wrong-headed to support a failed political movement.'

'That's the rub of course,' Grace chimed in. 'Had the Reformers succeeded, Timothy would have been lauded to the skies for his perspicacity.'

'Maybe so. But I was still guilty of the sin of pride.'

'Pride?' Alice was puzzled.

'Of intellectual pride, Alice. Of trying to hobnob with the great and convert the powers in the land in a manner positively Jesuitical. How I bustled between Kang and the *Tsungli Yamen*, full of my own importance! I blush to think of it. Lin noticed, didn't he? I understood months after why he was impatient with me.'

'Well yes, he did. But you weren't the only sinner in that regard, Timothy. You could say intellectual pride defeated us all.'

'Partly, yes—we weren't sufficiently in touch with the masses, indeed almost scorned them.'

'Still no use crying over spilt milk,' Grace exclaimed briskly. 'Fortunately we've survived and now it's time for a new approach. We're starting a junior college for the better understanding of western sciences and languages at the old Mission in Paoting-fu, Alice. Timothy managed to win over the old fogies on the Board eventually and we've been allotted funds for books and instruments. It's going to be exciting and constructive, in a humbler way.'

'We're wondering if we can count on your help at all, Alice?' Timothy appealed.

'Me? I'm sticking to the lucrative business of selling jades from now on. No more politics, and I've never been a true supporter of missions, as you know.'

'Come dear, that's just a reaction against what's happened,' Grace protested. 'There's so much to be done in education that isn't directly political. We want to start again with bright young students.'

'And I'm sure Lin hasn't given up?' Timothy asked slyly.

'No, I heard from him again recently. They're still agitating for peaceful reform, still can't agree with Sun Yat-sen's crowd.'

'Quite right too. Bunch of revolutionary hotheads—they "look at an egg and immediately expect it to crow." And that's not the way. Anyway, please think it over, Alice. We desperately need your help. I know of no one better qualified to teach our advanced language courses and help me on the science side. As for the Christian teaching, we'll see to that, with Jessie's help.'

'Jessie Reeve, who's been holding the fort in our absence,' Grace explained. 'She's a treasure. New England farming stock. She left the American Baptists because of their narrow methods and came to us. One of God's naturally anointed good, isn't she, Timothy?'

He smiled warmly at the thought of her. 'She is. As you'll agree when you meet her, Alice.'

'But I haven't said . . .'

'Say nothing definite just now, Alice,' Grace advised, as she moved into the courtyard, and lifted her face to the sun. 'It's spring—the mimosa's in bud again. New promises, new hopes. Come and visit us in the summer when this city's unendurable anyway. Think of it as a little teaching holiday. Paoting-fu is less than two hours away now there's the rail link. Please, you've so much to offer, dear,' she turned to Alice, smiling hopefully. 'And don't be so disheartened: change is wrought slowly and painfully in human affairs, but it does come to pass. Remember the redoubtable Hsuen Tsang: "Ten thousand setbacks left him unruffled."'

Alice laughed. 'Oh I ruffle very much sooner. I'll think about it, Grace, and maybe I'll come when you suggest, if business picks up here.'

Trade did indeed pick up that spring when foreigners of wealth and taste visited the capital; but by July they'd fled to cooler climes and business sank to its usual mid-summer doldrums. Alice arranged for a cousin of Benjy's to come and take charge of what business there was, packed her lightest, native-style robes and departed for Paoting-fu. She had warned the Barlows by letter that she was making no commitment whatever to their college, and indeed only went because no more tempting prospect presented itself.

Paoting, the capital of Chihli province, about 120 miles south-west of Peking, was now the junction of a railway line eventually intended to stretch as far as Hankow. Its foreign population was quite large, and consisted of two disparate groups: missionaries and railway men. The two most prominent missions, set in large compounds, belonged to the London Missionary Society, headed by Mr. and Mrs. Coxhead originally from Walthamstow, and the American Mission Board, headed by Dr. and Mrs. Pike from Ohio.

The Barlows' college was on the outskirts, a ramshackle, single-storey building with a notice above the arched gate announcing in Chinese and English, 'Society for the Diffusion of Christian and General Knowledge.' Its outer walls were of mud-bricks which tended to dissolve into their original element during heavy rains; but such inconvenience would have been positively welcomed that summer, when the whole of Chihli was in the grip of a severe, long-lasting drought.

'Just look at Jessie's flowers,' Grace said, clambering from the Mission cart in which she'd met Alice at the station. 'It's her single indulgence—her father sends packets of seeds each year, and usually they do well, but . . .' She gestured at the shrivelled plants drooping in the baked soil. 'Ah, there you are, Jessie. Do meet my good friend, Mrs. Greenwood-Grant. I was just showing her your poor little petunias.'

'Yes, it's a shame. I feel quite guilty, thinking how they would have flourished back home. So happy to meet you.' Jessie Reeve was of broad stature, and wavy blonde hair framed a wide-open broad face with clear grey eyes. She held out a thick, strong, pink arm, 'Do let me carry the bags; it's so hot. As for the flowers, that's the least of our worries really. There'll be real hardship hereabouts soon if no rain comes.'

Alice's room was spare, neat, clean; a beautiful patchwork coverlet on the bed. She fingered it appreciatively, 'Who made this?'

'Oh I did,' Jessie smiled. 'I've got awful busy fingers, into everything. You'll want to wash up and then come and have tea. Mr. Barlow is just longing to show you his new scientific instruments. I'm too much of a duffer to understand them, but you will, I'm sure.'

'I'm not much good at science either, I'm afraid.'

'But you're clever.' It was said without malice; a statement of fact.

'Really? Whoever gave you that idea? Phew . . .' Alice took off her travelling jacket. 'I'm going into sensible native robes like yours.'

'Mr. and Mrs. Barlow both say so. And you'll be such a blessing for the advanced students, they've been looking forward to your coming.'

'But I haven't made any promises to . . .'

Jessie bit her lip. 'Oh, I know, I'm sorry. I get so carried away thinking how much needs doing. But the students will win you over, they're so eager to learn. Mrs. Barlow and I have a struggle to keep up with them, what with the Mission work. But you can just teach. I'm not supposed to talk to you about Christianity, which will be difficult because I dwell on it so, but I'll try.' She looked wistful, thinking that Mrs. Grant looked so pleasant she might relax that prohibition then and there.

But Alice merely chuckled, 'So the Barlows have been putting you right about me, have they?'

'In the nicest possible way. They admire you and so do I for being so loyal to the Reformers. You've had a difficult time, haven't you? And we all want you to be happy here. So if there's anything special you want, just ask me, I'll do what I can.' She bustled out, pausing only to flip dust from the washstand in housewifely fashion.

A treasure indeed, Alice thought, suspicious at first of quite so much frankness and concern. But she was soon won over to Jessie and, as Jessie had predicted, to the college's students. For the majority, the main attraction of the place was not the Mission chapel in the forecourt, but the 'laboratory' in the hall behind. Here stood examples of Western scientific instruments whose miraculous powers could be demonstrated and tested: a spectroscope and a dynamo, a galvanometer, the newest type of camera, pocket aneroids and a magic lantern with slides showing European capitals.

Timothy lectured on electricity, magnetism, chemistry to

students who, though well-grounded in the classics, had little understanding of modern scientific method. They were pale, eager, anxious young men, uncertain if they'd been well-advised to forsake the well-trodden academic paths for these strange processes of measuring, calculating, experimenting; unsure too if they could succeed, and if so, where success might take them. Alice, attracted by their uncertainties, soon found herself teaching language classes as Timothy had hoped.

Jessie was a born housekeeper who, in Alice's private opinion, had been perversely and inexplicably deflected from her motherly-wifely role in life by visits, at an impressionable age, to the Young Ladies' Mission Board in Portland, Maine. She seemed to have no regrets, though, simply bringing to Paoting all the skills and virtues of her upbringing and ancestry. She could sew, garden, clean, nurse and the larder was packed with neatly labelled jars of her millet syrup, gooseberry jam, melon pickles, beancurd pastes, long white 'finger grapes' preserved in earthenware pots. She worked as the Lord wished her to from dawn till bedtime and Alice often heard her singing one of Moody and Sankey's popular hymns as she did so:

'There are foxes to take, there are wolves to destroy.
All ages and ranks I can fully employ.
I have sheep to be tended, I have lambs to be fed,
The lost must be gathered, the weary ones led.'

The lost whom Jessie gathered were mostly the girl-babies left outside the compound gate in unusually large numbers that year because the continuing drought brought deeper poverty to the hard-pressed peasantry. She was mother to them all, in whatever filthy, scabrous, afflicted state they came, and Alice could only marvel at the seemingly bottomless well of her loving kindness.

'You know, Grace,' she said one morning as the two of them left the kitchen for the schoolroom, 'Sometimes I think there has to be a Heaven after all, so people like Jessie can go there.'

Grace smiled, 'There is a Heaven, otherwise people like Jessie wouldn't exist.' They smiled understandingly at each other and went their ways, having long before ploughed the theological furrows without conversion on either side. Going into the class, Alice noticed immediately that Yung-choon Wen hadn't yet arrived. Yung-choon was her favourite student, amusing, clever and Forever Handsome, as his name suggested. He had a certain similarity to Lin, and could have been that treasured Eldest Son she'd probably never meet.

Yung-choon was actually Third Son of a minor mandarin, a Strict Confucian, she'd been told, who didn't wish his son to be contaminated by the foreigner's religion while in pursuit of their knowledge. Accordingly the boy absented himself from Bible classes whenever possible, which annoyed the Barlows and amused Alice. He came in now, bowing with profuse apologies, saying his mule was lamed; then, at the class's end, lingered.

'Respected Teacher, my father asks if you will come to visit our humble residence?' he asked abruptly.

'How kind!' She was astonished by the unusual request.

'He seeks your acquaintance. I told him you are not a missionary. You will come?'

'It will be a pleasure,' she replied, and the arrangement was made.

Mr. Wen lived in a dignified house on the city's outskirts and Alice was shown into its main reception room one afternoon a week later. Inevitable was the row of high-backed chairs, the calligraphic scrolls that elegantly conveyed commonplace Confucian teachings. 'A thing unknown is a scholar's shame,' claimed one; perhaps that partly explained Third Son's presence at the college. The head of the house appeared, a lean, grave man with little of his offspring's looks or verse. After the customary pleasantries, the offerings of refreshments, he said abruptly, 'Honourable Teacher, Third Son is a frivolous, insincere student, is he not?'

'No indeed. He is sometimes lighthearted, but is that not a pleasant quality in youth?'

'His manner is over-animated. He does not persevere.'

'You are hard on him, Honourable. I don't find it so.'

'That is good. I do not know the correct behaviour required of students in your schools, even though I send my son to learn foreign matters.'

'You are wise so to do. Foreigners are here to stay, the clock cannot be put back to the seclusion of former times.'

He smiled at her for the first time. 'Third Son tells me you are not of the missionary persuasion?'

'No. I teach at the college, because, like you, I believe it is most important that the Sons of Han learn new ways. You'll be familiar, I'm sure, with Chang Chih-tung's recent *Exhortation to Study*? As he explains, many branches of Western learning have no essential connection with Western religion.'

'I am relieved to hear that. Morally speaking, the teachings of Master Confucius are sufficient for us.' She inclined assent. 'But speaking of morality, it greatly puzzles me that your missionaries extol the virtues of goodwill and human kindness while your politicians and soldiers seize our lands, undercut all our traditional trades?'

'I wish I could justify it, Honourable, but I think the powerful nations of the West behave outrageously towards the Chinese.'

'Ah. So you will understand why there is growing hatred of Europeans among the common people. I've heard recently that the sect called the Righteous and Harmonious Fists is increasingly active in neighbouring Shantung, since the Germans occupied a port there. They are a secret brotherhood, sworn to exterminate every foreigner in the land.'

'Oh yes, I've heard Mr. Barlow speak of them. The Boxers, we call them. You think they are dangerous?'

'I fear so. I've been informed that the contagion of their ignorant hatred is spreading here in Chihli. You and your colleagues should be warned.'

'Thank you, Honourable. I did not consider—one gets accustomed to upheavals of one kind or another.'

'It was not always thus. For centuries we Chinese were tranquil.'

'And yet, in our minds, "the past is always quieter than the present," is it not?' she quoted.

'You are well read for a foreign woman.' It sounded rude, but he intended it as a compliment and she accepted it as such, leaving soon afterwards with polite protestations of mutual esteem.

Dusk was falling as she was driven from Mr. Wen's residence in the college mule-cart; there was no sign of a cloud in the clear, lemon-pink sky. As she rode, thinking over what had passed, she heard gongs and rattles ahead, saw a procession of swinging lanterns. The weird, discordant sounds, the people wailing in unison made her uneasy. 'Another rain procession?' she asked the driver.

'Going to pray at the Temple of the Five Winds—one of them must bring rain, they think,' he snorted derisively. A devout convert, he no longer believed in such primitive superstitions.

Without another word, he deflected the animals down a side-street.

'Where are you going?'

'This way is better. People are saying that foreigners have irritated Heaven and that is why there is drought. Where there are floods, they blame foreigners for disturbing the natural balances of land and water. They are stupid, ignorant fools, but it is wiser to go another way home.'

Returned safely, Alice intended to talk over the day's experiences with the Barlows, but Jessie met her in the hall saying that Grace was in bed again, and Dr. Pike of the American Board had just seen her. Grace had been suffering recently from indigestion and bowel trouble, Alice knew, but she'd put it down to the heat. 'She must have felt poorly to call the doctor.'

'She's really ill, Alice, collapsed soon after you left. We're very worried.'

'Oh dear, talk about troubles coming by the dozen . . .'

'Why, what else is wrong?'

'Nothing—at least nothing urgent.'

While Jessie and Timothy hovered about Grace, Alice had a solitary supper and retired to her room. Sleep eluded her, for the day had been filled with menace—Mr. Wen's warnings, the rain procession, Grace's illness. She'd come to Paoting in search of peace, and was bitter that it again proved elusive, as was sleep itself. In a few days, however, things seemed to improve: rumours of unrest dissipated, rain clouds rolled a promise over the parched plains, Grace rallied considerably, and Alice decided to return to Peking.

'We'll keep a room here for you in case you come back—as we all hope,' Jessie said warmly. 'And here's some home-made buns and jams, and this . . .' she handed her a lumpish object wrapped in cheese-cloth.

'Jessie, thank you so much . . . but what is this?'

'A Christmas pudding, dearie. Even has a little brandy in. I thought you could share it with your relatives.'

'Jessie, you're sweet. I shall miss you,' Alice kissed her cheek (thinking, Christmas again, oh dear).

In Peking Alice took up the customary threads: business flourished during the autumnal tourist season: Benjy's cousin, nicknamed Sprig because he was small, wiry, wily, and a dandy dresser, had served her well and she kept him on. He had a disarmingly persuasive way with foreigners, and the two of them were engaged, one morning, in the leisurely, profitable sale of a jade vase to the wife of an American shipping director, when the shop door opened and Timothy hurried in. He looked very agitated and Alice ushered him straight into the sitting-room, leaving Benjy to clinch the deal.

'What is it, Timothy?'

'It's Grace. She's very ill.'

'Oh dear, what is . . . ?'

'Sprue, Dr. Pike has decided. He thinks she contracted it years ago when we lived in the South. She's lost so much weight, it's dreadful to see her—no appetite, can't swallow, bowel trouble, anaemia too, Dr. Pike says. The upshot is, if I don't get her to proper medical care in a temperate climate he won't give her three months.'

'Oh Timothy, how dreadful.'

He looked up, distraught. 'She is my—Grace. The greatest one God has vouchsafed me. The thought of losing that gracious soul fills me with such desolation I don't think I could endure. All my ideas, efforts—nothing matters now but to save her precious life. Is that wrong? I don't know. I don't even care. I'm taking her Home.'

'Is she here with you?'

'No, I've come rushing up for two days to get our passports in order, and to see you.' Her heart sank as she guessed what was coming. 'I've come to ask you, to beg you Alice to keep the college going in our absence. No one else can or will. The Pikes are already overstretched, and there's Horace, their new baby. Anyway, as you know, for the other missionaries, the simple Milk of the Word is sufficient and they'll have no truck with our teaching of "foreign matters." If you won't come, I must close the college and our promising start will be lost.'

'Timothy—what a way to put it! I have my business here to attend to, how can I come?'

'You sell jade for profit,' he interrupted flatly. 'That is the beginning and end of it, is it not? There is a saying, "A yard of jade is of no value compared to an inch of time." You know my students—clever, eager, anxious young men, wanting something new for themselves, for China. Think of Yung-choon. If we close now, we will lose him. I'm asking you to help Jessie hold the fort for them, for us. A few months only, while I try to save the life of my best-beloved. Will you say no because you have to sell more jade?'

She wailed at him, 'Timothy, Timothy . . . you are black-mailing me. Why do I have to be faced with these dreadful choices? Choices so many others seem to escape.'

Alice looked through the lattice into the grey-cold court-yard, thinking, incongruously, of missing the awfulness of another Peking Christmas, of the pudding Jessie had made for her, which, now, the two of them would share.

'You must have some tea,' she said.

'Quickly then, I have so much to attend to.'

She ordered tea, then took pity on the anxious pleading in his eyes, 'I have to arrange things here first. There will be an interval between your going—and my coming.'

He jumped up and put his hands on her shoulders, 'Alice, my dear, I knew you . . . no, I didn't know. I hoped and prayed. Grace will be overjoyed: she's been saying we mustn't go if it means closing the college. But we have to, Alice. It's her life at stake, and even then we are in God's hands. And so are you, though you don't recognise it. You will be aided by a stronger hand than mine, Alice.'

'I hope you are right, Timothy. My deficits are so many, I badly need a few credits to balance the final account.' She grinned.

'That is rather flippant.'

'I cannot, and will not, always be serious. If the serious don't laugh they are lost.'

'Perhaps, but I find it hard just now, I'm so terribly worried.'

She soothed him. 'You mustn't fret, dear. Take Grace away at once. Give the students a little break, and I promise to be there before Christmas.'

Alice kept her word, returning to Paoting-fu to share Christmas puddings not only with Jessie but with the Mission's orphans on the appropriate day. And it turned out to be quite a jolly one because the Pikes arrived, bringing a cured ham and jars of pickled walnuts. Their daughter Mabel helped feed the babies with broth; she was only seven and already a little mother to the manner born, Dr. Pike said proudly. After the meal he raised a glass of ginger wine and proposed a toast, 'To absent relatives, friends, the quick recovery of our dear Mrs. Barlow, and, if I may add, welcome to the promise of the twentieth century that is almost upon us. During it, I am convinced, we shall see greater progress than ever before towards the

574

health and happiness of mankind. And I confidently predict that the Word of the Gospel shall spread to all corners of the earth, bringing peace and good-will among men.'

Alice, about to slip away to spice her drink with some 'medicinal' brandy, wondered where the good doctor found his confidence. From her vantage point, the outlook for herself personally, for China, even for the wider world, looked anything but rosy. Opposite her, Mabel choked over the thimbleful of wine she'd been given.

'It's horrible—why do we have to have a twentieth century?' she gasped.

As Mrs. Pike wiped her daughter's mouth, saying that she'd grow up into a modern twentieth-century lady one day, Alice gave a sickened shudder and slipped from the room, helping herself to a double tot from the medicine cupboard to blunt the prickles of her inexplicable foreboding.

Certainly, the new century didn't show much early promise, even for the sanguine Dr. Pike who, soon after its beginning, found that his most trusted convert had been stealing medical supplies and selling them to the 'foreign goods shop' for a handsome profit. But such minor tribulations were soon overshadowed by the news of increasing outbreaks of violence instigated by bands of Boxer outlaws against native Christians. Earlier trouble had been confined to Shantung, but now it was spreading, aggravated by suspicions that missionaries were the secret advance guards of China's concerted take-over by foreigners.

Hundreds of Boxers drilled openly in the streets, armed with swords, spears, old-fashioned guns. Many were illiterate peasants dispossessed by a recent host of disasters—floods, droughts, and plagues of locusts; some were secret society adherents dedicated to the destruction of all foreign influences; some rowdy xenophobic braggarts who boasted of their supernatural powers. Eyes rolling, brandishing red banners, they stomped about the countryside, looting and bullying, swearing no weapons could harm them, that they could kill every barbarian pig in the country by directing a lethal light on them from their nostrils or fingertips.

Those foreigners who preached an alien faith, or who dislodged the spirits of land and air with their iron rails and overhead wires were their most hated targets. Next were the Christian converts, the 'secondary devils' who had eaten foreign rice and refused to take part in the time-honoured community festivals. Ominous yellow cards were delivered to them stating that Boxer 'representatives' would soon call unless they paid a ransom and recanted of their alien faith. Some did; some who refused were killed; others fled for their lives.

The provincial authorities attempted to quell the violence, but they were often half-hearted because orders on the subject issued by the Government were equivocal. In April, a Court Decree was circulated that the organisation of militia 'for the preservation of communities should not be prohibited.' The Governor of Chihli, guessing from this the Empress Dowager's secret sympathy for the anti-foreign factions, remained on the side-lines while the emboldened Boxers intensified their attacks. During that same month they pressed northward through the province and groups of refugee converts came seeking protection in the Paoting missions.

Until then, Alice and Jessie had managed to keep the college going, hoping the fearful rumours were exaggerated or false. When the first refugee family limped into the courtyard, dishevelled, scared, and battered, Alice knew they were true, and even as she listened to their tale of woe, the question throbbed in her mind, 'What shall I do now?' The family had received a dreaded yellow card a few days before, the Boxers had surrounded their home that same night, beating gongs, yelling insults. When their house was set a-fire, the converts fled screaming and were only saved by yamen guards. Bereft of everything, they'd walked for four days, kept alive by the charity of other converts. Now they wanted succour, reassurance that their losses would be redeemed, their loyalty rewarded. Jessie did everything she could, and Alice found herself helping.

But that arrival was only the beginning; soon every mission in the city was crowded with persecuted refugees, and at the college every space was occupied, every store-cupboard bare. In the evenings anxious groups gathered in the court-yard praying for guidance from the Lord. Should they seek the safety of the capital? Fly towards the coast? Stay and hope? And every night, Alice went exhausted to her bed, asking herself the same questions. It was becoming foolhardy to stay, but she had her escape route planned: if the Boxers threatened the city, she would simply take the train to Tientsin, then a boat to the safety of Shanghai. It was just a matter of telling Jessie and the devoted converts that she was not of their number, was not prepared to risk a martyr's death. Each night she planned to face their wounded bewilderment on the morrow; each morning slipped by in a bustle of coping and caring.

So the news that reached Paoting later in May was a body-blow: the Boxers were now attacking railways and telegraphs. Stations, bridges, engineering works had been burned and the recently forged lines of communication between Paoting, the capital and the coast all severed as the Boxers converged on the city. A frail sense of peace fell on those converts who had decided to remain and were thoroughly cast upon God's mercy. As sunset glowed pink on the mud-brick walls that evening a pastor held a prayer meeting for his flock, his blessing ringing strongly over their bowed heads,

'God Himself be with you. He can be, and is in ways we cannot trace. May the silent dew of the Spirit rest on you, my children. Light of the heart, illuminate them. Unseen Wing overshadow and protect them.'

Alice, standing near the gate, listened with detachment, unable to share the uplifted calm the words invoked among the faithful. She was frightened, already recalling the echoes of enraged mobs howling: 'Kill, kill . . . burn, burn . . .' As voices were raised in the final hymn, 'How sweet the name of Jesus sounds in a believer's ear,' she heard a whisper behind her.

'Honourable teacher, please let me in.'

She turned, 'Yung-choon, yes, wait a minute.'

She unbarred the gate and he handed her a note from his father: 'Honourable teacher, rowdy gangs of Harmony Fists are almost upon us, and I am informed the authorities will do little to protect foreigners. You came here purely to instruct our youth in foreign matters, but now you are in grave danger of falling victim to this ignorant rabble who would not distinguish you from Jesus-men and have cast aside the universal laws of courtesy towards strangers. I beg you therefore to at once accompany Third Son to my humble dwelling, where I may hide you. None will suspect your presence here, and you will be safe till we see what the next wind blows.' Yung-choon grasped her arm, 'You will come?'

'Oh yes, yes Third Son, and I thank you. Wait, I'll collect my things.'

Hurriedly she stuffed a few possessions in her travelling

bag, then went to find Jessie. She was standing by the stove ladling out the supper's thin gruel, and Alice beckoned her into the courtyard.

'Jessie, I'm leaving, deserting the sinking ship. Mr. Wen has offered me protection.'

'Oh, I'm so glad . . . the Lord be praised. I have prayed so often that you, at least, would be spared.'

Alice gasped. 'But why?'

'You are the clever one, Alice, more rare than those of us who do the donkey-work. We can easily be replaced.' She patted Alice's hand.

'What nonsense. I'm going because I'm a coward, that's all.'

'No indeed, you've already shown great courage.'

Alice sighed. 'I have the courage of no convictions perhaps, but that's as far as it goes.'

'And that's why you must leave. You see, Alice, if I am killed I know absolutely that the Lord has a place prepared for me in Heaven.' She drew a breath of intense devotion that was almost longing. 'He has one for you too, Alice, but you don't yet know that. I pray you will. But for you, not knowing, the sufferings of persecution and death would be much harder to bear. I have hated to think of your going through it, whereas for me, for the other devout here, it would be as nothing—so do go quickly now, for God has answered my prayers for you. Have you a guide?'

'Yung-choon is waiting at the gate.'

Jessie picked up her bag and almost ran to the gate. 'There Yung-choon, she is going with you. Blessings on you and your honourable father for this kindness.'

Alice kissed Jessie on the lips, fighting back her tears, 'And a blessing on you, sweet Jessie. Be of good heart, and all may yet be well.'

Jessie smiled radiantly, squeezing her arm, 'All will be well, Alice. Whatever happens, all will be well.'

Wrapped in a concealing cloak, Alice rode through the disturbed streets and was admitted into the Wens' house by a side entrance. Third Son took her to an attic where food was brought; obviously most of the residents were to remain unaware of her presence. In the distance were noises of riot and confusion, and her own inner turmoil made rest impossible until dawn, when she slept exhausted for several hours. While she dozed, Boxer bands surged into the city. They marched through the streets howling like dervishes, brandishing their blood-red banners on which were written 'Death and destruction to the barbarians from without.'

The first target was the London Missionary Society, where the mob broke through the gates, looted the downstairs rooms, then set fire to the whole. Mr. Coxhead fired on them with a pistol till his ammunition was exhausted and later eye-witnesses described the last view of him and his wife walking the upper verandah together till flames engulfed them. Later that day, the Boxers went on to the American Board and the Barlows' college. These they also fired, slaughtering some converts on the spot, and herding all the foreigners into a guard-house near the south gate. For two days they were kept prisoner, while the Boxers stormed about the city and Alice remained immured in Mr. Wen's attic.

On the third morning, crowds gathered early to watch as the pale, calm missionaries and their disciples were hustled along the streets, each attached with a rope-halter round the neck to the person in front. Dr. Pike headed the procession, followed by his wife holding baby Horace in her arms; then walked Jessie Reeve, her arm round the trembling shoulders of Mabel Pike. They prayed and sang as they walked, their heads held high, and Jessie sang loudest and sweetest of them all. On an open space outside the city gate they were executed one by one, and their heads, spiked on poles, dripped blood in the sunlight for hours afterwards.

7

Alice, still hidden in the attic, was told the next day of the missionaries' fate. The news stunned her and filled her with sorrow, but not surprise, and she accepted it with the fortitude that Jessie would have wished. Was it true, she pondered, that for the truly dedicated martyr, the actual time of death was irrelevant? 'Ripeness is all.' Had Jessie been ripe for Heaven? Had Alice's own father been when he was killed long ago? And dear Han-li, the sliced-in-half? Certainly there was a sense of dedication and cohesion about their lives that hers lacked. For didn't she, Alice Greenwood, keep stumbling through the years in a makeshift, aimless fashion, until almost by chance, she'd reached the twentieth century—still alone, uprooted, uncertain. In her youth, the twentieth century had seemed immeasurably distant, a haven for a secure and tranquil middle age. What vain hope, when already, of the company who had raised their glasses to toast its advent barely six months before, only she remained alive. For Jessie and the Pikes, death had held great meaning, martyrdom the ultimate crown. But try as she might, Alice had no ultimate faith in anything beyond life, and how to stay alive was her most urgent problem.

She paced about the attic, knowing she was entirely at Mr. Wen's mercy, wondering if he would help her further. She wasn't long in suspense; the following day he came to explain the position, which was grave. Chihli itself and the neighbouring provinces were reputedly overrun with Boxers, but he had it on good authority that a foreign force had landed at Tientsin and was fighting to reach the capital to protect its foreign community. Alice's best course therefore was to make for the capital also, considering the disturbed state of the countryside, and he proposed that Third Son should escort her thither. Alice, thanking him warmly, suggested it would be safer if she travelled disguised as Yung-choon's aboriginal servant. It was, she added, a role to which she was quite accustomed.

Disguised thus, she left Paoting with Third Son the next day. They travelled by cart across the sun-cracked Chihli plain; in the villages people were edgy, fearful of many things—the magical powers of the Boxers, the foreigners' reprisals, the Court's dictatorial edicts, further hardship, greater poverty. They did not welcome strangers in their usual fashion, and Yung-choon had often to resort to bribery and bullying to get them safely through.

Fortunately, the Boxers had hurried eastwards to intercept the foreign troops, and it was only on 13 June, as they neared the capital, that Alice fully realised the seriousness of their activities. In the late afternoon they halted at a vantage point from which the south-west walls of the city were clearly visible. As they watched, the distant crackle of flame and rifle shot seared the air and a glow that grew redder and more ominous than the approaching sunset stained the sky above the rooftops of the capital. Carts, riders, bands of men could be seen jostling at the gate to the Chinese City till it shut for the night. They had seen no sign of foreign troops, but Alice, ever-optimistic, decided that the firing suggested they were already in Peking, routing out the rebels.

She slept uneasily nonetheless till Third Son woke her at dawn. He was clearly nervous, wanting only to see the last of his honourable teacher and return safely home, for which she didn't blame him. So, without more ado, they rode to the nearest gate and passed inside without any question from the drowsy guards. Once inside, where smells of smoke and charred buildings hung in the early mist, Alice felt greater misgivings. But what was the alternative? She could trespass no longer on the Wens' goodwill and must seek again protection from her own kind. Just another turn of the coat, she thought bitterly, as she took her bag from the cart and urged Yung-choon to leave at once.

Still in her blue robe, she hastened towards Pumpkin Lane taking comfort from the surrounding quiet, the magnificent domes of the temples of Heaven and Agriculture shining as usual in the strengthening sun. Nearing the Ch'ien Men gate, she was just beginning to indulge the hope of a substantial breakfast in her own courtyard, when she heard shouting and chanting nearby. Peering round a corner into a square she saw an extraordinary scene—a band of Boxer militia were performing their ritualistic morning drill. She'd not seen the rebels at close quarters before and her first reaction was almost of disappointment—they looked so scrawny, unkempt, their weapons ridiculously primitive. They wore lengths of red cloth round their heads and waists, squares of flannel over their chests, supposedly making them invulnerable, and red-cloth shoes which they stamped rhythmically as they stood in lines facing the sun.

At regular intervals they waved their swords in the air and yelled, then stamped each leg, rolled their eyes and fell to their knees, knocking their foreheads on the ground and chanting,

'Cannon cannot injure, water cannot drown, knife cannot wound.' Then, jumping up, they twisted their hands towards the sun and chanted again,

'In the northern region open the mouth of the cave, let the iron gods come forth—temple of iron gods, seat of iron gods, iron our protection.' As they chanted, their leader leaped about, waving two red banners that proclaimed, 'Spirits and fists mutually assist' and 'Sweep the country clean of the devil-dogs.'

Alice watched, aware of the danger, yet curiously unafraid, for compared to the steely hordes of Japanese soldiers she'd seen, these Boxers were parody-warriors. The true menace of the scene, she realised, was that it could actually be happening, that in the very streets of Peking these men could flaunt their savage hatred without anyone attempting to prevent them. Indeed, the few citizens watching were cowed and respectful, and as their exercises ended, the Boxer leader turned to them, yelling truculently,

'Have you seen any big-nosed barbarians, any hairy secondary devils? Bring us rice and we will butcher them all.'

At these words Alice fled, not daring to speak to anyone. At the Ch'ien Men gate she bought a basket of fruit and, head concealed by a cotton shawl, stepped boldly past the guards. Inside the Tartar City the burning smells were stronger, and among the few people abroad, not one was foreign. What if they had all been exterminated already? Not here in Peking; surely it wasn't possible. She hurried down Pumpkin Lane, longing to talk to Snow Duck, but to her dismay the shop and house were closed and shuttered, as were the neighbouring premises. The only remaining inhabitant, crouched in a corner, was Tiger Blossom, who rubbed against her, mewing piteously.

'Where have they all gone? What is happening?' she asked the animal desperately. 'Who can I trust to tell me? Here, let's have something to eat, puss.'

The kitchen was fairly well stocked and she and the cat ate ravenously—a meal she'd long remember. Then, patting the cat, she hurried off to find William, taking nothing but her handbag and the fruit, for she expected to return in a few hours. The lanes were quiet, but the main thoroughfare was massed with Chinese hurrying in the opposite direction, and to the left rose billows of black smoke. A rifle cracked behind her and she crouched against a wall, wondering whose finger was on the trigger.

To her astonishment, a squad of white-uniformed foreign soldiers came pushing through the crowd at a brisk trot, rifles at the ready. Behind them trailed some Chinese nuns with their converts, carrying bundles or babies; old crones hobbling on sticks; one youth held a blood-soaked cloth to his jaw, a man carried an unconscious woman. Alice grabbed a soldier as he passed.

'Hello, do you speak English? Please help me.'

He stared at her. 'Hey . . . why yeah, I'm American. And who are you?'

'Mrs. Greenwood-Grant, though I don't look much like it. I'm trying to reach my brother William Greenwood who lives in Customs Lane. I've only just arrived and it's such chaos. What's happening?'

'The Boxers, ma'am, that's what's happening. They're massacring every convert in sight and we're on a patrol sent to rescue some of them. But you'd better come right back with us, to the Legation Quarter where all the foreigners are. How come you've only just got here?'

'I fled from Paoting-fu. All the missionaries were killed, but I managed to escape.'

'The lucky one, hey?'

'Yes—but I'm not a missionary, not a missionary, not a missionary.' In her pent-up tension she was suddenly screeching.

'All right ma'am, you're not a missionary. I expect you've had a rough time. Your brother will look after you.'

'I'm sorry. It's been a bit . . . difficult.'

Near the western end of Legation Street a barricade of carts, beerkegs and old furniture had been erected; on its far side stood armed American and Russian sentries. The soldier pushed Alice forward.

'This is Mrs Greenwood-Grant, sir. A British subject come to find her brother. She's not a missionary, sir.'

The officer-in-charge looked puzzled, but when Alice produced her passport waved her through, saying, 'Go directly to the British Legation ma'am and look up your relatives.'

'But they live in Customs Lane.'

'Not now they don't. It's been evacuated.'

Alice gasped at the speed with which things were disintegrating. She rushed along Legation Street; the Chinese houses and shops were closed and empty; turning left along Canal Street she reached the British Legation's main entrance. It was an imposing edifice, formerly a ducal palace, protected by high walls, its upper storey topped by the British royal arms.

That day its large compound was in uproar. Fighting men of several nations were milling around, unloading carts, cleaning guns, shouting orders into the din of snorting horses, barking dogs, and crying babies. On a patch of dusty lawn groups of just-arrived converts squatted passively, waiting to be put somewhere, and where that would be depended on a number of civilian gentlemen in white topees who were scurrying about with lists looking harassed. Among all this a few dazed ladies were resting in whatever shade they could find, and from one of them Alice learned that the Customs families had been billeted in the Escort Quarters north of the main gate. She hastened there yearning for a familiar face.

'Aunt Alice—oh, it's you, it's you . . . thank goodness!' Polly, on the point of coming out, flung her arms round her neck, hugging her. 'We've been so worried about you. Father tried to get news. Come and see them—they'll be so relieved. We've been given a tiny room for all of us, it's too ridiculous. Pappa says it will only be for a few days though. Oh, you can't imagine how pleased I am to see you safe and sound!'

Half-laughing, half-crying, Polly dragged her to an upstairs room where Isabel and William were sitting on mattresses on the floor; twelve-year-old Tommy was pointing a toy pistol through the window and shouting,

'Boom, boom, that's another Boxer killed, Pappa!'

'Look who's come, look who's come,' Polly cried happily.

'Alice, my dear. Thank goodness!' They hugged and kissed her, and Tommy pulled her skirt asking,

'Did you see any Boxers out there, Aunt? What do they look like?'

'Oh do be quiet, Tommy.' Isabel mopped her brow. 'I suppose it's as well he thinks it's just a game. But we heard dreadful stories about the Paoting area, Alice, and were so anxious. Sit down on the only chair, dear, and tell us how you got here.'

Alice gave them brief details of her escape, ending, 'As for the rest, I'll tell you later.' She glanced at Polly, who was all ears. 'But now please tell me what's going on here? Isn't there supposed to be a Relief Force? And what are the Imperial Forces doing? I didn't see one on the way here. And how could things have got to this pass?'

William snorted. 'You might well ask. Heaven only knows— certainly our so-called diplomatic corps don't. There were warnings, rumours of killings in the provinces—probably true?' he raised an eyebrow and she nodded. 'But nothing was done here. The foreigners in Peking were supposedly inviolate. And then, on the 9th wasn't it dear?—some Boxers burned down the racecourse grandstand. That really got the big white chiefs going—firing off telegrams for immediate armed support.'

Alice chuckled. 'How typical—converts slaughtered, missionaries attacked, but the grandstand really is a call to arms!'

'Well that's how it was, except the arms haven't come. A small mixed contingent—Brits, Americans, Japs, Russians, French—came in at the end of May and we're daily expecting a large force to arrive from Tientsin, but all rail and telegraph lines were cut a few days ago, and no one knows where they are.'

'I heard heavy fighting was going on between here and the coast.'

'Oh dear, I hope they arrive in a day or so. It's terribly stifling in here.' Isabel fanned herself vigorously. 'And we didn't bring many clothes, we were ordered to come in so quickly. But I'm glad we did, there were terrible fires everywhere last night.'

'Apparently foreign churches were burned and converts killed, that's why the patrol you met was bringing them in,' William explained.

'And our summer residences in the hills have been ransacked. Lady Maclaren is quite desolated, she had a beautiful porcelain collection,' Isabel added. 'And a few days ago they murdered the Japanese Chancellor in cold blood—it's all quite astonishingly awful.'

'Looks as if I better go back and get a few clothes and supplies,' Alice rose.

'Oh the soldiers won't let you out once you're in. Far too dangerous. Now you're here, here you stay!' William told her.

And so it proved: only military patrols were allowed out; only refugee converts were allowed in. There being no room for them in the already overcrowded buildings, they were quartered in the grounds of an adjacent palace called the Fu, and the defence lines extended to protect them. But those were the fortunate ones: many others were roasted alive when the cathedral in the southern city was burned down the night after Alice's arrival. Two days later she watched from a roof-top as a tremendous conflagration destroyed acres of shop-houses and spread to the Ch'ien Men tower; its ancient rafters crashed to the ground, roaring flames shot like arrows through its old slit windows. Alice, watching the fire's progress, wondered if she would ever see her little courtyard, its pond and mimosa tree again.

At that juncture however, Alice assumed that order would very soon be restored, and was therefore as shocked as everyone else by what happened next. On 19 June the foreign representatives received ultimata from the *Tsungli Yamen* that the entire foreign community was to leave Peking by four o'clock the following afternoon; safe escort to Tientsin was offered; it was stated that catastrophe might not be avoidable otherwise. Everyone spent a disturbed night; some packed bags in readiness; others prayed for guidance. There was no clearcut verdict, but it was generally felt that, if to stay might mean massacre, to go meant destruction, not to mention the abandonment of the Chinese Christians to certain death.

The next morning, after a stalling reply to the ultimata had been sent, the German Minister, Baron von Ketteler, set out alone for the *Tsungli Yamen*—and was murdered by bannermen of the Chinese Imperial Forces. This killing, which violated all rules of international diplomacy, convinced every foreigner that they could no longer put any faith in the Chinese

586

authorities. Their only recourse was to stay put and fight till help arrived.

That afternoon all the non-combatants, numbering some nine hundred, sought the comparative safety of the British Legation compound, which was the largest and best protected from outside assault. At four o'clock precisely heavy firing began to the east of the Legations and was responded to by volleys from the nearest defending garrison. Alice and Isabel, standing at the door of the newly-designated Customs Quarters, shuddered at the warlike sounds; Tommy capered about shouting, 'They're firing at the old Boxers.'

And when William came up he was actually smiling, 'Well at least it's really started and we know where we stand.'

Where they stood, Alice thought, was in an overcrowded, high-walled trap. It was bound on the west by the Imperial Carriage Park, on the north by the famous Hanlin Academy. Across the main canal to the east, a bridge led to the Fu, where the converts were herded, to the south was a jumble of deserted Chinese houses fronting Legation Street where combatant Americans, French, and Germans were holding out in their respective legations.

From the beginning of the siege all these perimeters were subjected to heavy onslaughts of gunfire and it was imperative to shore up the barricades strongly. Sandbags were the order of the day and non-combatants were put to the task of providing them, with Mrs. Hortensia Brown, indefatigable wife of an indefatigable American missionary, as self-appointed organiser. Alice long remembered the sandbagging scenes on the Legation lawns, for their mixture of farce and pathos was typical of the siege's earlier days, when everyone was still relatively clean and cheery and many still dressed for dinner in the evenings.

Piles of materials were dumped on the grass—wine-red damask curtains and monogrammed sheets, brocaded hangings from the Fu palace, striped flannel and native homespun, embroidered tapestries and humble strips of rough linen, swathes of grey and purple velvet, and yards of cobalt-blue Ningpo silk, intended for the Minister's wife's next ballgown. Mrs. Lister, young wife of the Legation's second secretary, fingering the red damask, said to Alice doubtfully.

'It doesn't seem right, does it, Mrs. Grant? Lady Maclaren received this only recently from Maples in Tottenham Court

Road. She just got it made into curtains in time for the Queen's birthday in May. Were you there? Such a lot of lovely coloured lanterns in the garden—this very garden. I remember her ladyship telling me about these curtains. Whoever dreamed that a few weeks later we'd be using them to make sandbags? It makes you shiver, it does really. What is the world coming to? I keep asking myself.' She held one up. 'Will each be enough for four, do you think?'

Alice considered. 'I should think so.'

Mrs. Lister began to rip the lengths of beautiful material, hesitantly at first, then with a certain vindictive vigour. 'You're not attached to the diplomatic side are you?' she asked. 'Between you and me, Lady Maclaren's very hoity-toity. Swanning round at the Queen's birthday and looking down her aristocratic nose at us lesser mortals.'

She chuckled as she ripped and Alice too began smiling. Timid little Mrs. Lister was having a field day. Who would have thought, as she herself said, that she'd be given licence to tear up the Legation's best curtains, and who would have thought she'd have so enjoyed it?

As Alice also got to work, bemused by the staggering unlikelihood of the scenario, the bell clanged from the Jubilee Tower near the main gate, the agreed signal for emergency action. She looked up and cried out, for flames were crackling upwards from behind the north wall.

'Oh no—they can't have. Mrs. Lister, surely they haven't set fire to the Hanlin? The savages, savages—surely not?'

But that was exactly what the Chinese soldiery had done, and one of the world's richest centres of accumulated learning was destroyed in a single afternoon. This, however, was not the prime consideration among the besieged, for the fire took hold of the venerable structure and, with a strong wind blowing from the north, quickly threatened to engulf the whole Legation. The imminence of the peril galvanised everyone into concerted action for the first time.

A mixed force of marines and volunteers battered a hole in the intervening wall and, under constant fire from the Chinese on the further side, tried to clear timbers and other combustibles from the flames' advance. Chains of non-combatants were formed to pass vessels full of water from the garden wells to the fire's heart. Buckets, pots, bowls, foot-tubs, jars of every description were pressed into use and Alice, carefully passing a filled chamber pot to an unknown Italian in a natty suit next in line, could only echo Mrs. Lister's earlier cry— what is the world coming to?

After about two hours, when the Italian's clothes and those of everyone else were soot-blackened and the leading fire-fighters bone-weary, parched and singed, the fire was pronounced under control. Released from the chain-gang, Alice rushed to the hole in the wall for a first, and last, glimpse of the famous Hanlin. It was a desolating scene: the ancient roofs broken and burned, the ornamental ponds choked with precious calligraphic scrolls and some 23,000 rare books scattered everywhere—torn, charred, soaked, their silken bindings in tatters, their long-treasured characters forever indecipherable. Creeping inside, Alice picked up a less-damaged volume and looked at its illustrated pages. A man lurched up to her, his arms laden with similar books.

'Dump that on my pile and find others worth saving,' he commanded. She looked up at a tall, stringy man with a long, narrow, soot-streaked face. His eyes were red-rimmed and a monocle dangled incongruously round his neck. Obediently she gave him the book and he staggered off cursing, 'The churls, the ignorant, loutish churls.'

A British soldier grabbed her arm, 'Not safe here, m'am, outside please. And no looting.'

'Looting! I'm trying to save . . .'

'Outside I said.' He was wearily impatient with these airy-fairy non-combatants more concerned with culture than defence. Defiantly she scooped up two more books as he hustled her away. In the garden, the man with the monocle was arguing furiously with a marine preventing his return. 'Barbarians,' he roared, 'the world's collapsing into barbarism!'

'Yeah, well you're not helping things, sir. So git off please,' The marine pushed the begrimed figure away from the wall so hard that he tripped backwards over the pile of books he'd rescued and lay on the ground, cursing more furiously.

Alice went up to him. 'Are you all right? I got two more, then they pushed me out too.'

He groaned and levered himself upright. 'Dam' roughneck soldiery. Dam' near smashed my monocle, and how would I replace that now?' He fingered it fondly. 'Let's get this little horde safely out of sight.' He ran for a wheelbarrow that had been used in the firefighting and they loaded the books on to it.

'And what's your name, may I ask?' he fixed her with a monocled stare.

'Mrs. Greenwood-Grant. I own an antique shop here. Or did, I expect it's a pile of rubble now.'

'How de-do. J.O. Bryant's the name. J.O. to everyone.'

'Oh, my friends the Blums know you. You've been a government translator for years, haven't you? They wanted us to meet because I do translating too.'

'Do you now? Here, let's take this lot into the Legation. I've got a whole cupboard to myself there.' He chuckled sourly. 'Can you imagine—*reductio ad cupboardem*. A very large cupboard though; I can sleep along the top shelf. Always been on the shelf—best place—keeps one out of trouble, what?' He cackled as they trundled the barrow to the main building and carried the books to a cupboard on the first-floor landing.

'There—these few saved for posterity,' he regarded them mournfully. 'Sacrilege, what? Mindless sacrilege. I saw it coming of course. Country was a tinder-cask. Here, let's clear out this junk or there'll be no room for me at all.'

They cleared the cupboard of its former contents—bowling alley pins, lantern slides of the Queen's Jubilee, Christmas streamers, fancy-dress masks—and piled the precious books inside. J.O. sat on a box of croquet balls.

'Phew—hot work. Here, let's open something nice.' He pulled out a bottle of white wine and mopped his face with a cambric handkerchief. 'Violence is always so abominably dirty. Here, take a glass. Cheers!'

As they drank, Alice asked, 'But how can you say you saw this coming when no one else did?'

'Because I work with Chinese officials who know a damn sight more of what's going on than these nincompoops in the Legations with their parties, picnics, and piffling papers.' He spat out each P with venom, wagging his finger at her. 'Court circulars went to the provinces, saw them months ago. Full of hatred and suspicion of foreigners they were. Then Yu Hsien came to Peking, a rabid xenophobe who'd like to see every foreign devil swinging from a tree. He got the ear of the Old Buddha and from then on the anti-foreign party went from strength to strength. All this I told Maclaren on the q.t. and what did he say, "Such a scaremonger you're becoming, old boy! We've got everything under control." Under control—and look at us now ...' His thin frame convulsed in humourless mirth as he poured more wine. 'So where are we? Trapped like fish in a stewing pot, as the Chinese say. And about to be either broiled alive—today's little conflagration was only the beginning—or shot to pieces when the formidable cavalry of Tung Fu-hsiang and the Peking bannermen make a combined onslaught. I hope, m'dear, you weren't counting on getting out of here alive? But you seem too sensible for that.'

Alice drew herself up. 'I'm not frightened, if that's what you mean. I was in Port Arthur when the Japanese captured it and this is just a picnic by comparison I assure you. But I've a young niece and nephew here too and certainly wouldn't like to think . . .'

'Ah yes, the young, terrible waste.' He screwed in his monocle. 'Then I'll say no more, Mrs. Grant, and I've only given you my humble opinion.'

She rose smiling, 'I wouldn't imagine your opinions were ever of the humblest, Mr. Bryant.'

'J.O. please?'

'J for Jeremiah?'

He chuckled. 'If you wish—but old Jeremiah was right you know, though he got scant thanks for it. Ah, before you go. You're fluent in the language, you say? Now the powers-that-used-to-be have given me a Committee to keep me quiet, and they've managed to find quite an unpleasant one. I'm head of the Labour Committee, detailed to translate lunatic orders from on high to those poor sods of converts who, being native, are naturally given the dirtiest jobs. Now the student interpreters have gone to the Volunteer Brigade, I'm a bit pushed and wonder if you might . . .'

'I'd be glad to do something more useful than sew sandbags.'

'Come to the Fu bridge tomorrow then. Not the safest place—unpleasant things like bullets fly about.'

'That doesn't worry me. If you're right and we're all doomed, we might as well go sooner as later.'

The following day, in spite of her bold words, Alice felt rather apprehensive as she neared the Fu, for the noise of gunfire was louder and spent bullets occasionally plopped in the canal. Hurrying across the bridge, she peeped into the park, a large expanse of grass, dotted with pavilions and stables. Groups of female converts were sitting in the shade quietly sewing sandbags, their children were playing in the dust. In a nearby pavilion, women were cooking rice in huge cauldrons and some skinny ponies, destined eventually to be served as 'Peking beef' atop the rice, were grazing under the trees. It all looked calm and settled, yet along the distant wall that formed the outer line of the Legations' defences, foreigners were exchanging cross-fire with enemy troops. The Japanese, who held the largest part of this sector, already had the reputation of being the toughest, bravest soldiers, and seemed to have everything under control.

'Ah, there you are, just the person I require.' J.O. hurried to her. His thin hair and droopy moustache were sandy-coloured again and he wore a straw hat which he swept off in welcome. 'Would you explain to the more able-bodied of these charming Christian ladies that we need the sandbags actually filled? They're rather fonder of sewing than filling, and all bag and no sand is the result.' He beamed cheerfully. 'Quite nasty today. The enemy have brought up a most unpleasant long-range gun, and the Japanese are organising some coolies to build a fall-back barricade. So if you'll excuse me.' He loped away rapidly, his monocle flashing, leaving Alice to carry out his orders as best she might.

She persuaded some of the women to return with her to the Legation tennis-court, where Hiram and Hortensia Brown had organised a line of people to fill bags from just-dug holes. Alice and the converts joined them and the filled bags were carried off on coolies' backs to the many parts of the defence in need of them. And which need was the greatest? The sentry posts along the Tartar wall? The hotel next to the French Legation, crucial to the southeast defences? The windows of the hospital set up in the British Legation Chancery? Sandbag fillers, of different nationalities and creeds, wrangled heatedly over the matter, and Alice found she was pleading the cause of the Japanese soldiers and Chinese converts at the Fu.

It seemed strange that this was so, but there was no reasonable explanation for anything anymore. So she simply worked, as did others, getting wearier and dirtier over the days, and amazingly accustomed to sights of priests filling sandbags, Chinese cooks in chintz aprons cooking horsemeat, and missionaries on bicycles inspecting fortifications. At night she slept, exhausted, on the floor in her relatives' room in spite of

592

the nightly fusillades of gunfire. During an unmarked day of this dreary routine, she was gladdened by a familiar voice.

'Alice, my dear, you are safe and sound. Praise be! But why haven't we met before?' Veronique rushed up and hugged her.

'Veronique—but I asked for you. Where were you?'

'Karl and I have stayed on in the Hotel Peking, helping brave M. Pelot with the food. But it's getting so dangerous now— bullets all the time—and they've sent me to find a billet with the non-coms.'

'A miserable category, isn't it? But I can't fire a gun, I fear,' Alice smiled wryly.

'Well, some of us have to keep the troops going and M. Pelot performs miracles with the food supplies.'

'So I've heard. But the soldiers won't let you move from here to go and see.'

'I have to return and collect my things now, so come along— they'll let you through with me.'

To reach the hotel, they crossed an area of half-demolished houses, passing en route loaded coolies, a stretcher bearing a Russian marine, three German soldiers enjoying an off-duty smoke in the rubble, an American gunner with a ladder, a tired-eyed British sergeant who tried to turn them back. Sporadic firing sounded from the other side of the high walls, and, in the silences, they heard crickets clicking away under crumbled bricks; on a clump of weeds an orange butterfly spread its wings serenely in the sun. Absurd, mad; everything's gone mad, Alice thought as she looked at it.

Inside the Hotel Peking a certain sanity prevailed. Catholic converts were milling wheat for the daily bakery round, cutting up horsemeat for the evening stews. In the adjoining room, Karl was slumped asleep over a sack of millet.

'Karly-kins, look who I've found,' Veronique shook him awake.

'Alice, good Lord, almost given you up for lost. What have you been doing?'

She explained briefly, adding, 'But you two make me feel quite lily-livered, staying near the front-line like this.'

Karl grinned, 'Ah, but the food's much better here and so is the drink! Let's open a bottle to celebrate your appearance. There's a practically limitless supply of champagne in the cellars here, so we can all go swimming into the last ditch on a tide of bubbly.'

The cork flew out with a bang as Veronique held a glass. 'Funny, I used to worry about corks popping—not anymore after all this racket!'

They drank a toast to mutual survival, and Veronique said with a sniff, 'Well, if we do survive, there'll be scant thanks due to some I saw this afternoon. As you suspected, Karl, several able-bodied men are doing nothing except organise committees—for food, for fuel distribution, for hospital supplies, Lord knows what else! Why don't the women run them and let all the men take duty at the barricades?'

Karl yawned. 'It was ever thus. A siege doesn't bring out the best in us all. Now you two get back while there's a lull.' He handed his wife a valise.

'Oh do come too, for God's sake, Karl. You've done more than your stint here.'

'I've told you, I'm staying as long as Pelot does.' As he patted her cheek, a volley of fire crackled very close and Alice jumped. 'Off with you now.'

'I'm so frightened for you,' Veronique clung to him, but he gently disengaged her.

'I'm not in the firing line, I'm in the feeding line,' he reassured her as he propelled them out of the back gate.

The following evening, as the Greenwoods were listlessly shovelling down the unvaried diet of horsemeat and rice, Alice broached the subject Veronique had raised in her mind. 'Are all the able-bodied men doing as much as they might, Will? Some, like J.O., are in the front-line helping with defences, while others . . .'

'Oh J.O.—he's an odd fish anyway. Turned up at the Queen's Birthday this year wearing a flowing scarf-tie of claret and blue silk—said it was the latest waterfall style, remember, Isabel? Always comes in something outrageous apparently, then disappears with his native cronies for another year.'

'Anyway, in answer to your point,' Isabel said, 'he's a bachelor remember, and doesn't need to be quite so careful as a family man.'

Will nodded. 'True enough. Still, I agree and, naming no names, there are some who do nothing but wring their hands all day long.'

'And don't some of the others show them up?' Polly broke in. 'There's Howard Thringer, for example. Have you met him,

Aunt? He's so enormously brave, and I do admire him. He works in the American Consulate normally, but he's been fighting in all the worst trouble spots. He was on that sortie yesterday that tried to seize some enemy guns in the Mongol Market. Three men were killed and one injured, but Howard came through without a scratch, thank goodness. A bit stiff he said afterwards, but he was so cool about it. I wish I could handle a gun and have a go at them!'

'You'll never be able to because you're only a girl,' Tommy jeered. 'I'm going to be an army officer like Great-Uncle Robert when I grow up and go shooting people all over the Empire.'

'What a dreadful ambition, Tommy,' Alice said severely.

He flushed sulkily. 'Well, if they don't behave properly and make wars you have to shoot them, don't you?'

'Not necessarily, my boy,' William corrected. 'It all depends on things you don't understand. I'd like it better if you helped to manage native affairs in a peaceful way, as I do.'

'But that's not so exciting.'

'Nor is being in the army,' Alice said. 'Uncle Robert spent most of his career shut up in cantonments feeling bored stiff.'

'Anyway, it's altogether finer to be a civilian and fight bravely in emergencies, like Howard,' Polly said.

'Oh you and this wonderful Howard!'

'Well he is wonderful, Mamma! You must meet him, Aunt. He's asked me to have supper at the American mess sometime and you can come too.'

'Take the chance and go, Alice,' Will advised. 'Rumour has it that the Yankees live in high gastronomic style compared to the rest of us.'

'Well this is certainly more disagreeable than usual,' Isabel pushed her plate away. 'Yes do go, Alice. Oh, wouldn't it be nice to go out for a good dinner and dress up properly for it, as we used to! Listen to those guns again. The noise makes my head ache here. I can't imagine how the men at the barricades bear it.'

'Sounds worse than usual, I'll just go and see . . .' Alice slipped from the stuffy room.

Outside, volleys of gunfire rattled in the warm, misted dark; Alice sniffed an unusual dampness—time for the summer rains. What difference would they make in this ludicrous situation? Probably delay the arrival of the Relief Force still more, if indeed it even existed, which the besieged were beginning to doubt. But at least rain would improve the water supply and they could wash. Oh, for a bath! While filling sandbags that day she'd begun to menstruate and there was a dire shortage of clean rags to cope with it. Never in her life had she felt so disgustingly dirty and smelly, so caged and helpless. Within the compound, buildings hemmed them in on all sides and no horizons were visible; instead there was the terrifying sense of being trapped—walls, walls within walls, as in the smallest of a set of Chinese boxes.

The usual stories of imminent relief from outside seemed ever less convincing and the news from inside got worse: more casualties in the hospital, fierce night attacks, growing exhaustion among the combatants, crumbling defence lines. Yesterday, the French Legation and parts of the Fu had been given up; after that the making of bomb-proof shelters had been ordered, presumably for the last stand. Would it really come to that?

She stared up into the dark sky, yearning for the lovely wide world beyond all these walls, that she could scarcely believe existed anymore. She thought yearningly of Lin, spared by exile all this present horror. His countrymen were now her sworn enemies, yet she longed to snuggle against him, hear him tell her what a sweet and luscious polished jade she was. Would he still do so, were he here? Surely he would never condone this mindless, savage hatred directed indiscriminately, it seemed, against the whole world? He would repudiate it as utterly as she—if only he were here!

She plucked irritably at her lank, dirty hair, wondering how it was that Lady Maclaren seemed able to keep hers clean. Of course her head was of more consequence than Alice Greenwood's . . . Surely by now the seeming disappearance of so many consequential heads in Peking must be causing an international uproar? And here she was in the middle of it; on the spot while history was being made. Only, she felt nothing except discomfort, uncleanliness, occasionally fear; no heroics, little drama even. There was a pause in the firing, and during it Alice heard missionaries in the nearby legation chapel singing 'Nearer my God to Thee.' She smiled, thinking of Jessie Reeve and the indomitability of the true Christian under stress. What a comfort such faith must be! It was Sunday of course; 1 July, start of a new month. Surely by its end, every foreigner in Peking would be either released or dead?

During the next few days the latter outcome seemed increasingly probable. Rain fell and hundreds of sandbags split; barricades were undermined, trenches water-filled, the canal was a raging evil-smelling torrent, and the air putrid with the stink of unburied corpses of enemy soldiers beyond the firing lines, the stench of overflowing sewers within. A Sanitation Committee was formed to deal with the situation, which J.O. volunteered to head, considering it the final task he could perform for the Celestial Empire.

'Let us bury what evidence we can of this sorry débâcle,' he pronounced grandly. 'So that when we are all slain and the Western nations come storming in thirsting for revenge, they may never see just how hard it went with us.' His view was, as always, eccentric, but as the work required of the Sanitation Committee was distinctly unpleasant, he was allowed to do it, for whatever motive.

Alice, now on the Labour Committee, was given the task of translating instructions to the coolies detailed to build a second line of barricades within the compound, using torn-down roofing, uplifted paving stones and half-burnt timbers. In the pouring rain the work proceeded slowly, and she was watching it from the portico of the former theatre, now the marine barracks, when Polly ran up to her. 'Aunt, there's a private feast at the American mess tonight because it's their Independence Day, and Howard's asked us to come. You will won't you? It will be such fun.'

Attracted less by the improbable idea of 'fun' in such a setting than the desirable word 'feast,' Alice accompanied her niece that evening. Howard met them at the threshold of the American quarters, a handsome, blond young man with blue eyes unclouded even by the present trouble.

'I'm sure pleased to meet you, Miss Greenwood. Polly has told me about you. Come right inside. I wish I could offer you the usual cook-up we Americans have on this day.'

'If you have anything other than stringy horsemeat I shall be absolutely delighted, Mr. Thringer.'

'We'll do you a bit better than that,' he promised, leading them along a passage.

'Tell him you're not "Miss Greenwood,"' Polly whispered.

Alice shrugged. 'Oh never mind. I feel as much that as anything else these days.'

There was a sense of well-being in the dining-room that immediately lifted her spirits, for the others present were manifestly enjoying themselves. Most of them were Americans, plus the German surgeon, Von Hague, who did sterling work in the hospital, and two Russian officers, for, since the Americans and Russians had been fighting side by side along the Tartar Wall, much soldierly camaraderie had developed between them. The guests, faces softened by candlelight, sat on rolled-up mattresses and trunks drinking champagne. A trestle table was decorated with crayonned American flags, and a delicious cooking smell came from the adjoining kitchen.

Mr. Hiram Brown was just expressing his belief that the Relief Force was only a day's march away, for its searchlights had been reported seen from the northern barricades. Why, or how, any Western force should approach from this most unlikely quarter was a mystery, but as champagne flowed, even the doubting Thomases were convinced and more bottles were opened in celebration of imminent rescue.

'I tell you one thing—the commanding officers of that Force will sure have something to answer for when they do arrive,' said the Legation's second secretary belligerently. 'How could they possibly take so long to cover a mere eighty miles? Beats me. And it's said there are thousands of properly armed men, while here we are, a handful of doughty, poorly equipped Anglo-Saxons holding out against the savage Chinese hordes.'

'And some on our side of the barricades must answer some questions too,' said Von Hague heavily. 'Our gallant Germans are always in the firing lines, but others have a most easy time by comparison.'

He glowered round, purposely including Alice, who felt uneasy, for she knew there was dissension over allocation of fighting men to various sectors, and that the British Minister as Commander-in-Chief was ultimately responsible for it. She buried her nose in her glass, avoiding the German's gaze and Howard broke the tension with,

'Say, have you heard about this old muzzle-loading cannon they found in Legation Street? They reckon it dates from the Anglo-French expedition of 1860. To think—the lime-juicers and froggies were here forty years ago! Anyway, our man Butler is chipping off the rust of ages and thinks he can get it going. So here's to the first blast-off of our secret weapon, the "International."'

598

As they drank to that, American ladies hurried in with steaming plates, and what a feast ensued: brown soup made with Liebig's meat extract and toast à la Hotel Peking; corned beef croquettes with tinned beans; the mess's last jars of Bishops Preserved Fruits with condensed milk. They ate in quiet rapture, hunched over, until Mrs. Hortensia Brown clasped her hands, exclaiming,

'My land! Hiram, it's disgraceful, we were so longing for a decent meal, we forgot to say Grace—of all times. May I beg of you, a minute of thanksgiving. Oh thank you Lord for this gift of food supplied to us now in our great need. And let us pray that, when we are safe home again, and our tables laden with the bountiful fruits of the earth, we remember this time of scarcity and hardship, giving double thanks for the blessings and comforts we nations of the West customarily enjoy. Amen.'

'Amen. Amen,' murmured the diners, setting to afresh till every plate was picked clean, every stomach churning happily. Into the contented silence burst a distant volley, and Howard stood up, reaching for his slouch-hat.

'Well fellas, there's some of us must return to duty.'

Polly, who'd been sitting beside him, listening devotedly to his every word, said, 'Oh no, Howard, surely you don't have to return to that dreadful Wall tonight? I mean, it could be unlucky.'

'Nonsense, little English Poll. No bullet would dare harm a true-blue Yankee on the 4th of July! It would bounce right off me.'

'A citizen of God's own country, hey, young man?' the German was a trifle sour. 'Well I hope that is so. I have more than sufficient to deal with in my hospital. I don't want other casualties.'

Polly turned to him impulsively, 'Let me help there, please Doctor. I'd do absolutely anything.'

'Anything and everything that is nasty you would have to do, young lady. And you are a little young, but if your Aunt . . . ?'

'Certainly, doctor. I'm a great believer in girls not being too sheltered from the realities of life. I'll accompany her myself, if we can be of use, and if Polly's parents don't object.'

After that the party broke up; Howard and his comrades returned to the treacherous shadows of the Tartar Wall and the doctor to his hospital. The ladies cleared up, chatting about the shocking state of their underlinen and the effectiveness of rice-water as a cure for dysentery from which several were suffering. Returned to the Customs Quarters, Polly regaled her parents with details of their gastronomic orgy and announced firmly, over-riding their protests, that she'd been summoned to hospital duty with Alice the next day.

By that time the siege was in its third week and fifty men lay in the hospital, formerly the British Legation Chancery. In the main office, Von Hague and his missionary assistants performed emergency operations on despatch tables covered with surgical cloth.

'So blood spatters where ink was spilled,' remarked the doctor one day, surveying the body of a man he couldn't save, 'and had the ink been used more wisely, the blood need not have flowed.'

But blood had flowed in considerable quantities, and now large black sticky flies buzzed round the torn flesh of the wounded as they gasped in the hot, dust-laden air, crying in several tongues for water or solace. Regarding the scene for the first time, Polly turned pale and gripped Alice's arm.

'Oh dear, this is awful. Can I possibly . . . ?'

Alice, more inured to the sights of battle, considered. 'You must decide if you can, Polly. I'll stay because help is obviously needed. But if you'd rather go . . .'

'Rather! what a silly word!' Polly laughed shakily.

'Yes dear,' Alice agreed meekly. 'But I don't know how to put it. I shan't blame you if you go, I mean.'

'But you'll be prouder if I stay?'

Alice nodded and they reported for duty. Having no medical skills, they were put to stuffing pillows with packing straw, cutting muslin dressings, filtering water, sterilising instruments and ministering to convalescents who lay in long chairs in the rear passage, there being nowhere better for them. It was there, on early morning duty a week later, that Alice experienced the most shocking moment of the entire siege, one which—as when she saw the child's head in Port Arthur— would remain in gruesome clarity when other siege recollections had distanced to a jumble of mostly meaningless and distasteful episodes.

The man was heard screaming before he arrived; the convalescents shifted uncomfortably, some turning their heads to the wall, for bad cases were often brought in past them. Alice simply stood, a feeding cup of bouillon in her hand, petrified by the snorting, piercing, mad shrieks of raw agony. Four soldiers came running through the passage with a stretcher; the victim on it was covered with blood—his trousers, shirt and what there was left of his head that had been partly blown open. The open mouth from which the dreadful sounds came was bright red and foaming and the face mangled almost beyond recognition, and yet Alice recognised it. Hand on her throat to suppress her own screams, she whispered to the officer following, 'Who is it? I think I know but . . .'

'Mr. Arthur Rawlins, one of the Customs volunteers, ma'am.'

The door shut, the screams mercifully lessened as the doctors reached him. Alice, having spilt most of the bouillon, drank the rest with shaking hand. Pink-cheeked, talkative young Arthur Rawlins; how he'd laughed from that same blood-filled mouth at the Christmas tableau. She had to tell William, for Arthur was a Customs man.

'You look pale, Alice. What's the latest disaster?' Isabel was sewing sandbags on Lady Hart's old treadle machine when Alice told her, adding, 'And perhaps you'd go and tell Will. And, Isabel, let him bring Polly away from the hospital. It's too much, too much. Thank God she didn't see what I just did. But she could have and it could have been Howard, say. She's too young for . . .'

'That's just what I said when she went there, but you supported her against us, as usual.'

'Yes. And I was wrong—as usual, you might add I suppose. I'm not always wrong, but perhaps I try to push Polly too far too soon.'

Isabel wound spare cotton on a spool. 'Oh you always have, Alice. Filling her head with the most gruesome Chinese fairytales and . . .'

Alice looked up in surprise. 'But that was years ago. When she stayed at Fairlawns?'

'Yes. Most unsuitable they were for a young girl. She told me some afterwards. They gave her nightmares.'

'You should have said something.'

The older woman snapped a thread, put the spool in a cloth bag. 'What was the point? The damage was done and I hate fusses.'

'Damage—oh, that's a bit thick, honestly . . . but this is quite stupid. Here we are confusing totally different issues, while poor young Arthur is in a terrible state and Polly should be brought away from the hospital.'

'That she certainly will, at once.' Isabel hurried out, leaving Alice to marvel, as she had before, at the way in which things had rankled with her over the years.

Arthur Rawlins died the next day and the Greenwoods attended his funeral in the Legation cemetery late that evening for, in siege conditions, bodies had to be disposed of quickly. J.O., on sanitary patrol smoking a black cigar, supervised the burial arrangements. The American chaplain read the funeral service; Arthur's body, shrouded in cloth and strapped on a plank, was laid in a trench next to an Italian soldier who'd died the same day.

'Was Rawlins a friend of yours then?' J.O. asked Alice as they left the melancholy scene.

'Not really. I only met him once, at my brother's house. He seemed a jolly young man.'

'Did he though? Never mind. "From the contagion of the world's slow stain, He is secure."'

'I presume that's a quotation?'

'Shelley. He's rather good on mortality, useful at a time like this, when we're all approaching ". . . that high capital where kingly death Keeps his pale court in beauty and decay." "Adonais", verse seven. Would you like a drink?'

'Very much please. We never see such luxuries in the Customs Quarters.'

'You wouldn't with stern Sir Robert in command. Poor old devil! He must wish he were dead. Thirty years' service in China and it's all ended in this bloody fiasco. I'm told the Chinese have made their headquarters in his compound grounds, where Lady Hart did but lately sally forth in a gilt sedan-chair on the shoulders of liveried bearers. Oh, life's lovely ironies!'

As they entered the Legation, she asked, 'You've put in many years' service here yourself, I believe?'

'Yes, but cynically. Unlike other old hands I never trusted the Empress or her ministers and never got mixed up in their politics. A snake pit, m'dear, of such venomous subtlety as leaves us simple-minded Westerners in a state of total obfuscation. Here, come into my cupboard and let's see what there is. Stores are dwindling sadly, but I think they'll see us through to the end. Ah yes . . .' He unearthed some red wine.

'I was quite involved in the Reform Movement,' Alice

volunteered, 'and its members weren't venomous.'

He chuckled. 'Nor subtle enough. One reason it failed.'

'I suppose after this furore only an outright revolution would work? Or nothing?'

'Probably nothing for a while. Immense staying power, the aged dowager she-dragon. 'Course, if we are all massacred. . . .'

He handed her a brimming glass. 'Cheers. Then I think she'd find it difficult to . . . er, sort of explain away. An "act of gross disrespect" would definitely have been committed, what? Naturally she'd blame the whole catastrophe on the Boxers, whom her gallant Manchu bannermen couldn't control. Heads of Harmonious Fists would roll and afterwards she'd still be there—sitting on the Peacock Throne with that basilisk smile intact!' He doubled into one of his long, mirthless laughs.

'In fact I hear Tung-Fu-hsiang's famous braves are firing on us from the front line, while the Boxers, having discovered themselves less bullet-proof than they'd imagined, have mostly vanished?'

'So I believe—and the Empress must make sure that none of us survive to tell that little tale.'

Alice chuckled. 'I think you rather relish the prospect of extinction all round.'

'Well, optimism has never been my forte, I must admit, that's why I'm so seldom surprised by life. Here, have a top-up. Case in point—ran into that old fool Maclaren yesterday, stepping from his dining-room into which a cannon-ball had recently dropped, and he simply couldn't look me in the eye. And why not? "Of all the horrid, hideous notes of woe, Sadder than owl-songs or the midnight blast, Is that portentous phrase, I told you so."'

'Not Shelley?'

'Byron, m'dear.'

'You're well acquainted with the Romantics.'

'On paper only, best place for 'em. Well, a last tipple, then I must go back to my ghoulish round.'

'Oh J.O., let me come with you.'

'You? It's not at all the sort of round to appeal to ladies, I assure you.'

'But it can't be worse than the usual evening—in that stuffy room listening to the guns.'

'Well it is worse, and I don't think you've the stomach for it.'

603

'I was in the massacre of Port Arthur as I told you and my stomach's been cast-iron ever since.'

He shrugged, 'Come on then, but if you faint I'll give you a heave-ho over the Tartar Wall with the corpses.'

'Whose corpses?'

'The Chinamen who creep up to our barricades in the night, trying to set us all ablaze. Our men pick 'em off and they lie there till the Sanitary gang chucks 'em back. It's smelly, so you'd better light a cigarette for a start.'

'I don't smoke.'

'You soon would on this job. And think what a smart line 'twould be for you next year in some grand drawing-room at Home, "I just *had* to take up smoking during the Peking siege, darling, to cover up the smell of putrefaction."'

She took one, dubious. 'Assuming I live to say it.'

'Aye, there's the rub. Come.'

The night was steamy from recent rain that had made the siege stench particularly nauseous and brought out clouds of mosquitoes. J.O. and Alice went back towards the cemetery, where some converts were throwing the contents of latrines into the canal. J.O. rushed up to them, waving his arms.

'Stop it, you stupid beggars. Non, no, I told you, all this must be buried. The canal's a cess pit already, breeder of God knows what foul diseases. Here,' he grabbed a shovel and began furiously digging; sullenly, the men followed his example. From where they stood, Alice could see the high black shape of the Tartar Wall, their most solid bastion of defence. But a mile to the west was Pumpkin Lane. She had a mad yearning simply to walk out over the top towards it; perhaps the soldiers would be surprised to shoot.

'Come, let's get this over,' J.O. led her across the canal that smelt as he'd described it, to the near side of the Fu, where some young Russian students, supposedly on fire patrol, were attempting amorous contact with some female converts. J.O. snorted contemptuously, then briskly rounded up some of them to re-bury two dead horses that had been dug up by scavenging dogs.

'I tell people to kill the blasted dogs on sight, but then they don't bury 'em so I don't know if they're worse alive or dead,' he explained as they left, stopping inside the main Legation gate to light up cigarettes.

'What's going on here?' Alice peered at a heap of metal.

'Little arsenal, making amalgam bullets out of brass pots, pewter mugs, any old iron. We're running short of ammo.'

'Things really are getting desperate, aren't they?'

'Ra-ther. Oh ra-ther,' he spoke with deliberately boyish glee. 'Well, off you go. I've got to inspect the barrack latrines—unless you'd like to do it?'

'No, I'll leave that in your capable hands, and thanks for taking me. Look after yourself, won't you?' she grinned and went back towards her quarters.

Rounding the corner to the entrance she almost collided with two figures standing very close together against the wall; she gasped in embarrassment, realising they were kissing. Then she gasped again.

'Polly—and Howard. It's you, isn't it? Whatever are . . . oh really!' Confusion, amusement, indignation made her stutter.

'Oh dear . . . Aunt.'

'Miss Greenwood, ma'am, please don't think we were . . . I mean, we are only . . .'

'Only kissing, hey?' Alice decided to be amused, as Howard's handsome face loomed over her.

'Polly's a lady, ma'am, and I wouldn't dream of taking advantage.'

'No, I'm sure not, Howard.'

'But please don't tell Mamma. She'd be so angry.'

'No, I won't, dear. But you'd better come in now, at once. It's not quite the sort of thing . . . And she's rather young, Howard.'

Polly snorted indignantly, then looked up at Howard, misty-eyed.

He kissed her forehead. 'I'd be awful grateful if you didn't tell her parents, Miss Greenwood.'

'Don't worry, I shan't.'

As they went upstairs, Polly whispered urgently, 'You understand, don't you, Aunt? It's not like normal times . . . I can't sleep for worrying, so I creep out when he's going on night duty, just to spend a few minutes with him.'

'Yes, well be careful, that's all.'

'Oh I will, and thank you.'

She squeezed Alice's hand and they crept to join the other, innocently sleeping Greenwoods.

The next day, 13 July, fully lived up to its ill-omened reputation by being the worst the besieged had yet experienced. Heavy firing continued the whole day on all fronts and shells landed on the grain store, the hospital roof, the students' mess. The French Minister, who'd long been forecasting inevitable doom, decided it had come and made a bonfire of his Legation's archives; the Japanese lost more ground in the Fu; a captured Chinese stated under cross-examination that about three thousand armed warriors were now attacking the Legations.

At four P.M. the Jubilee Tower bell warned of grave emergency, and the women with children huddled together in sheltered corners, praying, comforting each other, or laughing it off according to their temperaments. At six, two tremendous explosions, caused by mines under the French Legation, shook the whole area. Karl Blum, buried up to his neck in rubble from the first explosion, was lifted clear by the second, as were three others. Shaken, with a wounded leg but otherwise unharmed, he limped away, carrying two bottles of champagne. He joined Veronique, saying God had obviously intended him to continue living purely for comic effect, and he wasn't going to tempt His goodwill any further.

Counting their considerable losses the next day, the besieged saw their position deteriorating rapidly. Men muttered about killing their families and then fighting to the death at the barricades; women also thought of death, and Isabel, watching pale-faced Tommy still valiantly playing wargames, had to turn away to hide her welling eyes. Heavy onslaughts continued for another few days and then, on 17 July, just as the besieged neared the tether's end, the Chinese unaccountably announced an armed truce.

In the eerie silence that followed, members of the diplomatic corps, better at wielding pens than guns, came into their own again, drafting a series of replies to contradictory notes sent in from the *Tsungli Yamen*. While this was in progress, fighting men of both sides laid down their weapons and peered cautiously at their enemies. By the truce's third day it was judged safe for non-coms to move around a little, and Howard took Alice and Polly on a tour of the defences. They scrambled up a ramp on to the Tartar Wall still stoutly bolstered with sandbags, their earlier brilliance blighted by sun, dust and rain into hues more befitting their sombre function. From the American outpost they could see the no man's land of demolished buildings and the flags of the eight nations still flying.

Polly held Howard's arm tightly. 'How frightening it must be at night—just a few of you up here in the dark with the enemy so close.'

He smiled indulgently, 'You're too durned tired to be scared. The other fella's lying there asleep while you're on the alert and you're just aching to do the same. Crazy, isn't it? I never envied the millions sleeping safe and sound in their beds all over the world, I just envied the men sleeping at my feet! And at the end of a watch, you give 'em a kick saying "time's up" and slump down in their place.'

Polly was starry-eyed with these tales of Howard's valour and Alice, watching, wondered how it would be with them when the excitement of the siege was over. Peering through loop-holes in the defences, she could see the Chinese lolling about on their barricades at surprisingly close quarters. Their uniforms, though dust-coated, still suggested the brilliant plumage of fighting cocks—the blue trousers with violet jackets of the artillery, scarlet and yellow tunics of the cavalry; cartridge belts gleaming round every waist. The soldiers waved cheerily at them as if no harm had ever been intended, and occasionally threw across melons that were eagerly scooped up by those who had tasted no fresh fruit for weeks.

Shortly after, two cart-loads of melons were sent into the Legation compound by order of the Empress Dowager herself and Chinese infantry began an illicit trade in eggs and vegetables with the besieged. Messages were also smuggled in by spies with varying assurances that a Relief Force was 'being mustered,' was 'on its way,' was 'reaching the capital.' Yet the hot days crawled by and nothing happened. People felt peevish, uncertain, bored, for, though no longer under constant fire, they were still trapped, still suffering from overcrowding, poor food, and general debility.

Alice, afflicted with these general woes, sometimes sought solace in the relatively undamaged Legation library on the second floor where a few torn, dust-covered magazines still lay on the tables—*Punch, Cornhill, Pall Mall*. These irrelevant publications had recently been ignored in favour of more apposite material, in particular Tennyson's *Ode on the Defence of Lucknow*, to which, it was hoped, their own ordeal would one day provide a parallel:

> . . . *Backward they reel like a wave, like a wave flung forward again,*

Flying and foiled at the last by the handful they could not subdue;
And ever upon the topmost roof our banner of England blew . . .

Tennyson made the event sound as fine and stirring as would the survivors of this siege, providing there were any, Alice supposed. But what about the filth and the boredom, the numbers of craven, hysterical, and useless, the bickerings between nations, races, creeds—all that was too ordinarily human, not the stuff of which either history or heroic poetry was made. She stared over the sandbags in the window to the scene below. It had no obviously heroic dimensions: some consular juniors were playing makeshift cricket on the square of dust that had been the Legation lawn; a few prams stood in the shade of the trees, each containing a pale, debilitated baby; a few tots armed with empty cartridges were playing soldiers on a pile of burst sandbags; an emaciated elderly convert from the Fu shuffled along the terrace looking for food-scraps; some coolies were digging a mine-trench along the northern defences, for the military commanders didn't believe the fighting was yet over.

They were right. The besieged woke one morning to hear trumpet calls blasting again from the Chinese lines as fresh detachments of troops were observed converging on the area. July ended—the month during which Alice, like everyone else, believed their fates would have been decided—and the next day a secret despatch was pinned on the Jubilee Tower noticeboard; it stated that Tientsin was in the hands of a strong International Relief Force now en route for Peking. Nevertheless, a few days after, enemy firing began again, interspersed now with messages from the *Tsungli Yamen* apologising for its occurrence, and polite condolences—to the Italians on the assassination of King Humbert, to the British on the death of the Duke of Edinburgh.

'And so, Alice—all happily collapses into comedy after all,' Karl Blum said, lying in a convalescent chair on the Chancery porch. 'A little while ago we were gambling in injury and death and now we hold raffles for eggs and melons. The livers of the last surviving horses will, I hear, be given to the one who designs the best siege medal. Shall we be honoured with them, ladies, do you think?'

Veronique sniffed. 'One thing I know—those who most

deserve medals won't get them, and several poltroons in high places will be highly commended for their valour.'

'Some of the older men have turned out to be much fonder of their shrivelled skins than I'd have imagined,' Alice agreed. 'And I don't think I'll ever believe a single word in the history books after this—Who really came out well and who badly, what really went on in the past . . . we don't know, do we? J.O. was talking the other day about all of us in a "great siege test"—it's been more of a siege muddle, right from the beginning.'

And that was how it remained to the end. On the night of 12 August, the Chinese mounted ferociously heavy and sustained attacks on the Legations. Metal whizzed overhead for hours, rifles cracked, Mauser and Krupp guns boomed. Barricades crumbled under the onslaught, shrapnel tore through roofs, trees, the bodies of several more defenders. Clearly the Relief Force was driving the remnants of the Chinese army back on the capital and it was touch and go whether the besieged could survive their last desperate offensive.

It continued undiminished throughout the next day, J.O., William, along with other civilians in the Last Reserve, were sent into the firing lines when the enemy launched an attack across the Mongol Market, where, in happier days, sheep-skinned traders sold prayer-wheels, brass teapots, silver bangles. No one could rest anywhere, and about midnight the alarm bell in the Jubilee Tower sounded yet again, and the Greenwoods joined the other women in the dining-room. At the barricades, exhausted men fired on in a mindless stupor, their rifles hot with use, and there was a long-drawn-out thunderous exchange between the homemade International and a Krupp gun atop the wall of the Imperial City.

The women stood together in silence; there was no point in shouting against the din; there was nothing to say. About two in the morning, during a lull, they heard the distant booming of a powerful battery from the East, followed by the rattle of Maxim machine guns. Near at hand, the enemy fire sputtered gradually away into a silence that seemed like dismay. A Chinese stretcher-bearer rushed into the room speaking excitedly in his own tongue. The women crowded round him.

'What does he say? What is it?'

'He says the Relief Force is almost here and we shall be saved,' Alice shouted.

8

Throughout the next morning the booming of the foreign guns drew nearer and look-outs saw shells bursting on the eastern plains. Fretful, tense, impatient, the besieged stood about in groups; some ladies put on the best dresses they'd been keeping clean in hopes of just such an occasion. About three in the afternoon, the actual breakthrough came and suddenly, miraculously it seemed, the Legation tennis-court was crowded with red-turbanned Sikh soldiers who had come in through the Water Gate and up Canal Street. People jostled round them, touching their dark, sweaty skins incredulously, cheering, laughing, crying.

Then came General Gasalee, Commander-in-Chief of the British Forces, red-faced, white-moustached, smiling broadly, shaking hands all round, gulping with emotion because he'd scarcely hoped to find so many foreigners left alive. A further burst of cheering heralded the arrival of a column of American 14th Infantry, dog-tired, their khaki uniforms positively clotted with grime. Soon every open space was choked with people, offering food and water to the soldiers, questioning them, congratulating them and each other, every heart hammering, every eye shining with relief.

Relief. It had come, at last, after all. Alice, separated from her relatives in the confusion, sat down on some sandbags, feeling weak and strangely devoid of emotion. An Italian lady with a parasol was rushing from one soldier to another, kissing them on both cheeks, offering chocolates. Men of the Royal Welsh Fusiliers who'd just arrived were discussing the merits of the recently-dug mine-trench; three American infantrymen were sleeping against a wall, brimmed hats over their faces; nearby a group of high-booted Cossacks were eating melons. The scene was such a kaleidoscope that it was fatiguing to contemplate it in the heat. She pulled herself together. Surely there was something she could actually contribute to such a momentous occasion?

As she rose, a man came hurrying to her, doffing his topee in salute.

'Well if it isn't ... It certainly is ... Mrs. Greenwood-Grant. Madame, I must congratulate you on your ability for getting yourself into tight spots and emerging from them unscathed.'

She blinked at him. 'Oh ... It's Mr. Galbraith, isn't it? The war correspondent from Port Arthur.'

'At your service, madam. I'm delighted to see you alive and well. Indeed all of you—there have been great fears for your safety throughout the entire world.'

'I suppose so, yes. One did think of it occasionally, but after a time the world went impossibly far away. Fifty-five days we were besieged and it seems like a life-time. At the moment, its's hard to believe it's all over.' She smiled at him, the very saying of it making it more real. 'You came in with the British Relief Force? I hear there was much hard fighting all the way from Tientsin? We couldn't imagine why it was taking you so long.'

'And you were calling us every name under the sun, I'll warrant! Look, I wonder if you could possibly find me a drink? The warrior heroes of the hour are being plied with refreshments and kisses from all the ladies. But to this obviously useless civilian they pay not the least regard. Yet I too am most extremely thirsty after so much hot marching.'

'What a shame! Of course—follow me.'

As they pushed through the throng, he said tentatively, 'And perhaps I can ask a few questions about your siege experiences, Mrs. Grant, before Mr. Risley comes pounding out of the rubble and sends me packing?'

She giggled. 'Oh, Mr. Risley. Why, I haven't seen him for years, not since he left Port Arthur soon after you.'

'Och, is that so? I thought maybe he was your lifelong protector.'

She tossed her head briskly. 'Not at all.'

She led him into the Legation and James peered curiously into the dining-room as they passed. The cannon ball had crashed through the ceiling, half of which had caved on to the mahogany table below; draperies had been ripped out, crockery broken. Above the mantel a gilt-framed picture of Queen

611

Victoria hung badly askew, covered with rubble-dust.

James smiled. 'The old Queen looks as if she's been in a spot of bother, but she's still there.'

Alice opened J.O.'s cupboard and produced a bottle of white wine. 'You won't believe it, but this was one man's quarters throughout the siege. He slept on the top shelf.'

'Good Lord!' James gulped the wine eagerly, then took out his notebook. 'Now Mrs. Grant, can you give me something of the non-com view? I've already heard something of the squabbles over men and supplies, but how did the ladies get on together?'

'There were very few disagreements among us, very few hysterics, and we all pulled together in a sensible way.'

'You're a wee bit prejudiced of course?'

'In favour of women? Indeed I am. It's men who cause their dreadful wars and women who suffer through them. But if you don't believe me—ask the men at the top. I often heard them praising the ladies, especially those who worked hard in the kitchens and hospital.'

'And what did you do, may I ask?'

'Interpreted instructions to the Chinese, helped a bit in the hospital, nothing special. We non-coms simply weren't allowed near the firing-lines, so, compared to Port Arthur, it was more tedious than dangerous. I suspect you were at more risk than I. The Force had to retreat to Tientsin after the first attempt to get here, I gather?'

'Yes, I hadn't arrived then. Came rushing up from Calcutta and was just in time to join the second force that left on the 4th. Deuce of a lot of international bickering and rivalry went on. That's one reason it took so long. And the Chinese kept tearing up the rail-lines, which didn't help matters. When we did get underway, the Chinese kept attacking, but they were poorly equipped and ran off eventually, just as they did at Port Arthur. It was damnably hot, thirsty work, and sunstroke accounted for as many deaths as bullets. Pretty disheartening too, because, even when we got to Tungchow three days ago, the stories were that you'd all been massacred. So—all in all—it was a very pleasant surprise to see ladies rushing out to meet us wearing nice dresses and garden-party hats. But if you'll excuse me, I must get back to the historic scenes outside.'

He drained his glass and stood up, just as a voice thundered, 'What the hell are you doing in my cupboard, sir?'

'Oh J.O., it's my doing,' Alice explained quickly. 'This is Mr. Galbraith, a war correspondent I met years ago and he was so very thirsty I took the liberty of . . .'

'Ho-humph, all right then.' J.O. tugged at his bright silk tie, which, in assembly with a white linen suit, straw hat and monocle, gave him also a distinctly garden-party air. 'Newspaper chappie, hey? And has Mrs. Grant been telling you the true story of our recent incarceration or the official version for the Press?'

'There's a difference, sir?'

'Ho, but my word there is. The last of the wine please. Know what my main function was? Dealing with dead bodies and—er—night soil. Never smelt such noxious odours in my life, sir, but what stinks much much fouler is the whole tale of our glorious siege—the diplomatic bungling, the backbiting and poltroonery, the sheer dam' fool muddles.' He took a deep draught. 'Not bad is it? Dead Froggie had three bottles in his knapsack. My siege employ had its compensations. Well, do you want the true story or not? Shall I divulge, for example, the name of a certain European plenipotentiary who emerged but once from his secluded lair in a certain safe quarter, and that to chase and kill a hen for private consumption by himself and his lovely lady-wife?'

'Come now, J.O., your jaundiced version isn't the whole truth, anymore than mine or anyone else's,' Alice protested. 'You usually saw the worst, I the best, and the truth lies somewhere in between.'

James bowed to her. 'That's where it usually lies, Mrs. Grant, and a slippery fish it is to hook when it's there too. I'd be delighted to hear your truth later, sir. But I really must find out what's going on. Has the French contingent come in yet, do you know?'

'Ah, who is coming, who going? That is quite unanswerable, Mr. Galbraith.' He waved his arms dramatically. 'Outside is confusion worse confounded. Bedlam is loose and Babel born again. There is infantry and cavalry and artillery and commissary of several nations all choked up together and people shouting orders and counter-orders, advances and retreats—in short, nobody knows what the deuce goes on. Only the sun is going down as usual as if nothing untoward had happened, as if we the besieged had not just been condemned to live on—

after all.' Carefully he removed his monocle and hat, bent to
unlace his shoes, and James asked, with a raised eyebrow at
Alice over his back,

'Condemned, sir? That's not the way you look at it I trust?
There's many men been risking their precious lives recently so
that you can be so condemned.'

'Ah yes, and I'm sure the great majority will be duly grateful to them. But when you've been in this wretched country as
many years as I and given as good service, and now see what a
shambles we're reduced to, and think on the future—the
recriminations, the retributions, the chaos still to come,—I
can only say "condemned" again. But my view has always
been a minority one. Take Mrs. Grant here on the contrary—a
fine woman, optimistic, resilient, overjoyed to be saved, hey
m'dear?'

Alice curtsied mockingly. 'Thank you kindly, sir. I suppose I
am. But I can't say I feel much of anything except an overwhelming desire to breathe really fresh air and have a bath.
We must be disappointments to Mr. Galbraith—not very good
copy. I'm sure you'll be able to find many more satisfactory
examples of the saved outside.'

'Perhaps, though not many more charming, I'll be bound.
The wine was much appreciated and I thank you both.' He
bowed and hurried away.

J.O. muttered, 'Good riddance—now I can take my little
nap.' Carefully he hoisted himself on to the top shelf, spread
his lank frame along it, covered his face with a spotted
kerchief.

Alice watched him in amusement. 'Sweet dreams J.O. and
cheer up,' she whispered, going out.

For the first few days after their rescue many of the
besieged didn't feel quite as cheerful as they'd dreamed of
being in such circumstances. For the duration of the siege,
they had developed certain routines, performed certain
tasks, established certain domains, however cramped; under
fire, their deprivations and discomforts had meaning. But
afterwards, a cloud of inertia and anti-climax settled within
the Legation Quarter. There was no logic, no discipline, no
purpose of any kind anymore and it was difficult to find out
what was happening because, as J.O. predicted, chaos
reigned throughout the capital.

Bewildered contingents of British cavalry and Italian

sailors arrived. The Japanese and the Russians, who didn't trust each other, quarrelled over the occupation of the Tartar City. Men of the French Infanterie Coloniale, coming late on the scene, peppered with shot the tiled roofs of the Imperial Enclosures already occupied by the Americans. Detachments of Indian soldiers marched into the Chinese City and bivouacked in the Pleasure Quarter. On the third day after the Relief it was deemed safe for civilian residents of the capital to go and find out what remained of their residences.

Alice and her brother went together, Isabel unable to bear the sight of so much cumulative destruction. There was not a building intact in sight and the bungalows in Customs Lane had been so reduced that only scraps of blue and gold hangings, a tangle of piano wires and fragments of familiar china remained to indicate the exact spot where Will's had stood. They did not linger, but trudged on in silence, past piles of rubble, walls without roofs, doorways without rooms.

At the burnt-out shell of the Ch'ien Men gate they walked west to Pumpkin Lane. 'The Polished Jade' was still just recognisable. Alice stepped through the ruined shop into the courtyard; the mimosa was a charred stump; the pond and well stank with broken objects and rubbish that had been dumped into them. From the surrounding rooms, every beautiful object had been looted. Alice prowled about, thinking that whether the plunderers had been Boxers or foreign soldiers mattered little. She sat down on a shattered urn and William said comfortingly, 'I'm sure you'll get some compensation eventually.'

'I suppose so. My only hope is that Snow Duck took some of the valuable pieces away with him. He'd already gone when I came in from Paoting that morning. It seems years ago, now.'

William kicked at a battered cooking-pot. 'This damnable country. Sometimes I wish we'd all settled at Home years ago . . . nice quiet country town, in Norfolk perhaps.' He patted Alice's bent head. 'I'm sorry. It's hard for you, a woman alone, who'd built up this little business.'

The pity was well-intentioned, but she said defensively, 'Snow Duck will come back and Benjy's probably all right in Shanghai.'

'You won't give it up then?'

'I really don't know, Will.'

'I wonder if there's anything worth salvaging.' As he moved

into the kitchen he heard a rodent-like scurry and raised his boot for a kick.

'Miaow.'

Alice jumped up. 'Tiger Blossom, oh Tigy, Tigy, Tigy, it's really you. You clever creature! How did you manage to survive?' She cradled the starveling bundle of bones and tawny fur in her arms. Then, quite unexpectedly, Alice began to cry. Having started she couldn't stop, weeping as she was, one copious draught, for all the pain, stupidity, fear, and savagery of the past months. William patted her shoulders, offered a handkerchief, then went in search of some whole object with which to console her.

'Jessie . . .' she snivelled at last. 'Jessie Reeve . . . I didn't tell you what a splendid person she was, did I? She used to make such delicious melon pi—pi—pickles. Such a good woman, such good pi—pickle.' She began mopping her eyes, aware that her brother was out of earshot, and Tiger Blossom was staring at her in alarm.

'Come here, I've found something they've missed, looks as if it might contain some valuables,' William called.

She went to where Will was trying to open the pigskin trunk with the ornate brass handles. She leaned against a wall, both laughing and crying.

'Oh Will, imagine! That's all that's left to me, Lin's trunk full of schemes for a wonderful universal world order!'

He stood up, disgusted. 'His! I'll be damned. You should have got rid of it anyway.'

She patted the trunk. 'Of historic import. Obviously meant to be saved—like Tiger Blossom.' She was feeling more cheerful already, some weight of her woe discharged. 'Hide it away again and I'll collect it later. I'll leave a note here for Snow Duck in case he turns up.'

The sun was setting hazily as they walked back towards the Legation, carrying a few rescued possessions and Tiger Blossom in a basket. Bugles sounded the evening watch in various military bivouacs where fires were being kindled for the evening cook-up, and the purplish twilight softened into melancholy the harsh, war-torn landscape. To the north, a flock of pigeons fluttered round some marbled pillars that had once adorned the portico of the Austrian Legation, and now stood proudly among the low-lying rubble like relics from some ancient Greek temple. It had all happened before of course, and undoubtedly would again. As they walked, gold light caught the buttons of a Chinese soldier's tunic; it's owner, once shallowly buried, had been dug up by dogs and the result was flyblown and obscene. Alice kicked some dust over the ravaged flesh while Will, less used to sights of war, pretended he hadn't seen.

She said softly, 'The trouble with growing older is that one understands so much less. Don't you agree?'

He stiffened with automatic rejection. 'Oh, I'm not so sure of that. When I think what a callow innocent I was twenty years ago. I knew so little.'

She was impatient. 'I said understand, not know.'

'Hmm. Come on, this stinks, and I'm not standing here philosophising.'

The base of the forty-foot-high Tartar Wall was in shadow, but along its broad top sentry figures moved in dramatic outline against the coloured sky. Just so, Alice thought, warrior-figures always looked on the war-torn walls of the world. At the base of a ramp, British, Russian, and German officers were engaged in a mutually incomprehensible acrimonious dispute; already the general bonhomie engendered by the Relief was evaporating. Tension and discontent were also rife within the Legation compound where the Greenwoods were obliged to stay for another week, because they, like many others, had no alternative dwelling place. Most women, children and the sick were sent off to the coast, but William had to help with the re-organisation of vital communications and the family elected to stay with him.

Slowly, news of the outside world filtered in, and first came confirmation that the Empress Dowager, Emperor and members of the Court had managed to escape from the capital just about the time the Relief Force arrived. The fugitives were reported to be travelling north-west in country carts, dressed as peasants. This information was greeted with angry incredulity by the foreigners and there was much argument about sending a force in pursuit. However, nothing was done and the Empress was spared to live, and fight, another day.

Much more welcome was the arrival of messages from afar—telegrams expressing joy at the siege's outcome from illustrious personages such as Queen Victoria and President McKinley, and long-delayed mail from the less illustrious. Alice received anxious letters from Frank and Adam, the

617

latter having narrowly escaped from dangerous anti-foreign riots in Manchuria. There was a letter from Timothy Barlow saying that Grace was recovering well and thanking Alice for her part in that, and one from Mary at Fairlawns to say that her daughter Lilian had been murdered by Boxers, one of several 'Shansi martyrs' as they were now being termed. 'Such a waste, such a dreadful tragic waste,' Mary wrote. 'It's terrible to have lost a child whom I never understood and now never will.'

Lilian, the pale-faced and studious, disapproving of so much. Alice remembered her own state of half-envy watching Lilian's late-night studies at Fairlawns, seemingly immune from and certainly contemptuous of the temptations and uncertainties that had beset the younger Alice. Even the knowledge of later martyrdom would have been unlikely to deflect her from her chosen path, and she probably died exulting, like Jessie. Should she try to explain to Mary the serenity of obsessed souls? It wasn't a subject they'd ever broached.

While she was pondering, Isabel hurried in waving a letter, 'My dear, such good news. Lottie's become engaged to Philip Brent of the well-known Singapore banking family. I mentioned him to you—hoping something would come of it. She'll be very well provided for. Philip is a pleasant young man and very ambitious I believe. Oh, I am delighted!'

'How lovely! Singapore will suit Lottie, don't you think?'

'And they want the wedding to be there. After all, no one in their senses would come to China after all this mess. So we shall go. Oh! at long last, something pleasant to look forward to—a summer wedding in Singapore!'

Alice laughed, 'Not to mention a future unclouded by horse-meat stews and sandbags.'

'Yes, marvellous. I think I shall perk up now. Have you seen Polly? I must tell her the news. She's probably trailing the handsome Howard. Really, she's quite shamelessly besotted with him—it will do her good to get away. Will is seeing Sir Robert today about a billet for us. Not that the great I.G. listens to anyone these days. Poor man—house burned, archives destroyed. I am amazed he bothers with anything.'

But Sir Robert Hart, like the Empress Dowager, was an indomitable stayer, and as determined as she to rebuild his life's work after the débâcle. To this end, he needed experienced men like William Greenwood, and two days later he and his family were allotted a residence commandeered by the military in the Tartar City.

James Galbraith brought Alice the news. 'I was having a chat with the I.G. and saw a paper on his desk with your name inscribed thereon. Kept trying to read it upside down, as in a doctor's surgery, but had to ask him eventually, and he bade me tell you. Quite a grand Manchu house, he said.'

'How kind of you to bother, Mr. Galbraith. We'll be so thankful to leave here. Talking of doctors, this Legation life is like having to stay in hospital after one's cured.'

'Aye, you must feel that way. Still, you've actually experienced the siege at first hand, and I wish I had. Take good old George Morrison of the *Times*: he'll do well from it, being here throughout.'

'He deserves to; he behaved admirably.'

'Oh quite, and I might not have, hey?' He turned on her quizzically. They were standing on the tennis-court where he had found her, when General Gasalee had ridden in triumph.

'I didn't mean to imply that at all. I should have thought you'd behave well too, you must be fairly used to tight spots in your job?'

'I suppose so, but you also get a little calloused, Mrs Grant—so much wanton destruction in so many places.' He began carefully refilling with earth one of the holes made recently in the cause of sandbag-filling, as if, by so doing, he hoped to repair all the world's damages he'd ever witnessed. Watching, she suddenly found him attractive, bustling about earnestly, directing soil into the hole with his feet, a man who did things and thought about them also. A small, self-conscious silence fell between them and Alice remembered that her hair and clothes were dirty and dishevelled.

She said eventually, 'You're determined to level it so they can play tennis here again one day I see? Another bunch of consular assistants and young ladies fresh from Home? People who'll know nothing of all this except what they read in the papers. Odd, isn't it?'

He stopped his self-appointed task, saying thoughtfully, 'Consciously I had no such exalted aim, Mrs. Grant. Maybe I was behaving symbolically, yes. Certainly I have a yearning for a return to normality, the levels of life. As I'm sure you do yourself?'

'Yes, except in my case it means a certain flatness of surface. My ordinary life is not as eventful as yours.'

His eyes twinkled. 'You amaze me. I had thought of your hurrying constantly from one crisis to another. So what do you do in the years between?'

'Sell jade curios mainly. I had a shop here. It's been destroyed, of course.'

'And you will set it up again?'

'I hardly know, at present.'

She was elusive, yet self-contained, and talked as if she had only her own decisions to make. He was reminded of their earlier encounter; in the years between he had not met another woman quite like her. 'You've not yet told me what happened after you left Port Arthur? Were your parents in Kaiping?'

'Indeed they were, and thank you very much for getting the news to me.'

As they strolled towards the Customs Quarters Alice told him how she and her mother had survived the rest of the war.

'An admirable story, Mrs. Grant. You should write your memoirs one day—experiences like that are seldom published.'

'In that case perhaps I will. But I shan't need to write of this siege, for everyone who's anyone will be doing so.'

'Aye, and it will be fascinating to read how much their accounts differ.'

'I hope J.O. writes something. Have you seen him recently?'

'Went off to breathe some fresh air with the non-coms. And, by the by, I'm on my way to Shanghai very shortly to send off red-hot despatches and steal a march on all these other diligent scribblers.' He held out his hand, which she took with a little sense of disappointment.

'We seem to meet only to part again, Mr. Galbraith.'

'Oh, I'll be knocking around China for a while yet—writing about this extraordinary situation. When I return to Peking perhaps I may call on you?'

'Please do. I'm sure to be here somewhere. Living à la Manchu, it seems.'

Alice hurried to tell the family the news about the new billet into which they all moved the next day. The house was located in the north-east quarter of the Tartar City, now under the command of the Japanese, as was evidenced by numbers of little flags hung above doorways and adorned with the legend, 'Compliant subjects of the Rising Sun Empire.' Alice winced when she read it, and Will said, 'There—these oily Chinks, just what you'd expect from them.'

Lilac House, now given over to their use, was in a long road flanked by similarly grand residences. Nearby were the Confucian Temple and the Imperial Granary. In the former, the tablets in honour of the ancient sage and his 'four great disciples' were still intact; the latter was now practically empty of grain, but full of fat rats. From the road, they could also see the artificial mound in the Forbidden City unromantically called Coal Hill; on its eastern flank stood a knarled pine-tree on which the last Ming Emperor hanged himself in 1644 when the Manchus conquered the capital. Also visible to the north was the top of the Drum Tower from which the five watches of the night had always sounded, until silenced by this most recent foreign invasion.

The house was large, its various pavilions surrounded by pillared verandahs, linked by walled courtyards and covered entranceways leading to inside gardens, where long-necked ornamental cranes stood beside round ponds. Its former inhabitants had fled so precipitately that signs of their recent presence were still scattered about—jewelled combs on a table, books thrown in a corner, pots dumped in a sack. The Greenwoods wandered round, bemused by its aloof dignity. Pillars were intricately carved, roof-ridges tiled, there were doors shaped like leaves, windows like petals or crescent moons. Carefully framed views of the house's manifold parts were visible from curious angles, yet all turning inwards upon themselves, upon each other.

'You can imagine the women passing their days here, can't you?' Alice was whispering, as seemed right, for they felt more like intruders than conquerors. 'Protected, sequestered, moving only from one verandah to another.'

'I'm not sure I like it,' Isabel was doubtful. 'There's no centre, no flowers, not much furniture.'

'Well I like it,' Polly said positively, both because she did and because she liked to contradict her mother just then. 'May I have those two rooms, Father, across the bridge there?'

'I don't know who'll have what yet.' He was irritable; it wasn't his idea of a home.

Taking mean advantage of the others' indecision, Alice and

Polly appropriated a pretty, airy pavilion in the second court-yard with a verandah overlooking a garden with shrubs and bamboos, while the others settled in the grander pavilion near the main entrance. That first evening, servantless, and feel-ing more homeless than in the familiar, if cramped, Legation, they spread their meagre supper on an exquisite lacquer table and ate in silence. The moon was sailing high; trees rustled in a cool breeze; crickets clicked in the bushes. It was the first time for weeks they'd breathed comparatively fresh air, walked about freely, talked in peace. It all seemed unreal, mysterious, strange.

'Life is so extremely odd these days isn't it?' Isabel voiced all their thoughts as she sliced melons for dessert. 'I do hope it will get back to something like normal soon.'

But the hope was vain, for nothing in the Chinese capital was normal. Even the conquerors didn't behave in a normal way, for none of the eight nations concerned had been given definite orders beyond the Relief. The Chinese government had simply disappeared, the Boxer chiefs were either dead or in hiding. In the absence of any other authority, the command-ing officers on the spot carved the city into nationally-controlled sections. The British and Americans who had the strongest forces and had arrived first, appropriated the Tem-ples of Heaven and Agriculture respectively for their military headquarters.

The Forbidden City was opened to foreigners' gaze for the first time, and they strolled about the Empress Dowager's reception rooms, awed by her priceless collections of lac-quer, ivories, bronzes, and porcelains. They went to the Win-ter Palace where the young Emperor had been held captive ever since the failure of the 1898 Reform Movement until he had fled with his Aunt. Imperial yellow carpets and brocades emblazoned with dragons still graced the room from which he'd long gazed on the rippling-jade lake, melancholy, fearful, disillusioned.

These royal treasures were carefully guarded by foreign troops, but elsewhere it was different. Cart and donkey loads of valuables looted from wealthy households and designated as treasure trove were sent to Tientsin on the railway for onward despatch to European markets. And a late-arriving contingent of Germans, not to be outdone, seized the ancient instruments of the Jesuit Observatory. For several weeks the nations looted, raped and ransacked, each accusing the others of the worst excesses and all of them guilty.

Eventually a semblance of military order was restored and two high-ranking Chinese officials—Prince Ching and the long-suffering Li Hung-chang arrived in extremely conciliatory mood to begin negotiations for peace. This made little difference to the ordinary residents, however, for whom life remained uncomfortable and disordered. Few shops were open, currency and fuel were scarce for the coal-camels from Mongolia did not appear in their customary plodding fashion as the weather worsened.

For Isabel and Alice, who suffered most from these diurnal dislocations, the first sign of improvement was the return of Snow Duck and his family. They had fled from the Boxers early, knowing they would be branded as foreign sympathisers, and had spent the intervening time living in a Hopeh village. They brought with them several of Alice's most precious jade pieces, and she, deeply touched by their honesty and loyalty, gave them a comfortable pavilion in Lilac House. After that, all was order and cleanliness within, and well-cooked meals appeared regularly.

'Your Mrs. Duck's a very good cook I must say,' remarked Will one evening, soon after the new regime had been established. 'But I suppose even she can't get hold of any decent meat? I'm so sick of the eternal horse.'

'They eat corned beef in the American mess at the Temple of Agriculture,' Polly volunteered.

'You've been seeing Howard Thringer again, I suppose?'

'And why not, Mother? He's a friend of mine.'

'Well, so long as that's all . . .'

'What do you mean by . . . ?'

'Oh stop, it you two.' Will got up and lit a pipe. 'And don't answer your mother so pertly, Miss.'

'Can't I even speak without getting called over the coals? I only mentioned corned beef and what's more Howard's asked me to a ceremony there tomorrow because a detachment of marines are moving out. I could perhaps bring a tin back.'

'Well we're not exactly reduced to corned beef bribes, and you're not going off there alone with all those American officers.' Isabel was still irritated.

'I'll go with her, I'd like some corned beef,' volunteered Tommy.

623

'Oh don't be stupid, Tommy. And American officers are perfect gentlemen, I really don't see why . . .'

'Let me go with her, Isabel,' Alice suggested. 'I'd like to see the inside of the Temple of Agriculture, and I'll make sure no officer eats her up.'

Isabel sighed. She was sick to death of these out-of-joint times. It seemed most unfair that so soon after they'd settled in their lovely bungalow, it should have been destroyed. 'Oh all right. You two go,' she capitulated.

True it was indeed that one lavishly decorated pavilion in the Temple of Agriculture enclosure contained not only stacks of tinned corned beef, but barrels of salt beef, rows of hams and cases of army beans.

'How is it you Americans always manage to eat so well?' Alice challenged Howard laughingly as they peeped inside.

'Our commissary's always been the most efficient, ma'am,' he replied earnestly. 'We spend more on it, and that keeps the men fighting fit.'

Polly sniffed wistfully, 'That ham smells so good!'

'Well, I'll see what I can get you later. But now, let's listen to the band.'

As they strolled to the main square, Alice saw what havoc had been wrought in this sacred place where, every spring, Emperors came to worship and perform the ceremonious cultivation of a choice plot of earth, thereby setting a royal example to the country's peasantry. Now, the Stars & Stripes fluttered from the topmost tower, the ancient halls were officers' quarters, and the marble altar where the royal head had bowed to the divinity of the soil was ranked with musicians, their instruments glinting in the sun. Precisely at noon they struck up the National Anthem, while the spectators stood with heads uncovered and the departing marines at stiff attention.

Alice glanced at Howard, stiffly standing also, looking solemnly patriotic; beside him Polly, in a fur-trimmed coat and bonnet, very much aware of his nearness. How was it between them, Alice wondered, now the drama of the seige was over, when every kiss could have been their last? Undoubtedly they were still on kissing terms. She frowned uncomfortably, thinking herself back to Polly's age, the intensity of those first passions, hoping her niece would not be overwhelmed by them. For Polly was, in her aunt's view, too intensely, intelligently alive, possessed of too much youthful promise to unite herself to the rather conceited, essentially conventional young man at her side. The anthem ended, everyone applauded and, as the marines marched off the square in tight formation, Howard explained that they had been invited to a buffet luncheon at the British mess across the square, to which they should immediately repair, because there would be a rush for the food.

Turbanned Sikhs stood smartly at the gate leading to the vast enclosure of the Temple of Heaven. The grandest of its temples was three-tiered and dedicated to the Ruler of the Universe, the Emperor of China; today it stood with such wide open doors that it looked somehow amazed. An adjoining pavilion was filled with cart-loads of loot to be sold at auction for the benefit of the British Army, the Emperor's personal apartments were officers' bedrooms, and luncheon was being served in the Temple of Fasting.

They joined the throng jostling at the food tables—officers of several nations, diplomatic ladies and gentlemen, people like themselves of no special account. Champagne flowed as always and by the time toasts had been quaffed to each of the eight nations (the Japanese, as always, being the oriental last) Alice had become fully aware of the intrinsic absurdity of the whole situation.

She turned to her niece, 'You know, Poll, we've been taking this whole thing far too seriously.'

Polly blinked. 'What thing?'

'The siege—it's really a choice piece of farce—a gem, a highlight in the low-level human comedy.' She stared up at the ornate ceiling. 'And it goes on and on, from one carnival to another, from a shoot-up in the British Legation to a feast in the Temple of Fasting. Wouldn't have missed it for the world! Ask Howard for some more champagne, dear.'

Polly looked dubious. 'Shouldn't you eat a ham sandwich first? They're very good.'

'Drink first, food after,' Alice held out her glass. 'I'm too serious, that's my trouble, Polly.' She stared at the pale gold liquid. 'I love champagne, reminds me how stupid seriousness is.'

Polly giggled. 'It does that for most people, till it wears off, then you feel even more stupid, or serious, than before. Isn't that so, Howard?'

'I guess it is. But it's good to see your Aunt so happy and relaxed, Polly, after all she's been through.'

'That's just it, Howard, I don't relax enough. Ah, that's what I need now, a dose of good wholesome cynicism as is usually dispensed by that gentleman over there.' Alice weaved in the direction of J.O. who was munching silently by a table. 'J.O. How are you? We've not met since the grand old siege days, when we all pulled together in the same boat.'

He grimaced. 'Good afternoon, Mrs. Grant.'

'Oh please call me Alice. I feel like that today.'

'Do you indeed? I wish I did.'

'Don't tell me your sense of the absurd has deserted you, sir.'

He beamed mockingly. 'Ah no. How could it when I dwell right here in the very Temple of Heaven itself, at the very footstool of the Divine Ruler of the Universe I eat my little ham sandwich. Oh, what ineffable bliss! Try one,' he handed her a plate.

'You're living here?'

'With the British top-brass, m'dear. Well set up too, some of 'em. Do my old eyes good. I'd no other billet—my 'umble' ome, all my worldly goods including many long-treasured translations, burnt to a cinder. So they took me in here, the Horphan from the storm. Same with you I suppose?' She nodded. 'Ah me—more champagne?'

'So what do you propose to do now?' His plight was similar to her own; she wondered if he'd found a solution for it.

'I'm seriously thinking of going Home, haven't been for twenty-five years. But no money. Got to get money first.' He lowered his voice. 'Velly nice little tlicky-tlade—I go to my Chinese neighbours and friends, people who know me. So scared are they, shake like leaves at the sound of foreign boots marching. I say, you get me curios and silks, I buy velly cheap and protect you from nasty foreign boots. So they bring me things, family treasures dug out from hiding, fallen-off-cart things, and I bring them here, get velly good plices from the officer-gentlemen.' He chuckled hollowly.

'J.O., how could you? They're your friends and neighbours.'

He looked savage. 'Were my friends and neighbours—the Chinese who burned my house and all my work. Killed my friends. All is fair in war m'dear, and don't you forget it.'

The bubbles of her day threatened to dissolve. 'Oh, I know,

but I still don't like the sound of your tlicky-tlade.'

'Well, I'm doing something else, might appeal to you, Mrs. . . . er Alice. Translating novels. There's going to be a huge demand for "foreign book things" when all this dies down. And it's an activity that takes the mind off the present— Hawthorne, Dickens, Trollope—peaceful times and places. Nothing political. Politics here was always a snake pit, I told you, well, it will be a cess pit in future. So steer clear.'

'I fully intend to. Novels, yes, I might, if there's money in it. Like you, I need it.' She sighed. 'Now I'm getting serious again.'

He was flagging down a servant for more champagne when Howard joined them.

'We're thinking of taking a ride along the Wall, Mrs. Grant. Polly and me with a few others. Would you care to join us?'

'I'd love to,' she set down her glass. 'I'm resolved to enjoy myself today. Excuse me, J.O. I hope things soon look better for you and I'll bear the novels in mind.'

'Enjoy your ride,' he turned back to his food with a stabbing heartache for a certain young Frenchman who had been killed in the siege with whom he used to ride along the Wall, before the deluge.

The riders along the Wall that day were a merry group— Alice, Polly, and Howard leading, followed by some young English and Americans who treated Alice with the deference due to an old China hand, for most of them were comparative newcomers to the city and had little idea of its former glories. Alice, only too familiar with them, found it hard to keep her spirits screwed high as she pointed out various ruined landmarks—desecrated temples and churches, burnt-out towers; even the cells of the Examination Halls torn down by troops. The siege barricades had all been dismantled, and when Howard pointed out their earlier locations, his hearers were amazed, so incredible did such an event seem to them.

'So that's the end of old Peking,' Alice said lightly, as they descended a ramp into the Chinese City. 'There's going to be a twentieth-century version now, with macadamised roads, electric lights, and a proper Foreign Concession. All quite marvellous, I'm sure.' Her listeners were most enthusiastic, but even as she spoke, Alice felt a violent headache coming on, and the champagne-lightness wearing off. She excused herself and rode home alone.

Modern Peking was indeed in the making that winter when, instead of its customary icy withdrawal, there was continuing change, upheaval, the coming and going of strangers. Never had the capital been so accessible, the restored railways running efficiently, larger entrances blasted in the ancient walls to accommodate widened roads. The occupying forces created their own open society—drinking parties, riding excursions, camp-hops where foreign ladies, being scarce, were much in demand. During New Year, a skating-rink was made on the flooded canal, strung with coloured lanterns and a hurdy-gurdy played popular tunes. Alice spent several evenings twirling round floor and rink in the arms of various officers, flirting and laughing, still dogged with a sense of farcical, temporary unreality.

When William and the family set off for Singapore to spend time with Lottie before her wedding, Alice accompanied them as far as Shanghai and stayed at Fairlawns. The 'Model Settlement' had not been physically damaged during the crisis, but there were scars: public buildings were heavily guarded, many shopkeepers and servants had fled; both foreigners and natives were still uneasy. Mary, still distraught at the murder of Lilian, had, as Robert put it, 'taken up religion.' Formerly, her piety had been of the conventional, lukewarm kind, but now she went to church daily in a closed carriage.

'It's quite rum,' Robert complained irritably to Alice. 'She was always most critical of Lilian when she was alive, now she's making a martyr out of her and can't spend enough time praying for her soul. Whatever for? As I keep saying, Lilian will undoubtedly have been saved, considering her blameless life.'

'Perhaps Mary feels a trifle guilty—and is beginning to worry about her own salvation?'

Robert chuckled. 'I suppose we all tend to do that as we get older, even find myself at it occasionally. But I don't think China's the place to work such matters out with diligence, and it's time we left. In fact, we're definitely going Home for good and all next year. Once Mary feels more like it, we're going to begin selling up and packing—which will take a while,' he indicated the size, extent, and material content of Fairlawns.

Alice bit her lip. 'I've always been so fond of this house, it's

628

been a haven, an anchor at times, Robert. And you and Mary have always been so welcoming. I shall miss it and you greatly.'

'Why don't you come Home with us, Alice? Great heavens, woman, when are you going to face the rest of the world? See your own heritage? And you could greatly help us in getting settled. Mary's lost some of her pep . . .'

He stared moodily into the lovely garden, and Alice followed his gaze.

'Perhaps I will, perhaps I really will. I've begun translating novels these days—lucrative and interesting. Dickens, the Brontës, George Eliot. It makes me think differently about what you call my heritage. I'll consider it seriously.'

It was partly that conversation that made Alice decide not to re-open her Peking shop during such unpropitious times. Instead, she drew up an agreement whereby Benjy controlled the Shanghai business. She took a percentage of the profits in return for its foreign name and goodwill. The day she signed it, Alice was tempted to take off for Home there and then, but the pull of the capital was still strong, and she returned there in the spring. She began a translation of *Mill on the Floss*, picked up the threads of her friendships, and assumed she had no other reason for being there.

James Galbraith came knocking at the front gate on a warm April afternoon. Over tea, he told Alice that he'd been in Western China looking at opium farms, as he'd been commissioned to write a report on the Far Eastern opium trade.

'Anti-opium societies are having a field-day at the moment—suggesting that China's present ills are mainly due to addiction, and that wicked traders here and in India are making fat profits from it. Not quite true, as I found out. The bulk of the stuff is home-grown—acres and acres of it, every farmer with his little patch, every magistrate his happy pipe in the evenings.'

'But the habit is increasing, is it not?'

'Rapidly. According to missionaries I talked to, about one tenth of the population is now smoking. They're trying to cure addicts with morphia pills.'

'Which usually leads them into morphia addiction instead?'

'Precisely, and there are firms now turning a neat profit in morphia imports. The wicked are always the most resourceful, as I told one Hongkong missionary, who didn't want to believe me. You know anything about opium yourself, Mrs. Grant?'

'You mean, have I ever indulged?'

'Oh, I wouldn't like to suggest that a lady . . .'

She grinned. 'My behaviour hasn't always been entirely consonant with that required of a perfect lady, Mr. Galbraith. I have smoked, yes. I've known the vivid dreams of the white nights, but in my limited experience, it's not necessarily addictive. Anyway, I was once given some very cheap stuff by mistake. It badly upset me and I never smoked again.'

He would have liked to find out more, but she had obviously closed the topic. 'So what's been happening in Peking? The new station is very grand—and lit by electricity.'

'Yes, the plant came from the Summer Palace, I believe, where it was never used. The Brits have been careful to take the new extension right through a famous burial ground, did you notice? I don't understand the need for such gratuitous desecration.'

'The very words I used in a despatch recently—it's the order of the day.'

'That and occupation. All the Legations have extended their boundaries, the Japanese are in the Board of Revenue, Indian regiments in the Board of War, Field Marshal von Waldersee in the Winter Palace, and an International Club in the former *yamen* for Mongolian Affairs.'

'I know that. I'm lodging in the annexe. Still smells of Mongol, but conveniently close to the best bar in town. Well, I won't detain you longer, Mrs. Grant. It was kind of you to take me in, arriving unannounced. And perhaps you'll allow me to repay the compliment by giving you supper at the grand International tomorrow evening?'

She accepted the invitation, entertained him and the Blums to supper in her turn. In accord with the free-and-easy atmosphere for the time and place, they were soon on first name terms and within a month seemed almost like old friends. It was, she assumed, in that spirit he turned up late one evening, bringing a box of French chocolates he'd won at poker. They sat together on the pavilion verandah, moonlight casting scalloped shadows from curved gables and open-work walls, and the air was heavy with the scent of white lilac.

'Nice to see flowers blooming, unusual for these Manchu gardens,' James volunteered. 'Why's that?'

'They prefer the beauty of rocks shaped by the weather, decorative walls like that one—which looks delicate as crinkled paper in this light, doesn't it?' Leaning over the verandah, she gazed at the wall, and continued softly, 'But I think sometimes of all the English flowers I've not seen in their proper setting. Primroses in woods, daffodils on grassy banks, even roses, I'm assured, only look their best in English country gardens.'

'It's time you saw the home-country.'

'You say home-country in the nice Scottish way my mother used to. Yes, studying these novels I'm translating makes me want to go.'

'You'll enjoy it. Even a born traveller like myself appreciates the comforts of the home-country occasionally.'

'And its certainties, I imagine—compared to China, where nothing seems certain anymore and the future is . . . anybody's guess.'

'Aye. I'm not sure China will be a very secure berth for the next decade, Alice, you might be wise to look elsewhere. Have another chocolate?'

She took one. 'But I've always lived here, you see. It's difficult. Where else is home?'

'Where the heart is, they say.' He looked at her keenly, but she continued leaning over the railings, not answering immediately, watching Tiger Blossom stalk a cricket, catch it, eat it. A tension grew between them and he was about to change the subject, when she said, 'The heart? I'm not sure where that is except somewhere between my neck and waist.'

'Which is the very best place for it.' He'd got up quickly and, as she turned, put his arms round her, squeezing the part of the anatomy in question. She was startled rather than shocked and 'Well, I'm blessed' was her first thought. It made her lips loosen in a slight smile that he took advantage of.

'Excuse me,' he said then. 'But you're an attractive woman, Alice Greenwood-Grant, standing there in the moonlight with your heart just in the right place.'

'It's sweet of you to say so.' She looked demurely into his eyes, which twinkled as he kissed her again. 'Well . . .' he ran his hands down her forearms, 'do you wish me to go or not? It's getting unrespectably late for us to be alone here together, though of course I have a thoroughly unrespectable proposal in mind.'

631

'I'm quite surprised, James. I thought of us simply as friends. At least, I did until a few minutes ago,' she added honestly.

'Friends and . . . what you will. There's another road we could embark upon. It is as you choose, of course.'

'Give me another chocolate.' She took one, thinking frivolously, 'If it's soft I will, if it's hard I won't,' and bit into a cherry cream. 'Embark upon,' he'd said, a good term for another voyage in a frail boat, risk of another shipwreck, another loss. And yet the season had been a long dry one; many moons had passed since she'd felt a man's hands on her as ardently as James' were now. She shivered, the cherry cream slipped delectably down her throat. She looked up at the moon, smelled the lilac, thought, as she leaned into his arms, that it was all rather romantic and how nice if he could sweep her off her down-to-earth feet.

He kissed her neck and fondled her breasts, 'Perhaps we'll get a wee bittie closer to where that heart of yours lurks, hey?'

She chuckled. 'James, you're speaking more Scottish-ly every moment.'

'It's the passion, my dear, brings out the native in me,' he replied, guiding her inside the bedroom.

The relationship thus started in a spirit of friendship, developed slowly into passion. At first, their lovemaking was conventional, but soon James was delighted to realise he'd found a woman of his own kind as well-versed as he was himself in the less decorous ways of oriental pleasurings. And she, who felt at first that James' freckled, brown-haired sturdiness, lacked the sensual masculinity of Lin's blackness and pallor, soon forgot the comparison, delighted in her turn by his uninhibited sexuality. Their shared enjoyment became a private corner of their separate lives and, for a while at least, the arrangement suited them both.

James had been asked to remain in Peking for the time being to report on the military occupation, the progress of peace negotiations, and the measures taken by the Empress Dowager during her exile to make amends for her former misdeeds. 'Adopt the strong points of foreign countries in order to make up for China's shortcomings,' she'd ordered as early as January 1901 and, with the guidance of stalwarts like Li Hung-chang and Jung Lu, proceeded in the following months to draft outlines of a reform programme which, ironically, was

632

similar to, though less radical than, that proposed by the Reformers two years before. One of the major problems, the Empress realised, was the low state of the nation's morale. The people had 'seen the strength of foreign soldiers' and the 'stern orderliness of foreign settlements,' and were 'sick and tired of their own discord and weakness.' The suggestion was, if the Empress herself were allowed to resume the reins of government, she—a reformed character, a chastened and enlightened spirit—would put China on its feet again.

'And what about the Emperor Kuang-hsu? Why isn't he returned to power? He's the anointed ruler, the true believer in Reform,' Alice demanded angrily of James and the Blums as they sat in the courtyard of the International Club. Along its front wall, flags of the eight nations hung limply in the heat; officers and civilians of those nations strolled about or sat at rickety tables drinking their customary beverages—beer, whisky, pernod, saké, vodka.

'Because the Allies aren't willing to get too embroiled in internal politics,' Karl said, 'They've got enough just squabbling among themselves and all they really want now is to squeeze a whacking war indemnity out of the bankrupt Chinese, get the guilty punished, and get themselves out of here.'

'I had a letter from Lin Fu-wei last week,' Alice said, and Veronique, glancing at James, saw the name meant nothing to him. 'He says the Empress's pronouncements are no more than eyewash to deceive the West and that no real reforms will happen as long as she holds sway.'

'Probably true,' James yawned. 'My, but it's hot . . . best thing is, though—leave 'em to work out their own salvation and get out, as Karl says.'

'How are the exiles in Japan these days?' Veronique asked.

'They don't like being there, but are coming round to Sun Yat-sen's view—it has to be revolution or nothing for China.' She sighed. 'Lin talks of Asia for the Asians and he's off to fight for the Filipinos against the Americans. That sounds awfully dangerous to me. Is it, do you think?'

'It's a tough and dangerous life anywhere for a dedicated Asian revolutionary these days,' James replied. 'I feel sorry for them—so much needs doing and so few sufficiently capable. This Lin a friend of yours, Alice? Well, I hope he manages to keep his head and his shoulders in the same place, that's all.'

Alice averted her face to hide her distress, both at his words and her recollection of the other news Lin's letter had contained. He and his fellow Reformers now realised that the struggle against the tyrannies of the reactionary regimes in Asia was going to be harder and longer than they'd earlier imagined. Life-long probably, and his sweet Uncut Jade had to accept that he might never be able to return to China. With obvious sadness, he said it would be better if she forgot him— not all they had shared, he added pathetically, but accept that it was probably past. 'The time has come to pour the wine in the dust,' he had written the same words that he'd spoken to her years before in Port Arthur. This time they sounded very final.

Veronique, sensing Alice's preoccupation, had diplomatically steered the conversation towards the latest of the capital's scandals: that the Japanese had seized cart-loads of silver ingots from the Revenue Board; that an eccentric Indian army officer regularly rode round the Carriage Park in a gilded imperial equipage with his Chinese concubine; that the Germans, in the course of punitive expeditions for the revenge of their Ambassador's murder during the siege, were tying strings of innocent villagers together by their pigtails and leading them to slaughter; that the Austrians had raped a houseful of female converts living near the American mission; that the Russians and British were almost starting a new war over the management of the railway to the north.

In the light of these disorders and uncertainties, the majority of Peking's residents, both native and foreign, were much relieved when the peace settlement between China and the Allies was eventually signed early that autumn—which included the former's promise to pay a ruinous indemnity. A week later the first detachments of foreign troops were moving out, the International Club was on its last days, and, in his room there, James Galbraith began writing his final despatches of the campaign.

Seeking inspiration, he went to the window, looked along a dusty, pot-holed, oriental street, half its buildings in ruins. An old man with a hand-cart and a whisk broom was sweeping the road very, very slowly, so bent over he was surely unable ever to stand upright. 'Nations come and nations go, but sweepers sweep forever,' he scribbled, then stood, whistling through his teeth. He was accustomed to the alienating boredom of solitary rooms in foreign cities, of desolate streets, the pointless detritus of human catastrophe. Sometimes, recently, it oppressed him. Time to move on perhaps? He was not compelled to leave yet, but would be turned out of this room shortly. Should he go and stay in Lilac House for a while? As Alice's relatives were still away in Singapore, she was living there alone and would presumably welcome his companionship for a while? Mustn't get too involved though; with women that had always been his rule. But Alice seemed level-headed, given neither to ensnaring feminine wiles nor embarrassing confidences. Indeed, during their congenial and ardent encounters he had found out little about her, for she had a self-containment rare in a woman. It was beginning to intrigue him, though he didn't analyse why; simply deciding that, when the time came to vacate his room at the Club, he'd go to her.

If James (at the moment he was watching the street-sweeper) could instead have seen the woman who was in his thoughts, he would have learned much more about her. She was lying on her bed, doubled in an agony of grief, the letter that had caused it crumpled beside her. It was from Lin's friend Crabbie, who reported that Lin had been killed during a guerilla attack shortly after his arrival in the Philippines; his death had been instantaneous. Her first hysterical outburst over, she now lay rigid in the aching grip of sadness, remembering their shared past, railing against the injustice of this sudden violent death, imagining his lifeless body sprawled on the ground—as she'd seen many of his country-men's in recent years. The arms that had so often held her flung out in some last gesture of despair, that black hair bloodied, that manly body war-torn and stilled.

She knuckled the vision from her eyes, only to see instead the handsome young fellow she'd first met on the *Mandalay*, brimful of confident enthusiasm for changing the world, he as leader-in-embryo. Then a succession of later Lins forced themselves so vividly and strongly upon her it was almost as if he, somewhere in an after-death, were making a last desperate effort to imprint his image on her mind forever. She accepted them in that spirit—the earnest lecturer and trans-lator, the persuasive and idealistic reformer, above all the private and passionate lover who had enjoyed the soft warm places of her sex.

His last letter had told her that their loving union was

ended, but then he had been alive at least, then she'd grieved only for their separation. Now she grieved even more deeply for his own loss of life, for the promises never to be fulfilled, the leadership never to be grasped. That sorrow weighed her down during the next dreary days as she moved like an invalid about the house, her ache sharpening into agony when, quite unexpectedly, she seemed to actually see Lin standing near— beside her desk, leaning against a verandah pillar with his warm eyes on her: 'Hello, sweet Uncut Jade' . . . Scalp tingling, eyes prickling with fresh tears, she rushed forward into the emptiness of his never-ending absence, and then cried again, or sat dry-eyed, rocking to and fro to ease the pain.

She was sitting thus one afternoon when she heard James' voice in the courtyard, and scurried to hide in her bedroom.

'Are you there, Alice?' he strolled inside.

'I'll be with you in a minute. Sit down.' He did so, watching Mrs. Duck hanging out some bed-quilts to air, thinking that Lilac House was indeed a pleasant and comfortable abode.

'Oh James, hello,' she greeted him coolly. 'Like some tea?'

'Please—some of us spent last night finishing up the oddments in the bar. The Club's about to close.'

'So soon?'

'Well, most of the military top-brass are away. Leaves me a homeless waif.'

He waited hopefuly, but she simply ordered tea.

He sat down; lit a pipe. 'What are you working on?'

'Hmm? Oh—work. Just finishing *Mill on the Floss*.'

'You don't sound very cheerful. Thought you'd be glad to see it done.'

'Oh, I am I suppose. Might get some money for it.'

'Are you short? I mean, if you're in any need, Alice? I've not mentioned it before, but don't think I'm a tight-fisted Scot.'

'Oh no James, I'm quite all right, thank you. My Shanghai business keeps me solvent.'

He liked her pride; of course he'd insist on paying rent; he waited to be asked about his next plans, but she merely said, 'Had a letter from my relatives yesterday. They're on their way back from Singapore. My niece was married there in the summer.'

'They lived with you here, didn't they?'

'Yes, but now they'll have a new bungalow in the Legation Quarter.'

'What about the Manchus who were here?'

'I've often wondered. No word, no sign. I hope they're still alive. The women must be unhappy—torn from this ancestral home so unexpectedly. I often imagine them here—sewing, gossiping, watching the shadows of the moon.'

She relapsed into dreamy melancholy as the tea was brought and she poured it.

'You make them sound a little creepy.'

'Who?'

'Those Manchu ladies. I'll keep you better company tonight, shall I, Alice?' He leaned forward and touched her hand, but she quickly withdrew it. 'Tonight? Oh no James, I don't really feel . . .'

'I'm sorry. You have another engagement?'

'It's not that . . .' she sat back, closing her eyes; in the lengthy silence he noticed her pallor. 'I might as well tell you, I suppose. I had some very bad news a few days ago. Lin Fu-wei, the Reformer I mentioned to you, was killed—fighting in the Philippines.' She didn't open her eyes.

'Och, I'm very sorry to hear that. He sounded a fine brave man. So many of these Asian revolutionaries get it in the neck before they can accomplish much. And he was a good friend, you told me?'

She replied in a low voice, 'He was my lover for—a considerable time. He was, in some ways, the most important man in my life.' Then she burst into tears, for the very speaking of the words aloud was so painful.

Awkwardly he offered a handkerchief. 'Oh dear, dear, I am so sorry. A heavy blow for you, of course.' He paused, at a loss.

'I didn't tell you about him before; it was all past history, in a way, and not many people knew about us. We had to be discreet, a most unsuitable liaison from everyone's point of view,' she essayed a sarcastic smile that turned into a sniffle.

'Is there anything I can do to help, Alice? Of course, in the circumstances . . . I mean . . . I'm a bit taken aback and . . .' he flushed slightly. Her grief was so genuine he did not voice any disapproval, yet he was undoubtedly a little shocked that Alice . . . with a native . . . none of his business, of course.

She looked up, sensing his coolness. 'In the circumstances there's nothing really you can do, or even say, thank you James. You probably can't understand and I don't expect you to.'

He pushed out his lower lip. 'Maybe you'd rather I leave you now?'

'If you don't mind. I'm afraid I'm simply not good company for a while. I shall recover of course,' she smiled bleakly.

'Well the Club's about to close as I told you and the campaign's over. So I suppose I'll be leaving Peking altogether any day now.' He waited, prepared to stand by her, if she begged him to do so. Even though . . .

'You disapprove of me now, don't you?' she flashed suddenly.

'Me? . . . Why . . . I suppose one doesn't quite expect . . .'

'Ladies to behave as I have? I've never been a very proper lady in that sense, James. But please go now, and I hope you won't exactly ostracise me if we ever meet again?'

'Why of course not, I'd not think of such a thing, Alice! And I hope indeed that we will meet again on some happier day. It's just . . . well, as you've said yourself, I can't be of any help to you for a while, so I'll be on my way.'

They shook hands quietly and he hurried away, thinking it was a blessing he hadn't actually asked to stay, for that would have been difficult in the circumstances. Surprising really, someone like Alice—but never mind, he was a wise laddie, not getting involved with the ladies.

James left the capital in a military train the following day. The platform was piled with bayonets, bedding, rifle-racks, folded tents, horse-troughs and field-ovens, and the train crowded with troops of several nations—lanky Yankees, swarthy sepoys, booted Cossacks, French Zouaves, German officers with spiked helmets, British ones with high-peaked caps. A few had fought heroically in the siege or marched in with the Relief Force; many, arriving later, had not fired a single shot, but turned a pretty penny instead. All of them seemed glad to be leaving the capital, for China was simply too enormous, too chaotic, too strong even in its weakness to be managed even by eight of the world's leading nations. The results of the Boxer revolt, of the siege, the Relief, and the occupation were inconclusive and unsatisfactory on every front. The country had still to be left to decide its own fate.

9

January 7, 1902, was the date pronounced auspicious by the astrologers of the Court for the official return of the Empress Dowager to her capital. And on the afternoon of that day she duly arrived, having travelled in considerable state for hundreds of miles from Hsian, her place of exile. The last stages of the journey were made by train, a modern conveyance in which neither she nor the Emperor had ever travelled before, but which she enjoyed immensely, seated in a specially-built, high-backed, throne-like chair.

The station outside Peking was canopied in yellow silks, the platform covered in red cloth to honour the royal coming, and dignitaries clad in brilliant robes made profound obeisance when their restored sovereign appeared in the doorway of her private car. She too was robed richly, jewels and flowers glinting in her oiled, winged hair; her square face was treble-chinned, her skin deeply wrinkled. Dismounting from the train she stood on the platform for several minutes, supported on each side by eunuchs. Utterly still she was, her stone-cold, black-ice eyes taking in the scene before her.

Those close enough to be encompassed by that pitiless gaze shuddered and felt similarly cold—at least Alice did, standing with Isabel, Polly and J.O. near a group of blue-buttoned mandarins. To her, the squat figure brought a ludicrous memory of Lydia Lawson in the Christmas tableau, and that conjured the faces of young Arthur Rawlins whose body now lay in the Legation cemetery, and of Han-li, the sliced-in-half. A smile of utter mirthlessness cracked the painted lips of the Old Buddha, returned to rule all China, as she tottered to a sedan chair and was borne away.

The Empress had much to smile about and be thankful for. To one of her implacable, long-lasting vengefulness, it must have been truly astonishing that, less than two years after her

639

ignominious flight, she'd been allowed to return unharmed, indeed feted. Defeated by the foreigners, she had triumphed eventually; she had even outlived the great Queen Victoria; she was invincible—in her age as in her youth.

'The incubus returns,' J.O. murmured to Alice, 'The evil elderly one, the demon dragoness.'

'You're hard on the old lady,' Isabel protested, over-hearing.

'In this case, madam, no hyperfole could overstate the hardness of that stony soul who is again permitted to direct the destinies of this wretched, shambling, decaying monster of an Empire.'

Isabel blinked at him. 'What was the alternative though? I heard it suggested that the Allies should have partitioned it among themselves and given it the benefit of enlightened Western-style rule for a while.'

He chuckled. 'The last colonial jewel in the crown of our late-lamented Queen, what?'

'Well, you'd surely agree that most of our colonies are much more orderly and secure than this country? We've recently returned from Singapore—such a pleasant place, and the natives are very contented under our rule.'

He pulled down his mouth. 'I wonder how much we, the rulers, ever know what the natives are, madam?'

Isabel turned away; J.O. was most difficult, he simply never agreed with anything. As he moved away to talk to Alice Isabel thought it rather typical that he should be a good friend of hers. Alice had been chatting to a mandarin while the rest of the royal retinue—Yuan Shih-kai's red and black costumed soldiers, minor courtiers in conical hats a-quiver with tasselling, attendants carrying coloured silk umbrellas—moved away in dignified procession.

She turned to J.O. 'The man I was speaking to said the Old Buddha maintained an extremely luxurious court even in exile. Yet he thought that was quite proper. I don't under-stand—incubus is the right word for her.'

He sighed. 'I find it all extremely depressing, so much so I've definitely decided to go Home.'

She looked up in dismay. 'Oh, J.O.—must you really?'

'All the old guard are dead, Li Hung-chang the last to go. And I simply cannot stomach this new bunch of toadies who'll lick the—er—feet of that dragon-bitch we just saw. And no only the Chinese, mark my words—foreigners will flock to do her honour. Within months she'll be the toast of the Legations, she who wanted every barbarian devil strung up on a tree. Can't stomach anymore Alice, too old for so much hypocrisy, corruption, mendacity, self-seeking.' He stared gloomily at the end of the splendid procession shuffling out, saying abruptly, 'I wanted to die in the siege you know. Did what I could to, wasn't foolhardy enough, the good Lord wouldn't have me. Took a young French friend of mine instead, he was foolhardy enough. Very fond of him I was; mustn't talk of these things. Though the Lord wouldn't have me, I find King's College, Cambridge will. I shall go back to teach Chinese there—where I started from.'

'J.O. I didn't quite realise. I'm sorry. I shall miss you terribly.'

Polly darted up and tugged Alice's sleeve. 'One of the Press gentlemen keeps looking at you. Isn't it someone you know?'

Alice glanced carefully. 'Why yes, it's Mr. Galbraith back again.' J.O. chuckled pointedly, and she said, 'Shall we go, Isabel?'

It had started to rain outside, where a positive encampment of yellow and purple tents had been erected to protect the most important heads, and now a mêlée of rickshaws, carts, chairs were all trying to leave at once.

'Wait a mo . . . I'll try and find chairs,' J.O. ducked away, and Alice, clucking with annoyance, turned brightly to her sister-in-law, 'Times like this you must yearn for Singapore, Isabel? So peaceful and easy to manage, you say?'

'Indeed I do, why . . .'

James appeared before them doffing his hat. 'Why, if it isn't . . . Good afternoon Mrs. Grant—er, Alice. And Mrs. Greenwood.'

Alice greeted him coolly, asking, 'And have you been in Peking long?' avoiding the difficult matter of naming.

'Just set foot. I was one of the Press allowed on the royal train last night, travelling with the royal personages themselves. Most entertaining. You should have seen the Court ladies running giddily about the platforms at every halt—and crowds making profound obeisances the whole way.'

'Extraordinary,' Alice murmured.

'Yes, isn't it? Good old inscrutable China.' He smiled at her. You're feeling better, I trust, Alice?'

'Much better thank you.'

There was an uncomfortable pause; Isabel looked from one to the other in perplexity. Having been absent from the capital, she had no suspicion of their earlier relationship, and now decided to make conversation. 'Do you always write about Chinese affairs, Mr. Galbraith?'

'Some of them, ma'am. Others aren't exactly suited to publication.' His eyes smiled and Alice turned away with a spluttering cough. 'Oh this rain! I'm sure it's giving me a cold. J.O.'s trying to find chairs, perhaps you might help, James?'

He turned to obey as J.O. panted up. 'Here we are, two is all I can find—we'll have to squeeze in. Oh hello Galbraith. Thought I might see you here. No room for you I'm afraid, old chap.'

He took Alice's arm, dashing through the rain to a chair. She turned back to James and, he, seeing, followed her to the vehicle. As she climbed in, he said quickly, 'I've booked in at what they call the "Little Bung" in the Legation Quarter. Will you join me there for supper tomorrow evening?'

'Well . . . I . . . er . . .' she was taken by surprise.

'Do you good, Alice, an evening out,' J.O. said quietly.

'Yes, all right, thank you.'

'Seven o'clock.' He stood hatless, watching her chair leave. The rain flattened his usually springy hair and made him look almost like a suppliant. And this disturbed her, for, during the intervening months, she'd resolved to forget him.

'A health to you, Alice, the lady I didn't forget!' James, smiling, raised a glass to her. They were seated in the poky dining-room of the 'Little Bung,' a makeshift building beside the Legation canal, used as communications headquarters during the occupation and now a temporary lodging for foreign visitors—and a draughty, damp, and dirty one at that, James had just been telling her.

She raised her glass. 'Nice to hear you say so, James. I assumed you soon would.'

'Forget? So did I, to be frank.' He toyed with his glass. 'One never knows about such things. And you? Forgot me, I presume? You had, after all, an unexpected sorrow that naturally overshadowed anything else. I felt a little guilty afterwards—going away when you were so distressed.'

'Oh it was the best thing, James. Because of—what had

happened between us, you couldn't help me then. I've recovered from my grief, though I shall always feel the loss sorely. And it seemed such a stupid, meaningless way for Lin to die—not even in the cause of China. Still, it's finished and one mustn't dwell too much on the past. I'm always telling myself that, though I don't always succeed in obeying my own orders.'

She smiled and he gestured for more wine, saying they needed it to drown the taste of the wretched food. 'I only wish I could take you somewhere decent, but there's no proper hotel yet and private accommodation's hard to find, now the locals are all coming back. You're still in Lilac House?'

'Yes. Safe for a while, I hope.'

There was another pause; the evening had been like that from the start; each tentative, skirting round precarious areas of disagreement or intensity.

'Have you finished your report on the opium question?'

'No, it's turning into a real "can of worms" as the Yankees say. And I have to be careful. Also I've another assignment—to see what the Russians are up to in Manchuria, now they're supposed to go away, but aren't. And what have you been doing?'

'Translating novels mostly. Quite enjoyable, not very exciting.' Again there was a pause, and she steeled herself to say the one thing she'd prepared in advance. 'Before we finally drop the subject of Lin, which we then will, James, I'd like you to know how involved I was in the Reform Movement—its aims and ideals. I put everything I could into it, and was loyal as long as it lasted. So the shock of its failure, and then Lin's exile and death was—cumulative. I'd like you to know that, because I've been what you might call a "trimmer" in so many other matters, never sufficiently convinced of anything for a life-long commitment, compromising again and again between the Englishness and the Chineseness in me.'

He looked at her meditatively. 'You make that sound like a confession, but it's people like us—for I'm of the same ilk—who keep the wheels turning. We're not fanatical, don't want to fight to the death, know the world changes slowly, and not always for the better when it does. Fully paid-up members of the Organisation of Innocent Bystanders, as a friend of mine puts it.'

Alice laughed. 'I like that, a good organization to belong to.

I've never thought of it so positively before, You make me feel so much better about myself, James.'

As she drank again her greenish eyes sparkled in that lively, attractive way he hadn't forgotten. 'That's better, don't take the world too terribly seriously. It's not worth it. And there's always something comical popping up. Case in point, I remember at Ping Yang in Korea, just before I met you at Port Arthur. There were the Japs out in full battle trim, rifles loaded, bayonets sharpened—and opposite them the Chinese, in brand new uniforms with large coloured circles on the front that made excellent targets for enemy sharpshooters. Then it began to rain and half the Chinese infantry, acting on orders from on high, mind you, dropped their weapons and put up umbrellas to protect themselves and a comrade and keep all their lovely uniforms dry! A fact. One knew from that moment who was going to win the war.' They laughed and he continued, 'Of course it isn't really funny, because there's going to be more trouble in that region one day, I'll warrant.'

As they continued discussing Far Eastern affairs, which greatly interested them both, Alice realised she was truly enjoying herself. One of the nice things about James Galbraith, she recalled, was his way of talking to her on an equal basis, without masculine pomposity—actually listening when she expressed her own opinions as vehemently as any man. And, sometimes, for light relief, laughing her out of her vehemence with one of his quirky anecdotes about the odd customers he'd met in his travels. She felt relaxed and cheerful, remembering, as he poured the last of the wine, the gentle surety of his hands on her body. The look he gave her suggested he was thinking along similar lines and she began to feel a stirring of the desire that had been stilled since Lin's death. They looked at each other rather seriously and she murmured with some reluctance, 'It's really very late, James, and Snow Duck's waiting in the cart.'

'Oh what a shame! Sure you don't want a strong white man to escort you home then?' He gave a half-comic, half-hang-dog look that amused her. She looked round the shabby room; the atmosphere reeked of kerosene, stale food, and the fetid canal nearby. 'Oh James . . . oh, all right. There's lots of space in Lilac House these days. You can come and stay for a while if you like. I mean, we've no need to . . . I mean, we can see if . . .'

He hugged her. 'Alice, you're a fine lass, yes you are. I'll be

644

along tomorrow, and, as you say, there's no need to . . . unless of course . . .' They laughed together then and she went home feeling light-hearted.

James moved into Lilac House the next day and into Alice's bed that night and it was only when they woke in the morning Alice remembered that Polly was coming to stay for a while to pursue her Chinese studies. 'It's most awkward, James,' she explained as they sat draped in quilts, drinking morning tea. 'I've had so many ups and downs with her parents in the past. But I'm very fond of them nevertheless.'

'Do you want me to go then?' He didn't conceal his disappointment.

'No, there's no reason. I've insisted on making it clear to them that I lead my own independent life, but that's difficult for a woman.'

'And quite unusual?' he suggested, probing.

'I chose to. Anyway, I'll just have to ride any storm there is. I'll tell Polly the situation when she comes. She can still stay of course.'

'Unless she decides to flee this house of sin?'

'Oh don't. I love her dearly, and she's just floundering through her own first affair of the heart. Still, we all have to go through it.'

He tweaked her ear. 'You make it sound like hell.'

'Sometimes it is.'

'And sometimes the other place, I hope?'

She kissed him. 'Now dear, I'd rather you weren't here when Polly first arrives.'

James obediently left after breakfast, and Polly arrived a few hours later. She'd seen little of her aunt since she'd returned and was longing to tell her about Lottie's wedding. 'It was very grand in a formal way, Auntie Alice. The Brents live in fine style with loads of servants and Mrs. B. is awfully regal.'

'Lottie rose to the occasion, I'm sure?'

'Oh absolutely. She looked tremendously beautiful and grown-up. But you could see just how she'll look in ten years' time. And the bridegroom, Philip, is much shorter than she.'

'No one told me that,' Alice murmured.

'And so bossy and possessive. Not good-looking either.'

'You mustn't judge by looks so much, Polly. It will do you no good.'

She grinned impishly. 'Which reminds me, Howard's just

back from his compassionate leave in America. Isn't that marvellous? I haven't seen him yet.'

Alice sighed. 'I'm sure you will. So you didn't much like the Brents?'

'Oh, I liked Mr. B. and Philip's sister, but it all made me think of getting married in a way I haven't before.'

'You're much too young,' Alice protested.

'Don't be silly. I'll be twenty next year.'

That was a jolt. Alice remembered holding the just-born Polly in her arms in the Customs House in Port Arthur. It seemed like yesterday. Well, it wasn't, so perhaps it was time Polly learned a few facts about life. . . . She tried to interrupt her niece's gay babbling, '. . . Not that I'd ever want to marry anyone like Philip. I think a man has to be a bit reckless and, well, manly, don't you?'

'You mean Howard again I suppose? Look dear, just because he behaved admirably in the siege doesn't mean he'd make a good husband for everyday.'

'I don't think he wants me. But I'd have him if I could. Well, you saw us together that night . . .'

'Kissing isn't everything and I'd say Howard is a fairly ordinary young man.'

'And am I not an ordinary young woman?'

'I'm not sure yet. You haven't had much chance to prove exactly what you are. But if you marry Howard, you'll never find out, I promise you.' She glowered at her niece, who got up, saying in a small, hostile voice, 'Oh. I'll go and unpack.'

'Yes dear, but there's something . . .'

'It's only because you want me to stay a child. You're as bad as Mother and Father. They're against Howard too, and yet he's perfectly gentlemanly and from a very good family. You're all being stuffy because he's American.' She pouted, because she'd counted on Alice's support, which was usually forthcoming.

'A child? No, I only want you to have room and time to grow up to be yourself, Pol. And that's hard for a woman to do if she marries very young and all her interests and talents are then supposed to be subordinated to her husband.'

Polly frowned. 'Yes, but Howard is all in favour of women having more say in things. They do in America.'

'I'm pleased to hear it.' She laid a hand on her shoulder. 'Dear little goose, you know I'm always on your side—really?'

646

'Oh I suppose . . . Well, if you are, then do one thing please, Aunt. Ask Howard to supper here with us. I'm longing to talk to him properly.'

'All right—just to show I'm friendly.' As she made for the door, Alice said, 'And there'll be another supper guest. Mr. Galbraith, the journalist we met at the station recently.'

'Oh good. He seems nice.'

'He's staying here. With me.'

Polly turned, wide-eyed. 'What do you mean exactly?'

'Exactly what I say. With me, day and night. You are not unaware of certain things, Polly, and I'm sure your parents have already hinted that your Aunt Alice doesn't always behave with total decorum?'

'I see,' she mumbled. 'Have you . . . I mean . . . just?'

'No, we came together when you were in Singapore and are simply together again for a while. There's no more to it, and no less. If you can't accept it, then you'll have to leave—but I should hate you to.'

'Oh, I'll accept it, only it's rather . . .'

'Shocking?' Alice smiled bleakly. 'Well, if you marry Howard and live happily ever after you need never know the troubles of an independent woman's lot. This may open your eyes a little—to the good and the bad.'

Polly rushed out, cheeks aflame, whether from embarrassment, anger, or distress, Alice couldn't say.

Whatever her emotion, Polly stayed and was soon won over to James, to such an extent that she soon decided he was quite the nicest Scotsman she'd ever met and her aunt should consider settling down with him for what she, in her cruel youthfulness, termed her declining years. 'Have you ever considered marrying him?' she asked. They were in the kitchen helping Mrs. Duck to prepare the reunion supper for Howard, which had been somewhat delayed because Polly, her resistance lowered by her recent tropical sojourn, had succumbed to a bout of flu.

'Marriage? Oh we don't talk of such a thing. He's not the marrying kind nor am I, now,' Alice replied, as if shocked. 'Though funnily enough your grandmother advised me once to marry a Scot. But James isn't quite the solid type she had in mind, I fancy! He's too bouncy and all-over-the-place.'

'But I rather like that about him, don't you?'

'Well yes, I suppose I do,' Alice was conceding when Polly

interrupted, 'Isn't that someone arriving? Yes—look, it's Uncle Frank!'

'No—really?' Alice flew to greet him. 'Why this is an unexpected pleasure. What brings you to the capital?'

'Just business,' he said vaguely. 'And I've brought Lily again for a change. Took her straight to Will's where we're staying, then thought I'd pop by to see you. Why Polly, you have grown up.' He kissed his niece. 'Quite the young lady now. Like my Lily. Seems incredible.'

'It certainly does. Like some tea?'

'Just had some at Isabel's. Have you anything stronger?'

'There's brandy or whisky.'

'Didn't know you imbibed the latter.'

'I don't. I've a friend staying, a Mr. James Galbraith, and it's his native beverage.'

Frank looked keenly at Alice, then at Polly, who dropped her eyes. 'James Galbraith, hey?'

'He's away at present, but he'll be back tomorrow evening when we're having a supper party. You must come, dear, and bring Lily.'

'We'd be delighted. Now pretty Poll, I wonder if you'd do something for me? Run home and keep my Lily company—she's a bit shy of her Aunt and Uncle, but wants to see you.'

Polly skipped off straightaway, and Frank wandered round the large garden.

'Quite an establishment, this. You're lucky to have the use of it.' He ran his fingers along a row of decorated wall-tiles. 'Used to be some quite similiar to these at the Chus—near the archery store, remember?'

'Vaguely. Still there I expect.'

They went inside and Frank poured himself a stiff drink. 'Still think of the Chus sometimes, don't you? Funny, even a row of tiles can bring it all back. Poor old Han-li. That was terrible, terrible. You know, Sis, I sometimes think he and I should have just stayed there. He the younger son of the house, me the horse-boy. Mucking out the barns with Spots; never been so happy since.'

'Oh rubbish, Frank, of course you have. Childhood always seems golden in retrospect.'

But he wasn't listening. '. . . Lots of good outdoor physical work, bit of sport, didn't know then what money could buy, and what it couldn't, no responsibilities or problems. Just "yes sir," "no sir," and keep your nose clean.'

'Well I daresay one of the Wangs would give you a job in the stables if that's your dream of bliss.'

He glowered at her. 'I'm little more than a servant there anyway. They all dislike me now, except Peachy and Lily.'

'But why, Frank? Why has it turned so sour? You've got your own villa, horses, carriage, a sweet wife—what you wanted.'

'And all to be paid for. And there's Little Nut, who hasn't helped. Now young Ken's going to finish his education in America—more expense. Still, I suppose you're right. Hunan couldn't be as good as I remember it. Certainly changed our lives though, didn't it? More than thirty years since we were bundled off there—couple of God-fearing missionary brats. And you can say we've never been quite right since. Not good on the straight and narrow, hey? More like over the ditches and down the hills, perhaps?'

Alice shrugged irritably. 'To continue your laboured metaphor, I've been good at the fences ever since—sitting on them, that is.'

'Me too. Lack of moral conviction. Little old business of right and wrong got confused in our tender years.' He finished his drink and rose at once for another, examining the whisky bottle as he did so. 'Who's Mr. Galbraith, then? Just a friend or . . .'

'He's living here for the time being, with me.'

'Is it serious?'

'Of course not. He's a newspaper correspondent, something of a rolling stone. And I lead my own life.'

'That will be harder as you get older,' he said brutally.

'Oh for heaven's sake Frank, if you're in the dumps that's no reason for putting me in them too.'

'I was just thinking of your future, Alice—ours, in a country like this. No security, totally unstable and corrupt, internationally a write-off. Robert and Mary are definitely going Home.'

'That'll be a pleasant bolt-hole closed. Actually, I intend to go to Europe for a long holiday anyway, perhaps with them.'

'Do you now? I'd come too, if I had the cash. But what a hope! The Manchurian rail deal has fallen through and I'm here to see if I can pick up any pieces.'

'I'm so sorry. You don't have much luck with railways do you?'

'Nor with anything else.'

'But I always considered you the lucky fish of the family.'

'That was years ago—look at me now.'

She considered him: he was forty-one, looked older, running rather to flesh, cheeks mottling, the same bewildered little-boy-blue eyes. Her heart went out to him. 'Is there anything I can do to help?'

'No. Just don't condemn me too harshly.'

'Why should I condemn you at all?'

'You think I lead a pretty useless sort of life for one thing.'

She sighed. 'What's useful? Or useless? Praiseworthy, blameworthy? I'm not always sure I know. Like you, I got a little confused in my early years, and the longer I live the less I understand. I remember saying that to Will as we stood among the ruins of the legations just after the siege. He didn't know what I was talking about.'

'Oh Will wouldn't. He's right up there on the straight and narrow. But I know, Alice. Yes I do. And it's just the same with me.'

They sat in silence, disheartened, and she waited, feeling a trouble, wanting to help. But he suddenly got up. 'Must get back. Lily always feels a little lost at first, unused to English home-life. That's why I bring her—for the experience.'

'She's well?'

'Oh yes, attracted to various young men. Some take her out, others don't.'

'You mean Englishmen?'

'Oh yes, she'll have nothing to do with the other team.'

'She's sweet, pretty and good-natured, Frank. She'll find a good husband one day.'

'That's what they said about Peachy—once,' he answered, moving out.

'And didn't she? Frank, what is it?'

'Nothing. See you tomorrow evening then.'

'Yes. It's Polly's occasion really. She's bowled over by a young American who's coming.'

'And there'll be your James? Sounds fun.' He kissed her cheek. ' 'Bye, Sis. It's always good talk to you even if we don't say very much.'

After he'd gone, Alice spent a restless evening, dissatisfied by their encounter. Nor was she any longer looking forward to the supper party; feeling somehow threatened by problems she couldn't define.

Polly arrived first the next day, bringing dried flowers to brighten the rooms, it being too early in the season for the romance of moonlight and lilac. James, who came soon after, was in a romantic mood however, wanting Alice to bed with him before the others arrived. Not sharing his inclination, she refused and he retired to the study in a small huff, while Polly began indecisively trying on different dresses and arranging her hair in different styles. Alice, climbing into an evening gown of dark moss-green velvet, felt threatened with a headache.

'He's here,' Polly poked her head round the door. 'You go, Auntie, please.'

'He's your guest and I'm not quite ready.'

'Oh, I can't. *Please!*' her dark eyes shone with shy agony.

Alice clipped on a brooch. 'Really Polly, for someone who keeps insisting how grown-up she is . . .'

She hurried to the door. 'Howard, how nice to see you again.'

'And a real pleasure to see you, Miss Greenwood.' Evening attire suited him well she thought as he bowed over her hand and she led him inside.

'A friend of mine, Mr. Galbraith.'

Tense-white Polly, who'd decided on a rather unbecoming yellow dress, joined them, accepting a sherry with shaking fingers, asking with immediate intensity about Howard's recent leave.

'Oh it was real great. Those of us who'd been in the siege were treated like real heroes. We had to keep explaining over and over what happened. The ladies especially found it very hard to understand how it could have been.'

'Still, I'm sure you enjoyed telling them over and over,' Alice said a little maliciously.

'Well, I didn't mind. I drew sketch-plans of the barricades, showed them around at parties, and they were a great hit. People kept telling me I should write a book.'

'Oh Howard why don't you?' Polly begged. 'I'm sure you'd do it so well—and I could help a little, as I was there too.'

'Oh but my book would be about the actual fighting, tactics, organisation of defences and so on,' he replied loftily.

'Well we made the sandbags for the defences, didn't we, Polly?' Alice interrupted and James, who'd been listening amused, added, 'Every sandbag had its heroine just as every barricade its hero. You can use that line in your book if you wish, Mr. Thringer.'

651

'Oh yes. I believe you write for the papers, sir?'

'A Grub Street hack, yes.' He moved to pour Alice a drink, grimacing at her. She smiled, knowing he shared her dislike of Howard's brash conceit, and the maring was a comfort, even though she feared the evening itself might prove difficult. It began to be a few minutes later—when Lily walked into the room looking radiantly beautiful in a white organdie gown with a crimson shawl round her shoulders, a camellia in her jet-black hair. Howard stared at her, drew a breath; as he bent low over her hand, the light shone on his lustrous blond hair. He raised his head, and his blue eyes held her blue eyes long enough for Alice to think—why didn't this occur to me?

'You certainly have an extremely lovely line in nieces, Miss Greenwood,' Howard was still looking at Lily.

'Thank you, I'm very proud of them all, and indeed there's an auburn-haired beauty as well isn't there, Polly? Recently married in Singapore.'

Polly agreed listlessly, knowing full well she was in neither Lily's nor Lottie's class.

'He's smitten with Lily, isn't he, Aunt? Isn't he?' Polly hissed a little later, following Alice as she went to check over the dining table.

'Don't say smitten, it's vulgar.'

'Smitten, smitten, bowled over, head over heels, call it what you like, that's what's happened.'

'Howard isn't head over heels for anyone except himself, though his head's probably been turned a little by all those admiring American ladies back home.'

'Oh I wish I'd worn my scarlet instead of my yellow,' Polly plucked miserably at her dress.

Alice said brusquely, 'Pull yourself together, Polly and just enjoy the evening, for heaven's sake.'

But that Polly couldn't do; she simply stood by the table, numbed by the hopeless tragedy of it all. Alice suddenly recognised the lineaments of Polly's Grandmother Eliza there—a suffering, stubborn, blind intensity of feeling, whether the unworthy object were Edward Blake or Howard Thringer. She sighed,

'Tell them supper's served, dear.'

It was not a success. Howard did little to conceal his fascination with Lily and there was something else—James and Frank who'd been talking quite amiably at first, were now defintely not. In fact, they scarcely exchanged a word for the remainder of the evening, during which Alice struggled valiantly to keep normal conversation going against undercurrents of flirtation, jealousy, and a disconcerting tension she couldn't fathom.

In these circumstances the party broke up quite early, with Howard attentively anxious to help Frank escort the ladies home. When they'd gone, Alice joined James for a night-cap. 'Not a sparkling success. I'll have a brandy now, please.'

'You look very nice in that lavender, dear.'

'Thanks. But what man could look elsewhere with the lovely Lily in the room? Certainly Howard couldn't. I'm sorry for Poll. But I hope that breaks it. I don't want her marrying that cocky Yankee . . . but there was something else wrong, between you and Frank?'

He pushed out his lower lip. 'Thought you'd notice. Have a drink.'

She obeyed, tensing herself.

'I'm afraid your kid brother's heavily involved in the illicit import of opium—Wang & Co. is one of the firms I've been asked to investigate secretly. I heard there was an English link somewhere, dealing with foreign merchants in India where the stuff's coming from. I started questioning him casually, and when he twigged what I was after, he shut up like a clam.'

'Oh Lord save us! So that's it. I knew he was hiding something. He's been so evasive and anxious about money. Then his talk yesterday about right and wrong—it all fits.' She sank wearily into a chair, her headache a throbbing reality.

'I'm sorry, Alice. I'd no way of guessing this before.'

'I'm not blaming you—just going about your journalistic business.'

'Naturally I wasn't going to press it this evening, but he's got to get out immediately. What he's doing is certainly illegal and in most foreign eyes highly immoral to boot. And there'll be a corking scandal when the story breaks.'

'Who's going to break it? You?'

'Sooner or later, yes. But even if I don't one of my rivals will.'

'Oh, Frank, Frank—you silly young fool,' she murmured, as if her brother were still ten years old.

James came over and stroked her hair. 'Look dear, I'm very fond of you, as I hope you know. I don't want to hurt you or be the cause of your brother being dragged through the law courts. What he's doing isn't very pretty, but not a heinous crime in my book. One of those shady areas I'd rather remain an innocent bystander about. See him tomorrow and tell him what I've said. Make it clear that he must get out at once, to save his own skin. As for my opium report—there's no hurry. Going to Manchuria first. I'll be away for a while, time for him to . . . if you follow me?'

She nodded. 'It's very kind of you, James. Frank has meant so much to me over the years. He's not wicked, honestly, just not specially dedicated to conventional morality I suppose. He likes a good time and he'll take the easy way to it. Not that it's made him very happy. He seemed quite dejected yesterday— guilt and worry, I realise now. But opium smuggling, what a stupid, stupid thing!'

'Here, come and sit on my lap and relax a minute,' he tweaked her nose gently as she did so. 'Poor old Alice, the burdens of being an aunt and an elder sister are weighing you down most dreadfully I can see!' He held a brandy glass to her lips. 'Drink this and remember, the situation is desperate but not serious.'

'Oh you're always saying that.'

'Part of my philosophy: it's got me out of several tight spots.' He began squeezing the soft velvet round her waist. 'I really do like this dress, but I think you've had it on long enough for one evening.' He moved her head back and flicked his tongue inside her mouth. 'Hmm! This is the way to get a taste of the brandy you have bought for the lady as well as your own, so the Scots say!'

'Oh James really,' she giggled as he began undoing her dress at the back. 'Shall we stay here—or in bed?' he asked softly.

'Oh in bed dear, it's easier afterwards.'

At that he swung her into his arms and carried her off, and, for the next few hours, she gave no thought to the misdemeanours of her younger brother.

The following morning however, she knew the matter had to be tackled and went early to Will's bungalow in the Foreign Concession.

Isabel greeted her in the morning room where she was again choosing upholstery patterns. 'Oh Alice, I'm glad you've come. Perhaps you can throw some light on Polly's mood this morning? Her very worst combination of tantrum and sulk.'

'Oh that . . .' the more urgent worry had pushed it from her mind. 'The handsome Howard was rather captivated by the lovely Lily last evening, that's all.'

'I thought Miss Poll's nose was out of joint. I'll be pleased if this ends her infatuation. He's not really suitable and she's far too young.' Alice agreed fervently, then remembered guiltily how, in her own youthful past, she'd loathed such sentiments. 'Is Frank up?'

'Just going out—in search of siege relics I believe.'

'Men never tire of playing soldiers in their minds do they? Anyway, I'll go too, I'm sure he'd like company.'

Normally Frank would have, but only at Alice's insistence did they walk out together that morning. The reconstruction of the Legation Quarter was well underway and each national residence was being built in an individual style, with Flemish gables, Gothic windows, Corinthian pillars, Venetian gateways and German turrets rising from the rubble. The main street was already macadamised and smart detachments of international guards patrolled the area in which the only natives now allowed to reside were servants.

'There's not much in the way of battle mementos,' Alice said. 'Just one little monument, I'll show you.'

They walked to the east corner of the British compound where a portion of shell-damaged, bullet-nicked wall had been left standing with the legend 'Lest We Forget' carved on a stone below. Frank stared at it. 'Must have been terrifying. Still, I wish I'd been there.'

'Huh—you'd only have been uncomfortable, dirty and tired like the rest of us. As Isabel and I were saying, you men never grow out of war games. If you did, the world would be a safer and happier place.'

'Perhaps happier still with no men at all?'

'I often wonder.'

'But what would you do without your loving brothers, and devoted suitors like Mr. Galbraith?'

He'd been casually teasing, but realised his mistake, for she seized the opening. 'Yes, I wanted to talk to you about what he told me last night after you'd gone.'

He groaned. 'About . . . ?'

'I don't want to hear the sordid details, but your opium-smuggling has got to stop at once, Frank.' When she repeated what James had said, Frank reddened furiously. 'And what right has this dam' Paul Pry of the press to blackmail me? Let him do his worst. How else am I going to keep things up to scratch, pay for Ken's education abroad? He's your nephew, remember.'

'Well, you're not blackmailing me with Ken's educational future. It's a dirty business and you know it.'

'I don't know anything of the kind. The Chinese have smoked—and grown—opium for centuries without our help.'

'Oh, I know and fifty years ago some very respectable British merchants made their piles from it. But attitudes have changed and if you're involved when this breaks you'll be legally charged and hounded out of the foreign community.'

'Sod the foreign community, they've never really accepted me because of the Wang contact anyway.'

'Look Frank, be sensible, you know I'm on your side and . . .'

'I know nothing of the sort. You're a turncoat like me, Sis. We're two of a kind, go to whichever side of the bread the butter's thickest. Only saying so the other day. Well, there's pretty thin scrapings left on my side, so I should get your hooks into that Galbraith bloke. His game of snooping and spying about must pay quite well with a little blackmail thrown in!'

'How can you, Frank? When we're both trying to keep you out of a mess? All right, go and stew in it then, and don't come running to me for help, as you have in the past.' She glared up at him; he dug his fists in his coat pocket and marched away. She stared for a minute, then ran after him. 'Frank—for your own sake, if you don't . . .'

He turned, saying in vulgar Hunanese that she perfectly understood,

'Piss off.'

After that, her pride wouldn't let her do any more. When she described the scene to James, he agreed to let the matter rest for the time being and Frank went away the next day, leaving Lily at Will's for a holiday. When Alice's anger cooled her usual love for her brother returned, mingled with a certain pity, as she remembered his bitter words about his present life, his longing for an imaginary golden past. Poor Frank, he'd never been quite so good at anything as when he had beaten Han-li at throwing the javelin in the paddock of the Chu. She wrote him a conciliatory letter begging him to change his mind. He didn't reply, but letter writing had never been his strong point either.

James lingered in Peking while waiting for permission to visit

Manchuria, which Russian forces had occupied in July 1900. Diplomatic negotiations for their withdrawal were in progress, but the Russian authorities were not keen on foreign journalists reporting how firmly they were entrenched there, because they intended, in some guise or other, to stay. Adam, a harmless doctor, had been allowed to return to his Mukden mission and told Alice in a letter that the town was still full of Russian troops and local railways were under their control.

'He sounds quite low-spirited, James,' Alice said. 'Mukden's such a hole, and must have so many dreary childhood memories for him. Please call and find out how he is.'

James sighed. 'All right. I don't seem to have had much success with your other brother though.'

'Oh, Adam and Frank are totally different. Adam's easily put upon, overconscientious, never thinks of himself, quite unlike our dear Golden Horseboy.'

They were standing in the verandah of Lilac House on the afternoon James' visa had finally come through and he was leaving for Manchuria the next day. Alice was busy withdrawing into herself as she always did when someone of whom she was fond went away. He looked at her tenderly. 'Rather a pity we've promised to dine with the Blums this evening, as it's our last for a while.'

'How long will you be there do you think?'

'Hard to say. Jobs of this sort, when the authorities don't want you there, take a time. About three months probably. May I leave a trunk here? There's no point in taking too much with me.'

'Yes of course. Put it in the store-room.'

He wandered off to pack and she stood looking out, thinking how much she'd miss his cheery company. He certainly had a way of charming people and even William and Isabel had accepted him, especially since he'd written a complimentary piece for a Shanghai paper about the Imperial Postal Service. She admired the professionalism of his writing, and also that it never seemed to obsess or over-burden him. Travelling lightly with his skill, he could remain unencumbered; he always had and, she presumed, always would. She leaned against the verandah rail, frowning at the thought of his departure.

He came out to join her. 'Is that your trunk in the store-room, with the brass handles?'

'Oh, I'd forgotten. No, that belonged to . . . the man who went away and never came back. Perhaps you shouldn't have your trunk there. It might be unlucky.'

'You mean I mightn't come back either? You want me to, then?' He put his arm on her shoulder.

'Yes, I'd like you to very much, James.'

'Then I will,' he kissed her and they made happy love on the strength of that promise.

James left the next morning and Alice, determined to carry on just as usual, settled down to work. Nevertheless, she found concentration hard and as lunch-time approached, wandered to the store-room and stared at James' trunk—a much-battered one compared to Lin's, its worn surface plastered with steam-ship labels—P & O, Mesageries Maritimes, Glenn Line, the German Mail, the Canadian Pacific. Suddenly she imagined them as coffins side by side. James' voyages as finished as Lin's; these trunks all that was left to her of two dead loves. A love? Was that what James had become? Anyway, she'd ask Snow Duck to move James', ridiculous superstitious fool that she was.

Returning to the sitting-room, she found James standing there, and blinked in disbelief because he was so much whom she wanted to see. 'James why ... is anything wrong?'

'No, I found I had time to spare before the train leaves, so I thought I'd share lunch with you, and perhaps a drink first.' He moved towards the gold and black lacquered cupboard where the bottles were kept, then paused. 'I've been thinking ...'

'Don't overdo it, dear,' she murmured, for he often claimed such activity was an effort to him.

He looked at her speculatively then, and for so long that she added, 'I was only teasing.'

He came and tilted her head up by the chin. 'That's what I've been thinking, that we joke pleasantly together, get on well generally, do we not?'

'Yes we do. And I was thinking I'd miss your company.'

'And I yours.' He walked back to the cupboard, saying, 'So I was thinking—when I come back from Manchuria and finish the opium report, then I'm planning to go Home for a few months. I've been here in the East three years without a break.'

'I see.' She lowered her eyes and he said irritably, 'I wish I knew what you are thinking at this moment.'

'Well I can't tell you, James, so please go on.' He took a deep breath. 'So I was thinking ... wondering, whether you'd like to go Home with me, as my wife?'

'Oh James, I hadn't really expected . . . at least not till just now I hadn't,' for she wanted to be thoroughly honest.

'You didn't have the notion of anything so serious between us?'

'Well you've always made it clear that you weren't interested in marriage, so I never even allowed myself to consider . . .'

He chuckled, 'Aye and I was remembering this morning a line of Shakespeare's, when Benedict proposes to Beatrice in *Much Ado*. He admits, in defeat, "When I said I would die a bachelor, I didn't think I should live till I were married." So there you are.'

She came across and hugged him. 'Let's have that drink. It's all a bit sudden.'

'That's why I've come back like this. If it's a definitely ir-rever-sible "no," Alice,' he rolled his "r"s, horribly, 'then please say so, and I'll take my trunk and not trouble to return this way after Manchuria. But if not, then you'll have time to think it over while I'm away. I'm not asking you to leave China forever, of course. The East will be my beat for years yet, I hope, and it can still be yours, with me, if you've a mind to it. And you're the only woman I've ever met who I think might do it. So it's up to you now.'

She smiled tremulously. 'Oh James, thank you for the compliment. Two compliments really—asking me, and thinking I could share your sort of life, which I'm sure I'd enjoy. So it's certainly not an "ir-rever-sible no" dear. But as you say, I must take time to think it through. I'm a little old to rush ahead heedlessly . . .'

'Mature rather shall we say, dear?' He grinned, then added seriously, 'And I'm too mature to have made my offer heedlessly, Alice.'

She squeezed his hand, then he poured drinks and they stood close on the verandah talking casually about his coming journey rather than the subject uppermost in both their minds. He kissed her lingeringly when he left, and she had an impulse to accept him absolutely then and there, but knew that should not be the way of it.

The way it was, however, seemed also rather unsatisfactory and Alice spent the first week after James' departure in very indecisive mood. His proposal, though unexpected, had not been entirely unsuspected and she was suspicious of it mainly because it seemed to solve so many of her future uncertainties, rather as her first marriage had been supposed to do. But, as James had said, she'd greatly matured since then, indeed found it hard to recall exactly the emotional frame of mind of the young woman who'd eagerly become the wife of Charles Grant without knowing him, or even herself, very well.

She knew herself now, and it was the threat to the territory of self that gave her most pause, for she prided herself on the emotional equilibrium, the independence of spirit she'd built up, very deliberately and sometimes painfully, during her years of solitary living. It had not been easy and she treasured her privacy. Did she really want to become more vulnerable again, more dependent, more selflessly loving—and more loved?

The lilac came into bloom, and one evening the moon sailed over it, casting its usual scalloped shadows on the garden. Alice stood alone on the verandah, staring at the crinkle-paper wall, thinking it through again, from the first occasion when she and James had become lovers on just such a night the year before. She found herself dwelling curiously on the little he'd told her about his family. He had two brothers who farmed, and an unmarried sister of whom he was very fond who lived in Edinburgh with his elderly parents. She smiled affectionately, thinking what a merry, cheeky broth of a Scottish lad he must once have been. When he grew up, he became the only wanderer in the family, slightly envied and resented when he came home from foreign parts with exotic presents and tales, but never yet with a wife. Wandering had made him resilient, resourceful and, by now, a little world-weary; yet he would continue to do it, he'd once told her, because he loved the feel and taste of so many countries, while settling down in one place simply to make money wasn't to his liking. Money for him was to buy steamer tickets, good meals, whisky, tobacco, a few clothes; he'd never wished for more, nor, he said, would he like to settle for less.

That he was sometimes moody, given to blasts of temper, she also knew, and he could be as stubborn and contrary as she. Living together would not always be easy, for they were both quite set in their single ways. But together she knew they could enjoy much, for they had passion, and laughter, and interest in common.

She looked up at the moon and smelled the lilac, realising

with an instinctive honesty that it was not really a question any more of 'wanting' to become more vulnerable or more loving again. She had so become. James Galbraith had come bustling into her life and made himself at home and she had chosen to ignore the fact partly to preserve her own territory and partly because she'd expected him to get up and leave anyway. Well, now he wasn't leaving unless she sent him away, and she was not going to do that because she loved him too much.

So then there was no more question about what her answer would be when he returned. Having made the decision, Alice settled lightheartedly to her translating work, and so absorbed was she in her own concerns that she rather neglected her relatives—as she was guiltily aware when she saw Polly hurry through into the courtyard one morning. 'There you are—I've been meaning to call,' Alice greeted her. 'Is anything wrong?'

Polly looked at her tragically. 'Oh Aunt, he's spurned me,. spurned me.'

'Spurned? Howard? Come and tell me all about it.'

'Lily was the trouble. You remember they were attracted that first evening they met here? He came to see us both very often after that, and she, well, she was flattered and encouraged him. My own cousin!'

'But Poll, there was no understanding between you and Howard, was there?'

'No, just the kissing which only you knew about. Lily went home last week and I prayed that we'd be all right again. But then he just didn't call. It was awful—like a slap in the face every day he didn't come. Mother said I was to be proud and forget. But I was so miserable, that yesterday evening I went to his lodgings, quite brazenly called on him. He was very embarrassed and so was I when I got there. Then he told me— he couldn't imagine anything serious between us ever, and Lily had made him realise that he wasn't worthy of my regard. That's how he put it, but only to be kind. Then I walked out, very quickly.'

'Oh Polly, I'm sorry, but that was the gentlemanly thing for him to do. Much better now than later.'

'That's what Mother said. I thought you'd be more sympathetic.'

'Dear, we are being sympathetic. One just has to carry on and eventually the pain goes away.' Alice talked more in this vein, heard her words as Polly was hearing them—as she, the

661

younger Alice had heard similar womanly advice. How true it was that in the course of love as in war, nothing much ever changed—the hurt eyes of a young girl; columns standing among rubble; bullet holes; wounds of the heart, that the years plastered over.

Eventually Polly, though unconvinced by her assurances, was persuaded to come and stay for a while. Work was a good antidote, Alice said briskly, it was time she improved her translating abilities so she could earn some money of her own. In such fashion weeks passed slowly for both of them, punctuated by occasional notes from James, riding picnics in the western hills, a farewell party for J.O. And that summer, as he predicted in his parting peroration—which was a positive cacophony of 'I told you so's'—the Empress Dowager succeeded in winning the trust and admiration of most of the foreign community.

To make amends for her earlier misdeeds, she invited the leading ladies of the diplomatic corps to the Imperial Court, presented them with pearl rings, jewelled bracelets, and little black dogs with bells round their necks. She clasped their hands, saying in a broken voice how grieved she was over the late troubles which, she vowed, would never recur. When the heat came the Empress moved as usual to her summer residence and the same ladies visited her there—where few foreigners had ever set foot.

Ensconced in Imperial houseboats, they drifted along canals, over the clear waters of the Summer Palace lake, under hump-backed marble bridges, past fairy-tale islands dotted with pagodas, statues, flowery grottoes. There were open-air picnics, teas larger than banquets, luncheons served à la barbarian with white cloths, knives and forks, wine-glasses. The ladies (and indeed the gentlemen when they attended) were bowled over by the Empress's graciousness, and told their friends she was quite a lovable person after all. She, like her nephew, still kept in the background, adored ornamental clocks and mechanical contrivances, theatricals and beautiful clothes; she ate heartily, conversed amiably, and even if somewhat capricious and misguided—were not these common faults of womenkind?

Thus did the old Dowager win back her former position of esteem, and even those who refused to sing her praises expressed admiration for her invincible staying power.

Realising, at long last, that the best hope for the survival of the Manchu dynasty was to tackle the modernisation of China, she rid her government of its ultra-conservative members and supported schemes for educational and military reform. While all this persuaded many foreigners that her heart was now in the right place, others, like J.O. and Alice, could not accept her assurances, and Alice was resolved not to have any truck with politics again as long as the Manchus remained in power. That they would be for some time to come now seemed certain, and this strengthened her desire to leave the country.

So in all ways she was ready for James when he returned from Manchuria in August. He arrived unannounced as usual and simply held out his arms to her. She rushed into them, so that he should know even before he asked, what her answer would be. William and Isabel were delighted, and Alice wrote at once to tell her other relatives. From Adam in Mukden she had no reply, which puzzled her; Peachy sent a warm letter of congratulation and so did Mary, who added what she termed a 'last request': 'My dear, you know it will be hard for me in many ways to leave the East after all these years—as it will for you, who have never yet left. So let us do it together, Alice. Come to Shanghai and be married from Fairlawns this autumn. Your wedding reception and our farewell party will be the last grand occasion we'll share in this lovely old house. And then we'll all sail away together and spend Christmas at sea. Would not this make a joyous and appropriate finale to our Chinese lives? Please Alice, Robert and I beg of you and your as yet unknown fiancé, to fall in with this.'

There was little need for persuasion, because everyone thought it a splendid idea, and Polly added a rider: now China held no more charms for her, could she please leave with her relatives and seek solace in other climes? And so it was agreed, although as Alice said, one wondered how China would manage to get along in the absence of so many Greenwoods. She and James packed up Lilac House and left the capital a few weeks later, and for Alice the first great wrench was the parting with Snow Duck and his family. In gratitude for their loyal service, she left a substantial sum for the education of all Ducklings present and to come, and promised to return to the capital one day, for, as she said, she couldn't bear to leave otherwise.

Once she and James were settled in Fairlawns she went to see Frank, for, as she told James, whatever her brother's decision, he would sulk in his lair till she routed him out. Though she arrived at the time he was due home, only Peachy was there. 'I don't know when he's coming these days, Alice, he never tells me,' she plucked her sleeve sadly. 'And he's had such quarrels with my brothers recently. I don't know why, and he won't tell me that either.' Alice expressed her sympathy, though thinking the last was probably a good sign. 'Lily is rather like him, secretive,' Peachy continued in a soft tone of complaint that was becoming habitual. 'She never would tell me much about her stay in Peking, yet I suspect there was some young man in the case?'

'An American, Howard Thringer, yes. Are they still in touch?'

'I've no notion. But then, I'd be the last to know, as usual. Now, tell me about your fiancé. I'm so happy for you.'

This Alice was doing when Frank arrived, and she hurried to him, determined to dispel their earlier disagreement. 'So you're going to marry the gentleman from the Press are you, Sis? Good luck to you, that's all I can say.'

'Thank you, Frank. You sound as if I'll need every ounce.'

'Don't know much about the fellow,' he mumbled, then jerked his head at Peachy. 'There's something I want to say to my sister in private.'

She rose at once, scurrying out quietly.

'Really Frank, there's no need to play the heavy oriental husband in that fashion.'

'I'll be what kind of husband I like in my own house.'

'Frank, you're extremely difficult these days.'

'If you're going to keep at me, I might as well not tell you what I'd intended.'

'Yes, please do,' she tried an encouraging smile, though she was annoyed.

'For your sake I've stopped that bit of undercover business with the opium, and I hope you're pleased, because it's cost me a pretty penny and a lot of trouble with the brothers Wang.'

'For my . . .' she swallowed. 'I'm delighted and thank you, Frank. But if we are to talk of "sakes," then I've done several things, and willingly, for your sake in the past.'

'That's what I told myself.'

'And when the opium story breaks here, you'll actually thank me—and James.'

'Huh, we'll see.' He slumped back, dispirited. She went over, taking his fleshy hands in her small ones. 'I'm so glad. I couldn't bear the thought of leaving China still in a quarrel with you.'

'Yes, I thought that too.'

They smiled at each other. 'You'll come and dance at my wedding, dear, please?'

'There's to be dancing?'

'James wants the bagpipes and the reeling, yes. It's his only request, so one can't refuse. You'll like him, Frank. Now this cloud is past, you can get to know each other. I'm so happy: please be happy for me.'

She kissed him, and he touched her hair, whispering, 'Uncut Jade. Over thirty years ago, wasn't it, when it all began? But now we are to be happy, both of us. Happy as bats! Let's start with a drink!' He gave her a little-boy grin and clapped his hands for a servant.

With that cloud dispersed, Alice could see no others on the horizon and she and Mary sent out wedding invitations for the chosen date—25 November. Mary's love of a grand occasion at last jolted her from the melancholy caused by Lilian's death and the first day she forgot to go and pray at the church was a happy one for Robert. Mary's valuable Japanese art collection was sold or sent Home, but most of the house was to remain untouched till after the wedding, then Mary decreed, 'We'll clear up in a great bustle and just jump on the boat—better not to linger.'

Checking through the guest-list three days before the wedding, Alice was again reminded that she'd not heard from Adam. James had met him briefly during the summer and reported that his life seemed devoted to work as usual, and living happily in circumstances that would send most of us batty, as he put it. James had said nothing of his intentions regarding Alice, for nothing had been decided at that time. Surely Adam wasn't so narrow-minded that he dispproved of newspaper men? Her half-brother was still much on her mind when she went for a final dress-fitting in Velvet Paw Lane, the following afternoon. So it did not seem specially strange when, alighting from the Fairlawns carriage, she saw him walking towards her.

'Oh, you've arrived! I'm so glad—you old dark horse,' she ran towards him. 'I was beginning to wonder if you'd get here in time.'

Reaching him she realised he was staring at her in stricken surprise.

'Alice—you here? In time? Time for what?' he backed away from her.

'My wedding of course, the day after tomorrow. I wrote and told you ages ago. Adam, what's the matter, you look quite ill? Didn't you know? Then why are you here?' She was holding tight to his arm now, for he was showing distinct signs of wanting to bolt like a rabbit down some convenient hole.

'I left the Mission quite a while ago. I haven't had any letters since,' he mumbled. 'Look, just let me go, Alice. I don't want to see you and I can't explain.'

'Don't want—but Adam, I'm getting married. I invited you to my wedding, I assumed that's why you were here.' She found herself almost shouting to penetrate what seemed a fog of pain across his eyes.

'Married? Oh congratulations, Alice. Very nice. Who to?'

'James Galbraith whom you met . . . but this is ridiculous. Get into the carriage and we'll go straight to Fairlawns, you look quite shakey.'

'Oh, I'm not going there!' he backed again.

'But what on earth has happened? Why have you left Mukden?'

'Please go, Alice—just pretend you never saw me. It's most unfortunate.' He started walking away and she had to put her arms round his waist and pull back to prevent his disappearing. Only after they'd progressed in such conspicuous fashion for several yards did he finally agree to take her to his lodgings and explain. He was staying in a third-rate boarding-house near the docks. His unmade bed was piled with his dirty clothes, half-eaten bowls of food stood on the table; a smelly kerosene stove in one corner.

'My dear, this is terrible,' she looked round dismayed.

'Better than I deserve,' he slumped down atop the clothes, waving her to the only chair.

'What do you mean?'

'I should never have been born, Alice. I was some sort of mistake right from the start. I've often thought it. When Sunny and I were born together, only she should have survived. She's a normal, sweet person, but I'm a kind of excrescence, a wart, a pustule—the unwanted lump of turtle shit, to put it in the Chinese fashion.'

His voice was low, resigned, as if repeating a familiar litany to himself. She jumped up and shook his shoulders, 'Adam, how

666

dare you say such things about yourself? You, one of the truest Christians I know, a dedicated doctor, a man of such caring faith! Are you going mad? What could have happened to get you into this state?'

'I've done one of the worst things a man can do, Alice.'

She looked aghast. 'You've killed someone?'

'Oh no, no not that.' For the first time the hint of a bleak smile. 'But how can I tell you? A woman, my sister, about to marry. I'm so glad of that, Alice. I'm sure you'll be happy.' He squeezed her hand and she saw his eyes moisten. 'Now please leave me to my shame.'

'Adam Blake, my half-brother, whom I held in my arms as a little baby, I will not go away till you tell me. If I have to sit here all night.'

There was a pause; he said, 'I'm a sodomist. They suspected me first at Changsha with Glow-worm. They were right to suspect. That's why they sent me to Mukden. After a while I did it again there, with someone else. They found out and I've been drummed out of the Mission in disgrace.'

At first she couldn't remember what such an unfamiliar sin was. 'You mean a man with . . . a man?'

He buried his head in his hands, his voice muffled. 'I can't help it. I can't, I just *can't*. I'm made that way, a hopeless aberration from the beginning . . . an unnatural excrescence.'

'Adam, please stop using those words about yourself.' She stroked his hair, it was sticky and dirty. He must be loathing himself to live in such squalor; he, who'd always been most fastidious. It was that word, one she'd often used about J.O., that brought her to a full, hitherto undefined understanding. 'Adam, what you've done, what you are, isn't so very terrible. I don't understand it, but I do know there are perfectly civilised, kind men who are like you. I had a good friend in Peking who is. It doesn't make him any of the things you're calling yourself.'

He looked up. 'He must be very miserable?'

'J.O.? He's funny, clever, rather cynical and perhaps a little bitter, but not always miserable, no.'

'But he's not a missionary—or an ex-missionary?' He was rubbing his eyes with a grubby rag.

'No. I wish he were here to help, though.' She went to the window; it was getting late. She'd missed her dress-fitting, and she felt a sudden stab of resentment at this totally unlooked-for intrusion on her happiness.

'Where is this friend of yours?' he asked.

She swung around. 'He's gone Home. And that is what you're doing, my little brother. You're coming Home with us—Robert and Mary, Polly, James, and I—we're all sailing a few days after the wedding. And you must come too. We'll look after you. We're your family.'

He jumped up quivering. 'You think I could face all of them? Tell them all what I am—my disgrace? They'd be outraged beyond words, disgusted, appalled. No, no, I'm an outcast from any decent society. That's why I've been skulking round the countryside ever since I left Mukden, living alone and rough. Then I came here to . . . to . . . never mind.' He sat down again, still shaking.

'To what, Adam?'

'To find a woman, a white woman . . . a white prostitute . . . to see if I could . . . but I couldn't.' Again he broke and she let him cry, thinking back over his life—the boy brought up under the oppression of his father's deep-rooted, passionate bigotry, taught to pray for salvation from the sins of the flesh before he knew what they were. She thought of her stepfather—his hand raised to whip her own bared buttocks, his penis raised to chastise and subdue her. She throbbed anew with revulsion and hatred of him—even now, after she'd put him in his grave. Mechanically, she began putting the dirty clothes of his son, his victim into a case on the floor.

'I'm not going with you, I'm not, I'm not.' He was shaking like a child.

'Yes you are, my dear. But I've worked out how it shall be. Nothing of this need be known to anyone else. It's quite simple—you have got a Home leave, and you've come here first for my wedding. You were delayed en route and so have arrived a little late, and dishevelled. I met you on your way to Fairlawns. And everyone will be absolutely delighted to see you.'

'You want me to add deceitfulness to my sins?'

'I want you to survive this, Adam. And if you stay here, battling alone, you might not. With our help, in time, you will. And there's something else I want very much—for you to come and dance at my wedding.' She raised his face and kissed both his damp eyes, feeling him surrender part of his great trouble to her care. Gently she led him downstairs and they drove to Fairlawns.

* * *

The sun shone on Alice's wedding day. It was the first thing she saw, pulling up the bedroom blinds and looking down at the early glint of light on the lotus pond below. The boys were already stirring, sweeping paths with extra care, gathering branches to decorate the house, and her heart leapt with anticipation. Later, the sun shone on the mahogany desk of the Shanghai registrar where she and James quietly solemnised their marriage, and it continued to bless the proceedings so warmly that the wedding guests, champagne glasses in hand, moved out into the Fairlawns garden, admiring the last of the chrysanthemums, exclaiming how beautifully mild it was for the time of year.

After the feasting and the toasting, Frank and Peachy presented the newly-weds with a surprise—a pair of beautiful ornamental mandarin ducks, symbol of marital bliss. Then the pipers of the St. Andrew's Society arrived and ranged themselves on the steps leading to the *p'eng* between the two rows of lucky dragon-dogs. And how they all reeled and jigged—to *Glenlogie* and *Glen Lyon*, to the *Corn Riggs* and the *White Cockade*. Alice twirled sedately with her portly brother William and cavorted wildly with her brother Frank; at slower pace she led the way through a country dance with her half-brother Adam, who'd given them all such a lovely surprise by arriving from Mukden just in time, and she tripped many a light fantastic with her brand-new husband, James, for the two moved well together.

Once the wedding was over, Fairlawns was dismantled, as Mary had wished, in all-day bustles of removal men and packers, of crates and carriers, while each evening was an equally hectic bustle of farewell parties. On 30 November, exactly on schedule, the stately P & O liner that was to take them to Southampton sailed up the river and into port, and later the following afternoon they boarded her.

Alice had not realised before the height of the promenade decks on these ocean-going vessels, how comparatively small and insignificant the shore and people on it looked from such a vantage point. In a small knot below stood William and Isabel, Frank, Peachy, and Lily, who, like everyone else, were calling up last messages of goodwill—to Robert and Mary, Polly and Adam, Alice and James. The six of them stood smiling and nodding in reply, gripping the deck-rails tightly as if for safety. At last, to everyone's relief, the anchors rattled up, coloured streamers were thrown from ship to shore, from shore to ship, whistles blew, bells clanged, the mighty siren of the liner boomed farewell. Alice, overwhelmed with emotion, stretched out her arms to Frank and he raised his to her, bellowing above the din, 'Good luck, Uncut Jade. Uncut Jade, goodbye!' Uncut Jade. Where she was going, no one would ever call her that again.

Slowly, the ship began sailing down the Hwangpo River towards the open sea. Soon, the groups on the quay moved off, but the six on board still stood, gripping the rail, tight with thoughts of their own. Alice looked back towards the grandiloquent façades of buildings along the Bund, now fading into twilight, saw, as it were, straight through them, miles behind and away from them in every direction. All she'd ever known in her life of people and places, from Port Arthur to Changsha and everywhere, everything in between jostled at her in that highly charged time of departure. And she wanted desperately to think of them all, to fix them all indelibly in her mind. She stared again at the water; drowning must feel like this, and she gasped with the suffocating intensity of it.

Suddenly, the ship's lights snapped on, a band struck up in one of the saloons. People began moving away, laughing and chatting, stretching their sealegs. James, the rolling stone accustomed to such scenes, broke their tension.

'Why don't we go to our cabins, unpack a little, then gather in the bar? Say about six?'

Alice looked at the others: Mary and Polly were damp-eyed; Robert and Adam stiff-backed and silent. None of them were truly familiar with that Home for which they were all bound, she herself least of all. She wanted to clasp them to her one by one in sympathetic hugs, and perhaps they did her. But in this public place, none of them moved or spoke, just smiled a little wanly at each other.

'Well?' James reminded them gently. Obediently the others turned from the heart-rending view. James touched Alice's arm. 'I'll join you very soon,' she whispered hoarsely. 'Just give me a few minutes.'

'Don't try and swim for the shore, will you?' he murmured, bending to kiss her cold cheek.

'No. Promise.' She smiled, reassured by his understanding.

Left alone, she stared at the shore where lights were now coming on—in the work-sheds, godowns, shanty huts, cotton mills along the lower reaches of the Hwangpo. She imagined all the lights behind them: paper lanterns strung on a thousand poles, smoky kerosene lamps and waxy candles, fragrant flames of incense sticks, wicks floating in saucers of rape-seed oil under roofs of mat-thatch. She could spend so long reflecting thus—hours, days, weeks awash with loving nostalgia.

Think one place only, she told herself with a firmness that was her habit. So she thought of the courtyard of the Chu on one of those hot summer afternoons thirty years before. The vases were filled with peonies, windbells tinkled in an occasional breeze, doves cooed on the curved eaves, butterflies flipped over the ornamental pond where golden carp flashed in the sun. Gardeners tended the flowers, daughters of the house sat reading in the shade, servants swept the paths. It was all expected to go on forever. Only it hadn't.

She wrenched herself back to the present, her last glimpse of the already-vanished Shanghai Bund. She remembered the first time she'd seen it as a girl, in the year 1876, when she'd drunk her very first glass of champagne with Robert in the Grand Hotel that had seemed so enormously grand then. And overlaying—memories piling one on another like layers of a cake—came the picture of herself sitting on the verandah of that same hotel when she'd returned to Shanghai as a widow, the future again an open book. On that second occasion, she remembered thinking of the first; she remembered too, that in spite of her precarious situation, she'd been very happy that day, thrilled with the great adventure of life.

As she was now, in this very minute that she must always remember. The vessel moved on slowly; at the river's mouth, two lighthouses flashed a warning to mariners of the treacherous sandbanks on either side and, passing them, Alice felt below the greater swell and surge of the open sea. She looked up at the string of lights jogging above her head in tune with the engine's rhythms, looked down at the reflection of them dancing on the waters below. Then, for the last time, she stared back at the fast-receding lights on the shores of China. 'Goodbye, Uncut Jade,' she murmured with a little twisted smile that was both pain and joy. She uncurled her stiffened fingers from the rail and went below-decks to join the others.

THE END